TRAITOR'S GATE

OTHER TITLES BY CHARLIE NEWTON

Calumet City

Start Shooting

TRAITOR'S GATE

CHARLIE NEWTON

THOMAS & MERCER

Text copyright © 2015 Charlie Newton
All rights reserved.

Newton

Published by Thomas & Mercer, Seattle

www.apub.com

Amazon, the Amazon logo, and Thomas & Mercer are trademarks of Amazon.com, Inc., or its affiliates.

ISBN-13: 9781477849361
ISBN-10: 147784936X

Cover design by Shasti O'Leary-Soudant / SOS CREATIVE LLC

Map by Mapping Specialists, Ltd., Madison, WI

Library of Congress Control Number: 2014957295

Printed in the United States of America

Dedicated to the Cushing Flash

Gentlemen, we stand not at the brink of war, but at the final abyss. The decisions made here today will set loose the deadliest conflict in human history.

—Anthony H. G. Fokker
North American Aviation Corporation

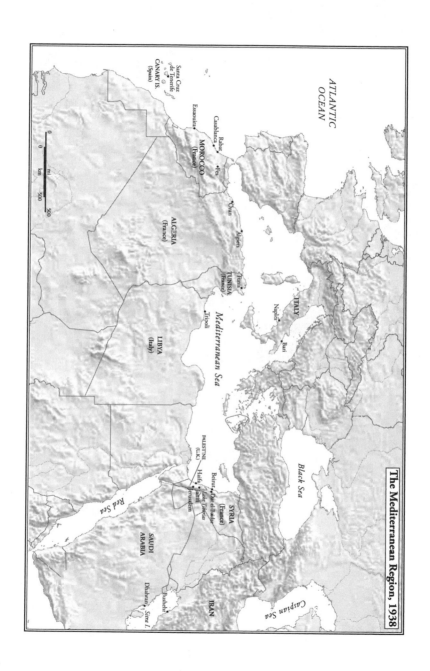

The Mediterranean Region, 1938

ATLANTIC
OCEAN

CANARY IS.
(Spain)
Santa Cruz
de Tenerife

Essouira
Casablanca
Rabat
MOROCCO
(France)
Fes
Oran
Algiers

ALGERIA
(France)

TUNISIA
(France)
Tunis

Tripoli

LIBYA
(Italy)

Mediterranean Sea

ITALY
Naples
Bari

Black Sea

Caspian Sea

PALESTINE
(U.K.)
Haifa
Beirut
Lake Dar el-Baidar
Jaffa
Jerusalem
Lake Tiberias

SYRIA
(France)

Red Sea

SAUDI
ARABIA

Dhahran
Bushehr
Sirri I.

IRAN

0   500
km
0   500
mi

THE ODDS AGAINST TOMORROW

The Roman Empire fell after eighteen centuries, the Ottoman Empire in six. The SS *Titanic* sank, and in 1929 so did the US stock market, taking with it the savings of a nation. None could happen and all did.

On July 4, 1933, the fourth year of the Great Depression, the fledgling government of the United States of America was 157 years old and teetering, the young nation's hopeful foundations assaulted by a global tide of economic despair. The daring democratic experiment had survived ten wars with others and one with itself, and now faced a frightened, disillusioned population whose grand aspirations had shrunk to food and shelter.

In Soviet Russia, after decades of violent political upheaval, the aspirations were far lower. Refugees described mass executions, political purges, and the ethnic "relocations" of entire regions. Soviet Premier Joseph Stalin's path to national stability had successfully terrorized the new union of republics into submission, but now confronted a vast internal enemy that no regime could silence: *famine*. Soon plague, possibly even cannibalism, would sweep the Soviet republics. This cataclysm, the dissidents said, was the true result of Stalin's forced reinvention of a war-decimated, agrarian society into an industrialized workers' collective. Before the coming winter was over, Stalin's political ideology would starve millions of Russians to death.

Stalin and the Communists' answer was that greed and "democratic" capitalism were the root cause of the world's poverty and hunger. Capitalism was a ruling-class lie of economic order. Capitalism enslaved and impoverished the worker, foreign and domestic. Capitalism and its sponsors—not communism—were the supreme threat to world peace and prosperity. Only a workers' revolt—a *global* economic reordering—would turn the current tide of despair before it caused a second world war. But should that war come, Stalin promised, Soviet Russia would defend herself and the Communist party no matter the cost to her or others.

On Russia's western border, Europe was not the horror of Russia's famine, but Europe was afraid. After fifteen years of postwar hardship and unfulfilled promises, much of the continent still struggled with rampant unemployment; uncontrolled inflation; and increasingly angry, battered populations ravished by the same Great War that had all but destroyed Russia.

In the beer halls and breadlines of many European cities, fascism rose as an answer to the hopelessness of the day, a workable defense against a total economic collapse that the Fascists warned was imminent. Economic collapse meant descent into another world war, this one on a biblical scale, a war the Fascists were certain the totalitarian threat of Russian communism sought to cause.

In the United States, many of the great industrialists agreed. They denounced Russian communism and the world slavery it would bring. Communism and socialism were *treason*—treason disguised as "labor unions" run by Communist-directed foreign agitators who freely assaulted the very underpinnings of the United States. These great industrialists swore an oath on God's bible that the free and democratic United States of America would not survive

President Roosevelt's radical-socialist reordering of the American Way. America desperately needed new leadership, not the "New Deal." America needed men who knew the truth and could light the way. Men like them. Prudent men like J.P. Morgan, John D. Rockefeller, and Randolph Hearst. Strong men like Henry Ford, Irénée DuPont, and Walter C. Teagle of Standard Oil.

These men, and others, stated a clear vision for the United States of America, a vision that would forge and maintain order to the benefit of everyone. The rich were not evil because others were poor. The rich were the absolute proof that American capitalism worked and Russian communism did not. If democracy and capitalism were to be saved for the common man, the United States must protect the fortunes of those who had earned them. The country must look beyond the breadlines, migrant camps, and cemeteries full of the common man and, if forced to defend freedom, fight another world war.

1929

CHAPTER I

Winter

The bluff was protection, just outside the Arab College in Jerusalem, and just high enough to be safe from the stones an angry elder might throw. Sixteen-year-old Saba Hassouneh crept to the edge, intent on her father as the crowd encircled him, his gentle professor's voice now raised in defiance: "We are not England's livestock! Your sons and daughters are not British slaves!"

The crowd of Arab men was ten deep and growing. Young and old, dressed in traditional long-shirt thobes, some with waistcoats, tarbush caps, and checkered keffiyehs, some in Western suits, they shouted and stomped their agreement, churning the parched marl until it rose as a blanket above their ankles. Ten years of drought were burning all of once-fertile Palestine into desert. Saba jumped to her feet and shouted support for her father. Precocious and feminine, the professor's daughter was a well-read, if starry-eyed, patriot, bilingual since age twelve and likely to die at the hands of her fellow Arabs for those offenses.

A half-hidden girl at Saba's knee tugged at her sleeve, cringing at Saba's display and the long chestnut hair that Saba declined to cover, even now with the clerics in plain view. "Sit. You are too bold. Sit before the men see us."

"*See*? I told you." Saba glowed with teenage pride. "My father is not afraid. He is a great man. He will liberate Palestine from England. And I will help."

Both girls were visible on the low bluff. Saba hugged an American novel to her chest, one of many she read to improve her English, stories that thrilled her with their adventure and romance. America! Victors in their fight for freedom!

"Saba. You must sit."

Sit? How could she? Her father openly confronted Great Britain, the largest, most ruthless colonial power on earth! It was not a time to sit. The very *existence* of Palestine hung in the balance! England's King George had made promises. Saba had read and reread every document, the promises of England's king explained in great detail by her father.

Before the Great War, the professor had trusted King George and favored the king's plan: "Join with England to fight the union of the German Empire and the Ottoman Turks who so brutally occupy the desert, and the desert will be free." The king's plan promised that those born to Palestine, be they Jews, Christians, Muslims, or no religion, would keep Palestine. The Zionists of Europe would have their Jewish national home in the states that would lose the Great War. The native Palestinian would have Palestine.

But now Saba's father decried England's new truth. With the Arab blood spilled and the Great War won, Palestine's sovereignty had been abandoned at the peace table by England's king, a heartless bargain to curry favor with powerful men and moneyed interests on both sides of the European conflict.

Professor Hassouneh waved a sheaf of papers above his face, red with sweat: "England's Balfour Declaration is a lie!"

The crowd shouted and Saba shouted with them. Now her father was a revolutionary—like the American heroes of her books—a quiet, principled teacher of history driven into the street to defend his home. Her father would rally Palestine to expel England's soldiers! Palestine would rise from the dust and ashes!

Saba grinned and made no effort to cover her face, a display that angered many who saw women as chattel, who feared the clerics and took England's bribes. But not her father—her father was a patriot and had raised her to be the same. Together, they had a grand plan: school next year in America—political science. She would graduate with honors then return to help free Palestine from England's army. A small band of Americans had outfought England 150 years ago and made history. History Saba had memorized by candlelight while she devoured the victories and speeches of America's founding fathers. America's heroes were hers, and one day Palestine would have her own. They would stand on every hill. America! What a grand adventure it would be. She would cross an ocean, see the vast, grassy prairies and buildings as tall as mountains. There would be suitors of every type. She might even find a boy like Nick Carraway from *The Great Gatsby* and bring him home.

Saba's father held the papers high for all to see. "This is British treachery! Three agreements—all lying contradictions that will drive the indigenous peoples of Palestine into the desert. The victorious nations of the Great War steal Palestine for Russian and European citizens those nations wish to expel!"

The crowd surged and yelled, swirling the dust.

"England, Russia, and Europe fear their Jewish countrymen, fear Jewish success and their politics. They deport them *in God's name* into Palestine!" Professor Hassouneh shook the documents at the crowd. "With these, England steals our land and kills our families. Let the guilty states of the Great War—Germany, Russia, and all others that robbed and murdered Jewish citizens—let those states, those villains, surrender their land, their territory to those they abused. But not Palestine! Palestine has wronged no one!"

The crowd roared again.

"The treachery of King George leaves the citizens of Palestine no choice! Who is England to grant ownership of our electricity to the foreigners? Our water? Even the salt of the Dead Sea! Rise up as Saladin's soldiers. Do not trust that this wrong will be quashed by the League of Nations. It will not be. In one generation, we will be servants on the lands of our fathers. There is no peace with England's king, only lies and slavery."

Saba pocketed her book. She clapped and yelled for her father. He did not incite the crowd with fiery religion—freeing Palestine was nationalism, land rights, and government. The clerics and their followers were not good because of their chosen God *or* evil. If you were a native Palestinian you were a *Semite*, the same as she—religion did not matter. Saba had friends, fellow students, and even suitors who were Christian, Muslim, and Jew. The turquoise stone she wore around her neck was a gift from the Jewish boy who shared her love of American books and, unknown to him, her dreams at night. Saba's peers were proof of what her father constantly asserted to all who would listen: "Palestine is the country of *all* Palestinians. It is the Zionists—the Europeans and Russians—colonizing under 'God's' flag who are evil in its purest form. See the Russians and Europeans for what they are, a colonial power that uses divinity as a land right for the wars they prosecute!"

Forty British soldiers appeared at the western edge of the college library. Saba's hands stopped midclap. More soldiers appeared at the dying orchard's eastern fence, their brown rifles and brilliant red tunics massing double time. Saba recognized the pincer formation from previous assaults, screamed, and sprinted downhill toward her father. The first rifle company charged. Her father turned as the red wedge split the crowd. Rifle butts cracked at heads and ribs. Blood splattered the white thobes. The second company of soldiers braced, then charged from the library.

Saba raced into the demonstrators and was knocked prone. A rifle butt slammed near her head. She rolled to her stomach. A boot lifted her to all fours and a boy's body piled her flat. Boots kicked dust in all directions. Men yelled. Steel bayonets flashed. Saba was kicked again. She rose to a knee, choking in the dust, and was slammed back to the ground. Special security police trampled past her; found her father, bloody, dust-caked, and ragged; and dragged Professor Hassouneh away by his feet. Saba yelled from her stomach, struggled to stand, and was knocked unconscious.

For seven days, Saba scoured for her father's location. She pleaded with the protectorate's court for his release until the officers beat and banished her. She implored the college—they could do nothing. She went shop to shop. Older Arab men beat her—an emboldened girl badly raised, one who refused to know her place, her behavior an insult to the dead and injured men. Finally, Saba groveled at the Al-Aqsa Mosque, and on the seventh day, her father was returned. He could not speak nor hear, his head swollen black and almost twice its normal size.

Saba ran half the Arab Quarter for the doctor. He arrived, looking over both shoulders, and warned the family to leave immediately. "Hide in Abū Dīs. All of you. The Haganah Militia have promised Professor Hassouneh's death. The Europeans are outlaws, professional murderers; you know this. They will kidnap the professor, if he remains here, and kill him."

Saba's mother argued that travel would kill Professor Hassouneh and she would not do this. Nor would she allow the family to be scared from their home. Saba's mother said she knew this tactic, a long-favored method of the English when dealing with public figures. "We will treat my husband here. We, his family, will be his guardians."

The doctor condemned the terrible risk of her choice, chastised Saba's mother without success, and left shouting dire predictions. Terrified, Saba promised her semiconscious father they would be vigilant until he was stronger, until the English released his fellow protesters and they could join in his protection. She would not fail him.

The night brought a strange silence and no breeze. Only one candle was burned. Saba and her younger brother guarded the door, exchanging glances and no words. Their mother tended their father. Early evening brought England's soldiers. They pounded the door, demanding to see Professor Hassouneh. Saba had her father's pistol—a British Enfield with three cartridges—and spoke through the door: "My father is gone, in Ramallah. They treat him for your beatings."

"Open the door."

"It is not yours to demand, butcher. Be gone. To the bastard you serve."

The door splintered off its hinges. Saba got the pistol almost to the first soldier's chest; he slapped it aside and her hard across the mouth. She clawed for his eyes. Her mother ran wailing into the room. A rifle butt flattened her. Saba sank her nails deep into the soldier's cheek and lunged to bite. He yelled and twisted away. Saba heard, "He's here. That's him, okay," and was punched to her knees. Another soldier grabbed her hair and snatched her to her feet. "Fuckin' quim. You won't be doing that again, will ya?" He punched Saba's stomach and threw her outside. Saba was dragged screaming and flailing to an alley where the soldiers beat her unconscious.

She came to on her back, screaming, a man crushed to her chest. Hips rammed hers. Whiskers scraped her face. A hand smothered the scream in her throat. Pain everywhere, her wrists clamped, naked shoulders gouging the dirt. The man finished with both hands clawed in her hair. Another soldier mounted her. He rammed and spit, then another and another . . .

Saba blinked awake. She was in an alley, far from her home. Pain shot through her private parts, then her jaw, then her legs. The stink of the men was all she could smell. She struggled to stand, fell, and rose again. No one was near. Her eyes tried to focus. Her clothes were bloody. She arranged them to cover what she could. Her hands were swollen and blue-black; she was dizzy . . . Memory flashed a soldier, and another and another. Shame engulfed her. She reeled and covered her face. Behind her hands, another memory: *England's soldiers have my father*. She shocked sideways against a mud wall, recovered, then staggered toward her uncle's house. Her uncle could help his brother.

Saba arrived her uncle's door, eyes swollen and down, voice broken, clutching shredded clothes across her chest and hips. Shaking outside his doorway, she spoke to his shoes. "Please, please, you must come. My father, your brother, they will kill him."

Saba's uncle called for his wife and daughter. A neighbor's wife rushed to Saba and, with both arms, clutched Saba to her chest. The woman's husband pulled the uncle away. The neighbor had information. His face was grim. Less than an hour ago, five men in hoods had descended upon Professor Hassouneh's home. It was very bad there. The men in hoods were Haganah. The names of six murdered Zionists had been nailed to the fragments of Professor Hassouneh's door. All inside were now dead: Professor Hassouneh, his wife, Saba's two brothers, and her eight-year-old sister.

Saba collapsed. Police arrived.

The police took her to the British Colonial Police Service compound on Jaffa Road, not a hospital. For an hour Saba sat alone and immobile on a worn wooden bench. Flies dotted her face and the rags that had been her clothes. An officer of the Palestinian police put down the Koran he was reading, made notes in the ledger on his table, then called her to stand before him. Saba did not respond. He told her that her family was dead. He added that her uncle and his family were also dead, and that her promiscuity bore the blame.

TWO YEARS LATER
October, 1931

Dawn's first gusts blew cold and strong through the mountain pass near Dhār el Baidar, Lebanon. The sprawling refugee camp shuddered, its canvas tents worn thin and brown. A hazy sunrise breached the pass. The muck began to thaw, as did the open latrines and last night's unburned dead. Saba moved toward the main gate, tracking a company of French soldiers as they slogged up the mountain road. The sun glinted on their buttons and bayonets. The military column protected a muddy truck and enough food for half the camp. Saba shivered at the outer edge of an anxious crowd queuing for a chance at food. The food she would never reach added to a hunger that drove many in the camp to stoop-shouldered madness. In this camp, the stronger ate first after fighting among themselves. They were elbowing past her to do that now. The weak died. Her education from sixteen to eighteen in the world's realities had left little doubt on how the infirm fared cradled in the hands of the strong.

Shouts erupted; men attacked one another, first with fists and feet, then the hungriest with crude weapons and hacking savagery. The soldiers fired level and just over their heads. Saba flinched and retreated to the camp's fouled Palestinian quarter. She watched the day's food divided, only the thin strip of her eyes visible, her head, face, and shoulders always shielded by a stained *haik* headdress. The hunger made her shake. She huddled with the older women warming in the sun, her arm and thin blanket wrapped around a frail woman trembling at her side. Saba had stopped crying after three months and stopped expecting to survive after a year and a half, now gripped by the slow death of starvation.

In Arabic she whispered the lie that began every day, "We will eat tonight; I will see to it."

The old woman in her arm rocked slowly without opening her eyes.

The camp was French-policed but self-segregated: Kurds from Turkey, Armenians, Assyrians, and Palestinians. The Palestinians were the least in number and mostly women and children. They bore the brunt of the camp's cruelty and its worst geography, sandwiched between the open latrines and the cremation pits.

Two men emerged from the fight bloody and empty-handed, both swearing oaths against the Kurds. They walked past Saba and the women, avoiding hog but staring at the group, searching for youth who could be sold or used. Finding none, they raised their soiled *jellabas* and straddled one of the slit trenches. Saba shrank into her shoulders and felt for the makeshift blade cold against her stomach. Shame had kept her once-proud face covered since she'd been dragged screaming into that dusty Jerusalem alley. The rage at the murder of her family still burned, providing bits of courage when there were food scraps to steal—when the hungry-eyed men roaming the camp were at prayer or the more violent disputes erupted. On the nights with the most violence, she would take the biggest risks, roaming the farthest. Twice she'd been beaten badly but had fed the entire tent and felt the strongest, remembering fragments of the girl she had been, the girl who would save Palestine.

Midmorning brought more sun and an unsteady calm; the food was gone, the hungry again resigned to beg, steal, barter, or die. Saba and the old women retreated to their tent. A man yelled.

Voices rose against one another. Saba half stood, sensing danger and opportunity. Uniforms blurred past. More voices, French and Arabic. A French soldier stooped at her tent's missing curtain.

"Up. The camp is being relocated." He tore tattered canvas and cloth from the poles until only part of the frame remained, then slogged to the next tent and tore it from its rigging. Saba turned; the action was being repeated throughout the camp—men being roused in bunches—soldiers yelled and pointed them uphill into the rocks and mud. Arab men yelled back, shaking their fists; women huddled or bent to gather their men's belongings. Saba glanced through the camp's wood-and-wire gate to the steep road bordering the fence. The old women of her tent could not climb such a road; they would perish going higher into the Lebanon Mountains. These women had protected her, scenting her robes with their open sores and infirmities, hiding her under their bodies when the men came.

Saba gathered those robes to her hips, knowledge and fear mixing with shame. There was a small chance she could save the women from the climb. Both hands trembled as she uncovered her hair and face. She dipped an unsoiled corner of her *haik* in their water jar and cleaned grime that hid an eighteen-year-old's smooth olive skin. Bile bubbled in her throat. She swallowed and forced tangled hair under the headdress. Sweat seemed to drench her. She steadied, then tied the *haik* bold as a half scarf.

The camp's perimeter churned with arguments and confrontations. Saba drew sharp, hungry glances from the men. She kept moving until she located a French officer giving orders from a truck's dented fender.

"*'Afwan*," she said, "the *ermile*, the old widows," and tried to smile, to be bold like her scarf, and pointed downhill across the camp's convulsions. "They cannot make the climb. You would please help them. Please?"

The officer listened, inspecting her features with interest, then winced at the odor of her clothes. He shrugged, said it was in God's hands, "*Insha'Allah*," and pointed her away.

"Please." Saba added proximity in spite of her shame, her eyes completely in his, something French soldiers understood.

The officer stepped back and around the fender, wrinkling his nose. He called two soldiers. Each cinched an arm and twisted Saba away. Saba clutched at her robe, raising its dirty hem. "Wait! There is more—"

The soldier grabbed a handful of Saba's tangled hair. She kicked and slipped, stumbling to a knee. The soldier fell with her into the mud. Saba fought her arm free. A bayonet sliced at her, chest-high. She raised both hands, trying to back away. "Wait. I can—"

A rifle butt slammed above her hip, a fist into her chin.

A rough hand woke her. A man's hand. On her face, then on her body. The nightmare: rough beards on her cheek, meat breath and saliva on her neck. She jolted into the hand and it flattened her. She clawed for British eyes. A face blinked into focus, leaning away, not British: Arab. Not young, not old . . . The hand pressed harder. She couldn't breathe—

"Gentle." He spoke in English. "No move. Injury."

Saba tried to fight but couldn't. Pain radiated from her hip. Her face wasn't covered.

"No move." The black eyes were squinting, furrowing already creased skin. Black wings were tattooed under the right eye. "Safe." He added weight to his hand, then glanced over a wide shoulder, then back. "For now. Safe."

Saba patted for a rock. He stood, quick and athletic, now staring down at her from six feet. She crabbed backward, forgetting the pain, her eyes glued to his and the black wings. He remained stationary, robed in dusty black. She noticed the night, then the smell of lamb fat and sweet peppers—glorious scents she hadn't tasted since . . .

Her hand touched a heated stone. "Ough!"

The Arab smiled. A British Army holster belted his tunic. A black keffiyeh covered his head and part of a muscled neck. Behind him, three horses stomped and whinnied. He spun, drew the pistol, and ducked. The black horse kicked. The Arab charged into the darkness, a dagger flashing in his other hand. He moved like an animal, so sudden that Saba did not consider escape until he reappeared with the pistol holstered, the dagger not. Her eyes jumped from face to dagger and back. She remembered her knife, reached for it, and found nothing. It would have to be the heated stone—

The Arab opened his palm and shook his head, reading her mind. "Burn." He nodded to the fire near her shoulder, but the dagger kept Saba's eyes. He walked to the fire's other side, then lowered to the ground using the strength in his legs. Saba jumped to her feet, staggered at the pain, and fell. He did not acknowledge her movements and served himself from an iron pot. Saba braced for a charge the Arab did not make, then registered that no tent sheltered him or his meal. She glanced fast past both her shoulders, then back at him now staring at her face, a small smile coming to his. She retreated, one hand rising to hide her features. She would make him pay for his pleasure, knife or not. The Arab did not move. If the black wings under his eye were true, she was doomed.

Saba baited him from a crouch, succumbing to fear and temper. "You are a *corsair*, a raider?"

He ate instead of answering the insult, his eyes glancing at the food, then her.

"The camp . . . What happened to the women . . . to me?"

"Ten French francs. I buy you."

Saba felt the soldiers on her again, felt power in the urge to kill him, hoped he would come closer now, wings or not. She shed fear for anger and new humiliation, and rose, keeping a small bend in her knees and a hand veiling her face. This corsair would remember this slave. She would mock him to her side of the fire, then rip out his eyes and eat them. "What happened to the old women? Did you not buy them, great Sharif? Were the mothers of the tribe not to your liking?" Saba spit in his fire. "You will not be the man who enjoys me, either."

The Arab nodded. "This I believe."

Saba glared, eager to kill him.

He ate until no food remained, then cleaned the pot as if he had been raised Bedouin and without women. This was as the legend said. She watched him walk to the black horse, retrieve a goatskin bundle from the saddle, then return to the fire and sit.

"You will not share my tent until you are clean. The river is behind the hill." He tossed her the goatskin bundle. "Clothes. You will wear man's clothes. Steal like a man, fight like a man. For you as a woman I have no use."

Saba caught the bundle and smelled the horse that had carried it.

"*Now.* Then you and I raise my tent."

Saba was dry and cold from the river and inside the coarse goat-hair tent. The clothes were heavy, unfamiliar, and too large. A tied-rope belt held the pants above her narrowed waist, further supported by suspenders that bowed outside her breasts. A man's keffiyeh covered her hair and face, draped across her nose. Saba was angry and frightened and hungry and it was the best she had felt in two years. The Arab had not transformed himself into the fierce black bird of legend. It was possible the wings under his eye were a lie.

The Arab spoke English. "I pay ten francs. They say you read and write English. You will teach." He threw her the last book her father had given her, one she'd managed to keep through the desolation of the camps. "I speak, not read, not write. I want read your book of . . ."

Believing it lost, Saba fingered *The Great Gatsby* while he fumbled his words, then interrupted him in English, an insult in their culture. "You are Bedu?"

He floated thick eyebrows above the searing black eyes. "I am Arab."

She frowned, her temper returning. The wings were a lie, the man wearing them a coward in masquerade. "You are a raider, a thief, an assassin maybe?"

"This could be."

"And I am your slave?"

He smiled and said nothing.

"Do not close your eyes tonight, great Sharif, if I am your slave."

His neck curved against his shoulder. "I must fight with dogs in my tent?" The dagger was fast into his hand, across her throat and gone. Saba lurched away. The slash of light or blade had long passed. Only his words were still in the air. "For saving a *kalb*'s life? For keeping a dog from the cold and the French?"

Saba felt her neck for the blood. Her fingers were dry; her neck uncut. She blinked, weighing an answer, stuttering between bluster and hope, fear and safety. The wings might not be a lie. No man could move that fast.

The Arab remained cross-legged. Two rifles were behind his right shoulder, one matching those England's soldiers had carried in Palestine, the other shorter and more menacing.

"I am not whore or slave." Saba raised her head and used her father's name for the first time in two years. "I am Saba Hassouneh."

The Arab nodded and did not ask about father or husband. "Read."

She bristled at the command, remembered the book in hand, then opened it. "'Before I could reply that he was my neighbor dinner was announced.'" She glanced at him, insuring his distance. "'Wedging his tense arm imperatively under mine, Tom Buchanan compelled me from the room as though he were moving a checker to another square.'"

"Is true." He laughed loud. "The old women do not lie."

The guilt of a survivor washed over her and her clean clothes. "What . . . happened to them?"

"The same as will happen to all Arabs in the invaders' desert. Your fate, if not for my ten francs."

Saba's hands closed the book. The Arab told her to open it, to read. Her eyes drifted to her knees crossed in the coarse wool pants. She said good-bye to the old women who had been her family, who had saved her, and wanted to weep.

The Arab went silent, then acknowledged her loss. "Life is not separate from death."

Saba heard words her father had also used, suddenly too tired to be afraid. The book curled itself to her chest and she rolled to her side, already unconscious. She dreamed of revolutionary America and three-pointed hats and half-British, half-French soldiers dying in large numbers.

They spent four seasons together before she knew his name, Khair-Saleh, and even then she was unsure. The wings were true, of that she *was* certain. And he was a man—a fearsome warrior man—but not the terrifying wraith of legend. At least she didn't *think* he was. He learned English at a slow pace and she often believed this was deliberate. Saba learned faster, became lethal with a knife and pistol and better with a rifle. He said she had the eye and, more important, the heart. They stole together, kept their tent and camp together; and when they sold their booty in the souks of Damascus, Beirut, and Amman, she hid her hair, chest, and face. She was treated as a man; could fight like a man; and, when challenged, could kill like a man.

Khair-Saleh's preferred targets were European soldiers who patrolled the Damascus-Haifa Road near the Syrian and Lebanon borders, the soldiers' British Enfield and French Lebel rifles bringing the highest prices, their deaths the most satisfaction. In Saba's second summer with the Arab, they had celebrated such an event, drinking *qumiz*—fermented mare's milk—under the canopy of gnarled oak trees, cooling their feet in the northern waters of Lake Tiberias, England's name for the Sea of Galilee. A false dawn had risen in the east.

"My homeland." Khair-Saleh nodded at the dawn, then shared pieces of a brutal history.

"In my eighteenth year"—his deep voice remained monotone—"I become a proud conscript of Transjordan's Arab Legion— the army of Amir Abdullah and the first Arab state to govern itself. I serve this new state with honor but fall victim to a boy's desire for promised glory, privilege, and money. When asked, I join England's new and elite Frontier Force. We hunt Arabs who oppose the Crown and its policies."

Of this he was not proud. He had hunted his own, pacified warring Bedouin camps with truck-mounted Lewis and Vickers machine guns, buried hundreds of Arabs for the good of England's empire and a crisp uniform. "I am wounded near Wadi Rum and I lay in the red sandstone to die. A shooting star cuts long across my final sky. In the star's light I see the great lie of my life—my need for embrace in the Europeans' culture. Embrace that will never come for the Arab. And if somehow I am remade European, how little this embrace will matter."

Khair-Saleh did not look at Saba and went silent. When he spoke again, he told their feet in the water, "As the star crosses the desert, I see it shine in the dead eyes of a fellow Bedouin I have killed. Fever days follow, not death. I wrestle unconscious with the Bedouin's eyes. Someone tends my wounds and gives me water. I awake protected from the sun with black wings beneath my eye"—Khair-Saleh touched his cheekbone—"and no dagger in my heart. Those who save me—only the Bedouin's tribe could do this, I believe—leave me the star's name: *Minchar al Gorab*—the Raven."

Saba sat silent, aware she was hearing the heart of the legend that no one else had.

Khair-Saleh inhaled a slow breath to finish. "I stand that day with life in me I should not have. I disown the gods who bless all sides and vow that no Arab will die at the Europeans' hand if I am witness. I promise to drive the invaders from the desert and share their spoils with those I have hunted." He passed Saba the last of the milk-wine, then, unsteady, stood and disappeared into the night. It was the most he had spoken at one sitting in the entire time she'd known him.

Another three seasons passed and they were once again camped above the rocky banks of the River Jordan near the northernmost tip of Palestine. Surrounding them was the mountainous confusion of French Lebanon and Syria, a forested safe haven for bandits and guerrilla fighters. Maronite Christians controlled the north, the Druze parts of the south and east.

Saba was comfortable here in spite of the area's violent population, maybe because of it. All this territory east of the Sea of Galilee and the River Jordan was called the Golan Heights. It remained under colonial French mandate but with only tacit French control outside Beirut and the main port cities, and then only when the occupying French army was patrolling at company strength. Saba trusted she could hear the feet of that many men even sound asleep.

The British patrols west of the River Jordan were more murderous but less worrisome. They rarely strayed this far north from southern Palestine. In reality, the northern reaches of the Sea of Galilee, and the malaria marshes beyond, were no-man's-land. "God's will" and man's laws were adjudicated here by brute force and without quarter. Yesterday had been such a day. Saba had been dressed as a woman stranded on the Damascus Highway. Four Legionnaires stopped to offer assistance, then decided to rape and rob her instead. The sergeant dropped his pants to have her first. He died by her knife, the others by gunfire. Half their weapons would be gifts to the guerrilla fighters, the other kept for sale in the Damascus souks.

Dusk's chill came with the setting sun. Saba tightened the blanket at her shoulders, warming herself with thoughts of the clean water, a wound that had been successfully dressed, and no ride in the morning. The noise came from the rocks behind her and then in front. She registered the uniforms before she knew they were French. Impossible, but somehow she had been tracked. Five rifles were pointed at her, bayonets fixed on three. The nearest spoke in French. She shook her head.

He used Arabic. "Where is he?" She shrugged, feeling the Frenchman's eyes on her naked face, her pistol covered by her shirt but too far to reach.

The soldier lunged his rifle at her mouth. "Khair-Saleh. Where is he?"

Saba said, "I do not know this man."

"The Raven. Where is he?" Four of the five rifles were mounted tight to French shoulders, fingers white inside the trigger guards, the barrels too far to grab. These Frenchmen were scared, anxious in their battle line. An incorrect movement by her and their fear would kill her. Saba stood with her arms extended, hoping the Frenchmen would not shoot her. "I am alone . . . with my husband." She pointed toward the water through the cedar trees on her right and covered her face with a black keffiyeh. "He swims the river."

Three sets of eyes followed her finger.

She ducked. The closest rifle fired flame past her face. Tree bark exploded behind her. The soldier unlevered his bolt but pitched forward, struck from behind. The rifleman on his right sprayed blood from his coat and snapped at the waist. An 8mm bullet grooved her shoulder. Saba spun sideways, reached her Enfield pistol, turned into a series of explosions, and fired. A soldier crashed at her feet, his face gone. Another charged, his bayonet slicing through her shirt. The knife was in her hand and buried in his liver before she knew she had done it. He screamed almost in her mouth. Saba twisted and fell under his weight, his hand clawing at her eyes. She bit at his face and stabbed through his coat. They wrestled until he quit and he was jerked dead from her chest.

The Raven tossed the soldier aside and scanned the others. His black robe was bloody, as was his face, the black wings under his eye all that remained of his cheek. He sank to his knees, his eyes not leaving hers, then relaxed until he rested on his boot heels. The exhale was deep, a wet, wheezing rattle. He filled his hands with his pistol, dagger, and a bloody ten franc note, then pushed all toward her.

"*Dayman*. Not for me. For Palestine."

EIGHTEEN MONTHS LATER
September, 1935

The rebel camp had been betrayed. Hidden under the cliffs and cedar trees of Lebanon's Beqaa Valley, they would be under siege by French mercenaries before today's sunset. Fawzi al-Qawuqji was the commander of this camp. He was a French-trained Arab and a decorated officer who had deserted the French army after the Great War to join what he passionately believed were "the Arab Nationalists" and what the French and British Authority defined, without exception, as a "murderous gang of terrorist criminals."

Looking beyond the hills, al-Qawuqji weighed battle options. To his north and west would be a fast death. To his east was to be pushed out of the fight. To his south, in the hills and cities below him, was the fight. Palestine was ablaze in civilian riots and strikes that had killed many but had not ended the League of Nations Mandate or halted England's plans for her desert territories. At his shoulder, an Iraqi mullah lobbied for al-Qawuqji's ear. "France and Great Britain warn all those with an interest in the region that you must be stopped, that you gather the 'zealots' of our many tribes into these mountains. They fear you will mount a second Arab Revolt."

Fawzi al-Qawuqji nodded but did not speak. It was true; his commanders and rebels had all sworn a blood oath with him to rally the factions of the desert against England's occupation, swearing to die fighting against the final phase of expulsion from their homeland. This mullah wished them to join a larger organization with Islam at its center, the Arab Higher Committee's Pan-Arab Army of God.

The mullah added, "Without us you will be alone and perish without success. Your focus in *Palestine* is too narrow, too—"

"*Here*, two hundred thousand *Palestinians* are deported to make room for the European colonists." Fawzi al-Qawuqji waved his hand. "*Here*, not Iraq, England imprisons and exiles *Palestinian* Nationalists. Here, the British Mandate Authority steals *Palestinian* land to give or sell to the European colonists."

The mullah stiffened but maintained his reasonable tone. "Yes. But your camp remains small and fragile. And England speaks daily in the Arabic, French, and English newspapers of the soldiers they are sending. The newspapers frighten your partisans back into their homes. To succeed you must join the Pan Arab—"

"No." Al-Qawuqji looked at the mullah. "Palestine must build her army *here, now*. Kill the invader in greater numbers than he kills the people of Palestine." Al-Qawuqji hardened his tone. "Send me weapons and ammunition, not words."

The mullah hardened his tone to match. "And the women who defame your camp? What of them?"

Fawzi al-Qawuqji allowed few women to train in his camp, and those were segregated, bound under the strict codes of desert traditions. Women were not men. And never treated as such.

All but one woman. She was tall for an Arab, olive-complected, and fierce like the desert tribe that had birthed her. The Enfield pistol in her left hand was smoking, the target at twenty feet had six holes in the center ring. The man to her left was on a knee and bleeding from his eyebrow, his checkered keffiyeh askew. Without looking, the woman hit him again, this time with the butt of the pistol, and knocked him unconscious. She spoke in Arabic, then English.

"I am Saba Hassouneh al-Saleh."

The men stepped back. Hers had been a trick, an exercise in new-world etiquette and combat. They had thought her a whore or lower, forced to wear a western man's clothes, her faced covered out of shame, not piety.

"In this camp, no man will place his hands on me. Until you are as I am, until you have killed thirteen with your hands, you are dogs—all temper and without talent."

The professor's proud teenager was now twenty-two. She wore suspendered pants and a warrior's calm. Her hip pocket held a bloodstained ten franc note pinned to the lining, a talisman from the man who had saved her. In his blood, tiny bird wings were tattooed black beneath her right eye.

She belted the Enfield and adjusted her black keffiyeh. The tail draped a powerful shoulder scarred twice by French bullets and hid all but her scorching eyes.

The men saw the bird wings and added distance, unsure if this could be her—the Raven—or another trick. None wanted to know badly enough to remain within reach of her hands.

Saba licked dust from her teeth. "There is no God here. If you fight for Him, take your holy book and leave. We fight for Palestine."

ITASCA, TEXAS

CHAPTER 2

September, 1935

E ddie Owen kept himself upbeat and happy; the alternative was beaten and unhappy and what did that solve? There were things twenty-two-year-olds could fix in a Dust Bowl Depression and things a fellow couldn't. Focus on the fact that you had a job today, no matter how hard or dangerous the work; outwork your boss's expectations so that you had your job tomorrow; and everybody wins.

The grizzled bosses Eddie worked for still had trouble figuring him. Pointing him out like a man would a good huntin' dog with three legs. "That boy there's one-of-a-goddamn-kind—a college-educated roughneck. So damn smart at books the college there at Norman had let him come for free. Hell, prior to the crash of '29, the boy woulda been called a liar even if he had the damn diploma in his hands."

September's last Friday was seven and a half hours old, the Texas sky blurred brown by the blizzards of overplowed land and the Great Plains blowing east. The radio was on, and had been all night because that's what the rig's driller wanted. The driller was

Eddie Owen's boss. His name was Thurman Deets; he'd be dead in one hour.

Eddie focused on the radio, happy that Thurman Deets and his fellow wildcatters had embraced the big wooden boxes. Walter Winchell's live staccato bulletins had finished long before midnight, but the harsh realities Winchell spoke about were being rebroadcast into the parched slaps of a sapless wind.

Thurman Deets swallowed the last of his chalk beers, listening to the broadcast a second time as was his way, no happier than before he'd started his beers. Walter Winchell warned that a second Depression was coming, this one the backbreaker. Winchell painted word pictures of America's industrial cities roiling right now with job riots and Communist agitators. Five years of hunger marches hadn't added hope or reduced the breadlines. Walter was scared for America—said that her great promise could come to an end right here and now—and wanted to know what President Roosevelt intended to do about it.

Deets spit on the drilling platform and answered the radio. "He intends to not get assassinated. If he can."

Behind the derrick tower and through the brown clouds, the sun hinted at Dallas to the east, a gambling town that Eddie hadn't seen and didn't figure he would, a town that Thurman Deets repeatedly said he could piss on or let burn. Deets turned up the radio's volume. Winchell was replaced by the News Cavalcade, rebroadcasting yesterday's presidential Fireside Chat. Sandwiched between the static and New Deal rhetoric, FDR offered little comfort or contradiction. He denounced the nation's bankers as "moneychangers and the privileged princes of industrial dynasties." *They and their scions*, not he, were the architects of the nation's ghost banks and the workingman's soup kitchens.

Thurman Deets spit on the deck, said, "Fuck them high-collar bastards, every goddamn one of 'em," and called for drill pipe. Eddie was already moving. Deets almost complimented Eddie's speed but didn't; not much out here warranted compliments. Deets watched Eddie work. Even the tired-ass business agent called Eddie Owen *the Cushing Flash*. Said it with a grudging pride, as the business agent was doing right now, telling the owners at the derrick's stairs whatever the fuck business agents told owners when they came to watch.

"Lotta gristle in that Okie kid," the agent said. "Lotta heart for a candy-ass college boy."

Thurman Deets half listened while he worked. His people were from Oklahoma, too, and dead since '33, buried by Dust Bowl wind and Great Depression reality. Eddie Owen wasn't all that special to him, just another starving wheat farmer's kid looking for food and a day's pay to feed the parents back home. Kid had a fast smile, though, and faster hands if you forced him. And the sumbitch didn't complain.

Eddie grinned at the agent labeling him "college boy." The best boots Eddie could afford were on his feet and held together with tape. Not exactly the "college plan." And not a girl to dance with within fifteen miles. A tremor rumbled the platform. The wind gusted out of the west. Eddie grabbed for balance. Thurman Deets's eyes sharpened, then jumped from workstation to workstation. Deets cupped an ear, sorting rhythmic banging from wind. His knees flexed—drillers listened for the really bad news with their feet—the last layer of Itasca, Texas, topsoil showered the platform and Deets covered his mouth. Eddie used a raised shoulder to block the same grit. A second rumble stumbled him forward. The drill pipe wrenched to a stop and the roughnecks flinched back from the wellhead.

Methane and sulfur.

Thurman Deets cut the motor and waited. The rumble quit. He pointed Eddie to the corrugated roof of the doghouse, waved the derrick man down from the top and everyone else to the stairs. Cochise No. 1 was a wild well, plagued with gas pockets, bent pipe, and broken men. More tremors. A chill straightened Eddie's back—not a good sign, not at all. But like Thurman Deets had said, "Where else you going? On the relief? *If* you could get on. Bakersfield? Wander two-lane highway outta the dust and into California's migrant camps? Ain't no money in the Hoovervilles and no damn victory in picking peaches."

Eddie smiled in spite of the chill. Peaches didn't sound all that bad; they rarely exploded, almost never flashed a hook knife after swilling bucket beer, and peaches tended to grow in the sunshine, usually beneath dirt-less air you could breathe. Eddie forced another laugh. It died in his throat. Best not to think about sunshine and dirt-less air. There weren't any paychecks in California. And from what he'd heard, nowhere else, either. A year ago, Eddie had been a graduating petroleum engineer with "brilliant" prospects—he'd been full scholarship/Phi Beta Kappa, top of his class at OU, class president even though he couldn't afford the suit and tie. Eddie'd had big plans then, big dreams that would send enough money home to beat the wind and the bankers, then carry him through far-off lands with oceans and mountains and exotic people of every shade.

Thurman Deets coughed dust and a string of profanity. Eddie grinned at the gruff old monster. Roughnecking was far better than your parents and brothers and sisters starving or begging in California—

The methane again. Another rumble.

The wellhead flashed and fire shot up the cable. Eddie stumbled sideways. He and Thurman Deets locked eyes when their knees buckled. Rumble became roar. The explosion blew the platform sideways and crushed two roughnecks scrambling off the stairs. Bolts snapped and buzzed bullet trails. Deets was chunk shredded in red mist. Flames erupted below the deck and the sky billowed black. Eddie braced to be buried in pipe and fire. A second explosion splintered the tower. From seventy feet up, wood and steel showered the well site in jagged spears and slugs of burning oil. Derrick to deck, Cochise No. 1 killed everybody it could.

On that same morning, Newt Owen, Eddie's forty-four-year-old father, coughed into his hands and fought another day to save his farm. All around him, Western Oklahoma was suffocating. As was much of Kansas to the north and West Texas to the south. Six years of drought and four years of the brown blizzards had reduced the landscape to a thick, dead blanket of surreal gray dust.

Another towering dust storm had just blown across the Owen family farm, uprooting hollowed-out cedar trees and stripping whole sections of barn from the wall studs. Newt and Mildred-Mae, his wife of twenty-five years, labored in the last of the sandpaper wind. Mildred-Mae shielded Newt while he hammered up barn siding long ago bleached of paint and any real job to do. Man and woman, they were frail at middle age. Everything was frail now, farm and family past their good years, rushing toward affliction and early death. The wind gusted and Newt clutched for Mildred-Mae, hugging her safe to his chest. The brown cloud rolled on to the far fence line and smothered the cottonwoods.

Their youngest children huddled on the gray farmhouse porch. Howard and "big" sister Lois wore goggles and wet-cloth masks and coughed into their shoulders. Howard and Lois were clothed and safe as Newt and Mildred-Mae could make them—there was victory in that—and fed three times on most days from the posthole and tin-can garden. The livestock was gone, all but the one cow dead to the elements or sold off for lack of feed—grinding the

Russian thistle tumbleweed hadn't worked as a feed substitute. The neighbors were gone, too, victims of their mortgages, or dead to the "dust pneumonia," or swept away in the never-ending drought.

Grit peppered Newt's neck and back. His wife's mettle, and maybe some of his own, had kept their family from the "terrible faith"—the road to California, and there was victory in that, too. The few neighbors who'd straggled back said it was better to die here, where there'd once been family and friends, and churches and pride. None of that existed in California; California was a lie, a desperate paradise fevered in your dreams but brutal as a slaughter pen.

Newt coughed and squeezed his wife, forgetting her bones had begun to hurt. Mildred-Mae winced and Newt gentled, looping his arms to keep the grit off her best he could. Their end here was close; he couldn't help but see it now, same as he'd seen the terrible faith settle into his neighbors. It was in his wife's silent shivers when she slept and their youngest child's cough every morning since the cold nights had come early. And once that terrible faith grabbed hold, it was a plague men with plows and sweat and pride couldn't overcome.

Newt tightened down the hat he'd worn every dawn since leaving the coal mines for Oklahoma. Thirty years of farming—first in Cushing, then this grassland ground—but now their fields were dead. Only charity or President Roosevelt might save his wife and children. The Owen family's survival—here *or* in California—would no longer hinge on how hard he and Mildred-Mae could work, and that was a bitter pill for a man to swallow. Now the survival of the family would be up to their oldest boy, Eddie. And a monthly bank draft sent from the oilfields of North Texas.

Sixty-seven days after the explosion on Cochise No. 1, its only survivor ended his hospital stay. Eddie Owen was only semimended and weeks earlier than the doctors felt was prudent. Eddie had sixty-two dollars—the last of the drilling company's hospital money—no job, no prospects, and a letter from his mother. The letter scared him. That's why he was leaving. It had a tone between the lines Eddie hadn't heard before. On his way out, Eddie stopped by the rehabilitation room to see little Colette Porter Weiss of Bayou Teche, Louisiana. Colette was with her "therapy nurse," a busty platinum blonde, ex-nickel-hopper (taxi dancer) from Bossier City hired special by Colette's father. She testified that Colette was the gutsiest twelve-year-old polio victim God ever made, and as in love with Eddie as a little girl knew how to be.

Eddie kissed Colette's forehead good-bye. Her cheeks were scarlet and Eddie told her, "When you walk outta here, and you and I know you will, you make sure they find me wherever I am. I'll be your date to the first dance." No one but Eddie and Colette believed Colette would live long enough for that to happen. Eddie said, "It's a miracle that I'm standing here. Don't forget that . . . when . . ." Eddie choked up. He tapped the brace that encased her withered leg. "Don't ever forget that."

Eddie wiped the tears out of his eyes; found Suzy, his favorite nurse; thanked her and the other nurses; and said good-bye. They snuck him food he'd likely starve without. Two men saw him off, both aged early from TB, one in a wheelchair, the other a maintenance man employed at the hospital. The maintenance man warned, "Don't stray off them highways, boy: desperate men in them fields."

From the wheelchair, the patient jabbed a gnarled finger. "And keep to your own self."

Eddie had taught the chair-bound patient how to play chess and helped the maintenance man fix the hospital's boiler so the state wouldn't fire him. The maintenance man was a tireless supporter of the American Workers Party. His health would fail him before he could attend his first American Communist Party convention in Madison Square Garden. The chair-bound chess player was a Great War veteran, a member of the American Legion, and an ardent believer that only fascism would save our democracy from the criminal subterfuge of Roosevelt and his Communists.

Eddie was the moderator. He confided to both men, "As God is my witness, gentlemen, I don't see how you'll get on without me."

"Don't need no damn boy talkin' to me like that," said the chair-bound chess player.

Eddie smiled to where the swelling had been the worst and raised his hands. "Guess we'll settle it fightin', then. Winner takes the nurses to the dance."

"The hell you say," said the maintenance man. "Suzy'd make pie outta you."

Eddie patted each man's shoulders and turned for the door. Both grimaced, mumbling confusion at why anyone with sense would leave a roof *and* food. The chess player rasped at Eddie leaving, "And keep your money in your shoe if you got any."

Eddie limped ranch roads north toward Fort Worth, hitching rides in the powdery all-day twilight. At the Highway 77 intersection, he bit into the first of today's bread, catching a miracle ride on a Standard Oil tank truck before he finished chewing. The driver made Gainesville at midnight. The town was dark from beginning to end and that's where the driver dropped Eddie, just south of the Red River Bridge. Seventy miles had taken all day. This close to Oklahoma, the air had heavy grit, drier, more parched. Eddie drank jar water that didn't help. The northbound Rock Island rumbled in from the dark, slowed for the bridge, and blew its whistle. A score of hard knockers scrambled from the trestles, elbowing and cursing Eddie out of the way. Eddie was too beat up to contest them for a space. Instead, he found shelter in an empty hay barn on the southern bank of the river.

Eddie woke with the sunrise, cold, hungry, and aching everywhere. Two families now shared the barn; one had a small pull wagon with a wheel gone. A hollow-eyed little boy sat at the heel of Eddie's boots; the boy cowed, staring through his eyebrows, but didn't speak. Eddie didn't, either. The boy extended his trembling left hand, palm up.

Eddie's stomach growled.

The boy used his other hand to hold up the arm.

"Where ya from?"

The boy's arm began to droop. Eddie smiled, kept yesterday's uneaten bread ration, and gave the boy all the food he had for today and tomorrow. "You share with your sister, okay?"

The boy scooped the food and froze when Eddie patted his head. The boy's father and mother pretended not to see.

Across the river, leery chalk-colored men walked Oklahoma's two-lane highway in greater numbers, bedrolls on their backs, dirty kerchiefs tied across their mouths and noses. Each mile that Eddie walked, the dust stole more of the landscape. By mile ten, the wilted wheat, corn, and cotton were gone, smothered beneath the gray drifts and foot-deep blanket. By noon, he began to pass half-buried fence lines and empty farmhouses smothered to their rooflines.

Eddie bought canned beans from a shack store near Davis and was advised to get off the road before nightfall. He did, spending the night shivering in the dried stock pond of an abandoned pasture north of Fort Cobb near Route 66, the road to California. For the first time, Eddie realized he heard no birds. There were men's voices, though, angry voices that carried from the vehicle camp he'd passed at dusk.

Two men appeared above him. They were a hundred yards west of his hiding place on the California road's shoulder. One man yelled, "Howdy," while the other man ran back down the road toward the vehicle camp.

Highwaymen. Men with hook knives and little sympathy. Likely they'd been hunting him since he'd passed their camp. Better to leave now, before full sunrise, so he wouldn't have to fight, not that he could in this condition.

Day Three. The fence lines Eddie walked were drifted ten feet thick and over the post tops. The piled dust and tumbleweed thatch were creating their own desert. High ground or low, two-lane or one, the smothered, lifeless landscape never changed. It was as if God had incinerated some other part of the world and dropped the ashes here. You couldn't kill a land any deader than this, not with gasoline, bombs, or the plague that had wiped out half of Europe. Western Oklahoma was just . . . gone, in its place a silent, barren, windswept graveyard.

Eddie arrived late that evening, pausing at the junction that led to the Owen family farm. He'd known it would be bad, but seeing his home in the colorless moonlight, it was obvious the farm was beaten to its limits. The barn he'd helped his father build, the machinery they'd run, the posts and wire they'd set and strung, all had finally succumbed to the battle. His baby brother, Howard, and little sister, Lois, ran to the road, coughing and churning great clouds of dust, grinning like it was Christmas snow. They shouted, "Eddie! Eddie!" and hugged both sides of him home every step.

His mother and father stood on the porch, kerchiefs tied across their faces, chins up but leaning on each other. Eddie walked toward the two strongest people he had ever known, he and his siblings shuffling through the dust, through a wasteland of family work and dreams. Eddie began to cry. He stopped and turned away, wiping mud streaks from his face. He was twenty-two. He had fifty-nine dollars left.

Inside at the table his mom tried to hide her concern for his condition. "You're fit, Eddie?"

"Ah, Mom, worry not." Eddie stroked her hair, no longer soft, and tried not to look out the window. The window had oiled rags stuffed in every edge. "Be back on top of it in no time. Same with all of us."

She coughed and said, "That's my boy."

Mildred-Mae coughed through dinner, too, and never stopped wiping dust off the table. Eddie noticed they all coughed. Out in the panhandle, young and old were dying of the "dust pneumonia"—coughing first, then a fever spike, then . . . funerals.

Newt wanted to know about Texas, the derrick explosion, the drilling business, the conditions in general; were there jobs for good engineers yet? For a farmer like him, willing to work at anything? For anyone? His mother wanted to know if Eddie had a girlfriend, if he ate properly in the hospital, was he going to church, when did the doctors say he'd be healthy again, and did anyone in Texas see an end to all this dismay?

Eddie delivered all the false hope he'd manufactured on the trip home along with the last of the drilling company's hospital money. He recuperated for six days, helping the family work hard at repairs that wouldn't slow or stop the inevitable. They did not discuss politics—communism, fascism—or California as an answer, but California was where the family was going, where they had to go.

Unable to sleep more than a few hours at a time, Eddie read his mother's saved *Amarillo Globe*s for the news that hadn't made it to the oilfield or hospital. The reports were grim. Millions continued to starve in the frozen, postrevolution, postwar Soviet Union. Their leader, Joseph Stalin, was "purging" his party's "Fascist traitors" and blaming Germany for repeated attempts to subvert the workers' revolution. Eddie's four years of history and political science had depicted Germany as decimated by the Great War, then plagued by rampant inflation. The *Globe* reports said Germany was once again plagued, this time by maniacal Fascist politicians, dangerous men bent upon rearmament and the expulsion of "all Communists and undesirables." In contrast, as Eddie read his mother's more recent *Globe*s, they reported that Germany was actually on the improve, a "Nazi economic miracle," the reporter called it.

Eddie had read and heard both opinions before. Sometimes in the same day.

Mixed into the yellowed stack of *Globe*s were recent editorials someone had torn from the *Tulsa World* and the *Kansas City Star* and sent to his mom. In the clippings, the newspaper editors admonished a number of world leaders for haranguing their hungry populations with incendiary speeches that demanded territory from their neighbors as an answer for empty bellies and what the newspapermen termed "incompetent leadership." A stated example was Italy had invaded a defenseless Ethiopia with France's concurrence. The editorials complained that not two decades had passed and the lessons learned in the trenches and mustard-gas battlefields of the Great War had been forgotten.

Eddie sensed there was more in the editorials than he'd actually read and reread for an answer. The newspapers mirrored the Walter Winchell radio broadcasts about the USA—soup kitchens and labor riots up north, drought down south and out west that Eddie didn't need a newspaper editor to see. The world was awash in bad news and blame. And had been—according to most of the newspapers and his professors at OU—since the Great Depression had begun the decade. Between the lines, the editors seemed to be saying there was worse on the way. Anonymous members of the banking and Wall Street communities were quoted in the *Globe* as saying how unfortunate it was that the assassination attempt on President Roosevelt had been unsuccessful. Eddie had to read that twice to believe it was *in print*. The same was true of the most recent "Prohibition" editorial *lamenting* its repeal.

Eddie shook his head. Hell, the only *good* news he'd heard in the last two years was the repeal of Prohibition—the Eighteenth Amendment that had outlawed alcohol was finally dead after fourteen years of forced temperance and tommy-gun headlines. At least now those without hope could drink, and any dog in this fight would be one more than most folks had. Eddie frowned. Except in Oklahoma and North Texas. Demonstrating the God-fearing tenacity that had sustained them thus far, Eddie's fellow citizens had chosen not to see alcohol as medicine. Their counties were to remain dry and heavily patrolled against the demon in the brown bottle. And according to the *Amarillo Globe*, that choice, however righteous and farsighted, was creating jobs that even in the Dust Bowl had no place.

More men than ever, the editorial said, some desperate, some who just lacked respect for the law, were becoming bootleggers, gangsters with the same violent flair as those Prohibition gangs who had serviced Chicago and New York. Eddie thought of Thurman Deets and his chalk beer. The driller had family in the illegal liquor business, had introduced Eddie to a thin, kind of frail fellow with three pistols and a dry sense of humor that didn't quite hide all the violence behind the words.

Eddie's mother coughed in the next room, dry and ragged. Eddie cringed. His mother coughed again. Was that God talking? *Everyone in this dusty farmhouse is going to die?* Eddie sat up bolt straight. *Die right here or on the road to California?* Eddie winced at hip pain, then stood fast onto the cold floor and straightened. Or . . . or was God saying that Eddie's family *shouldn't* have to die, here or in California's migrant camps?

Eddie blinked at the dark, then at the wall between him and his mom's ragged cough. *I'm fit enough to drive—but am I willing to break the law? Risk prison? Die in a hail of FBI bullets?* The Barrow gang had been shot dead, as had John Dillinger, Pretty Boy Floyd, and almost every other outlaw or bank robber the Great Depression had birthed.

But even if I am willing to break the law and risk prison, I'd have to know someone who had that kind of job, then convince him to give it to me instead of fifty other fellows in the same situation. And a job like that requires none of the skills I worked three jobs and four years to acquire.

Yeah, but it is money. Eddie's mom coughed again; a muffled sob followed, then his father's reassuring voice. Eddie glanced out a window that overlooked nothing but moonless dead and dark. Does God owe the Owen family one? Eddie waited for a discount revelation, "a burning bush," the glory shouters would've called it. His mother coughed again. The farmhouse went silent, only the wood walls creaking against the sixteen-penny nails.

Eddie stood still in the cold, silently asking for an answer, silently explaining to his parents a decision they could never hear out loud and would never accept. Hard times did not break a man's faith in God or family, his father would've said, faith in God and family were often all a man had. Grip both tight, go to work the next day in a coal mine or wheat field, and go an hour early. A man won 'cause he didn't quit what he believed.

At breakfast, Eddie held his mom's hand and smiled into his father's proud but wilted brown eyes. Then lied to the people he loved most. Eddie told his father there was a man he'd met on the rig, a man who owed him a favor; the man had work near Fort Worth, with automobiles. Eddie felt his mom's grip tighten on his hand. His father's eyes didn't blink. Newt studied his son. A year ago, Eddie would have had to defend the decision to his father's protective questions—who was the man? What was his history? How would he pay? But not in 1935; the dust had erased the luxury of protection.

Eddie added his best grin, said not to worry, there'd be no going to California. He kissed his mom Mildred-Mae good-bye, hugged

Newt, Lois, and Howard, and three days later talked his way into the only job that paid oilfield wages and could be done sitting. Driving a very fast car for one very dangerous man:

Lester "Benny" Binion.

March, 1936

Tonight, Eddie was using both lanes of the Jacksboro Highway, the real Thunder Road if you lived in North Texas, his boss's turf for the foreseeable future until Benny would kill two rivals and move west to open the legendary Horseshoe in Las Vegas, Nevada. Eddie was doing ninety in Benny's fresh-off-the-lot 1936 Lincoln V-12 Zephyr Sedan, risking a twenty-year prison sentence for the second time this month, like he did every month. The Lincoln was full, packed with forty cases of bonded Canadian whiskey headed for the blue-blood Petroleum Club in Oklahoma City.

It was early 1936 and while not a good year, it was *for sure* better than 1935's hospital bed and fear for his family. There'd been no letup in the dust-bowl weather, and everything Eddie's conscience had warned him about this rumrunner life had been true. Benny Binion's ten dollar bills kept the Owen farm away from the bank and the family together, but Eddie's Phi Beta Kappa key still couldn't open an office door or start a car, and the Colt .45 nervous in Eddie's belt could do both.

Eddie jiggled the custom Motorola radio, attempting to tune in Tommy Duncan's voice, decided two hands were more useful on the Lincoln's wheel, and quit jiggling. Eddie's headlights split just enough dust and dark that he mashed the brakes before rear-ending the stalled Buick Roadmaster and the two dusty citizens arguing behind the trunk. All four of their hands were visible in his headlights and empty, and all punching each other with a drinking man's late-night precision. Eddie stepped one work boot out onto the cold concrete, drew the Colt he forgot to cock, and finally fired two rounds in the air. He and the men cringed at the first shot and the men staggered apart at the second.

Probably not highwaymen.

Eddie leaned into his best Cushing accent: "Forty of them assholes from Dallas headed this way, fellas. I'd be home protecting my property if I had any."

Both men hitched suspenders and stuffed at tattered shirt-tails. "Dallas assholes" in North Texas meant the federal law. Eddie tipped the short-brimmed fedora favored by schoolteachers and the deceased Clyde Barrow, slid into the Lincoln, hit first gear like he meant it, and squealed around the Buick. He sincerely hoped the boys would move before they added to the Jacksboro's every-weekend death toll.

The next twenty miles required fifteen minutes and a fair amount of steering to avoid withered tumbleweeds and herds of jackrabbits waiting for their chance to die. A last-second swerve missed the fender of a lightless, slow-moving Model T tied together with cords and hope. In the far-off night-covered nothing to Eddie's right, specs of light glimmered. Another three miles and the road bent right. The glimmer became neon. Blue, red, and green tubes lit the eaves of a low-roofed roadhouse set back deep from the road and semisurrounded by cheap transportation: Pappy Kirkwood's Four Deuces. A man with money could gamble there, and legal, too, because Pappy lived in the back—in Texas it was legal to gamble in your house. Pappy's house was big by Depression standards, held three hundred, had five bars and twelve tables, ten poker and two dice. Pappy also seemed to know a number of women who wore makeup and would dance with a stranger. Sally Rand in particular. And on a weeknight when she wasn't headlining in Fort Worth, Sally was known to hold court at the back bar, smiling her way through the pocketbooks of oilfield gentlemen and occasionally a roughneck's affections. Eddie slowed and considered stopping to see if Miss Rand was in and if he was sufficiently mended to dance. He'd lack money to spend, but Miss Rand had smiled at him last month just beyond Pappy's front door like that might not matter.

Eddie wrestled with a young man's hormones, decided it was too risky with forty cases of whiskey aboard, found a sweet spot in the Lincoln's seat, and nudged the gas pedal. Twenty car lengths after he passed the Four Deuces's lot, headlights swerved out onto the road behind him. Eddie added gas—seventy, eighty, ninety. The Lincoln had a hundred and fifty horsepower in an eighty horse-power world. If the headlights didn't fade or turn, it was hijackers or the law. Benny Binion didn't run from either, but his drivers ran from both; stand and fight was for the newsreels.

The headlights stayed in his mirror. Eddie's heart added beats. He nudged the gas. The lights stayed bright. Exhale. *Time to earn your money.* Eddie's foot asked for it all. The V-12 shoved him into the upholstery and straightened his arms. He checked the needle—full-out one-twenty—then the mirror. The lights went high beam and charged at his bumper. *Whatever it is, it's fast.* Eddie clenched the wheel, hoping to steer darkness that killed people at half this speed. In tandem, he and the other car veered past slower traffic and roadkill. Eddie's breath came faster. *Twenty years in prison. Family loses everything.*

The curve at Springtown almost killed him. Twenty miles, then twenty-five . . . another curve, this one with a dead piece of live oak in it. Eddie slid, the tires buckled, he righted and risked the mirror. *Please be just a bar asshole playing chicken . . .*

And . . . *shit*: more sets of headlights, flashing lights, too. That'd be the law. More than a hundred miles of Texas left. Make the Red River and be fine. *Unless there's a roadblock.* Eddie's mirrors glared. The Lincoln's interior flashed blue-red from behind. They'd be shooting soon. Man, this was a hard way for a "brilliant" engineer to make a living. Eddie grimaced. "Brilliant" seemed a bit overstated just now. His lights struck a dented farm truck bent down over its rear axle, the bed loaded with— Four people at the shoulder, two of them making *X*s with both hands. A kitchen apron in blue checks, a rail-thin man in a beaten hat . . . then a kid, scruffy and frozen midroad grabbing for a dog—

SHIT— Eddie picked stupid and swerved. He may have missed the kid, but not the bar ditch, and at one twenty, in Benny Binion's new Lincoln loaded with whiskey, that was the definition of stupid. The big sedan's headlights corkscrewed into the night. The Lincoln landed hard and began to roll.

CHAPTER 3

March, 1936

The room was dim for heaven, bright for a jail cell, and white. It had nurses and sheets and tubes . . . and handcuffs. Eddie tugged his left hand. Yup, handcuffs. The body parts he could feel announced themselves by shooting various levels of pain. He decided to remain still until the hard-eyed man sitting on his bed quit shaking him and said something.

"Eddie?"

"Ah . . . yeah?"

"You seeing me okay?"

Eddie nodded, seeing at least two.

"Time's a wastin'." The man speaking was Floyd Merewether, Benny Binion's top lieutenant, a 170-pound ex-Gulf-Coast stevedore who legend said John Dillinger chose not to fight with his hands or a gun. Behind Floyd were two policemen with their backs to Eddie's door, their uniforms covering two sets of broad shoulders.

"There's an engineerin' job for you up north with something called the Culpepper Oil Products Company. Long way away and

$115 a week. Room's a dollar a day; same for the food, leaves you $55 clear. A teacher of yours from that college, Harold Culpepper, asked somebody up there at the Petroleum Club. They sent this Culpepper to Benny; man said he's been hunting you since December last. Benny planned on telling you after Okie City."

Fifty clear meant the forty a week Eddie was sending to Oklahoma would continue—the bankers could kiss his father's ass. Eddie's face wondered how that would fit with the handcuffs connecting him to the bed.

Floyd said, "Talked to the sheriff—my uncle by my dad's sister. I'd be on the Rock Island for Chicago, ten a.m." Floyd Merewether did not give idle advice. "You got an hour. Benny says you owe for his Lincoln. Stay out of Texas awhile. Stay in touch, but no telephone. *Ever.* Don't know why, Eddie boy, but Benny thinks you got talent." The lieutenant smiled like he agreed, then unfolded to his feet. Two nickel-plated Smith revolvers were tight between his belt and wool vest. He patted Eddie's leg and tossed a handcuff key on the bed. "Me? I think Benny always wanted to be a farmer."

Eddie palmed the key. "Hey, Floyd, the kid with . . . the one in the road. I missed him, right?"

Floyd Merewether's eyes narrowed. "Yeah, you missed him." He nodded at the uniforms in the hall. "Copper's car didn't. Benny's paying your respects to the family. You be gone on the Rock Island, Eddie. They hang people in this county."

At the same moment that Eddie stepped off the passenger platform and onto the Rock Island train, Montague County impanelled a jury of temperance-minded citizens who intended to charge Edward Fred Owen with manslaughter and bootlegging. If the temperance-minded prosecutor could elevate the boy's death to murder—and the prosecutor thought he could—Eddie Owen would hang.

Eddie took a nervous window seat for his two days and nights aboard the rackety rolling stock of the Chicago Rock Island. A Texas Ranger boarded the car and rode from Sanger to Gainesville. God and luck kept the Ranger occupied with the constant conversation of a man and his two daughters, the man wanting to know who was at fault for all this misery. The car grew colder as they rolled into Oklahoma, the dust thicker, the sun a heatless glow. Whistle stops produced a trickle of new passengers. At each stop, armed deputies stood the platforms, hard-looking men, rangy and under-paid, pistols high on their hips and bandannas across their noses and mouths. The Rock Island made Missouri at sunset. Floyd had said, get this far and you're likely jake.

Leaving Joplin, Eddie quit imagining prison and the gallows, but safety and night produced no sleep, only endless replays of the little boy and his dog. Eddie realized he didn't know the boy's name.

A frosty dawn broke across the Midwest. Eddie washed his face in the train's lavatory, straightened clothes he'd slept in twice, and stepped off the Rock Island 1,200 miles north in Chicago, Illinois, no more comfortable than when he'd boarded. By now there would be wanted posters in Texas. It didn't matter that he had parents and siblings to support—Eddie Owen was a fugitive, *a gangster* by proper standards, and, he guessed, deservedly so. His reunion with a college professor who couldn't find "integrity" with a microscope somehow seemed fitting.

A thunderous, modern metropolis did Eddie a favor; Chicago forced him to deal with Chicago instead of thinking about the dead little boy and his dog. *Everything* here was moving—trains, people, cars, trucks, wagons—all in different directions. Even at a distance the buildings could block midmorning sun. These were the "sky-scrapers" of Louis Sullivan and Daniel Burnham, in person and three times as tall as any structure Eddie had ever seen. Chicago truly was a "World's Fair City." Engineering theory brought to life.

Eddie bumped and bustled through jammed boulevards filled to both curbs with cars and trucks and oogle horns and exhaust. He marveled at almost everything, unembarrassed, bumping shoulders with flannelled, rough-shaven men, caps tight to their eyes, their accents fast and Irish. And a lot of them angry. Eddie apologized as often as he said hello.

Separating two of the impossible skyscrapers was a mammoth brick warehouse constructed on an entire city block. Along the east wall, men of every size and shape inched forward in a line that reached the whole block from corner to corner. The men were broad and narrow, stooped and straight, their clothes clean and dirty. Some wore hats like Eddie's father. All were silent. The effect was ghostly, a combination of overall quiet defeat and the occasional glare of real violence. The crowds walking the sidewalk pushed Eddie forward and paid the line of men no notice. Eddie followed the line around the first corner and down that block, then around a second corner and another city block. The line of men ended around a third corner midblock at a foggy storefront serving soup through one open door. Walter Winchell's "soup kitchens" in person.

On almost every Winchell broadcast that Eddie'd heard, Winchell warned President Roosevelt that soup kitchens were not the answer to no work. Americans wanted an honest future, not communism and charity. Eddie wasn't sure Mr. Winchell had ever been hungry. Opposite the soup kitchen's serving door, a crowd had gathered and spilled into the street. Vehicles belched exhaust and honked to push the crowd back. The crowd shook their fists at—or maybe with—a man on a soapbox shouting, "Roosevelt's the devil, boys! He's to blame! The New Deal is No Deal!"

Eddie kind of liked Roosevelt, the Fireside Chats for sure, and moved on. At the intersection, two lantern-jawed fellows pushed pamphlets at his chest. Swastikas were emblazoned across the headlines:

JEW BANKS & COMMUNIST MASTERS.
IS THAT WHAT AMERICANS WANT?
SAVE AMERICA!
JOIN THE GERMAN-AMERICAN BUND

Two blocks farther down, five men in clean work clothes stood boxes and waved papers, asking everyone who passed or stopped if they valued workers' rights and democracy. The man on the tallest box shouted: "Do you fear J.P. Morgan and his foreclosure banks? DuPont and his strikebreakers? Rockefeller and the Wall Street speculators who put us in breadlines? Stop the Fascists before they destroy us again! Join the American Communist Party! No more lies!" The Communists' crowd was growing, spilling deeper into the intersection. Men came from across the street and began to argue and shove, forcing Eddie to dodge horns and bumpers and more shouters until he found the front door of the Carbon and Carbide Building. Eddie the engineer grinned at all forty stories until his neck cramped and the sun blinded him into the lobby.

The ornate elevator was a rocket compared to the two he'd been in, and he said as much to the black operator. The outer office of Culpepper Oil Products Company was no less ornate, staffed with a smiling, stylish receptionist and furnished with ox-blood leather furniture. Behind the receptionist's red hair and wide shoulders, two windows overlooked endless green water that met the horizon in three directions. Lake Michigan had to be a misnamed ocean.

Eddie turned . . . and froze.

A policeman's pockmarked face and brushy mustache shadowed in the far corner. The lamps on either side of the man's wing chair were turned off. Eddie faked a smile. *The Montague County police couldn't get to this office this fast. Could they?* The policeman leaned into the sunlight. His uniform was Army Air Corps—not the police—a major, and a hard-looking one. But the mustache? Did the Army Air Corps allow mustaches?

Harold Culpepper rushed into the space between them, his hand extended to Eddie. "Welcome, Eddie. Welcome to the *Windeee Citeee*." Culpepper pumped Eddie's hand and circled an arm around Eddie's shoulder.

The greeting was too theatrical to be honest, but definitely not how anyone would greet a fugitive if he knew a fugitive was what Eddie was— "C'mon in, we're in the swim."

Eddie shied at the familiarity and the lingo. Forty-three-year-old Harold Culpepper seemed awfully juked-up for an ex–college professor. His expensive tricolor sweater-vest and billowy trousers were what Clark Gable wore in the *Hollywood On Parade* newsreels. When at OU, "Professor" Culpepper had avoided flash like it was tenure poison. The new Harold Culpepper herded Eddie away from the Army Air Corps major and into a magnificent office. Culpepper made pistol fingers toward Eddie and an empty chair like he and Eddie were jitterbugging.

Eddie sat, tried to sneak-eye back to the major but couldn't. Harold Culpepper rounded a leather-topped desk to his chair and tossed Eddie today's *Chicago Tribune*. "Take a look." The March 7 headline read: HITLER MARCHES INTO RHINELAND, VERSAILLES TREATY BROKEN. The second sentence explained "the Rhineland" as a slice of Western Germany taken and kept by the victorious Allies after the Great War. The slice of former German territory had been reconstituted as a demilitarized zone, a buffer for France's protection. Germany's new Chancellor/Führer Adolf Hitler had charged that France intended to occupy and steal the territory, so, today, Germany had invaded first. The French were furious and massing tanks at their border.

Okay . . . I'm sure that matters to France and Germany. Eddie checked Harold Culpepper, now mesmerized by his own fingernails.

Maybe I'm supposed to keep reading. Paragraph two said the Treaty of Versailles also covered armaments outlawed after the Great War, armaments Germany had been mass-producing in open defiance of the USA, England, France, and Russia. The reporter seemed pretty concerned about this now that the Germans had actually marched somewhere.

Eddie was an ominous three lines into a list of those armaments when Harold Culpepper said: "That Hitler and his Nazis are plenty rugged, eh, man, unifying Germany's territory like that? Fine with me. Somebody's got to stop the Bolsheviks from overrunning Europe. France and England won't. Wouldn't want to be a Jew, though, not in that spat—Hitler and Joe Stalin don't care for . . ." Culpepper extended his nose with his index finger. "*The bankers of Judah.*"

Culpepper's caricature and emphasis on "the bankers of Judah" sounded like an indictment, although Eddie wasn't clear why. Eddie wondered out loud at the professor's newly hip diction and political interest, given that the professor's history had neither.

Harold Culpepper pointed down toward the street instead. "Labor Communists on every other corner. Unionists, the whole lot"—Culpepper made the index finger by his nose into a conductor's orchestra baton—"singing breadline ballads to you and me and the apple tree."

Eddie took a wild guess that this was a criticism of the country's two largest labor federations, the AFL and the CIO, and their reported infiltration by the Communists. "Unionism" was being assailed by the Hearst newspapers and Wall Street bankers as grossly un-American and, in some cases, treason.

Harold Culpepper said, "No AFL or CIO in this shop, not as long as this American has the right to vote." The juked-up ex-professor beamed and grabbed a golf putter leaning against his desk. "Now to business, Eddie-boy. Your employer, and mine, the Culpepper Oil Products Company, has the *refinery modification* patent for catalytic cracking. How about that?"

"Ah . . . congratulations?"

"Catalytic Reforming. Alkylation and isomerization. Platinum platforming, the undergrad project I had you working on in '33 and '34. That's the ticket behind the grind."

What the "ticket" was to, Eddie couldn't guess. "Behind the grind" implied that Eddie had been late with his participation in the platinum platforming project, when in fact *Eddie's* theoretical refinery designs had been on time and all Eddie's.

Professor Culpepper had taken the credit. The program then received a substantial increase in funding from the US Army Air Corps, giving the university a reason to look past some very troubling allegations regarding their professor's private life. The program's expansion benefited so many at the university that Eddie had swallowed hard and remained silent, the smart thing for a scholarship undergrad to do in the Great Depression.

"Ticket to what?" Eddie asked, allowing himself to wonder if the engineering profession he'd worked day and night to join might actually have a spot for him.

"AvGas. Aviation gas, 100-octane, your future. And mine." Harold Culpepper extended the woven-leather grip of the putter past Eddie's shoulder toward the major in the outer office. "And his." The Army Air Corps major and his hip now shared the corner of the receptionist's desk. The major's eyes weren't on her and should've been; they were on Eddie. Eddie summed his surroundings: ex–college professor, big-city oil-company office that lacked any other part of an operating oil company, and a high-rank Army Air Corps officer cooling his heels who emanated enough threat to be a coiled diamondback. Eddie turned to Harold Culpepper and went with the obvious question first. "There aren't any engines that burn 100-octane, as in none."

"Are now." Harold Culpepper nodded toward the major. "A company in New Jersey used our designs to commercially refine

100-octane gas last December. Gents from the Army Air Corps like that major out there have been designing and redesigning engines night and day since."

Eddie glanced at the *Chicago Tribune* and a picture of Hitler congratulating Mussolini on Italy's air strikes in Ethiopia, then back to Harold Culpepper, the unmarred soles of Bass Weejun loafers Harold shouldn't be able to afford now crossed on the desk.

The new 1936-model Culpepper adjusted expensive argyle socks that matched his sweater-vest. "This 100-octane AvGas produces a thirty percent increase in engine power but no increase in engine temperatures. Adds range, just like we suspected, even to existing engines."

Eddie processed the "we" without changing his expression, then cocked the side of his head at the major beyond the doorway. "And the Army Air Corps will need range?"

"Soon, so they say. *Lots* of range." Harold Culpepper made a grin functional drunks reserved for the first drink of the night. "Ever been on an airplane?"

"Can't say as I have."

"Ever ridden a camel?"

Eddie added a small, very tentative headshake, thinking *steady job* and *wanted fugitive* thoughts. "They have camels in Chicago?"

"You'll go to Indiana first—run the tests at the refinery there." Culpepper pointed over his shoulder southeast. "Lots of disbelievers on that payroll. If you can prove Culpepper Oil Products Company has the answer, then you've got a job. You'll be the next T. E. Lawrence."

Job sounded great. *Engineering job* so grand it was hard to believe. But T. E. Lawrence was "Lawrence of Arabia." The Great War, camels from Wadi Rum to Aqaba—

Culpepper widened his eyes and bobbed his head . . . as if being shot at by Turks and Arabs would be the most fun a guy could have.

April, 1936

Indiana's spring had broken but turned cold as winter. Eddie had spent his first thirty-three nights sleeping on clean sheets at Chicago's Allerton Hotel and fourteen-hour days at the Standard Oil/Royal Shell refinery in East Chicago, Indiana. The men and bosses Eddie worked with were hard, serious fellows who kept their hands busy, their mouths shut, and their political opinions to themselves. Only the three foremen knew what they were building and testing, the secret structural modifications that Eddie'd helped invent. Eddie kept that pride to himself, but it was there. He'd found a key others couldn't and he'd muddled through theoretical designs that could make his key work, or so he hoped. Eddie's modifications were dangerous and had never been attempted outside a laboratory. Modifying a facility of this scale was testimony to *someone's* urgency. It was an engineering leap from a circus cannon to Jules Verne's Moon Gun.

June, 1936

Eddie arrived at Standard of Indiana's downtown Chicago offices straight from the work deck of his two-hundred-foot cracking tower. In twenty-four hours the tower would go online. Seated at the long table in Standard Oil's boardroom were ten somber men in dark blue and dark gray suits. The man at the head of the table was Standard Oil's senior vice president and responsible for the refinery that housed Eddie's modifications. It was one of the largest refineries in the world. The men continued their discussion without acknowledging Eddie's arrival. Eddie's fingernails were dirty, his work pants stained, his stack of papers and folders wrinkled. He dropped his papers on the table in front of the chair where the secretary pointed him and sat down.

A gray-suited and silent Harold Culpepper sat alone at the table's far end. Eddie recognized three others. Two of them were

Engineering Fellows from Johns Hopkins University. Their 1933 textbook on petroleum engineering was considered the industry bible. The most important of the three was Conrad R.L. Chenoweth, the Babe Ruth of mechanical engineering. Large in size and bearing, Mr. Chenoweth pointed down the table at Eddie. Eddie scrambled for a fountain pen to get his first autograph.

Mr. Chenoweth said, "Mr. Owen's *collegiate* spirit and accolades have their place, as does his pursuit of gainful employment. That place is not here. Mr. Owen's calculations are flawed or they are outright fabrications. Your East Chicago refinery will be a ball of fire. There are no circumstances where I, or my colleagues"—Chenoweth gestured across the table—"will sign off on *anything* other than a complete halt to the Culpepper/Army Air Corps project."

Harold Culpepper exhaled but offered no rebuttal. One Johns Hopkins Fellow turned his slide rule toward the senior vice president and two corporate oilmen at the table. "Simply put, the 'controlled' reaction in Mr. Owen's tower cannot produce the desired catalytic alkylation and isomerization result . . . other than on paper, and even there, it is sufficiently questionable as to imply dishonesty."

The senior vice president kept his hands folded in front of him and shifted just his eyes to Eddie for his answer. Eddie looked at the best minds in engineering, then his stained papers stacked between his dirty hands, then his hands. "Um . . . ah, with all due respect." Eddie cleared his throat. "Mr. Chenoweth and his esteemed colleagues"—cringe, dry swallow—"are wrong."

Chenoweth sipped coffee, set the cup down, and turned to excuse himself. The vice president said to Eddie, "And your proof, Mr. Owen? These notable men in your field do not see it. They see naiveté *or worse*, and grave, grave consequences."

Eddie dry swallowed again. He would have eaten live centipedes to work for any of the three engineers at this table. Eddie inhaled and said, "The best men Standard Oil has built these modifications.

We ran all these tests." Eddie tapped his folders. "Ran them *live*, not on *paper*. The welds are perfect. They will hold; the vessel is tuned. The project is complete. It will work. The slide rules are wrong."

The Johns Hopkins Fellow shook his head and lowered his slide rule. He said, "Gentlemen. Sadly, the stunning lack of competence demonstrated here is why the USA is still lost in the Great Depression while Germany has risen from the rubble of the Great War."

The senior vice president thanked Eddie and dismissed him. Harold Culpepper was asked/told to stay. On his way out, Eddie stopped at the door, turned to the men at the table, and said, "I can *see* the reaction inside the tower, inside the chamber—the heat, the colors—I can *smell* it. The modifications will work. No one else has to be there; I'll throw the switch myself."

Sunset was flattening Lake Michigan to dark. Harold Culpepper's secretary showed Eddie into her boss's office. Culpepper sat behind his desk wearing the same somber gray suit from earlier in the afternoon. There was no jazzy patter, no argyle socks. Culpepper said, "Do you know the term 'savant.'"

Eddie shook his head.

"Two of the plant's three foremen were called in after you were dismissed. The foremen think that's what you are. A version of James Pullen, the asylum carpenter who builds the impossible."

Eddie declined a compliment he didn't deserve. "The *foremen* are your 'savants.' They built it; they oughta know."

"The VPs grilled both foremen, as did Chenoweth. Credentials were challenged. Dire consequences were, and are, predicted." Culpepper stared. "Are you *sure*, Eddie?"

"Sure enough I'll throw the switch myself."

Culpepper swallowed, looked around the room, then at the document on his desk. He looked like a man in a corner, exhaled deeply, and sighed. "If you fail, they will own all my stock in Culpepper Oil Products Company, all my rights to all our patents. I will have nothing."

Eddie shut his eyes, said a silent, *Thanks, I think*, and nodded with all the confidence he had. "It'll work, Mr. Culpepper. I need this job and the next one. And I can't afford to die."

Tonight was Eddie's last Tuesday in the USA. Earlier this morning a jubilant, sweaty, relieved Standard Oil senior vice president had told Eddie, "pack for Bahrain." The SVP and the two foremen had dutifully witnessed Eddie's two-hundred-foot cracking tower go online, not explode, and produce Standard Oil's first gallon of 100-octane aviation gasoline.

While the crews were still cheering from the far fences, Harold Culpepper whisked Eddie to the Culpeper office, presented him with a multi-page employment contract, then shared a glass of bourbon and pointed at a globe next to his desk. Culpepper told Eddie his first stop would be ten thousand miles east in Bahrain. "Bahrain is a group of thirty-three desert islands on the western edge of the Arabian Gulf. Standard Oil of California and the Texas Company are building a refinery there after signing a 'need to know' agreement with 'someone.' This agreement allows for a portion of the refinery's design to be modified so AvGas can be produced by 1937. And no, Eddie, you don't need to know who or why to do this job. Oaky-Smokey? A twenty-four-hour bodyguard will be at your side. Just be glad you're the cat's pajamas, the first person on planet Earth who the moolah men believe can make these modifications without incinerating their *very* expensive refineries. Or crashing all the test pilots who'll test the gas."

Eddie balked big. "Pilots will fly my gas before I know it's consistently good?"

Culpepper shrugged. "We live in troubled times, Eddie. Your green light to throw the switch this morning was all the proof you'll ever need." Culpepper wiped theatrical sweat from his brow.

The news abroad *was* bad. Unfortunately, Eddie's family in Oklahoma had no hope but him. And if the Texas Rangers working Montague County decided to track Eddie Owen outside of Texas, Bahrain would be a long, long way to reach. The incredibly good news was Eddie was about to be given the keys to the kingdom, not the keys to a jobsite latrine to clean. Eddie signed the contract, drank the bourbon, and called his folks. God bless Standard Oil, the Owen family had a job, a job his parents could know about.

Ten hours later, Eddie was in the Allerton Hotel's plush elevator, awash in equal parts success, relief, and trepidation, a guest of Harold Culpepper for Eddie's *bon voyage* dinner in the Allerton's world-famous Tip Top Tap. The saloon and its intimate tables were on the twenty-third floor, crowded with swooning Northwestern coeds and their trust-fund dates. Perry Como sat a stagy barstool crooning "Lazy Weather," the pin spot tight on his extra-large head and pink V-neck sweater.

From the table to his left, Eddie heard, "German-American Bund," and, "We must stand *together* against the Communist Internationale." He turned to three men and a woman deep in discussion instead of swooning. The woman's glance landed, then lingered, unruffled and smoky. Her hair was tight dishwater blond above Joan Crawford shoulders. A gold ring circled a long finger sheathed in a black velvet glove. The finger slowly traced a high cheekbone; she looked like she might purr but didn't.

She said, "*Guten Abend.*"

Before Eddie could answer, she was tugged politely back into her companions' discussion. Eddie felt the room temperature rise and grinned to ask the woman to dance—

A man eased into the empty seat across from Eddie that Harold Culpepper had just vacated. Three months ago, Eddie had seen the man in Harold Culpepper's office. Now the major was sans his Army Air Corps uniform and summoning a waiter to their table.

The major leaned into Eddie's face, forcing Eddie back in the previously comfortable chair. "You're shipping out under contract tomorrow, New York, London, Istanbul, Baghdad, then Bahrain. Don't contact your family in Oklahoma; I'll handle that."

The major nodded Eddie at an oblivious, half-drunk Harold Culpepper buying tobacco he didn't smoke from an almost-dressed cigarette girl. "Actually, Harold will. Forty a week of your check goes direct to Oklahoma like you been doing."

Eddie glanced back to the table on his left. The German woman was no longer smiling at him; she was staring at the major, her mouth a tight line. Eddie followed her eyes to him. "How's it you and the Army Air Corps know when and where I'm going? Or where my family lives?" Eddie leaned forward. "With all due respect, Major, my family and where they get their money are none of your concern."

A hint of North Texas drawl came with the major's answer. "I know a lot about you and your family, Mr. Owen. And Harold's. In fact, I know enough about Harold and Oklahoma that he made this job for me. Pays well and requires so little effort I can spend my nights in places like this."

That sounded like blackmail. Of Harold Culpepper for sure. Eddie tensed for the consequences that might come with the North Texas drawl. The major's other hand rose to the table. The hand was a claw, the first three fingers missing at the second knuckle. *USMC* was tattooed small on the inside of his wrist. The waiter the major had summoned arrived and bent at the waist. The major stared at the blond woman while he whispered to the waiter's ear.

The waiter stiffened so quickly it flapped the towel covering his silver tray. He located Harold Culpepper's shape in the crowd, mouthed, *Yes sir*, to the major, and heel-turned in Harold's direction.

The major pointed Eddie toward the elevators. "Harold's gonna be busy with our waiter. Let's you and I take a walk. See what part of your life I can concern myself with and what I can't."

Eddie checked the blonde, then Perry Como, then the least pleasant of his new companions and his claw hand. Their walk finished in the front seat of the major's coupe, stopped and parked just shy of the Biograph Theater on Lincoln Avenue, the now infamous theater where John Dillinger had been shot dead by the FBI two years ago. Nothing had been said about Eddie being a fugitive, but the major's chosen parking space couldn't have been an accident. Eddie read the marquee backlit in black: *Frankie and Johnny*. Under the bright lights, fur-collared swells huddled out of the drizzle and away from the less fortunate.

The major lit a Chesterfield using the mangled hand as if it weren't. "Three years ago, gangsters from here—'the Italian Mafia' as we call 'em—assassinated Chicago's mayor Anton Cermak in Miami."

Eddie had read about the assassination in the Oklahoma City papers. Big news because Cermak had been standing next to President-elect Roosevelt.

"The Miami police said the gunman 'confessed,' said he was paid to kill Cermak by Al Capone. That confession never happened. Cermak was window-dressing and Capone had nothing to do with it. The real target was President-elect Roosevelt. It was a coup d'état."

Eddie turned back from his window. "What?"

"The assassin wasn't supposed to survive the attempt. When they got him to Washington, he told a different story, said he was there to kill Roosevelt. Elements inside our federal government were pressured to sequester him, which they did. They held his trial, convicted him of first-degree murder, and executed him . . . all in thirty-three days."

The major's eyes moved across the couples under the marquee, his tone deteriorating.

"Four months later President Roosevelt rescinded the gold standard as part of his 'New Deal' promises and began printing money to kill the Depression and help the little man. The same conspirators tried again that November and they'll keep trying till our president is dead and their man's in office."

Eddie wide-eyed the revelation.

"But Eddie Owen and I aren't gonna let that happen."

"Me?"

"World's nothing like you think, Mr. Owen. It's crumbling again, coming apart, worse than what makes the radio and the papers." The major drew a triangle on his windshield and pointed at the corners. "Pay attention. This information is gonna keep you alive or kill you: Present day, 1936, there are three major powers— us; the Russians; and the big dog, England. Real soon there'll be two more—Germany and Japan—five total by 1937 or '38."

Eddie imagined the five-sided triangle. He'd listened to the radio and read the Chicago papers all spring like anybody would— from an interested distance. That distance had just been shrunk to zero. Eddie did the math: AvGas. The major continued.

"Three months ago the Jap military attempted a coup d'état. They killed a bunch of politicians but didn't get the prime minister. Didn't matter. What the Jap army did get was lots more power. If you're a Russian Communist, a militarized Japan is not a comforting thought. Why? Japan has close ties to Germany. Germany is rearming fast and furious, massing an illegal, mechanized, Fascist army that ain't a fan of Joe Stalin, either. Hitler says Stalin and his Red Army plan to invade Europe, colonize it into their 'Communist workers collective.' Hitler plans to be ready."

Eddie could guess what "plans to be ready" meant.

The major confirmed Eddie's guess before he could finish the thought. "War's coming . . . on a scale a college boy can't imagine. The stakes are who rules the world—the Capitalists, the Fascists, or the Communists. The Capitalists are the swing vote. If they side with the Fascists and win, the world gets one system of interconnected strongmen. If the Capitalists go with the Communists and win, the world gets border and trade fences and an uneasy truce that won't last. Whoever wins, the strong will eat the weak 'cause they always do. But you know all about that, don't you."

Smeary headlights half lit the major's thick horseshoe mustache and the pockmarks that marred his face. When the lights passed, he continued.

"Powerful interests in this country are picking sides in the coming fight and you best understand they ain't picking the same ones. That is a serious goddamn problem . . . a problem that kills presidents, builds factories, and marches armies."

The major dragged on the Chesterfield, then cut his eyes to Eddie and added a small, unpleasant smile.

"Not much different than the Jacksboro Highway. Put a federal revenuer warrant on somebody and a sharecropper's dead nine-year-old." The major shook his head at bad luck. "That'd be a serious goddamn problem, too. And tough to explain to a fellow's family, them takin' blood money and all."

Eddie flushed. His eyes narrowed.

The major nodded to himself. "Heard an escapee can do twenty years on a road gang in Montague County . . . or hang, depending on the mood of the day. Suppose a fellow'd be lucky if the nine-year-old were a Jew, although I can't see how that should matter."

The money Eddie had sent for the sharecropper farmer and his family was all Eddie had that didn't go to Cushing, and not much considering their loss. Floyd Merewether had sent the money back with a note saying to move on, that Benny had taken care of it. Eddie did get the boy's name and where he was buried. Franklin Nadler, age nine.

"We understand each other, convict?"

The major pulled a Colt .45 from his belt and pushed it at Eddie. "They say you boxed light-heavy in college and know how to use one of these. You'd better where you're going." The major checked another set of headlights, these in his rearview mirror, and waited until the glare and car passed. "In Bahrain you'll meet a Brownsville cowboy named D.J. Bennett. He'll work with you on the refinery, although he couldn't pump gas if you gave him the handle. Bennett will see to your protection when your ass is in the fire. And it will be."

Rain rivered on the coupe's windows and Eddie heard Benny Binion in his ear whispering, *No point in being somebody's sucker. The short money's always that, and usually expensive.*

Eddie said, "Why do I need an army-issue Colt and a body-guard to be a petroleum engineer? Didn't when I graduated."

The major frowned. "Your problems in Texas are serious, Mr. Owen, as are Mr. Culpepper's in Oklahoma. Very serious. Worse, as I explained, I know all about 'em. Worse, still, I know men in authority who'd be eternally grateful if I handed your asses to them."

Eddie kept the Colt in his lap.

"*Technically* speaking you're working for Harold Culpepper's company, but all his money comes from another company in that Carbon and Carbide Building that I don't care for much, either."

"Standard Oil? What's wrong with Standard Oil?"

The major frowned an already soured face. "Regardless of the crap you hear and read in the Hearst papers, Roosevelt will be reelected in a landslide. After he's sworn in, he'll be assassinated in favor of his vice president, John 'Cactus Jack' Garner. Although Garner has never said it in public, Garner hates everything about the New Deal, labor unions, and Communists. When he's president, he'll admit it, return to the gold standard, and side us with Germany."

Eddie shied, like you would from a loud drunk with a broken bottle or a mental patient who should be in a straightjacket but wasn't. "Ah . . . *someone* intends to assassinate President Roosevelt so we'll side with the Fascists . . . in a war . . . that hasn't started?"

The major turned just his head like an evil Charlie McCarthy ventriloquist dummy. "And you find that hard to believe. Because of your vast fucking experience outside Oklahoma and Itasca, Texas."

"Well, I—"

"Listen, sonny, our Wall Street bankers and captains of industry are just fine with Hitler. They say *someone* has to stop the Communists and their labor unions or the Communists will bury the world's democracies in another Depression." The major pointed at the triangle of his windshield. "And for the record, the big dog king of England agrees."

Eddie said, "My family's still in the Depression, Major. So *any* answer that ends it is a damn good idea. And from what I've read and heard, Stalin's Communists seemed dead set on pouring fire across Europe, so stopping the Communists might be a good idea, too."

The major's cheeks reddened, pushing heat into his scars. "I've seen the Jerries in person, college boy, in the trenches steel to steel. Seen towns after Jerries' been there."

A long silence followed, as if the major were deciding whether to continue. Finally he flexed his neck, raising the square chin, and said:

"We're having this conversation because somebody found an ocean of oil under the desert where you're headed. Keeps getting bigger . . . fuel the world's moneymen want worse than male children. All the oil the Fascists, Communists, and Capitalists will need to march their armies at one another. And once these dumb bastard bankers and munitions makers start this war—in Europe or Russia or maybe the Balkans again—it'll spread . . . like a plague. No way these turncoat sons-a-bitches here will be able to stop it where and when they want. Your aviation gas is the antidote. With luck, Mr. Roosevelt can be protected, kept alive long enough to try these Wall Street and Detroit bastards for treason. Then we'll use your gas to bomb their Nazi friends back to their fucking castles."

"*We*, meaning the Army Air Corps?"

The major didn't answer.

Eddie felt the noose around his neck but couldn't see who held it. "Who wears an Army Air Corps uniform but has USMC on his wrist? And how's it you have the inside scoop on the world's politics?"

The major inspected his USMC tattoo. Chesterfield smoke hid his expression. "You and the rest of this democracy's citizens aren't paying attention. It's a bad habit."

"I pay attention."

"Yeah? Like that blonde and her playmates speaking German tonight. Six to five she's Nazi Luftwaffe and you'll see her again, somewhere, an accident, but she'll be there, on the arm of somebody you trust . . . You don't have a clue, Mr. Owen, but your ass better get one."

Eddie cocked his head to answer.

"And you better get it soon, 'cause the USA won't be neutral forever. 'Our side,' and whoever ends up deciding our nation's intentions, needs 100-octane AvGas if we figure on being anything but prisoners of war to the winner, and we need 100 octane before these treasonous bastards kill Roosevelt and give everything you know to the Nazis."

Eddie tried to figure how "these treasonous bastards" could get AvGas if "a company in New Jersey" that ten to one *had* to be Standard Oil had the only formula? Or the small detail that only a handful of Americans knew how to *theoretically* modify the current refinery equipment to make AvGas. And so far, only Eddie Owen and East Chicago, Indiana, had actually done it. And *no one* knew how consistent the run would be until several runs had been completed. And that hadn't happened yet.

The major said, "When asked what you're doing—by anybody, *including Americans*—you're in Bahrain for the start-up, trying to fix a temperature problem. You've heard of 'cracking' but know nothing about it, think it's bullshit, in fact. Don't know nothing and ain't interested." The major's eyes were just slits now and not much goodwill left. "Think you can follow that, Eddie the Cushing Fucking Flash? Or do we need a map to Montague County?"

Eddie had a burning desire to get out of the car but didn't. "So we understand each other, Major, my family matters to me more than *I* matter to me." Eddie tapped the .45 he'd been given. "I do know how to use this. Threaten my family again and I will."

CHAPTER 4

June, 1936

The Arab Revolt was in its sixtieth day. To Saba's south and west, Palestine was open war. The Revolt had begun in Jaffa as a national strike organized and initiated by the AHC—Arab Higher Committee—an uneasy alliance of Arab kings, sheiks, and emirs headquartered in Iraq. Saba agreed the national strike had begun in Jaffa, but "uneasy alliance" was the Red Crescent and Red Cross description of the AHC. She knew the AHC for the violent factions and open betrayals that it really was.

Spread beneath her and her partisans was the French detention-refugee camp at Dhār el Baidar, the camp where she had been sent to die seven years ago. The camp's forced relocations up and down the mountain each winter had thinned the constant flow of refugees expelled from Palestine and displaced from Transjordan, Lebanon, and Syria. "Thinning" was the French intention, a practice also employed by the English. Despite its death rate, Dhār el Baidar remained crowded to its limits, the stench stronger than last week when Saba had secreted herself inside the fences to plan the raid.

Tonight she would pay a debt long overdue. Tonight would be a message to Paris and London and those who believed they could spend Arab lives as worthless chattel. Saba touched Khair-Saleh's ten franc note pinned inside her pocket, repeated his mantra "For Palestine," and gave the signal.

She and twenty-one partisans descended on the one hundred French guards, soldiers, and their Arab collaborators. The initial attacks were silent and with knives, then gasoline bombs in the garrison tents, then close-quarter pistols, and finally rifles for the French cowards and Arab traitors who ran. By first light, the camp was free. Saba stood in the smoke rising from the French garrison tents. The air around her was cordite, humid with blood, and almost soundless. The blood on her face was her own; the blood on her knives, hands, arms, shirt, and pants was French. As the light spread across the camp, Saba scanned what remained. The power of the moment shook her far beyond her expectation. She had done many raids and those raids had successfully continued the terrifying legend of the Raven, but this . . . this was somehow the full circle of her rebirth.

Saba walked through the muck and smoke, unaware her keffiyeh was loose, her face covered but her hair exposed. As she entered the fouled Palestinian quarter, two old women pointed, then helped each other to their feet. They pointed again, women who had replaced those who had tended Saba the teenager and whom Saba had not saved. The bolder of the two hobbled in front of Saba, staring at her hair, the pistol and knife in her hands. The woman feebled a hand forward as if to reach. Saba stepped to her. The old woman raised her hand, touched the black wings beneath Saba's right eye, and wept. Another came forward. Soon there were ten. Saba's breath caught in her throat.

Movement behind her in the marl.

A wounded Arab collaborator stretched for a bloody revolver too far to reach. Saba spun. The camp's self-appointed Muḥāfiẓ jumped between them—a pious and brutal Assyrian who Saba had not expected to find when the fighting was over. The Assyrian cleric forbade Saba to harm the guard-collaborator and shouted for her submission—the camp was his to govern, his leadership ordained by Allah and the Arab Higher Committee and beyond challenge by a marked woman infidel. He grabbed for Saba's hair to jerk her to his knees. "No whore will—"

Saba slammed the cleric's head with the butt of her pistol, then kicked his collaborator away from the revolver. Straddling the cleric from above, she belted her knife, grabbed his wrist, and twisted his arm in its socket. He screamed. His male followers reached for rocks to stone her.

Saba yelled, "I am her. *Minchar al Gorab*. Know this now and forever. You have seen her." Saba slammed her pistol against her chest. "A woman! And the women of this camp are mine." Saba wrenched the holy man's arm out of its socket. He screamed again and she shot him dead. His followers ringed back. She shot the cleric's collaborator, then raised her pistol to the sky. "*My sky. My women*. You will protect them with your lives until I return. This is so because I, the Raven, say it."

Tonight's ambush would be in minutes, a high-risk trap sprung in the moonless dark and parched July heat of the Transjordan border. Saba finished reassembling her Schmeisser MP18 submachine gun, cleaned sand from each 9mm bullet, and loaded her drum magazines. If successful, she and the partisans would capture a weapons shipment bound for the Haganah militia, men from the same outlawed militia who had murdered her family in Jerusalem. Masked, nameless men who continued to kill Palestinians and Englishmen in order to birth a Zionist state.

On a mission such as this, the partisans' risk of betrayal was constant, the Transjordan desert full with treachery, propaganda, and conscription. The desert had always been so, though worse now. To arrive here undetected, she and her partisans had been forced too close to England's patrols of special soldiers and Royal Marines. For the three years that France, England, and the special soldiers had been hunting her, their traps and ambushes had been numerous and lethal, but to date had produced only near misses, mistaken identities, and dead English soldiers. Saba hoped tonight would be no different.

The Arab Revolt that had begun sixty days before her assault on Dhār el Baidar was now in its ninetieth day. What had begun as a national strike had been a strike in name only. Saba knew this because she had been there. The AHC's demand for an Arab government in Palestine had instantly degenerated into hand-to-hand combat among England's occupying army, Zionists, and Arabs. The death and destruction spread from Jaffa to Jerusalem, where the fighting was house-to-house, and then everywhere amid the gunfire, billowing smoke, and funerals of Muslim and Jew, European and Arab. Hundreds were dead and thousands displaced. The Red Cross reported only England's truth: England's "security forces" were the victims of terrorist attacks, first by Arabs, then in quick succession by Zionist militia gangs. The Red Crescent reported only the Arab truth: Arab civilians were the victims, murdered by an unholy alliance of England's occupying army and Zionist militia gangs utilizing superior arms and assassinations to drive out the Arab.

Saba knew all of it to be true, and in far worse volumes. Moving through the fighting always dressed as a man, she had seen the Red Cross and Red Crescent often, but always at the periphery of the carnage. Their access to the actual Revolt remained limited by the English to inspections and triage in the refugee camps. En route to tonight's ambush, Saba and her partisans had encountered two Red Crescent workers at a well near the refugee camp at Irbid. Both men mentioned they had encountered an odd, new defiance in the old women of the camps. The women whispered as they always had, but the whispers had pride now. The old women said their children would not die as slaves or refugees in their own land. This was possible, for some had actually seen her. *Minchar al Gorab*, the Raven.

According to the women, the Raven was not a child's lie, not the myth that for three years England had promised she was. Their *myth* had risen out of the night and raided the French camp at Dhār el Baidar, a camp where the Raven herself had once been a prisoner. The camp's armed soldiers who did not die in the raid had fled, their food stores looted and distributed throughout the camp—personally, the old women said—by the Raven herself, and first to the old and the weak. The Red Crescent workers said the story was being passed from camp to camp along Palestine's borders. When the women whispered the story, it seemed to glow in the low fires and their children's eyes.

Saba's fingers tightened on the Schmeisser's magazine.

Her return to Dhār el Baidar had proven costly. The anonymity and self-control that were her hallmarks had melted when the old women approached. Many in the camp had seen her emotional display. Their descriptions had produced waves of undeserved adoration coupled with expectations far beyond the achievement of anyone but a myth. A high price for anyone who believed in her. France and England could no longer deny her existence and now admitted her, labeling "the Raven" a terrorist bandit, nothing more. The occupying armies and their bounty hunters openly circulated Saba's given and surnames. England could not afford a champion of the people to emerge—of the Arabs *or* the Zionists. Successes like the assault at Dhār el Baidar could not be tolerated.

Unknown to England and France, Saba's strike against a French camp was seen by the AHC and the Pan-Arab Army of God as a significant tactical blunder bordering on treason. Her murder of the Assyrian cleric could not be verified or she would already be dead. The AHC funded Saba's partisans. Furious, they placed her unit under the stern Iraqi wing and the direct control of King Ghazi bin Faisal of Baghdad—the Pan-Arab Army of God. Bin Faisal and his holy-men mullahs made Saba ill and she avoided their main camp at all costs. The Iraqi boy-king had recently declared that one day *he* would unite Iraq, Syria, Kuwait, and Palestine into one great, powerful country. *His* country. Saba spit into the marl. When the Palestinians finished fighting the Europeans, the Palestinians would face their Iraqi benefactors. The Iraqis' orders for tonight had forced her partisan unit out of Lebanon's Beqaa Valley and into the furnace of the Syrian Desert. Tonight's ambush would intercept an arms and explosives shipment from England's Royal Marines in Transjordan destined for the Haganah and Irgun militias in Arad, Palestine, near the Dead Sea. Saba understood the tactic—militias could kill in ways that even the English could not openly sanction.

Saba set the Schmeisser across her lap and surveyed the layered marl rock. A new moon's first bit of light added little to the desolate, rugged nothing that rose above the East Desert Road to Irbid and Al Hosen. Four men sat with her. They were unusual for Arabs, seeing only minor insult in female authority and little blasphemy in Saba's denouncement of all gods. The same was true of the other fourteen men in her unit who waited beyond the rise to cover the ambush's escape. Her new Iraqi commanders were far less tolerant. They were men of God, fervent believers and openly hostile toward Saba and her partisans. She and they were infidels, allowed to live only because of Saba's successes against the English.

Saba spoke with controlled calm. "There will be two trucks if our Iraqi brothers in bin Faisal's camp do not lie. The lead truck will be smaller; the second truck will carry the arms." She handed two grenades to Safiy, the twenty-four-year-old on her right. "Murad and I will stop the first truck when it slows to enter the second turn." Saba pointed to the serpentine road below them and a tight hairpin curve with no shoulder, a thousand-foot drop from the out-side edge. "Find a grip at the edge. When the lead truck arrives, roll one grenade underneath."

Safiy glanced at her instructions to hang off the road's thousand-foot edge.

Saba smiled an inch. "You are young and strong, Safiy, or so you tell all the women we encounter." She turned to the remain-ing two men, brothers older than she who had been with her since Fawzi al-Qawuqji's camp in the Beqaa Valley had been overrun and al-Qawuqji killed. "The arms truck will be forced to brake or stop behind Safiy's explosion. The truck will be trapped between the two turns." Saba pointed at the older brother. "Khalid, you charge the arms truck from the front, and you, Jul, from behind. If possible, do not disable the truck or we become the camels carrying the arms on our backs."

The brothers nodded. There were no safe jobs in this type of ambush, the notice and planning too short, the equipment limited, death a certainty for the losers.

All five waited in silence, Murad at Saba's shoulder, fingering his submachine gun. The small sliver of desert moon rose higher in the east. Saba allowed herself the moment before the battle, as was her way. She thought of school in America instead of war in Palestine, of green ivy climbing brick walls, black gowns and graduation hats—pictures of hope her father had provided, leafy pathways that ended in powerful orations and the liberation of her homeland. Then the drunken English soldiers, as also was her way, ripping at her clothes and hammering inside her. She remembered the camps and the old women no English or Zionist or Arab neighbor cared about, and what precious little she had accomplished for them herself. Her last thoughts were always of the man who had saved her and what he had asked. Saba touched his pistol and the bloodstained ten franc note pinned inside her pocket, then the wings beneath her right eye.

She checked his star in the sky and said, "For Palestine."

Headlights flashed low and distant on the mountain's serpentine edge. Saba sprang to her feet. The headlights were two sets, possibly fifty yards apart, and traveling faster than caution would dictate. She listened to the engines whine up the steep grades and coast down the dips. Not amateur drivers. Few were familiar with driving in the desert, unless they were English or their collaborators. Saba and the partisans descended the cliff's face to the narrow road. They landed just past the road's second serpentine turn. She pointed Safiy and his grenades to the canyon side of the road and a few feet down grade closer to the turn. "One grenade, as soon as the first truck reaches you."

She told Khalid and Jul, the brothers who would confront the arms truck, "Your truck will stop. Kill the driver and guards, not the truck."

The brothers ran down the road. She and Murad ran fifty feet up road from Safiy, the grenadier. Saba cocked the submachine gun, touched her hand to her heart, and told Murad: "For Palestine."

They would stand into the headlights and empty their Schmeissers into the radiator and windshield, then attempt to duck below the road to avoid the grenades' shrapnel. Saba rechecked the road and debated her decisions. Experience was a hard teacher and she had been well schooled, had learned to be far more careful and better prepared, but her new Iraqi superiors wanted action at any cost, wanted blood on the sword for their orations in the mosque—

Engine whine. Louder. Close, the gears grinding. Headlights washed the rutted road two turns down the canyon's face.

Saba exhaled, patted Murad's shoulder, walked to midroad, and shouldered the weapon. The windshield was hers. The English soldier or conscript behind it would die without trial. She would likely die as well and felt the emptiness and adrenaline that accompanied these moments.

Headlights beamed into the sky, then made the turn and blinded her. She fired thirty-two rounds. The truck's windscreen disintegrated. Twenty more banged from Murad, shredding the truck's hood and radiator. The truck charged forward. Saba jumped toward the abyss and the bumper missed her. A blinding white explosion flattened her. Shrapnel and fire ripped overhead. She clawed into the road. Gunfire erupted down grade behind the curve where the arms truck would be. Saba rolled to the road's cliffside edge. Everything was on fire—the explosion far too massive. She sucked a breath, ejected the drum, and slammed another. More gunfire below. *Trap.* The Iraqi king, or those he trusted, had set this. The driver she'd just killed would be an Arab tricked into his job of driving a bomb. The burning hulk of the truck bomb blocked the curve and illuminated her section of road. Murad and Safiy were in pieces. The arms truck would be English special soldiers or Haganah, and swarming up the road toward her.

MOVE.

Saba scrambled for the cliff she'd descended moments ago. Higher ground. From there she could support Khalid and Jul down grade between the two curves, if they were still alive. She reached a shadowed ledge above the precipice. The second truck was visible below, undamaged three hundred feet before the curve. Nine men stood the road, none in uniform. They slow-scanned the cliffs and searched the road's edges. Khalid and Jul were prone, their mangled bodies illuminated in the headlights. She swallowed hard, but dead was better than captured.

Five of the men approached the rock face that hid her. She scrambled ten feet higher and ran out of handholds. Two men climbed on her left. She dropped toward them in the dark, then edged right and climbed higher. Marl chunks bounced down the face. A man yelled in Hebrew, then another.

Haganah or Irgun.

More yelling from men Saba could no longer see. She spidered up the rock, the Schmeisser slung over her back. The militiamen were close. Her fingers bled on the rocks; she was panting and almost to the ledge she and the partisans had originally occupied. A last lunge upward and she was over. Saba clawed, rolled, found the two grenades left for this purpose, pulled the pin on one, counted, and dropped it.

The explosion shattered the dark. A man was screaming when she dropped the second grenade. She huddled until it exploded, then ran night-blind toward a barren hill. The hill hid five camels; four would run without riders. If she could make the escape position, the partisans waiting there could encircle the Haganah chasing her and kill them in their own trap. To know which of her new Iraqi commanders had betrayed the partisans, she would have to survive this chase. Saba ran behind the hill, turned four camels loose, and mounted the fifth. This was her desert; these mountains were hers. She rode hard into both, heart open to any outcome.

SITRA ISLAND, BAHRAIN

CHAPTER 5

July, 1936

H ot—no, strike that. Really, really hot—North Texas if there were two suns and more tent preachers. Eddie wiped his forehead and face. And salty. Loud, too, as if most of the old Spindletop oilfield was being erected here on a one-day calendar. England's heavily armed Royal Marines glared at everything that moved, hard-jawed fellows who looked rough enough to police most of Texas on a bad day. The "Arab Revolt" was a good five hundred miles of desert away, but nothing here looked or acted like that was enough. For sure, Floyd and Benny could use a few of these guys.

Eddie strained to hear Foreman Bill Reno's drawl over the screech and clatter. Reno was explaining what it was like to build a refinery in the middle of nowhere using drunken fuckin' Irishmen and illiterate East Indians. Best Eddie could decipher, Bill Reno was behind schedule, didn't approve of young men on contract from Chicago consuming time he didn't have, and had zero interest in decoding what the papers in Eddie's hand would explain was the reason.

"Consulting fucking engineer, my ass." Foreman Reno spit tobacco juice on his floor. "College boy no fucking less."

Bill Reno put a small hand in Eddie's face before Eddie could answer and told the Irishman behind Eddie to move his ass out of the trailer and onto the crane or go the fuck home and sing limericks. Reno reconnected with Eddie's eyes and asked what the fuck Eddie wanted. Eddie showed him the papers again, suggesting Mr. Reno might want to read them this time—the first part for sure and maybe the last page, the one with the signature.

Bill Reno seemed surprised, bordering on wary, and not laughing. He took the papers. "Where you from, sonny?"

"Oklahoma."

"Too stupid to find Bakersfield?"

Eddie stiffened. His family wasn't going to California. Eddie knew the risk but was ten thousand miles from Texas and said it anyway. "Got lost on the Jacksboro Highway."

Bill Reno paused again, longer this time, his eyes taking in all six feet of Eddie Owen, the burn marks at his temple, the scarred knuckles and thickened nose, then took the papers and read only the signature. Reno glanced up, then down at Eddie's worn Wellington boots, then the signature on the papers again. "Jacksboro Highway, huh? Down there slummin' with your college chummies?"

Eddie added an unspoken *Fuck you* to the respect in his posture.

Reno said, "You know Pappy Kirkwood then, and Sally Rand, up there to the Four Deuces?"

"Yes, sir, I do."

"And Floyd—"

"Floyd Merewether: two pistols, both nickel-plated. And I know his boss, Benny."

The foreman's shoulders responded to Benny Binion's name.

"I've been to college, Mr. Reno, but I've been to work, too. And so you know, *my* family isn't going to Bakersfield."

Bill Reno wrinkled the papers in his hand, his eyes wrinkling the same—then closed the gap between he and Eddie so yelling louder than the din wouldn't be necessary. "Floyd Merewether like to drive?"

"Floyd prefers to shoot people. Fellows like me do Benny's driving."

Bill Reno leaned into a drafting table stacked with dog-eared folders and shook his head. "Things so damn bad Benny Binion's down to college-boy rumrunners?" Reno glanced at Eddie's hands again, the scars and the burns. "Bring any a Fort Worth with you?"

"Two fifths of JTS Brown. Your name on both of 'em. Sir."

The weathered foreman fought a grin, the dry skin stretching wrinkles grooved deep from frowning. "Guess one of Benny's boys can stay." Reno shoved the papers back into Eddie's hand, then pointed to a round-shouldered, almost-black Arab robed in some sort of traditional dress. "Wander some with Hassim here. Then you and me'll have a drink at the shift change, talk about home a sentence or two. See what the fuck you're really doing here in God's country." Reno squinted at him. "And don't start no shit with the Limeys or the Irish. Rest of us got honest work to do."

They shook. And Eddie took the Hassim tour—dodging heavy construction vehicles belching exhaust and others with folded-open engine compartments and shirtless men banging wrenches. Burlap-belted material pallets were stacked everywhere and made the hardpan work yard part maze, part obstacle course. Towering above everything were the refinery's main tank components until the main tank disappeared into the brown dust cloud hanging at thirty feet. The dust cloud multiplied the heat, suffocating everyone under it.

Closer to the refinery's core, gangs of men heaved and hammered in the spiderweb of pipes and valves and iron rigging. Grease and rich-burned gasoline fouled what passed for air. Welding torches whooshed and married molten metal under billows of acrid smoke. Oily sweat was the best part of the odor. Eddie noticed two armed

85

Arab guards following them, their expressions almost contempt. The one making hand gestures seemed to be mocking Hassim. Eddie asked who they were.

"BAPCO." Hassim looked elsewhere. "Bahrain Petroleum Company."

The Arabs' leather-holstered sidearms rode high on their hips, hanging from gun belts cinched across flowing white robes. Both guards moved with affected importance. Eddie wondered out loud, "We . . . ah, need Royal Marines and pistol guards to build a refinery?"

Hassim squinted. He seemed confused for an Arab who spoke English a minute ago.

Eddie asked him directly.

Hassim checked the guards and told his boots, "There are classes in the desert, as in the West. There is also trouble. BAPCO is the partner with the American oil companies. These guards are Bahrainis, blood relatives to the Shaikh, Hamad bin Isa al Khalifa. I . . . you are not. They protect the Shaikh interests . . . and England's. Bahrain is a British protectorate. These Arabs wear King George's guns."

"Protection from who?"

Hassim glanced toward a knot of five rough-skinned Irishmen in cuffed denim jeans and yellow hardhats with *Sinn Féin* scrawled on the sides. They crowded and yelled at a bearded, midsize Irishman also wearing a hardhat. His hat was white with nothing written on it.

Hassim whispered, "Mr. Ryan Pearce. He is the line boss for the Irish."

Mr. Ryan Pearce's feet were set wide and his jaw jutted forward into the five-against-one argument like he might fight. His hands gave the opposite impression, resting nonchalantly on his hips. He cocked his head back to hear over the din and his hardhat appeared about to fall. Pearce's left hand steadied his hat; he glanced toward Eddie. Could've been a smile there—

Pearce's right hand exploded into the nearest head. That angry Irishman went down. Two fast left hooks cracked the second man's ribs and eye socket. He crumpled. The remaining combatants stepped back. Eddie would've stepped back, too. It wasn't hard to recognize real good hand speed and plenty of power. The bearded Mr. Pearce didn't look angry, just busy. Two KOs, three punches total.

"Asses to work, lads, I'll look after your mates. You're buildin' a refinery for the *Yanks*, not the Brits, and I'll hear no more of the politics on a man's work hours."

They backed away. Hassim snuck a glance at the Bahraini guards trailing him and Eddie. Hassim's posture, almost a cower, seemed to apologize. He told Eddie's shoulder, "Mr. Ryan Pearce. From Belfast; 1925 All-Europe Middleweight Champion."

Eddie nodded to the bearded Irishman. Ryan Pearce saluted two casual fingers, then reached for the first man he'd dropped. The man staggered to his feet, swaying while Pearce dusted him from shoulder to chest. Pearce spoke to the man's ear and smoothed the matted hair, then stepped back, allowing room between them. The man rubbed at glazed eyes. Pearce buried a boot in the man's groin, found a length of board he liked, and pounded the man into the dirt, savage blows that continued until Eddie charged and shoulder-blocked Pearce eight feet back. Pearce stumbled over his own feet but did not go down. Pearce leaned on the board and sized up Eddie, his clothes, his white skin. "And who would you be, lad, to be in my business?"

Hassim jumped between them. "Please, sir, Mr. Pearce. He is Mr. Reno's guest—"

"The man's done," blurted Eddie. "You can't . . . you can't just beat him to death."

Pearce dropped the board, retrieved his white hardhat, and walked calmly into the maze of pipes and tanks.

Hassim spun to Eddie. "This is very bad. An unfavorable man to provoke, Mr. Ryan Pearce."

Eddie said, "No shit," and glanced at the three British Royal Marines with both hands on their rifles but doing nothing for the two unconscious men on the ground. "C'mon, let's get these boys some help."

The remainder of the tour was less entertaining but no less troubling. Funny how the job counselors at OU's engineering school had declined to mention the foreign intrigue aspect of the career. The amount of work being performed by the throng of workers could have been completed by half as many men. The Irish were organized in ten-man work gangs, the East Indians in great blobs of brown humanity. The East Indians were achieving more, albeit at the cost of materials disappearing into their dirty tunics and pants. The Indians' line bosses seemed to notice but not care.

Eddie slow-walked past the section of the completed refinery that he'd be modifying. His stomach fluttered. This was the real deal, "chance of a lifetime" and all that. *Gulp.* His section had much less activity but no fewer guards. The new Ford trucks were there and waiting, outfitted with the latest arc stud welders and their constant-voltage generators. The good stuff, the giant leap from rivets and boilerplate to oxyacetylene welding to electric arc to arc stud. Eddie asked how long ago the section had been completed.

Hassim furrowed his forehead. "Two months."

"Been tested?"

Hassim checked beyond both his shoulders, then behind his back. "Who are you to ask this?" It was the most direct the Arab had been.

Eddie blinked confusion—maybe the section wouldn't run. A ten-thousand-barrel refinery of this design would be tested in sections, then retested, then all the sections brought online together after they were proven. Kept down the explosions and rivers of fire. Killed *a lot* fewer people.

"That's my job, Hassim. What I'm doing here. Has it been tested or not?"

"Yes. There are problems, small but—"

"Like what?" Eddie faced him. "Show me."

Hassim stepped back, not forward.

Eddie looked around and saw no threat. "C'mon, show me."

Hassim shook his head, some nervousness affecting his speech. "I am not an engineer; I cannot show. Mr. Reno must discuss this."

"Need a hand there, lad?"

Eddie turned to the soft Irish lilt and stepped back fast. Ryan Pearce was at a respectful distance, the white hardhat covering his left hand. Eddie stuttered, "N-no; well, yeah, actually I do."

"That'd be my pleasure, then, wouldn't it." He took two steps to Eddie and extended his right hand. "Ryan Pearce, Belfast, Republic of Ireland."

"Eddie Owen, Cushing, Oklahoma." The Irishman's grip was strong but reasonable, a workingman's hand. "Nice to meet you, Ryan."

"And yourself."

"Sorry about the, ah, intrusion." Eddie nodded back to where they'd met.

Pearce smiled. "I'll grant you one, Mr. Owen. But that's all it'll be. You mind your flock; I'll mind mine."

Eddie nodded a wary *okay* and angled his head at the gauges next to his shoulder. "This ready to go?"

"Right as rain last I heard." The Irishman smiled at Hassim. "A flap with the cooling tubes, but nothin' to fret. Be fixing it in the morning if we've the parts."

"How about the rest of the place? We on schedule?"

Ryan Pearce blinked dust out of his eyes and licked it off his lips. "And who might you be, Eddie Owen, if you don't mind my askin'?"

Eddie explained the maintenance modifications, start-up function agreed upon as his cover. Ryan Pearce nodded while looking away and in both directions. Royal Marines watched from a distance; BAPCO guards watched from closer. "We're getting there, we are. Be movin' to the next'on soon."

"You build these monsters for a living?"

"That I do, Eddie Owen, that I do. Spain's Tenerife be next, off the coast of Morocco. Be pleased to buy you a pint in the canteen this evenin'. Bring yourself in; you can tell the lads about the Alamo in Oklahoma." He patted Hassim on the shoulder the way a father would a favored child, then stepped into the spaghetti of pipes.

Hassim smiled and nodded until Ryan Pearce was a troublesome memory and the closest BAPCO guard had quit inspecting their conversation. "You must be very careful. There are too many secrets here and little safety. *Insha'Allah*, God willing, we build this plant and move on to better camps . . . if there are such places."

The heat dropped twenty degrees when the sun finally set, but Eddie still had to wipe sweat out of his eyes. He stepped into the large plank-floor canteen with the same uneasy respect he offered a Fort Worth roadhouse. Could've been one, too, if Texas built them with army tent poles, green canvas roofs, and the Irish had settled Tarrant County instead of Ireland. Naked lightbulbs were strung overhead above the din, hazy and half shrouded in cigar smoke. The Irish fiddles were faster than Bob Wills, and men jig-dancing with each other was new. The grit, sweat, and beery humor gone edgy wasn't.

Ten of His Majesty's Royal Marines filled the tent's farthest corner, out of uniform but all with sidearms and none with their backs exposed. The Marines occupied two tables, both cluttered with empty bottles like each Marine had been at it awhile. The empty bottles hadn't added revelry to their demeanor. Eddie smiled. World travel: gotta love it. At the opposite corner thirty feet away, a glot of East Indians was three deep over and around their long table, yelling and jumping, intent on a gambling game of some type.

Bill Reno waved at Eddie from the near corner on Eddie's left. Reno's corner was just beyond the smoky glare of naked lightbulbs. His three empty tables were separated from the saloon's dust and fray by a row of fifty-five-gallon drums and a drooping rope gate. A bottle of J.T.S. Brown was his centerpiece. Eddie stepped over the rope and added one of the bottles he'd promised.

"Compliments of the great state of Texas, Mr. Foreman."

Reno stayed slouched in the chair, feet on the table, boot soles facing Eddie. "How's it you know I drink fact'ry liquor? College finally teachin' something that matters?"

"Harold Culpepper, my college prof. He knew you were the boss here, said you and he go way back in Oklahoma."

Reno spit a brown stream sideways without looking. "Harold fucking Culpepper. Dumb as a fuckin' post, that boy—rich daddy, mostly. What the fuck did *he* teach that you couldn't learn on a playground?"

"Not so much teach as organize. Undergrads could work with him on postgrad projects . . . I had some potential so they let me work on—"

"Cracking. Army Air Corps contract. That what's in those papers?"

Eddie stopped the wince before it showed. "No, not cracking, exactly. Maintenance modifications. I—"

"I been on a fast train, sonny. Think I don't know how to build a refinery? Call your modifications whatever the fuck you want, but I know different, and so do you." Reno took a sip from a dirty glass. "So, you'd be the 'asylum carpenter' who did East Chicago?"

Eddie couldn't answer and didn't.

"Yeah, I heard. Heard the kid who pulled that off was some kinda freak." Reno waited for a reaction. "Some kinda 'England savant,' whatever the fuck that is." Reno waited again. "You drinking, Mr. Savant?"

"Ah, one or ten'd be good."

Foreman Bill Reno pushed Eddie a glass. Clean didn't seem to be an issue. Eddie poured a half inch and watched the dust it dampened turn to a light mud. He toasted Foreman Reno. Behind Reno, just outside the canteen tent, guards with bright lights swept them across a makeshift boxing ring, the corner posts set in fifty-five-gallon drums painted the same as the ones Reno had inside. Eddie smiled. "We're a sporting camp?"

Reno frowned. "We try to settle the disagreements with hands as opposed to knives or bayonets." He frowned deeper. "I told you no bullshit with the Irish."

"I didn't start—"

"Talk to me, Mr. Owen. What the fuck are you doing at my refinery with a Standard Oil high-hat VP's signature on your papers? And it better not be nothing to do with East Chicago, Indiana."

Eddie pulled the papers from his shirt.

Bill Reno drank the last of his glass and knocked the bottom on the table harder than necessary. "Out here, among the natives, friends are the difference 'tween getting your job done or not, maintainin' your employment or not. Assuming I'm willing to read that nonsense in your hand, you best get the lay of the land or men like Ryan Pearce will put you under it."

"Not sure I follow."

"I'd say that's painfully obvious." Reno acknowledged Ryan Pearce entering the canteen. "They still teach geography at that fucking college in Norman?" Reno nodded toward the knots of

Irishmen, a few still wearing *Sinn Féin* hardhats. "Know what that means, that writin' there on their hats?"

Eddie read *Sinn Féin* for the second time today. "Nope."

Reno glanced at the armed Royal Marines. "*Sinn Féin* means those boys are no friends of the Brits. *Sinn Féin* means you're a republican, the IRA. You're trading bombs and bullets with the Brits in Ireland for Ireland's independence . . . and you're trading blood with 'em here, whenever the sneaky Irish bastards get the chance." Reno nodded toward the East Indians. "Same for the Indians, they hate the Brits with both hands, death-fightin' His Majesty's redcoats from Bombay to Calcutta."

Eddie took a new look at his fellow workers. "Ah, not sure I get it, boss. These fellows are working for us, right?"

"Us?" Reno snorted. "Who's 'us'?"

"Standard Oil, the Texas Company . . ."

"Brits are the landlord for a quarter of the world, sonny, half a billion people, and not many of 'em like His Majesty's boot on their necks any more than you would if the sons-a-bitches were running Texas. Used to be the Turks were boss here, but they got their asses pasted twenty years back in the Great War. Standard Oil and the Texas Company have to keep the Brits happy or all of King George's protection and this oil goes to somebody else." Reno smiled at his empty glass. "And we wouldn't want that, would we?"

"Suppose not. But if we need to keep the Brits happy and they don't like the Irish, why hire—"

"Irish don't like the Brits. But so what? Brits don't give a fuck who likes 'em as long as it's the Brits running things and England is making money." Reno did a bad English accent. "The Empire and all that."

"Why not hire someone else?"

"Brits with the talent and stomach for this kind of work are busy elsewhere . . ." He glanced at the East Indians again. "Colonizing

India, the Philippines, Singapore. And the Irish work cheap, real cheap, always have."

Eddie considered the slow work he'd seen today and wondered.

Bill Reno poured another drink. "How long you got to get your new component online?"

"If that's what I was doing, I'd probably have six months. From what I saw today, it doesn't look good. What I'm here to do looks like a year, maybe more."

Bill Reno straightened in his chair but left his feet crossed on the table. The butt of a revolver protruded from his shirt. "That's what you think, huh? 'Cause you been buildin' refineries all your goddamn life?"

"You asked. That's what I think."

"About right, actually. Fucking micks work hard to be slow . . . it suits 'em." Reno smiled. "See, we got us a war coming—you probably been told that. A big war: that's the big picture—you'll believe it when you start working with the RAF test pilots." Reno nodded to himself, then cut his eyes to the Irish. "What you *ain't* been told about is all the little wars that go on inside the big war. That's where you find yourself this evening, son, inside two or three of the nasty-ass little ones."

Eddie shrugged, not sure how much more he wanted to be told about wars he'd like to avoid. "Mr. Reno, I mean no offense and I sure hope you know that. The last guy in this lovely country I want to insult is you. But I, ah, need to see a fellow working here named D.J. Bennett. Right after you read these papers and Mr. Bennett and I talk, I can answer your questions better." Eddie added an apologetic grin. One he used to no great effect on girls who often harbored higher hopes for his behavior than he had behavior.

"Bennett, you say?" Reno eased back an inch, then shook his head. "Hooked up with that bunch ain't healthy, sonny. Word I hear is Bennett and his kind are walkin' in the wildfire." Reno's eyes lifted toward the bar and two men leaving it, one with a cock in his hip, his head shaved, and a brushy mustache that horseshoed his mouth. The man walked with a tilt, a horseman's amble, like he carried more weight on his right leg.

Eddie mumbled, "Holy shit."

Reno took time to stare. "D.J. Bennett would be the one who looks like a fucking broke-down bull rider. Broke down he ain't, but the jarhead, cowboy cocksucker hasn't worked a lick since your Professor Culpepper put him on this job and that don't seem to matter to anybody on this side of the ocean but me."

D.J. Bennett stopped at the gate, patted the dusty Arab he walked with on the back and away, then turned to Bill Reno and his rope gate separating them. "Come by to see ya, Bill. Seems you and me the only fellas out here know Texas from tarpaper."

Reno didn't speak, the caution evident in his silence and posture.

Bennett grinned under the mustache. "Who's your young friend there?"

Eddie stood, eyes wide, and offered a very confused, tentative hand. "Ah . . . Eddie Owen, we met in . . ."

Bennett shook hands. His grin quit and he said: "Give the ol' bastard your papers and answer his questions if he's dumb enough to press 'em, just don't do it in here." Bennett turned and limped back toward the bar, avoiding Irishmen dancing the jig, stumbling drunks, and other workers paying him no mind.

Eddie glanced at Bill Reno. "That's *my* D.J. Bennett?"

Reno nodded. "Need his permission, do you?"

"Sort of. I think he's my, ah, company bodyguard."

"Well, he might could do that. They say he got that leg in the 'labor riots' after the war; I hear he was good at both, the war and the riots." Reno tipped his glass an inch but kept the caution. "All them trench fighters come back from the Great War, nowhere to go, living in the mud and shit and tarpaper—'Hoovervilles,' not much different than you Okies trying for California." Reno drank the whiskey. "Stood their fucking ground, though, Bennett there one of the leaders, against ever-damn strikebreaker, goon, goddamn marshal law them rich bastards and Herbert Hoover threw at 'em. Gutless sons-a-bitches, them bid'nessmen." Reno spit on the canteen floor. "And now we're all working for 'em."

Eddie wondered if he was hallucinating. How many guys had pockmarked faces *and* claw hands? The shaved head was new, but in Chicago, "the major" had worn a hat. But why throw the who's-who curve? Curve or no, the blackmail/fugitive threats probably still applied.

Reno interrupted Eddie's puzzle. "So you and Bennett and your papers got something cooked up for me? Goddamn East Chicago, Indiana? What a fucking surprise. You two taking over?"

"Huh? No, not hardly. I'm in and out. Have zero to say about how you do things, Mr. Reno, or who you do 'em to. I need help to do my job and my folks in Oklahoma need the money. Need it in the worst way." Eddie's eyes were steady on Reno, not begging him and not bullshitting; Eddie had come to work and expected to earn his wages.

"Imagine that. A college boy listening to reason." Bill Reno poured Eddie a drink. "Tell me it ain't your East Chicago aviation gas; I got a wife and a kid. Wanna live to see 'em both."

Eddie faked a smile.

Reno sighed, finished a drink he didn't appear to need, palmed both J.T.S. Brown bottles, and walked Eddie out of the canteen to the trailer. They passed Royal Marines and BAPCO guards and shadows that drew Reno's attention more than once.

Inside his trailer, Reno bent just one light closer to his drafting table and flipped it on. Somehow he didn't seem as bourboned as he had in the canteen. "Show me the goddamn papers."

Eddie did. Reno read them twice, wrote down the vice president's telephone number in Chicago, then burned all but the signature page with his lighter. "About what I figured." He exhaled, walked to a small concave sofa, and sat in the deep shadows. Elbows on his knees, Reno's rough hands massaged both temples, then patted his thin hair back into a semblance of place. Reno told the floor between his shoes: "You and Bennett bein' together don't fit. Harold Culpepper's dumb, that's a natural fact, but he don't choose Bennett to be your chaperone."

Eddie's face soured. "Not sure Harold 'chose' Bennett."

Reno looked up. "This ain't a game, sonny. Put the wrong people in it, *none* of us finish." Reno nodded out the trailer's small window toward his refinery. "Once we modify, be easy to change the entire production run to AvGas. Pump 100 octane into the right kinda airplane and . . . change the balance of just about every-fucking-thing in this neighborhood." Reno cocked an ear to a noise outside. "There're people on this job—Irish, Indian, even some Arabs—who ain't gonna like that. Not even a little."

CHAPTER 6

April, 1937

When in America, Nazi Luftwaffe Oberstleutnant Erich Schroeder enjoyed baseball; the American stadiums possessed an operatic elegance that a well-born German could appreciate. When not supporting America's pastime, Erich Schroeder was a criminal, a killer, and Reichsmarschall Hermann Göring's man in the field if the business involved aviation gasoline, Capitalists, or violence for profit.

Schroeder was seated among the baseball memorabilia at Al Schacht's Restaurant on Manhattan's 52nd Street. Midway through a delightful roast beef lunch and the Mutual Broadcasting System's *World Events* radio show, Dr. Joseph Goebbels, Nazi Reich Minister of Propaganda, announced to the restaurant and the world's press: "Tonight, Germany will own the skies of Europe."

Schroeder pushed back blond hair that had fallen over his right eye and checked his watch; the Junkers Ju 52s would already be in the sky. In approximately thirty-seven minutes, three Nazi Luftwaffe bomber squadrons would incinerate Guernica, Spain. Basque Nationalists (who the world press would undoubtedly label as "defenseless civilians") were the target. Schroeder finished his lunch, complimented the waiter, and paid the bill. As Schroeder moved through the bar, he thanked the grinning former-baseball-player owner, Al Schacht. Behind Mr. Schacht, the RCA radio on the bar broadcast a second announcement from Reich Minister Goebbels: "Adolf Hitler has this hour come to the aid of Generalissimo Francisco Franco in his courageous fight against the Communists."

Al Schacht lost his grin.

Schroeder walked out onto Park Avenue and turned north. Al Schacht was a Jew whose parents had fled Russia on the eve of Emperor Alexander II's assassination. Schacht's reaction to the Guernica bombing did not surprise Schroeder. Jews had odd antennae, both predator and prey. Their union with their surroundings was primal, as if parts of the Jew had not evolved as homo sapiens.

In the lobby of Schroeder's hotel, the very same model of RCA radio that graced Al Schacht's bar was already broadcasting France's outrage at Germany's actions, accusing Nazi Germany of battle testing illegal Nazi warplanes outlawed by international law. This was as expected. Schroeder knew Goebbels would soon answer through diplomatic channels, stating in Hitler's name that the devastating raid was notice to the Old World Order: Germany, with or without international blessing, owned the sky.

Ten days later, the Hindenburg exploded.

Seven million cubic feet of hydrogen illuminated most of Lakehurst, New Jersey, in volcanic white light. The massive red swastikas adorning the tail fins burned last. Schroeder watched without comment, then woke Reichsmarschall Göring with the Hindenburg news before the fire was out. Göring was a loud and vocal champion of the Zeppelins. As the president of the Reichstag and the minister of Aviation, Göring believed the Zeppelins to be priceless Nazi propaganda and a reasonable addition to an air force that "did not exist" but could already threaten all of Europe and half the Soviet

Union. Schroeder thought the Zeppelin airships more theater than weapon. But theater had its place, and Reichsmarschall Göring was not frivolous in his endeavors, nor in the friendships he cultivated in America to make those endeavors successful.

Schroder spent the evening on station, then drove across the George Washington Bridge into New York City the following morning, stopped at his hotel for a clean suit, then on to Ebbets Field in Brooklyn. By late afternoon, Schroeder's beloved Dodgers had won their contest. From box seats behind home plate, four of Reichsmarschall Göring's "cultivated friendships" had watched the Dodgers' catcher Babe Phelps go four-for-four, before being chauffeured to dinner in the Cloud Club high atop the Chrysler Building. The radio announced that DiMaggio and the Yankees were now twelve games into the Yankee Clipper's second season and had just lost to the Detroit Tigers, 12–6. Schroeder was a Dodgers fan and any pain to the Yankees was to be applauded.

As part of Schroeder's mission in America, he had accompanied Reichsmarschall Göring's friends to Ebbets Field, maintaining a respectful distance, as he was doing now inside the Cloud Club. Two of the four friends were Americans; one was a German national, the other an Englishman. All were seated at the window table overlooking a troubled Manhattan and the choppy gray Atlantic beyond.

These men had invested heavily in President Roosevelt's defeat, but Roosevelt had been reelected, crushing Republican candidate Alf Landon in a populist landslide. It seemed the battered population of America so desperately wanted to believe Roosevelt could end their eight years of despair and 25 percent unemployment that all common sense and clear thinking had been lost, replaced by an ever-growing blend of utopian socialism and Communist dogma.

There was no mistaking it for Schroeder or for the four men at the table—Roosevelt was a dangerous man in dangerous times.

America's president was a charismatic liar whose constant rhetoric unfairly blamed greed and America's industrialists—many of whom were also seated in the Cloud Club's comfortable leather chairs—for the failures of his New Deal government. At heart, Roosevelt was a Communist, on this Schroeder would wager all the gold in the Reichsbank. Roosevelt's policies threatened the United States of America's very survival as a capitalist democracy. And therefore threatened Germany.

The four diners Schroeder had accompanied to Ebbets Field were not delicate flowers. They held strong opinions on the lie of communism and labor unions, and it was clear to Schroeder they intended to see their opinions acted upon. The largest of the four was an American, bombastic, well over six feet and two hundred pounds. He smoked a Havana cigar in a pretentious amber holder. The man on his left was the German whom Schroeder watched over in America—Teutonic, stubby, and dour, as if unhappy with the meal or the company. He was neither. The third was so obviously British that the Savile Row suit, mutton-chop sideburns, and banker's bearing seemed a caricature. The fourth diner was the other American, younger, Midwestern, and spindly, and a touch aloof. His eyes wandered to the towering art deco murals while the much larger American pontificated, waving the cigar and holder in a striking mimic of President Roosevelt's theatrical gestures.

The four men could have been discussing yesterday's Zeppelin crash or the Yankees' fourth loss of the season, but they were not. They were discussing the world's future, because they held a very direct say in it.

Erich Schroeder watched Reichsmarschall Göring's friends finish their meal while he sipped a cosmopolitan at the Cloud Club's gleaming Bavarian oak bar. His manicured nails on the glass's stem a sharp contrast to his large scarred knuckles and the starched French-cuff shirt. The foursome dined in unhurried comfort, unusually comfortable for men whose governments privately planned the other's destruction. Erich Schroeder saw no incongruity with the rapport; at this level, men made decisions based upon relationships more important and long lasting than government. Schroeder smiled at his civility, a quality he believed as useful as violence when in the hands of a professional. And he was a professional. Unfortunately, the newer members of the Reich's junior officer corps were not. Feral cunning seemed their dominant quality. These new aspirants to power saw his civility and restraint as weakness, an unnecessary humanity. Schroeder widened his smile. Misjudging his "humanity" would be costly. His was feigned, practiced—the professional's failsafe between emotion and action. He understood torture, as well as murder's decisive punctuation, and used both when appropriate. A loved one hung from a lamppost was a tool, no different than a fountain pen or a shovel.

The barman smiled his own practiced smile, straightening his shirt too late to hide a Star of David, and asked Schroeder if he'd enjoy another. Schroeder declined with a laugh and sparkling blue eyes, displaying manners learned postwar at the third-best schools of Germany and Austria and survival instincts forged in the bloody alleys of Berlin and Munich. A bastard nephew to the Krupp Dynasty, Erich Schroeder had spent most of the 1920s (and his twenties as well) defending the Krupp factories and foundries by any means necessary, helping the armaments and steel giant decapitate a fledgling labor movement they depicted as "Jews and Communists threatening one of Europe's preeminent industrial empires."

Schroeder had done the dirtiest of the dynasty's business to be acknowledged a Krupp, but in the end the family monarchs chose not to allow a bastard at their table. The great inflation and the rise of the Nazis had offered Schroeder another option: Reichsmarschall Hermann Göring. Göring's professional and personal interests were the reason Erich Schroeder tolerated transatlantic travel and New York. This week those interests included accompanying the Reich's leading indus-trialist now stripping the bones of a Cornish hen with his teeth. That stubby and dour man's name was Hermann Schmitz, president of the Nazi chemical and drug consortium I.G. Farben. With the assistance of the Nazis, I.G. Farben had surpassed Krupp and now reigned as the industrial colossus of Germany. The company was driven internally by Heinrich Himmler's Gestapo and externally by powerful foreign stockholders and sponsors. Schroeder frowned at the thought of Himmler, an emotionless chicken-farmer opportun-ist whose unwavering quest for Aryan racial purity had made him the most feared man in Germany.

The bombastic American seated next to I.G. Farben's Herr Schmitz was both an I.G. Farben sponsor and stockholder, and still waving his amber cigar holder. Born to wealthy parents in Cleveland, Ohio, the American had graduated from Cornell before going to work for the Rockefellers. His name was Walter C. Teagle, chairman of the largest petroleum corporation on earth.

Standard Oil of New Jersey.

While most of New York and his charge slept, Erich Schroeder had his driver slowly recircle the block of midtown Manhattan. Schroeder was much less familiar with Manhattan than Detroit, having assisted Irénée du Pont there in 1936 shortly after du Pont's acquisition of Gen-eral Motors. Schroeder had helped du Pont form the American Liberty League and the now unfortunately infamous Black Legion, the latter to terrorize GM's autoworkers away from unionizing and any possible connection to the Communists. The campaign had gone well, partially because Schroeder and du Pont had worked together since 1933 when Irénée and his father began smuggling arms to Hitler in partnership with I.G. Farben.

Schroeder nodded to himself. Profit had been simpler then. He had piloted barges of war materiel up the unpatrolled rivers of Holland, the risk minimal. Tonight was different, the Luger in his hand no small proof. Schroeder's concern lay with Hermann Schmitz and the English banker with whom the president of I.G. Farben had dined in the Cloud Club.

The English banker was a representative of powerful British banking and chemical interests. According to Reichsmarschall Göring, the banker was also a user of morphine and an unexposed homosexual whose lover was a London actor in the private employ of the Communists. The actor was passing the English banker's most private information directly to Moscow, and that could include I.G. Farben's plans.

Schroeder's black Mercedes touring sedan eased west, slick with cold rain and almost invisible without its headlights. This was a touchy business—the English banker had powerful sponsors in the Reich, Germany's ambassador to England, Joachim von Ribbentrop, being the highest placed and most vocal. Schroeder's German driver reflected Schroeder's caution, but for different reasons. The narrow streets he drove were mostly mud and overworked sewers. Construction debris littered the stoops of brick tenements fronting the site of the new Lincoln Tunnel. According to the newspapers, Hell's Kitchen had been selected for the tunnel's terminus because it housed Manhattan's poorest and most desperate citizens in a city rapidly filling with the same. The driver slowed. Three prostitutes huddled at the edge of an iron streetlamp's murky light. Their cigarettes glowed in the mist, dingy coats held open as Schroeder's Mercedes passed.

Schroeder waved his driver on without speaking, then tapped the driver's broad shoulder and pointed him at a doorway announced only by a small blue light. The English banker's car waited twenty feet beyond. A man in a raincoat sat smoking on the car's fender, his eyes on Schroeder's Mercedes as it approached. Schroeder frowned. There were much better neighborhoods for homosexuals less than a mile north. The banker's stop here was either business or morphine. Either way, Reichsmarschall Göring had spoken.

"The man on the fender?" Schroeder asked his driver. "He is the one you paid for our Englishman's location?"

"*Nein, Oberstleutnant*. He drives the Englishman."

"Carefully, then."

Schroeder's driver rolled to a stop midstreet and dropped his window. He spoke German, his right hand hiding a Luger that matched Schroeder's. The man on the fender shrugged. Schroeder's driver switched to abrupt English. "This is the place?"

The man drew on his cigarette.

"The bridge? We seek the bridge to Brooklyn."

The man pushed off his fender, shook his head, and pointed around the corner as if the bridge were a long way off. His hands were visible and empty and the driver shot him in the chest.

He fit nicely in the large trunk, as did the English banker when Erich Schroeder felt he understood all the banker's secrets that might assist a bastard who one day would be king. The English banker's segmented body was found in Manhattan's Five Points, his mutton-chop sideburns hacked out of his face. Six days later, Erich Schroeder's driver died at sea, as did the actor in London the day after Schroeder arrived. London was abloom in an uncommonly beautiful May. Schroeder had the good fortune to remain a few days and enjoy a grimy industrial city suddenly festooned with multicolor flora. Paying him a silent, but much appreciated, homage to his skill as an assassin, England and the rest of Europe had not focused on Schroeder's murder of the English banker in Manhattan nor the murder of his actor boyfriend in London. Europe's focus—and Schroeder agreed—was on England's soon-to-be monarch, George VI—new king of England, emperor of India.

George VI would be the replacement for his older brother, Edward VIII, abdicating the throne under mounting rumors of treason. The House of Windsor countered the rumors every hour or two with "affairs of the heart," constantly refocusing the public on the American divorcée Wallis Simpson. And as one would expect, it was working.

Schroeder found his way to the coronation while half the world enjoyed the fairy tale and the other half held its breath, hoping the new sovereign of the most powerful empire on earth could force calm and reason on the world's flashpoints. Schroeder saw no basis for such hope. The coronation, though, was wonderfully entertaining pageantry/propaganda, much cheerier than the gothic epics produced by Goebbels, and Schroeder was thrilled to have seen England in all her finery.

On July 7th, two months later, Schroeder was in the blast-furnace heat of Iraq. At noon, while waiting on his meeting with King Ghazi bin Faisal, the newly militarized Japan attacked China. First Peking, then Shanghai. According to the radio broadcasts and newspapers that arrived Baghdad, the Japanese Imperial Army had manufactured an incident on the Marco Polo Bridge, then went on to commit the *Rape of Nanking*, "the blood of raped and butchered Chinese women so deep it overflowed the Yangtze River." Schroeder tried to picture slaughter on that scale but could not. He could, however, picture the Communists of the world press corps twisting Japan's self-defense into an indictment that only the noble Communists could adjudicate.

The Nazi Reichstag answered the press on Japan's behalf, stating that Germany also had a right to protect its borders and citizens. Reichsmarschall Göring added an announcement—the opening of Buchenwald concentration camp—then demanded further political concessions from Austria, or Germany—like Japan at the Yangtze River—would be forced to invade. As anticipated, the world press had vomited their disapproval and recriminations. Schroeder did not relish the negative publicity of open war with Austria, but the intellectuals and illuminati of Vienna and their deepening flirtation with communism could not go unanswered indefinitely.

Fortunately, Austria was not his theater; his summer and autumn had been busy with problems and opportunities in the desert state of Iraq and the Mediterranean states of Lebanon and Palestine. While he had been busy building the Reich's influence in the desert, the Reich and Imperial Japan had signed a political and military treaty. The new king of England chose not to comment on the treaty or his deposed brother—the now retitled duke of Windsor—or the duke's trip to Germany, or the clandestine meetings held there with Joachim von Ribbentrop, Hermann Göring, and Rudolph Hess, meetings designed to forge an alliance between England and Germany, a masterstroke of statesmanship from a dethroned king that Schroeder and his superior, Hermann Göring, believed could avert a world war.

The new king of England *did*, however, choose to comment on the issue of Palestine and the Zionist movement. With his parliament and prime minister's guidance, Great Britain's King George VI forced the dissolution of all Palestinian political organizations.

Schroeder was sipping coffee in a Beirut seaside café, thrilled to be out of Iraq's sandstorms and religion maze, when George VI's decree was reported. Schroeder was stunned silent. Two royal brothers—the dethroned king a master statesman, the new king a fool almost beyond understanding. Schroeder loved the new king. In George VI's single stroke of blind British hubris, the new king had delivered Erich Schroeder his empire.

CHAPTER 7

December, 1937

Dried blood spotted the *London Times* in Saba's hand. If the yellowed pages of England's newspaper were to be believed, the "Christmas season" had begun a month ago and brought snow, sleigh bells, and a "blind man's nervous peace" in Great Britain. Palestine, the *Times* reported, was open war.

Saba frowned her assessment of England's venerated newspaper, a propagandist's lie of bad faith and colonial hypocrisy from first page to last. England knew nothing of the conditions or people here. Their king's dissolution of all Palestinian political organizations had silenced the Arab leaders as desired, but it had not shrunk the war nor silenced the partisans. Only the king's bounties had risen. And with them, the death toll on both sides. It was Saba's deepest hope that England's cold-hearted arrogance would one day kill the English in their cottages and homes the way the English killed the Palestinians in theirs.

The partisan stronghold where Saba camped—like all the battered but surviving partisan enclaves—was held together by a tenuous bond of food, ammunition, and hate. Tribal animosity ran especially deep in this camp, as did clashing objectives should the English ever be driven out. The camp was financed and controlled by the Pan-Arab Army of God, the same Iraqis who had betrayed Saba and her partisans eighteen months ago on the East Desert Road. The Iraqis remained the strongest and best financed of the AHC factions, ruling by zealot religion and Pan-Arab nationalism.

Her association with the camp and its commanders was a marriage of convenience both would end at the first opportunity. As Saba had vowed after the betrayal at East Desert Road, she had returned to find those responsible. Fourteen days after the Zionist militias and Iraqi mullahs had declared her killed in the ambush, Saba rose from the dead and killed the two Pan-Arab Army of God commanders responsible for the betrayal/ambush. Both men were killed in their tents inside their heavily fortified camp, their throats cut, Palestinian daggers left in their hearts. Saba and her surviving partisans then made camp inside the stronghold and waited to be discovered behind the camp's defensive perimeter.

Within the hour, Iraqi sentries discovered her partisans at their fire. The sentries inspected the partisans at gunpoint. Saba rose behind them, weapons in both hands. The sentries realized it was a dead woman they faced in the firelight, some kind of Samarian demon, and ran screaming into the night. Saba and her ten partisans filtered through the sprawling camp, then regrouped to confront the remaining commanders and their mullahs at the morning meal. Rifles to their shoulders, she challenged the seated men to die with her, today, if reprisal was what the brave and devout wished.

The brave and devout did not wish to die. The murders of the two commanders were deemed tribal assassinations, physically impossible to have been committed by a woman, even this woman. The Army of God's surviving Iraqi leadership stated unequivocally that it was so, because King Ghazi bin Faisal said it was so. The men of the camp faithfully repeated the same words, but none of the mullahs nor their righteous soldiers strayed anywhere near Saba's section of the camp.

Saba had spared King Ghazi bin Faisal . . . but not forever.

Outside her goat-hair tent, Saba considered the geography in every direction, then sat away from the other partisans, as was her custom. The night sky was clear, sharp, and she scanned for the three brightest stars, whispering names as she found them. The sky was her cemetery, the stars her gravestones, the names her nightly ritual.

On her lap, she smoothed the crumpled copy of the *London Times* two weeks after its stilted articles made news in the western world. Using the brilliant moon, she read every page aloud, stopping to consider why Japanese aircraft would attack an American oil tanker convoy being escorted up China's Yangtze River. The American boat had been sunk and the Japanese pilot had machine-gunned the survivors. Why would Japan wish to fight with a power so great as America?

Her eyes drifted to the paper's edges; she noticed her hands, the desert grit caked under her nails, and the roughness of her skin. In truth, the reading was only part practice; she still longed to know of the world outside Palestine, to feel its pulse and someday see its people. The irony did not escape her, that what she could know of the world would be filtered through the liars and slave owners of England. In her darkest moments, she wondered if that would change, if she and her people had the will, if Arab leaders could see past the centuries of tribal war to focus on a single enemy.

England's formal dissolution of the Arab Higher Committee and open support of the Zionists had helped. The *Times* seemed to agree and predicted a bloody year in the desert, blood that could reach well beyond Palestine. By reading all the books and newspapers she captured, Saba had begun to understand why. Oil. The recent discovery of oil in Bahrain, and the expectation that huge amounts would be found in Arabia, had changed the value of the southern desert from sand to gold. England, France, and Holland were competing with one another and the Americans for control of the desert. Germany was new to the competition. Saba had not encountered Germany's efforts but she had heard them spoken. The Germans labeled Zionism the new Crusades and England its colonial pope. If this comparison were well presented, it would be a persuasive argument with the sheikhs, emirs, and their mullahs. Especially persuasive in places like Iraq if accompanied by weapons and ammunition.

The *Times* on Saba's lap accused the Germans of just that, offering Arab factions munitions from the outlawed Krupp armament factories, gold from the Reichsbank, and intelligence from the Abwehr. In return, the Germans would want dead English soldiers, something many misguided locals—Arab and Zionist—were already pleased to provide. Saba considered the word "misguided." Had the readers in the great and powerful England ever wondered if they would become "misguided" should their land and families again fall under the boot of another king, another nation? The sound of footsteps broke her concentration. One hand quit the paper for the pistol under it. Three heads appeared at the ridge below her low hill, then their torsos. The three men stopped at forty feet, hands clearly visible in the moonlight—two armed Palestinians from her unit and an unarmed blond European wearing a dusty suit and fedora hat. Saba covered her face. The Palestinian on the left approached to twenty feet and used Arabic to break the silence. "We have the visitor."

Saba nodded. She'd been instructed to talk with this man, had watched him inspect their camp during the day, following him at a discreet distance. He had inquired about her personally, asking the Iraqi commanders to arrange this meeting. Saba cocked her head in invitation, the pistol still aimed from under the paper. At seven feet, the Palestinians dropped comfortably to the rocky marl; the European remained standing, removing his hat.

"I am Erich Schroeder," he said in courtly English. "An honor." He bowed only his blond head, none of his six-foot athletic frame. "I extend personal greetings from our Reich president, Reichsmarschall Hermann Göring. Your long list of successes, including Dhār el Baidar, is the subject of much envy and appreciation."

Saba smiled at the German's eyes, blue as Circassian cloth. She had not seen blue eyes before. The smile quit as she read the remainder of him.

He said, "May I continue?"

"Our custom is to share our tents." Saba bent her empty hand to the low stool on her right. "Not our lands. Do you come to speak of this, Herr Schroeder? Or is it something else that matters to the butchers of Europe and not to me?"

The German nodded and sat the stool, his hands cupped on his knees and empty, the suit wrinkled but well cut.

"The Reich wishes Palestine, Arabia, and all of the desert to be free of Zionists and their British protectors."

Saba considered him and his noble wishes for a people he could not know. "And the Germans? Are we to be free of our princely benefactors when this is accomplished?" She glanced at the *Times*. "Your Führer offers flowers to the English, a grand partnership against Stalin in the East."

Herr Schroeder smiled, his skin as colorless as the English but brighter. "Like Palestine, we are a small country; one devil must be confronted at a time." His face attempted fervor. "But eventually all territory enslaved by the British Empire should be freed of their king and his Jews."

Saba glanced at the Palestinians, turning her half-closed hand at her stomach, a gesture of disdain meant to teach them something about all Europeans, the shifting loyalties of treacherous men who would "help" the people of the desert.

Erich Schroeder followed her glance, then returned with more real respect in his voice, less noble alliteration. "The oil of your deserts can make the Arab servant or king, prisoner of the Jew or his master—"

"I have no quarrel with the Jew, unless he is German or Pole or Russian and he would colonize my homeland." Saba leaned closer. "His god, your gods, do not interest me if you stay in your forests and out of mine."

The German smiled and nodded again, his blond hair falling over one eye. "May I ask where you learned your English, your politics? Quite impressive."

"The desert is full of teachers, Herr Schroeder, and of thieves and patriots dying for the causes of others." Saba stood and folded the newspaper one-handed. The pistol eased to her hip, finger still tight on the trigger. "You waste your words, bright eyes, and handsome smile. I fight for no one but Palestine." She stayed in his face. "And for her I will kill you, your Führer, and the children of your precious Reich . . ." Saba allowed that to hang in the air. "If their deaths drive the invaders from this desert."

"Please." He motioned for her to reconsider, to sit. "I have traveled a great distance and at great expense. We have common ground, you and I, if you will listen."

Saba checked the seated Palestinians; two sets of brown eyes implored her to listen. In truth, she had no choice. She could listen now or in the morning after her superiors commanded her again to do so. Benefactors with quality arms and budgets as large as their mouths were in short supply, and without the support of the despised Iraqis, her unit would be forced away from the fight and into the piecemeal bandit tactics where she had begun.

Saba offered coffee from her fire and invited the three men into her tent.

Inside, the partisans sat away from her—this invitation was a first—and allowed the German her right side, both out of courtesy for his money and respect for her temper. She was lightning with the dagger and favored her right hand. Saba watched her men scan the interior without moving their heads, examining her small stack of captured books and newspapers, the worn pillow of her sleeping rug, and two rifles with a leather ammunition belt strung over the barrels.

The German spoke without honoring her tent. "It is said that you pass well for a man, although I'm confused at how this could be."

Saba frowned. "I do not hunger for attention, the affection of men." She nodded at the two Palestinians. "I am surrounded by them and their odor."

Herr Schroeder stayed silent, his bright eyes trying to read her.

"Your business, Herr Schroeder. Your time in my tent is short."

He cleared his throat. "The refinery at Sitra Island, Bahrain. It produces gasoline, in theory for automobiles that are almost nonexistent in the desert—"

"I have no fight in Bahrain. My enemy is here."

Schroeder smiled. "Your fight requires resources, no? And your enemy is most assuredly England, and she is everywhere."

Saba had no argument for that and didn't.

"Final tests on this refinery are complete. The gasoline will support England's mechanized battalions in Palestine and elsewhere in Arabia, *not* automobiles. It is a specialized refinery, one that will also produce fuel for airplanes, planes that one day soon will bomb your villages and cities."

Saba had never flown, but understood and feared superior industrial armament such as tanks. She had seen planes over the desert and read of them in the *Times*. "I know nothing of refineries."

"But you will, through me. The English have completed a large plant in Abadan, Iran, and are building another in Palestine, not two hundred miles from here in Haifa Bay. The Haifa plant is to be secretly modified during its construction and modeled after Sitra-Bahrain, immediately after Sitra-Bahrain proves successful."

Saba shrugged, wondering aloud why this was in her tent.

"England has centuries-old networks throughout the region. She uses those networks to reward and protect those desert monarchs and their families who select *England's* surrogates to develop the oil reservoirs. As you have seen, England's military and monetary resources are deployed against *any* rival who opposes these corrupted monarchs and, by default, England."

"Why tell me how the great nations of Europe poison the wells of others?"

"You read and write English. You can travel as a Bedouin man or woman as needed. This refinery in Bahrain is a partnership of American oil companies and the shortsighted sheikh in Bahrain, both protected by England's navy and air force. We wish you to assist a skilled team of Arabs who will cripple the refinery but not destroy it."

"Why Arabs? And why only cripple it?"

The German nodded a slight congratulation. "The Arab must be seen as fierce, too potent for the English to subjugate further. Nor should the desert appear safe for *American* investment without the good will of the region's true owners, the Arab."

"This benefits the Germans?" Saba remembered their part in the American Revolution, 30,000 mercenaries fighting for the British Crown. "Do Göring and Hitler wish to be peacemakers or reign in the desert as they would in Austria?"

The German seemed confused, either at her meaning or her command of strategy.

He spoke deliberately. "Germany, and all of Europe, faces the great Bolshevik threat massing in the east, an army of millions. It is in Germany's national interest, and the world's, that the desert states rule themselves, forming alliances with those who would benefit their future. The Reich wishes to be remembered as one who helped you fight the colonial powers in Palestine and throughout the region."

"For that you would be remembered."

He settled, comfort returning to his posture.

Saba said, "It is your weapons that arm this camp and bin Faisal's mullahs, yes?"

Schroeder nodded.

"And for that you expect me to agree? To attempt a bombing for which I have no experience? I am a desert fighter and nothing more."

The German added twinkle to his blue eyes. "There are many ways to fight *all* the invaders." He glanced toward the Iraqi section of the camp. "We wish to arm and teach the Raven, add new weapons to her arsenal." Erich Schroeder leaned closer, but not close, and whispered, "That is my offer . . . *to you alone*. A payment you may one day spend as you will, against *anyone* you will."

CHAPTER 8

December, 1937

M erry Christmas, gentlemen." Eddie wiped sixteen hours of sweat and grease and tired from his face, grinned at D.J. Bennett holding a dirty glass, then at Foreman Bill Reno offering the bourbon bottle. It was the three Americans' second Christmas together at the end of the earth: seventeen months and none of them easy. Eddie's thrill at bringing his designs to life had been more than tempered by the harsh realities associated with actually doing it.

Eddie, Reno, and D.J. clinked glasses, pleased that the evening's efforts hadn't killed them or anyone else. The radio chirped on Reno's desk: "Little Orphan Annie" was looking everywhere for Santa Claus. Eddie poured himself another shot. You'd have to drink a great deal of Bill Reno's J.T.S. Brown to mistake Bill Reno or D.J. Bennett for Santa Claus.

But that's who D.J. was. Had it not been for the often hardnosed, narrow-focused, oddly perceptive King Ranch cowboy, Eddie would be long dead. Eddie knew it; D.J. Bennett knew it; Bill Reno knew it; God knew it. What had begun with blackmail and suspicion in front of the Biograph Theater—Eddie a fugitive/D.J. an outlaw in uniform—had become a partnership: Eddie worked sixteen-hour days to duplicate what he'd accomplished as a test in East Chicago and D.J. kept the desert from killing him.

And it was clear the desert wanted to kill Eddie Owen. Redesigning a refinery while you built a refinery that had never been built before was either a bold act of innovation or, as some said, an overt preparation for war. Building said refinery in one of the most inhospitable deserts on earth was, well, troubling.

Eddie's weekly letters home couldn't do the desert justice even if he'd wanted to be truthful, which he didn't. Three British RAF pilots were dead and three badly injured. Nine Spitfire and Hawker wrecks dotted the sandy bottom of Bahrain's gin-clear Tubil Bay. Eddie's AvGas was the reason. Eddie had duplicated his construction success at East Chicago, but his AvGas production runs were hideously flawed, his attempts at correction and balance far from complete in spite of double-shift days and relentless pressure from every direction. At the demand of its oil company clients, Culpepper Oil Products was actively recruiting other engineers and attempting to train them in East Chicago.

So far, and with great effort and probably personal risk, D.J. had kept Eddie from being replaced and Eddie's family off the road to California. How D.J. had accomplished this he repeatedly declined to share, saying, "Just be glad your boy Culpepper's got some character flaws." D.J. pointed Eddie at Bill Reno's transatlantic radio. "You're on."

"On what?"

"Our foreman set up a call to your folks."

Huh? That would be a week's pay. The Owen family used paper and pen. It allowed everyone to eat.

Reno barked, "Bullshit I did. Mr. Goddamn Mayhem Bennett here said the call was part of your contract, that I'd be on the wrong side of all things clean and holy should I object." Reno eyed D.J. "Not that the risks somebody's been takin' on your behalf are approaching clean and holy. Or smart."

Eddie looked at D.J. D.J.'s face was blank.

D.J. said, "Your ma's got 'em all waiting by the phone at the general store in town. You bought 'em a tree, a turkey, and a gift or two for the kids."

Eddie blinked. His family hadn't had anything approaching "Christmas" in seven years. He looked at Reno. Reno shrugged. Eddie looked back to D.J. Eddie's eyes began to mist. "You did that?"

D.J. drank bourbon. "Santa Claus." D.J. chinned at the radio. "Use the fuckin' thing; we ain't got the whole goddamn day."

Eddie hugged D.J. hard. "Thanks." He clamped D.J.'s arms to his side and choked out, "For everything."

D.J. said, "You don't get extra for being a girl."

Seventy-five days had passed since Christmas.

D.J. didn't see how Christmas had helped a damn bit. He spit by his shoe, watching Eddie pace the marl inside the boxing ring behind the canteen. The kid probably wouldn't fold—Eddie'd shown no quit thus far, and a reasonable man would've—but the kid was right up against it. Times like these, a conscience worked against a man.

D.J. said, "Tomorrow's gonna happen whether you worry about it or not."

Eddie's gas was crashing RAF planes pretty regularly now, four more in the last thirty days. Two more pilots were dead, boys Eddie's age, boys with families just like his.

Eddie exhaled, rubbed his face, and kept pacing the ring.

"You're the best at this, kid; exact science, it ain't. A new man comes in from Culpepper, he'll have to learn what you already know, *if* the sumbitch can learn it. Either way, there's gonna be dead planes and dead pilots. Just lots more of 'em with the new guy."

Eddie rubbed his face again. "I can't kill these RAF pilots anymore. Someone else has to be able to do this better. Let 'em fire me. I'll go home; the family, we'll do something, somehow." Eddie looked at D.J. "I'm sorry, I can't kill any more pilots. We'll stop tomorrow's test—"

"Nobody's stopping nothing. Hitler's on the march. You and me can cry all night but the RAF is flying your gas tomorrow. One of these days the gas will work—maybe that day is tomorrow, maybe it's next month—but it'll happen because we didn't fold when it got bloody." D.J. stepped inside the ropes and into Eddie's way. Eddie stopped and looked up. Twelve inches separated the two men. D.J. said, "I'm proud of you, kid. And we both know I don't say that easy. Tomorrow's a trench fight. If we lose, we take the beating, stand up, and go again. We do that because we're made outta the same stuff that kept your pa on that farm, your ma there with him. Your people don't run. Your people don't quit. And neither do we."

Eddie exhaled.

D.J. said, "Pick your head up, goddammit. I'll not have these miserable bastards see you wonderin'. C'mon. Around the corner— we're drinking to tomorrow. She'll have winners and losers, but she ain't putting nobody we know on his knees."

Morning came because it always does, this one with a hangover. Eddie glanced at D.J., stoic behind the wheel of a parked 1936 Ford convertible the hipsters back home called a "breezer." Eddie sat in the passenger seat, staring across the bay at the runway of

Shaikh Hamad's new airport. Eddie squeezed at the tremble in his hands. The tremble should've been directly related to tomorrow's bare-knuckle contest with Ryan Pearce, troubling for sure, but not the reason for today's stomach or last night's D.J.–Eddie, father-son chat in the boxing ring and canteen. Eddie'd had another "vision," this one now titled Mixture 41. Across the bay, an RAF pilot selected by loser lottery was about to bet his life on it. Mixture 41 was an off-balance blend that had appeared in Eddie's head three weeks ago while lying on his cot trying to imagine the girl he'd fall in love with. Two girls actually, one for him, one for D.J. The nightly search for "happy ever after" was a ritual, the only break in an endless chain of heat, hate, failure, and death. The worst nights were a cauldron of guilt and self-doubt, and of late had required more and more of D.J.'s father-son chats. D.J.'s uncanny ability to shift from his hardass "major" persona and its bare-knuckle protective perimeter to a genuine, almost gentle, South Texas cowboy was a thing of beauty. Eddie was pretty sure there was no better living creature than D.J. Bennett. Odd, that God packaged this way, but then God had made dinosaurs, animals with jaws full of teeth but who only ate when hungry and never their own children.

Although D.J. was absolutely positive a war to end all wars was coming, Eddie's "happy ever after" was just as positive that he and D.J. would be alive when it was over. They'd sit down with Benny Binion and Floyd Merewether, probably out in Nevada, far away from the rubble and disease D.J. said would be the postwar future for much of the world. With Eddie as his sidekick, D.J.'s postwar future wouldn't be like what D.J. had faced at the end of the last war, his wife and only son lost to a range fire, the "Hoovervilles," and the labor riots. D.J. liked to play cards, loved horses and outside. The Eddie-and-D.J. show would set up in Nevada as part of Benny's plans for legalized gambling. Eddie'd had a vision for Benny's gambling, could now see how engineering and mathematics and a sense of fair play would be a good use of a first-class education, university-taught and otherwise. There'd be no dead pilots. Eddie and D.J. would import the scrub mesquite so D.J. could cook his jackrabbits. The entire Owen family would relocate to Nevada and be safe. It would be aces.

Yeah, it would, if Eddie could stay the course. If the RAF pilot about to fly Mixture 41 survived the next ten minutes in his cockpit, betting the rest of his life on Eddie's vision. Eddie squeezed his hands whiter. He'd "seen" the entire formula, the combustion colors, all the way to the engine tones. His slide rule couldn't prove it and he'd fallen asleep still trying. Unconscious, he'd dreamed the vision all over again. Eddie told no one, including D.J., and spent part of the next fourteen nights making the modifications in secret, then ran the gas and hid the liquid. On night sixteen, he began to test, and the RAF group captain had somehow found out. The group captain told Eddie, "Prudence and caution are not attributes of the victorious; they are sedition. If you won't do the job, there'll be new engineers here to replace you who will." Eddie's "vision gas" passed the ground test. The RAF group captain ordered it put in the Spitfire and a young pilot/lottery loser into the cockpit.

On the north side of the bay, a lone Spitfire leaped off the runway and wheeled high into the morning sun, one bad gallon from exploding or splattering into the Gulf. Eddie tensed, bracing one hand against the dashboard of D.J.'s parked convertible. The Spitfire climbed toward 15,000 feet. Eddie concentrated on the engine tone. The Spitfire topped out . . . then broke screaming into an eighty-degree dive. Eddie's eyes squeezed shut. These RAF pilots had balls like you couldn't believe and a fatal good humor that made most people cringe. The pilots kept to themselves out on their base at the airport, but as Eddie had written Benny and Floyd, if they could convince these pilots to take up driving, whoever employed England's RAF would own the Jacksboro Highway.

D.J. grumbled. The plane screamed toward the water. Eyes shut, Eddie focused on the engine tone—still steady, thank you God, but louder, louder, and louder still . . . and for too long. "No, goddammit!" Eddie's eyes popped open, glued to the blue-water intersect where the crash would happen.

D.J. said, "Pull out. C'mon, Beethoven. You got the gas."

The Spitfire roared toward the water. And pulled out.

"Oh, yeah! Oh, yeah!" Eddie slapped the dash, then D.J.'s shoulder hard enough to wish he hadn't. "It worked!"

D.J.'s mustache rose above a smile that pushed his scarred cheeks high enough to wrinkle his eyes. "Edward my man, congratulations. I do believe you've done it." He slapped Eddie's knee. "Your gas may actually kill the right people someday. Be the blood in Roosevelt's veins if we can get it to the deservin'."

Eddie didn't want to think about "killing the right people," just that his gas hadn't killed anyone today. "Wish our RAF boys would wait till I worked out the kinks."

"No time." D.J. frowned. "We'd all be living in the Hoovervilles and speaking German."

The Spitfire topped a second climb and dove toward the water. Eddie held his breath. The Spitfire . . . pulled out. Eddie shuddered. "Jesus Christ, man, park that thing. I can't take another dive."

The pilot did a third dive, survived, banked, and landed. Eddie let his head roll on his neck. D.J. put the convertible in gear and tapped the accelerator. Eddie's bodyguard/pal/desert-swami drove them onto Shaikh Hamad's nearly finished causeway. Ultimately, this drive wasn't just to watch this morning's test flight away and apart from those it might kill, it was also another father-son chat. Eddie's mouth had placed him in a pickle and he had respectfully declined D.J.'s offer, then demand, to intercede.

D.J. was not partial to unaccepted wisdom. He tapped the pistol on the seat between them, then inhaled to begin his "grow the fuck up" speech and his "operational plan" for how this would be accomplished.

Eddie looked away—never a good idea to antagonize a mountain lion. Eddie hid a grin, checking the Gulf that didn't require checking. *The gas worked. We did it.* Eddie patted D.J.'s arm. In spite of D.J.'s temperament on days like today, D.J. was the difference between how bad it was and how bad it could be. He was mysterious when it suited him, disappearing into thin air when oil company executives from the USA were visiting, then reappearing without explanation. According to letters from Eddie's mom, D.J. had repeatedly reached deep into Oklahoma's Dust Bowl to help the Owen family and even some of their neighbors, and D.J. had never mentioned that, either. He was always armed, asked for no quarter, and gave none when challenged. D.J. was a pal—that was for sure—but a pal who, unfortunately, saw a cold-blooded, merciless future with the absolute clarity of an Oklahoma tent shouter.

D.J. tapped the pistol again. "I'll be taking your notes and papers for safe keeping. Anything you got written down, give to me."

Eddie saluted.

D.J. frowned. "Pay attention, wiseass. We're settling tomorrow, today."

Eddie braced for the discussion of his immediate future. Avoiding D.J.'s grim predictions for mankind while building a refinery that would aid in this extinction had been easier than avoiding the endless Indian and Irish friction with the Brits. Eddie had not proven adept at minding his own business. The *Sinn Féin*–related arguments usually turned violent, always slowed construction, and, in the end, had snared Eddie a second time.

Eddie focused on the Shaikh's steel rigging, not "tomorrow's business." The Shaikh's suspended steel and concrete causeway was a staggering achievement, lauded as one of the new wonders of the Arab world. And who wouldn't agree? There was nothing like this in Dallas or even Chicago. Maybe the new bridge spanning San

Francisco Bay, but it was only nine months old and having trouble, and loads of smart money was betting that the "Golden Gate" Bridge couldn't/wouldn't hold.

"You can't fight him," D.J. said, breaking the silence. "Ryan Pearce will kill you. And you know I can't let that happen; we've got bigger fish to fry."

Eddie settled into the leather and casualled an arm over the convertible's door. Casual lasted two or three seconds until, just ahead of them, armed Royal Marines signaled them to stop.

D.J. stopped the convertible.

Eddie said, "Someone has to fight Pearce, but you shooting him isn't an answer I want any part of. Not 'cause of me."

D.J. sniffed one side of his lip.

Eddie said, "The man's a bully. Just plain mean. And not as tough as y'all think. Make it a fair fight and I can handle him—"

"Fair fight?" D.J. spit tobacco juice as the Marines approached. "It's bare-knuckle here and you know it." D.J. showed Eddie blotchy, knotted hands. "Like the picket lines. Better you get on one of these airplanes like Bill Reno said, 'head to Bakersfield, pick some fucking fruit.'"

"Like you'd let me? Hell, I haven't been in a *car* in a year and a half. I've been handcuffed to a refinery cracking tower."

"Hands up!" A British sergeant squared up to the convertible's front bumper and jabbed with a big pistol. "Out!"

D.J. showed his hands and craned around the windshield. "D.J. Bennett, from the refinery."

The sergeant sidestepped and wheeled the pistol at Eddie.

D.J. yelled, "He's okay! Calm the hell down."

"Move your arse, Yank. Bomb on the deck." Five rifles behind the sergeant were pointed at the windshield. "Out! Now!"

D.J. opened his door and nodded Eddie out. Eddie looked past the rifles to the uniformed Brits clustered farther up the causeway. "Blow this bridge? Jesus, it's a work of art."

D.J. spit again. "Shooting that *Sinn Féin*, IRA motherfucker won't send the proper message. *One* of us is fightin' him now; put that in the goddamn book. He and his fucking mates ain't blowin' my refinery."

Two Royal Marines rode in the jeep's front seats, Eddie and D.J. in the back. The borrowed convertible had been lost to impound and bomb search. Eddie built queasy on top of nauseated. D.J. broke twenty minutes of bumpy silence as they approached the refinery gate, "Brits and the Shaikh are some lucky sumbitches. Fifty sticks of dynamite and a bad blasting cap. As our Irish friends would say, 'She'd have been a banger.'" Eddie focused on the refinery's twelve-foot chain-link fence bristling with three shifts of BAPCO guards. All had rifles now and combat stances. Every worker who approached the gate was braced and searched. Eddie's stomach rolled again. The jeep passed through the gun barrels and grumbling Arab day laborers queuing.

On the paycheck side of the fence, nobody was working. The Brits stationed at the refinery's working perimeter used bayonets to ring back anyone who stepped near. Intel officers questioned East Indians with loud rebukes and occasional punches. Unhappy Irishmen who weren't already handcuffed inside interrogation rooms faced British officers and BAPCO guards outside who waved cocked pistols and wanted to use them. D.J. and Eddie's escort delivered them to the infirmary.

In the treatment room, the American doctor slapped Eddie's back. "First class, Eddie. First class. It's New Year's Eve in the RAF barracks, pilots drinking your gas from champagne glasses."

Visualizing a glass of gasoline made Eddie's stomach churn. The doctor tonic'd Eddie, then asked D.J. a question about the diffused causeway bomb that D.J. didn't answer. The doctor commented on tomorrow's fight with Ryan Pearce. "Your stomach will be fine. Tomorrow, though, that's another thing entirely."

Eddie tried to chuckle. "Who'd you bet on?"

"Gave the four to one. Sorry, I've stitched up eight or nine of Pearce's disagreements." The doctor bit on his lip. "Wouldn't have provoked him, had there been an alternative."

"*Provoked* him? Those half-breeds were dumbass teenagers working the cafeteria. Pearce baited them into that fight for nothing more than them saying, 'Talley ho,' after he told them to button up waving a Union Jack patch. I stepped in because the whole goddamn tent was just watching him beat them half to death."

D.J. said, "What you 'stepped' in *again* was none of your damn business."

A snarling Bill Reno stormed through the infirmary door and glared at Eddie. "Now we *all* got your damn problem."

Eddie shook his head. "How is it that the Brits are always the bad guy? Who the hell are the Irish to decide you get your butt kicked if you wave the Union Jack? Jesus, what about the Japanese? Or the Germans or the Russians? Assuming the newspapers are true, those fellows aren't fooling around. Especially if you're Chinese or your family goes to church on Saturday."

The doctor said, "The Nazis and Japs aren't occupying Northern Ireland, and Ryan Pearce isn't Jewish: good Papist boy, I'd imagine."

Eddie checked his hands. "Who took me at four to one?"

Bill Reno answered. "Hassim took the four to one. Seems the sandys like you. Probably because them boys you saved got part Arab blood." Reno looked at D.J. "We got us a situation here—to finish this refinery we gotta have labor and we gotta have sponsors. We can't have bombs, can't have labor fighting one another wholesale." Reno nodded at Eddie. "Gotta have their champions fight instead. Our boy has to fight, or at least show up to fight. Up to you, Bennett, to see Eddie don't die." Reno looked at everyone in the room. "Y'all think today's test was the beginning of the good times, don'chya?" Reno stopped at Bennett and said, "I *know* you know what's coming. Be just goddamn swell if you took your foot off the gas long enough for us to get out of here alive."

Ten goddamn hours. Bill Reno snarled into his coffee. *Good, goddamn these sons-a-bitches.* An entire day wasted to wrestle control of *his* goddamn refinery from Brit and BAPCO officers. A bunch of uniformed piss squeezers whose only corporate authority to impede him was their numbers, weapons, and willingness to use them. And the Irish couldn't be outdone. Hell no, the mick bastards were threatening to strike, maybe kill them a foreman, too. Again, all because of Eddie goddamn Owen.

Reno frowned till it hurt. Eddie goddamn Owen. Ten thousand miles west in the Carbon and Carbide Building, Eddie Owen wasn't a fucking white-knight idiot; he was a goddamn hero. The coded field report Reno had submitted this morning on Eddie's Mixture 41 had generated confetti parades on Standard Oil's executive floors. And when the test rumors hit Wall Street later today or tomorrow, those execs and stockholders would be neck deep in AvGas money. If the sons-a-bitches got their air war, they'd be the richest men on the planet.

Bill Reno surveyed his refinery from his trailer's window. After Eddie and Bennett left the infirmary, the Royal Marines had gone after them a second time. The RAF group captain got the Marines to stand down before Bennett could shoot the Marine hostage he'd taken. Within minutes of the group captain cutting Bennett and Eddie loose, the Royal Marines began arresting *all* members and associates of *Sinn Féin*. Every goddamn one of the Irish bastards. Eddie Owen's release had nothing to do with the Brits' *Sinn Féin* dragnet, but that was a fact no Irishman in camp would ever believe. An hour ago the Brits had pronounced the refinery clean of bombs, then finished the *Sinn Féin* arrests by beating twelve Irishmen unconscious and almost to death.

Reno rubbed feeling into his face. Somewhere in the day's "lesser" events were options he was having trouble locating. Bahrain was a British protectorate, an important detail a guest or guest worker wanted to remember when King Georgie felt threatened. Tomorrow would be worse than today, the micks swearing blood for their jailed and beaten mates. Allowing Eddie's fight was bad; canceling it would be worse. Fucking Okie had to square up on Ryan Pearce over some Arab kids no one gives a damn about in their own fucking countries . . .

Reno paused. A bad thought trumped other bad thoughts.

What if it had been Pearce who picked Eddie? Pearce wasn't a flag waver, for Ireland or anyone else. Ryan Pearce was a hard-knuckled line boss who worked for money, fought for money, and probably killed for money. A fucking mercenary. Reno's stomach knotted. Better stop the fight; the fight could be some kind of diversion . . . Sabotage? Like the causeway bomb? Who? Arabs? A family squabble—princes taking down the Shaikh? Hell, it could be Nazis. No, today's successful test wasn't known when Pearce's fight started, but it for damn sure put this refinery on every chessboard from here to Iceland . . . True enough, but no Nazis would ever get in past the BAPCO and Royal Marine guards, not now or tomorrow during the fight.

Reno yelled for Hassim, standing just four feet away and waiting. "We got work to do. Make sure there's plenty of whiskey drunk in the canteen tonight. I wanna see boys with hangovers. Make noon tomorrow as painful as possible. You read me, Hassim?"

Hassim nodded and extended an empty palm. "This will cost. The Irish have a strong thirst."

●●●

Eddie hadn't slept well. High-noon sunlight ricocheted off the sand behind the infirmary. A homey West Virginia drawl lingered in his face. Eddie listened and wished he'd made other choices.

"Ring's leveled out and ready. Gotchya four fifty-five-gallon drums, brand-new posts cemented in their centers. Those are the corners. Stay out of 'em. Them drums'll break a bone. Crowd'll be close and just as dangerous."

Those bits of bare-knuckle wisdom belonged to a cauliflowered Logan County miner-turned-pipe-fitter, scarred arms and torso not much tighter than the steel cables Eddie had admired on the causeway. Eddie flexed his hands. The pipe fitter unwrapped Eddie's knuckles, the smell of pickle brine so strong it made everybody's eyes water.

"Use his body." The pipe fitter threw two soft punches at Eddie's gut and glanced at D.J., frowning agreement. "Won't break your hands on the body. Bust up his breathing apparatus. Step back and knock his block off. Simple as that."

Eddie nodded, staying with the fantasy that he could beat the Middleweight Champion of Europe.

The miner-turned-pipe-fitter glanced at D.J. again, then Eddie. "Norfolk Railroad brought in fellas like ol' Pearce. Called 'em 'detectives,' used 'em to break our strikes." He bent his head into Eddie's face, then turned to D.J. "This boy ain't you in the day, Bennett; hell, he ain't even *me to*day. Ryan Pearce gonna kill this young fella if you let him fight."

Eddie couldn't help the smile.

The pipe fitter eased back from Eddie's smile. "Funny? Them Belfast fellas think you yellow-dogged 'em to the Brits. They got kin beat half to death, others jailed up in that Naval Yard suffering God and Mother Jones knows what. Sure as I'm standin' here, that Irishman's gonna beat those Oklahoma kidneys outta your body."

"No he ain't."

Eddie glanced up at D.J.'s comment. D.J. winked. "You stay away the first two or three rounds, that mick motherfucker will be begging for a trip to the barn."

"And how's that?"

D.J. patted his stomach. "Something the dumb sumbitch just ate."

The crowd was loud, drunk, and Irish, except one tiny wedge behind Eddie's corner. From Eddie's corner the crowd looked like slaughterhouse workers who'd run out of animals. Across the ring and naked to the waist, Ryan Pearce spoke with his three handlers. The Middleweight Champion of Europe was about one eighty, only twenty of that fat and well distributed. His wide shoulders were marked and blotchy from backslaps and rope burns. When he turned, he broke into an honest, unshaven grin and his typical two-finger salute. A nice fellow from twenty feet.

Eddie heard encouragement above the general bloodlust. He turned and glanced over his shoulder at Hassim ringed by six Arabs in traditional dress and Bedouin keffiyeh. Crushed in behind them were a horde of Irishmen and a few BAPCO guards. Beyond them at the farthest of the crowd's backs, Royal Marines edged in closer from their posts. Hassim shook both fists above his head, yelling something in Arabic. Eddie winked, scared shitless but ready to execute Mr. Pearce if the opportunity arose. Eddie was the bigger man, probably stronger, too, but not the more skilled or confident. Bare knuckles wasn't really boxing, it was a roadhouse fight without weapons. Eddie checked the crowd again and figured the next three minutes would prove somewhat painful.

The bell wasn't as loud as the roar. The referee tapped Eddie's shoulder, then pointed at Ryan Pearce, his hands up and ring center.

The pipe fitter peeled Eddie's robe—Bill Reno's memento bathrobe from the Adolphus Hotel in Dallas. Eddie went left; Ryan went right. Two steps and they were throwing.

Pearce looped a feint disguised as a right and hooked hard with his left. The fist caught Eddie's shoulder and jarred his spine. Eddie spun and set his feet. A straight right from Pearce landed high on Eddie's chest, knocked him back a step, and helped him duck a left that could've broken his jaw. Eddie countered from his crouch, landed underneath, and threw a left high and hard for Pearce's chin. A right dug deep into Eddie's kidney. He buckled, tried to stagger back, and took a hook square on the temple. Big white flashes and Eddie was breathing dirt. He rolled to his shoulders. Sun stung his eyes. Boot tops and hairy white legs provided some shadow.

"Four." A hand went by his face. "Five." Another hand. "Six."

Eddie rolled and made a knee. Blinks added less fuzz. "Seven." Ryan Pearce materialized in his corner, arms over the ropes. "Eight."

Eddie stood, wobbled, blinked for depth perception. The referee checked Eddie's eyes from kissing distance, paused, then waved at Pearce. Nice smile, hands up, and here he comes. Eddie waited. Pearce dallied leaving his corner. The crowd roar registered, as did the feeling in Eddie's feet. Lots of information all at once.

Son-of-a-bitch Irishman can hit, can't he?

Pearce circled. Eddie blinked. A jab snapped in Eddie's face, then another. Eddie ducked the first, slipped the second, intending to eat the third. Would hurt but be worth it. Pearce's jab landed; his timed follow missed. Eddie hooked him chin-high and hard, threw the follow right and another left. Bang, bang, bang. Pearce buckled, tossed a nothing right, and tried to unravel away on his heels. Eddie nailed a straight right that split Pearce's eye. Pearce staggered into the ropes, blood gushing. Eddie charged. Pearce bucked off the ropes, bent low and head rising. The head butt caught Eddie under the chin. He was conscious, staring into the sun again. Both hands hurt. The blood in Eddie's mouth made him cough and roll.

"Two." A hand in his face. "Three." The damn hand again. "Four." Eddie rolled to all fours, wincing from the weight on his knuckles. "Five." He straightened to his knees. "Six." Got to a foot. "Seven." And stood. His chest was blood paste and dust. The referee said, "Hands up." Eddie did that; the referee stepped out of the way and Ryan Pearce replaced him, one hand after the other. Eddie ducked; Pearce's chest slammed Eddie backward and they both fell wrestling into ring center.

The bell and the referee's giant hands ended round one.

Eddie staggered to his corner. The pipe fitter greeted him in the ring, fronting the rusted drum with a stool and towel. He sat Eddie on the stool, then doused him with a water bucket.

Behind Pearce's corner, the crowd tried to kill one another. Eddie watched thirty men fighting and BAPCO doing nothing. D.J.'s horseshoe mustache appeared and began moving around his mouth. Eddie picked up the words midsentence. " . . . the Cushing Flash, huh? Ain't gonna last three like that. I'll have poisoned the worthless sumbitch for nothing."

Eddie concentrated on breathing.

"Chickens run when there's a rooster in the pen and you ain't the rooster in this pen. That Irishman means to hurt you, bad, and the United States of America can't have that. You didn't want me to kill him, but that's what's gonna happen." Bennett tapped the pistol in his belt. "Lotta these people gonna die when I shoot him."

The pipe fitter nodded, thumbing Eddie's knuckles.

"Ouch!"

The pipe fitter frowned at D.J., then Eddie's left hand. "Use the other'un."

The bell for round two was the referee waving.

133

Ryan Pearce no longer looked friendly or like a fellow who had extra time. His right eye was closed and he was moving with his left hand up, the crowd screaming on all four sides. Eddie noticed the Arabs had added East Indians to their numbers; an entire side of the ring was now full-sleeved white robes and Indian tunics. A straight right whistled by Eddie's ear. Eddie countered to the body. Pearce headlocked him and dug fingers for Eddie's eyes. Eddie grabbed at the hand trying to rip him blind. The referee slammed a forearm that loosened the headlock. Eddie spun away, the ref between Pearce and him.

Debris sailed into the ring. Eddie ducked and checked his corner. East Indians skirmished with Irish. More Arabs and East Indians filed in, hundreds maybe. *Strange . . .* The ref pushed at Eddie's shoulder, yelling about fouls. Pearce's good eye was a coal boring in on Eddie. The ref's eye-gouge lecture didn't seem to be registering. The ref stepped out of the way and Pearce threw across the ref's chest. The punch mashed Eddie's lips and knocked him sideways into his corner on all fours. His face scraped the drum. D.J. yelled something. Eddie's eyes fluttered. Hassim was leaving, his head turned back over his shoulder as he and his Bedouins were swallowed by the crowd.

Hassim's leaving? I'm doing that bad?

The ref was counting again. Eddie swiveled before he stood, making sure Pearce wasn't waiting. He was, his boot tops shuffling just behind the ref's. Eddie faked left, stood right, then slid out on the ropes past the ref's shoulder. Pearce lunged wrong and Eddie was behind him, the remainder of the ring open to Eddie's back. Pearce turned into a mouthful of hard, overhand right. He staggered. Eddie dug two to the body. The ref stumbled out of the way. Pearce swung wild. Eddie floored him. *Like that, tough guy?* The ring ropes began caving in near Pearce's corner. Eddie staggered backward into hands pulling at him from his corner. The pipe fitter yelled in his ear: "Nice work, boy, nice work. Stand off him now, pound to the stomach. Boy'll be dog-sick soon."

The bell ended round two.

Eddie collapsed on the stool and nodded at the instructions being yelled, his eyes fixed on the crowd roiling behind Pearce's corner. Could be Hassim bailed on his gambling losses a bit early. Eddie's ear felt D.J.'s mustache before Eddie heard him talking.

"Damn, you can fight for a college boy." Bennett surveyed Eddie's face. "How's the hands?"

Eddie remembered how much they hurt. "Maybe another round or two if I don't use 'em."

The pipe fitter threw water in Eddie's face without warning D.J., soaking them both, then knelt and clasped Eddie's face with his left hand. "He'll be gunning for ya this round. Micks got tempers. Be careful; move to his right where he's blind. He's a man and you ain't."

The referee pointed Eddie out of the corner because it was too loud to hear the bell. A wave of number ten cans high-arced in from behind Eddie's corner, falling like ten-pound bombs on Pearce and his supporters. The Irish answered with beer bottles from three sides. Half landed inside the ring, the other half on the Arabs roaring behind Eddie. Eddie covered his head, as did D.J. and the pipe fitter. The referee drew a revolver, fired five shots in the air, then fanned the gun at the crowd. The cut on the ref's forehead was almost as bad as Pearce's eye and Eddie's chin. Six Royal Marines sliced into the crowd to separate the Arabs and Pearce's Irishmen. Rifle butts and rifle barrels beat back the hand-to-hand combat into a skirmish line, extending out from the ring's corner. Men shouted in languages Eddie'd never heard. Prone bodies appeared above the crowd, bloody and ragged. Hand to hand they were shuffled overhead away from the ring.

The referee reloaded his revolver, kept it in his hand, and waved Eddie and Pearce out of their corners, yelling, "Round three."

Eddie took two steps and the ground knocked him off his feet. A tower of orange fire mushroomed above the refinery's southern corner. Heat blast poured across the four hundred yards and into the crowd. Four thunderous explosions followed. A mountain of black smoke roiled up out of the pipes and tanks. Eddie tried to stand. Smoke swallowed the refinery and churned toward the ring. Another explosion, a blinding orange flash, then brilliant red flames. The ring crowd reeled and fought for balance using the shoulders of those jammed next to them. Smoke blocked the sun. The crowd panicked and shoved for room. Airborne fire burned through the canteen toward the ring. Eddie felt hands on his shoulder and turned to a USMC tattoo and D.J. yelling, "*Tank fire*. Get your ass outta here."

Eddie stumbled up as the dense smoke engulfed the ring. D.J. helped him through the ropes. The ring shielded them from flames and stampede like a dam about to collapse. Hands and elbows flailed in the new darkness. Men screamed. Eddie coughed, staggering behind the stampede, stumbling over men already unconscious underfoot. D.J. ran Eddie out past the main gate. The wind was out of the Gulf and blew the smoke back over men still trapped inside the refinery's fence.

D.J. leaned Eddie against a vehicle covered in soot. Men straggled out of the smoke shell-shocked, soot-covered, shirts and robes shredded. Most finished on their knees puking beer, oily air, and blood. D.J. pushed Eddie off the fender and farther away from the survivors. Bill Reno staggered out of the smoke wiping at grease and blood streaks on his face. Two Royal Marines were with him. Reno said, "You fellas all right?"

Eddie choked, trying to nod. D.J. glanced at the Marines flanking Reno. "Know something I don't, Bill?"

"Just about every-fucking-thing."

D.J. stepped past Eddie to Reno's shoulder. "The AvGas? Eddie-boy's section didn't blow, did it."

Reno nodded an inch, adding a street cop's frown. "Like somebody wanted to miss it." He glanced behind his shoulder at the Marines and spit. "The Brits are looking for Nazis. Could be their aspirations of becoming the Shaikh's new protector is more 'n a rumor."

"Nazis?"

Reno nodded. "Hitler just now invaded Austria."

D.J. took new stock of their surroundings. "The little house painter did it?"

"He did." Reno and Bennett stared at each other while the camp emptied, a Civil War battle scene with Arab and East Indian extras. Reno checked Eddie, Eddie's swollen hands patting at a swollen face. Reno said, "Whoever's responsible, Eddie's their target, too. Best he be moving away from Pearce and the lads as well. I'll call into Harold Culpepper, tell him his star refiner ain't protectable here for now."

"Who final tests Eddie's . . . section?"

Reno screwed his face into D.J.'s. "You gonna sacrifice that boy for Roosevelt? Who looks after your boy's people in Oklahoma when you goddamn heroes are all done fightin'?"

D.J.'s eyes narrowed. "What and who I am ain't no stranger to you. That war brewing out there starts . . . there won't be much anywhere to look after when it's over."

"You asshole freedom fighters actually give a shit about Eddie surviving till tonight, his next contract in Haifa best be startin' today. The Brits in Haifa got good reason and plenty of horsepower to keep Eddie whole. I'll get the tests done here; you got my word on that. If we need Eddie back, we'll deal with Pearce and the lads then when their blood's lower."

Bill Reno pivoted, looking into the stragglers as they dragged out through the main gate. He spit soot and wiped at the acrid smoke in his eyes. "Anybody seen Hassim?"

CHAPTER 9

March, 1938

S aba had seen the Palestinian, Hassim Dajani. It had been three days ago in the refinery flames. The IRA's causeway bomb had initially complicated her mission. But once the refinery had been pronounced secure, the bomb proved a benefit, the Marines focused on stopping an attack from without, not within. Saba replayed the bombing, searching for errors then that would kill her now.

The prizefight was ending its second round, the American bloody but rallying after a fierce beating, the crowd pressing and drunk with the blood. Saba, the explosives team, and Hassim had turned away to snake through shouting Arabs and Indians, then past an outer ring of British Marines and BAPCO guards standing on pallets and intent on the contest. Filing toward the worker billets, the men with Saba were loud, complaining of their gambling loss. Bahraini guards acknowledged Hassim without respect or courtesy, one guard grabbing his crotch and hissing. Another said, "*Kwanii*," calling him weak, a homosexual, an insult reserved for servants or prisoners. Palestinians, even those with education, were considered refugees who lacked the will and courage to hold their own land. Hassim averted his eyes and added nothing to his stride that might provoke a lesser man's betters, a signal to Saba's men to show no anger at the insults. They required no such signal. When all were safely past, Hassim whispered toward Saba's shoulder, "Bahrainis. The guards believe themselves royal, their Shaikh's uniforms and oil a way to shed the Arab skin and be as the English."

As they walked, Saba whispered through her teeth, her tone and inflection that of a man. "The Arab day is coming; it blows down out of the Beqaa Valley and up from the Sinai." She checked the gate ahead. "I have seen this wind, smelled it, sown it."

Hassim shied at her tone, unusual for a woman, even dressed as a man. And harsh as if her teeth had bitten many. There were stories of such a man-woman, but that is what they were, stories. Saba glanced at a guard, his disdain for them obvious in how he mishandled his weapon. The guard's disdain mocked men who were twenty-year guerrilla fighters, trained as sappers by the English in the Great War. The same men who had driven the kaiser's feared *Deutsches Asienkorps* from Palestine by bombing the Turkish/German outposts and mining their heavy convoys. A lifetime ago when England had been the Palestinians' trusted ally.

At the worker billets' gate, two Bahrainis argued instead of guarding, neither interested in the seven men strung out in a fifty-foot line. Saba and Hassim passed without speaking, as did their third man. The fourth stopped and spoke an insult to the Shaikh's wives. Both guards snapped to his face, one swinging his rifle. From behind, Jameel Nashashibi looped the rope from his keffiyeh around the guard's neck, spun to cinch it, and snapped the Bahraini's neck. The other guard slapped for his pistol. A dagger was driven through his heart. The bodies were dragged three feet to the guardhouse, stripped of their weapons and headdresses, and Hassim restrained from pounding the faces unrecognizable. Saba donned one set of guard clothes, Hassim the other. As guards, they walked the remaining members of the team into the tanks. The shaped charge took one minute to set. The explosion's chain reaction would pour fire across the refinery. The sappers added two minutes to the timer, engaged the clock, and the entire team sprinted through the mammoth oil tanks toward the prizefight. It took one minute to reach the last oil tank. Beyond the tank, two Bahrainis patrolled the road that separated the tank from the prizefight that was now a riot. Saba stopped her men behind the last tank. She shed the guard's headdress and the robe covering her laborer clothes, wiped sweat from her eyes, added a keffiyeh to re-cover her hair, and drew the guard's pistol. His belt fell to her feet. She checked the weapon's cylinder loaded with six rounds.

Hassim stared at the wings now partially visible beneath Saba's right eye. His eyes added white; he stuttered as he tried to speak. Saba grabbed a handhold on the last oil tank and waited for the first concussion. A thousand feet behind them, the sappers' bomb rocked the refinery. The Bahraini guards in the road staggered, fighting for balance. They turned toward the tanks using their rifle butts to remain standing.

Rushing at them had been the myth the strong chose to believe was a lie, her pistol tight in both hands and firing.

Saba finished the replay . . . reasonably confident the bombing had no errors that would kill her when she exited the car she sat. The bomb had done less damage than planned, but she was alive, as were all members of the team. All had crossed the fifteen-mile Arabian Bay without being accosted by England's Royal Marines. The last three nights had been spent hiding in Dhahran, Arabia. Two of those nights involved heated discussions with an Iraqi representative of Ghazi bin Faisal's latest reconstruction of his Pan-Arab Army of God and Erich Schroeder. These discussions had not gone as well.

The memory whitened Saba's hands; she glanced at Erich Schroeder. They shared the rear seat of a car outside Dhahran's tiny airport. The blond German was far more dangerous than the Iraqi representative, a self-important pig. For two days she had listened to both men praise Arabia's new king—their host, King Abdul Aziz Ibn Saud—and Ibn Saud's open hatred of all Jews, his fondness for the Führer, and Ibn Saud's private fear of England's domination. The Iraqi and the Nazi fed her hate as if it were lamb, as if she were a child who could not see past the garnish to the meat. On the third night they had offered her today's mission, it more foreign to her abilities than the last, and again baited her with the benefits. Trusting either man's final intentions was as laughable as their entrée, but the German's private promises of support against the Iraqi mullahs and the seed money he had already placed in her hands were another matter. So here she sat in the German's car, preparing to be someone she had no desire or tools to be—a woman of interest, a seductress, a woman who enjoyed the attention of men.

When she exited this car and walked inside the terminal's tent, she would be a Bedouin woman of means, her face veiled by a silken yashmak and the hood of a cloak-like burnouse covering her hair. Jameel and a second armed Palestinian would act as her Bedouin escorts. This airport was her third in as many weeks. A silver de Havilland airplane waited on the runway, its giant propellers silent, the desert sun glaring along its enclosed fuselage. She adjusted the veil already covering her face and demanded calm.

Erich Schroeder tapped his finger near Saba's arm but not on it, gently reinforcing the mission confidence she lacked. Schroeder said, "The flight is full. Sit one of your men in Eddie Owen's seat. The only empty seat will be next to you. He will be yours for half the day."

Saba's skin flushed; this would be the closest she had ever been to America. The anticipation surprised her. Minutes before the prizefight, she had stood within hearing distance of the American, the first of either she had seen. What struck her more than how the American looked was how he sounded. Not at all like she had imagined when reading America's history. Her Americans had Palestinian accents.

"And I am to do what with this man, Eddie Owen? Kill him? Have his child?" Saba moved her arm farther from Schroeder's fingertips.

"We have been through this. You and I have an agreement and it is your superiors' wishes."

"My superiors." Saba would have spit had there been no veil. "Zealot fools who see God on every sword and Palestine as their future colony. I return to the desert, to fight with those who would liberate my people."

Schroeder leaned away. A reassuring hand reached for her knee, hesitated, and stopped. "Liberation is expensive. Succeed in my missions and you will have your own camp, your own supply, your own war outside, or against, the Army of God. As promised."

Saba heard, again, what she wanted to hear.

The German continued. "We wish to know what this very special petroleum engineer Eddie Owen thinks of the Arab, the Germans, the English. You are a woman; in America he is comfortable with women, curious with foreigners. You speak the language and are not German. We suspect Eddie Owen does not yet understand the Nazi mission against the Communists and thinks us cruel to the Jew."

Saba understood the German mission. It was, in the end, no different than the Iraqi or English mission: *rule.* She read the Nazi's lifeless blue eyes instead of answering and wondered if all German skin had the frigid shine of a high mountain lake. His glance lingered again beneath her right eye, the tiny wings hidden by a mixture of kohl makeup and marl paste and covered by the silk yashmak. The tattoo could be covered for a brief trip or souk/medina visit, but she had never intended to hide the wings from close inspection. Sweat would always be a threat she could not control.

"You are nervous; I understand. This is not your usual terrain." Erich Schroeder nodded to the de Havilland. "With all due respect, you are a compelling woman, quite capable of gaining and holding a man's attention for a moment or a day or likely as long as you wish."

Saba accepted the compliment as a lie and prepared to face the airport and its American petroleum engineer, Eddie Owen.

Inside the Dhahran airport, the structural tents were crowded for the twice-weekly flight to Basra, Baghdad, Damascus, and finally Beirut. Flying was an event, flying in the desert more so. For every passenger braving the air, at least two Saudis or Germans or Americans were seeing them off. A woman aboard was most unusual and the cause of much comment among the Arabs inside and outside the cavernous black pole tent adjoining the runway. For this reason, Saba sat away from the others, shielded per Bedouin custom by her two escorts. From behind her veil she watched Eddie Owen. He talked with a mustached, bald man wearing similar clothes. This must be Eddie Owen's protection, a man named Bennett who the Nazis feared. Eddie Owen touched at his bandages and un-bandaged cuts. Most of his face was discolored and swollen, as were his hands.

He glanced toward her often but never stayed, never challenged her men as others might. Men were boys, prone to show their strength. She would be civil and ask about America and accept the insults of his hands and breath if that was what was to be. She would suffer this for Palestine. Then she would kill him for treating her with such liberty. She felt her teeth grinding and stopped, breathing deeply enough to raise the fabric covering her chest. Jameel locked on her eyes, then scanned for the threat, then back to her after finding none. Saba looked away, something she never did, then flattened a hand over her knee, a gesture that said, *It is nothing*. Jameel turned back to face the crowd.

•••

Eddie couldn't tell she was a woman even though D.J. said she was, possibly a Bedouin princess or the daughter of a wealthy merchant. Undeniably someone special if only because she was a *she* and waiting to board an airplane. Eddie had seen Arab women in Bahrain but not often—like Texas, the ladies were kept pretty close to the house and away from strangers. Culpepper's next paycheck for him was in English Mandate Palestine under contract to M.W. Kellogg, the Texas construction company hired by Shell Oil to build the Haifa refinery. Eddie had big aspirations for the young ladies of Haifa, hoping there was truth to the rumor they could at least drink coffee and talk to you.

The Haifa contract paid the same but had a drawback or two. Shell Oil was a Dutch/British partnership formed to *compete* with Standard Oil. Standard Oil and Culpepper agreeing to lend Eddie was, D.J. said, absolute proof that there was collusion among the big oil companies of Holland, England, and the USA. Those companies would produce AvGas and distribute it to the Nazis, thereby forcing the governments in England, Holland, and the USA to side with the Fascists against the Communists.

D.J. made it clear he did not intend to let that happen. How he planned to intervene was beyond what D.J. thought Eddie needed to know. The politics of oil and war was a cesspool. Girls over here were no easier to figure but a whole bunch more fun to think about.

Even from this distance, the Bedouin girl's black robes and cloak seemed expensive and exotic, catching the light in the folds, the flowing headdress hiding everything but her eyes. Eddie looked away, not wanting to stare, then back. She moved very little, shielded by the two men almost completely. Quite the picture if you'd been to a library and had an imagination—Eddie smiled back to high school English in Cushing, Oklahoma—the unapproachable princess of the *Arabian Nights*. The beautiful black mirage coming to life. The smile hurt his face all the way to the ears. And not a dime to show for the beating, the fight unfinished, the supposed insult to Ryan Pearce and Eddie's treachery to Ireland unresolved. Eddie inspected swollen knuckles. Man, his hands hurt . . . but at least Pearce no longer mattered. Pearce would be at the Sitra refinery for another six months or more before going to a Spanish plant, and by then Eddie could be anywhere.

To Eddie's left, a loud cluster of what looked like German businessmen in high-cut European suits were chatting with an equal number of Americans, some in cowboy boots, others in felt fedoras, briefcases in everybody's hands. D.J. elbowed Eddie, then nodded at the cluster. "The assholes with the American assholes are Germans." The cluster of Germans and Americans patted one another's backs. "Awful chummy, ain't they?"

Eddie smelled warning. D.J.'s warnings tended to include nasty predictions that, so far, had always come true. Eddie focused on the Bedouin princess instead.

"Hey, stupid." D.J. nodded Eddie toward two Saudi robes joining the Americans and Germans. "Being alive is about being awake. *All* the fucking time. And we both need your dumb ass alive."

Eddie tried to look less stupid.

D.J. frowned. "Notice there's no Brits in this tent. The American oil companies have the drilling concession in Arabia *instead* of the Brits. And the Brits have been in Arabia a long, long time . . . actually granted independence to this country. In effect *gave* Arabia to Abdul Aziz Ibn Saud and made him king . . . but the king didn't give the Brits the drilling concession. He gave it to Standard Oil."

Eddie thought about that. Wondered how Standard Oil had pulled a coup of such magnitude and why the Brits had accepted the outcome, so far.

D.J. continued. "Great Britain and the USA as *governments* are allies in the 'world problems' we read about every day against Germany, Japan, and Russia. Right?"

Eddie answered. "Yeah."

"But here in *this* desert, those same Brits are Standard Oil's direct competition for the oil rights. That puts Standard Oil in Ibn Saud's pocket. If Ibn Saud favors the Nazis—and the bastard does—then Standard Oil favors the Nazis or Standard Oil loses all Ibn Saud's oil. That puts Standard Oil directly at odds with President Roosevelt, his allies, and their policies—just like I told you." D.J. nodded at the oilmen. "And in that clusterfuck of assholes you're looking at is *proof* I ain't wrong."

Eddie glanced at the Saudis, Americans, and Germans chatting as if they knew one another well, not one Brit inside the tent. "Why are you always so sure our oil companies are for the Germans? The Germans don't have desert territory or desert oil fields for Standard Oil or the Texas Company to drill."

"The Nazis have guns and money. They need oil for their future plans, oceans of it. Standard Oil operates the oilfields in Hungary and Romania that supply Germany today, but there ain't near enough oil there. Out here where the real oil is, the Nazis got cow shit. Standard Oil hasn't found oil yet, but it's here." D.J. nodded again at the German and American cluster. "And all them sons a bitches know it."

Eddie looked confused or disbelieving, or both.

D.J. frowned. "Make it simple. The Arabs and their oil company partners sell oil for money. The Nazis burn oil in their factories, tanks, and planes. Our oil companies and industrialists are afraid of Roosevelt's New Deal and the 'Communist' unions, *not* the Nazis." D.J. glanced close over his shoulder and leaned to Eddie's, waving off any further discussion.

"There'll be people to meet you in Damascus. They'll drive you an hour drive through Syria—it's French, fucking assholes, too—but shouldn't matter. Brits will pick you up at the Transjordan border. Haifa's two hours south of there."

Eddie nodded, wondering how weird this travel segment would get.

"Don't say shit on the ride in. There'll be an MI6 man in the car. He won't identify himself, but he'll be the one to chat you up."

"You're not coming? I thought—"

"And like I said, when it comes down to the nut cuttin', nobody really knows which way the Brits are gonna go, but pick they will. Between the Nazis and the Russians, and soon. The king of England favors the Nazis but only half the politicians agree—a fucking mess for damn sure, inside the empire *and* out." D.J. pointed in Eddie's bandaged face. "Remember, you're not an AvGas man, just a special engineer trying to fix a temperature problem design before it gets built."

"But, shit, D.J., everybody in Bahrain knows—"

"These dumb shits don't know anything for sure." D.J. frowned at Saudis in traditional dress. "Who knows what you've been doing in Bahrain all this time? Any of them towelhead assholes look like college graduates?"

"The Irish knew. Ryan Pearce for sure."

"Maybe. But that mick's got his own problems now, probably headed to Pentonville where the Brits teach their hangmen how to hang. You make this trip nice and quiet and I'll see you in Haifa—"

"So you *are* coming to Palestine."

D.J. nodded. "Somebody's got to look after you."

"But you're not getting on the plane?"

A loudspeaker called the flight. D.J. said, "There's business back at the refinery that I don't want following us. I'll see to it, then to you. Don't get killed this week or I'll be out of work." They shook hands and D.J. pushed him toward the plane. "Be alive when I get there or you'll be facing one mad fucking cowboy."

Inside the plane, Eddie shuffled and sidestepped down the crowded aisle, apologizing to men speaking German as he passed. The princess was seated at a window, shiny black robes covering her in her seat. The adjacent seat was vacant. Couldn't hurt to ask, could it? Well, maybe it could, but no more than he already hurt.

"Excuse me, ma'am, this seat taken?"

Up close, her eyes were a brilliant brown—no, hazel—and they actually stopped him from talking. Wrapped in the cloak, she looked more deadly than attractive, her head rising to consider him without effort or trepidation, her shoulders flexing back on the seat. Nothing demure or angelic was in the posture, even seated. Annie Oakley in a satin bedsheet. Eddie smiled—no fringe, though—then swallowed further comparisons. *Better watch it, hoss.*

"You may." The voice was strong like her posture.

Eddie sat without touching her arm, then noticed the younger of the two men who'd been with her now standing at his shoulder. "Oh, sorry, this your seat?" The man was oddly weathered for his age, a smallish man with hard eyes and strong hands. Eddie followed the man's eyes back to her waving the man off. The young man bowed slightly and moved down the aisle. He was young, but not.

"Did I make a mistake?" Eddie used both hands to apologize. "Shouldn't I be here?"

"An empty seat. You are . . . an American?"

He smiled. "The accent, isn't it?"

"The bruises, I think."

Eddie laughed, noticed her eyes again. Man, she could look at you. "Sorry." He offered a hand. "Hi, I'm Eddie Owen."

She nodded and did not take his hand. "Calah al-Habra." She leaned against the window, squaring to scrutinize him. "You are injured?"

"Yeah. A bit." Eddie grimaced, which hurt and wasn't supposed to. "A prizefight, bare knuckler between two fellows who should know better."

"You were the winner or loser of this contest?"

He laughed again. "Tough to say. Didn't get to finish. Maybe it was a draw."

She squinted.

"A tie—no winner, no loser."

Two men bumped his shoulder, both apologizing in German, the second man a cold, blue-eyed blond who seemed to stare at the princess. Eddie turned to her, wondering what she looked like, if her face matched her eyes.

"Do all Americans prizefight?"

"Nah. Just the stupid ones."

The stewardess stopped at their row, explained oxygen masks in Arabic, then English, then spoke Arabic to the princess and English to Eddie, a bit of concern for Eddie's condition in her face and voice. "Would you care for water before takeoff?"

The propellers spun, vibrating their wing, and he wasn't sure he'd heard the stewardess right. He nodded because Calah with the hazel eyes had nodded. They buckled seat belts and he noticed her hand. The skin matched the strip of her eyes, olive and almost glowing, but rough for a princess, the veins standing all the way to her knuckles. She tucked the hand away and turned to watch the propellers.

"Fly a lot?"

She didn't answer, evidently intent on the engines. He touched her to ask again. She snapped from the window, the eyes serious as Fort Worth February. Eddie swallowed and eased back without realizing it.

Through the veil, she said, "You spoke to me?"

"Ah, yeah, I asked if you fly a lot?"

"Three occasions." A blink with eyelashes. "They are . . . a fearful thing."

The eyes hadn't looked fearful. More like a diamondback coming out of your boot. "Me, too, my second. You're going to Damascus?"

"Yes. And you? To the hospital? The French have a good hospital there for their countrymen."

"Jeez, I'm not hurt *that* bad." He patted his face with a lumpy hand. The stewardess brought their water. The princess declined hers by shaking her head. Eddie took his and drank, thirsty every day since he'd arrived.

"Is America as it is in the books?"

"Depends on the books. Which ones?"

"*The Great Gatsby.*"

Eddie smiled; somehow F. Scott and Zelda had made it to this girl's planet. "I live in Texas. You've heard of Texas? Cowboys, the Alamo . . ."

He could tell she was smiling, a sparkle in the eyes that hadn't been there before.

"Yes. Yes. We read of cowboys. And Indians. The Apache, Cherokee, Seminole—"

"That's a lot of Indians. Most people at home couldn't name two tribes, let alone three."

The plane began to taxi and she adjusted in her seat, then answered as if she were reading out loud. "The native peoples to parts of America, one million on a vast land mass, herds of buffalo that stretched from dawn to sunset."

Eddie grinned, amazed.

"Then the Europeans came." She stopped and the sparkle left her eyes. "The Europeans occupied the land, claimed it for their kings, drove the Indians west, and finally drove the English into the sea. For the latter you deserve the compliments America often receives."

That sounded *odd*, but then he had only her eyes and a foreigner's inflection to go by. Eddie smiled, hoping to hide his confusion, and felt the plane's engines rev higher. "America's a big place; I haven't seen most of it, just Oklahoma, Texas, and Chicago."

She brightened, adding posture, almost girlish. "Chicago. The skyscraper. Yes?"

"Yeah." Big smile. "Just the way I felt. You can't believe how tall the buildings are." Eddie held his hand above his head. "Five hundred feet or better. Huge. And they're all over the city. I was in—"

The de Havilland backed off the brakes and lurched forward. A slight gasp from the cabin, then another lurch. Eddie said, "Guess it's time to fly."

The princess had turned toward the window and remained in the large oval while the plane gained speed down the runway, bouncing over the concrete's expansion joints faster and faster, and then heaved into the air. Eddie's shoulders hit his seat back. The plane smelled like . . . perfume? Did Arab women wear perfume? Pain rushed up his arm. His knuckles were white on the armrest; a grimace replaced the grin. Big leap, then a shudder. He almost yelled but squeezed both armrests instead. Another shudder and they jumped higher. Jacksboro Highway at too fast for conditions. He said, "Holy sh—" before he knew it left his mouth.

She turned, no fear evident, composed in the seat belt. "Excuse me?"

The de Havilland rattled into the climb, adding steep to loud. "You are all right?" she asked.

Eddie thought of Flash Gordon on Saturdays at the Bijou, turned just his head, and answered through a badly hidden grimace and serious reservations. "Can't get enough of this, actually. You?"

Her eyes locked on his, strong but tender, almost maternal, and stared until he was too embarrassed to keep thinking about the plane bouncing and rocking and dipping—all things that must add up to "fly." She said nothing but had his full attention. The perfume again, light, but right there. Exotic but . . .

The plane was level. He heard conversation on his left, felt rested and just a steady vibration in his seat. "I'll be darned . . ."

She blinked, eyelashes again.

". . . you hypnotized me."

A laugh puffed her veil and she turned away, asking the window, "Are all Americans so . . . imaginative?"

Eddie unflexed his hands, wishing they hurt a lot less. The rest of him felt pretty good, considering. He would have touched all his parts, but that would've added stupid to an already brimming performance, then remembered she'd asked him a question.

"Ah, no . . . well, maybe. Jeez, how'd you do that?"

She faced him, the eyes the same, just a strip but luminous. "I think your contest has injured your brain."

"Possible. Heck, probable." He tried to laugh but he'd been out for however long it took this monster to reach level and had no idea whether that was an hour or a minute. Almost two years without women was a while, but he couldn't afford to get all drifty every time—

"You are all right?"

Shit, he was drifting again. Maybe the altitude. "I, ah, think I'm gonna take a nap."

Saba watched him sleep, his breathing normal, the discolored hands limp and comfortable. It had been the strangest thirty minutes of her life. America—right next to her! The boyishness in his laughter, the scent of soapy skin. America was real. *They had driven out England's army, yet he was afraid of flying.* She wanted to dance like she had as a girl, smiling at the boys, enjoying the air and the music.

Americans were no different than her! They had faced setbacks, too—Philadelphia, Germantown, Fort Mercer—but America had regrouped and found the will to win. And their victories—

"... *min wayn inta?*"

Saba jolted out of America to parry a blow. The stewardess stumbled backward in the aisle. The American still slept. No passengers watched. Saba answered the stewardess by lifting her head and saying, "No."

The stewardess passed to the next row.

Saba eased deeper into her seat and covered her hand. She checked the seats again, then the American, then allowed herself room to turn. She glanced at the window and the Persian Gulf below. The water asked her the question: *Who hypnotized whom?* The feelings were ... were more than the joy of American victory. An event so small but so immense. She had spoken to a man about something other than war and had enjoyed it. The thought of defending against him or killing him, and how she would accomplish either, had not crossed her mind. Neither of her hands had touched her weapons, nor had she considered asking him the German's questions as instructed. She'd just talked to him. Person to person.

Girl to boy.

Saba shivered and drove that away, brought the rapist Englishmen's faces to hers. They had been young, too. And brutal, and had shamed her for life, taken her family, her joy, her desire ...

The shivering stopped. No, they hadn't taken her desire; it was intact, just different. She had enjoyed watching the English soldiers die; it was her communion, her present, what she had to offer. Saba glanced at Eddie Owen and resolved to ply the forgotten questions. Had her father lived longer, he would have explained how alliances worked at the higher levels. She would be far better prepared and wondered if this American understood the battle plan, how all this was being organized by unseen men with unspoken ambitions. A small shudder interrupted her thoughts. The shudder vibrated down her side of the plane. The plane dipped left, dished, then righted. She heard the engines steady, then a jolt and the plane bucked. Eddie Owen stirred, his hand clutching for balance. Saba checked the wing, then the cabin, the passengers all frozen as if listening to a noise in the night.

The stewardess walked the cabin, a gentle hand touching each aisle seat. She offered a smile and occasional wink. "Turbulence. Sometimes the air above water is like a bumpy road. Nothing at all to be worried about."

Saba checked her window. The plane seemed no closer to the water or the Iran coastline. She felt disgust instead of comfort. The coastline was part of England's Empire. Iran was England. Why had neighboring Iraq been granted independence by the French; Saudi Arabia and Transjordan by the British; but not Palestine, Iran, and Bahrain? Syria, Lebanon, and so many others? Who were the Europeans to decide who went free and who remained a slave? The plane lurched hard right, throwing her shoulder into the window. Yelps echoed behind her. The plane shuddered, dished, then dived left. She pitched forward, belted in at the waist. The plane leveled but the engines coughed, then high revved on her side and steadied.

Eddie Owen said, "What the—"

They dipped, then swung hard right again and back. Burning oil? Saba turned, watching Eddie Owen turning to look behind them in the cabin. He said, "Uh-oh, there's smoke back there."

Saba checked the engines. No smoke, both propellers turning. A sharp jolt threw her and Eddie into their seat belts again.

"Damn." Eddie reached for her. "You okay?"

"Yes. You said smoke?"

He undid his seat belt and stood to look. The plane bounced and buckled his knees. "No one's out of their seats."

The loudspeaker announced the pilot. "We are experiencing a minor difficulty in the rear of the aircraft and, although minor, we think it best to land. Please keep your seat belts fastened and remain in your seats."

Their stewardess appeared with a small fire extinguisher and a frazzled expression. She asked Eddie Owen to sit, said not to worry, that they were making an emergency landing on the coast in Bushehr, Iran.

Saba almost bit through her lip. *Bushehr, Iran.* The British Political Residency: seat of all British power in the Middle East. Bushehr was a massive navy base and antiguerrilla training facility. She had fought the special men who trained there on three occasions, dangerous men who had killed many partisans and rebels in the mountains. A number of these antiguerrilla fighters had come close to killing her, and although she had wounded them badly, they had escaped, backed by reinforcements from England's regular army. Bushehr would be where those she had wounded had recuperated while others trained for the hunt.

The plane bucked. Saba realized she was rigid in her seat, Eddie Owen staring. She relaxed and sat back, steadying her breaths. The coastline was closer, the mountains of Iran adding color and shape. There would be no way out of Bushehr if she were recognized, if the mixture of marl paste and kohl makeup covering her tattoo was exposed.

The flat blue water speckled to white, the waves running west to east—

"It'll be okay."

Eddie Owen's voice surprised her, as did her panic. She had been confined before and escaped. This metal tube was no different. They could not know her on the plane, could they? Only on the ground, only after an inspection that revealed the wings— The engine drone changed pitch. Saba turned. The inside propeller on her wing was still. The plane yawed right and lower and began to vibrate. She gripped her armrest, noticed her hand, and retracted it under her robe.

The loudspeaker said prepare for an emergency landing, heads between your knees.

Saba looked at Eddie Owen, most of the blood gone from his face, an Englishman's lying smile forced over his mouth. Through the shudder raking the plane, he forced out, "Hey, you're a princess, right? *Arabian Nights*. I read the book. She didn't die on an airplane."

Saba softened behind the veil; she had read the book also. The smile fell into a frown. There was no bounty on that princess, no torture cell waiting with its leather restraints and hairy soldiers. Saba palmed the Enfield pistol under her robe. She would die proud if this plane did not kill her, take the highest-ranking British officer with her. Saba closed her eyes and said good-bye to the three stars in the sky she would not see again. The de Havilland hit the runway like a bomb. A collective yell muffled the impact. The plane bounced, slammed again, and seemed to warp on its frame. G-forces ripped wing passengers from their seats. The plane slid almost off the runway. Screams echoed from the tail section. Tire screeches drowned their panic and engine roar rattled the fuselage. A window shattered.

And then the plane slowed. The G-forces eased, the plane running straight and higher on its tires. The metal body relaxed and passed that sensation to the passengers. Hands began to release death grips on their armrests, first in silence and tentative, then clapping, then yelling.

Saba took a breath, thought of boys riding horses. Scared of not going fast enough, scared of going too fast, jubilant that they could posture their courage now, puff out their chests and demand respect for their brave endeavor.

"Man, that was fun."

She glanced at Eddie Owen, her hand on her pistol, muscles rigid in her jaw. Bushehr awaited. Her time in this life was short. Was there something she wanted America to know?

"You okay . . . Calah?"

Honest concern filled Eddie Owen's eyes as his fear faded. What was not present was the false pride she hated, the superiority. The plane stopped. Saba turned to her window and two men in overalls pushing a stairway toward the plane. Behind them were eleven armed English soldiers and four men in suits. The loudspeaker explained that all passengers must deplane; arrangements would be made for overnight accommodations, then transport to Abadan two hundred miles north, then Baghdad.

"Guess we have the night off." Eddie Owen laughed with split lips. "Could I, ah, interest you in dinner, coffee, or something?"

Saba was intent on dying well, on killing as many of England's soldiers as possible, before killing herself and avoiding the finish England enforced for guerrilla fighters. A hand touched on her arm. She scorched him with her eyes. Eddie Owen flinched, bending into the aisle as his right hand blocked the punch she hadn't thrown.

He spoke softly, maintaining the distance. "Hey, just dinner. I meant no disrespect if that's what I did."

"You are gracious. Thank you. That will not be possible."

The older of her escorts snaked through the full aisle to their row. He spoke Arabic, almost a whisper, asking for instructions. Saba glanced at Eddie Owen and his seat.

"Oh. Sure, no problem," he said, and stepped into the aisle.

Saba concentrated on her escort's questions but noticed Eddie Owen smiling back toward her over his shoulder as the crowd jostled him down the aisle. She wasn't smiling. Saba and her men carried Transjordan passports. Although they were still considered British subjects, there would be scrutiny for two reasons: She was a

Bedouin woman traveling anywhere, and the bombing in Bahrain four days prior. Saba whispered that surviving this encounter would be accidental. They would pass through the English together; the men would not speak. If she fired or stabbed, they would do the same. She touched near the man's hand and reminded him what the English did to prisoners, what they had done to his family in Ramallah, then rose with him into the emptying aisle.

CHAPTER 10

March, 1938

Bushehr's tarmac radiated heat under Saba's shoes. Armed red uniforms were everywhere. The plane's passengers were being funneled into a "welcoming line" that for her would lead to gun muzzles and bayonets. Saba forced a soldier's calm. The passengers in front of her wore suits with the coats draped over their arms. Behind her the group was the same and included six Arabs in traditional dress, their robes all white, hers all black. All were "wogs" to the English, no better than vermin. Outside a door to the terminal, an English soldier with a clipboard separated the passengers based on eye contact or a short question, Saba could not tell which. Eddie Owen went left. Erich Schroeder went right. A tall, rigid man was pointed right.

He barked, "*Nein!*"

The man with him complained in English. "Herr Strobel is with me." The accent was like Eddie Owen's.

"A formality, sir. Please move left. Herr Strobel will be with you on the moment."

"But—"

"Left, sir. Immigration. Germans to the right, Americans to the left." The officer smiled above his clipboard, his eyes hard and humorless. He confronted Saba and said, "Passport."

Jameel stepped forward with three booklets, all fakes, then stepped back. The English expected respectful distance from Arabs. The officer studied each fake, then said, "Right," and handed the passports back, eyes moving to the next passenger. Those forced into the "Right" line were escorted inside by armed guards front and back. The concrete hallway was short, no doors. It emptied into a cavernous, arched hall and men working on airplanes. Jumbled echoes mixed with gasoline fumes. Three doors were punched into the hall's longest wall, each doorway bracketed by two armed British soldiers standing at attention. A long table separated the passengers from the doors. Seated behind the table were two British sergeants, also armed, and backed by more soldiers. The sergeants beckoned the crowd forward.

"Form two lines." One sergeant pointed them into line, his tone curt and military. "Please."

Blood pumped in Saba's neck. She picked the Englishmen who would die with her. Ten against three. Saba and her men could win the opening salvo, at least one, maybe two of her unit surviving to reload. If only she could get—

"Passport."

Saba's men shuffled to her side. Jameel produced the documents. The sergeant frowned at three people fanned instead of an orderly line. "You are . . . ?" He was staring at her.

"Calah al-Habra."

"You are Jordanian?"

"Bedouin."

He flipped her passport front to back. "You are Jordanian?"

"Bedouin."

The sergeant next to him glanced at her, then back to his business with a German national.

"Where did you learn English?"

"Amman. A tutor of the Emir."

"The Emir." The sergeant nodded and frowned as a schoolmaster would. "What was your business in Arabia?"

"A private matter."

His eyes rose from her documents. "A private matter? I'm afraid that won't do. Were you in Bahrain?"

Saba slipped her finger inside the trigger guard. Her back muscles tightened and both ears began to ring.

"I will be forced to detain you"—the sergeant's eyes went narrow—"and your associates if you do not answer my question."

Saba inhaled, quieted herself for this final act, and answered. "The English lack respect for the desert and its people. You will do what you will do."

Both standing soldiers fixed on her. Their sergeant inspected her more carefully, then said, "Wait over there," and pointed to a bench against the wall. "Next."

She had trouble hearing. *Decide. Close is better*; the bench against the wall would be a firing squad. *Shoot him now.* Better to die here with their blood on our clothes.

"Over there." The sergeant barked as if she were his servant or wife. "Others are in the queue."

The ringing in her ears built to a roar. *Shoot him and die here—*

Eddie Owen appeared in one of the three guarded doors. A British officer had a hand on his shoulder, smiling as both turned toward her. She hesitated. Eddie Owen walked toward her, the officer pulling him back, explaining something . . .

"Miss al-Habra," was shouted in her face. "Move aside to the bench. Now."

Saba's pistol slid to leave her robe. Eddie Owen loped past the sergeant ordering her to the bench. A soldier heel-turned toward Eddie. The shooting triangles were changing too quickly. Eddie Owen stopped at her chest, blocking her line of fire. "You okay, princess?" The seated sergeant glared from behind Eddie.

Blood and adrenaline reddened Saba's face; the shiver she trapped in her shoulders. "The English are forceful when they have servants in the house . . . the pride of small men."

"See here, Mr. Owen, you must not interfere with the Crown—"

Eddie touched the tunic of the officer who had followed him from the doorway. "Calah's a friend of mine. These are her escorts. If not for her, Lieutenant"—Eddie touched the bandages on his face—"I wouldn't be going to work for you guys. Young lady saved me from the Arabian nurses."

"You know this woman, these men?"

"Absolutely. The al-Habra family are friends of my employer. My guides when I visit Petra and the Dead Sea." Eddie smiled and patted the air near her shoulder.

The lieutenant seemed genuinely concerned. "I see. Could you wait a moment?"

"Sure."

The lieutenant walked to the table and the sergeant glaring their way. Eddie turned into Saba's eyes and those of her men. "That ought to be worth dinner or at least coffee, don't you think?"

Saba prepared to kill the next soldier who approached her. "If the benevolent British allow it."

"*If*? You're kidding, right?"

CHAPTER 11

March, 1938

Eddie made himself look as pretty as he knew how, given his current condition. "You're not much of a fan, huh? The Brits, I mean?"

The Arab princess said, "And would you be? If they had crushed the rebellion that birthed America?"

Eddie took a wild guess on what she wanted to hear. "Probably not."

They were on a hillside cliff, a mile north of Bushehr and its tan, geometric buildings. Her two escorts sat the edge of the rock buttress, out of hearing distance but sharply silhouetted in the moonlight. The Persian Gulf glistened below, the air better without the burned diesel and vented gasoline; the terrain was better, too, absent the bustle of a city originally designed for camel traffic.

Eddie offered her wine provided by the British. She declined and ate dates with one hand, spitting the pits quietly behind her. She was like a ghost wrapped in black, wrapped in a starry night and a little boy's imagination.

"What does a princess do?"

She shrugged, or he thought she did.

"Really. What do you do? Is it like in the book?"

"For the emir's children, maybe yes, but for us, no."

"You're not a princess?"

"No. A teacher of the emir's students. The daughter of a teacher."

Eddie nodded. Finally she'd told him something. "Teachers in Transjordan have bodyguards?"

She took a while to answer. "This one does."

Eddie smiled. She said, "Do you work for the English in Haifa?"

"Yeah. Well, no. Actually, I work for an American oil company that's loaning me to that refinery; I'm supposed to fix a temperature problem they'll encounter because of an original design mistake. Kind of complicated, but . . . It's not really complicated. It's boring. Nothing like the *Arabian Nights*. Tell me about the desert."

"The American wishes to know the desert?" She waved her hand behind her. "Then you must go. The desert will teach you or it will kill you."

A pistol flashed into her man's hand, the arm rigid. He was already standing when Eddie flinched. She extended her hand flat to the ground and he sat, covering the weapon as if nothing had happened.

"*Jesus.* Your boys are serious."

She stared.

"You must be some teacher."

He thought the moonlight caught a glint in her eyes. It had, and both stayed with him when she spit a date pit just past her shoulder. He imagined an ingénue's smile on her lips.

"Is America cold? Valley Forge and the Delaware. Is it cold most of the time?"

"You know about George Washington?" Eddie snuck a glance past his shoulder.

"Patrick Henry. Bunker Hill, Ticonderoga, Concord. Burgoyne surrenders at Saratoga."

"Wow. They . . . You teach American history over here?"

She shook her head.

"Then why—"

"England no longer rules America. Here, England continues to rule, my people subject to today's treatment, or worse, had not an important American rescued us in our homeland."

Eddie could taste the bitterness even though she wasn't emphasizing it. He glanced again at her bodyguards paying no overt attention, but able to react at her smallest hand motion. Eddie thought about the airport and the soldiers there if they had put their hands on this woman. Would not have been pretty.

"How long have the Brits been here?"

"All my life. And before the British, the Turks and the Germans."

"You said 'homeland.' You're from Transjordan, right? Not Iran." He patted the ground, meaning *here*, then wished he hadn't. The bodyguard didn't flinch.

"History. The English draw lines in the sand to make states to their liking, to fit the Europeans' way of things. That is not how it is in the desert, nor how it will ever be. My people do not come from European blood, do not eat, sleep, or marry as they do there."

She leaned closer and Eddie could smell the perfume again, see the fire in her eyes. The treble in her voice rose and she pointed at the ground he had patted. "This place *is* a place, not a land waiting for the European to come and change it to his. We *live* here, and have for thousands of years. The English have England; why should they have my country or the right to give it to others?"

Eddie wasn't aware the British were giving away Iran or anywhere else.

"Ibn Saud is given Arabia, Hussein is given Transjordan, the Zionists are given Palestine—who are the British to effect such things. Are they gods?"

Eddie wanted to answer but didn't have one.

"Do they have a right to empire? One that makes me slave or servant because I am not as you or they?" Her voice was getting louder and both her men were staring. That wouldn't be good if they got mad, even worse if they were just nervous because their boss was about to go off. They didn't look like fellas who scared easy.

"No. No they don't. No one does. If it's your country, it's your country."

"And the Indians in yours?"

"Lots of rich Indians in Oklahoma and Texas. Whole bunch of 'em. Lots of poor ones, too."

The princess-schoolteacher eased back, collecting herself the way rattlesnakes do on hot days, her eyes staying with his, her posture softening, the threat moving away, under a rock but not gone.

"Sounds like you really don't care for our hosts—" Eddie choked on the word *hosts*. "Shit. Sorry, I didn't mean to imply this was theirs . . . or swear, either. Got a lot to learn. You can tell I'm not quite as historically proficient as you."

She pointed at the wine. He set it as near to her as he could reach and watched her raise the bottle and sip behind the veil. She sat with the bottle between her legs crossed as an Arab man would, the bottle resting on her robe. She pointed at the sky.

"There are three stars in a row to the left of the moon and below. Bright ones, all together. Do you see them?"

Eddie didn't but said yes. The sky in the desert was so bright it hurt his eyes.

"Those are my family. The dead who keep me company. Every night they never fail to visit me, wherever I am." She sipped the wine again. "Tell me about your family, Eddie Owen, American."

His name felt strange in her voice, fluid, exotic, better than his name usually sounded when said by roughnecks, gangsters, and drunk Irish construction workers. Eddie laughed, almost asked her to say it again.

"This is funny, your family?"

"No. My name, it sounded . . . nice in your voice. Hadn't heard it said like that in a long time." Eddie thought about Oklahoma, the Dust Bowl, the letter from his mother thanking him for the money, telling him it was enough to keep them in food and the bank receiver away every month. The news about his father hadn't been as good. Newt was failing, the Dust Bowl and the depression killing his father's heart, the money from his son good, as was all the help from D.J. Bennett, but painful for a proud working man to take.

"My family's okay; they live in Oklahoma. Things aren't good there now. No rain . . . they call it the Dust Bowl." Eddie raised his hand carefully above his head. "Big clouds of dirt blown across hundreds of miles . . . It's bad in Oklahoma now."

"Why are you here, then? You do not help your family when in need?"

"I send them most of my paycheck; I don't need it, and it keeps the bank from taking the farm."

"Taking the farm? The government will take their land?"

"If my mother and father can't pay, the bank will sell them out, hold an auction."

She couldn't quite grasp the concept. Eddie explained how foreclosure worked and why it was happening to thousands of Americans. Shock was burned into her voice as if he'd poured gasoline on her dreams.

"But how could this be to America? You defeated the English, settled a civil war. How could this happen? Do the rich in America suffer, too?"

Eddie laughed. "Probably not. The rich tend not to suffer anywhere."

Headlights.

Her two men were standing, both with pistols drawn and held behind their robes. The lights above them on the seaside road fanned past them, then stopped. Two voices spoke in Arabic. One of her men returned. Eddie saw a hand signal that seemed almost military and Calah the princess-schoolteacher stood. She pointed the man to the headlights and stepped sideways, putting the moon at her back.

"I must go."

"Go? The Brits won't have our car caravan available till tomorrow."

She stepped into his face. Eddie noticed both her hands were visible, a fingertip rubbing wine under her right eye. Her hand dropped; there were black . . . He leaned closer, for some reason afraid to step . . . *Wings* tattooed under her eye. Small black wings.

"It is possible you and I will meet again in Haifa, Eddie Owen, American, to speak again of America and your family. This"—she tapped the tattoo—"is how you will know me."

Eddie said, "I—"

She put a very fast hand in his face. "No. I must go. Do not speak of me to others; it will not be good for you." She climbed uphill. "History, Eddie Owen. Ask your English employers why they have a right to an empire and I have rights to nothing."

And then she was gone. Like she'd never been there. Just a car from nowhere, its door closing, engine noise, and then nothing. Fast, fluid exit. He'd seen them before, in the newsreels, guys with fedoras and Tommy guns.

She was a schoolteacher, right?

Sure she is.

Eddie rubbed his forehead. It hurt and reminded him he wasn't a genius with England's world politics and those it affected, the Irish for sure. The desert was strange; he was smart enough to figure that. Eddie glanced at the sky beginning to lighten behind him and realized she had hypnotized him again. They'd spent the entire night out here, her explaining the desert, him walking her through Oklahoma and Texas. He smiled; his first date in almost two years and he'd only seen her eyes. Well, her hands, too. Awfully rough for teacher's hands. Eddie sipped the wine and thought he could taste her mouth on the bottle. Her stars were still up there somewhere; excellent place for a cemetery, actually. He toasted the stars on their choice of girls. God knows she was potent when you couldn't see her. No telling what she'd be like if you could.

Daylight came with a gruff British accent.

Eddie blinked at nine uniforms blocking most of the sun and tried to shield his eyes. "Huh?"

"Up fast and standing, Mr. Owen. The cap'n's waiting."

Eddie stood, dusting what he could, and checked his surroundings. Last night's events still lingered. The lieutenant pointed at the empty wine bottle and barked, "And the wogs are?"

"Sorry, I didn't get that."

"The Arabs, man. Mates of yours, their whereabouts?"

Eddie shrugged, surprised at the tone. "Don't know?" He noticed the soldiers all had rifles and the look of fellows who'd used them before.

The lieutenant's voice hardened further. "On the hop, Yank, Captain Wingate is waiting. Your bunch travels on the hour; whether you're with 'em is up to him."

The soldiers packed Eddie into a jeep and rode downhill into town. Bushehr, Iran, looked different in the early daylight. Ancient buildings blended into the landscape in grand and humble ways and made a curious sense with the roadway and the seafront. Then, suddenly, there'd be structures that could've been dropped in from Charles Dickens. Very odd. But odder still were the people on the street. Most were light-skinned men in western clothes or British uniforms. This was the port of Sinbad the Sailor—minarets and domes topped with the crescent moon and star—where were the Persians?

Captain Orde Wingate's office had no Persians present. The office was large and so was Captain Wingate. Two rows of decorations marched across a stiff red jacket, the collar tight under a jutting chin. A fan slowly revved above him and a palatial wooden desk. Middesk, a green leather blotter supported the captain's clenched fist, a folder, and a single framed picture. The photograph framed two chubby children and a severe-looking wife, hair so tight in a bun it hurt Eddie's eyes to look.

From behind Eddie, someone stern said: "Your Arab chums appear to be truant."

Eddie turned to a five-foot-nine bespoke suit lighting a pipe with a stick match. The man puffed apple tobacco into the air as if the smoke were a gift. He wore a silk bowtie; his bearing suggested enmity, and not altogether latent.

Eddie extended his hand. "Hi, I'm Eddie Owen."

The man didn't shake. Eddie forced bravado. "Nice suit. They sell those here?"

A fist hammered a desk and snapped Eddie back to Captain Wingate. "*Mr. Owen.* The Crown does not tolerate sedition or spies. We execute them."

"O . . . kay?" Eddie tennis-matched between the two men, not sure where this was headed.

The civilian behind the pipe spoke first, his face a sharpened wedge and a disturbing blank. "Our desert has harsh realities, Mr.

Owen, as will Haifa. There, and here, Great Britain has a mandate: Curb the wogs from murdering one another and any foreigner they choose."

Eddie nodded without agreeing.

"The wogs are children, Mr. Owen, *obstinate* children; the sooner you understand that the better. The threat of a European war makes our already onerous governing situation here worse. Your Nazi and Arab friends wish that to continue." The civilian paused for a long draw on his pipe. "As in all governance, treachery among the masses requires a decisive hand." He curled a bony finger at Eddie, summoning him to the window, then pointed his pipe at a blond man waiting to board the first of the passenger transports. "Erich Schroeder. You are familiar with him? A friend of yours and the Arab girl?"

Eddie had seen the fit, blond fellow at the airport and on the plane. The fellow moved stiffly as if his back had been injured. "Nope. Not a friend of mine."

"Herr Schroeder is Hermann Göring's man in America and the oil fields of the desert. You do know of Reichsmarschall Hermann Göring."

Eddie didn't and said so.

"President of the German Reichstag, Reich Minister of *Aviation*, and the first successor to Adolf Hitler. You've heard of Adolf Hitler?"

"Oh, yeah." Eddie knew he was being mocked and, deserving or not, had lost his inclination toward further bravado. Cottonmouths near his face had always had that effect.

"Herr Schroeder was in Arabia, a mere fifteen miles west when your refinery exploded and our causeway was sabotaged. Schroeder had high tea with Ibn Saud, the Nazi-sympathizer king of Arabia. Then Herr Schroeder vanished for three days . . . before arriving at the airport for his flight here."

Eddie nodded, not knowing what else to do.

"The three Arabs for whom you vouched yesterday? There is no record of their entry into Arabia, yet they were aboard your plane from Dhahran." He fanned three passports at Eddie's face. "Forgeries."

"Sorry. I sat with her on the plane; your sergeant was giving her a hard time for no reason, so I helped her. I didn't know."

Captain Wingate slammed his desk again. *"For no reason?"* Wingate rounded the corner, aiming for Eddie. "That Nazi down there and his Führer have been busy, possibly you've heard?" Wingate stopped eight inches from Eddie's face. "Hitler has pushed France out of the Rhineland and remilitarized the entire area. Five days ago he seized Austria. Now his storm troopers threaten Czechoslovakia."

Eddie learned better from a distance but there didn't seem to be much. Possibly his "for no reason" was a poor evaluation of the Brits' airport police work. The Brits were nervous about threats to the empire and there seemed to be a number of them from several directions.

The civilian waved his pipe for Captain Wingate to disengage. Wingate stepped back three feet. The civilian pointed it at Eddie. "Our meeting here is fortuitous; I had planned your education for Haifa for Friday after you arrived. Your mission in Haifa is important to the Crown and the stability of the region. We will not have either jeopardized by recklessness or stupidity."

Eddie flinched at "mission." He let "stupidity" pass.

"Hitler may or may not be the answer to the Bolshevik threat, that is for Parliament to decide. Clearly, France will not draw the line; their weak-kneed performance in the Rhineland makes war in Europe almost inevitable. And the Hun at war, like the Arab and the Bolshevik, is no humanitarian." The civilian relit his pipe, eyes on Eddie, not the bowl.

Eddie felt the big finish coming, could feel the safe falling out of the sky, just couldn't see it yet.

"You have much to learn, Mr. Owen, as do most Americans. All of Europe is now threatened by two great powers, Nazi Germany and Communist Russia. Aviation gasoline will defend Britain. France will have no defense. Their Maginot Line is folly." The civilian and his pipe stepped closer to Eddie. "This year your American petroleum companies have tripled oil sales to Nazi Germany and now have more refineries operating there than anywhere in Europe, the Middle East, and Asia. Who do you think will receive the gasoline refined in Nazi Germany, Mr. Owen? And if it is aviation gas, what then? What then, Mr. Owen?"

Prior to this job, Eddie'd understood oil as an American commodity, his perspective the Great Depression and the Dust Bowl. The world politics of oil was a brand-new concept unless you worked inside the boardrooms of international corporations and government offices. "I'm, ah . . . just fixing a potential temperature problem—"

Before Eddie could finish lying, Captain Wingate stepped forward and punched a fountain pen in Eddie's chest. "You are under British jurisdiction here and in Haifa. The Crown enforces stiff penalties in the possessions we administer—even on *American oil company engineers.*"

Eddie was now as confused as he was uncomfortable. The civilian with the pipe and bow tie made no second move to restrain Captain Wingate, but did offer explanation.

"The refinery in Haifa *that you will convert to aviation gas* is owned and defended by Great Britain. Among those who would forcibly supplant British rule throughout the region *and* commandeer our refinery are the Nazis and the Pan-Arab Army of God." The pipe lowered. "The latter is a bafflingly well-funded coalition controlled by Iraq's King Ghazi bin Faisal and his mullahs." The civilian paused to control his tone. "The Pan-Arab Army of God is comprised of self-rule murderers and Islamic fundamentalists, including a smattering of Palestinian guerrillas . . . as were the three *you vouched for* yesterday."

Eddie choked, trying to swallow. "I didn't know. Honest."

"You have heard of the Raven?"

Eddie shook his head. "He's a Palestinian?"

The civilian paused again. "He is a she, or so the stories go. A guerrilla fighter of some repute."

Captain Wingate looked past Eddie to the door. A uniformed man there said, "The call for the bus, Captain."

The civilian with the pipe pointed Eddie toward the door. "The bus will take you to Abadan at the top of the Gulf. A commercial plane will complete your transport to Damascus. Once you are in Haifa, I suggest in the strongest terms that you mind your affairs and the Crown's carefully. We will. And His Majesty's police shall take a dim view if we confront your Arab self-rule sympathies again . . . or *any* harm to our refinery."

Eddie said, "I don't have any sympathies; I have a job. My company lent me on contract to the refinery to help . . ." Eddie stopped before stupid overtook him. "To fix some temperature problems before they happen."

"Your government—those loyal to President Roosevelt—used duress to present you on *England's* behalf; your *government*, Mr. Owen, is who demanded your participation, not your company. England and your president fear that Standard Oil, like you, has other loyalties."

Captain Orde Wingate walked Eddie to the bus. At the door, Wingate said, "Make no mistake, Mr. Owen. We will hold no trial for sedition. I will personally place my pistol to your head."

Eddie boarded the bus, found an empty seat, and checked for the British tail he had to have. *Hell, I'd be happy to have the company. I'd buy the Brit drinks all the way to Haifa, ask about Communists, Nazis, Zionists, the Pan-Arab Army of God—didn't they sound special—self-rule sympathizers, and His Majesty's police. Don't think I'll ask about the Raven of Palestine, though.* Eddie rubbed his swollen face. At least with Ryan Pearce and Benny Binion back in Texas, you knew who was on your side and who wasn't. Over here, every road you drove led to the barrel of somebody's gun.

Erich Schroeder glanced out the bus's window. Iran's dusty lowlands' plain was turning to rock. He had not enjoyed the previous evening as a guest in the British Empire. All night, the six-officer interrogation team had questioned him, wearing him down with adrenaline, caffeine, anger, and compliments. The fact that the English had a brief dossier on him and that the dossier was in this Persian Gulf outpost was more than mildly disconcerting.

His interrogators praised Hitler as a defender against the Bolsheviks and their Communist Internationale, then insulted Hitler's government as drunken street rabble. Schroeder politely disagreed, suggesting that his current geography held better examples of failed government. The lead interrogator had laughed before he swung the baton. As always, Britain's minions saw a fundamental difference between their actions of the last two centuries and the Reich's plans for this one. Schroeder smiled, then winced with the pain. Theirs was a poor performance, really; these Englishmen were a laughable imitation of their forefathers. Two decades ago the British would have killed him. The iron will that had carved a world empire out of barbarians and continually crushed their revolts now lacked the stomach to defend it.

British weakness would please Reichsmarschall Göring, for if the highly placed British politicians did not deliver England as an ally against Russia's Red Army as secretly promised, Göring's Luftwaffe would one day meet Great Britain's lords and ladies on their side of the Channel. The bus bounced. Pain shot up Schroeder's back and gurgled his bruised intestines. Schroeder had discussed these very same British politicians with Göring immediately after finishing the Reichsmarschall's business in New York eleven months ago.

The discussion occurred at Karinhall, Göring's baronial estate that began forty-five miles northeast of Berlin and stretched forever, almost to the Baltic Sea. The five-man hunting weekend was a distinct reward and proof that Schroeder's star continued to rise with his mentor's. It was Schroeder's third weekend at Karinhall and had, like the previous two, produced many candid conversations among the guests, including a violent argument between the uninvited and mercurial Reich Minister for Foreign Affairs Joachim Ribbentrop and Hermann Schmitz, the president of I.G. Farben.

Reich Minister Ribbentrop had stormed into the lodge flanked by no aide-de-camp, furious at the slaughter of his English banker in New York. Ribbentrop did not accuse anyone present, although his suspicions were obvious. Ribbentrop railed at Hermann Schmitz, and by default, the American Capitalists who were Schmitz's partners. "Herr Schmitz trusts that Roosevelt will be assassinated. Ridiculous! The International Jew and the Communists will never allow it. Roosevelt is their man! Herr Schmitz, at best, you are a fool. Or you are a traitor." Reich Minister Ribbentrop turned to the others. "Herr Schmitz asks us to trust his American Capitalist friends and their pledge of continuing support for Germany and Göring's Luftwaffe, but where is the promised formula for 100-octane gasoline? The refinery modification schematics?" Ribbentrop spun to face Schmitz and shouted: "Your *friends* in America are Jew-controlled whores. Only money moves them, not honor or fair treatment of the German people."

"The formula and schematics will come." I.G. Farben's president checked with Göring before continuing. "I have returned with the patents for tetraethyl lead, the crucial ingredient of aviation gas, and the promise that Standard Oil will also slow their research to develop synthetic rubber while we increase ours. A strong Nazi Germany is in Standard Oil's interest. Stronger Communists are not. The rest will come."

Ribbentrop bristled. "Will it? Roosevelt plays God from his wheelchair while the German people eat rations and prepare to face the Bolsheviks alone. What good are trucks and tanks and rubber if others rule the skies? If you and the Americans eat caviar?"

Schmitz sipped coffee and glanced over the cup at Schroeder. In spite of the foreign minister's recriminations, recriminations that could land even a powerful businessman like Schmitz in the hands of other powerful men, Schmitz's hands remained steady. He enjoyed strong connections inside the Gestapo, and his personal relationship with Himmler's deputy, Reinhard Heydrich, would likely be sufficient protection, unless failure or Ribbentrop brought Hitler into the argument. Then nothing would be enough.

Ribbentrop glared, waiting for an answer. "We must have 100-octane gas *now*, before the fight with England is unavoidable. If we do not have 100 octane, England will be brave and we go to war on two fronts. And when war comes, the Jew-controlled businesses of America, supported by their very-much-alive Roosevelt, will abandon us."

Schmitz set his cup on its saucer. "Not all Germans fear war. Those of us who have tasted it."

Erich Schroeder hid a fast smile with his hand. Ribbentrop collected himself, his anger pushed beneath his words. "I have been the Führer's ambassador to England and know well their fear of the Communists massing to the east. England can become our friend and ally as easily as our enemy." Ribbentrop stepped directly in front of Schmitz's chair. "I have also been to Russia and seen the Red Army, Herr Schmitz. I have seen Russian winter. The future of Europe and the Fatherland lies in the Red Army's complete and utter destruction. Victory, our very *survival*, will hinge on the sky."

Göring stood and embraced the much smaller Ribbentrop, gently turning him away from I.G. Farben's president. The two men walked to Göring's private offices and left the others to the fire and more bottles of Moselle.

An hour before dinner, Schroeder was summoned to Göring's private offices and given his rumored, hoped-for mission in the Middle East. Alone with Schroeder, Göring confirmed that what Ribbentrop had said was true, in part. Göring did not discuss the planned assassination of President Roosevelt and Schroeder did not ask. These were delicate matters that often killed the successful operatives, secrecy and denial being crucial for the state.

Göring did agree with Ribbentrop's charge that Germany's future would hinge on the sky, but before the sky could be Germany's answer, Germany must dominate the desert oil fields—eventually from Morocco to Iran. Schroeder's part in *this* plan was imperative and immediate. Reichsmarschall Göring used the thickened fingers of his left hand to list Schroeder's responsibilities: "First, you will ensure that British Mandate Palestine remains a cauldron of hate, mistrust, and murder. Second, you will degrade England's refining capacity and undermine their relationships with the desert kings. Third, if the Americans decline to provide Herr Schmitz the 100-octane technology as promised, the technology *must* be acquired by other methods—any methods."

Erich Schroeder had not been able to suppress the smile he had hidden earlier. In any scenario, the Middle East would be a slaughterhouse. And in this slaughterhouse, irrespective of Germany's goals, Erich Schroeder would be a king.

A hard bump in the cliffside road jolted Schroeder back into the present. He claw-gripped the bus seat against the pain. His beating at the hands of the English would require proper medical attention, and soon. Stomach blood bubbled into his throat. Schroeder's jaw clamped and he swallowed. The English had won the night, but it was he, Erich Schroeder—"the bloody fuckin' Nazi bastard"—who continued to win the contests, contests that would, very soon, wipe England off the map.

Schroeder's lips pursed crooked into the pain. Eleven months ago at Karinhall, Reichsmarschall Göring had demanded that *British* Mandate Palestine remain a cauldron—and it had. Nazi armaments—*Erich Schroeder*'s armaments—and Iraq's mullahs had incited another bloody Arab Revolt. Göring had demanded the *British* refining capacity be degraded—and it had. Britain's Sitra Island refinery was offline and smoking, and Britain's Haifa refinery would be next. Göring had demanded an alternative source be found to acquire 100-octane aviation gasoline—and that source, Eddie Owen, now sat within reach on this very bus.

Much had been accomplished, too much to die now. Schroeder hugged one arm around his stomach and glanced out the bus's window . . . at *British* hegemony . . . that the once-feared power was about to lose . . . to a "bloody fuckin' Nazi bastard." Schroeder's eyes narrowed. His breaths were short and painful. He focused on Eddie Owen, the young man who would make Erich Schroeder king.

Eddie Owen had first come to the Luftwaffe's attention in Chicago. Eddie's bold success there and his immediate mobilization to Sitra made him an attractive target. Schroeder summed what his operatives had reported: Eddie Owen had family in dire circumstances. He had an active criminal history—the death of a Jewish sharecropper's child that would matter not at all in the Reich but remained important in Jew-addled America. Eddie Owen also liked women and had been swayed by several, according to friends at the University of Oklahoma. This was a great deal of weakness for one young man once the pressure was brought.

And the pressure had already begun. Slowly those who supported and protected Eddie Owen were being removed. The British were beginning their significant role, questioning Eddie Owen's allegiances, and would soon threaten him with corporeal wartime penalties. And at home in America, the police in Texas would find new evidence and begin new enquiries. Eddie Owen's family would suffer calamities as well. Yes, it would soon be quite terrible for the young man. Much tougher men had succumbed to far, far less.

But I will befriend Eddie in his time of need. Schroeder exhaled and leaned against the bus window. It would be good if he could sleep part of the all-day trip across Iran to the airport at Abadan and the medical attention available in Baghdad. Iraq had a young Nationalist king not much older than Eddie Owen and not much wiser. It would be good to see Iraq's king Ghazi bin Faisal again. The young king fancied powerful sports cars, young German women, and Pan-Arab aspirations he would never see. Schroeder shut his eyes against the pain. Very soon there would be no place in the desert for Pan-Arab—or Pan-any—aspirations except Germanic. And more precisely, the aspirations that the new king was already forging into reality. Erich Schroeder would be the new king. And *his* aspirations already had many friends in Iraq.

CHAPTER 12

March, 1938

Bushehr and the British were one hundred miles behind her on the cliffside road. Abadan, at the top of the Persian Gulf, was still a half day of heat and dust to the north. Saba jarred in the passenger seat of the salt-rusted truck. Her black Bedouin robes and hood covered all but her eyes. Jameel and Rafid rode in the open bed separated from her and the driver by a glassless back window. She had been silent the entire seven hours. Iran's bleak Zagros Mountains were a wall on her right.

The two-lane road was narrow but well kept, likely for routine British transport. A series of tight, exposed turns wound higher, then lower, then higher again. Saba analyzed what she saw and startled behind her veil—with the proper weapons and the element of surprise, her partisans could kill *hundreds* of the special soldiers on this road. This narrow, exposed road would be the only road from their base in Bushehr to Abadan. She could kill the special soldiers *before* they could slip into the mountains to hunt the partisans. Adrenaline pumped through her. Engage the English on their "home" ground.

Saba calculated the requirements. To accomplish such a bold strike, she and Jameel and Rafid would first have to escape the British soldiers no doubt swarming to hunt them *now*, then acquire heavy weapons that the German must agree to provide, then survive a return trek across Iraq and part of Iran overland in winter with twenty men and heavy weapons. But with careful planning and the proper provisions . . . hard, committed partisans could do it. Attack the English where they were safe. Make their houses and their roads the fearful places that hers had become.

Saba imagined England's forced response—troops would be deployed to defend their main base of operations and its two-hundred-mile road of overland access; those troops would no longer be available to hunt the partisans and rebel units or murder Palestinians. Saba blinked at the simplicity of the plan, wondering why her Iraqi commanders had not undertaken this long ago, then wondered, as she often did, why they were the commanders.

In Arabic, she told the driver to stop. He threatened a cuff with his hand, told her women did not speak to men in the Army of God, that this road was not safe, his risks high to serve the wishes of Ghazi bin Faisal.

Saba paused, then backhanded him with her fist. His truck lurched. Her dagger finished tight to his throat. The driver jammed the brakes, his eyes wide and fixed above the knife. Saba waited for a response that did not come, then pressed the blade harder to his neck. "You do not know me, servant of Faisal, nor do you wish to."

Her partisans behind him reached through the glassless back window and patted the driver's shoulder, assuring him that this was best. Saba stepped out of the truck to the rear and removed her cloak, veil, and then the robe. Her men stayed in the truck. Her garments were once again those of a man; she wound a black keffiyeh across her face and scaled forty feet of rough granite bordering the road. At the top, she scanned the road, then the horizon—

It would be good. Each dipping section of road was isolated by the previous turn. Much better than the road had been near Metzada. Here, late afternoon would have the sun glaring off the Gulf. Her men could attack in two groups and do tremendous damage. Should the road continue in this fashion, they would have a hundred kilometers to choose from. If she could acquire the weapons from the German, the main issue would be coming overland in winter . . .

She slipped. Fell hard and teetered at the edge. A thought blocked the pain in her knee and almost made her laugh. What if Britain's lord high political officer traveled this road? Or his generals? *Oh, that would matter*, if they died at the hands of Arabs, the Englishmen who had thought it best for her family to die. Oh, that would matter a great deal to the masters of the Empire.

Saba descended to the truck. Before entering, she donned the robe and cloak and added the veil. The driver glared when she took the passenger seat. He slammed the gearshift and proceeded toward Abadan in silence. Saba grinned behind the veil.

The British roadblock was a surprise.

Saba's driver slammed the brakes with both feet, stopping just before he hit a Willys MB patrol truck. Saba bounced off the windshield, her hand taking half the blow. Four rifles, no bayonets, all pointed. An Arab's English accent demanded they exit and lay facedown in the road. The Arab who spoke was not visible.

Saba spoke without turning. "Do not be taken alive." She dug her hand into the driver's thigh. "Speak a word of any language, servant of Faisal, and one of us will kill you." Jameel and Rafid would not quail; the driver she did not know. She told both partisans, "Exit as they ask. Drop only to your knees; say you have a woman and will not have her lie as a dog in the street."

Both partisans climbed out of the truck bed into the road and sank slowly to their knees; Rafid repeated Saba's instructions in Arabic. The hidden Arab voice commanded Jameel and Rafid to lie facedown, then commanded Saba and the driver out of the truck. Saba scanned the roadblock for the voice hidden among the rifle barrels. She and the partisans had no travel documents. Chill climbed her back, part fear, part hate. She stepped into the road, leaving her door open, then limped a pace away on her injured knee as if trying to comply.

"Hands up! On your knees!"

Saba showed her hands but remained standing, risking the bullet for the mobility.

An English voice bellowed, this one with no Arab accent: "ON YOUR KNEES."

Her driver crawled out and to his knees, then facedown flat to the road. Only Saba stood. A grizzled sergeant appeared from behind the Willys, his tunic off. His roadblock vehicle was dipped down over two flat tires. He led with a huge, cocked .455 Webley pointed at her chest.

"DOWN, WOG."

Saba lowered her head and curled her shoulders; the Webley was powerful but not accurate. Behind the veil, she struggled to mount womanly submission, the hate and fear so strong . . . *Control*. Her ears were ringing; if the ring became the roar . . . these Englishmen would end her grand plans here.

The sergeant cursed, but his eyes never left her. He motioned a uniformed Arab forward, barking at him in English. The Arab translated into Arabic for the driver, believing the driver most prominent. "Your truck will be returned tomorrow. We will need your water also." The Arab did not look sorry about the robbery, dooming them unless they were very lucky and willing to become road pirates also.

Saba's driver edged a silent glance toward his passengers. The Arab followed his eyes. "I will take your water." The Arab walked to the truck, eyeing Saba stoop-shouldered in the sun and her partisans on their knees.

The sergeant ordered his soldiers to board the commandeered truck. All four lowered their rifles to parade arms and walked toward Saba, the sergeant at their front. He stopped in Saba's face and raised his pistol to her head. In broken Arabic and meat breath, he said, "On your knees, wog." Then added in English, "Wogs're good there. You can scrub or suck."

A horn blared behind the soldiers. Three of them turned to an approaching F30 troop transport. Saba stared into the .455's barrel. Sweat beaded on her forehead and temples, running past both eyes. The roar building in her ears replaced the memories that proximity to English soldiers always triggered. The sergeant's grin faltered. He squinted and stepped back, adding his other hand to the pistol.

"Well I'll be damned—"

He squeezed. She ducked to a knee; the explosion scorched her keffiyeh and boomed her ear deaf. Saba sprang to strike but the sergeant was airborne past her and landed on his face, a rifle butt behind him finishing its swing. A Royal Marine officer yelled and pointed the rifle he'd just swung. Saba cut to her men—they had not drawn weapons, their angle of understanding offering a reason to hesitate—then cut to the sergeant unconscious on the road and the Marine officer above him, her hand on her pistol covered by her robe.

The horn again, loud and repeating. Fifteen Royal Marines double-timed from an F30 and half circled them. The Marine lieutenant standing above her asked one of the original soldiers, "And what's this about?"

A private stopped gaping at his sergeant prone in the road and snapped to attention. "Nothing, sir. A vehicle inspection."

Saba pushed up from the injured knee but spoke English to the dirt. "These men meant to steal our truck and water, and leave us to die."

The private backhanded Saba off her feet. She rolled with the blow. Jameel dived, covered her clamped in his arms, whispering in Arabic.

The lieutenant barked, *"Private."*

"Sir!"

"Desist."

"Yes, sir!"

Jameel helped Saba to her feet. Both finished with pistols tight in their hands but hidden. They faced twenty soldiers. Their driver spoke from his belly, apologizing for the woman's behavior. It was unfortunate the Bedu knew little of the English ways. He apologized again and said the private was within his rights.

The lieutenant frowned almost to his collar, then ordered the men to carry the sergeant into the troop carrier. The private hesitated and the lieutenant barked close enough to bite him.

"Now."

The Marines and soldiers double-timed past the lieutenant. Only the uniformed Arab remained with the lieutenant. The Arab inspected Saba, approached her perimeter with some caution, and said, "You speak English. Your documents, please." He extended a weathered brown hand.

Saba had forced her head down, her eyes locked on the ground, her hand clamped on the pistol. She demanded that she breathe instead of fight. Her robe rustled. The lieutenant slapped the Arab's extended hand away from Saba, then pushed him aside as a royal would a beggar. The lieutenant's voice added measure; his eyes fixed on Saba's dusty cloak. "You are a troubled, insolent people who would do better to stay with their camels. Make no attempt at communion with Europe; it is beyond the pale. Be on your way and grateful officers of the Crown see no glory in punishing the insipid."

Saba half turned, caught Rafid's glance as he touched his cheek, and moved to the truck. The driver hesitated; Rafid eased him in from behind. Jameel and Rafid loaded in, then Saba. She told the driver, "Drive. Do not speak," her Enfield pushed into his ribs. The fear carved into the driver's face was new; likely the Royal Marines had scared him with their fast feet and good weapons. The truck did not move. Saba dug with the Enfield. The driver apologized without looking at her. He started their truck, looped the damaged Willys patrol truck, and then the troop carrier.

They rumbled a mile in dusty silence and the driver apologized again. Saba wedged her back against the door, staring through the rear window, hoping they were clear. The road bounced her cloak's hood from her head, spilling chestnut hair. She replaced the hood and touched her veil. Chalky. Saba touched the cheekbone beneath her eye, remembering Rafid's signal, then grabbed the driver's rearview mirror. The driver shrank and swerved the truck.

One wing was visible; the kohl and marl makeup had flaked. Enough for the English sergeant to know, or to think he knew. But her driver, an Arab, he would have no doubt. Saba raised her pistol to his head. "You know me?"

"It is . . . an honor." He got smaller behind the wheel. "Please do not kill me."

"But I am a woman and you are a man; how can this *honor* be so?"

"On my mother's name, I—"

"You are what tribe?"

The driver answered, trying to be respectful and small, naming a tribe in the southern Euphrates Valley, the same tribe as Ghazi bin Faisal.

"And how is it I am known here in Persia?"

"The Raven is"—the driver rushed the words, then grimaced and lowered his voice to a whisper—"is much discussed by the English, *Minchar al Gorab*. A high price is offered for her head, a thousand gold dinars . . ." He shied. "If she is no myth."

Saba considered the sum, enough to buy a hundred rifles, double what she had last heard. "And you would collect this?"

"No. No. No. I would not. This could not happen."

Saba recited the myth: "The Raven is of the night, the sky. She can kill an entire camp or one enemy alone in his sleep, eat his eyes in front of his children." Saba watched the driver wilt, glad the veil hid her smile. "This I have done." She glanced at Jameel and Rafid behind her, each with a hand covering his mustache and yellowed teeth.

"If I am her, know that you will never speak of me. And never insult another woman. For I will be her also and from her chador I will bite out your eyes." Saba poked her Enfield's barrel against his temple and he veered them almost off the cliff.

"Yes. Yes. It is so. As you say."

Saba nodded that it was so, that one day the women of the desert would kneel to no man, no religion, and to no foreign invader. She turned back to the black granite cliff walling the road. Where the wall met the road, she saw the lord high political officer's future. His assassination in England's colonial stronghold would be headlines in England's national newspaper and read around the world. Yellowed copies would be read aloud at campfires under the desert sky and in black tents. Saba glanced at that sky where her stars would be tonight then touched the ten franc note pinned inside her pocket. She could, and would, kill the man responsible for much of Palestine's suffering. The reality made her shiver. The promise she had made Khair-Saleh and the old women of the camps was within reach. Saba squeezed the revolver, then whispered to her window: "*Dayman*. Not for me. For Palestine."

SIX MONTHS LATER

CHAPTER 13

September, 1938

S aba scanned the Huleh Valley going to shadow beneath her; the village buildings she had refused to attack were coming to light. Desert Jews were not the enemy and never had been. English garrisons and Zionist militias and lord high political officers were the enemy. And to fight them you could not rely on God or be a coward.

The months since Saba's return from the Bushehr-Abadan road in Iran had been bloody defeats, angry accusations, and the treachery one would expect of cowards and clerics maneuvering for position. While her Iraqi commanders and German bene- factors postured, the English continued to deport thousands of Palestinians into the squalor from which Khair-Saleh had saved her. Five hundred more had died in skirmishes; a like number of European Zionists and militia; and, as always, far fewer of England's soldiers, less than one hundred.

Three of Saba's in-camp altercations with the Army of God had drawn blood, all over Saba's refusal to attack indigenous Jewish villages. The first altercation had been the worst. Saba had beaten an Iraqi recruit unconscious after his hands had followed the insult on his lips. She was chided by the camp's Iraqi commander, then threatened by his cleric. Saba challenged both at the evening meal, calling the commander and Ghazi bin Faisal cowards for targeting civilians and refusing to support her return to Iran. A *man's* God, she told them, did not favor cowards or slaves. Weapons were drawn, death threats made. Saba shouted the truth for the entire command staff to hear, all eighteen of her men at her back but facing fifty. The clerics were braver than her last gun-barrel confrontation with them and this time demanded her death. Erich Schroeder had risen to her defense, brokering an accommodation.

The German's accommodation had two components and Saba had quickly agreed to both. First she would train a select group of Army of God fighters who would combat the fearsome special soldiers from Bushehr. During this period, Saba would receive training of her own—hers in the ways of Abwehr spies and provocateurs. The second component, unknown to the Army of God, the German reiterated his promise to supply Saba the resources required to splinter into her own camp. She and her partisans would be free to kidnap or attack high-ranking British officers as they saw fit, first in Palestine and then, if she were successful, her audacious, spectacular return to Bushehr, Iran, for the lord high political officer himself.

So, on the last sunrise of the first month, Saba set about training thirty men and two women to hunt, trap, and kill the special soldiers from Bushehr. Over the five months that had followed, the women had performed poorly, her anger with them obvious and occasionally brutal. Those who would free Palestine from England had no rights to morals or codes taught in other times. War meant death, and on the partisan side, almost always.

Saba stared deep into the Huleh Valley. Tomorrow's mission would be Herr Schroeder's final test, proof that Saba could operate independently—a bold kidnap for ransom that, if it did not kill her, would set her unit on a path teeth-to-teeth against the English, the best equipped she had ever been, and far away from the Iraqi's Army of God coward war.

Higher behind the cliff where Saba now sat, the western face of Mount Hermon and the 9,000-foot Jabal Ash Shaykh guarded her back and flanks. Directly below her cliff to the south and east was the Golan Heights. Saba had not been in the Golan Heights since the French had killed the man whose name and life were now hers. She checked Khair-Saleh's star in the sky, then his burial ground due west where he died. Silently, she spoke his name, then told him and all of their country suffering beneath her, "Tomorrow, it will not be you and your children who kneel."

Saba tapped two fingers on his wings beneath her eye. Her target was sixty miles due south in the Valley of Jezreel, well protected and sitting behind an elevated mahogany desk: the district commissioner in Janîn, Palestine. Generations of farmers had nursed Janîn into a harvest city of 30,000. Saba's pride in the people here was total. They had survived despite British tyranny to push their crops under, Zionist murder to push them out, and another ten-year drought that had again decimated much of the country. Janîn's year-round market of olives, figs, dates, and carobs was often meager but never empty. The British had added a market in suffering. For a price, everything they had, Palestinians could avoid being deported to the camps. Saba had an appointment to see the district commissioner on such a matter.

Movement at her shoulder.

Saba spun. Two squirrels topped the limestone ledge, staring at her and the revolver now pointed at them. They stood on two feet, craned their necks, and scampered away. She kept the Enfield trained on the rock and the shadows behind it. Tomorrow's mission required skills not used since she was a girl flirting with schoolboys, other than the day and night spent with the American, Eddie Owen. The memory materialized before she could stop it. Some for America, some for the first man who had pierced her armor. All he had seen were her eyes and hands, but somehow he had done it. She thought of Eddie Owen more often than she cared to admit, had been harsher on the women in camp because of it, her weakness automatically theirs.

Eddie Owen was in Haifa; she had seen him shirtless there in her binoculars while she scouted the refinery by boat and again from the roof of a café north of the harbor. A refinery the Germans would no doubt level soon, killing everyone in it, deaths of Palestinian collaborators she had not yet determined how to prevent, or if she should. There was no question the Germans intended to deny England the gasoline produced there, gasoline that could help free Palestine if it could be controlled by Palestinians, not Europeans. Saba spit between her feet. But that would never happen; her countrymen lacked the will and foresight to think larger than the moment, larger than their own tribal disagreements and whatever God they picked.

The squirrels returned, interrupting her thoughts. They crept closer until she frowned, used names she had given them, and shared her rice. She had brought them from the camp. They would be the last inhabitants of the camp to see her alive.

At noon the following day, Saba was one of many crowding the dusty narrow streets, her right eye covered with a patch, her robe and shoes those of a shopkeeper. As she walked deeper into the city, the buildings gained menace. Her usually cool skin began to sweat. Saba glanced at shadowed doorways, then the alleys, and for too long. The hills and deserts had become home; these cities all bristled with her memories. Saba willed herself cold, adding confidence in skills she did not possess.

Two blocks from the commissioner's grand residence, armed men, European men, stood near the corners eating falafel they were not eating. Saba lowered her head, shuffling with the other Arabs, and affected a slight limp. The Europeans' attention stayed too long. The familiar fight or flee rose in her blood. The instinct was old and controllable. She turned away from the commissioner's residence, following three boys running toward the market just passed. Saba palmed the eye patch off her face, fearing the patch would mark her.

Another pair of Europeans eyed her, then another.

Trap—Irgun, Haganah, or England's special soldiers. A man shouted in English, possibly at her. Saba hurried around a building's plaster-spalled corner. More shouts followed. She sprinted between two buildings, then through an open gate into a courtyard filled with noisy children. Another gate led into a crowded street. Horses neighed, bothered in the dusty commotion. A mare bumped her off balance. The crowded street fed the market square and was shoulder-to-shoulder with first-harvest buyers and sellers. Saba joined the throng. She inspected dates with one hand, her revolver in the other hand under her robe.

European men—at least three—in the square but not shouting. All three turned toward a confrontation in the street Saba had just left. The Europeans drew revolvers. The crowd behind her was large and she shrank into the crush, most of them dressed exactly as she was. The crowd flowed her deeper into the market. Under the canvas awnings, men and children offered all manner of vegetables and fruits. Saba shuffled, head down. Bumps and jostles pushed her to the square's farthest edge. The Europeans held their stations, disciplined; discipline meant English. And it meant they were unsure if the figure near the district commissioner's residence had been her. They would guess soon. By then her partisans who waited there would be gone, melting away to regroup when she did not appear.

Saba and her partisans re-formed in the hills outside the city.

They hid for seven days and six nights while British patrols combed Janîn and always in groups of four or more. The pursuit was an expensive use of manpower and absolute proof the English believed the Raven was there. Instead of retreat, Saba reconstituted the kidnap plan. She did not inform Schroeder or her Iraqi commanders. As always in the desert, war meant religion, and religion always meant men, men like bin Faisal and his camp commanders, men who feared her popularity in Palestine, men who despised her as an infidel woman who would not bow and would not worship. Men who had betrayed her. Again.

When she had the commissioner in hand, Schroeder would know it had been her and they would proceed with his ransom plan. She would prove this to bin Faisal as well, in person, at night, and soon. At sunset of the seventh day, Saba put her plan in motion, dispatching Rafid back to the Iraqi camp and Jameel to Jerusalem. Rafid would arrive at the Iraqi camp at dawn of the following day. He would inform the camp commander and his mullahs that Saba had been fatally wounded in a bandit skirmish outside Janîn and had been taken to a safe house in Jerusalem. There was little hope for her survival. Rafid would give the mullahs her safe house so the Pan-Arab Army of God might render Saba assistance and comfort. Rafid's reward would be lamb and milk and great praise for his journey. His risk was that the mullahs would have him murdered in his sleep. Rafid was told this. He said his good-byes, asked to be remembered if this was to be his end, and accepted the mission.

Jameel and two partisans waited at the safe house in Jerusalem with a badly mutilated and beaten corpse, the right eye tattooed to match Saba's wings. Jameel was told to expect assassins, not assistance and comfort. The mullahs' representatives arrived. Jameel would not acknowledge Saba's death, nor show the corpse, until he had negotiated to collect England's bounty, finally agreeing to share the bounty with the mullahs' representatives.

Once the bargain was struck and the mullahs' men satisfied that the corpse was indeed the woman whose face the mullahs' men had never seen, the mullahs' men conscripted three farmers to show the corpse to England's Royal Marines and claim the bounty. This was done on their farm outside Janîn and included Saba's clothes, weapons, and personal belongings. The farmers told the story of her bandit skirmish on their road, her men calling her "*al Gorab*" and weeping at her death. The Raven's men had run off without her body when a company of Royal Marines had driven into the area.

Word spread like fire throughout Palestine: the Raven was dead.

Black wings began to appear on walls in Janîn and Jerusalem. For ten days the Raven was mourned and the English gloated, one more wog myth put to the sword. The Pan-Arab Army of God publicly mourned her passing but privately would be hunting her infidel partisans. Saba waited in hiding. She did not relish adding to the sadness of her people, nor did she relish her popularity and the pressure it brought, but the Raven's death was the only way she could approach her target and the only way to gain German money from Erich Schroeder.

On the fourteenth day, the East Indian maids at the commissioner's residence reported a return to normal security. Through intermediaries, Saba facilitated an appointment, but as a woman this time, one of some means, desperately trying to save her children from the camps, a woman who could pay with property. The Raven was dead; the Europeans did not fear a lowly Arab woman, although it was unusual for a woman to speak for a family. Her story was not unusual—no brothers and the father dead in the fighting outside Haifa.

Saba concealed a small pistol and two knives, the hope being that she would not be searched thoroughly, and the tattoo beneath her eye covered by two layers of marl and kohl paste. If she were discovered, she would assassinate the commissioner in his office, an act that in the previous plan had been strictly forbidden by the German. She would kill the commissioner and what soldiers she could, then herself before she could be captured. If she were successful, she would run through the rear of the residence dragging the fat English pig to a narrow alley and her escape team waiting there.

"Wait for me with the cart, here." She pointed a young man at an intersection just past the commissioner's two-story residence. "They will chase me and be shooting. You cross the road and fall there."

The young man she had trained all summer fingered his food cart then his disguise, trying to hide his worry. Three of her six partisans would provide cover fire from the rooftops.

Saba reiterated, "Have no weapons. Make no statements and mount no defense. The English will beat and accuse you; they know of the camp and our Iraqi benefactors there. Your comrades from the camp are gone and only the traitors remain. Any admitting will condemn you to English prison and death. The English lie; you know this. Their promises of pardon will be as empty as all the others."

The young man agreed, his death almost a certainty, and stepped back. Saba scanned the alley beyond, straightening her black robes and the keffiyeh covering everything but her eyes. She stopped him with a hand to his shoulder and thanked him: "*Shukran.*" Her heart was in it. "You are my one success among the Iraqi pigs. Be brave, for you are." Saba worried for him, and herself, and all of them. She signaled Jameel and the others to the rooftops, then walked three blocks out of her way, gathering her nerve.

At the front wall of the residence, two British soldiers barred her path. Large men with rifles, red tunics, and narrow eyes. She provided proof of her appointment and shrank from the leering, prodding inspection. A third soldier, an older corporal, his jacket sweaty and tight to his belly, escorted her up a long walk, through a garden without flowers, and into the grand residence's anteroom. The interior was opulent, more so than any Saba had seen. Huge floor tiles three times the normal width spread out in all directions, alternating green and a silver-veined black. Woodwork edged the floor and ceiling; two stairways wound upward under hand-carved balusters, a red carpet covered the treads.

This had been the house of Fahmi Abboushi, mayor of Janîn, and still employed the same East Indian maids. An ornate double door finished the anteroom; two dwarf date palms guarded either side. Her chest tightened. The corporal used accented Arabic, instructing her to wait. He turned and knocked on the double doors. Saba scanned without moving her head. The left door opened. In English the corporal discussed her as if she were not present. Saba wanted to rub the sweat from her eye but did not.

The corporal told someone inside the door, "She's the wog from Haifa, the shopkeeper's daughter. By the look of her hand and eyes, I'd say she's done a bit a farmin'."

"She's been checked, has she?"

"Not by me."

"Then be to it, corporal."

The door shut and the corporal heel-turned. He used three disconnected Arabic words to explain he had to search her. She extended her hands and arms, the small pistol high in the crotch of her legs. From behind, he patted her hair under the keffiyeh, then her neck and the length of her shoulders, his hands following down her arms to her hands. Saba began to tremble, felt him staring at her hands, his fingers lightly testing the skin and muscle.

His breath was wet, the smell of meat . . . He pushed the heavy fabric of her robe against her ribs and brushed the weight of her breasts, then felt the curve of her waist and the outside of her hip. Saba's trembling became a series of shivers, his breath close to her neck again. His hands went to her thighs, her knees, her calves, and finally her boots. He lifted her robe from the floor and she jerked away, eyes averted, head down, the panic real. Sweat beading across her forehead into her eyes.

The old corporal apologized and reached again. She jerked again and stumbled into the stair, tears forming in her eyes, hands forward to stop further contact. There were knives in her boots. She fumbled English. "Must go. No more hands." She fought the panic, eyes wide, the terror not an act. "No more."

The corporal straightened, confused. "You won't be seeing the commissioner, missy, unless you're searched."

Saba waved both hands and edged toward the outer door, ashamed at his effect on her, the memories she couldn't bury heightened by women's clothes and English hands.

The corporal blocked her exit. "Calm it there, miss. S'okay. You're okay, then. I'll tell 'em."

Saba stopped; the trembling did not. She tasted kohl makeup. The corporal backed to the double doors, smiling her calm, and knocked with the knuckles of his hand. The door opened and he told the space she was unarmed. The space widened and a tall, rigid sergeant bent only his neck to inspect her, then waved her forward.

For Palestine. She added dignity to her posture and walked the twenty paces. The sergeant allowed her to pass the doorway. A mammoth desk and painting dominated the room from the far wall. The desk was elevated and leather-topped, eight feet across and ornamented in gold leaf. To its left, on a ten-foot standard, rose a British battle flag at rest. Next to the flag, a single door was embedded in the wall just as the East Indian maids had told her. Behind the desk, a fat man sat as if he were on a throne, his reddish face too small for the body, the sagging cheeks those of a hound. His feminine hands had papers in one, a doily or napkin in the other. The belly vest had bits of his lunch. He did not honor her with an invitation or coffee.

An Arab interpreter, an Egyptian by his color and bearing, stood to the commissioner's right, both men framed by the life-size portrait of England's king. The Egyptian asked her business, barking, "*Matha tureedi?*"

Saba turned her entire body away as if cowed by his tone. The tall, rigid sergeant blocked the now closed double door. His sidearm was holstered, the flap undone and tucked behind, his eyes glued to her hands. The Egyptian asked her again. Saba turned to the voice, trying to hide her eye, and began to stutter.

"Speak slower, woman."

Saba fell to her knees, bending at the waist to touch her forehead to the floor, then stuttered in Arabic, apologizing for her family, begging they not be deported. The camps were cold; they would die.

"What have you to offer? Many costs must be paid."

Saba unbent, her hands clutched at her waist.

"What?" The Egyptian added measured volume. "Speak or we have no time for you. There are many who wish to stay and few spaces."

"Bu . . . but it is our country, my family's shop—"

"Silence!" The Egyptian's shout raised the commissioner's rheumy eyes from his desk.

He licked his lips and glanced over her head to the sergeant at the door. Saba rose from her knees, sensed the room shrinking, her eye paste dissolving, an attack coming. She backed away and bumped into the sergeant. His hands gripped her shoulders and pulled her back into his chest, his pelvis against her buttocks. Saba spun on the sergeant, buried the .32 in his chest, and fired twice. He banged into the polished white door and bounced back toward her. She ducked his hands, pivoted, and charged the commissioner's desk. On her left, the Egyptian fired a pistol. She ducked a bullet that had already missed her and fired the .32 empty. The Egyptian twisted into a tall row of plants. The commissioner stumbled up out of his chair. Saba lunged across the desk and rammed her empty revolver in his face.

"With me. Now."

One double door slammed open. Saba wheeled and threw the knife. The old corporal recoiled and fired wide. She rushed him. He sidestepped the dead sergeant but stumbled to a knee. Saba kicked at his gun hand, drew a second knife from her boot, and slashed. His pistol discharged past her face then bounced to the floor. She slashed again and the corporal fell to his back, his arm cut to the bone. Saba grabbed his revolver, aimed it at his face. He screamed, *"Nooo,"* and blocked at the barrel with a blood-gushing arm. Movement behind her. Saba spun and fired at the Egyptian aiming at her. He splattered the wall red. She spun to the corporal struggling to hold his bloody arm together and push away. She didn't fire. A gun cocked, *click-click.* Saba jumped left and fired three rounds through the commissioner's fortress desk. The commissioner fired back. His first bullet missed, the second tore her robe at the shoulder, the third hit the metal flag standard, knocked it into her forehead, and blew her backward. From the floor, she emptied the corporal's revolver into the desk, then wrestled out of the flag and pole, stood— surprised she was able—and ran through the single door embedded in the wall. It led into the residence and past two maids cowering behind furniture. Saba jumped a low table, bounced off a chair, and scrambled for the door she had been told would lead to the alley.

The alley was quiet. Blood streamed from the rip in her forehead. Saba ran toward her young man with the cart. "Run! Follow me!" Rifle fire erupted behind them.

"It was her, I tell ya. Plain as day and right in front of me." The corporal was in a hospital bed and put his hand ten inches in front of his face.

Captain Orde Wingate listened to the bandaged corporal, then glanced to a fellow special-branch officer, then back to the corporal.

Wingate had come all the way from Bushehr. "A ghost shot three men and sliced off the better part of your arm?"

"She did."

"Black wings under the eye, you say? A woman, not a man? And you didn't search her?"

"Felt her, I did. Polite, but a full search—"

"How could that be, corporal? This dead woman—*the Raven*, you say, as if the dead can rise—assassinated the Crown's district commissioner, killed a battle-tested sergeant and an Egyptian security officer using only a revolver and two knives. One of which remains stuck in the door you guarded."

"She's alive all right, and I searched her, Captain. I did. She had no weapons." The corporal shook his head and squeezed his bandaged arm.

"You were the man who searched this woman and you were the man she allowed to live. Do you find that strange, corporal? I do." Captain Orde Wingate pointed out the window. "The wogs rally at their Robin Hood's return." Wingate summoned two armed guards to the hospital bed. "For your efforts, Corporal, you will be court-martialed tomorrow and shot as a traitor. It is treason to give aide and take money from the enemy."

CHAPTER 14

October, 1938

Eddie had been regaled, lectured, and preached to about "the Holy Land" since he was three feet tall. Palestine was a bit different in person. He hadn't shared that in his letters home to his mother and father over his six months here; best for them if they thought he was on some glorious adventure holiday that included a paycheck. In Haifa, Eddie's "home" since March, it was no longer a good idea to close your eyes at night. So Eddie did his dreaming about her, the Arab princess-schoolteacher, during the day. Without her to think about, all he had was Haifa. And Haifa, like every square inch of British Mandate Palestine, was a mess, an unavoidable hate triangle of Jews, Brits, and Arabs that was now open warfare in two-thirds of the country. The Brits had just gone semi-insane over an assassination in Janîn—the district commissioner himself—thirty miles southeast. Royal Marines and Palestinian police had systematically detonated ten thousand pounds of explosives throughout the city over the last two weeks. Most of Janîn's population was now homeless. And so far no one knew, or no one was saying, who'd done the assassination.

British convoys were openly tying the wives and children of known combatants to their bumpers as human shields or force-marching the captives up ahead as human mine detectors. According to the truck drivers, the desert between the refinery and Janîn was littered with captured combatants who had been tried, sentenced, and shot on the roadside as examples. The message: "Don't come to Haifa." Vlad the Impaler had nothing on the Brits.

"Eddie!"

Eddie snapped to his name. His British boss waved at him to come down from the refinery's pipes. Eddie tapped the arc welder's shoulder next to him. "Take a break; the lord high and mighty wishes to have a spot of tea. We'll do the crane when I get back."

Eddie's boss did not offer tea. He was less happy than usual and presented Eddie with a telegram from Chicago. "You are being transferred to Tenerife in the Canary Islands."

Eddie grinned. He would attend church every day for the rest of his life.

The foreman scowled. "Our contract with Culpepper is a binding agreement and not yet complete. Breaking this contract will have serious repercussions for this refinery, our companies, and you as an employable engineer."

"Ah . . ." Eddie tried to cover the grin. He shrugged his best disingenuous apology and opened his palms. "Not up to me, sir, first I've heard of it."

"If this cannot be changed"—the foreman shook the telegram—"you are to present yourself at this office for departure: 0-700 hours on Thursday."

Eddie quit fighting the grin. Three days and he'd be on a plane, a ship, a camel—good-bye Promised Land, hello Canary Islands. He ran back through the refinery pipes, did a jig in the dust at the cab of the refinery's forty-foot crane, jumped onto the crane's work platform, and pointed up. The crane operator hoisted Eddie into position. A thunderous blast rocked the platform. The dust layer levitated off the spaghetti of pipes and tank. Eddie gripped the platform's rail against a fall he wouldn't survive. Beyond the refinery fence, smoke boiled into the sky above the ancient part of Haifa. A shocked stillness radiated through the refinery, Eddie and everyone else bracing for . . . Had to be the Arab market again. The last explosion was a double car bomb that killed twenty-seven.

A shout, then another. Distant voices began to yell in Arabic. Eddie blocked glare with his work fedora and scanned for D.J. Bennett. Eddie didn't see D.J. and waved the fedora at the crane operator to lower the platform. Palestine was no place for a sane person with options. The crane eased Eddie to thirty feet. Turning to the sea didn't improve the view. The Haifa harbor and this refinery were an armed camp and had been since the Arab Revolt had begun two years ago. But since the assassination in Janîn, the harbor and the refinery were on full battle alert all day, every day. The very few Arabs with whom Eddie worked whispered that any Arab suspected of participation in the Arab Revolt or loyalty to a group called the Pan-Arab Army of God were being forced into British detention camps, and behind the detention camp fences those Arabs were tortured for information, starved, and more often than not, shot for "attempting" escape. Eddie had pressed for details and his Arab associates quit talking to him entirely.

Eddie 360ed for D.J. Usually mayhem of any sort brought D.J. running from somewhere. And from day one of their six-month tour here, there'd been plenty of mayhem. Britain's battle cruiser, the HMS *Repulse*, had arrived in July to protect the refinery's Mediterranean exposure with her fifteen-inch guns. Five hundred Royal Marines patrolled the razor wire that fenced the harbor's land side. The Brits would not discuss the refinery with anyone but officially stated that the harbor was central to their control in the region, their "mandate" confirmed on them by the League of Nations.

Numerous Arab factions charged that what the harbor was central to English domination of the Arab desert and illegal Zionist immigration. Charges and countercharges were the extent of "conversation" between Arabs and anyone affiliated with the British. Anything beyond that was "treason" to your side or an insult to the other. One fact was for sure: The harbor represented work, and in a farming country dying of drought, work meant food, and like the desperation of the Dust Bowl, food mattered more than tomorrow's politics. For 176 days Eddie had watched the Palestinians who stevedored at the harbor strip-searched every shift, same for those building the refinery . . . had to be tough putting up with that in your own country no matter how hungry you were.

Eddie had tried to imply as much when shopping in the market and out of D.J.'s earshot, hoping to make an acquaintance who might help locate the mysterious hazel-eyed teacher of the *Arabian Nights*. Calah al-Habra had promised to come and hadn't. Daydreaming about her felt beyond good, why, Eddie wasn't entirely sure, nor did he wish to cross-examine. Better just to find out in person.

As the weeks passed, Eddie'd been seriously tempted to mention the wings beneath her eye, wings similar to some Eddie'd seen scratched into a wall after a partisan fighter had been killed, but heeding her warning and the cold stares of every Arab in the market, he had not. Eddie guessed her tattoo meant she was part of, or born to, a religious sect or a Nationalist faction of some kind. After seeing the wings on the walls, Eddie'd asked British soldiers and was told it was "wog mythology." The single Arab Eddie felt he could approach and not die told him, "Your questions are an insult to our sorrow." From there the Arab Revolt had grown even bloodier. Any Arab who willingly engaged an employee of the British outside the refinery in anything other than a shouting match risked being stoned to death by his peers. And since Janîn two weeks ago, any interaction with the locals had become just as physically dangerous for Eddie. No question, Eddie had seen all the hate he needed.

The refinery whistle blew shrilly, ending another shift in paradise. Three more to go. Can't wait to tell D.J.—the Canary Islands, exotic, pirate port o' call off the coast of Africa—Morocco to be exact—D.J. will swoon. We'll be swashbuckling Errol Flynns. No doubt plenty of backroom dealings involved but that will all come out in the wash. Out of here is the main thing! Eddie jumped off the crane ten feet from the foreman's construction trailer. The foreman's end-of-shift report would have to wait till D.J. heard the news. Eddie checked D.J.'s trailer, then the canteen. Nope. Kinda odd . . . maybe the café Mataam Cairo; it was D.J.'s spot for a pint.

Eddie negotiated through shift-end workers being searched prior to exit. At the fortified main construction gate, Eddie tipped his fedora to the Royal Marines. Their response was grim eyes and bayonets. After showing his identification to a sergeant he saw every day, Eddie was allowed out into the road. The dusty ribbon of concrete separated the refinery from the old part of Haifa—a maze of narrow cobblestone streets and plastered buildings stacked uphill toward Mount Carmel and the olive trees. Eddie's name sounded behind him.

D.J. Bennett. Finger in the air beckoning Eddie forward. D.J. was wearing work clothes that hadn't seen any. Not that unusual given that Eddie had never actually seen D.J. work. They met midroad, dodging a pipe truck about to lose its load. D.J. eased Eddie left toward the seaside cafés three blocks away, the café umbrellas adding color dots to the tan-on-tan plaster cityscape. "Pick 'em up 'fore we get our asses run over."

Eddie squinted in the sun ricocheting off the bay. D.J.'s pocked face was creased awfully somber. Eddie stopped. "Bad news?" The letters from Eddie's mom were stoic, but they didn't lie. What wasn't in them was impossible to miss. Eddie tried to get ready but wasn't.

D.J. looked past one shoulder, then at Eddie. "Nah. Same old shit." D.J. frowned. "Could be there's some new shit, too."

Eddie beamed. "Did you hear?"

"Hear what?"

"Tenerife." Eddie slapped D.J.'s shoulder. "We're outta here in three days. Good-bye Dust Bowl, hello Errol Flynn."

D.J. hardened. "Says who?"

Eddie nodded toward the refinery. "Telegram from Chicago. Foreman's none too happy. Hell, I thought you'd be thrilled."

"Show me."

Eddie shrugged. "Foreman kept it."

"Who signed the telegram?"

"Harold Culpepper, I think. Why's that matter?"

"*Why's that matter?*" D.J. shook his head. "Goddamn bastards." This would be the backroom dealing. "What? Why?"

D.J. walked two blocks along the harbor's edge without explaining his response, then stopped at the first of three café outposts enjoying some disconnect from the troubles and a saltwater breeze instead of diesel. D.J. pointed at the only empty table in café Mataam Cairo. Eddie eased into a chair with his back to the sun and water. D.J. waved two fingers at a dark Egyptian sidestepping their way and fixing his apron. The Brits at the next table were Royal Marines in civvies and didn't care who heard their conversation. "Wog bandits are payin' for Janîn. Assassinatin' bastards murder a district commissioner *in his own flat*. Wogs will be tastin' His Majesty's guns till we've tired of loading. And about bloody time."

Another Marine at the table lifted his glass. "Buggers all." He chinned at the smoke above the city. "Who's our freedom fighter this afternoon?"

The Englishman closest to Eddie replied, "Not the wogs according to the captain—Jews. Zionist militia. A grenade." The Englishman frowned distant recognition at Eddie and kept the tone. "Captain's hunting the Jew Nancy-boys now."

Eddie turned away. Gosh, and the Brits wondered why *everybody* hated them.

The pints arrived. D.J. shuffled his chair until his back would shield his words from the Brits. "Think about this before you answer." D.J. waited for Eddie to nod. "Anybody been talking to you I don't know about? Asking questions about gasoline, this refinery? American oil people in particular?"

"*Talking to me*? I ran out of pencils keeping track of who hates me and who intends to kill whom on what day. Thought you'd be thrilled to get the hell out of here."

D.J. said, "Three years ago, the president of the Canary Islands was assassinated. The islands are now a staging ground for General Francisco Franco's Nationalists in mainland Spain's civil war. Franco and his Nationalists are Fascists. Evil sons-a-bitches."

"We're building a refinery for the Fascists?"

D.J. nodded. "I heard Culpepper might be moving you. Got a call through to our good friend Harold an hour ago. Took the whole goddamn day."

"And . . ."

"Harold suddenly thinks he's stronger than he is. Told me you were headed to Tenerife. I told him that he and whoever thought they were moving you better rethink the proposition. Made it crystal fucking clear that Harold could not afford to piss me off, that his problems in Oklahoma hadn't gone away. Harold said I wasn't welcome at the Tenerife refinery and there's nothing he, or I, could do about it. Six months ago Harold Culpepper never would've said that."

Eddie frowned. D.J. had just admitted, not inferred, that he'd blackmailed Professor Culpepper—why wouldn't that blackmail matter now?

D.J. continued to process today's news. "Bastards get you out there all alone . . . Could be their plan for Eddie Owen and his talents . . . You'd be ripe and ready when the serious hostilities break out in Europe."

"Are you saying . . . What? Kidnap me? If a war starts?"

"I told you before, it ain't *if*. They got you taking over for the fuck-up engineer who was poisoned—"

Eddie's eyes widened at *poisoned*.

"*Fish* poisoning, a barracuda. Flew your predecessor to a special hospital *in Berlin*." D.J. tapped the table with his claw hand. "Guy trained at East Chicago, had 'em all believing he was an Eddie, but he couldn't get the job done."

Eddie said, "The foreman didn't mention that. He was pissed, though, inferring that Culpepper and me would have hell to pay if we broke this contract."

D.J. swallowed a quarter of his pint. "Bill Reno's dead. An East Indian with a pipe wrench."

Eddie jolted back. "No . . ."

"His office was ransacked; files are missing. Yours and mine, some others, but not the AvGas schematics. Bill's copies we let him have were in the safe where your personnel file was supposed to be." D.J. checked his shoulder again. "Indian said it was self-defense and didn't know nothing about the office. Brits have him; don't figure he'll see daylight again."

"When?"

"Be a week this Sunday. Same day your counterpart ate the barracuda in Tenerife. Culpepper shipping you to the Fascists to finish up their AvGas modifications is a serious statement, especially so since it means you're leaving the Brits tits-up here. Bill dead and our personnel files missing in Bahrain ain't good, either. All of it five days apart."

Bill Reno dead? Eddie slouched back in the chair, limp to his feet. Bill was a damn decent fellow. Never occurred to Eddie that Bill wasn't West Texas invincible—hard, weathered leather that couldn't be worn beyond anything but shiny or dry. Beat to death with a pipe wrench. *Shit.*

D.J. raised his pint. "Salty old son of a bitch. Went down fighting, I'd promise. Maybe for us."

Eddie winced, then raised his pint. The world was a fucked-up place, that was the long and the short of it. "To you, Bill."

D.J. sipped his, then set it down. "Our files are missing, Eddie. You heard me?"

"Yeah."

"All of that in five days is too fast to be an accident. That war triangle I drew for you back in Chicago is about to collapse into two sides. When that triangle collapses, the war starts."

D.J. used three fingers to make one point.

"One: The oil companies are a 'country' of their own. And now making open votes. By moving you to Tenerife, the oil companies are siding with the Nazis.

"Two: France is workin' three shifts a day building an armored tank barrier along their border with the Nazis. Call it the Maginot Line. Lotta goddamn money France doesn't have . . . unless you actually expect a tank attack. France goes it alone behind their wall or they have to side with Russia.

"Three: Spain's civil war is Communist versus Fascist. When Franco wins, and that'll be soon, Spain sides with the Nazis. That gives the Fascists southern Europe." D.J. frowned at his own math. "On the day Franco wins, the Canary Islands—where Culpepper is sending you without me—becomes the AvGas trophy. When Hitler has her, he has an Atlantic port to receive crude oil *from anywhere* and the refined gasoline to march across the rest of Europe. That includes England."

Eddie's shoulders flattened. "Bill was a good fellow."

"That he was, son. Did you hear what I just said?"

Eddie nodded, lost in . . . everything.

D.J. raised his chin at the almost full café next door to theirs, the only separation between them a mostly dead potted hedge. "See the girl reading the book?"

Eddie looked. Hard to miss the only girl there, black hair swept back over her shoulders. European, maybe late twenties.

D.J. said, "And your Lieutenant Hornsby a table away from her pretending he ain't interested?"

Lieutenant Cornell Hornsby was an MI6 intelligence officer who Eddie's foreman occasionally hosted in his office trailer.

D.J. chinned at the girl again. "Dinah Rosen. Been in town a couple of days. Says she's got something important for us, life-or-death important. Asking about the refinery, too, about the Americans working here. Do you know her?"

Eddie didn't. "Who do you mean, *us*? Asking what?"

"Be sure, Eddie. Have you ever seen her *anywhere*?"

"No. Not like there's so many single women here a guy can't keep 'em straight."

D.J. chewed on Eddie's answer. "Our skirt there is a musketeer of some stripe; don't know who she shoots for, but given the timing of the last five days we better know before we have the serious chat with her." D.J. sipped the pint. It coated his horseshoe mustache white. "Roosevelt and the Brits can't have this refinery carbonize like your last one. Best we know what interests her and why."

"We? I thought I was an engineer." Eddie private-eyed his sweat-stained fedora over his eyes.

D.J. hardened. He emptied the jar between them of its book matches. "You best be real careful, Eddie boy . . . *everywhere* you sleep from today forward. Bill Reno was no accident. People with that kinda reach gotta be respected. And people with the balls to shoot a US president won't hesitate to leave you in a bar ditch"— D.J. nodded to include Dinah Rosen—"should you begin associatin' with folks they find offensive. I ain't saying we kneel; this Marine ain't begging at J.P. Morgan's soup kitchens a second time. I'm sayin' be careful."

D.J.'s tone meant that conversation was over. His claw hand carefully lined up book matches like dominoes on the table, fat end down. "Like I said, our Dinah Rosen there says she's got something life-or-death important. Don't know what that would be, but she's only gonna give it to one guy. Can't say I'm happy about sending you out alone, but—"

"Sending me out? Alone? I'm an engineer, remember?"

"Miss Rosen wasn't using my name."

Eddie imagined a Buddy Rich rim shot and cymbal.

"And careful with her, son. She's a Czech, got a dog in this fight now. Sky ain't falling on Chicken Little anymore."

"Huh? What happened in Czechoslovakia? Hitler and Chamberlin were on the radio yesterday saying everything was Jake—"

"Yep, you're right. British prime minister announced 'Peace in our time' at Munich yesterday. Said him and Hitler have everything calmed down. Hitler said thanks, then took western Czechoslovakia this morning while you were out there in the rigging." D.J. flicked the first matchbook. One after the other, the matchbooks tumbled. D.J. stood, then stepped through the potted hedge that separated two of the cafés. He grabbed a chair and engaged Lieutenant Hornsby at his table. Their loud, rather spirited discussion included England's objectives in India and Prime Minister Chamberlin's deft handling of

Hitler's aspirations to subjugate the part of Europe the Nazis didn't already own.

When the argument had Lieutenant Hornsby's full attention, Eddie walked to Miss Dinah Rosen's table. He said, "Hi," and removed his fedora, then extended the hand without the pint and hat. "I'm Eddie Owen."

Her eyes rose from the book, taking in his belt, his shoulders, and finally his face. "That you are." Her accent was difficult to place, but her English was British. She returned to the book. Eddie left his hand there, lonely in the air between them.

"Excuse me. My hand; don't know what to do with it now."

"It may fit in your pocket?"

Eddie waggled his hand. "Allow me to try again. Hi. I'm Eddie Owen, Cushing, Oklahoma, USA."

Dinah Rosen glanced through the café by shifting in her chair, added a smile, closed the book, and shook hands. "Dinah Rosen. Munich by way of Prague, Czechoslovakia."

Eddie pointed at a chair. "Now that we've been properly introduced, may I sit?"

Eyelash flutter. Twinkle. "A pleasure, Edward. Tell me all about Oklahoma." She patted the closest chair.

A siren wailed, then another; Eddie glanced toward the smoke still hovering over the rooftops. Her voice followed his eyes. "The initial reports suggest Arabs bombing Arabs, a bloody ploy designed to blame us, the Jews." Dinah Rosen rolled her eyes. "Only my fellow zealots believe that."

"You're a zealot?"

She smiled. "That would depend upon who might be asking and why." Her eyes wandered to Lieutenant Hornsby and her grin faded. She quickly marshaled another and raised her pint. "Cheers, Eddie Owen." Smile and eyelashes. Not bar-the-door pretty, but the twinkle added a lot.

"That's everything I need to know about zealots? This wonderful country and its happy people?"

Miss Rosen spit part of her beer on the table. She dabbed at her lips and made a face. "Sorry."

Eddie toasted her again and drained his glass, enjoying this detective business much more than expected.

Miss Rosen finished dabbing and stood. "I was off to perform a commission—sorry, that would be 'run an errand' in American English—in town. Care to walk along and protect me?"

Damn, that was easy. "Sure."

The breeze plastered a thin dress to a very impressive figure. Miss Rosen wrinkled her nose at Eddie's admiration. "I'm not ever the prettiest girl at the dance but rarely fare poorly on the beach." She grabbed his hand. "Possibly we'll find one for a dip."

Eddie and Dinah walked a block of cobblestones into the city before she released his hand and reached for a flower she decided not to buy. "I am a teacher. I understand you are an engineer."

"Me? I didn't hear anyone say that."

"You weren't around when I attempted to arrange this accidental meeting."

Eddie laughed. She was direct, too. "So this is a blind date?"

"Ah, that American wit one hears so much about."

Eddie stopped, realizing her English was as good as his. He furrowed his forehead and asked.

She said, "I teach English. Why I was allowed to immigrate under the current policy. Teachers and students aren't required to sneak past the Nazis or swim in to the beaches of Palestine."

An Arab man stumbled toward them, bandaged and humped over, assisted by another Arab in the narrow street. A group of young boys followed behind, shouting and waving fragments from the explosion. The lead boy looped the men, charged Eddie, and spit in his face. In Arabic, the boy shouted accusations. Dinah grabbed

Eddie's arm and pulled them through an open storefront full with ring doughnuts and platters of falafel.

Eddie wiped saliva as the angry crowd passed. Dinah bought two stuffed pitas and pulled him deeper into the shop. "Glorious, no? Haifa was once their home; now it is England's sea route to the treasures of India—'the Empire's silken highway.'"

Eddie thought about the "Vlad the Impaler" highway to Janîn. "Pretty sure the Brits intend to keep their highway."

"That they do." Dinah leaned to Eddie's ear. "British policy, in this wonderful country as you so eloquently put it, is based upon 'divide and rule.' A simple design that fans fear and hate between Arab and Jew. It assures Great Britain the position of arbitrator and master."

As Arab men passed, they stared into the Arab bakery at two people who weren't Arabs. Dinah eased behind Eddie's shoulder. The men hauled damaged baskets from the market, the fruit and vegetables ripe but stunted from lack of water. Drought, same as Oklahoma . . . Eddie asked Dinah Rosen, "So why'd you come here?"

"Munich is worse, far worse, and sadly, now Austria and Czechoslovakia, too. Here, Jews have a chance, a history. But we need friends, friends like America . . ."

"Europe must be as bad as they say to think Palestine is better." Eddie stepped out of the shop. "This place is on fire."

Dinah stepped out to his side, taking a nonhungry bite of pita. "Come." Her hand reached for his. "Possibly we will be allowed through."

Closer to the market, their street added more glares and angry postures. Rumblings and shouts trailed them on both shoulders. They approached the market from the west side but were stopped short on the crowded cobblestones. Eddie asked a well-armed member of Britain's hated Palestine Police Force what had happened.

The policeman was alone, nervous, and had his pistol in hand. "Grenade. Could've been two. Killed two dozen, I'm hearing from me sergeant major, and started the fire. You and your bird clear off, find somewhere else to be." The policeman wiped at his forehead, then pointed them back the way they had come. "There'll be trouble with the wogs after dark."

"Who did it?"

"Arabs dead today, Jews tonight or tomorrow. What's it matter to a refinery man? A smart bugger just does his day's tour and stays well out the way."

Dinah Rosen said, "Irgun," as she scanned the claustrophobic intersection.

"What?" The policeman glared at her. "You said what?"

She explained to Eddie instead. "Irgun. The militants. They want Britain gone with the Arabs. Not at all shy about how."

The policeman reddened, patting for his whistle. "Terrorists, that's what your Irgun are. Murderin' Jew bastards. Keep your feet, woman." The policeman couldn't find his whistle and hard-eyed Eddie. "I know who you are. Keep your Jew here. The sergeant major'll be having a word with her."

Eddie agreed, almost saluted. The policeman double-timed around the corner. Eddie grabbed Dinah and ran her north through a perpendicular alley. He veered them left; she stumbled and ran right, waving him to follow.

Been here "a couple of days" and she *knows where to go?*

They weaved through a confusion of streets and population, running seven blocks until Dinah stopped them near a jail converted to a synagogue. Eddie caught his breath first, looking in all four directions. "That the magic word, 'Irgun'? And if so, how's it you know?"

Panting, hands on her knees, Dinah Rosen scanned the streets and didn't answer.

Eddie said, "Honey, I don't know how long you've really been in the country, but you don't want the Brits mad at you here. This isn't England. Whoever's been killing the Brits the last two months has their attention—Jews and Arabs. I hear the Marines talking at work and they're looking sideways at *all* y'all."

Dinah grinned at the uneven cobblestones, hands still on her knees. "Always . . . wanted to hear . . . Rhett Butler say 'y'all.'"

Eddie didn't want to confront angry Royal Marines or Palestine Police. "C'mon. Scarlett O'Hara and I will have a beer somewhere inside; she can explain that policeman's sudden interest in you and *Irgun*."

Dinah Rosen straightened, still grinning, then squinted past Eddie at lengthening shadows. "The men in Munich and Prague prefer their women silent and pregnant. How do they like them in Oklahoma?"

"I'm not kidding; we better get inside somewhere."

Dinah pulled them deep into the synagogue's outer doorway and opened the door. The building's interior was musty, too dim to navigate, but large enough to echo. The section Eddie could make out was a wall of plastered sandstone bricks that rose to a high roof of old timber. Water dripped somewhere and sounded like slow footsteps. Eddie waited for his eyes to adjust, then cut to the chase. "My friend said you were asking about me? Said you had 'something important.'"

"He did?" Dinah did not seem particularly shaken by the revelation.

This wasn't how the Q&A went in the Dashiell Hammett novels. Eddie tried again. "I wasn't the only American you were asking about, right?"

No answer, just the eyelashes.

"C'mon. You have to help. I'm new at this."

"Never would have guessed. You seem so . . . authoritative. Quite masculine."

Eddie held up both hands. "I surrender. Please tell me why you're asking questions about me, what you want to know; and

221

if there's anything secret-agent-ish about you, please include that, too."

Dinah patted her dress into reasonable order that Eddie hated to see added, then pointed deeper inside the synagogue. "There."

"We're going to church? What happened to the beach?"

Dinah laughed, both hands reworking her hair. "That wit again. Amazing the American girls ever get out of bed." She led Eddie to an undersize doorway. A bearded man watched him. The man was in his late twenties but weathered, like he'd spent most of those years outside, a farmer maybe. He was the same height as Eddie and wearing a New York Yankees cap.

"Tom Mendelssohn," he said with no discernible accent. Tom Mendelssohn offered a hand. Eddie noticed the other hand wasn't visible, above it a leather shoulder holster only partly covered by the unbuttoned work shirt. The holster was empty.

Dinah said, "I had trouble in the square. Military police heard me mention Irgun to my friend here. We were not followed, but . . ."

Mendelssohn frowned, waved Eddie to follow through a doorway, then another, then another—each doorway progressively smaller—and finally into an office cluttered with papers. The desk had a pistol atop its corner.

"Have a seat." Mendelssohn grabbed the pistol and holstered it. "Keep forgetting this thing."

Eddie checked the room instead of sitting. Just the one Tom Thumb doorway they'd squeezed through and no windows.

"Please." Mendelssohn gestured at a worn captain's chair. "You're from Oklahoma? Small world, huh? I was born in Joplin, grew up in Tulsa working at the Greyhound track."

Yeah, Eddie thought, *awful small*. He glanced at Dinah Rosen and sat.

"Well, Eddie—I can call you Eddie?"

Shrug and another glance at Dinah Rosen. Eddie didn't remember his name being introduced.

"I'll make this short, then you'll want to ask questions and I'll try to answer, okay?" Mendelssohn smiled at Eddie, then Dinah. "Had to do this quickly. You're being reassigned in a few days—we didn't know—to Tenerife, to do the same work as here—"

"I'm being reassigned? Says who?"

"I'll get to that. When you get to Tenerife, you'll see proof, incontrovertible proof that your employer there is in league with the Fascists and Hitler's Nazis, conspiring against the US government's official policies and objectives."

Eddie held up a hand. "Ah, who, exactly, are you?"

"Me?" Mendelssohn patted his chest, offering an innocent smile. "An American just like you." Mendelssohn's fingertips bumped the pistol under his shirt, "Well, maybe a little different."

"Why am I here, Mr. Mendelssohn? I think you'd be better off with Nick Charles."

"We were talking about Tenerife." Mendelssohn stopped. "Forgive me. I'm doing a bad, hurried job of recruiting you."

Eddie shifted in his chair. Maybe he'd missed some of the conversation. Maybe he'd dozed, because this was left field all the way to the fence. "Could we go back just a question or two? Start with who you are?"

Mendelssohn folded his hands on the desk and smiled again. "You're right. Sorry. I'm a smuggler. I smuggle Jews. From Europe to Palestine via Marseilles; Lisbon; and, as of this morning, overland from Prague." He stroked his beard once. "If you're a Jew, hospitable Europe shrinks every day."

"You smuggle people, Jews."

Tom Mendelssohn nodded. "There's an annual immigration quota here set by the British. Completely separate from being allowed *in* by the British, there is a cost *out* paid to the Nazis.

In order to legally emigrate from Germany, Austria, and now Czechoslovakia, personal property must be forfeited to the Reich and bribes must be paid to Reich officials. Unfortunately, after the property is transferred and these bribes are paid, the Jews in transit often disappear. One begins to fear identification as a Jew, even as a departing Jew."

Eddie listened to the pleasant monotone, thinking it odd that anyone could be calm and pleasant explaining what Mendelssohn was explaining, assuming it was true.

"And when the transiting Jew arrives here, he fears identification as an arriving Jew. Hence, we smuggle out *and* in."

"Big world out there. Why fight the British quota here? Why not go somewhere else?"

"Not so big a world if you are a Jew, my friend. Even the USA has very strict immigration laws for foreigners—our Congress's stated intent is to 'not upset the current racial balance.'" Mendelssohn grimaced, small but obvious. "And anywhere the Nazis and Stalin's Bolsheviks reach in the next few years will become a tolerance graveyard . . . then just a graveyard."

Eddie looked around. "The Nazis can't reach this far?" He thought of Erich Schroeder in Iran and Bahrain. "I've seen 'em here."

"True. Nowhere is perfect. But in some European capitols there's support for a Jewish homeland in Palestine—get us out of their hair forever." Mendelssohn laughed and looked both happy and not. "The more we mass, the harder it'll be for the West to look the other way if things begin to . . . deteriorate."

Mendelssohn removed two books from his desk and laid them flat, his hands covering both. "Here goes, Eddie. Not my best recruiting job, but neither of us has much time." He inhaled all he could. "The Nazis intend to murder all the Jews of Europe, roughly eleven million people."

Silence.

Echoes of water dripping.

Eddie looked at Dinah, then back to Mendelssohn and tried to keep a straight face. No reason to insult this guy. He had a gun and was obviously crazy.

Mendelssohn eased back in his chair. "Twenty years ago when Hitler was still campaigning in the beer halls, he laid out a plan to deal with the *Judenfrage*, or Jewish Question. Hitler blamed us for the spread of bolshevism, calling us racial tuberculosis. His plan's first stage was Exclusion, then Expulsion, and finally Removal. At the time, Herr Hitler did not define 'Removal.'

"Presently, Hitler and the Nazis are well into phases one and two—Exclusion and Expulsion via the loss of citizenship and the sanctioned theft of property. Phase three, the final phase, is now receiving the funding and full attention of highly placed officials in the Nazi government." Mendelssohn cleared his throat with some difficulty, glanced at Dinah Rosen, and continued.

"The first written draft of phase three, now called *Die Endlosung*, or Final Solution, was completed last November right here in Palestine, and just after the Reichstag added the 'racial purity' amendments to the Nuremberg Laws. Two low-level SS officers of the Jewish Section authored the Final Solution at the request of Reinhard Heydrich, chief of the Gestapo.

"The authors were SS men Herbert Hagen and Adolf Eichmann. Eichmann has since been promoted to Special Officer for Zionist Affairs. Before he became the special officer, Eichmann was a salesman." Mendelssohn smiled for effect. "For an American oil company, *your company*, Eddie, the one that first made your AvGas modifications work—Vacuum Oil Company A.G."

Eddie had never heard of Adolf Eichmann, but Harold Culpepper had talked about Vacuum Oil Company. He'd also mentioned "the bankers of Judah."

Mendelssohn continued. "In brief, the Nazis' Final Solution outlines a way to steal all the wealth of every Jew who falls under Nazi territorial control, then exterminate them. *Genocide*, Eddie, much like what the Japanese are doing to China right now." Mendelssohn paused. "Make no mistake, the Nazis are building the infrastructure to *systematically* murder eleven million people, exterminate us as vermin."

Eddie stayed blank. Not too many responses for that kind of statement, at least none that he knew. He checked Dinah Rosen again to see if she looked any crazier.

Mendelssohn said, "I mentioned Industrialists who are betraying our government in the USA. They support this genocidal policy by association and default—"

"C'mon." Eddie's skepticism got the best of him. "I can't believe any US company would—"

"Wouldn't think you could. *I* didn't." Mendelssohn smoothed his beard again. "Hitler's architects and engineers have worked months to design and fail-test these facilities to meet the genocide timetable. Actual blueprints, Eddie, full construction plans with schematics and flow charts and rendering capacities of how these Nazi facilities will 'process' vast quantities of human beings. *People*, Eddie, with names and families." Mendelssohn nodded at Dinah Rosen. "Like her and me."

Eddie thought of Franklin Nadler, age nine.

"There are copies of these blueprints and I've seen them, with complete cost and operation budgets. The first extermination camp is already built, Buchenwald near Weimar, ostensibly for 'political prisoners.' Other camps are under construction contract to Topf and Sons and I.G. Farben. You've heard of I.G. Farben?"

Eddie had, but still thought Mendelssohn had logged too many days in the sun.

"After the Rockefellers, I.G. Farben is the largest stockholder in Standard Oil of New Jersey. And Standard Oil owns a large share of I.G. Farben."

Eddie couldn't hide the frown. The implication was ridiculous.

"I.G. Farben has an American subsidiary, American I.G. On its board of directors is Walter C. Teagle, chairman of Standard Oil and Edsel Ford, son of Henry Ford, the chairman of Ford Motor Company."

Eddie shook his head. "No. Bullshit—"

"Bullshit?" Tom Mendelssohn handed Eddie one of the books on the desk, a first edition copy of Hitler's *Mein Kampf.* "Look at page 639; Hitler has high praise for our famous car builder/philanthropist and his views."

Eddie rolled his eyes, happy Mendelssohn was crazy, gun or not. "Right, Hitler's a fan of Henry Ford." Eddie flipped to the marked page, read Ford's name and Hitler's opinion:

> . . . It is Jews who govern the stock exchange forces of the American Union. Every year makes them more and more the controlling masters of the producers in a nation of one hundred and twenty millions; only a single great man, Ford, to their fury, still maintains full independence.

Eddie checked the book's binding, obviously a fake, a trick to discredit a man who back home was considered close to a saint. "No way Henry Ford, Sr., thinks Hitler's plans are the right idea. We'd lynch him."

"You might want to reconsider." Mendelssohn handed Eddie another book, a bound set of four booklets. *The International Jew: The World's Foremost Problem.* Circa 1922.

In print below the title was, *By Henry Ford, Sr.*

Eddie opened the book and scanned three pages. No way. Not possible. "Sorry, this has to be a fake."

Mendelssohn continued. "Ford owned a newspaper in Michigan, the *Dearborn Independent*. He used it weekly to blame us for anything he didn't like, including starting the Great War to make a profit." Mendelssohn tapped Henry Ford's book in Eddie's hands. "Try page twenty-two."

Eddie flipped and read:

> All over the United States, in many branches of trade, Communist colleges are maintained, officered, and taught by Jews.

Eddie skipped and tried again.

> Until Jews can show that the infiltration of foreign Jews and the Jewish Idea into the American labor movement has made for the betterment in character and estate, in citizenship and economic statesmanship, the charge of being an alien, destructive and treasonable influence will have to stand.

Eddie looked up at Dinah Rosen. Mendelssohn said, "Page thirty-one, under 'Name the Enemy.'"

Eddie skimmed the marked paragraphs:

> Judah has begun the struggle. Judah has made the invasion (immigration) . . . Let . . . civilization . . . know that the attacking force is Jewish . . . It is against this that the Jews protest. 'You must not identify us,' they say, 'You must not use the term Jew.' Why? Because unless the Jewish idea can creep in under the assumption of other

than Jewish origin, it is doomed . . . It is an invasion, nothing less, and it is inspired and helped by influences within the United States. When it is not secret it is thinly cloaked with sentiment 'these people are fleeing from persecution.'

"Jesus." Saint Henry seemed to think and believe a great deal like Hitler sounded. "Henry must not want to sell any more cars."

"To Jews." Dinah Rosen half laughed. "Already translated into sixteen languages. Very popular in Germany, as you might imagine."

Mendelssohn continued. "Ford has said worse, but you get the idea. Henry's not a fan. And he's not alone. Lots of politicians and industrialists, both in America and Europe, fear the Communists first, and Hitler second or not at all." Mendelssohn pointed at the two books in Eddie's hands. "These men and those pages say seventy-five percent of the Communists in America and Europe *are* Jews bent on taking over their business empires or governments."

"Glad I'm Presbyterian; nobody's afraid of us."

"*Afraid* might not be the only benchmark. What if a specific group of Americans became a *burden*? The Nazi's solution for Jews has been previously applied to Chinese and Africans for their lack of value to the 'new way.' Why couldn't the Nazi solution be applied to 'Okies'? Families like yours or those already on the desperate trail to California? Labor camps have already been proposed. What happens when those people can no longer work?"

Eddie palmed his forehead, sick to his stomach. "Don't imagine I'm here for the history lesson, so . . . why are you showing me this stuff? Your extermination-camp evidence should be in front of the FBI or Congress or Walter Winchell."

"You're at my table, Eddie"—Tom Mendelssohn unrolled a large set of architectural drawings and schematics—"because you are very valuable to the oil companies, Standard Oil in particular;

you'll be in the Canary Islands for at least a year, and you can read complicated blueprints. You'll know these are authentic. I'd like to trade these very unpleasant documents"—Mendelssohn tapped the blueprints—"the already-built and to-be-built plans for *extermination camps*, facilities with railroad spurs, gas chambers, and four-story ovens. I'd like to trade these architectural and engineering plans stolen from Standard Oil's Nazi partners . . . return them, *in principal*, to the Rockefeller family and their senior executives at Standard Oil."

Dinah Rosen handed Eddie a half-inch-thick, ten-by-ten envelope.

Mendelssohn tapped the horror documents on his table. "In exchange for not making these public, we'd like you to help facilitate Standard Oil's participation in our human import/export business . . . starting next week, via your next stop, the Canary Islands. You can smuggle these documents out of Palestine and into a very threatening position. You won't be searched." Mendelssohn paused. "Or executed if you're caught."

Thirty very troubling minutes later, Dinah Rosen and Eddie walked out of the synagogue. Eddie had the large, incredibly damning, sealed envelope of papers flat against his back under his shirt, doing his best to calm his stomach and pass for stable. What he'd been shown and read would be devastating blackmail if a guy had the balls to play it against the biggest oil company on planet Earth, guys with Nazi partners who invaded other countries and built human extermination camps as . . . a goddamn business.

Mendelssohn had tried to run the blackmail himself from Palestine, but the response he'd received from his target had scared him, he said, and then almost killed him. Mendelssohn wanted an intermediary; no more negotiations that were "close to home where the blackmail target could compromise my entire network."

Eddie had hedged participation, not out of principle—because on principle he thought the blackmail scheme was a damn good idea—but out of confusion, unsure if Tom Mendelssohn and Dinah Rosen had just conned a guy from Oklahoma who'd never seen pure evil in blueprints before. But Mendelssohn had picked the right guy to recruit—Eddie could read complicated blueprints. He understood engineering—temperature management, burn limits, the movement of material through a system. These plans were for a high-volume rendering plant, an interconnected series of intake, processing, and killing-floor stations . . . with a new twist that *burned* the finished product to ashes.

Not a slaughterhouse. It was a disposal system.

The oven designs were a first of their kind. The plans were undisguised, unapologetic. They were *signed*. The ovens were *patented and trademarked*. Eddie shook his head as he walked away from the synagogue, struggling to absorb the scale, the *moral comfort* with systematic murder as a business.

Beyond the nearest corner, two men moved fast, as if something were chasing them, one checking over his shoulder . . . Eddie followed the guy's eyes back to the synagogue, said, "Shit," and grabbed for Dinah. An explosion flashed white, sucked the air off the street, and knocked Eddie flat. The synagogue's roof erupted red; the front wall drove across the street as a solid piece then burst into massive blocks of stone and mortar. The largest section missed Eddie by three feet and knocked down the wall behind him. He rolled. Flaming debris rained on him and the pavement. The smoke mushroomed. Eddie sucked air, couldn't hear, and blinked for focus. His clothes were scorched and smoking. The ragged crater that used to be the synagogue pumped dense, greasy smoke at the sunset. Eddie blinked left then right . . . more scorched plaster, gaping holes in walls. He patted cobblestones and touched

Dinah's dress. Part of her dress. Some of her was in it, about half. Vomit choked him and Haifa went black.

CHAPTER 15

October, 1938

E ddie patted at his head for the spike that had to be in it. No
spike. His eyes semifocused through the throb and blur—empty
metal beds, white tile, blade fan rotating slowly overhead. Infirmary?

"He'll live, has a concussion."

Eddie refocused on the voice, then two shapes beyond the
soles of his boots at the foot of the bed. MI6 Lieutenant Cornell
Hornsby and a uniformed British officer. Eddie blinked. The officer
was . . . Captain Orde Wingate? Eddie flashed on diagrams. Death-
camp patents. The envelope. He gushed: "Brits have to stop the
Nazis. Have to. Quit wasting time here; fly every Spitfire you've got
to Berlin, and—"

"Your orders"—the Captain Orde Wingate lookalike spit each
word—"from the Palestine police were to detain Dinah Rosen
where she stood at the Arab Market, where neither of you should
have been."

Eddie's head hammered. The explosion at the synagogue. Dinah Rosen's body. Next to him. Then hands, searching his clothes . . . Eddie squeezed his eyes shut.

"Mr. Owen!"

Definitely Captain Wingate. Wingate had been in Iran six months ago.

"Mr. Owen!"

Eddie opened his eyes.

"Your orders were—"

"*My* orders?" Eddie lifted his left hand to point at his chest but couldn't. His wrist was handcuffed to the bed rail. "Did I join the redcoats?"

"You are in a Crown colony," said Wingate, "the guest of H. MacMichael, high commissioner for Palestine. While here, you are subject to British colonial-mandate law in its totality; this was explained in Iran. You can, and *will*, be shot as a spy if I decide a spy is what you are."

"*Spy?*" Eddie looked to Lieutenant Hornsby, hoping for a sanity moment. Hornsby was MI6; he knew Eddie was no spy. Hornsby stared bullets. Eddie cut to Wingate. "Fuck you, Captain. I'm an American. I didn't do anything. Took a walk with a Jewish girl that ended up at a synagogue. It was your goddamn job to protect her. Remember? You're the big deal masters of British Mandate Palestine."

Hornsby said, "A bomb was planted, either by the Arabs or their Nazi benefactors. You were there; you alone survived."

"You don't believe I planted the bomb. What's this really about?"

Captain Wingate turned his squarish head to Hornsby. New scars crisscrossed Wingate's right cheek, extending to a now wilted ear. Wingate told Hornsby, "Mr. Owen wishes to emigrate to Tenerife, to assist General Franco's Fascists with their refinery modifications."

Hornsby nodded, his mouth hardening at new "evidence."

Wingate returned to Eddie and continued. "Mr. Owen continues to associate with rabble who incite against the Crown. The Palestine police have documented trips through the Arab Market, questions Mr. Owen attempts to ask after 'Calah al-Habra,' a teacher he *knows* is no such teacher. Did you have a look under your teacher's right eye? She had the wings."

Eddie's headache hid his surprise. He'd never heard a British soldier, or anyone else, mention Calah's tattoo, the sect she must belong to.

Wingate read Eddie's face for the answer, then spoke to Hornsby. "Have this spy-collaborator escorted to the brig. Show him the wall where we executed his fellow travelers. The charges will be along shortly." Captain Wingate heel-turned and marched out down the aisle separating the beds.

Eddie shouted at Wingate's back: "*I* bombed the synagogue? That's the best you can do? March your goddamn Marines to Berlin! That's where the fight is!" The yell drove the spike back through Eddie's head.

Hornsby slapped the bed rail. "Button it up. Be pleasant marching to the brig and you might not be shot during the exercise." Hornsby bowed his neck and added, "At best you are an American oil company pawn on loan to the Crown today, eating schnitzel tomorrow. At worst, you are a spy-collaborator."

"Spy? Me? If walking a Jewish girl to a synagogue is a crime on your watch, you and Hitler will get along fine."

"Your *job*, Mr. Owen, does not include—"

"I *am* doing my job. Try doing yours . . . instead of pounding on these people in their own goddamn country. You're MI6: Have you looked at the Nazis? I mean *really* looked?"

Hornsby made his expression professionally unreadable. Eddie inhaled to scream "extermination camps" but the pounding in his head stopped him. Something here was out of sync. MI6 *should* know . . . if the extermination camps were true. MI6 would have to know, wouldn't they? They really *were* spies. Maybe MI6 did know and didn't care? Was MI6 part of the England who wanted to side with Germany?

Hornsby stayed blank.

"Fuck you, then. And your captain and the horses you two brave bastards rode in on."

Hornsby uncuffed Eddie's hand. "On your feet."

Eddie semistruggled to sitting, his clothes scorched from the explosion, then hesitated. Tom Mendelssohn's envelope wasn't gouging into his back. Wingate and Hornsby hadn't mentioned the envelope, but that didn't mean they hadn't taken it. Eddie started to ask—*The wall, Eddie, where they execute spies. Spies deal in secret envelopes. Do not be a spy in British Mandate Palestine.*

The walk out of the infirmary went past the execution wall, one of four walls enclosing a twenty-by-twenty courtyard. Set out three feet from the wall was a post with metal cuffs. Bullet holes pocked the plaster behind the post. Eddie had the odd thought: How could anyone miss from seventeen feet? Did the firing squad play with the condemned? Like cats in the market did with the mice they ate?

The brig was jail, but British, and hence lacked the noise and commotion associated with most jails. This jail was also empty, testimony to how serious the Royal Marines it was built to house took their mission. The silence left Eddie alone with the four-story ovens, railcar sidings, and conveyer belts. The plans were *signed*, for God's sake. How do you tell that story without the envelope? Who'd believe it? And if MI6 didn't have the envelope, who did? Eddie leaned back on the hard bunk. *Man, D.J.'s gonna be pissed.*

Eddie's first and only contact with the outside world arrived in the afternoon, an American, an angry one with a south Texas cowboy accent. The guard opened the cell door and allowed in D.J.

Bennett. When the guard was gone, D.J. said, "Stupid don't begin to explain your actions, Edward."

"*You sent me*, for chrissake—"

D.J. patted the air to cut Eddie's volume.

Eddie's jaw clenched. He lowered his voice. "I took a walk, pure and simple, like you fucking wanted. From here to there." Eddie spread his index finger and thumb. "Talked to her about being a Jewish girl, and this hellhole blew her up."

D.J.'s lips remained flat under the horseshoe mustache. "What'd she say *exactly*?"

"Say? The fucking maniacs blew her in half. She was a teacher for crying out loud. And a nice one, too. Like your fucking sister or girlfriend. I knew her an hour, maybe two. And this lice-lousy fucking country blew her up." Tears rolled off Eddie's cheek and he didn't know why and that pissed him off as well. "That fucking captain comes in here alone, running his mouth about me being a 'spy-collaborator,' it'll be his last fucking time."

D.J. stood and stepped back, staring like he was having trouble seeing in murky light. "You all right, Eddie? Saddling that white horse ain't too hard; it's ridin' her that gets a bit lonely."

Eddie wiped his face and shrugged, not quite ready to explain. "Guess two years in the sand wears on a fellow. Hate sandwich for every goddamn meal."

"Haifa's not the only spot on the planet where folks ain't getting along."

"Only one I'm in."

D.J. nodded toward the jail's main door at the end of the cell line. "Orde Wingate's no piker. He's running an outfit here called the 'Special Night Squads.' Half British, half Haganah. Goes out after dark, pulls Arabs from their houses, and executes 'em. Brits donned this suit a' clothes once before, back in Jerusalem in '29. Started a full-on revolt, same as the one they got now."

"Wingate does *what?*"

"He and his believe themselves antiguerrilla fighters and maybe they are. But for fuckin' sure they're no better and no righter than the boys they're hunting."

Eddie looked away. There were no good guys here, only ovens and gas chambers and railcar sidings and pieces of Dinah Rosen on the sidewalk. Eddie wiped at his cheeks and inhaled to recount the horror diagrams he'd seen, horror that no longer had any proof.

D.J. interrupted. "How 'bout I get you out of here? We go see a friend of yours in from Bahrain."

"Who?"

"Hassim, his own self. New assistant to the foreman's assistant here; he's gonna help calm the Arabs."

"Bahrain's finished?"

D.J. nodded. "All fixed. Your section's in the third round of retests; ol' Bill was saying good things about you, same as the RAF pilots."

Eddie checked the brig bars behind D.J. "You can get me out of here? Wingate says I'm a collaborator, a spy. Showed me the goddamn post where he intends to shoot me."

D.J. shrugged. "Are you gonna calm down, tell me what the schoolteacher said?"

Eddie frowned. "Somehow my bodyguard has the horses to override the lord high commissioner of Palestine and a captain of the British empire?"

"Funny how I can do that, ain't it?" Cowboy lean, adding nonchalant. "Lieutenant Hornsby and I can speak the same language . . . when it suits us."

Eddie liked that and didn't.

D.J. said, "It'll help if you explain your Bedouin girl, this Calah al-Habra you forgot to mention to me."

Eddie balked. "Why?"

D.J. waited. "Because I asked."

"You saw her. She was in the airport in Arabia. I sat next to her on the plane. We talked; I helped her in Iran and Wingate didn't like it."

"It's more than 'didn't like it,' Eddie. Lieutenant Hornsby was surprised as I was that I didn't know about her." D.J. added concern to his creased face. "Your Bedouin friend ain't who she said she was."

"So? Who do you know who tells the truth over here?"

D.J. hardened his frown. "Your girl was in Arabia but not there with who she said she was. And not there legally. That's a serious set of circumstances, Eddie. Only a special kinda woman can bounce around this part of the world AKA."

Eddie shrugged.

"Your girl's a musketeer, same as Dinah Rosen and that Nazi blonde sitting next to us back in Chicago."

"You don't know that."

"I don't?" D.J. paused. "Remember us discussing that the Nazi on your plane from Arabia had a serious interest in aviation? There ain't no aviation in Arabia, but Erich Schroeder's there three days after our aviation gas refinery explodes next door. Not too hard to imagine your Bedouin girl and the Nazi were debriefing after she'd blown Sitra-Bahrain for him."

Eddie's eyes rolled to their limits. "Every bit of that could be coincidence or bad facts or just plain bullshit. There isn't anyone over here who tells the truth about anything. Ever."

D.J. nodded. "That's a fact, son. Tell me what the schoolteacher said, what else you saw, then get some sleep. We'll cover your Bedouin girlfriend again in the morning. And don't hit that fucking captain if he comes back. He'll kill you. We'll give MI6 your Bedouin's particulars and I'll take care of this if you don't make it any worse."

Eddie's jaw dropped. "I'm not giving these assholes *anyone*'s particulars. You just told me the Brits are killing Arabs in their houses. What the hell's wrong with you?"

"It's war, son, and you better get used to short life and fast death; gonna be a bunch of both."

"Trading Calah to MI6 is the only way you can get me out of here?"

D.J. read Eddie. "*Spy-collaborator* carries a death sentence; you do understand that?"

Eddie mugged. "The Brits won't kill me."

"Yeah they will . . . if they think you're arming the enemy." D.J. curled the fingers of his good hand. "Talk, son. I don't have the whole day to salvage your ass."

Eddie looked at both sides of his cell. "No. If they want a coward, the bastards can look in their own barracks."

D.J. frowned until his lips peeled and teeth showed. "Bowing your back, are ya boy?"

Slowly D.J.'s frown quit and a smile crept across under the mustache. "Guess we'll see if I can sell an accommodation—MI6 lets you out to me; we take a day or two by the beach before you leave; I get your white horse–ridin' noble ass to give me your Bedouin's particulars." D.J. flashed both his hands. "I know you won't, I know. We'll cover the price for that later—and there will be a price."

Eddie's jaw unclenched. "I hate this goddamn place."

D.J. replaced the smile with sarcasm. "Is it okay to ask what Dinah Rosen told you?"

Eddie walked past D.J. to the bars, checked for the guard, then pointed D.J. to the back wall. At the wall, Eddie whispered, "Dinah wanted the USA's help against the British. Said her people, the Jews, were being used to destabilize the Middle East, human bombs designed to die and drive the Arabs—and their oil—into England's pockets."

D.J. squinted. "That ain't news, Eddie; everybody's playing everybody right now. She's supposed to have something 'life or death' for us. What?"

"Not her. A guy named Tom Mendelssohn, an American. He smuggles Jews out of Europe and into Palestine. He, he . . . It's bad, D.J., bad like you can't believe. Remember when you said 'Erase'? Out front of the Biograph Theater in Chicago? How'd you know?" Eddie didn't let D.J. answer. "I've seen the plans—full construction blueprints, schematics, build budgets, operational budgets, quotas—the whole nightmare."

This time it was D.J. who balked. "You saw actual plans?"

"Government stamped. *Signed* by architects and engineers. A company named 'Topf and Sons' had *trademarks* on four-story ovens. *Trademarks*. And, and I.G. Farben, Standard Oil's goddamn *partner*, is—"

"I know about Farben, Standard Oil, and Ford Motor Company—"

"Do you know it's *I.G. Farben* that's building the extermination camps?"

D.J.'s eyes widened. "No. I didn't. You're sure, dead sure?"

"Farben's name is all over the plans and papers I saw." Eddie detailed the envelope and papers Mendelssohn had given him and watched D.J.'s face fall when Eddie explained he no longer had the envelope.

D.J. said, "Why you? Why give the papers to you?"

Eddie explained Tom Mendelssohn's blackmail plan to smuggle Jews via Tenerife with Standard Oil's help. "Mendelssohn thinks I'm too valuable to kill as the messenger and for a year I'll be in the Canary Islands when his Jews pass through . . . like that might reduce the chance his people don't transit the islands alive."

"The out islands, maybe. Nobody'd be safe on Tenerife with no transit papers and 'Jew-Communist' in his or her history. Was Mendelssohn gonna transit the Jews here, to Palestine?"

"Don't know. He said I'd be contacted on Tenerife. I figured to find you and you'd know what to do . . . but I never made it that far."

D.J. frowned. "Awful lot of explosives to kill a schoolteacher and her boyfriend . . . when bullets would do. High-power explosives that are hard to come by. I could've leveled that building with one-tenth. Something was in there that someone did not want to see loose out in the daylight." D.J. considered Eddie. "Tends to make me believe what you saw was the real McCoy."

"Mendelssohn said he'd made contact with the 'targets' of his blackmail plan and since then people had tried to kill him twice— he implied it was Standard Oil but didn't name them. Mendelssohn said he couldn't risk running the blackmail from Palestine or it might compromise his entire 'network.'"

D.J. nodded. "That explains the explosives. Somehow someone, maybe folks from Standard Oil, knew those papers were there; Mendelssohn and Rosen were just a bonus."

Eddie swallowed.

"Either someone took that envelope off you in the rubble or the Brits have it. If the wrong Brits have it, they'll bury the proof to protect the oil companies and their partnerships. If the right Brits have the envelope, they'll use it on Standard Oil for Britain's own purposes . . . which would be oil and AvGas. Neither bunch, good nor bad, will use it for this eon's Exodus."

"The plans are a 'how to' that will murder eleven million people. Even these assholes couldn't stomach that."

"War, Eddie. A million Jews and a million dollars is a lot today, but when what's coming is over, it won't be. Every country, including ours, will be protectin' its own. Won't be much budget for gallantry."

Eddie inhaled to argue, but D.J. waved him off, pointing to the sound of boots in the aisle outside the cell's door. D.J. patted Eddie's shoulder. "Careful, son. I know you're hurtin'. But spilled secrets kill people out here. They surely do."

"Get me out. I ain't letting this lay."

D.J. tapped his claw fingers to his lips and mustache. "For now."

A guard arrived, told D.J. his time was up, let D.J. out, and locked the cell door behind him. Eddie paced until the headache and pain faded the anger. The air was better by the small window. The execution post was below. How many people had died on that post? How many posts? All sides would have posts. Who was Eddie Owen to think he could stop entire armies—he couldn't save one farm or one Jewish girl. Who the hell was Eddie Owen when D.J.'s dominoes began to fall?

Eddie dropped to his metal bunk, head pounding in his hands. He rolled to the wall, his last thought a collage:

Dinah Rosen's dress, Topf and Son's patented ovens, the ashes they spewed covering the farm in Oklahoma. And the eyes of a mysterious Arab princess-teacher-who-wasn't.

All of it on fire.

CHAPTER 16

October, 1938

Erich Schroeder fought the urge to shoot Saba Hassouneh. Uncontrolled anger was not his trademark, but there was a point where even he could succumb. With great care and focus, Schroeder inhaled the seaside air of Beirut, then flattened both hands near his small cup of thick local coffee. Three weeks ago his brilliant strategy for dominion in the desert had been maimed and nearly destroyed by Saba's assassination of the district commissioner in Janîn. The agreed plan had been to *kidnap* the district commissioner, then drag out the high-profile ransom. This would focus British resources away from the refinery while it was sabotaged, *then* Saba Hassouneh could kill the commissioner, capping a hugely powerful series of Arab victories.

Schroeder glanced at her seated alone at the adjacent table on his left. In her defense, the Army of God's attempt to sacrifice her to the English had not been agreed upon, either. As a result of these Arab-driven fiascoes, all borders with Palestine were now closed. All mail was inspected; all telephone and wireless-telegraph contact with neighboring states had been outlawed to all but the British military. The Haifa refinery, and Schroeder's plans for it, was now beyond the reach of Arab or German saboteurs. In order to retard the refinery's progress and defend Reichsmarschall Göring's long-range plans for the air war, the only option had been to remove Eddie Owen from Haifa. But it had to be *unharmed* and *unaware*. If Eddie could be kept safe but secure, he could still be the trump card that would deliver 100-octane gas to Reichsmarschall Göring and the desert kingdom to Erich Schroeder. Risky but possible. And now in progress.

Schroeder fingered the sealed Luftwaffe pouch that had brought Reichsmarschall Göring's titanic displeasure over Janîn, debating whether to show the document to Saba. He would not show her the document that stated Reichsmarschall Göring was to be given full charge of the "Jewish problem." Göring's orders assured Schroeder his place in the Reich's solution to the Jewish problem would be an important one, but not until Oberstleutnant Schroeder crippled the Haifa refinery and then only if Schroeder could regain control of his operatives in the desert. No matter what others in the Reich argued, *the desert* and her Arabs was the proper killing ground for Europe's Jews. Schroeder must regain control!

Control. Of Arabs . . . Schroeder sipped the coffee, wishing to butcher, not control them.

Thankfully, the British army had done significant butchering for him. With the British incineration of Janîn, the British had resuscitated their long-established colonial identity. *Bravo*—this was the Great Britain Schroeder knew and Britain's adversaries feared. Orde Wingate's Special Night Squads had begun dragging men and boys from their beds and shooting them in the streets. The price on the heads of the partisans and rebels in the hills had been doubled again and a promise made: For every partisan brought to the Crown, a family could buy their deportation documents back and be removed from the list. The price on Saba Hassouneh, *his* Arab, was the highest.

Schroeder admired the return of England's will. He did *not* admire Saba Hassouneh's temper, nor her mulish stupidity over the aftermath of Janîn. She sat coiled in her chair, her eyes on the sea and not him. Her keffiyeh was tight across her face, the breeze rustling it on her shoulder. Two Arab men stood across the street, their backs to Beirut's harbor and ninety feet apart. They were hers, although she had not said as much.

"Make me believe," she said, "the men of the Nazi Reich would run from your homeland if the English murdered your women and children."

Schroeder affected his well-crafted civility, the veneer of his humanity stretched tight across his skull. "You will die if you return to Janîn and it will accomplish little. The bounty on your head is too high, the sentiment too strong. A number of Palestinians blame you for the reprisals. *You*, not the Iraqis and their mullahs—you, the Raven."

Her eyes turned to his and her tone hardened. "I have no fight in the Canary Islands. No interest. Give me the funds for Janîn and I will kill them all, the British first, then the Iraqi fools you arm"—she spit on the ground—"bin Faisal and his mullahs."

Schroeder bit his tongue. Arabs were the bastard children of conquerors and camels. To keep bin Faisal and his mullahs in line, he, Erich Schroeder, must remove Saba and her myth from Palestine. Use her for a last mission to kill D.J. Bennett and drive Eddie Owen into complete helplessness, then kill her in a place where her death could be assured. Tenerife in the Canary Islands was such a place—a volcanic island of pirates and smugglers blood-drenched in the intrigues of Moroccan Nationalists and Spain's civil war. Killing Saba there served his grander purpose of dominion in the desert, but given her skill as a warrior and the loyalty of her partisans, it was an unfortunate expense. Such were the ever-changing bedfellows of war.

Schroeder said, "The Canary Islands first. A man will soon be there, on Tenerife, a dangerous sympathizer to the Communists who maintains far too much influence over our American engineer. It is important this man be taken, kidnapped by Arabs, Arabs demonstrating a long reach." Schroeder added fuel to the lie. "This man has information we must have; he plans operations against our American friends and the Tenerife refinery."

Saba barked: "One man on an island makes no difference. The English are in Palestine; they kill us in Palestine. The Iraqi king whores for your money; I do not. Find another spy."

Schroeder noticed two coltish girls near the water, adolescents carrying their shoes. The morning sun sparkled in their hair. One glanced at him. He tried to imagine her as Saba, a ploy to invest a pleasantness in this negotiation that would help him keep his hands off Saba's neck. Schroeder patted Saba's hand. She jerked. Schroeder parried to defend. Her men charged. A man five tables away short-armed a Luger at her back. Saba snarled, then waved off her men. They halted midstreet, pistols extended at Schroeder. Saba glared from behind the keffiyeh, half the knife visible in her hand.

"Do not touch me. Ever."

Schroeder eased away, lowering his hands, adding apologetic emphasis. Pulse pounded equal parts anger at her threat and anger at the mistake, the murder in this woman very close to the surface.

"My apologies, I meant to offer comfort to my message."

Saba did not sheath the knife. Schroeder considered how much additional weight to add to his mission. "The Canary Islands first, then the Haifa refinery. Haifa's special gasoline must be taken from the English and given to the Arab. Do you understand the importance? That you are one of the few who could accomplish this?" Schroeder added what he hoped was a lie. "Without action, the

English refinery at Haifa will be completed earlier than anticipated, earlier than we can reasonably remove its control from the English."

Saba shifted in the chair. Slight, but her movements were few and always meant something. Schroeder kept his eyes cold, marshaling restraint. An unusual woman, this Arab, fraught with sexual disconnects, Teutonic in her anger and buried rage. A woman who would die badly and in a cause that would betray her. She should see one German opera before this happened, hear the music climb the walls and explode out over the audience. Her death would be like that. The thought calmed him.

Her eyes went to the street and the harbor beyond. "What is this man's name on Tenerife?"

"D.J. Bennett. An American. You saw him in Dhahran."

"I have no quarrel with the Americans."

"Nor do I. Soon the Americans will be our friends against the Communists—after we have crushed the English empire in your desert." In that moment Schroeder decided to tell Saba pieces of the problem and the plan. He began with, "Our engineer, Eddie Owen, is bound for Tenerife. You must see him there, further his interest in you as a woman. Your ability to help dissuade his interest in the Zionist cause—"

"*What* interest?" Saba's eyes flashed.

Schroeder hesitated, processing her reaction. "Eddie Owen is currently under arrest in Haifa . . . as a suspected . . ." Schroeder chose his words carefully. "Spy. Eddie Owen was injured leaving a synagogue run by the American Zionist Thomas Mendelssohn."

Saba's eyes chilled but hid whatever her thoughts were.

Schroeder continued, "We suspect D.J. Bennett was using the Zionists to disseminate false documents, papers that would recruit Eddie Owen against us—the Arabs and the Germans—and induce Eddie Owen's support of the Communists. It is vitally important to *all of us in the desert* that this very special engineer knows the true motives of those around him."

At eight p.m. Lieutenant Hornsby stood with Eddie in front of the execution post and unlocked Eddie's handcuffs. The shadows at the far corner produced D.J. Bennett. Hornsby faded; D.J. pulled Eddie close. "Walk natural, next to me, like you're free to leave."

Eddie slapped his fedora against his thigh to knock the scorch and dust off, then pulled the fedora on. He squared shoulders that hurt, set his jaw, and began walking. Hornsby was already at the outer gate and pointed two armed Marines to open it. They did; neither made eye contact or spoke.

Outside the compound, D.J. steered them downhill toward the Arab market and the refinery beyond. "The longer we stay in Palestine, the less likely you'll leave. Hornsby was a whole lot harder than I expected. Don't pack. Take what you can wear and what fits in your briefcase. We're gone in an hour."

"Where are we going?"

"North to Beirut. It's French. Got them a brand-new airport. Once you're out of the Brits' jurisdiction we'll figure what to do next. If we decide it's Tenerife, we'll catch a plane or a ship across the Mediterranean to Morocco. French control it, too, most of it."

Eddie glanced toward the neighborhood where the synagogue had been leveled. "What about Mendelssohn's . . ."

"Brits didn't take the papers off you. Hornsby didn't ask me about them and had he seen those papers, Hornsby would've put you on that post till you blabbed everything you knew."

"So it was someone from the neighborhood, had to be. We could go back there, the synagogue. Mendelssohn's people might be—"

"No. If Wingate and his squads find you back there, don't know that you'd survive the encounter."

A block downhill from Eddie and D.J., four uniformed Palestinian police came together in the narrow intersection, looked uphill, and marched toward them. D.J. shouldered Eddie and himself into an alley and pointed Eddie back uphill from the alley's other end. "Go. Could be the police have had a change of heart. Take the long way; meet me at Hassim's room in an hour." D.J. hugged the alley's corner, shielded from the police by the building. "Move."

Eddie bolted uphill, turned at the first corner, dumped D.J.'s warning, and made for the synagogue. Six men and women picked through the stones and timber shards. Behind them the building was a jagged heap. One of the men looked up as Eddie approached from the shadows. Eddie spoke English. The man pointed to another man. Eddie stepped over the smaller chunks of stone and wood. The next man wore a dusty Orthodox Jew's hat and waited for Eddie to speak.

"My name is Eddie Owen. I—"

"We know."

"Do you know Tom Mendelssohn?"

"Yes." The Jew looked into the heap. "Thomas Mendelssohn is here."

Eddie said, "Tell me something about him. Prove it."

Dark brown eyes studied Eddie. The Jew touched his hat and said, "Tenerife."

Eddie nodded, surprised. "Right. Tom Mendelssohn gave me an envelope and instructions. Somebody took the envelope off me after the explosion. I need it back—if you want me to do Tom's business—I need the envelope tonight. Now. I leave in an hour."

The man looked past Eddie to the left and right, then pointed Eddie into the dark. "Wait there."

Eddie climbed over and through mammoth chunks of wall and roof and into almost complete dark. He squatted, leaning against scorched tile and concrete that might have been uprooted floor. Ten minutes passed. Figures appeared at the downhill corner of the small square. Eddie squinted through the debris. Policemen. They watched the Jews comb through the black char and gray everything else. The policemen left.

Stones toppled behind Eddie. He turned. A voice in the dark said, "Here." Something touched Eddie's arm before he could see it. The scorched ten-by-ten envelope slid into his hands. Eddie put it inside his shirt without looking inside. The stones behind him tumbled again, then silence. Eddie stood, exhaled slowly, climbed down to solid ground, and walked into the shadows. Time to be Nick Charles. Make a brisk walk through town to the refinery, meet D.J., and disappear.

A uniformed policeman reappeared one hundred feet downhill. Eddie pivoted to backtrack uphill. Fifty feet uphill, a second policeman blocked Eddie's path. Both British. The downhill Brit already had his revolver out. He stepped toward Eddie and said, "As I live and breathe. On the wall, Yank." Eddie waited until the Brit was within reach, stepped into the gun, and threw a left hook over the top. The Brit's head snapped back. His revolver fired. Eddie spun. The uphill Brit's revolver was cocked and about to shoot Eddie in the stomach. D.J. Bennett hit him from behind. The revolver fired as the Brit crashed to the pavement. D.J. stomped the Brit on the head and kicked his revolver into the cobblestone street.

Eddie said, "Oh, shit," and dropped to his knees.

The first Brit gushed blood, shot in the chest. Eddie covered the hole and pumped the Brit's lungs. D.J. yanked Eddie to his feet. "He's dead. Wash up at a mule trough. Tell Hassim I said get you to Beirut. I'll catch up." D.J. shoved Eddie hard. "Move, goddammit! You may be too fucking stupid to save."

CHAPTER 17

October, 1938

Yesterday, the day before Saba had met with Erich Schroeder in Beirut, she had agreed to meet Hassim Dajani there as well. Via intermediaries in Haifa, Hassim's request was to be valuable to Saba inside the Haifa refinery, as he had been inside Sitra in Bahrain. Saba believed Hassim could be valuable. Or Hassim Dajani could be arranging her murder for bin Faisal and the Pan-Arab Army of God. Today, Hassim would arrive the southern outskirts of Beirut. Jameel would meet Hassim at the construction zone of the new Bir Hassan Airfield. In an old truck, they would drive a circuitous route above the city to Beit Mery, an old Roman stronghold of Christians and Druze, very difficult to penetrate for the Muslim jihadists if that was who Hassim Dajani had joined.

She would trust her instincts, as she had with the German Erich Schroeder yesterday. The German was as angry over Janîn as she was sickened by its aftermath. To his credit, Erich Schroeder understood the root cause had been Ghazi bin Faisal and his Pan-Arab Army of God. To Erich Schroeder's discredit, he would lie and attempt to keep his Iraqi pig-king as an ally in the desert. Saba clenched her jaw. Until she and the partisans could kill the pig-king with his own sword.

Kohl and marl paste hid the wings under Saba's eye. She wore a western man's pants covered to the knee by a robe. A red checked keffiyeh covered her head and face. Hassim's words shocked her, but she hid it. "Eddie Owen is here, in Lebanon? With you?"

Hassim answered, marshaling respect reserved for an emir's tent. "No, he is not with me, but yes, he is here in Beirut, down below at the Hotel Royal."

"And he is here alone?"

"I bring him, yes. The British consider his exit a Crown deportation . . ."

If this were so, Eddie Owen was lucky to be alive. Saba weighed for treachery. "The British grant his freedom. And he asks for me?"

"Eddie Owen tries for conversations in the market, too many. For six months he searches for a teacher, a Bedouin who teaches the emir's daughters. He met her on the plane that crash-landed in Iran. I know this plane, this teacher."

"How is it he asks you, Hassim Dajani?"

Hassim checked his shoulder and whispered, "The day I arrive in Haifa, D.J. Bennett—a dangerous man even as a friend—tells me Eddie Owen is in Haifa. Hours ago Eddie Owen tells me he must leave, that a British policeman has been shot. Eddie Owen must come here to Beirut; I must take him. I drive him here; he tells me of the Bedouin teacher, that she is possibly marked under the eye, although he has said this to no one else and does not know its significance." Hassim swallowed. "He thinks this mark may be religion or Palestine freedom."

"And you know of his friendship with the Zionist militia?"

Hassim jolted. "I know of no such friendship. Never does he speak such words to me. And I know him two years in Bahrain."

Saba nodded small. "Go down the mountain. Give your American to Jameel and remain at the house where Jameel and the others will take you. I will see Eddie Owen. You and I will speak after."

Hassim bowed. "The people of Palestine forgive you for Janîn. It is the British we hate, the Zionists and their murder militia. For us, you are the victories that will turn our tide."

Saba belted the revolver Hassim had not seen, shamed by his faith and her weakness, then motioned two weathered Arabs closer. To the older, she said, "Take our friend Hassim to eat and rest. Keep him safe until I return." The Arab left with Hassim. To Jameel, she said, "You remember the American?"

Jameel nodded. "In Iran. He risked the British guns."

"Bring him to the rock beach at Byblos, the north point. Sit him alone with food and wine. I will watch, and you will watch me."

Alone, Saba looked beyond the city's rooftops to the Mediterranean Sea. Was her American a convert of the Zionists? Is that why Eddie Owen asked for her every week in the Arab market at Haifa? If so, the Irgun or Haganah would be with him. They would kill her. Or try, as they had many times before. Or was he bait for the British night squads, trading his freedom from their jail for her life? The American Eddie Owen did not know her ability to smell a trap, and his puppet masters would not warn him. Saba rubbed her upper arms. And what of her heart? Her shoulders tightened. She felt lightheaded from wine un-drunk. Would she touch her American's hands on purpose; would she . . . kiss her first man? The thought made her shiver in a way she liked and hated. The flash of hate brought her back. Eddie Owen sought to betray her. For that, she would kill him.

Eddie was free, but he was worried. D.J. hadn't arrived Beirut yet and whenever he did, he'd be one mad cowboy. Hopefully, Eddie having the Mendelssohn papers in hand and out of Palestine would ease D.J.'s anger. Whatever D.J. had done to deal with the dead policeman in Haifa had allowed Eddie to pass through the cliffside border check at Ras-A-Nakura and into the French Protectorate of Lebanon. Speed and time had been an ally for Eddie. He checked his watch: eight p.m. Now that almost twenty-four hours had passed, time would be the opposite for D.J.

Eddie concentrated on the beach instead of D.J.'s absence and the death sentence for millions in the ten-by-ten envelope taped across his broad upper back. Eddie had seen moonlight on the Mediterranean, but it had been in Haifa and nothing about Haifa was romantic. An hour ago he'd watched two women splashing naked in the waves of the Mediterranean, enjoying the moonlight and calm, clear water at Byblos. Women; warm, clear water; and moonlight . . . he'd found the one spot where the world hadn't lost its mind.

Well, *he* hadn't actually found this spot or set up the picnic. Two young but leather-skinned Arabs had transported him from the Hotel Royal, frisked him for weapons Eddie didn't have, looked inside the envelope at the Mendelssohn documents they couldn't read and *thank-you-God* returned it, then left him, his elevated heart rate, and picnic basket alone on a rocky point. Eddie could handle himself with a blanket and a picnic basket, but this was his first picnic with an armed escort team instead of a girl. One of the Arabs looked familiar, like he might've been on the plane and in Iran six months ago. But all that had happened so fast it was hard to say, and when asked, the Arab didn't answer. The Lebanese wine they'd provided tasted good and was helping with the cuts, lumps, and bruises from the synagogue explosion.

Eddie sipped then extended the bottle to toast Dinah Rosen, German-Czech schoolteacher, a little package with a lot of life, dead now because she wanted to stop mass murder on a scale the

Romans couldn't have conceived. "*Lekhaim*, Dinah. *Lekhaim*, Tom Mendelssohn." The dark bottle hung heavy and Eddie added the dead British policeman. Eddie shut his eyes. The vision came through anyway—the towering storm walls of the Dust Bowl rolled in across the two girls splashing naked in the sea, clouds of human ash from the extermination camps that would suffocate everything, everywhere. For those who'd done nothing to stop the ovens and smokestacks there'd be no explaining . . . no matter who won. The papers taped to his back were *evil*, the absolute clear-cut horror of it, nothing else you could call it. The Indians in Oklahoma told a similar story, and as a boy it had made Eddie so sick he'd wanted to be deaf. And he had been. If he made it home, he'd no longer be deaf to the Indians or anyone else under cannon.

Eddie forced his thoughts to the schoolteacher he was about to meet a third time, Calah al-Habra, princess of the *Arabian Nights*. Who wasn't. The stars she'd pointed to at their second meeting in Iran would be almost directly above him when the moon was finished rising. Sometimes he looked at her stars—okay, maybe more often than sometimes—knowing that somewhere exotic she would be doing the same. It felt . . . interesting.

"You remember, Eddie Owen."

Eddie jolted but didn't drop the bottle.

"This is good, an honor to my family." All black, like before, but much lighter-weight material; moonlight silvered one shoulder, half of her in the light, the other half not. She walked to the side of him and sat, farther away than necessary, the strip of her eyes locked on his.

Eddie found taking a breath useful. He sat, then added, "Ah . . . hi." He wasn't absolutely sure it was her.

His finger rubbed under his right eye.

She didn't respond.

Eddie offered the wine.

The woman in black waited until he set the wine closer to her knees. She lifted the thin veil and sipped. "So, the American wishes to see a teacher." She seemed to be studying his lumps. Her voice was cold but not frigid. "Much effort to see one teacher."

"No kidding. You gotta be the most secret teacher in Transjordan."

She placed the bottle between them. "Possibly you have learned more about me, Eddie Owen?"

"If you're asking have I had the odd thought about the mysterious princess, well yeah, I have. Maybe once in a while . . . maybe a little more often than that."

"We know that is not what I mean."

Eddie smiled a schoolboy smile.

Her eyes looked away but returned quick and confident. "Boys and their teachers."

Eddie beamed and reached inside his shirt next to the tape that held Tom Mendelssohn's envelope— The barrel of her revolver finished four feet from his nose, hammer cocked, her eyes ice-cold behind it. She didn't speak. Didn't blink.

Eddie didn't breathe.

"Ah . . . I . . . ah, brought you something?"

She said, "So it would seem."

Eddie finished extracting a small box and set it between them. She lowered the revolver but didn't uncock or holster it. Her finger remained on the trigger. "You were in an explosion?"

Eddie eyed the pistol. "A synagogue two white guys blew up."

"You are Jewish?"

"No. A girl took me there. We were running away from British soldiers and the Palestinian police . . . after the bombing in the Arab Market. She said something they didn't like."

"This girl, she was—"

"A teacher, like you." Eddie frowned at the pistol. "Sort of. Is that gun necessary?"

She kept the cocked revolver in hand on her knee between them. "All people are not who they seem. Even Americans." Her empty hand retrieved the box. She considered the lid, then used two fingers to flip it open.

A gold ring. Wings across a raised center.

She tilted the ring in the moonlight and used just the fingers of her empty hand to slide the ring on her finger. "Very beautiful. The first I have ever owned."

"You're kidding."

Her eyes flashed, suggesting she wasn't.

"Sorry, thought you were making fun of me."

No telling how to flirt with an armed princess-schoolteacher-who-wasn't.

"You like it, though? The ring?"

"Yes." Her interest remained with the ring, but her tone lowered. "These wings, you have told others of me?"

"Just Hassim, but not 'wings.' I said 'tattoo.' I was sorta desperate. Not having much luck finding you and I was leaving . . ."

She retrieved the wine bottle with her ring hand and drank again, her movements masculine and direct. She twinkled her ring above the revolver in her other hand, the movement feminine, almost girlish. Eddie registered the combination ten seconds apart. Very strange. He extended his hand for the wine bottle. She passed it without setting it down.

This time he was sure he could taste lipstick or some type of sweet, softening oil. He licked his lips. Exotic for sure, sharing wine in the moonlight on windswept rock at the far end of the Mediterranean Sea. Long, long way from the Dust Bowl. A ghost woman next to you wrapped in black, obviously not who she said she was. When Eddie had pressed Hassim about the tattoo, Hassim had admonished Eddie to discuss the tattoo with no one and Hassim hadn't been kidding.

"Tell me about the wings." Eddie touched his cheekbone. "I think I saw them scratched on walls . . . in the market."

"You do not know, Eddie Owen?"

"Wouldn't ask if I did. Hassim didn't want to talk about the wings, either."

"The Bedu say it is a wise man who keeps his own tent." She looked toward the sea, deciding something, then backed to him. A deep inhale raised her chest, the curve of her breasts evident for the first time. "If I speak of this, much will change. Possibly when we say our good-byes, yes?"

"Fair enough." Eddie wasn't saying good-bye and reached for the wine bottle just as she did. He touched her hand for the first time. She snatched hers away, spilling the wine.

"Sorry." Eddie righted the bottle, embarrassed at her reaction. "Didn't mean to—"

"I am cautious with strangers." Her hand tightened on the revolver.

"Yeah. I can see that." Eddie slowly extended his hand, flat, palm up. "I've never touched a princess."

No movement. Even her eyes.

"C'mon. Think of me as an American, not a stranger. You know more about us than I do." He edged his hand an inch closer. Her hand materialized from the folds of the thin robe. She hesitated and placed it on top of his, the weight almost nonexistent. Eddie sensed he was reaching out to an animal in the wild, one that would fight or flee at the first impulse. Instinct told him not to move, to let her do it.

And she did. Gently at first, then more, her fingertips tracing the curve of his hand. Either he had the most erotic hand God had made or the princess didn't get out much. He heard her speaking but hadn't caught a word.

"Sorry, you said—"

She removed her hand so slowly that it was almost sexual, the way it'd been for him when a woman's touch was all brand new. She said, "I am a soldier."

Eddie heard himself say, "A soldier," before he could mask the surprise.

"Yes. Do not ask which army; it would be dangerous for you to know."

Eddie heard a rumbling in the back of his brain, distant but there, and not an alarm. More like a library's hum when the study desks were full.

"Could I . . . ah, touch your hand again?"

She laughed, he was pretty sure; it sounded honest but not quite confident. "You are forward for a boy."

But she offered her hand and he touched her again, his fingertips doing the tracing this time, past her hand and to her wrist. Eddie felt the sexual adrenaline that pumped when clothes were coming off and all he was doing was tracing her wrist. Was she trembling? He glanced at her eyes and she pulled her hand to her chest. They stared in silence, the air electric between them.

"*Man.* It's either you or Lebanon." Eddie took a deep breath he needed. She seemed pleased with the compliment. It was heartfelt, so she should be. But out here, no telling what people thought when you mentioned anything close to sex.

"Possibly the weather." She was staring right at him.

"I . . . ah . . . have no idea what to do." He laughed and meant it. "At home, I'd lean over and kiss you. But here—"

"No." But she didn't lean away. "Here it would not be right. I am married."

"No you're not."

She stiffened.

"No offense. But you're not." He showed her his palms, a submission of sorts. "Look, I won't lie to you if you won't lie to me. It's so strange here, I'm lost most of the time, but I want to know you. A lot. And I'll be careful and I won't press, but I'm serious, I want to know you."

She made no movement at first, then dropped her veil. Eddie almost fainted. Holy shit was she pretty. A girl, too, no older than he was. She removed the headdress, shook out chestnut hair, and wiped some kind of paste from under her right eye.

"Now you know me, Eddie Owen." She seemed almost naked and acted it, as if this were a huge decision on her part.

"My God, Calah, you're beautiful."

Her hands went to her face. He reached for them and she pulled away, adding her veil. "Calah is not my name."

"You don't need the veil." Eddie was shaking his head. "You're . . . you're staggering." Her comment finally registered. "What's your name, then?"

"Just know that it is different; for now that is enough." She unfolded her legs to stand. Eddie reached, laddering up to panic.

"*Wait.* Wait, you can't go. Please don't go."

She hesitated, then eased back to sitting.

"Don't go, okay? I'll be as nice as you want. Anything, okay? Just talk to me. I'll sit in the water if that's what you want."

She laughed and reached for the wine, the motion masculine again. Eddie watched, afraid if he spoke she'd leave. It *was* like being with a wild animal. She handed him the wine and checked behind her.

"Soon I must go."

"No. Don't. I can tell you all about America, more stuff than last time." Eddie had reverted to thirteen and his first real date, losing years of experience because she'd dropped her veil. He was *sooo*

CHARLIE NEWTON

glad they didn't have veils at home; lotta power in those little strips of cloth.

"Tell me, then, all about America."

And he did. Eddie shared his world outside the desert. She was wary, smart, and brutally short in the opinions she offered, not those of a young woman but of an older man who'd been hardened by what he'd seen. Still, America was her hope for everything, her interest and questions boundless.

Predawn hinted behind the Lebanon Mountains.

Saba said, "Once again, we have talked all night."

"Spent the night together, a second time. We're almost married."

She blushed and raised both hands to her face.

"Sorry." Eddie laughed. "Kinda new at talking to a princess."

"I am a soldier."

"Right. Right, a soldier." He paused. "Sure seem like a princess."

She exhaled as tired but not altogether displeased parents sometimes do, the pride overriding their judgment. "I am a soldier and all that this entails. For good and bad, life and death, of mine and others."

Eddie blocked most of that, no longer wanting to ask questions about politics and Palestine. "With me, could you just be the girl who was before the soldier? Beautiful girl, smart American historian . . . can she and I climb in those mountains behind me or swim, even?" Eddie pointed at the water. "It'd be fun, but you couldn't wear the robe."

She shook her head like an American girl would. "If my father were alive, he would shoot you for suggesting such things."

"Sorry, I didn't know about your dad . . . Was it . . . recent?"

She looked away, but not far. "Yes and no. He is one of many." She pointed at the stars. "There he is, watching you ask me to swim without clothes."

"Think he's mad?"

Her smile came after a rugged trip across her mouth, a fight she finally lost and seemed happy about. "Yes, he is angry with you." She blinked once, not an eyelash flutter but something. "But I am not, and for now, Eddie Owen, that is more important." She stood so fast it was a blur. Before he could speak, she said, "We will meet again; I will see to it. And we will climb or swim, yes?"

Eddie stood. She stepped back. Eddie said, "Deal. Tell me what dark alley to be in and I'll be there."

Her eyes narrowed. "You make light of my precautions but know little."

"No. No. No. Tell me to march naked and I'll be doing that." Eddie stepped closer and she didn't move. He stood still while she added the keffiyeh, her eyes not leaving his. Finished, she tossed the keffiyeh's corner over her shoulder the way a woman flirting would toss her hair. He wanted to kiss her more than he wanted to breathe.

"Don't. I am not what you think."

"Could I find out on my own?"

She hesitated. "No. Yes." Then ran up the hill.

Eddie had never been so stunned by so little. So stunned, he hadn't moved and now she was gone, not a trace of her other than the basket her guards had given him.

Predawn began to shadow behind him and Eddie leaned against the rocks. Tom Mendelssohn's envelope creased into Eddie's bruised spine. He jolted at the pain. If the papers were true . . . then the money he sent home every month from Culpepper and Standard Oil, money that kept his parents, little brother, and sister off the road to California, was the worst kind of blood money.

Did the papers have to be true? They could be elaborate fakes; it was possible. Dashiell Hammett could write a plot like that. Where was D.J.? *Fine, you're mad, get over it. You have to look at these. Explain how we prove they're real. Or not. Then we—*

Eddie looked at the rocks to his left. Bury the envelope here? Only require one search in one of the four countries he would have to transit en route to Tenerife. The Brits thought he was a spy. The Nazis would kill him to recover the papers. And Standard Oil probably would, too, if they knew he had them. If they were real. Eddie glanced up at Calah's stars going dim. *I guess the Brits are right. I am a spy.*

The question was, for whom?

CHAPTER 18

October, 1938

Eddie hitched in from Byblos just as the sun topped the green mountains that hugged Beirut to the sea. The truck dropped him near the port at town center. Six steps into the marble lobby of the Hotel Royal, he was intercepted. The gloved bellman presented a silver tray, on it a yellowish telegram envelope. Eddie's second-ever international telegram read:

> "URGENT." *STOP* "PROCEED TENERIFE ON FIRST AVAILABLE FLIGHT." *STOP* "URGENT YOU ARRIVE IMMEDIATELY."

The sender was the foreman of the Tenerife refinery outside Santa Cruz de Tenerife, not D.J. Bennett. When asked, the Hotel Royal manager said there had been no telegrams or notes from a D.J. Bennett. Eddie spent twenty minutes deciding, then scribbled a cryptic West Texas note D.J. would understand (Eddie had the

Mendelssohn papers), put the note and the telegram in a sealed hotel envelope, and asked the manager to hold it for Mr. D.J. Bennett.

The road into Beirut's new airport had been staked and cut but wasn't paved. Everything about Bir Hassan Airfield was loud, dusty, and noxious with diesel and green-gas exhaust. The three-story terminal wasn't completed but the tower on top was, and they were landing Air France planes on the runway. Eddie talked four mailbags off and himself on, a three-engine Bloch 120 bound for Casablanca via Algiers and Oran. Twenty hours of Mediterranean Sea and North Africa later, plane, passengers, and mail landed without incident at Anfa Airport in Casablanca.

According to D.J., Casablanca was no place to dally; everything in North Africa was bought and sold here—weapons, camels, hashish, opium, slaves, children, murder—anything. Eddie had time for five words: "Holy shit, I'm in Casablanca," then ran for and missed the ferry to Tenerife just as it left the dock. The vaunted Casablanca Ferry did not appear to be seaworthy, although it had plenty of passengers.

Plan B was a Latécoère seaplane beached on a purpose-built embankment inside the jetty at Casablanca's harbor. The flight saved a full day and four hours later landed Eddie on blue water 650 miles out into the Atlantic Ocean beneath his very first volcano, a volcano that . . . holy shit number two, actually *puffed smoke*. The pilot puttered them across eight-inch waves toward the Tenerife dock and motioned Eddie and the other two passengers to drop their windows. A steamy, sulfuric breeze filled the plane. Eddie eyed the volcano. Okay, island plus volcano . . . what does one do on an *island* if a volcano erupts?

Horns sounded at the dock. A large ferry was mooring on the far side. Passengers lined the rails; most appeared to be Arabs. A gangway was extended. It touched the dock and a squad of plain-clothes gunmen rushed up the gangway, guns drawn. The passengers crushed backward. The gunmen grabbed a middle-age man and dragged him fighting and shouting down the gangway to the dock. They beat and wrestled the man into a six-by-six cage.

Eddie glanced to the pilot for an explanation. The pilot was intent on a small wooden boat motoring toward them. The pilot looked wary. He wiped his mouth and nodded toward the plain-clothes gunmen on the dock. "*Policía Judicial.* Careful with them. The PJs."

Eddie did not want to be the man in the cage. The ten-by-ten envelope taped across his upper back might be tough to explain to the PJs. Eddie checked the ferry. The passengers there were motionless. Not a good sign. Arabs used their hands when they spoke but they were statues on the ferry deck. At the bottom of the gangway, the PJs waved all the passengers to debark. Single file and slowly, each one began the trip down the gangway, papers in hand.

The wooden boat arrived under the seaplane's wing. Eddie and the seaplane's other two passengers climbed in and motored in to the dock. Two steps onto the concrete, Eddie was pulled aside by a plainclothes *Policía Judicial.* Sunglasses hid his eyes. In Spanish, the PJ said, "Hands up," and reached to frisk him. Eddie knocked the PJ's hands away. Mendelssohn's envelope would mark Eddie as a spy. The PJ drew his pistol, stood back, and— A second PJ brushed the pistol aside and motioned for Eddie's briefcase. Eddie surrendered his briefcase. The PJ opened it, checked Eddie's passport, eyed him like he recognized Eddie's name, held up D.J.'s .45 as if it might be a problem, then motioned for Eddie to raise his shirt.

Eddie raised his shirt to show his beltline held no weapon or contraband. The PJ motioned Eddie to turn a full circle. Eddie tightened his shirt against his skin, turned, and hoped his heart didn't explode. Silently he repeated, *no envelope, no envelope,* then dropped his shirt and waited.

The PJ with Eddie's briefcase said, "You are to come with us." He tight-gripped Eddie's left arm; the other PJ gripped Eddie's right arm, and they walked him to the cage. The ferry passenger in the cage shouted in Spanish, shaking the cage with his hands. A bolt-straight PJ wearing a formal red-yellow beret and far better clothes shouldered past Eddie and spit fast French/Spanish at the prisoner in the cage.

"CAM. *Comité d'Action Marocaine.*"

The prisoner barked back instead of quieting.

Red Beret un-flapped his leather holster and drew a pistol. The caged man continued to tirade. The senior PJ shrugged and spoke benign Spanish to his subordinates who gripped Eddie's arms. The two PJs released Eddie's arms, set their shoulders against the cage, and pushed it off the dock. A length of heavy ship chain ran past Eddie's feet and the cage plunged underwater.

Eddie rushed to the dock's edge. "Are you nuts? He'll drown!"

The senior PJ did not holster his pistol. "You are a red shirt? A fellow Communist? You are here to fight against Generalissimo Franco?"

"Pull him up! He's drowning!"

Red Beret leaned over the pier and fired four rounds into the flesh-colored shape fighting beneath the surface. "Now he is not. Are you Communist, Mr. Owen? A member of the International Brigades? In league with the *Comité d'Action Marocaine*?"

"*What*? What the fuck is wrong with you?"

The senior PJ nodded. Hands grabbed Eddie's arms. The senior PJ repeated, "Are you a Communist?"

Eddie glared. "I'm an American. We're neutral in your war, remember? I'm here to build your goddamn refinery."

"The British say you are not neutral. You are a Communist, a Zionist, a murderer of policemen. They say you are a known protector of terrorists. The Raven of Palestine."

The papers of Zionist Tom Mendelssohn creased into Eddie's back. Eddie bluffed: "And you care what the Brits say? If any of that were true, would I be here? No, I'd be tied to a post in Haifa, shot dead by the miserable bastards. Like . . . like you just did."

Three serious-looking civilians hurried up the pier. They wore pressed work clothes from the refinery and stern expressions. The senior PJ glanced at the civilians, frowned, then squared up in Eddie's face. "Spain is not for Communists or Arab terrorists who wish to 'liberate' Morocco." His breath was sharp, his skin oily. He pointed behind Eddie into the bloody water and two sharks nosing the cage. "My police do not fear their responsibilities to the nation. You will do well to remember this. If the Raven of Palestine is *seen* on this island, I will personally bait the cage with your body parts."

CHAPTER 19

October, 1938

Spindrift sprayed over the wooden bow of the Casablanca Ferry. Saba steadied against the rusted railing. After thirty hours at sea, her legs were still unaccustomed to the light pitch and roll of her first ocean voyage. She inhaled into the saltwater wind, enjoying the relative safety of the Spanish flag and the last of her time on the water. The journey from Lebanon to Morocco, utilizing Erich Schroeder's Abwehr network, had required ten arduous days and delivered her into Casablanca dressed as a man. Saba severed her connection after being warned that the British bounty on her head now included an equal amount, tripled recently by the French. Saba did not require the warning. Casablanca and all of Morocco that was not under British rule was under French rule, policed by hard, sullen-eyed Legionnaires, soldiers reminiscent of those who had policed her as a teenage orphan refugee in Lebanon.

Once aboard this ferry, caution had forced her hand to her pistol only twice. It had been an exhilarating night watching the stars, reminiscing with remnants of a young girl's dreams and days of no price on her head. A wave dotted her with saltwater. This was the Atlantic Ocean. If crossed, she would be in America, far from her partisan life of Spartan rebel camps, parched-marl hate, and blood religion. The thought of America's possibilities was wistful but rich with temptation and it shamed her. And then there was the boy . . . She felt Eddie Owen in her chest, that shame even greater, then finally smiled and allowed it as if she had the right. Eddie Owen had not sought to betray her to the Night Squads or the Haganah in Haifa; his mission was to swim with her naked. Saba blushed crimson.

Her mission, the mission that was no young girl's fever dream, was to kidnap his Communist friend, the Zionist sympathizer whose plotting worried the German and had almost resulted in Eddie Owen's death at the synagogue in Haifa. There could be no future with the boy, and in many ways this would make her life much simpler. She would see to Eddie Owen's safety, though. Removing the Communist-Zionist sympathizer who used him as a pawn was something she could do, and would do. The sun hinted from behind Saba's left shoulder. Dead ahead, an island silhouetted in the predawn haze. The sun's first glare raced past her west across the three-foot waves toward a great volcano that centered the island of Tenerife. The volcano towered as massive as she'd been told, its peak piercing above long clouds and reaching, some said, to four kilometers.

The ferry deck came to life under the brightening sun. Sleeping passengers stumbled to their feet, adjusting their robes. Men began to line the leeward rail and urinate under its peeling paint. Saba considered how she had accomplished the same while they slept. To be a woman in the desert was to be less. The thought darkened her mood and she became a soldier again, glancing at the ferry's enclosed section.

Two classes of passengers filled this ship, Arabs and Europeans, the Arabs almost exclusively segregated from the Europeans and their comfortable seats. Saba frowned and touched the dagger hidden on her leg; here, too, the Arab was servant. More men grumbled awake; she listened to unfamiliar desert dialects with bits of Spanish and French. Saba had accepted the German's mission as a prerequisite to funding her partisans, and only after he again sanctioned her grievances against Iraqi King Ghazi bin Faisal. She had also demanded, and received, a guarantee that the Haifa refinery would only be attacked by her partisans and on a day that all Palestinian workers would strike. The attack could happen no other way and she remain loyal to the Tenerife bargain.

The ferry closed on Tenerife. Saba and four partisans remained near the stern and away from the others. She was dressed as a man, her face and eyes covered by keffiyeh, her shoulders square and unapologetic. Her group offered no responses when approached by Moroccans selling *griouches* of honey bread, packets of dates, and mint tea. The Moroccans lingered and sold to others; she heard bits of Arabic conversation—a man pantomimed a radio with his hands, then pointed toward the ferry's bridge and began to shout in loud, angry blasts. Another repeated his words as fact. Saba's knees buckled. She turned away toward the sea; both hands clutched for the rail.

The Haifa refinery had been bombed. Three hundred dead. Her fingers clawed into the rusted metal. *Three hundred.* Haifa was her target; *Schroeder had given his guarantee.* She and her partisans would risk the mission; their payment would be the lives of their people. *Three hundred.* One of her partisans stepped closer, his eyes wide at the news. He had family in Haifa, two still living, the rest dead in last year's fighting. Saba's whisper choked her as she tried to speak. Both fists slammed the rail. She beat back a shriek and pushed the words through her teeth: "The Nazis, our benefactors."

The cords rose in her neck. *My benefactors.* Saba squeezed her eyes shut. Saba bent double over the rail and vomited into the sea. Her partisans surrounded her, their backs to the sea. She shrieked at the water until her lungs were empty, the pitch so high the wail was almost silent.

Sea spray washed at her tears. She began to breathe and slowly a grim control shut down her emotions. She wiped her mouth and turned to face her men. "If Haifa is as they say . . . it is our benefactor who will die on Tenerife. We will make Herr Schroeder the lifeless pawn he has made the Palestinian." Her men patted agreement near their hips. Saba told them to circulate among the Arabs, learn what they could of Haifa. The ship rolled on a wind gust and she turned to face the sea again, tears running the makeup off her cheek and onto her lips. She checked stars no longer there and apologized to her family, then to her mentor, Khair-Saleh. Saba touched his bloodstained ten-franc note pinned inside her pocket and wanted to die. Soon and fighting. This she promised on the name of her father.

Day twenty-three in paradise.

Eddie's elbow bumped the 9mm under his shirt. His new boss in Tenerife had issued him the pistol immediately after extricating him from the PJs on the dock. Eddie's boss said the pistol was licensed (only government-licensed weapons could be owned or carried) and instructed Eddie to carry the weapon at all times. He warned Eddie that the Canary Islands was a nation founded on the profiteering of smugglers and pirates—many of whom were related to the workers inside the refinery's barbwire fences, workers who would know Eddie was the new "special engineer." To mitigate the threat of kidnapping for profit, or politics, or personal harm, Eddie would have around-the-clock security. It would not be D.J. Bennett.

Bennett would be arrested if he set foot on the island. Eddie's boss finished Eddie's introduction to the Canary Islands by explaining that all movement (by anyone) was subject to restriction if the *Policía Judicial* deemed such restriction necessary. There were no circumstances where complaining about the *Policía Judicial* would be beneficial. "The PJs speak for Generalissimo Francisco Franco." Eddie's boss added inflection. "So we understand each other, the Generalissimo rules without humor. Before his coup d'état on mainland Spain, he was the commander of the Spanish Foreign Legion."

Eddie said, "Never heard of the Legion."

"They *slaughtered* Morocco during the Rif Wars. *Anyone and everyone* they considered a threat."

The remainder of Eddie's first day on the job was better than the dock but not without additional conflict. After being issued a package of lightweight work pants, shirts, and boots, Ryan Pearce, the Irishman Eddie'd fought in Bahrain, had stopped by to say welcome. While Eddie held his clothing package with both arms, Pearce complained about being poisoned for their fight, said, "Can't have a pup such as yourself parading about after lockin' down so many in the king's jails," and punched Eddie unconscious. Eddie's "around-the-clock security" applied to the Irishman—but only after his first punch had landed—or Eddie would likely be dead. The fact that Pearce hadn't killed him didn't mean the refinery wouldn't.

Eddie spent the next seventy-two hours completing a system-wide inspection and evaluation. To quote the dumbed-down translation of Eddie's inspection report, the refinery was "a precarious production environment." Eddie's predecessor had completed 95 percent of the modifications, but his preliminary test runs had failed to produce 100 octane and had put several of the mainline systems into borderline failure. Angry accusations had followed, focused on the engineer's politics rather than the man's inability to translate academic theory into field reality. Shortly thereafter, the engineer contracted Ciguatera Fish Poisoning. He was still alive, convalescing at a special Berlin hospital in Friedrichshain. The refinery he left behind was a bomb and Eddie was leg-chained to it with too many fuses to count.

Today was the all clear. After three weeks of nail-biting, high-temp, almost certain death-by-fire, Eddie had given the all clear four hours ago. His success was equal parts skill and luck and he'd take it either way. Eddie adjusted the 9mm in his waistband. Tonight, he was headed into town to drink a beer or seven, smile at as many girls as possible, and show the flag. If Mendelssohn's people really were on Tenerife, they weren't inside the refinery, and the narrow streets of Santa Cruz would be their best chance at contact. Better still—whether they were there or not—four days ago there had finally been contact from D.J. Bennett, angry ex-bodyguard and Tenerife *persona non grata*. D.J. had made it out of Palestine and was on the island.

D.J. could prove or disprove the Mendelssohn papers. And D.J. could safeguard them if they were true. Every day Eddie had been here, the extermination camp plans had been taped across his back, burning against his skin. A D.J.-Eddie plan would be crafted. Together, they'd make something good happen. Eddie considered what *might* happen in a pirate town and reset the 9mm a third time. The clean refinery chinos were the best pants he had. His one and only civilian shirt he adjusted to cover the gun, then headed for the main gate and was immediately picked up by a refinery security man. Eddie'd have to shake him on the two-lane road into the capital city of Santa Cruz or in the maze of streets when they got there.

Outside the refinery's greasy rumble and constant tumult of workers, Tenerife bristled with the potential for disaster, natural and otherwise. The massive red-gray volcano that dominated the night sky set the tone for everyone and everything. Since Eddie's first introduction on the dock, the volcano's tremors had topped Eddie's list of things to not think about. The heat, though, you couldn't deny; it emanated from every direction—under your feet, above your head, from the refinery, from the ocean. Even the odd mix of French, Spanish, and Moorish buildings of Santa Cruz de Tenerife radiated heat. So did the people, everything and everyone brimming with Fahrenheit soaked up during a long day of sweltering subtropical sun and five centuries of colonial conflict.

Eddie turned a corner at the Bar Atlántico. A drunken crowd of Spain's Nationalist soldiers filled the café's outdoor tables. Fifty more jammed the sidewalk four deep and half the street, Calle San Jose. Loud guitars played inside the café. Eddie craned over the crowd toward the café's open doors but couldn't see the girls or the musicians.

Tenerife's uniformed police, the Armada, began pushing through the soldiers. General Franco's plainclothes gunmen, the *Policía Judicial*, watched the Armada's efforts. Eddie waited for a PJ to quit looking at him, then glanced left across Calle San Jose to a plaza on Calle de Miraflores and the stern Portuguese facade of Les Demoiselles. Les Demoiselles was a brothel run by a friend of D.J.'s, an Algerian woman named Doña Carmen. D.J.'s cryptic message had said to meet him there tonight, around midnight.

Cymbals crashed. Eddie flinched. A women yelled, a shriek the Moroccan singers made . . . according to the man at Eddie's shoulder, a German, blond hair and blue eyes. Eddie spooked, then recovered, like being too close to a train that roared past out of nowhere. He'd seen this guy twice before, once on Calah's plane and a day later standing in an Iranian courtyard with a coat draped over his arm. No doubt about it, in the flesh this was the Nazi, Erich Schroeder.

The Nazi extended his hand. "Erich Schroeder." A smile and happy eyes came with the hand, his other hand grabbing his hat to keep it from the gusts. He didn't look like the papers taped to Eddie's back, someone who'd murder a Jewish schoolteacher, someone whose intentions were to systematically incinerate much of Europe.

Eddie took the hand, concentrating on not crushing it. "Eddie Owen." The German's wrist was encased in a high-quality linen cuff. Eddie added, "Not from Tenerife, huh?"

"Berlin. And you are an American? Your champion Joe Louis was too much for ours this last time. Most impressive."

Eddie made a careful smile and stepped sideways, checking behind him. His security man was watching, unconcerned.

"Yeah. Joe Louis can hit. Schmeling took a twenty-year beating in two minutes." Eddie sounded harsh like he felt but added honest respect. "Not a thing wrong with your man, though. His corner threw in the towel, not him."

Schroeder nodded and craned his neck, scanning the crowd. "Thursday nights and the Spanish tango. These brave *godos* are too wounded to fight for their country against the Communists but not too wounded to dance. They should learn from our boxers what it is to commit, to honor and protect their nation."

Eddie guessed Schroeder meant that the Nationalist soldiers were tangoing inside Bar Atlántico, because out here the crowd of scrubbed but frayed Nationalist uniforms was drinking and shoving, not dancing. Schroeder seemed civil, unbelievably delicate for a Nazi who the Brits in Iran had said worked for Hermann Göring, the Luftwaffe boss who, according to Tom Mendelsohn, had commissioned plans from architects and engineers to rob and murder every Jew alive.

Schroeder touched Eddie's arm and angled his Aryan chin across the smooth-worn pavers of Calle San Jose. "The Café Los Paraguitas. Better to have a drink and sit until the Armada sorts this out." Schroeder laughed, floating manicured eyebrows for punctuation. "Possibly you and I can solve the misunderstandings about our countries that the politicians cannot."

"I'm, ah, meeting a friend." Eddie checked the street for more Nazis, then scanned for D.J. Bennett. "He's late and usually isn't."

"Your friend will see you better across the street. We'll sit there." Schroeder pointed to an empty umbrella table. Adjacent were two radiant debutantes encircled by a group of Armada de España naval officers, high-power uniforms Eddie'd seen once at the refinery. "Come, Mr. Owen, our chance to discuss the madness circling the globe. Possibly you have some suggestions?" Big smile again and a polite nudge as Erich Schroeder stepped them into the street.

Eddie'd done dumber things, all involving debutante/belle-sirens, too. A whole bunch of him wanted to rip the envelope off his back and confront the Nazi. But Schroeder would say they were fakes. What else could he say? Get the papers in front of D.J., that was the mission. Prove they were real or not. If they were real, then get them to President Roosevelt.

Eddie followed Schroeder into Café Los Paraguitas, its Moorish facade fronted by candlelit café tables, potted palms, and vested men in maroon fezzes. Schroeder bowed slightly to the debutantes' five-person table, turned, and took one of the two empty seats at the umbrella table, motioning Eddie to the other. They sat facing the street and Bar Atlántico, the view interrupted by passing horse carts and one chugging motorcar. Schroeder ordered *mistela*. He explained it as a German mead made with palm syrup. Eddie ordered a beer, a *jarra* pint of Las Palmas Tropical, wishing he were in Pappy Kirkwood's.

The debutantes laughed on Eddie's right. He glanced at their clothes and faces, the combination far more fanciful-aristocratic in the candlelight than what could be local girls from a blustery volcanic speck. The beer and *mistela* arrived. Schroeder tapped near Eddie's arm, then explained the debutantes. "The daughters of Señor

José Ramón Batabanó, the CEPSA counsel general, your American employer's partner in the refinery with the South Africans. Señor Batabanó is also General Franco's ambassador to Morocco and these Canary Islands. The *Comité d'Action Marocaine* has twice tried to assassinate the ambassador." Schroeder nodded at the crowd in the street. "And from somewhere on this street they watch his daughters now."

Eddie sipped his beer, forcing calm into his hand as he set down the glass. A lone Arab beggar sat against a wall across the street. The candle next to the glass flicked. Silverware rattled on their table and others. The ground shook once, hard.

Conversations stopped.

Schroeder smiled and chinned at Mount Teide. "Mother Nature tells us to hurry our discussion. She sees mankind's hubris and laughs."

"You're German. Would've thought you believed you were above that."

"There are those who would take insult at your suggestion." Schroeder smiled wider. "In the future, I suggest you confirm your audience before implying their national character is lacking." Schroeder nodded almost imperceptibly at the military men in the café. "Especially our hosts." He paused then added, "America will soon recognize Franco's Fascist government, as will the English. Such are the realities of the day. Although Roosevelt and Churchill fear the Fascists, they will fear the Communists more. As they should."

"Why fear the Fascists?" Eddie had no idea why that came out of his mouth.

"An excellent question. I am a National Socialist, a Nazi if you will—at heart, a Fascist. Merely a simplified form of democracy with a powerful central government and leader. Better than a monarch and far superior to the lie of communism." Schroeder shrugged. "I see nothing to fear and everything to gain."

Eddie almost blurted *Jews*, but said: "Someone must disagree." Eddie nodded toward the Spanish soldiers crowding Bar Atlántico. "They're Fascists, fighting in Spain when they're not dancing here."

Schroeder grimaced. "Stalin is a beast. I have seen his work in the unions, in Germany and America—slow the production lines, sabotage the products, threaten the workers who would work a full day. It weakens a nation, adds hunger and misery to the population, softening them for the Communists' arrival."

"The unions do that?" The lone Arab beggar was still seated against the wall. D.J. in disguise?

Schroeder followed Eddie's eyes to the beggar, then the crowd. "It is difficult to be lost in Santa Cruz. Perhaps your friend is at the brothels on Calle de Miraflores."

Eddie turned at the word "brothel." He hadn't mentioned Les Demoiselles.

Schroeder laughed and raised his glass. "A business here for centuries, since the time of the pirates. And quite good."

The guy was congenial, not the outright Nazi monster they all had to be. "If Germany's worried about Communists conquering Europe, why'd you invade Austria and Czechoslovakia? How's that help?"

"Invade? *Anschluss* was not an invasion; it was a popular invitation. Germany has merely reestablished its historical borders. We unite to protect a common people with a common language threatened *yet again* by France, Poland, and Russia." Schroeder leaned closer. "Stalin builds a three-million-man army and it is not for use in Russia. And France—the habitual *provocateur* of Europe's wars—France has more tanks than Germany could build in ten years. Oddly, we Nazis never hear of that fact."

A man in a white T-shirt and well-fitted denims approached their table and stopped short, almost military in his precision and distance. He offered a respectful nod to Eddie then spoke to

Schroeder in German. Schroeder answered in English. "Tell them I will be only another moment."

The man turned with the same precision of his arrival and disappeared beyond the café's corner.

"My apologies." Schroeder stood. "Duty calls. Possibly tomorrow . . . here again, we can discuss your thoughts. Tonight we sadly only hear mine. The authorities here tell me that you worry for the Zionists. They are a powerful force for their interests; an interested party need only ask the Arabs and the English."

"I'm asking you," said Eddie, unable to keep his mouth shut. "What about the Nazis' plan to—"

"Again, my apologies. It must be tomorrow." Schroeder stood with an athletic grace, then angled his head left and winked. "Tonight, try the Casa Habana on the Barranco de Santos. My favorite."

Schroeder crossed the street. Eddie's security man spoke to the Nazi, then turned and left without looking back. Eddie mouthed, *That's odd?* then raised his Las Palmas Tropical to finish it. D.J. was still not out front of his brothel. Eddie put down the beer and reset the 9mm gouging in his waistband. Tom Mendelssohn's papers itched against his back. Eddie rubbed against the chair back, then jolted when he realized what he was doing. An ugly thought struck him. What about Mendelssohn's Jews who needed transit? Technically, these horror papers were theirs, their blackmail ticket out of hell. What if D.J. and Roosevelt chose to focus the blackmail for a larger goal? Consider Mendelssohn's Jews casualties of war. Hadn't D.J. said as much? *What do you do then, Eddie?*

Erich Schroeder's presence lingered. Eddie swallowed. Maybe "lingered" wasn't the right description. Schroeder had to be a monster . . . if Mendelssohn's papers weren't fakes. If the whole story wasn't a ruse designed by talented, desperate people who'd have no problem defending the end justifies the means.

Eddie rubbed his eyes. He was way out of his league. The boldest of the ambassador's daughters was looking at him. Her eyelashes fluttered. Eddie dropped his hands and smiled. Must be D.J.'s brothel, for damn sure not the ovens and rail spurs . . . The navy fellow with the ambassador's daughter turned; his glance wasn't pleasant. Eddie toasted him. The Spaniard stood, adding glare as if he'd been glove-slapped by Errol Flynn. Eddie lowered his beer bottle. The Spaniard's two friends stood. Eddie stiffened—*Shit, not again*—backed his chair away from the table, and stood into—

Ryan Pearce. Pearce twisted Eddie off balance, out of the way, and faced the three Spaniards. A bolo knife flashed in Pearce's right hand. "Aye, ya shower a savages. Wouldn't be thinkin' about three against one, would ya?" Pearce balled his left hand. "Be brave. Step to the blade and defend your lady's honor."

The lead Spaniard hesitated. His friend circled to Pearce's left. Pearce pivoted. Eddie sidestepped to Pearce's exposed right. A police whistle shrilled. The lead Spaniard charged. Eddie dropped him with a right cross. A fixed-blade fighting knife clattered on the pavers at the feet of an Arab beggar. Suddenly *right there*. Eddie reset to drop the beggar—

Loud police Spanish: "*Alto! Alto!*"

Pearce grabbed Eddie's arm. They bolted past the two naval officers, ducked around the café's weathered corner and into a puddled alley. Eddie and Pearce sprinted two blocks of fetid garbage crates and broken barrels until the alley T-boned a seafront street. Pearce looked right, then left. He seemed confused in the dark, the moon obscured by sagging timber balconies overhead. Whistles shrilled. Pearce pointed them right. They sprinted shoreline. Three intersections. One-story shacks on one side, beach on the other.

Pearce stopped and turned, checking behind them. Eddie ran three strides past Pearce, stopped, and turned to do the same— No PJs, no navy men, just moonlit waterfront and the dead edge of

El Cabo de los Pescadores, the fishermen's barrio Eddie'd been told to avoid. Eddie caught two breaths, said, "Thanks," and dropped Pearce with a straight right. Pearce landed hard, rolled to his stomach, but stayed down.

From his back, Pearce said, "You're learning, Yank," and wiped blood from his nose. "Could be ya broke it."

"Don't get up till I'm finished talking. Afraid I'd have to use my boots." Eddie moved closer. "I'm tired of all the bullshit. I have a family and a job, and both matter. You have arguments with the Brits, those arguments are yours; I don't give a damn, okay? No more fair fights between us and no next time."

"Eyes behind ya, lad, from now on. You and the Brits'll be havin' a bit a business, too, mark my words. About Haifa. The jackets figure you for the bomber and they'll be comin' to visit."

Half the words were undecipherable in Pearce's accent and phlegm.

"Bomber?" A noise distracted Eddie. Three men appeared from the shadows. Erich Schroeder silhouetted first. He had a rolled newspaper in one hand and a slouch hat in the other. The hat was a huge jolt, a familiar hat, sweat-stained from years of work in Oklahoma. Eddie felt the jolt mix with fight-or-flee and backed away, trying to add information that didn't add.

Pearce stood, mopping blood with a handkerchief and rearranging his nose. The two men with Schroeder blocked a street intersection no wider than a double doorway. Both were armed and seemed comfortable with the military pistols, both wearing denims and white T-shirts. Sailors? Submariners? There'd been German submarines off the coast of the refinery.

Schroeder stopped six feet from Eddie, hat in hand, silvered by moonlight. "My apologies. This location is more appropriate for us, now that you are a . . . suspect." Schroeder smiled as he had in the café. "My association with you could be costly for me as well."

"Suspect?" Eddie glanced at Pearce, then the submariners blocking all the exits. "The Brits' opinion of me shouldn't mean a damn thing here."

Schroeder shook his head. "The refinery at Haifa."

"Haifa?"

"Bombed by saboteurs earlier today. Possibly three hundred dead. Not that the British worry with such casualties, but the loss of their refining capacity is another matter. Britain's ability to prosecute the air war they plan is central to Britain's control of her colonial possessions."

"*Haifa was bombed?* And they think *I* did it?"

Schroeder grimaced. "You left your position quickly . . . after a similar bombing near the market, yes? You were jailed. Your release was affected without proper protocols; a policeman was shot while detaining you. You travel by night to Lebanon with a Palestinian, then immediately come to Tenerife? Even I would find that suspicious after the explosion at the Bahrain refinery. As do the officials here."

"How do you know when I left Haifa? Or where I went?" Eddie wanted the answer but half his focus was how to survive a four-against-one that he couldn't.

"A British agent who sees his country's interests aligned with Germany's, not the Communists. Several elements of the British services have been watching you since Iran. They questioned me about you while we were their guests." Schroeder touched his ribs. "A similarly severe group is en route here to mount an interrogation at the full demand and complaint of the British ambassador. And if our Nationalist hosts here allow it, you will be returned to Palestine or, worse, to London as a spy and stand trial for murder."

Ryan Pearce added, "You'll share bunks with the Sitra-Bahrain lads you helped lock down in Pentonville, I'm hopin'. Make their day having you in their cells before the jackets hang you."

Eddie stared at the hat. His father wore a slouch hat like that, pulled down low to his ears when he plowed, and had for as long as Eddie could remember. Schroeder said, "This hat, you recognize it, yes?"

"Maybe."

Schroeder said, "Oklahoma is a distance away, but in the end, not so far. The farm is not good there. The wind, the bank, your father's health." Schroeder shook his head. "Sad. And then your troubles with the police there as well—the killing of the Jewish boy in Texas. This is also sad. And now the British paint your actions in Haifa with a similar brush."

Eddie choked down adrenaline, trying to listen while his eyes looped over the men between him and safety. "What do you want?"

"To help, of course. If you will allow me."

"How?"

"Possibly with your . . . situations?" Schroeder inspected the hat. "Soon you will receive a very sad letter from your mother—your father's health has taken all the money you send, and the bank now takes the farm. She is quite frightened for your siblings. In just weeks they will be out . . . with nothing. Your father will die without treatment, as, quite possibly, will the remainder of your family when they reach the migrant camps."

"Die? Of what? What're you talking about?" None of this was in his mother's letters. And D.J.'s people had been right there every time—

"A lung problem is the diagnosis." The German shrugged. "From the years of dust storms and medicine your family could not afford if they wished to also feed you, your brother, and your sister. Sad. And I notice no one in the United States has seen fit to offer assistance—possibly they already know you are running from the authorities . . . in Texas. Is this possible?"

Eddie set his jaw. No possible way this bullshit was true. But if somehow it were true, there was no chance Newt would die from lack of money. Eddie turned to sprint. The Nazi submariners blocked his path. Schroeder said, "Eddie. Eddie. Please, I wish to help, not hurt you, or your family or your great country for that matter. But the world moves quickly and I lack time to be as polite as I wish."

Eddie glared. "I'm gonna deal with my family. If your submarine boys here wanna give it a go, then we'll do that first. Either way, I'm leaving."

Schroeder held up both hands. "Please, just a moment, then . . . then it is up to you. Please?"

Eddie checked Ryan Pearce staring at him, then fixed on Erich Schroeder, Nazi.

"Mr. D.J. Bennett and his friends are not who you think. They are Communists, angry over their treatment as returning soldiers of the Great War and angry over the 'plight' of workers the unions represent against the industrialists, the very men who built your great nation. Bennett has blackmailed your professor Harold Culpepper for a position in your company so that he might push you toward the Communist objectives."

"D.J.'s the guy who's helping my family."

Schroeder blinked confusion. "Then why are they in such dire conditions?"

Schroeder handed Eddie the rolled newspaper—a copy of the *Daily Worker*, the newspaper of the American Communist Party. "Your Mr. Bennett's champion is featured, a General Smedley Butler. It is their agents, the Communists, who sabotaged the refineries in Bahrain and in Haifa, and they will do the same here. D.J. Bennett traps you and your talent, keeping you from the truth that Roosevelt and my government plan to make peace after the Soviet Union is defeated. The cooperation is called the Munitions Treaty of Geneva and is already being drawn. Germany is not the enemy; Russia is."

Eddie rolled the paper. "Get outta my way."

"Please. Allow me to help, to explain—"

"Explain what? That Nazis are killing Jews because they're Jews. That Nazi Germany invaded Austria and Czechoslovakia. That you're threatening Poland, now my family—"

Schroeder stepped back, indignant. "No. Not your family and not our neighbors, nor our citizens. The business with the Jews is propaganda, first by the English—they cleanse their skirts in the desert and Africa. The Soviets paint the Nazis with a brush that hides the Russian purges—it is Stalin who robs, deports, and murders Russia's Jews. Ask yourself why we never hear of that?" Schroeder added emphasis. "Look deeper, Eddie. Germany's 'threats,' as you call them, are reunifications combined with offers to defend those countries from Russia—if Stalin attacks we will defend. But this cannot be done at a distance against such a monstrous army. As we speak, Stalin masses his tanks on the Polish border. If we do not help now, the Poles will be slaughtered and Germany will be next."

"Get out of my way."

Schroeder stopped Eddie with his chest. "Your British interrogators will be here soon, tomorrow morning at the latest. You must listen *now*, if only for a few more minutes. Your decisions here will affect all those you care about."

Eddie tried to read the icy blue eyes. Somehow Standard Oil—a USA company—was partners here with Franco's Fascist government, a government that was openly supported by the Nazis. If Eddie could see U-boats in the harbor on his third day at the office, pretty good chance Roosevelt and his agents could, too. What the fuck did that mean other than it was, *in fact*, okay with Roosevelt? How would D.J. explain that?

Schroeder said, "All I wish is that you listen. Do nothing, just listen and look. And if you wish to discuss what you see, I will be pleased to explain. If not, well then, that is your choice, and I will honor it. Although it is my opinion that President Roosevelt requires your help."

Eddie started to speak and Schroeder stopped him. "Please. To show my good faith, I have already assisted your family in Oklahoma. A specialist visited your father"—Schroeder checked his watch—"twenty-five hours ago. The bank will not be a problem for this month or the next." Schroeder showed his hands again. "You owe me nothing. Who you owe is Roosevelt. And to him I advise you, in the strongest possible terms, to be faithful."

Schroeder handed Eddie a card. "My number at the Hotel Mencey," he said, and waved his men out of Eddie's path.

Eddie was running toward the refinery before the submariners had finished moving. His boss there had a special transmitter and radiotelephone that could make transatlantic calls; Eddie'd seen him do it. A transatlantic operator could route Eddie's call direct to the farm— Except his parents no longer had access to a phone. Eddie kept running; he could call the federal bank in town; they worked late doing foreclosures. Or the Bryant Grocery on Main Street, they had a phone and would be open if they were still in business.

Sweat-soaked, Eddie reached the refinery and the office trailer. The door was locked and wouldn't budge. Lights were on, but the foreman's assistant who had to be on duty was not. Eddie scrambled for the foreman's two-room apartment and knocked on the door until his boss answered. The foreman was equal parts angry and nervous. Haifa wasn't mentioned but it was right there between them. Eddie convinced his boss the phone call was an absolute emergency. The foreman told Eddie he would have to listen in,

Eddie would have to pay, and it would be a day's pay, or more, for a very few minutes.

Eddie's call to Oklahoma required three operators and finally got through to the store owner at Bryant's Grocery. Elijah Bryant's news wasn't short-winded or good. Bryant reported that most of the Custer and Dewey County farmers had been tractored off by the bank. Cotton pretty much everywhere now was the bank's answer. Eddie's people hadn't been set off yet, but Newt had been ambulanced to the St. John's Hospital up there to Tulsa. A specialist come down all the way from Kansas City and looked in on your father yesterday noon. The family was gone on to Tulsa, too, just Old Tom staying back to hold down what the dust and goddamn tractor men hadn't killed.

Eddie said thanks, wished the Bryant family the best luck available, then called Tulsa. The last English-speaking operator said the wires were down outside Bixby and Oklahoma City—a tornado moving through northeastern Oklahoma, the dust clouds so thick not even the tumbleweeds could roll—please try again in twenty-four hours.

Eddie hung up the radiophone. How could something this expensive not answer your questions? Eddie's boss said, "Haifa will require answers in the morning. Get some sleep and prepare. Tomorrow, if you survive it, will be a long, trying day."

Eddie thanked his boss for the phone. For an hour, Eddie walked the fence line, Tom Mendelssohn's papers sticky against his skin, the 9mm useless against the Haifa accusations and the wind and dust five thousand miles away in Oklahoma. Guards watched him. Workers eyed him. Eddie's security man reappeared with two others.

Protect the family, Eddie. Do something.

Five soldiers and the captain of the guard surrounded Eddie at the fence. The captain apologized, then ordered two soldiers to disarm Eddie and search him for bombs or detonators. There was no fighting the search and Eddie didn't. They found the papers taped to his back. The captain told Eddie to remove them.

Eddie waved off any value to the captain. "Just my passport and personal papers; don't want them stolen."

The captain wasn't interested in papers that could not detonate the refinery. He kept the 9mm but allowed Eddie to go to his room. "Many are concerned. Do not give us a reason to shoot you, the PJs in particular."

Inside his room, Eddie locked the door, ripped Mendelssohn's papers off his back, and looked for a place to hide them . . . that didn't exist. Eddie dropped onto his cot, then rolled to his back. His head hit a lump under the pillow—a brown box of .45 shells and the Colt government .45 that had been in his briefcase since he'd arrived. And—wow—a note that had to be from D.J. Bennett. In pencil the note read, "Missed you at Doña Carmen's. Things are popping; be back in forty-eight hours—keep your head down and don't talk to strangers." *Strangers* was crossed out and replaced with *anybody* underlined four times. "I hear you are with child. Stay ahead of wolves for forty-eight and I can take it from there."

"With child" had to mean D.J. knew Eddie had the Mendelssohn papers. Eddie jolted.

Schroeder's copy of the *Daily Worker*.

It was back at the foreman's office under the radiophone. A Communist newspaper in a facility protected by Fascists. The fast track to the PJs' cage. Especially after Haifa. Eddie bolted off the cot— He'd need the office key that he'd returned to his boss. His boss's trailer was a hike down the fences. The captain had been clear on what would happen if they found Eddie at the fences again. Eddie paced. He stuffed Tom Mendelssohn's papers in his pants. Three hundred dead at Haifa. Eddie's room shook him sideways. He steadied, grabbed D.J.'s .45— No way D.J. was a Communist; no way he did Haifa. D.J. *had* helped in Oklahoma; the letters from home said so.

Yeah, but somehow home had gone all the way bad.

CHAPTER 20

October, 1938

Nine hours ago at midnight, Saba's chance to kill Erich Schroeder had come as hoped. Had her plan held together another four minutes, she would have cut his throat midstreet where he stood. At midnight, Santa Cruz de Tenerife's cobbled Calle San Jose had been alive with soldiers and police, women and tobacco, men drunk with wine and beer and possibilities. Guitars played behind open windows and doors. Men shouted, "Flamenco!" as if it were their anthem. Saba tracked Erich Schroeder from behind. She would die on this street tonight but it would be with the Nazi's blond, blue-eyed head in her hand. Saba gripped the straight-blade fighting knife under her beggar's clothes. Her other hand gripped the cocked revolver. The Nazi wished to "prove the Arab's long reach." She would murder him here in the next few minutes and make his wishes fact. Others would see the symbolism as irony, but Palestine would see it as the truth of who had bombed Haifa, that the Nazis were merely another European invader, a competing colonial master who saw the Arab as fodder.

Schroeder was alone, fifty feet ahead in the loud, crowded street. A man jostled him. Schroeder shoved the man away. Four bodyguards materialized on Schroeder's perimeter, two ahead, two behind. The bodyguards were discreet, ordinary to the untrained eye. Saba hung back. She had anticipated one bodyguard, two at the most, not four. Four would be impossible to defeat and still kill the Nazi. A revolver bullet from outside Schroeder's perimeter could not be trusted. Gun or knife, it had to be with her hands on him. There would be but the one chance.

Schroeder continued up the narrow street. Saba allowed him to extend the distance between them. He passed the loud commotion and Nationalist soldiers and Armada police outside the Bar Atlántico, then stopped and spoke to a young man. Stoop-shouldered, Saba mooched through the crowd, her hand extended, closed the distance, and glanced at Schroeder from behind.

The young man facing him was Eddie Owen.

She stumbled, stepping back. Eddie here was a complication, not an improvement. The Nazi and Eddie walked to a café across Calle San Jose. Saba found a beggar's wall at the mouth of an alley opposite the café. She squatted there, unimportant and unwashed in the brown on brown, hands under her robe on her knife and revolver. Arab and European men passed her but said nothing.

To the Nazi's left, a table of polished military men and attractive young European women enjoyed their night of finery and laughter. A strong young man, in denim pants and a white T-shirt, approached the Nazi's table. The young man's posture was military. He spoke. Schroeder made what appeared to be apologies to Eddie Owen, rose, and walked toward the waterfront. The Nazi's four security men closed around him. Saba rose to follow. An Arab man interrupted her line of sight. He spoke to her in caustic Arabic, the dialect unknown. Saba squatted back to her original spot and did not answer. The man kicked dust on her robe, speaking louder. Two men stopped behind him. The Arab tired of her silence and moved on, as did the others.

Across Calle San Jose, the café's candles shimmered in the faces of the fortunate and their conversations. The guitars here were melodic and mixed with the sweet scent of lamb and spices that drifted beyond the flowered terrace. Without the Nazi present, Saba focused on Eddie Owen, her thoughts shifting from revenge for Haifa to . . . To what? She had no right to die in failure, distracted by a boy's touch, his gentle hands, his words, his future in America. Her eyes cut to her stars and she promised this would not be so. She would retreat her alley as soon as she deemed it safe. Across the street, Eddie shared glances and flirtations with the attractive European women at the next table. Saba darkened, angered by his attentions, then by her reaction. Who was she to think these thoughts . . . of boys and America? But the thoughts did not stop and they saddened her for all that she and her people would never have in this life. What she had were weapons and the blood of many on her hands.

And yet she had saved no one.

Two of the polished military men rose from their chairs. Eddie Owen did the same. Another man came at Eddie's back. Saba jumped to her feet. The man confronted the military men, not Eddie. A knife flashed, then another. Saba charged across the cobblestones. Eddie hit the military man just as she arrived, knocking him to the street and the knife from his hand. Whistles blew. Police shouted. Saba backed away to the beggar's wall and shrank to her crouch. Eddie and the man who sided him ran toward the waterfront, away from the police. The police surrounded the military man on the ground, blew their whistles again, but did not chase Eddie into the dark.

Saba's shock was almost total. Only twice in seven years, and both times over the old women at Dhār el Baidar, had she reacted out of pure emotion. Eddie Owen was not the mission. She was not a girl—

An Arab appeared at her feet. The Arab who had bothered her before. He demanded sex and threw a coin on her robe. Saba stayed within herself, disgraced. The man again kicked dust on her robe. She stood, hands under her robe on her weapons, looking past the man without moving her head. He pointed her to follow him deeper into the alley. The rage that burned in her face was not for this man; he was correct at his assessment of her value.

In the dream, Eddie kept smelling the Moroccan mint teas and hearing the Arabian princess say, "The British are coming! The British are coming!" Eddie was at Newt's funeral service holding hands with Adolf Hitler and Josef Stalin in a California migrant camp, and both his hands hurt. Eddie's head began to pound. The pounding was the door to his room challenging its hinges. Eddie said, "Yeah?" and cringed at the sunlight filling his dirty four-pane window.

A muffled Spanish accent said, "Please hurry, the door must be open."

Eddie stumbled to the door, opened it, and sat back on his cot. The foreman's assistant was nervous, harried, flailing his hands as he spoke. His accent was Canarian and difficult to follow: Three out-of-uniform British military men were in the compound. The foreman, Eddie's superior, had spoken on the transatlantic phone with the refinery's owners. High government representatives were involved, ambassadors and others. Additional armed guards were now at all entrances—

Eddie held up a hand to stop the torrent. "Which government's representatives are we talking about?"

This assistant did not know, but he did know that the PJs had escorted the British men into the refinery. The PJs were keeping an unusual distance by order of Madrid. But this would not last. The assistant flailed his hands again. It was nine o'clock a.m. and Eddie was two hours late to explain himself and all the tribulation. Eddie must hurry to the office, immediately, now, or sooner. Yes, and there was a call from a hospital in Oklahoma.

Eddie exploded off the cot. "What?"

The assistant fell backward avoiding the door. He answered in Spanish, caught his breath, and added in English. "I have the number is all I know." The assistant pointed. "At the office where everyone waits."

Eddie bolted. Halfway to the office, Eddie slowed. Would his boss allow the British interrogators to pull whatever bullshit they intended to pull? Before a call to the hospital? The assistant caught up. Eddie stopped. He told the assistant, "Have the Brits meet me at the canteen. I'm having breakfast."

"No, no. You must be at work." The assistant tapped his watch. "There is much trouble."

Eddie patted his stomach and turned toward the canteen. The assistant swore and fast-walked for the office trailer. Eddie stepped out of sight and sprinted, circling back near the backside of the office to watch the assistant arrive. The Brits left with him to find the canteen, big fellas all three of them. Three PJs materialized and followed at a distance. Eddie ran for the office trailer door.

Inside, Eddie apologized to his boss, said he would explain what he could after he called the hospital in Tulsa. His boss pointed at the *Daily Worker* on his desk. "Eddie, you better have a first-class explanation for a Communist paper. Men were dying in Spain fighting against the Communists and we're standing on Spanish ground. The PJs will not be gentle." The foreman leaned closer. "*This* refinery, Eddie, is not going to blow like your last two."

The transatlantic operator said she could make the connection to Tulsa and would call back. Eddie's boss tapped the *Daily Worker*.

"You don't seem to get it. This refinery, *my* refinery, is owned by men who are mortal enemies of the Communists. I will not allow you to remain on premise another hour, no matter *how* vital your skills, if you harbor sympathies that jeopardize this enterprise and the people who staff it."

"Honest, Mr. Paulsen, I—"

"The PJs will kill you, Eddie. There won't be a trial. There'll be a cage."

"I'm trying to do my job in . . . in a universe that changes every damn day. I don't know whose side anyone is on. And I'm not real sure any of them know, either."

The foreman started to bark, exhaled instead, then said, "England may side with the Russians against Germany or she may do the exact opposite. It's fifty-fifty no matter what you hear. And whichever way England goes, so goes America. But none of that matters to you where you're standing. Understand? None of it. You'll be dead before the story's written."

"What I heard was that England will follow *America's* lead. You work for Standard Oil and the Texas Company, right?"

"For thirty years."

"And you can see those Nazi submarines laying off our fuel dock."

The foreman waved off the question. "You better have answers for Haifa. The damage was substantial and costly. The British are blaming Arab Nationalists—a terrorist they say you know, the Raven of Palestine. The Arabs blame the Zionists. The Zionists blame the Nazis. The Nazis blame the Communists *and* the Zionists as a singular cancerous entity. Get it, Eddie? *Communists*, the mortal enemy of the Fascists, *our government protection here* and the mortal enemy of our President Roosevelt if he'd wake up . . . completely. You cannot be seen as a Communist and survive."

The office phone rang. Eddie answered while his boss was still talking. The doctor in Tulsa spoke in a calm voice. Each sentence shrunk Eddie deeper into the desk's chair, all of him heavier with each pronouncement. Eddie asked his last three questions, then set the phone in the cradle and exhaled. He glanced to his boss.

Three British men had replaced him. Eddie had been so intent on the call to the hospital that he'd missed their entry. The nearest Brit barked: "Edward Fred Owen?"

Eddie's eyes were wet. Fred was Eddie's dad's name. Mom and his friends called him "Newt." A quiet tear dribbled down Eddie's cheek. Newt had stood up to everything God and man could throw, all with a quiet kindness that had absolutely no right to kill him now.

The Brit laughed rough and sarcastic. "Tears from a fifth-column bastard." The Brit's pie-face was hard, red, and angry. The other two faces were the same.

Eddie wiped his cheek and stood into what little space the Brits allowed. "Be with you fellas in a minute; have to talk to my boss first, in private." Eddie angled his head at the cradled phone.

Eddie's foreman told the Brits, "Make yourselves comfortable outside. We'll be just a minute." The Brits took Eddie's measure, then the trailer door outside.

Eddie told his boss, "My dad, back in Oklahoma. The doctors don't think he'll make it. There's a slim chance, though—lung surgery, a new procedure. I need a two-thousand-dollar advance right now and a telegram guaranteeing the money's arrival in Tulsa."

Eddie's boss patted Eddie's shoulder. "Sorry about your father. But I can't authorize an advance. It'll have to go through Chicago. I'll call, see what they say, but that's five months' pay—"

"Maybe you didn't hear me; it's my dad's *life*. I don't want you to *call* Chicago; I want you to guarantee the hospital the money so they can operate *now*, not tomorrow or the next day."

Tiny but firm headshake. Eddie's boss eased back, adding respect for Eddie's bad news.

Eddie said, "You know D.J. Bennett, right?"

Foreman Paulsen opened the *Daily Worker*, pointed at a USMC general pictured on the second page, and hardened his eyes. "Is Bennett how you came by this paper?"

"No. Maybe now's a good time for you to explain why D.J. wasn't allowed to be my bodyguard."

"That's between Bennett and the owners and General Franco's PJs, and you'd better hope the reason, or anything close to the reason, has nothing to do with you."

Eddie leaned in at his boss. "*Why*, goddammit? What's everyone's problem?"

"As long as Bennett doesn't set foot on this property, or *threaten* it, Bennett and his politics, *and his murder warrant in Palestine*, aren't my concern."

Eddie ran through options for his father's surgery. Without D.J., there weren't many. Harold Culpepper had to be the answer. Except Culpepper was not climbing out on a limb for $2,000, not with two bombed refineries, "spy" accusations, and the British ambassador demanding an interrogation for Haifa. Nope, not without blackmail pressure from D.J., which, according to D.J. in Haifa, was no longer as potent as whatever else Culpepper now faced.

Eddie's boss stepped to the door. Before he turned the knob, he said, "Remember what I said—the Brits can go either way—with Germany or against her. Germany wants England as an ally in the war they're plotting against Russia, and *oil* is Germany's leverage." His free hand pointed at the floor. "This is oil. And this is Fascist ground. America has declared herself neutral in Spain's affairs, but the owners of this refinery, in spite of being 'Americans,' are not neutral. Understand? Our owners have picked their side."

Eddie nodded. "Could I, ah, make a private call? For my dad? Just take a second. Tell those Brits I'd be happy to talk with 'em after?"

Foreman Paulsen shook his head at Eddie's use of *happy*. "Those Brits are out there because their *ambassador* demanded it of the US *ambassador*. That's high-level stuff, Eddie. I've been told I cannot interfere." Paulsen narrowed his eyes. "Your importance to this refinery and its ability to produce AvGas is the only reason we, *I*, could force the Brits to do their interrogation here, where we can keep them from . . . who knows what. But your next interrogation with the PJs . . ." Paulsen opened the door and pointed at the *Daily Worker*. "Surviving the PJs, if they believe you are in league with the Communists, will be far, far more difficult. The modifications you're completing on this refinery are imperative, but the two governments you are about to confront—England and Spain—may not be that farsighted. Good luck." And Foreman Paulsen was out the door.

Eddie locked the door, pulled the Mendelssohn papers from his pants, and opened the dustiest of the foreman's file cabinets. The ten-by-ten envelope fit inside a thick file labeled CORRESPONDENCE 1936. Eddie shut the drawer, then called Les Demoiselles.

No, they knew no one named D.J. Bennett. And, no, Doña Carmen was not in.

Eddie heaved an exhale. If the three Brits outside decided to be ugly— Eddie pulled the .45 from his belt. Full clip, a round in the chamber. If the Brits got ugly there'd be no more paychecks, no more money home. Everyone he cared about loses. The .45 slid back in his belt. Eddie's hand withdrew a card from his pocket. His stomach knotted. And he dialed the number.

The situation required only limited explanation to gain a commitment for a $2,000 wire, no further questions asked and no promises requested. Evidently Germans were like that—prompt and efficient when they did their business.

● ● ●

At six p.m. Eddie's interrogation was in its eighth hour. So far, the Brits had focused their efforts on pain with side discussions about Eddie's connections to a smorgasbord of Arabs, Nazis, and Communist-Zionists. The discussions were being held aboard a British flagged trawler that appeared to be overcrewed and underfished. In between the punches and slaps and threats and sun glare, Eddie caught glimpses of Tenerife's volcano and troubling smoke puffs above it. It'd been a long day on deck without food or fresh water.

The interrogation had begun in the refinery canteen. Gunfire erupted almost immediately at the nearest gate and drew away Eddie's PJs. The Brits chloroformed Eddie from behind, then loaded him loopy into a refinery panel truck—obviously the plan from the beginning. And obviously the Brits had paid someone at the refinery, or a group of someones, to look the other way.

Aboard the boat, the afternoon faded and the clouds dissolved. The least-violent Brit intervened when his associates unsheathed knives. The Brit sent the others forward and offered Eddie a clandestine drink.

"I tell ya, mate. We could do with a bit of the truth. Those boys have stamina . . . and the mean one lost friends at Haifa, burned into crispies, all of 'em."

Eddie felt the water burn, then heal his throat. The Brit gave him another cup that Eddie drank with a shaky hand, the hand sunburned like the rest of him from hours of exposure. The shore bobbed in the distance; it would be a very long swim in two-foot seas. Big fish in this part of the world, too.

Eddie swallowed, smelling the fish guts in the chum buckets. There'd been the inference his captors needn't guard against an escape; Mr. Eddie Owen would likely finish in the water anyway. "Like I've been saying since you *kidnapped* me, I was in the Haifa market with Dinah Rosen. She's the one who said 'Irgun,' not me. She took off, I followed, some sick bastards blew her up.

Your Captain Wingate let me go because he had no choice—I'm an American citizen; try to remember that—then I went to Beirut for two days. The guy who took me was Bill Reno's assistant from Bahrain, that's how I knew Hassim. That's it, whether you believe me or not."

"I think *I* believe you, the majority of the tale. My associates, however, sense your sympathies lie with the Arabs and their Nazi puppeteers." The Brit shook his scarred head. "My vote? You and the Jew Zionists—bloody Communists the lot—would dearly love to steal the Haifa refinery for their state of Israel . . . that no king I serve will ever give them."

Eddie felt at his face and ribs. This was the same *all sides against the middle* that he hadn't been able to decipher since he got off the train in Chicago. "We have anything to eat?"

The Brit looked impressed that Eddie could eat and offered a banana. "Local. Tasty if an eater favors the local worms."

Eddie favored anything that wouldn't bite back. The boat's engines revved and the bow turned out to sea. Eddie asked.

The Brit shrugged, adding the *fait accompli* grimace. "You've something to say, Eddie, now'd be the proper time."

"Any more bananas?"

The Brit sat back on the gunwale shaking his head, possibly at the humor attempt, possibly not. He considered Eddie as they split waves rolling in from the east. "When you were on holiday in Iran you vouched for a woman and two men. By evenin' you were with her on the Abadan Road along the Gulf." The Brit floated brushy eyebrows. "How'd I know? Your bird had a driver who saw you. He drove her into Iraq after they had a spot of trouble on that road. On his return, the wog driver was angry with your bird and looked up the prefect of police, shopping to collect a reward."

Eddie checked the horizon, trying to appear a lot less interested than he was.

"Had a tattoo, didn't she? Little black wings under the right eye. Nice girl, interesting sort if you like 'em rough-and-tumble." The Brit paused and licked a bit of spray. "They call her 'the Raven,' after an Arab Robin Hood named Khair-Saleh who was likely more myth than man. She, however, is no myth. Has *personally* killed between fifteen and twenty professional soldiers, and likely an equal number of your Zionist militia. Then there's the district commissioner in Janîn and three of his armed bodyguards, the ten Arab policemen in Bahrain, and the three hundred civilians in Haifa."

Eddie looked away before he could stop.

The Brit smiled and nodded like they'd just agreed.

Eddie snapped back. "That's bullshit. The girl I know is a teacher in Transjordan."

"She's a wog all right, a Palestinian, though; family was murdered in Jerusalem in '29. She was buggered, and more'n once I'm hearing. Either by your Zionist militia or, regrettably, British troops. Ended up in the French refugee camps—bad awful, those camps. Somehow she survived, was picked up and trained by the bandit I mentioned whose name she took after the French said they killed him in the Huleh Valley." The Brit laughed. "Only bodies they found were dead Legionnaires. Not much in the way of proof by my way of thinkin'."

Eddie cringed at the history—the gang rape, the murder of Calah's family, the refugee camps he'd also heard Hassim talk about. Part of Eddie admitted something like this was true, or partly true—the tidbits after Janîn, the way she moved, the things she said, the ferocity in her eyes. But she'd been so gentle to touch, almost a fawn . . .

The Brit continued. "Her name's Saba Hassouneh al-Saleh, grown into a bit of a legend herself, by the by, and very, very few have seen her face. So tell me, mate, what's your bird look like?"

"Never saw her face or the wings you're talking about. The woman I met was Calah al-Habra, a teacher in Transjordan."

The Brit extended one hand with his fingers spread. "The ring you bought in Haifa at the market? Had 'em make the face with wings as I'm remembering. Let me have a look."

Eddie realized he hadn't read quite enough Hammett to notice the tail he must have had all day, every day. "It's in my bag, in my room."

"We've been through your room. I'm thinking the ring's on her finger, that you gave it to her in Beirut along with the plans to our refinery, then came out here to the beach while she killed three hundred innocent people."

The banana Eddie'd just swallowed rose into his throat. He swallowed it again, eyes shut seeing the faces he'd seen every day for six months. "Were they . . . British, or the Palestinians I worked with, the ones she killed?"

"Wogs, almost the lot." His face blanked for an instant and he blinked like the spray was in his eyes again, but it wasn't. "Nine out of ten."

Eddie lowered his head. "You don't *really* believe a Palestinian *legend* is coming out of the mountains and doing that, do you?"

"Odd we hadn't thought of that. What'd she have to say in Beirut?"

"Nothing in particular—" Eddie stopped himself three words too late.

The Brit fractured a smile. "I chat with blokes like you for a living." Then he nodded toward the shore. "Guess it'd be ten miles now before a fellow could stand sandy bottom. We'll toss you in, add those chum buckets, and run alongside. If you talk about her, the Zionists, and the Nazis, we'll fish you out. If not, the sharks will have ya."

Eddie was airborne before he could respond.

The splash was more like a full-body slap. The chum slick followed: four, five, six buckets. Eddie ducked underwater, hoping to rinse and add distance. The deep water was clear like the Arabian Gulf, but he couldn't see bottom. Side-to-side visibility was thirty feet. His lungs burned for air and he surfaced. He wasn't in the chum slick but he was still close to the boat.

The "good" Brit was staring from the deck, comfortable against a barrel. "Sometimes it takes hours to bring 'em round; sometimes the big ones, hammerheads, come right round in seconds."

Eddie 360ed like it would help and began paddling toward shore he'd never make. The boat came about and ran up to his shoulder. The Brits added a bucket of chum to Eddie's head before he could duck under. He surfaced and they sloshed him with another. The process continued until Eddie quit ducking. The smell was awful; oily blood filled Eddie's nostrils and fish chunks his mouth. Treading water, his feet were wiggling bait beneath him. Swimming would be better even though it exposed his stomach. Eddie turned for the shore and stroked slowly, never checking the distance, feeling the boat's rumble and the sun's heat on his back.

He swam until he couldn't. Then he quit and would have drowned had the Brit not tossed a life preserver. Eddie crawled into the floating circle, too tired to care about his feet dangling or his head and shoulders and hands coated in fish guts.

The Brit shielded his eyes toward a dropping sun. "Won't be long now, Eddie Owen—American citizen. The big fish start feeding soon, chum or not. Won't care you're a Yank, or a fellow traveler for that matter. Eat you either way. From the bottom up is what the local boys say."

Eddie tried pulling his feet closer to the surface and couldn't. "It's not what you think. I'm on your side. America, Britain—Roosevelt, Churchill—aren't I? The AvGas is for you guys, your Spitfires. Why else would I have built Bahrain?"

The Brit emptied the chum barrel into the water. "No telling. You're lying to me, though, cocksure of that."

The sun glared off the fish-gut slick. Eddie began to shiver in the warm water. "Tell me what you want for chrissake."

"What I want?" The Brit took his time. "The truth, I'm guessing . . . or your life for those we lost in Haifa, for those we'll lose in Europe and London once this war begins in earnest."

"I told you the truth."

The water underneath Eddie seemed to quiver. He ducked underneath the chum and saw nothing, spun and did the same behind him. Just water getting darker with the sun's low angle.

Eddie breached the surface and heard, "Company?" as he wiped fish blood off his face. He checked for fins and did another 360. This really bent the beets. Something big was going to bite off his feet.

"The hammerheads are twice your size, Eddie. Teeth like razors, rows and rows of 'em. Once one hits ya, the rest come and take chunks. Nasty buggers. Like the wogs and Nazis and your sufferin' Jew Zionists. Hard bastards, those Jew militiamen, kill a hotel full of British civilians without blinkin'. 'Cause it's God they're serving, building His homeland one murder at a time."

"I don't know any Zionists."

"Know any Nazis?"

"No." A low wave bobbed Eddie with chum. "Yes. Met one. Your chief in Iran pointed him out: Erich Schroeder. Blond guy, about six foot, blue eyes. He's here on Tenerife; saw him yesterday."

"Where?"

Eddie splashed. The water near him moved again, like a river current. He curled his feet and ducked under the life preserver to look. A shadow passed. Eddie spun, tried to follow and couldn't. He spun back to check behind him. Panic. Bogeyman. Something in the water with him.

He dug his head out to breathe and heard, "Better hurry. 'E's a big one, 'e is."

"Big what?" Eddie splashed to spin again, fish pieces peppering his face. *"Big what?"*

"The Nazi, Eddie, what about him? He and your bird working together? What'd they promise you for Haifa? The same thing you got for blowing Bahrain?"

"I built Bahrain—I didn't blow it up!" Eddie squirmed out of the life preserver and kicked with his feet. He made the hull and reached. "Lemme up."

"Sorry."

"Lemme up! Before this thing eats me!" A shadow passed and brushed Eddie's feet, a tail maybe, fanning away. Eddie spun his back against the boat's hull and scooped his knees and feet up to his chest.

"C'mon, Eddie, you can do better." The Brit waved Erich Schroeder's card that had been in Eddie's pocket. "You have Herr Schroeder's telephone. Why would that be?"

Eddie saw the shark. Gray-brown and turning near the top of the water, the tail fanning chum.

"Get me up!"

A horn blew loud. Another boat, its bow high and charging. The shark swerved and lined up in Eddie's face. Twenty yards or less. God, it was big. Horn again and a gunshot. Then a series of gunshots. The shark bucked coming right at him. Its wide back twisted out of the water. A machine gun roared. The shark pumped blood and veered off the bow of the Brit's boat.

The charging boat had a deck gun and a wide red stripe across a bow that bristled with Armada police. A yellow and red Nationalist flag fluttered above loud commands. Eddie checked for the shark's return, then back to the police boat, his head bobbing against the

Brits' hull. Above him the Brit had both hands in the air. Armada police waved Eddie to swim over.

Eddie did and was hauled aboard by two workers from the canteen who'd witnessed the kidnap at breakfast. Erich Schroeder wrinkled his nose at Eddie's chum odor. "Lucky for you, my friend, that these workers decided to come forward. And that General Franco frowns on British subjects murdering Americans."

Eddie stood and lost his balance into Schroeder, then glared across the narrow chum slick at the bobbing Brits. "What the fuck is wrong with you people? You hate Arabs and Jews so much that you'd kill anybody who's nice to 'em? They're fucking people, too, you fucking assholes."

It was more profanity than Eddie used in a week. He glanced past Schroeder to the deck gun. If Eddie spoke Spanish, they'd be firing it. The Brit said, "Nice mates you got there, Eddie. Ask 'im how they're doing in Austria and Czechoslovakia."

"They just saved me, remember? Wasn't them feeding me to the fucking sharks."

The Brit nodded. "You're no better off now. Just don't know it."

Schroeder asked Eddie, "Our Armada captain wishes to know if you will press charges? It is a delicate matter"—Schroeder shrugged—"given the US and British ambassadors' involvement."

Eddie reconsidered shooting the Brit. "Give me a gun."

Schroeder spoke to the boat's captain, who ordered an Armada policeman to give Eddie a pistol. Eddie aimed at the "good" Brit. "Three against one is how the Brits do it, huh? How you ruled the fucking world. I don't care who buries your fucking country— Arabs, Jews, Germans—I just hope I'm there to watch."

The Brit nodded. "As we suspected."

Eddie glanced at Schroeder. "Can the PJs put these bastards in the cage?"

Schroeder shrugged. "Should Madrid allow it. Again, Eddie, it is a delicate matter; addressing it formally will have complications." Schroeder turned his back to the Brits. "The British are a tenacious sort, especially so when they are misguided as to their true friends. These gentlemen intend to harm you or at the very least affect a kidnap to British soil. Were it my choice I would sink their boat, allow them the same chance they allowed you."

Eddie aimed at the hull below the waterline. For some reason he thought of his father's surgery, his mother, his brother and sister. "I need to call Tulsa, the hospital. Will these policemen ferry me to the refinery?"

Schroeder bowed slightly. "And our British friends?"

"To hell with 'em. Let 'em run for the mainland."

Schroeder nodded. "I honor your decision. But this is one you will regret, Eddie Owen. A sense of fair play in this part of the world is a distinct liability."

Eddie's boss wiped sleep out of his eyes and took in Eddie's condition. Foreman Paulsen was not happy but he was willing to walk Eddie to the office trailer and unlock the transatlantic phone. Eddie made a furious series of calls. The news in Tulsa was a combination of better and bleak. Newt was alive, his condition "stable," the lung surgery allowing him to breathe but the effort so strenuous Eddie's father was encased inside an iron lung in the polio ward. Eddie's mother had collapsed under the strain. She was on oxygen in isolation, diagnosed with consumption, tuberculosis, her lungs weakened to the bacteria from all the years in the dust. Her treatment was temporary. Additional money must be wired to pay for the surgical collapse of her lung and a recovery in a TB sanatorium. Eddie's brother and sister were too young to understand and too young to stay alone. The hospital had surrendered them to the state home at Henrietta.

The hospital gave Eddie the number of a Tulsa lawyer. The lawyer was willing to intercede for Lois and Howard (on the promise of payment in no more than ten business days); the lawyer would try to court order Eddie's brother and sister to a foster family in Tulsa or Cushing. Eddie hung up the phone. Two weeks' pay had been spent on phone time and Tuesday wasn't over yet. Eddie looked at his boss. "What'd they say about my advance in Chicago?"

Forman Paulsen blew air through his teeth. "Lotta money, Eddie."

"To a goddamn oil company? Who the fuck are you kidding?"

Paulsen frowned. "I'm doing what I can."

Eddie ripped the phone out of the cradle and shoved it at his boss. "Call Chicago. Tell 'em if they don't help me my mother will die. Ask 'em if they want me working here after they let that happen."

"Meaning—"

"What the fuck do you think it means? Call the bastards now if you want me on the job in the morning." Eddie slammed open the door and walked out. His adrenaline quit halfway to his room. He resisted the urge to curl up on a bench and dragged himself the rest of the way. The infirmary for his ribs and stomach would have to wait.

His room was an oven. The ceiling had no answers written on it, but Eddie kept looking between the fan blades. His family had a fighting chance; his chances were less attractive. According to Foreman Paulsen, the British attaché in Morocco had filed formal charges of sabotage and murder for the Haifa bombing and a demand that Eddie be immediately ferried to the mainland and surrendered to the Crown. The extradition demand had also been filed with the United States consulate in Madrid. Eddie's hosts, the representatives of General Franco, were considering their response and Eddie's future under the Nationalist flag of Spain.

Eddie rubbed his face. He'd taken $2,000 from a Nazi, a highly placed Nazi. The same Nazi who'd bought his parents medical attention they would've died without. The same Nazi who'd saved him from the sharks. The same Nazi who'd kept the PJs from doing their interrogation when he got off the Armada boat— Eddie rolled to his side and yelped at the pain. His parents were on life support in a hospital he couldn't pay for beyond today. His sister and brother were abandoned to a state home, and the girl he dreamed about at night to escape everything else was a partisan bandit . . . who'd killed more gunmen than Floyd Merewether and Benny Binion combined.

Happy Halloween.

On cue, Eddie's bed began to tremble. The refinery lights flickered, then quit, and the hum of generators stopped. D.J.'s .45 rattled on the nightstand; Eddie palmed the gun and laid it on his chest. He stayed flat on the bed and let the tremors vibrate his bruises. D.J. and his magic had picked a lousy time to go AWOL. Doña Carmen at the brothel had taken Eddie's final call. Doña Carmen said she had never heard of D.J. Bennett.

Eddie shuffled cards he had no idea how to play and redealt.

D.J. did not like the Nazis, that much was twenty-four carat. D.J. did not like Standard Oil or any of the big oil companies. Unfortunately, Eddie's current salvation was a Standard Oil paycheck and a Nazi who supported Standard Oil, a Nazi who Tom Mendelssohn's papers would surely destroy. Erich Schroeder's name wasn't on Tom Mendelssohn's papers—that was worth something. And according to Henry Ford, the Jews were exceptional advocates for their causes. So maybe, just maybe, Mendelssohn's papers *were* a lie—not just because Eddie needed them to be a lie but because they actually were a desperate ruse by the Zionists to gain sympathy for the migration to Palestine.

Eddie had been down this mental track once before. In the six months he'd been in Palestine, the Zionists had matched the Arabs and the Brits, bomb for bomb, bullet for bullet. The Zionists had plenty of blood on their hands, just like the Brits said. And Mendelssohn's papers foretold a story so hideous it *was* almost inconceivable . . . Maybe the Communists *were* the *real* enemy to be feared. Eddie shut his eyes and rubbed at his head. A knock startled him. He fumbled for the pistol on his chest and said, "Yes?"

"A message." Strange accent, muddy and quiet.

"From who?"

"*Altair*. A bird."

Eddie aimed the .45. "It's open."

Nothing. The knob didn't turn. If this were PJs—

The knob turned and the door eased open. Slow and deliberate. Backlit in the moonlight, an Arab stood with his face covered. The Arab dropped the black-checked keffiyeh—one of Saba's men from Iran, the older one. He checked Eddie's small trailer, then waved at Eddie to follow. Eddie's .45 didn't seem to matter.

"Calah?" Eddie's pulse rate blinked his eyes. "She's here?"

The Arab nodded, then waved Eddie outside.

Eddie added clothes and shoes and more than one groan, belted the .45, and stepped outside. They approached a guard who on cue turned to look up at the volcano smoke. Eddie walked three paces behind the Arab to a shielded section of refinery fence. At the pole, a rod had been secreted into the fencing. The rod allowed a section to be unhooked from the pole and rolled back. Eddie marveled. Nationalist Spain could marshal all the PJ cages Franco had, but they wouldn't end a *culture* of smuggling and pirates. That thought didn't bode well if someone wanted to bleed this refinery . . . or level it.

A roomy light-gray convertible appeared—an *auto de turismo* taxi—engine rumbling, lights off. Both passenger doors sprang open. The Arab pointed Eddie into the backseat, then slid into the front. The driver was the Arab's duplicate. They drove too fast and west toward the moon, the breeze drenched in the sweet intoxicating smell of oleander, then north into and away from tiny banana plantations in what a sign said was the Orotava Valley, then higher on a nasty, narrow, serpentine road cut into the dark mountains. Eddie was nervous for a number of reasons, not the least of which were the blood-bleeding dragon trees thrashing the car and a mule-cart road too dangerous for fast mules.

No headlights tracked them.

No Englishmen or PJs was a major accomplishment in Eddie's new life as a spy. He put that in the "good" column. The big convertible spit gravel in the rutted hairpins, hugging the inside edge at the limits of what a burning clutch and old tires would allow. Eddie closed his eyes and white-knuckled the seat until he felt the car descend and could smell ocean instead of laurel and pine and radiator steam.

And there the ocean was under a yellow moon and a forever of black sky. Long white waves rolled in from . . . somewhere, maybe South America; Eddie wasn't strong on latitude geography. The driver stopped on the ocean side of the road. The road's edge was a sheer drop down a rough lava-rock seawall to a black sand beach. A bleached-out sign where the driver stopped read: PUERTO DE something, 11 KM. Eddie followed the driver's finger pointing out of the car at the ocean.

"The beach? She's out there?"

The driver pointed again. Eddie opened the rear passenger door and stood to the road's edge. The older Arab was out and waiting. He disarmed Eddie with two fluid motions, stood back with D.J.'s .45, and nodded Eddie toward the water. Eddie frowned at his repeated encounters with people who did what they did better than he could.

"Make sure you leave that in the car, okay? I need it at work." Eddie frowned, said, "And probably everywhere else," then climbed down the seawall buttress. He was too wasted from the day to be excited, too worried for his family to do much more than hear why she was here. Whatever the reason was would be swell if it weren't to bomb the refinery. Eddie's frown remained until he saw the figure shadowed in moonlight shimmering off the ocean. He knew it was her from thirty feet. She turned, dressed as a man, the keffiyeh leaving her face, the wind catching her hair. The wind pushed the white shirt against her breasts and the thin pants against her hips. Eddie suddenly felt better than a fellow in his circumstances should.

He stopped at five feet and said, "Hi."

She smiled like before, feigning comfort with her face exposed, the effort so endearing Eddie almost flinched.

"Man, you're beautiful here, too. That's two different continents. Can't be a fluke or the light."

"How are you, Eddie Owen?"

"Been better." Eddie was semimesmerized by the first silhouette of her body without a robe. "But sure glad to see the Arabian princess. Can you swim in those? You promised, remember?"

The smile stayed but shrank. "Yes, I remember."

Eddie wanted the smile to be her answer, but turned to look for her bodyguards on the excellent chance it wasn't. "Ah . . . we're going swimming, you and me?"

"A climb in the mountains was also discussed." She angled her head at a choice of volcanoes and mountains. "The mountain may be angry, although I know no such mountains. Swimming is possibly better for you."

Eddie thought so if it included her. "And the water's closer. How about we take off our shoes and walk in the surf, take it from there. You can talk to me about the desert and why you've moved to the islands."

She broadened the smile and he was glad. Glad because he wanted to know what she was doing on Tenerife and glad because she was absolutely breathtaking when she smiled. They left their shoes on and walked north with her nearest the water, a place she chose by stepping in behind him.

"I have never seen this ocean. It goes all the way to America." She pointed northwest. "Washington, New York, Ticonderoga."

"I missed you in Beirut, had big dinner plans for you both nights."

"There were no others for good company?"

"Sure. But not a princess. Not with hazel eyes and chestnut hair and—"

"You go too far and my father will be unhappy." She smiled at her stars.

"I'm going further this time."

She turned, looking down her shoulder, surprise but no concern in her eyes. "Boldness is often the little boy's answer."

"I'm okay with that if you are." Eddie glanced at the black-lava bluffs that hid them from the road. "And your bodyguards."

She told the ocean, "They are soldiers, like me, not bodyguards." Then told the sand, "They are most confused with how I . . . act with you. It is foreign to them . . . and to me."

"That's gotta be good. Isn't it?" Eddie touched her shoulder.

She spun sideways, eyes wide in his face. They burned right there. She glanced away. He'd forgotten that touching her had consequences. And, *man*, she was fast, like the cougars he'd heard about eating pachucos down in the Big Bend.

"Possibly, it is good. Yes." Her eyes came back wary, but not of him.

"Do, ah, soldiers ever hold hands or anything . . . like that . . . ever?"

She stepped past Eddie's side and waved at the bluff. Eddie turned and saw only rocks, then turned back. She'd taken a deep breath, pushing her chest at the limits of the shirt.

"I will try." Her left hand rose, not quite sure where it should go.

Eddie reached, not squeezing or trapping her hand, just there, like before. "I'm, uh, going to hold it now, like you'd hold something very valuable but fragile." He cupped her hand and felt it tense, then relax and cup back.

He grinned at her looking away toward the water. "You have on my ring. That's wonderful. You like it. Right?"

"Yes." She sounded out of breath.

"Don't slip; your hand'll break doing this. It's tricky the first couple of times."

She laughed but still didn't look at him.

"See, this is how it starts. If it lasts more than ten minutes, you're married."

She jerked her hand away. Then laughed and lowered her head the way a young girl would, caught herself again, and raised her chin, adding pride and control.

"Can you ask a princess how old she is if you're standing at the ocean?"

She held on to her own hand as if restraining it. "This one is twenty-five. And you?

"Me? Let's see, I'm, ah, twenty-five, too. How about that?" He reached for her hand. "It's customary. In America you have to hold hands at the water if you're the same age."

Frown. It didn't fit her eyes, though, more of a dating frown.

"Honest. Really. I'm not gonna lie to you out here. You have friends and I don't."

She let him take her hand again but didn't move. "Where are your friends, Eddie Owen?"

"Only had three and two of them are dead. An East Indian murdered Bill Reno in Bahrain. Just found out Hassim was killed in the refinery explosion at Haifa . . . and D.J., well, missing I guess you'd call him." Eddie felt the strength of her hand when he mentioned Haifa. "I understand you lost a lot of people. Sorry."

She let go but didn't turn away, becoming a man while he watched. "We are dead, standing between Europeans fighting over land Europeans do not own. One day the desert will swallow them all. After I die, but I will be there." Her face looked so hard it could have been a statue. "This I promise."

Eddie stood still, not afraid but absolutely sure she was what the Brits had said she was—maybe not the murderer, certainly not the bomber of Haifa, but the outlaw-bandit-corsair genuine article. They didn't make movie pirates more real than this woman. His mouth started before his brain could stop it.

"The Raven. They said you were the Raven."

She squared her shoulders, one hand near her hip, one not. "And if I am, Eddie Owen?"

"You'd be the prettiest blackbird I've ever seen or God probably ever made."

"Who told you this?"

"Three Brits who tried to feed me to the sharks today." Eddie pulled up his shirt and pointed to his ribs. "They said I gave you the plans to the Haifa refinery and the one in Bahrain." Eddie smiled at his bruises. "I told them they were full of shit. The girl I knew was a princess."

"And you believe this?"

"No way you killed those people in Haifa. They were your people."

Her posture softened, or at least Eddie thought it did. "Yet you are here. How did you get away?"

"Spanish police boat and a Nazi . . . Fellow was on our plane after Bahrain and in Iran when we were. Erich Schroeder. Big-deal Nazi who supposedly works for Hermann Göring." Midramble, it dawned on Eddie that the princess and the Nazi were both in three of the four places he'd seen her, at the same time. He tried to swallow that thought because it didn't taste as good as the others.

"The British who say I am the Raven, did they tell you my name?"

Eddie nodded. "Very pretty. Saba. I like it, suits you, in the moonlight especially."

She frowned, fighting the compliment. "You are a boy, no matter what the news."

"The news isn't going to change. And right now, right here, I'm standing with you in the moonlight. Forgive me, princess, I don't get to do this often."

"They told you what about the Raven?"

"The day I landed, the PJs said they'd feed me to the sharks if you were so much as *seen* on the island. The Brits said she killed twenty men and—"

"Eighteen."

Eddie tried to get past that without stumbling. "Ah . . . and she's sort of a legend among the Palestinians; raised by a bandit after her family was murdered—"

"Did they tell who committed these murders of women and children?"

"Either Zionist militias or British soldiers."

"Both." The word was gravel in her mouth. "And what else did they say of the Raven's past?"

No way Eddie was going to mention the gang rape. "Ah . . . she lived in the refugee camps, that the camps were bad. Few women survived them." Eddie lowered his head without realizing it. "They said almost no one has seen her face."

"You have."

Eddie raised his eyebrows at the admission. "They think you assassinated the district commissioner in Janîn. And for what it's worth, the PJs and the Brits are scared shitless of you and what you represent."

Saba nodded. "As the English should be. All of them." She held out the hand he'd held moments ago. "I am Saba Hassouneh al-Saleh."

Eddie shook her hand, but softly, not man-to-man. "Like it or not, you're the princess, too," and let go.

Her cheeks flushed, but she made no attempt to shield her face. "I have never been with a man . . . of my own choosing." Her chin was high and defiant, violence and affection in her eyes. "I . . ."

Eddie allowed her to keep his hand or let go. She kept it. He leaned in and kissed her cheek as lightly as he could and remained next to her until she exhaled. He felt a tear leave her eye and stepped back, smiled, then kissed her again, tasting the salt this time. "I think you've seen a lot for a princess and for a soldier."

She had tears on both cheeks and no words.

"I'm going to put my arms around you, okay?"

She didn't move or speak and Eddie hugged her as softly as he knew how, felt her breasts and her hair and the handles of weapons in her clothes. Eddie's embrace grew to include his family losing their battles in Oklahoma and the Nadler family on the Jacksboro Highway, losing their boy. Then Eddie was crying, too, squeezing harder than he planned. Her head fell to his shoulder and he touched her hair, the thick silk of it a surprise, and she pushed gently away.

Both were embarrassed, first-time lovers after the passion had passed. She left the tears on her cheeks and said, "You are sad as well, Eddie Owen?"

"Think it's the salt water." He kept wiping then admitted it. "Yeah, but I'm glad, too. Glad you're here. I feel better every time I see you."

"Your other friend, the one who is missing. His name is?"

"D.J. Bennett." Eddie felt a twinge, like he'd given a clue. Maybe not to the wrong person, but . . .

"He is your good friend and what has happened to him?"

"Probably my best friend. And I don't know."

New headlights interrupted. Eddie squinted at the road then turned back. Saba's revolver was between them. He started to speak; she crossed her lips with the barrel and ran inland from the water. Eddie followed, not sure why they were running, but sure cover couldn't hurt. At the rocks of the seawall buttress, Saba patted him into a crouch. They listened, but only to wind and the surf breaking. She crawled to the top of the lava rocks, scattering rock crabs in waves, peered, and dropped back to the sand.

"The police stop to investigate your taxi. The Spanish grow nervous with Arabs. There is much trouble with the Europeans' hold on Morocco."

Eddie noticed her revolver was British and could imagine how she'd gotten it. "While we're waiting, could you tell me why you're here—not that I'm unhappy in any way, 'cause I'm not—just be nice to know, since I can't figure out anything else."

Saba considered him at her shoulder, his eyes close to hers. "In my group, in the Arab states, there are factions. To some I am valuable; to others I am valuable also, but as something to trade. They wish to be rid of me and the attention I bring."

"You're here to hide? From your own people?"

"Yes." She stared hard at him. "No. I am here to kidnap your friend."

Eddie blinked his way through the silence that followed.

She added, "You are the bait."

"Bullshit."

Saba looked at him with hazel eyes somewhere between man and woman.

"C'mon." Eddie touched her arm, no flinch, just the hazel eyes holding his and his future.

"You're not kidding, are you?"

"No."

"O . . . kay. I guess since you told me that, you intend to tell me why?"

"I am here to kidnap D.J. Bennett. When I deliver him he will be tortured, he will talk, and he will die." Her tone was military, matter-of-fact. "You, I am to . . . corrupt . . . with the many womanly ways I do not have."

Eddie leaned away, not that he thought it might help save him, but to help process her words. The scariest thing was his hormones were still dealing with her as a woman. "Why, ah, are you telling me this stuff? You shouldn't be, should you?"

She inhaled to answer, reconsidered, and said one word: "Haifa."

"You're not gonna blow Tenerife—" Eddie felt the pistol at the back of his head, then heard Arab-accented English in his ear. "Do not move." The hand on his neck was tight and slowly tugged him backward.

Saba watched the road and did nothing to help him. She glanced, then said: "Do as you are told and we will not harm you. Do otherwise and you will die." She spoke brief Arabic to the figure holding the gun behind Eddie, then turned back to face him. "I am ashamed for our time together, and yet I wish it. Do not think you were the cause of my death." She removed the ring. "Keep this and remember me."

Before Eddie could speak, she ran toward the taxi and the new headlights.

CHAPTER 21

October, 1938

D.J. Bennett was worked to death, King Ranch tired. He sat in the transom of a *falúa* contraband boat as it approached the far south end of Tenerife Island. The boat was more shadow than shape, gliding low in the oily water. D.J. found himself in a pirate boat, although he was not a pirate, wanted for murder and sedition. Nor was he a Communist, although he'd fought alongside them. He'd fought against them as well but now found his sympathies, in some areas, to be once again in line with theirs. ("Politics makes strange bedfellows" was not mindless chatter.) Nor was D.J. a Fascist. Nor was he a blind believer in capitalism at the expense of the little guy—the working guy—or the nation he'd sworn to defend. And *survival of the nation* was what he believed to be at issue.

Had he been inclined to describe himself, D.J. would've used "realist." The facts were what the facts were. And the facts were that the world had become increasingly cruel during his lifetime, each and every decade producing more misery than the last. And the war that was about to engulf mankind—a mechanized, airborne slaughter D.J. could see just beyond the horizon—had no precedent in western history—history that included the Great World War to end all wars that he'd fought steel-to-steel in the mustard gas and trenches not twenty years ago.

A lone thunderclap shook the air and rattled D.J.'s boat as it motored nearer to Los Cristianos. An odd cross current slid the stern seaward. D.J.'s Canarian captain eyed the oily water, then the island of Tenerife to their right. The city of Los Cristianos was quiet, too quiet. And dark, as if the power were down. D.J. squinted beyond the city to the volcano silhouetted high and lethal in the moonlight. A powerful force, volcanoes.

Ahead, two long deep-water docks bracketed the main harbor of Los Cristianos. Beyond the docks, the beach was lined with the silhouettes of un-motored *lanchas*, honest fishing boats, their only equipment unlit carbide lamps. D.J. refocused on the two deep-water docks. Bobbing there were gray-and-black silhouettes. Larger boats. These boats were not honest, all had motors, no names, and pirates for owners. A silent gull sliced above the boats in moonlight too dim to reach the water. The hair stiffened on D.J.'s arms. He focused for the threat that would be well placed on any of those boats, his fingers sliding to the .45 in his belt. In the last twelve hours D.J. had learned that his death had become mandatory, the failure of his mission a priority of powerful men with empires at stake on both sides of the Atlantic.

The dock up ahead and its risks would end a grueling twenty-day trek from Haifa that had required far more personal risk and mission risk than he would have allowed a subordinate to accept. From Haifa to French Beirut had been by truck, then Beirut to Alexandria, Egypt, by steamer. A smuggler's coastal boat carried him across the Southern Mediterranean to Tripoli, then a caravan from Tripoli across French Algeria into French-British partitioned Morocco, and finally a car to the ferry at Casablanca. Far too many participants had been paid, trusted, and eventually outrun. The truth was he'd taken some of the risk because he wanted Eddie to survive. A combat line officer could not feel this way, yet D.J. did.

The capper for the father-son trek was yesterday's forty-mile boat trip to Gomera Island and forty miles back, separated by a night trek up and down the Hermigua Valley that had tried to kill him twice. The objective had been a crank-antenna radiophone at three thousand feet, placed there in 1937 by Communist remnants of the International Brigades—American fighters from the Abraham Lincoln Battalion who had survived Franco's prison ships. The Americans had reorganized with Gomera's smugglers and pirates, hoping to interdict the next flotilla of prison ships before the 100,000 prisoners aboard could be murdered.

The Americans had been unsuccessful. But their phone still worked.

While at three thousand feet, D.J. cranked the phone, hoping to make three life-or-death calls that could not be monitored or reported by any overseas operator. The first call was to Palestine. The news in Palestine was bad: D.J. was still wanted for murder, as was Eddie Owen. Rather than a British retraction of the charges that D.J. had been promised, an "eye witness" to the policeman's death had been added. D.J. was squarely on Great Britain's wanted list and that reduced the navigable world by one quarter. D.J. was also considered a prime suspect in the Haifa bombing. That put him in the "Black Book" of the major oil companies, almost as bad as being wanted by Great Britain, and further reduced the navigable world by another quarter.

Great Britain's wanted list included a price on D.J.'s head, an accolade the Brits reserved for known IRA bombers, White Chapel slashers, and "colonial terrorists who incite violence or sedition against the Crown." D.J.'s bounty was likely levied at the request of the oil companies. The death of one Palestine policeman left no London parliamentarian in tears. The death of a refinery was another matter. Protecting Eddie would be very difficult now, if not impossible. And that created another problem—there was no possible way Eddie could be allowed to fall into the hands of the Nazis. Even D.J.'s people would view Eddie training Nazi engineers as too dangerous to allow. They'd kill him. Sure as shit, they would. Eddie would have to run. But still make AvGas for the good guys. To accomplish either, or both, would take some doing.

D.J.'s second call produced better news, "heaven sent" if one believed in such: Eddie Owen's note left for D.J. at the Hotel Royal in Beirut inferred that Eddie had the Mendelssohn papers. The only surviving copy. If Mendelssohn's papers were as Eddie described *and* they were genuine, the papers could be used a number of ways, including, but not limited to, keeping one Eddie Owen alive, free, and working for the defense of a nation, the nation that D.J. saw as mankind's salvation if her soul could not be stolen by the oil companies and their support for the Fascists.

D.J. made the third call, now harboring the grandest expectations he'd had in this decade. Mendelssohn's papers felt like Resurrection—again, if a guy believed in such. The third call failed. D.J. cranked and tried and cranked and tried. Somewhere along the line of extended relays to the USA, the magic would not connect. There would be no cavalry for Eddie Owen, D.J., and the papers. No Roosevelt or his champion, Smedley Butler. The papers could still do their magic, but only if D.J. could grab Eddie and the papers tonight, get them all the hell out of Dodge before the flotilla of bad guys could slam the door. D.J. had finished that thought already running downhill through the jungle.

The lone gull cut across the moonlight again. D.J. thought, *Albatross?* His captain cut the engine and they drifted to the dock at Los Cristianos. The captain was a third-generation smuggler from Fuerteventura and skilled at night maneuvers. He squeezed them between a fat wooden trawler and an island-green skiff crowded with rope and shallow barrels. Two gulls spooked near the shore. D.J. gripped the .45 he'd already drawn. A shape materialized on the road beyond the beach, a man in western clothes, both hands visible. The man made himself plain, then walked three hundred feet to where D.J. had left the old truck provided by Doña Carmen. The man stopped and stood next to the fender.

D.J. exited his boat when it touched the dock. The air above him was oddly still and reeked of sulfur. The volcano. D.J. cocked and leveled the Colt for his dock walk. The weathered wood creaked under his feet. Each boat he passed could kill him. None did. The man at the truck raised both hands when D.J. arrived. "I am Moshevsky, a friend of Tom's."

D.J. made "Tom's friend" as some kind of European mix—ruddy, maybe a Jew, and sturdy, about five-foot-eight. The man affected "reasonable" with his posture and expression, but not "defenseless." D.J. said, "You don't know me. And I don't know anyone named Tom."

"The papers. Your Eddie Owen was given them the day he left Haifa for Beirut."

"Step away from the truck. Keep the hands up. You're a Jew?"

The man nodded small.

"Are we alone?"

"No." The man glanced toward the shadows across the road.

D.J. didn't look. "Why are we talking?"

Moshevsky short-versioned a story of Jews in Germany and her territories, adding bits of detail to what Eddie had repeated—loss of citizenship and theft of property. Formal Jewish ghettos being demarked for those who could not escape. Once in the ghettos, Jews would be sent to forced labor camps, then to extermination camps, and finally mass executions. Eleven million Jews. All of Europe. And if Russia fell to the Nazis, all of the Soviet Union as well.

"And if I had something to do with these papers of 'Tom's,' what would you have me do with 'em?"

Moshevsky explained a blackmail plan against Standard Oil and its primary stockholders. Standard Oil would facilitate the transit of Jews out of Germany. In return, the documents would remain out of public view. Standard Oil and Vacuum Oil were important partners of the Nazi war machine. It could be done easily.

"You don't know Standard Oil. Or its partners."

Moshevsky said, "Eddie Owen is under grave suspicion for the events in Haifa. He remains free of the PJs' cages here, but only with the sponsorship of Nazi Oberstleutnant Erich Schroeder. Twelve hours ago, Eddie Owen was abducted by the British but freed by Schroeder."

D.J. frowned. The Brits had taken off the gloves. The dumb sons-a-bitches were playing the Nazi's cards for him. D.J. knew the game, had played himself, and likely so had Moshevsky. Maybe this guy knew where the Brits had Eddie. That would be a start at least—

"My people in Tel Aviv," Moshevsky continued, "were unaware of Eddie Owen's . . . friendship . . . with Saba Hassouneh. She is most dangerous and would not wish Eddie Owen to help our cause. Now our documents may be lost." Moshevsky eyed D.J. for a reaction. "Eddie Owen was rescued from the English by the Nazi and the Armada police who Erich Schroeder pays. Eddie Owen was put under guard at the refinery where he makes many telephone calls to America, but as of one hour ago, he is absent without permission and no longer there. I may lower my hands?"

"No."

Moshevsky frowned and reset his shoulders. "Your interests and ours are compatible. Your assistance now, before it is too late, is beneficial to everyone."

"How'd you find me?"

"Doña Carmen. She directed me here to wait for your return . . . from . . ."

D.J. cut just his eyes to the shadows and squeezed tighter on the trigger. "Don't think she'd do that."

"Yes. Our network has assisted her many times on the mainland in Algiers. Like you, we share alliances and goals."

Algiers was French. Doña Carmen had serious underground connections in Algiers and French Morocco. Doña Carmen was also a Palestinian, although almost no one, including this Zionist, would know that.

"What'd you tell her? Why were you looking for me?"

"The Brigades. Americans who are attempting to evade capture by the Spanish in Morocco."

D.J. wagged the .45. "Maybe we'll talk. Be where I can find you if I have something to say. Hit the road."

"Do you intend to help us—"

"Hit the road."

Moshevsky lowered his hands. His face lost the practiced softness, replaced by the same resolve D.J. saw in his own mirror every morning. Moshevsky's diction hardened. "An exodus for eleven million can be built, Mr. Bennett. By just you and me and Eddie Owen . . . if we choose." Moshevsky waited, then added, "If the Final Solution is allowed to begin in Europe, no one will stop the slaughter until the continent is a cemetery. For everyone."

D.J. nodded. Moshevsky wasn't clairvoyant, just pragmatic. Murder on the scale being organized by the Nazis would empower leaders in the lesser ethnic conflicts once the war started—places like Yugoslavia, Czechoslovakia, Armenia would become the bloodbaths of Nanking. Europe would be the white man's turn at the plate.

"So, Mr. Bennett, you will help?"

"We ain't at 'the beginning,' son." D.J. wagged the .45. "Get outta here. Gimme a day or two and we'll see what we see."

Moshevsky started to speak.

"Move."

Moshevsky didn't. D.J. began a silent count. Moshevsky turned and walked toward whomever was in the shadows. D.J. watched. He suffered no confusion about the value of an exodus to those it might save or what they would do to achieve it. Nor did he harbor illusions that Moshevsky's reasonable tone was an accurate representation of Moshevsky's capabilities or intentions. Saba Hassouneh was a capable enemy. Before allowing Mendelssohn's documents lost to her . . . or to Erich Schroeder, or, for that matter, to D.J. Bennett, the Zionists would kill Eddie, recover their papers, and start over. Such were the realities of war and genocide.

D.J. walked away from his truck into the dark and waited for the headlights of Moshevsky's vehicle to pass. Moshevsky represented a tribe of survivors who hadn't accomplished that by quitting. Very soon, if not immediately, Moshevsky would be everywhere there was a chance to interdict the Mendelssohn papers or convert Eddie to the cause. And that included tonight. D.J. stayed in the dark, waiting for a trail car that did not materialize. An Arab did. On the beach, his robe and headdress silhouetted dirty white against the dim moonlit sea. The Arab did not approach the dock or its boats; he walked straight toward D.J.'s empty truck. At the truck, the Arab stopped and turned to face where D.J. hid in the dark.

D.J. stepped out, .45 extended, and backed the Arab up on his heels. The Arab flattened against the fender and opened his palms. "I am fighter for *Comité d'Action Marocaine*."

The "*Comité d'Action*" were Moroccans—some Communists, some not—looking to take back their country from Spain and France. This Arab's accent fit neither. D.J. said, "*Al Gorab*, the Raven."

The Arab reacted, then recovered. "The place of our meeting is there." The Arab pointed north on the road between the sea and

Mount Teide. "We have Eddie Owen. You will follow me now or he will be sold to Berlin or London."

"What is it you *Moroccans* want?"

"His life depends on a ransom you pay."

D.J. nodded. "So will yours, son," then waved the Arab away from the truck. "Make your radio call. Tell the Raven I'm on my way."

D.J. allowed the Arab a mile lead.

Hopefully the Arab had no idea who or what Moshevsky was back at the dock—the Raven would not see a Zionist involved with Eddie, *here*, as anything but a massive threat. It was out of D.J.'s hands, no matter what. For two hours of coast and mountain road, the Arab's and D.J.'s headlights dipped and turned in tandem, hugging the southern and western slopes of Mount Teide. If the electricity was working anywhere, D.J. didn't see it. And when the wind didn't gust in off the sea, the air smelled and tasted like a sulfur mine. No tremors, though. That was *probably* good. D.J. checked his mirror on the switchback turns. Occasional reflections in the dim moonlight might be a vehicle . . . Moshevsky without headlights. If Moshevsky were the professional he seemed, he'd lay back and watch for opportunity. Once Moshevsky saw Arabs, he would know that Zionists in person would add nothing to the discussion but bullets. Those conditions might, or might not, stop him.

Approaching the ransom location, D.J.'s lone headlight swept across a long black-sand beach with white lines of waves breaking. Dead ahead, a light gray convertible was parked alone on the road's seaside shoulder, lights off. D.J. pulled Doña Carmen's truck to the mountain side of the road and stopped opposite the convertible. Good place for a kidnap or killing. Spanish PJs were good killers and they had no soft spot for Americans who might be with the Brigades. The PJs would be happy to collect the British bounty on one D.J. Bennett.

With his back to the taxi and road, D.J. slow-scanned the myriad of places where kidnappers could be hiding. If he hadn't passed Eddie's kidnappers coming in, then Moshevsky's tail car couldn't run into them either and get everyone killed. Unfortunately, all D.J. could make out was a volcanic, scrubby ridgeline, then another, rising higher in a hurry. A gust laced with sulfur and iron blew down from the mountain. The roadside trembled. Somewhere in the dark a far-off, low-pitched rumble shook his feet. D.J. started to turn.

Movement to his right—

Saba scrambled over the seawall rocks toward the man she believed was D.J. Bennett. Erich Schroeder would be somewhere close. After her aborted attempt to kill him in Santa Cruz, Saba had dispatched one of her partisans to speak with Erich Schroeder. As anticipated, the Nazi was vehement in his denials of Haifa. He would see Saba tonight after her successful kidnap of Bennett and bring absolute proof that the bombing in Haifa had been the Zionists. Making herself plain, Saba walked toward the convertible taxi her men had stolen. The man she believed was D.J. Bennett stood at the taxi's fender, his pistol facing her. In the dim moonlight, he looked unafraid, although Bennett could not know the figure who approached him was a woman. Nor would he know that Erich Schroeder had been radioed when Bennett's contraband boat had docked at Los Cristianos or that Nazi submariners were at this moment rafting in from a U-boat waiting a half mile offshore.

"You are D.J. Bennett?" Saba closed the distance. He was the same man she had seen with Eddie in Dhahran.

"Where's Eddie?"

She began her answer. He aimed. "Where's Eddie or I put a bullet in your head."

Saba stopped, just her eyes visible under the keffiyeh. "That will not bring your friend."

"Can't hurt. They send the expendable ones out to talk."

Behind her keffiyeh, Saba smiled at the truth. Bennett was her second American and he did not disappoint. "I am his friend . . . from Iran and Lebanon."

"You? You're the Raven?"

"Yes." She had maneuvered a knife into her right hand, the blade tip up and resting on the inside of her forearm.

Bennett stepped right and removed her options. "Too bad. Drop what's in your right hand or we're both dead."

Saba sensed Bennett was about to fire and dropped the knife. This American had little of Eddie's naiveté; he would know others aimed weapons at him.

"I am not here to harm him. He is bait for a bigger fish."

"Get him up here."

"No. We talk first."

"Got no burning desire to go fishing. Get his ass up here. I ain't asking again."

"If it is true that you know who I am, then you know dying with you does not frighten me. And you know others will still have Eddie. They do not feel about America as I do; they are better, only Palestine matters to them." She paused to let Bennett fire. He did not and she added, "Like you, we are at war and our friends are also our enemies. Our fight is not with you."

"Since it ain't about a free Morocco, what's it y'all want?"

"From you, we want—"

The flash from the water reflected in Bennett's eyes but he didn't look. He said, "That Eddie's ride to Germany?"

"The ride is for you."

"For me?" Confusion, then understanding lit his face. Bennett frowned. "Then we'll be going together, honey."

"Return to your truck. There will be shooting. Eddie is safe. I mean him no harm."

Bennett blinked, his eyes searching for the target if it wasn't him.

Saba said, "I do this for Haifa. Those who come for you. I come for them. You were my bait. If you do not wish to be swallowed, now is your time to leave."

Bennett wrinkled his eyes. "The Nazi, right?" Bennett cracked an honest smile behind the .45. "Guess my boy Eddie ain't that stupid after all. No wonder the sumbitch acts like a teenager about you."

Saba grinned with her eyes, something like a teenager's response captured in a soldier's moment. All these gifts on the day of her death. "Eddie will be returned to you one kilometer south. On the beach. Go now. Our fight with the Nazi will kill him and likely us as well."

D.J. Bennett stared at her and didn't move. "You really twenty-five like the Brits say?"

Saba nodded.

"You're a goddamn handful for twenty-five, honey. You survive the next twenty minutes and got any interest in comin' to America, we got plenty of places could use you. That's a bona fide offer, ma'am, any way you'd like to take it."

Saba registered the compliment and an old dream she would never attain. "We will free Palestine first."

"Well, that one may take some doin'. Win or lose, my offer stands."

Another signal light flashed from the ocean, this one closer to the beach and bright.

Saba said, "The Nazis from the submarine. Go now. Our friend Eddie Owen must be kept from them."

D.J. Bennett squinted at the water.

Behind Bennett, a shape lunged for him and his weapon. Saba sidestepped but slipped in the oily gravel. Bennett slammed his .45 into the attacker and fired. Two more attackers knocked Bennett off his feet. Boots landed square to his head, then his groin. Saba rolled to her knees. Erich Schroeder faced her, Luger in hand, shielded by his men. One of Schroeder's men flashed a light to the approaching submariners. Saba expected to be shot by the other man and was not. No one leveled weapons at her. Schroeder pointed his Luger at Bennett's prone body, then glanced through his men at her as she climbed to her feet, her pistol behind her leg, heart pounding, waiting for Schroeder to move from behind his men so he could pay for Haifa. Saba stepped sideways for a headshot. A third man materialized and blocked her.

"Well done, Saba, as usual," said Schroeder, then shot D.J. Bennett in the spine.

Saba shifted her weight to one heel. Her first shot knocked the man blocking Schroeder off his feet. Schroeder pivoted. The man next to him stepped in front and took her next two shots. Schroeder fired twice. Both hit Saba. She pancaked, unconscious before she landed.

Schroeder kicked at Saba's pistol but it stayed death-gripped in her hand. Rifle fire exploded at him from the beach. Schroeder jumped over the bodies and behind Bennett's truck. Bullets banged into the metal. Saba's partisans. A line of Nazi machine guns charged in from the ocean, engaging the Arab rifles on the beach. Flashes lit the beach—stop-action stills of Arabs and Nazis fighting in the blood puffs and roar.

Then it stopped. Cordite lingered; Schroeder couldn't hear. He crawled into Bennett's truck. Bennett's starter wound and wound, then finally engaged. Schroeder ducked below the dash and steered blind. The truck left the road and veered uphill into the scrub where he wanted it to go. His shoulder throbbed; his ears rang and he could taste copper. The truck stalled. Schroeder rolled out and ran scrub until he found the small car he and his men had hidden an hour ago.

The driver's seat was tight but it offered a clear view of the road and littered beach. Best Schroeder could tell, he hadn't been hit, but everyone else had. As planned, Saba was supposed to die here, as was Bennett, leaving Eddie Owen isolated and alone on Tenerife. The dead submariners were an unanticipated cost. Reichsmarschall Göring would be angry. The evidence of the submariners and their involvement would be cleared quickly by the sailors from the submarine. There would be police and PJ cars soon. Fear would grip the island that an attack of some kind was imminent. Schroeder released the brake, coasting out of the scrub and onto the road. Before he could fire the engine, two men in the road waved at him to stop. One was five-foot-eight and shouted in English. Schroeder slowed, shot them both, fired the engine, and steered without headlights. At the first steep curve uphill into the mountains, he allowed himself the headlights and a smile. Eddie Owen was the prize, the final card, the trump card for a kingdom. And now Eddie was all alone.

At the seawall rocks, Eddie clutched Saba's ring in his fist, ears ringing from the machine guns. He squinted behind him. No movement on the beach—five, maybe seven corpses. Eddie pocketed the ring, fingertipped up the rocks, and eked just his head above. No movement on the road. More corpses were scattered facedown on the pavement. *Jesus.* Eddie felt at his torso, then the lava chips in his face; somehow the crossfire of bullets had missed him. He swallowed a breath, then another, then crawled along the rocks, staying just below the road, moving toward the bullet-riddled taxi.

Saba was sprawled near the front fender, pistol tight in her hand. Eddie jumped up onto the road, then fell to his knees. "No, baby, no." Both hands patted her face. No reaction. Saba was sheet white but breathing and not spraying arterial blood. Eddie scooped her off the pavement into the convertible's front seat and ripped open her bloody shirt. A hole bled lightly above her collarbone and one below the breast. The chest shot was aspirating. Eddie wadded her singed keffiyeh over both holes, tore off his belt, and cinched it around her torso.

"Don't die, baby. Don't die."

Eddie fished out D.J.'s .45 he was sitting on and mashed the gas downhill, swerved to miss two more bodies in the road, realized he was going the wrong way, braked hard, spun the wheel, and headed back uphill. Saba's head bounced in his lap, Eddie trying to shift and steer the mule-cart road, no clue what to do other than find D.J. Did D.J. know someone had paid Saba to kidnap him? *Where the fuck is he?*

Whorehouse? No, no one at Les Demoiselles had ever heard of D.J.— But, but that was right after things had begun to get ugly. D.J. wouldn't risk using Doña Carmen's place and her name if he didn't know her—D.J. was in country illegally and wanted for murder by the Brits just like Eddie was. The road dipped left. Eddie missed the curve. The convertible's headlights fanned the ocean. A boulder banged the front wheel and saved them. Saba's head rolled limp on her neck.

"Sorry, baby. Sorry." Eddie tried to steer and think. And breathe. Doña Carmen was said to be a *chicharrero*, a mixed-bred native. Someone like that could put her hands in a lot of pots, get a doctor for sure. *If* she wanted to help hide Saba from . . . just about everybody. Big, big *if*. Anywhere else that Saba went for a doctor she'd be dead in an hour. Eddie patted Saba's neck. "Doña Carmen will help. She will, trust me."

Eddie mashed the gas again. Doña Carmen and her whore-house would find a doctor. Doña Carmen would have to, because she was the only chance Saba had.

At four a.m., Santa Cruz was a mob scene. Eddie weaved and honked, then looped back out of the narrow streets and finally into the alley behind Les Demoiselles. Half the population of Tenerife's capital city seemed to be in the streets and pointing at the sky. Inside Les Demoiselles, everyone who wasn't horizontal by drink or choice was yelling back at the huge wooden radio set up on the front bar. Eddie fought through the crowd while the radio confirmed that space-men were attacking America in huge fiery balls. Saucer landings and death-ray massacres continued in New York and New Jersey. Eddie found Doña Carmen, cut the *patrona* from the hysterical crowd by using D.J.'s name and an American accent, then fast-talked her and him into her private quarters in the basement.

Doña Carmen did not comment on Eddie's bloody clothes, his accent, or his offer of money. Eddie didn't have to fake desperate; he told her he needed a room and a doctor *now* and no PJs. PJs would kill him on sight. After a too-long inspection that lasted sixty seconds and included her sniffing his collar, Doña Carmen asked who Eddie was to this man D.J. Bennett. Eddie explained while the *patrona* dialed her radio to the same broadcast as upstairs. Unable to locate the broadcast, Doña Carmen quit, pointed to a small bed-room, and told Eddie to lie down, she would return in a moment. Eddie allowed Doña Carmen to disappear into the bar and hysteria above, then climbed the stairs and out a back door into the alley. Eddie carried Saba in from the car and had her on the bed when the *patrona* returned.

Doña Carmen balked at a second person and almost spilled the bowl of water. Eddie said, "I can get two hundred dollars, I think, back at the refinery. D.J. has more. We need a doctor or she'll die. Please, it's my . . . wife."

The *patrona* frowned at a heartfelt lie, set the bowl on a table, pushed Eddie aside, and sat on the bed. After a tentative look at Saba's wounds, she stopped, then traced the wings tattooed under Saba's eye. Doña Carmen carefully removed the chestnut hair matted in Saba's face.

"Your wife, yes?"

Eddie nodded, edging sideways to block the door.

"Do you know who your *wife* is, Señor Friend of D.J. Bennett's?"

"She's a friend of D.J.'s. His best friend. His sister, I think." Eddie touched D.J.'s .45 he'd stuffed in his belt.

"You threaten me, *godo*?" *Godo* was an insult reserved for the Spanish high-and-mighty of the mainland.

"Not unless you make me." Eddie's hand stayed on the pistol. "She needs help; I'll do whatever you ask. If you say no, I'll do whatever it takes."

Doña Carmen huffed. "Americans. As you say, she requires a doctor . . . the lung. There is a *mora conejo* at the Hotel Mencey, a rabbit from French Morocco." She cupped her breasts. "If he could be persuaded."

"Great. Good." Hope rushed into Eddie's blood. "Wait, he can't talk, though, can't say we're here, to anyone. D.J. wants us to hide until he arrives."

"This man D.J. told you this?"

"Yeah." Eddie kept lying. "Said to bring her here and that you'd help."

Patrona Doña Carmen swore quietly, said *men are children* in Spanish, and told Eddie to apply pressure on both wounds. And do not answer her door. And cover your woman's eyes completely when I return with the doctor. And do not talk no matter what you are asked. Doña Carmen wheeled for the door. She pulled it open—tumult roared in from the ground floor above—she slammed the door behind her and the silence returned. Saba rustled. Eddie kissed her face and pressed her chest with his weight. She moaned.

"It's okay, baby. It's okay. Doctor's on the way." He pressed harder, trying to believe it. "Don't die. Hold on."

Upstairs, the whorehouse crowd hammered boot heels across the ceiling and dragged furniture like someone was building barricades or bonfires. Eddie remembered spacemen were attacking America. Must be the Italians or the Japanese somehow—maybe dirigibles like the Hindenburg at night or something.

Saba moaned again and stuttered. One eye opened then shut and opened again. "Dead."

"You're not dead, baby. Quiet, okay? Don't worry. I knew you weren't there to kidnap D.J. I knew you wouldn't hurt me or him." Eddie patted her forehead and felt the air leave her chest. "Shit." He pressed back hard with both hands. "Don't worry, okay? I trust you . . . Hell, I think I love you."

She rustled, trying to breathe.

"I know, I know. Kinda surprised to hear it out loud myself." He stumbled for words, needed to talk, burn time, keep the injuries busy, keep Saba from dying. "So there it is. I said it. First time for me. Not saying it again, either. So don't ask." He waited for a response, something. "Okay . . . I love you . . . naked, swimming. Head-to-toe naked. Go ahead, get mad." He bent to her lips and kissed her, tasting blood and sand. "Don't die." Eddie started to choke because that's what was about to happen.

The door opened before he could draw.

A man, dark and nervous, possibly the French Moroccan. Eddie had the .45 out in the man's face as the door swept shut, Doña Carmen now inside as well. Eddie remembered Saba's face and covered her eyes with the bloody keffiyeh compress. The doctor pointed Eddie away, spoke Arabic to Doña Carmen, and inspected the wounds, then Saba's breathing. Eddie slid to her shoulder, one hand still holding the keffiyeh across her eyes.

The doctor cut off Saba's shirts, bathed her chest in water and colored antiseptic, and went at the wounds. His attempt at saving her took an hour. One bullet had cracked a rib. Both bullets had passed through, exiting her back. He worked in silence broken only with Arabic commands to the *patrona*. Doña Carmen translated some of his statements as she assisted—the muscles below the shoulder were shredded. The left lung had collapsed and needed to be reinflated. Her blood loss was substantial and they had none to give; infection was almost a guarantee without better drugs than the doctor had.

Eddie said, "How about the refinery clinic?"

The doctor nodded, finishing the last of his sutures. He eyed Eddie and his pistol but didn't ask how the shooting occurred or who was responsible. In English the doctor said, "Bring her these medicines." The doctor listed four. "Her chances are poor, but she is very strong and that, until now, is the only reason she lives." The doctor waffled his hands in the air, meaning fifty-fifty. "She must not be moved. Travel of any distance will kill her. *Insha'Allah*. It is in the hands."

Eddie thanked the doctor's back as the *patrona* took him out. Eddie washed Saba's face and covered her. Too pale and too cold. And too quiet. He rummaged and found another blanket. Now he'd wait in "God's hands," holding Saba's, staring at her lifeless face. Eddie looked at the ceiling. "I know you hear this all the time, but name it. Line me up for a lifetime of whatever you want. My word's good. You know that. Save her, please. Please."

The door opened. Eddie quit God and drew the .45. Doña Carmen was already inside and the door almost closed behind her. Anyone from Zionists to Brits to spacemen could come in and kill Saba because Eddie Owen just wasn't capable of mounting a defense.

"She can't move. You gotta help us."

The *patrona* floated her eyebrows without much conviction.

"I can get the drugs and money. D.J.'ll get you whatever you want. I'm not negotiating. You say it, I'll do it."

The silence stretched. The *patrona* said, "You have brought great peril to my home." The *patrona* pointed at Saba on her bed. "You know who this is, yes?"

Eddie shrugged a cautious "Maybe."

"My father was Algerian, fleeing the French from Oran to Santa Cruz; my mother . . . was not the Canarian I suggest." She offered no further explanation. "She may stay. You may not. Find the medicines. Leave them in your room by dinner tonight. I will have them removed—"

"Ah . . . the camp's guarded real well. Maybe—"

"Do as I say, yes?" No hint of discussion. "Do not come again. You will be told of her condition only when I feel it is safe. Any attempt to see her will kill us all. If you agree to this, we will try. If not, take her now."

Move her and she'd die; leave her and . . . Eddie squeezed the pistol like it would help. "How about . . . Look, promise me I'll hear something in a week, okay? Just something. You need anything between now and then—*anything*—to keep her alive, I'll get it." His voice cracked. "If . . . she doesn't make it . . . somebody'll tell me quick. You can do that?"

"Something, yes. Now go."

Eddie bent to Saba's face. "Don't die. We'll go to America. You'll be a Texas princess. Don't die; I'll take care of everything else." He eased her ring back on to her finger and kissed her so lightly on the cheek he couldn't feel her move if she had.

CHAPTER 22

November, 1938

Eddie ditched the bloody, bullet-riddled convertible outside the refinery, crept to the section of fence he'd exited, and snuck back in. Steal drugs was the mission. He avoided his room and the guards who might be there, grabbed a bottle of sulfuric acid from the maintenance Quonset, and poured half on the infirmary's rear-door lock. The bottle's other half melted the cheap locks on the medicine cabinets and filled the small infirmary with acrid smoke. Eddie bolted before it blinded him. When the smoke cleared, searching for labels in a foreign language required thirty minutes of squinting by flashlight.

The drugs had to go under his pillow. Eddie reappeared at his room with the drugs in his pockets and socks. The same guard who had looked away when Eddie and the Arab had left didn't shoot him. He looked away as if Eddie weren't there. Eddie stuffed the drugs in his pillowcase; hugged it to his chest, hoping to add his heart and soul to the medicine; then slid D.J.'s .45 under the mattress and hauled his completely exhausted self to the refinery canteen for a dawn breakfast, then a confrontation with his boss over the advance that might save Eddie's mother. Saba had to live; she just had to. And so did Eddie's mom.

Without being asked, Ryan Pearce sat at Eddie's table. Eddie clutched his steak knife.

Pearce said, "Had you Yanks goin', he did."

Eddie leaned back, adding all the distance the table allowed.

"The radio, lad, the spacemen last night." Pearce's face was lit up red and fraternal. "*War of the Worlds*. The whole of America gacked wise by a stage actor."

Right, right, someone had attacked New Jersey from the sky. "That was a trick?"

"Halloween, trick or treat. Had you Yanks for smarter." Pearce grinned and took a slice of Eddie's bread.

"Nobody bombed New Jersey?"

Pearce shook his head. "Killing 'em here, though. Someone had a go with the local sandys . . . dead, four of 'em south of here. And two Europeans, Jews they're thinkin'."

Eddie scooped his hardboiled eggs with the fork in his left hand; the meat he left alone, keeping the knife blade up between him and Pearce.

"Seen your mate Bennett? Heard he was on the island."

Eddie ate, eyes on Pearce not the eggs.

Pearce pulled at his beard. "Mr. Schroeder would like a word with you. Says it's important; the Brits he ran off may be back lookin' for another dance."

Eddie shrugged.

"The harbor out by Puerto Orotava. Asked me to drive."

"Can't do it."

"The man saved you *and* your da. And he might have to do her again. I'd be granting him the time."

Eddie pointed his knife at the refinery that employed them both. "I've got finals to run on section one and the pretest on two and three. Happy to meet him in Santa Cruz after work, say Los Paraguitas at five o'clock."

Pearce stood and cracked his knuckles. "Mind your back, lad. You're on your own and the wolf's at the door. Our German friend's why you're not nailed to her."

Eddie watched Pearce walk away, thoroughly confused by every single thing the Irishman had said.

"Ough!" Eddie's eyes blinked open. Somebody had kicked him. His boss's assistant and two plainclothes PJs with pistols stood over him. One PJ said: "Up. You are under arrest."

"Huh?"

"Up. Now."

The sun was wrong. Eddie checked his watch: six p.m. Jesus, his "nap" on the shaded backside of his two-story converter tubes had lasted six hours. He'd worked half his shift then folded; Eddie checked his watch again. Culpepper had promised the money would be in Tulsa by now—

The PJ kicked harder. "Up. Now. The American Communist, D.J. Bennett, is dead. The auto de turismo you drive last night—there are bloodstains and bullet holes. Admit what you know about both."

"*Whaaat?*"

"Tell us."

Eddie pushed his aches and bruises to standing, wiped his pants and shirt, and said, "D.J.'s not dead. And he's no Communist."

The PJ shoved Eddie hard face-first against the pipes and frisked him. The PJ's partner added handcuffs that he cinched down until Eddie's knees buckled, then spun him back, face-to-face. Their commanding officer arrived, the same Red Beret official who'd ordered the cage murder on the dock the day Eddie had arrived. He stopped twelve inches from Eddie's nose, then spoke with definition. "D.J. Bennett provided assistance and support to the International Brigades. Therefore, he is a Communist. D.J. Bennett *is* dead and two Communist Jews with him on the west road. Shot last evening with four other foreigners, Arabs all. Now you must tell me what the Arabs and the Jews and the International Brigades plan for Tenerife."

"It isn't D.J., not out there. I was just—" Eddie stopped arming his firing squad. "I was just with him."

"When and where."

"A . . . I don't know. Three weeks ago in Haifa."

Red Beret frowned and pointed at the ground. "Bennett is here. Shot dead in the back. The automobile, Mr. Owen, it is here also. Witnesses saw you at the wheel. Explain the blood and bullet holes."

"I rented it from a . . . a cab driver, drove around looking for spacemen landing. Didn't notice the blood; didn't see any spacemen, either." Eddie stomped dust from his pants. "Why am I in handcuffs? D.J.'s not dead. I know nothing about Communists and Jews or any 'Brigade.' I'm an engineer, for chrissake. And you goddamn well know it."

Red Beret slowly lowered his chin. "I will grant you one opportunity to tell me the truth, Mr. Owen. Choose to protect the red shirts and their plans for Tenerife, and I will feed you to the sea. Tonight." The PJs marched Eddie in handcuffs through the refinery to the infirmary he'd burglarized fourteen hours ago for Saba's medicines. A body was on the exam table, the skin yellow and cold, personal items piled near the shoulder, a two-finger hand outside the sheet.

"Jesus, no . . ." Eddie shut his eyes and rocked back on his heels.

Red Beret spoke. "As I said. And you will fare no better. Why is this Communist on the west road with two Jews and four Arabs?"

Eddie tried to swallow and couldn't. *D.J. can't be dead.*

"Why are the Jews fighting the Arabs here? On Tenerife? They are Palestinians, yes? Or Moroccan? All of them together in this?"

A hard slap jolted Eddie's eyes open, spraying the tears on his cheeks.

Red Beret slapped Eddie again. "The Arabs are *Comité d'Action Marocaine*? They plan an attack on the refinery, yes? What did you show them? Where will the attack come?"

Another slap.

"The Raven of Palestine shows them the way, yes? You showed her at Sitra Bahrain. At Haifa. The *Comité* brings her here. When is her attack?" Slap. "On our refinery?"

Eddie blinked at D.J. and locked his knees to stay standing. *Saba did not kill you. God is my witness that can't be true—* A gut punch doubled Eddie over. From behind, kidney punches dropped Eddie to his knees. Two PJs lurched him up by the handcuffs and into D.J.'s table. D.J.'s personal belongings splattered to the floor. The PJs beat Eddie until he collapsed. The clinic doctor shouted for them to stop. He complained about the mess they were making and a break-in early this morning they'd done nothing about.

Eddie balled and sucked air. Red Beret kicked Eddie in the hip. "And the Communist Jews? Why do the Arabs kill them and not you? We know why. The Raven uses you!"

Eddie's boss banged in through the infirmary door. He shouted Spanish at the PJs. Red Beret closed a notebook he'd opened. In English he said, "And to whom is *your* loyalty, Foreman Paulsen?" Red Beret chinned at Eddie on the floor. "That you employ and protect a dangerous red-shirt coward?"

Paulsen shouted, "I'm not an enemy! Of General Franco or Spain. We are his *partner*."

"Your *employer* is Generalissimo Franco's partner. But like this man"—Red Beret pointed across his chest at Eddie on the floor—"who I will execute tonight, *you* are an American first, one who knows *nothing* of the struggle with the Communist. On España, in Morocco, everywhere."

Foreman Paulsen marshaled calm and stood to his full six feet. "*My* employee must be released to work on the refinery's critical systems. Systems that only *Eddie* can repair and complete. Systems that are *crucial* to protecting the Generalissimo's interests on Tenerife."

Red Beret stared at Paulsen, then Eddie getting to his feet, then spoke harsh Spanish to his two officers. One unlocked Eddie's handcuffs. Red Beret told Eddie: "Make no attempt to leave the island. You will be fed to the sea. *Before* any calls can be made to Spain." The barrel of his pistol pushed Eddie's chin higher. "You are a Communist, Señor Owen. You and your *Raven* will die in my cage."

Eddie wiped blood from his mouth and nose. "Brave motherfucker, aren't you?"

Red Beret pointed out the window. "The cage." He and his two officers walked out.

Eddie turned to his boss. "Is the money in Tulsa?"

Paulsen nodded. "It's promised for today, tomorrow at the latest. The hospital will telegram as soon as they have something to tell you."

Eddie clenched his teeth. That was not a "yes." He turned to the exam table, on it a prophet the world had finally killed. Eddie sniffed at the blood dribbling over his lips and stroked D.J.'s cold forehead. Hadn't required men from outer space, although it goddamn sure should've, just a gun and mankind's all-encompassing need for murder. Tears ran down Eddie's cheeks. D.J. Bennett, West Texas cowboy, best friend and protector, explainer of worlds. Eddie tried to say thank you out loud and couldn't. Tears and blood drops spotted his arm. God damn this place and these bastards. Eddie cupped D.J.'s two-finger hand and stopped a sob by biting his lip. D.J.'s hand was cold and stiff and yellow, like he was already part of the rock. Eddie inhaled and made a silent promise, the same promise he'd made to his mother and father; turned on leaden feet; and walked empty to his room.

The drugs for Saba were gone. The *patrona's* people had displaced nothing else. Eddie mashed his pillow over his eyes, his head mostly fog, and memories, and fear of how fast and how bad things changed everywhere he'd been the last three years—Bill Reno, Hassim, Dinah Rosen, Tom Mendelssohn, now D.J. and quite possibly Saba. *Time to go home, Eddie; get Saba and D.J. and go home; let these crazy motherfuckers kill each other until they're all dead.*

Eddie began to sob. The sobs hurt everywhere there'd been punches. In the pain and tears, he finally faced what couldn't be. That D.J. had been lying on that beach road with Saba—maybe dead already, maybe not—and that Saba had used Eddie Owen to put him there.

CHAPTER 23

November, 1938

E rich Schroeder stood his suite's high terrace at the Grand Hotel Mencey. The five-story Spanish colonial hotel dominated the skyline of Santa Cruz de Tenerife in the quiet but threatening way powerful noblemen dominated their subjects. Fitting for the residence of a German who would be king. A bastard Krupp who the noble family would very soon rush to claim.

The tops of tall canary palms rustled along Schroeder's railing and brushed his hands. A salt-water breeze carried faint echoes of city life from beyond the hotel's palatial gardens. Schroeder returned to the Mendelssohn papers stacked neatly on the cherry-wood desk. His fall from grace had now ended—Thomas Mendelssohn had been correct; these papers were incendiary. Fate had kept them intact despite the best efforts of the oil companies, whose agents, posing as Zionist sympathizers in Haifa, had failed to recover the papers, then detonated the synagogue as a fallback solution. Americans had much to learn and little capacity. Schroeder's total cost had been one bribe to one Canarian national.

Schroeder traced the raised seals with his fingertips. With these papers, his climb into the hierarchy of Göring's staff would rocket. Erich Schroeder was now important in the boardrooms of the United States as well as the blood-cauldron of the desert, a man capable of destroying reputations and realigning allies— Personal triumph brought the nag of caution and stopped Schroeder's lips short of the grin. The last two men he'd shot had been identified by the PJs as Jews, no doubt chasing these very documents. And if there were two Jews, then there were more Jews. A sound jumped his eyes to his suite's door, then to his Luger. Schroeder stepped to the Luger, palmed it, and aimed at the door.

Saba Hassouneh was dead, or at death's door where he'd personally put her. But her body had not been found. Someone had helped her and that someone might save her. Doubtful, but worth a concerted effort to determine—Saba Hassouneh al-Saleh was a dangerous woman, even mortally wounded. She'd risen from the dead twice before. Schroeder had allowed the PJs to learn of her involvement. They had resources on the island that he did not. The unintended consequences of providing that information was the background check the PJs had done on Eddie Owen and his ties, albeit tenuous, to the Raven. The combination of those ties and two incinerated refineries had reestablished Eddie's place at the top of the PJs' agent provocateur pyramid.

Eddie's circumstances were rapidly strangling him. And once Eddie accepted Saba as Bennett's killer—and Eddie would—Eddie would have only Berlin to protect him and his family, and Berlin was represented by the soon-to-be king of the desert oilfields, Erich Schroeder. Schroeder found his grin again. The sound at the door became a knock—too soft to be German. He answered, "*Ja?*"

Almost a whisper. "It's Eddie Owen."

Schroeder folded the papers into the desk's drawer and mounted the narrow table by the door. Beneath the louvered transom, alone and nervous in the hallway, was Eddie Owen. Schroeder dropped to the floor, hid the Luger with his leg, and opened the door.

"Come in, my friend, come in. I was worried when you did not arrive at the café earlier this evening. Is there trouble?"

"Yeah." Eddie hurried to the middle of the room.

Schroeder motioned Eddie to a chair and took one himself; Schroeder's chair faced the door with Eddie as a shield.

Eddie remained standing. "Somebody murdered D.J. Bennett. I wanna know who. You said he was a Communist. The PJs say he's a Communist, with the International Brigades, and that I am, too. And they'll shoot me first chance they get. I don't give a fuck who thinks what; I want to know who killed D.J."

"My condolences on your friend, Communist or not. Please." Schroeder motioned Eddie to the chair. "Sit. How may I assist you?"

"Tell me who was out there on the west road last night. The PJs found four Arabs, two Europeans they say are Jews and Communists, and D.J. The PJs found a hundred 9mm parabellum shell casings in the sand and tracks that led to and from the water. The tide was out. I wasn't there but I'm willing to bet submarines were."

Schroeder nodded and kept the sympathy in his face. "Submarines? Doubtful. Pirates. Smugglers are far more likely. Both cooperate with the PJs and the Communists when a profit can be made. And unfortunately, and I mean no offense, your friend would have reason to associate with any, or all, of those parties."

"No. Bullshit. D.J. was here to protect me. Period."

"None of those I mention are trustworthy." Schroeder held up his hand. "I have heard something, although I do not know its authenticity." He paused to add concern to a well-crafted lie. "Those dead on the west road were said to be arranging a trade for papers. Papers procured in Haifa that purport to implicate Germany in mass murder. Documents that you, Eddie Owen, brought to Tenerife."

Eddie froze.

Schroeder shook his head. "No, please, Eddie. I am not angry. If these papers were true, who could blame you?"

"They're not true?"

"I have not seen them. But if they infer that Germany plans to 'murder all the Jews of Europe,' I can unequivocally assure you they are a lie."

"An American in Haifa died giving them to me . . . Pretty detailed for a lie. Blueprints to kill eleven million Jews in Europe—"

"Nonsense, my friend. Propaganda and an insult to my countrymen." Schroeder allowed his face to lose much of its compassion. "The Jews who have driven Russia to revolution and infiltrated Germany are our enemy, this is true, but they are also yours—they are a nation within any nation who hosts them. Parasites, but not a shooting enemy who must be killed, only recognized as a tribe who works against the host."

Schroeder sipped a glass of water and continued.

"Should the international Jew have his own country? I am not opposed. As long as it is not mine. Some may prefer it be America? England? Palestine?" Schroeder opened his hands and shrugged. "See the problem? Germany's plans, as *announced to the world press*, are to deport our Jews to any country that will have them. It is as simple as that."

"You don't plan to kill them."

Schroeder exhaled. "Imagine the world outcry? Our position is much better served if we offer our Jews safe passage to any of the *noble* countries that disagree with us. Within Germany there are less than four hundred thousand Jews, a flyspeck within the entire population of America or the vast empty spaces of Australia or Russia."

"Other than you, a German, who could prove the papers are fakes or real?"

Schroeder sat back, pretending to consider the question. "First, I would have to see these papers." He frowned. "Somewhere where you felt safe that I would not abscond with them. Depending upon what they depict, we could determine *where* this atrocity was taking place. From there it would be simple—have a look."

"You could do that?"

"Not could; it would be imperative that I undertake such proof in defense of my country." Schroeder paused. "Eddie, the Jews in my country do not wish to relinquish their hold and they fight accordingly. The 'religious paradise' their Zionist segment wishes to build in Palestine they undertake in the most violent of fashions. You have spoken with Saba Hassouneh. She no doubt explained the breadth and depth of the conflict—the *European* Jew murdering his way through her homeland, claiming it as his own based upon a book of rights he *himself* has written."

Schroeder read Eddie for a reaction to "Saba Hassouneh," unsure of what he saw or the depth of Eddie's interest in her as a woman. Lacking the context to press further, Schroeder could afford to wait; Saba could not have spoken with Eddie regarding how Bennett actually died. Saba was either dead or dying herself. In due time, Eddie would be told that Saba was Bennett's killer.

Eddie rubbed his face. "If the papers are real, you'll shoot me and take them. You have no choice."

"Shoot you? My God, Eddie, you understand so little. I intend to shoot *no one* over the Jews. We don't rebuild our Army and Navy because of Jews. Germany fears Russia. We must have a partnership with America. *Shoot you?*" Schroeder shook his head. "I wish to help you. Tell me how and I will."

"Tell me who killed D.J."

Schroeder nodded. "I will inquire. For now, I think it best I request an audience with the PJs at the highest possible level. In the field, you have seen their eagerness to murder. I would not find it surprising that they organized your friend D.J. Bennett's death and that they plan yours as well."

Eddie walked two miles of beach around and over rocks, through seaweed clusters and carpets of sea pigeons. The shadows that tracked him could be PJs or Brits, or just goddamn shadows. The confusion that had followed him out of Erich Schroeder's hotel had not cleared. Eddie touched D.J.'s .45 cold against his belly and veered off the beach toward the waterfront rubble of Castillo de San Cristóbal. Schroeder had known about the documents but had never asked Eddie's help to locate them. He mentioned Saba but didn't know she had been on the west road with D.J. But Schroeder might find out when he inquired about who had done the shooting. What would that mean? Saba had said she was there to kidnap D.J. For whom? Damn sure not the English. Arabs? Oil companies? Schroeder? What would Arabs or Schroeder want with D.J.? Eddie neared Plaza Iglesia and the city's lights. Dawn in one hour. He hesitated, checked the shadows for anyone watching, then sprinted into the old quarter's arched stairways and narrow slate-paved streets.

This was stupid in a big way, but he had to know if Saba was okay, had to know if she shot D.J. Eddie cut into the maze. At least anyone following him couldn't do it unseen. Eddie ran the mud-walled narrows up and around, then skidded to a stop three strides into a dead end. Children, odors of laundry, fried maize, and spicy fish stew. Santa Cruz was coming to life. Eddie backed out, veered right, and ran alleys and steps until stupid overwhelmed him and he stopped. *What? Like Saba will admit killing D.J. if she had? Your need to know is worth exposing her and Doña Carmen? Or you being kidnapped by the Brits again? Or murdered by Red Beret?*

Eddie didn't know what was worth what, but unshifting ground was mandatory. Just one little piece. One person a nonspy

Oklahoma engineer could trust. Eddie ran the list of candidates and ended with zero. That left Saba. And he was in love with her, right or wrong. *Right or wrong?* Jesus Christ, he had to be the dumbest son of a bitch on this island. Eddie cocked a hard right for a mud-brick wall. Doña Carmen saved his knuckles. She was one block up and approaching. Two Moroccans trailed her, a leather-handled canvas bag heavy in each of their hands. Doña Carmen noticed Eddie, spoke to the Moroccans, and entered a dry goods storefront alone just as it opened. The Moroccans inspected a street vendor's fruit they had nowhere to put. Eddie guessed this was a signal, or at least an opportunity.

Inside the shop, Doña Carmen glanced, then asked the shop-keeper for something in the back. He disappeared.

Doña Carmen told a huge sack of beans: "She is not well but alive. Not much longer I fear. She repeats words for which I have no translation or understanding. You are to stay away; she is in Allah's hands. I have new British customers and PJs and Germans; all sniff the ground. Some for you; all for her. Go away."

The shopkeeper returned, startled at Eddie's proximity to the *patrona*, then smiled and bowed slightly. Eddie smiled back and asked about . . . flowers? The man said no and told Eddie where he might find pink canary orchids after the sunrise.

Eddie wedged out through the Moroccans and fruit seller blocking the door and up the windblown street. Weather was com-ing and the sellers' lean-to tents fluttered as they erected them. A group of children bumped him, laughing and pointing at his lumpy face. Frustration and fate balled his hands—"kismet" the Arabs called it—Saba fading alone in a whorehouse basement . . . maybe a murderer, a victim for sure; D.J. dead in this strange volcanic oasis, Newt and his mother fighting the bankers and tired lungs for every breath in the Oklahoma dust.

Sure there was a God.

CHAPTER 24

November, 1938

Five humid days and nights had passed without a telegram from Tulsa, the hospital or the lawyer. Eddie couldn't call; he had no money in his account and there'd be none until his paycheck two days from now. And when he spent that on the five phone minutes, there'd be nothing left to send. Not knowing, not helping was killing him. Had his mom been operated on? Did the lawyer find Lois and Howard? Was Newt stable in the iron lung? If Culpepper folded or Eddie's threats to quit lost their value, the last shot for the Owen family would be Benny and Floyd, two bootleggers who were already owed a small fortune for the wrecked Lincoln and the payments to the Nadler family.

Eddie was trying to pay attention to his own safety as well as the refinery's, and having serious trouble with both. Twice the PJs had told Eddie's refinery bodyguard to leave and both times the bodyguard found somewhere else to be. This was not comforting; Eddie tried to concentrate on work that paid the bills in Oklahoma and on never being the last worker in any area where the PJs were. That included the canteen, where he was sharing his lunch with an oddly heavy assault of flies and mosquitoes—a bad sign for the volcano, according to the locals.

Eddie pushed his lunch around the plate and glanced the canteen. Animated conversation spilled across the Spanish tables. News of some kind was afoot. He asked. An Irish pipefitter explained. "A Polish Jew, no more'n a cub, shoots him a Nazi diplomat this morning in Paris, Ernst vom Rath. Krauts're barreling savage, threatening to run every Jew outta Europe if their diplomat dies."

A mosquito bit at Eddie's face. He slapped both. "Hitler's been saying that for a year. Why's that news now?"

Foreman Paulsen's assistant came to the table. The last time Eddie had seen the little bastard, he'd led the PJs to Eddie sleeping in the pipes. The assistant passed Eddie a note. The note read: *Please meet Herr Schroeder at 7:00 p.m. tonight, the gardens, Grand Hotel Mencey.* Eddie folded the note into his shirt pocket. "This your other side job? Other than working for the PJs?"

The assistant harrumphed, turned on his heel, and strode toward the office in his most official manner. The pipefitter said, "Scummers, the lot. Will work for whoever's throwin' money at 'em that day."

At seven p.m., Foreman Paulsen strongly recommended Eddie not leave the refinery. Eddie said, "Great. Let me use the phone."

"You know I can't do that. Not without authorization. Tulsa said they'd telegram as soon as there was news. That's the deal we made with Chicago."

"Then I'm going into town."

In town, Eddie now had two refinery bodyguards, both scanning the Grand Hotel Mencey's gardens. Eddie pulled a chair from Erich Schroeder's table and sat. Schroeder appeared troubled. "I have spoken with the *Policía Judicial* commander for all of the Canary Islands. My influence there is . . . *felt* . . . but not without limits. Generalissimo Franco cannot afford to lose this refinery, nor can he afford a Communist victory of the proportion its loss would represent. Consequently, Nationalist Spain is most concerned with your plans and actions." Schroeder nodded toward the four PJs who had tracked Eddie to the meeting and Eddie's two refinery bodyguards who stood just out of earshot.

Eddie said, "Thanks for trying. Who killed D.J.?"

Schroeder frowned, didn't look away, but didn't answer. He tapped his right index finger on the table. "We inhabit a harsh world, Eddie. To some degree, I realize that you know this . . . Your family in Oklahoma, your situation here, the things you have seen in the desert—"

"Yeah. Who killed D.J.?"

"The Raven. Saba Hassouneh al-Saleh."

Eddie shut his eyes.

"She was paid to kidnap him and recover the papers that her employers believed Bennett had or could produce."

"Who?"

"King Ghazi bin Faisal of Iraq, the young patriarch of the Pan-Arab Army of God. The king intended to use the papers as a tool to rid the desert of the Jew and the Briton. How he intended to do this would have been some form of byzantine blackmail only an Arab could conceive but never prosecute."

Schroeder patted at Eddie's hand. "Your brief encounters with Saba, in Saudi Arabia and Iran, were memorable events I am sure, but they cannot prepare you, or anyone for that matter, to understand the Arab, and in particular the Palestinian. Saba Hassouneh fights for a cause that consumes her soul. And her personal history . . . it is a scar that never heals. Although I doubt you can forgive her, the quest for freedom in the colonial nations outweighs her commitment to any other cause or person. These Arabs are a proud people who now scrape for food and the pity of far-off monarchs."

"Saba didn't shoot D.J." Eddie let his confusion bury half the glare. "Who said she did? Where is she?"

Schroeder formed a small, sad smile. "If it is better for you today, then no, she did not. It was an accident of her argument, one I'm sure she wishes she could take back."

"She didn't shoot him."

Schroeder allowed the silence to hang between them.

"Be very careful, Eddie." Schroeder pushed an envelope to Eddie. "I do not know where Saba is or whether she is alive or dead. Some reports say Bennett wounded her in the fight. I will be away in Munich and sadly of little benefit to you from that distance. My number there is in the envelope. Only use it in an emergency." He paused, fixing his eyes on Eddie's. "Saba did not kill your friend out of anger or disrespect. It is part of this terrible game we play. Forgive her if you can or choose to, but do not deny who and what she is. It could very easily be fatal to you as well."

Eddie's "breakfast" was presunrise after another night of watching his ceiling fan. Two PJs stood at the canteen's center pole, watching Eddie look at a cup of coffee he wasn't drinking. The canteen was empty other than the PJs and two German submariners, clean and crisp in their white T-shirts and denim jeans. The submariners weren't eating and there was no submarine near the fuel dock. Eddie's refinery bodyguards were gone. An hour later the submariners were on the gangway road where Eddie was working. Throughout the morning the two Germans were always in his field of vision if there were PJs present. Eddie did the bodyguard math. Schroeder hadn't been kidding that he was worried.

At lunch, Eddie looked inside Erich Schroeder's envelope. Schroeder's envelope had the phone number in Munich, but it also had a voucher/receipt to sign like the one Eddie had signed for the two thousand that had gone to Saint John's hospital in Tulsa for his father's surgery. The second voucher/receipt was for an additional $1,000. Nine hundred had been wired to the TB sanatorium for Eddie's mother and her surgery. One hundred dollars had gone to the Tulsa lawyer representing Eddie's little brother and sister. When they were safely in a Tulsa foster home, an additional one hundred dollars would be wired.

Eddie choked. His roughened hands covered his face and the tears as they dribbled down his cheeks. It no longer mattered if Culpepper or Standard Oil had sent the money as promised. The Owen family had a chance because a reprieve had fallen from heaven. Eddie wiped his eyes and said a prayer of thanks he didn't know he knew. Three goddamn years of hate and derision, and the one guy who comes to the dance, *unasked*, is a Nazi.

Eddie read the remainder of the note. Underneath Erich Schroeder's Munich phone number was another phone number. This one Eddie could use as a billing number for one five-minute call per week to the hospital or the lawyer in Tulsa. Eddie sprinted for Foreman Paulsen's office. Lacking direct permission from Foreman Paulsen, the foreman's assistant denied Eddie access to the phone. Eddie threw the assistant out the door, turned the lock, pried and hammered the phone cabinet until the locks snapped, then dialed the international operator. She said she would call back. While he waited, Eddie paced the trailer. The phone rang.

A nurse at the Tulsa hospital explained, "Your father is stable in the iron lung but not sufficiently strong to talk. Your mother . . . had her lung deflated this morning. She is also stable. Their prognosis is undecided and will be for the foreseeable future. The hospital and sanatorium have been paid. Your parents will remain under our care and attention—"

The connection quit.

One minute of transatlantic time remained. Eddie tried the Tulsa attorney. When the call went through, the attorney was unavailable. His secretary said the attorney would telegram Eddie the details of his siblings. They had been located at a county orphanage, not Henrietta, and were now in Tulsa, in a good foster home but it had no telephone.

The connection quit. Two calls—a week's pay had it not been for Erich Schroeder. Eddie glanced at the file cabinet that held Mendelssohn's papers. *What do I do? If the papers are fakes, I don't have to do anything. If they're real, I have to do . . . something. But what? With whom? For whom? Maybe the papers are the real reason Erich Schroeder is helping me. He wants them; he's just playing it slow. I'm so buried in everything else, I didn't see it.*

Eddie jumped to the file cabinet.

The papers were gone.

Eddie ripped through the cabinet. Every file in every drawer. The papers couldn't be gone. But they were. Eddie stumbled backward into the wall. Foreman Paulsen? His fucking assistant? The PJs? A siren wailed. A *system* siren—Eddie banged open the trailer door and bolted for the cracking tower.

CHAPTER 25

November, 1938

M obs of civilian militia rampaged through Munich's streets. Erich Schroeder's airport taxi changed direction. Parts of the city were on fire. Glass shards covered the sidewalks. Diplomat Ernst vom Rath had been murdered. By a Jew. Schroeder's skin tingled. Bands of proud young men and women brandished red swastika flags and smashed windows, shouting: "*Juden raus! Juden raus! Auf nach Palästina!*" What looked like out-of-uniform SA troopers swung ax handles, beating shopkeepers the troopers dragged into the street. Schroeder smiled at the "spontaneous" eruption of sentiment. Ernst vom Rath was a diplomat so minor most Nazis in the Foreign Service had never heard his name. Now vom Rath was a hero.

A boy dropped from the sky and thudded in front of Schroeder's taxi. The driver swerved. A girl smashed to the pavement next to the boy, her dress shredded and limbs askew. Cheers followed. Schroeder craned out his window at a rooftop crowded with Nazi youth shouting and shaking their fists at the two corpses. *Not smug any longer, are we, Juden?* Schroeder's taxi continued south, past synagogues ablaze and fire brigades sitting idle. Swastika flags billowed everywhere. More Nazi youth spilled into the streets. More *Juden*, beaten bloody, would follow.

It was a wondrous homecoming.

Schroeder demanded the taxi veer into the mayhem. The driver did, until proceeding deeper was impossible. Schroeder struggled out into the mob on Fasanenstrasse—old Jews were being run like livestock—blond boys waved flags and clubs, glass crunched under their boots . . . smoke, shouting, blood.

Schroeder pounded his fists on the taxi's hood and screamed into the sky: "*Sieg Heil! Sieg Heil!*"

His release was almost sexual. The crowd herded his *Juden* past. *His Juden* who would fertilize his desert. Where he would be king, a monarch beyond the Krupp Dynasty's imagination. Destiny had finally called and Erich Schroeder wept.

All night Schroeder listened to the reports of *Kristallnacht*, a glass-shard tornado rampaging through the streets of Nuremberg, then the Rhineland, then Vienna and what had once been Czechoslovakia. Two hundred synagogues were flame-blackened rubble. Seven thousand shops were gutted. Thirty thousand Jews had been arrested. Across the entire nation the rioters had chanted, "*Auf nach Palästina!*" Their spontaneous solution to the Jewish Question redefined the national imperative to match Schroeder's. "Jews out! Out to Palestine!" Only Hitler could have orchestrated a stronger endorsement for Schroeder's empire. Himmler be damned, the people of the Fatherland had spoken!

Two days after *Kristallnacht*, Erich Schroeder was summoned to Karinhall. There, in private, Schroeder was informed that five men had concluded a secret meeting in Munich with Reichsmarschall Göring. They discussed new options for the Jewish Question. Three of Göring's participants were Propaganda Minister Joseph Goebbels, Deputy Chief of the Gestapo Reinhard Heydrich, and

Reichsbank president Walter Funk. The two-day, nationwide riot of *Kristallnacht* had been the Jews' final indictment.

Reichsmarschall Göring received Erich Schroeder upon his arrival at Karinhall. One lamp lit Göring's study, shadowing it in faint orange. A small fire smoldered in the hearth and added neither heat nor light. The Reichsmarschall seemed uneasy, his hand massaging the obvious bloat of his right leg. The wide face peered out of the shadows; the eyes were deep set and cautious. Reichsmarschall Göring motioned Schroeder to sit. "In one day of riots, Himmler and Heydrich have filled Buchenwald with thirty thousand *Juden. Ein tag.* Goebbels succumbs to Himmler's vision, bleating their heroic headlines—an impotent cripple's way of gaining fame and protectors."

Schroeder offered the nod that was expected and nothing more. The Reichstag and the Chancellor's Hall were a king's court of vicious intrigue and constant maneuvering. Propaganda Minister Goebbels was one of Göring's many adversaries campaigning for Hitler's ear.

Göring inhaled, stretching the powdered skin of his cheeks, then leaned in for effect, focusing eyes unclouded by today's morphine. "Tonight I have fined the whole of Jewry one billion reichsmarks for inciting the riots. All Jews will be banned from German economic life and their children from our schools." Göring made no attempt to hide the pride of great men facing monumental tasks. "But this is not enough. The Führer has made his final decision. I alone am entrusted with *Endlösung der Judenfrage.*"

The words entered Schroeder's head through his chest. *Ja!*

Göring gently lifted a biplane replica from his desk. "First and foremost, I am an aviator. But the Jews, *we must finish with the Jews.* Only then may we concentrate on the air war, the aviation gasoline that vanquishes Germany's hopes or makes us gods." Göring offered the biplane on his palm between them. "Which will it be, *Oberstleutnant*? Vanquished or gods?"

Schroeder could not stop the grin. "We will be gods, Reichsmarschall. Our American progresses daily with the Spanish refinery. There were many failures by his predecessor. But *our* American is brilliant. Final tests are planned in March, four months."

Göring bellowed, "*Four*? Chamberlain flies his British spitfires in my face *now*. I see Sitra-Bahrain in my sleep. Four months is too long for Tenerife."

"The aviation gasoline made at Sitra-Bahrain is high quality, yes, but limited in amount and cannot supply the British on even a small scale. Haifa is at least a year away if you do not wish it bombed again."

Göring returned the plane to his desk and his hands to his leg. The bloated fingers matched the girth of his other appendages but in miniature. The crimson socks were a surprise even for a man known to be a peacock. Schroeder said nothing, watched the massage, and waited. Göring found the measured, threatening tone he was known for. "Himmler believes you handle the desert gasoline poorly. He and Heydrich believe you have 'other' interests or are not up to the responsibility. A 'gangster,' an 'amateur,' a 'third-class bastard of the Krupps' you were called. They politick Hess and the Führer, suggesting the Gestapo be charged with protecting the Luftwaffe's gasoline." Red blotched Göring's neck until it filled his face and the blue veins spidered near his eyes. The fat hand rose off his leg, curling into a hammer. It hesitated with a slight tremor, then smashed the desk.

The biplane splintered and he screamed: "*My Luftwaffe. Mine!*" Plane pieces sprinkled to the rug. "*My Luftwaffe, Oberstleutnant.* While I fought and bled in Germany's skies, Himmler and Heydrich made speeches to children and policed shopkeepers!"

The Reichsmarschall sucked a long, labored breath and pushed his substantial weight almost rigid in the chair. "Tenerife is crucial. Once the technology is in place, we must control it, then duplicate those modifications in Germany. *Immediately.*" Göring stabbed a meaty finger at Schroeder's face. "You must succeed before the Jews of America turn the sleeping monster against us. Tenerife will force our partners in America to end these piecemeal business negotiations and take an open stand."

"I will, Reichsmarschall. The American engineer is under my control. Should the American corporations and I.G. Farben fail you, I will not. My American will produce for Germany what others cannot or will not." Schroeder cleared his throat and stood rigid. "I have no other interests but yours and mine, and they are the same. SS Reichsführer Himmler is wrong."

Göring inhaled through the beginning of a grin.

"And should you ask for Himmler's head, Reichsmarschall, I will bring it on a plate, tonight."

Göring horse-laughed. "Such an act would be treason."

"What one would expect from a 'gangster.'"

Göring darkened. "As von Ribbentrop worried, Herr Schmitz of I.G. Farben continues to guarantee America's participation in the Blitzkrieg but fails to deliver its final components as well. In three days he travels to New York to pacify his Jew bankers in New York, then to conspire with his Capitalist partners in Detroit. I fear things in New York and Detroit are not the rose garden that Herr Schmitz reports to the Reichsbank and Berlin. You will attend Schmitz's meetings as my direct representative. The bankers you cannot mollify. Bring me their true temperament. Detroit will be different. Your 'gangster' history with the Irénée DuPont should prove . . . helpful."

"*Jawohl*, Reichsmarschall."

"The Capitalists in New York and London have invested heavily in Germany's rearmament. Their money will be lost if the Reich does not receive the aluminum supply promised from the Alcoa monopoly. Alcoa's aluminum supply is worthless without Standard Oil's synthetic rubber formulas. And without promised production quotas for truck and Panzer equipment with Adam Opel—*80 percent owned by your DuPonts of General Motors*—the rubber and aluminum will produce only bicycles. Herr Schmitz still represents that these agreements are signed and sealed, but von Ribbentrop and I fear the agreements are now pawns in the negotiation for aviation gas." Göring tapped a telegram on his desk. "Make no mistake, the Capitalists, here *and* in America, *are their own country* with no allegiance to the Reich or any other government. And *here*, their would-be Führer is Hermann Schmitz."

Göring handed Schroeder the telegram. It was signed by Fritz Kuhn, the Bundesführer of the German American Bund. "While you are in New York assessing our banker 'friends,' speak with Herr Kuhn. *Before* his rally. If Kuhn will not cease his claims that our Führer is the force behind the American Bund, silence him. The Reich can ill afford *any* unwanted attention to our handling of the Jewish Question."

"Yes, Reichsmarschall. It will be done."

Göring pointed Schroeder at a roll of plans leaning against the ornate desk. "Open those."

Schroeder did—full-size schematics and stamped originals of the Mendelssohn papers. His pulse hammered and he almost stuttered. If he were caught withholding original duplicates of these papers, he would be shot as a traitor on the same day. Such was the risk of empire.

Göring explained that SS Untersturmführer Adolph Eichmann had authored the documents—an interesting plan, actually a memorandum of modification—for the complete "removal" of Jews from Germany and Europe. There were logistical problems with Eichmann's plan, as well as political. This was to be expected.

But the memorandum had been enough for Eichmann to convince Himmler and Heydrich that deporting the Jews to Palestine for eradication there would not work. Eichmann wanted to eradicate the Jews *here*, where they were. Hence these blueprints for modifications to camps such as Buchenwald.

Schroeder considered how quickly he could kill this Adolph Eichmann.

Göring tapped a fat fingertip on Eichmann's plans. "Jews must go to Zion, to Palestine. Himmler and Heydrich are fools; they do not understand the consequence of Eichmann's plan if executed on European soil. The *Juden* must be deported to their sacred "homeland" and dealt with there, the 'great and noble' Arabs the arbiters of the Jewish fate."

"Without question, Reichsmarschall."

Göring told Schroeder that an inspection had been scheduled for him at Buchenwald with the camp commandant, Standartenführer Karl Koch. "Review the existing construction and human data carefully, then the designs for the crematoria. According to Standartenführer Koch, Eichmann's burial component for such high numbers will not work; the bodies must be burned." Göring pointed to the plans. "These test ovens could be in place by January 1, 1940—thirteen months. Should Eichmann and his SS masters convince the Führer, there will be no support for my Palestine solution." Göring tapped harder. "These test ovens must be in Palestine, built by you but in the hands of Arabs, not Germany. Palestine and the Arabs are the proper answer to the *Endlösung der Judenfrage*."

"*Ja. Ja.*" Schroeder restrained from demonstrating his joy as the wealth of the fleeing Jew poured back into his third-class bastard hands. "I agree."

•••

The last leg of Schroeder's trip to Buchenwald was from the train station in Weimar. The serene mountain road climbed north to Thüringen through dense birch, oak, and beech, ending at a fairy-tale break aflame in color. Nestled at the valley's center were the baroque ramparts and minarets of Ettersburg Castle, a grand Germanic change from the smoldering, barren bickering of Iraq; Palestine; and, most recently, volcanic, sulfur-choked Tenerife.

Downslope, Schroeder exited the car out of the castle's sight. The hard-packed ground under his boots was desolate and dead. The mid-November air was brisk, clean of any death or decay but not construction. There was much construction.

Schroeder faced the *torgebäude*, the main gatehouse. It resembled a long gray train passing through a lifeless two-story barn, half the train visible on either side. A wide center entrance had been cut into the barn's side and gated in reinforced black iron. *Jedem Das Seine* was shaped into the gate's teeth, *To Each His Own*. Affixed atop the barn was a stubby clock tower with a hole for the clock but no clock. Time wasn't important here. Buchenwald was no longer a prison.

A puffy-faced man in a white uniform continued to point and explain.

Schroeder scanned the orderly low roofs above drab, mouse-colored brick buildings. There were also frailer structures of similar dull shape, but constructed of wood and already faded in color. *Faded?* Buchenwald was a prototype and not yet two years old. Smoke rose from the chimneys of the brick buildings but none from the wood structures; they had no chimneys. He counted twenty-two concrete guard towers, three guards in each, all pointing machine guns, all intent on the inside of the camp as if trouble were a constant expectation. The towers anchored an electrified-fence perimeter. Fang-like posts curved up and out of gravel that was the fence line's foundation between each tower. Ten braids of barbed wire were strung taut through the posts. Not a jail—Schroeder had been in jails, always tall or deep medieval affairs. This was different: a square, bald scar hidden in an otherwise rich landscape, an installation with a single purpose: answering *der Judenfrage* in Germany, not Palestine.

Standartenführer Karl Koch was still babbling about efficiency and projections and problems and *Juden* and . . . Schroeder asked about the crematorium, about *the system*.

"Ah, *ja*, the system. This is the beginning of a good plan, the Eichmann plan. And none too soon." He walked Schroeder to the burial grounds. "Here four die per day—the *Juden* cannot stand honest work, only complain. When our winter comes it will be ten per day—with luck, more. But where to put them?" He fanned his hand at the forest hillside. "We have no room *now*. If these numbers were to increase"—he glanced at the plans he'd put in Schroeder's hands—"we would require quarries deeper than ours, forests wider . . . it cannot be done in the old way."

"The *system*, Standartenführer."

"*Ja. Ja.*" Koch pointed at the top of the slope inside the fence just left of the main entry gatehouse, his pride obvious. "The new crematorium will be there, built by Topf and Sons. The dream of I.G. Farben and the SS. Let the *Juden* see their future when they enter . . . others disagree and wish to trick them: an unnecessary expense." The commandant shrugged narrow shoulders almost to his ears. "What do they know in Berlin? They answer the Jewish Question from their desks."

Schroeder spent the remainder of the afternoon touring through a proposed process not unlike a stockyard, listening to Koch's complaints and suggestions. Guards moved lines of prisoners at a distance, the prisoners' breaths clouding above shaved heads and gray stripes. Koch explained construction times and costs, the collection and cataloguing of valuables. He answered questions about efficiency in hot weather versus cold, dirt versus sand, oil-fired crematoria versus coal and kerosene.

At dusk Standartenführer Koch offered wine and dinner, possibly sensing an ally at Göring's court. Schroeder accepted the invitation as he glimpsed the commandant's wife, Ilse, regal and brazen astride her chestnut stallion. It had been rumored among Schroeder's network that Ilse Koch had developed "interests" while a camp guard at Sachsenhausen and that she freely exhibited these same "interests" here at Buchenwald. While waiting to board his train to Weimar, Schroeder had considered how Ilse Koch's "interests" might be used to subvert her from Himmler's cause. Ilse Koch properly terrified or rewarded, or both, could be a useful informant on Himmler's progress to steal Jews from their rightful owner.

It was said that Ilse Koch had a taste for death on a . . . personal scale, unlike Himmler, whose interest was sociopathic, empty of pleasure. Himmler was in the *business* of eradication. Schroeder's interest in death was no less patriotic, only more directed. He was about the *harvest*, the financial transfer *caused* by eradication.

Dinner with Standartenführer Commandant Koch and his young wife was average and long, the potatoes not firm and the roast meat no better than the Spanish beef on Tenerife, a disappointment that Frau Ilse was not. While Commandant Koch pontificated on the Jewish Question, his wife entertained long glances at Schroeder, finishing the last by wetting her lips and touching a napkin's corner to her bodice. Koch drank heavily throughout all three courses until he openly railed about *the fools of Berlin*, then fell into a mushy stupor. Ilse had glanced at her husband only occasionally, her eyes focused on Schroeder and mostly his mouth, her white teeth biting at a lower lip she now caressed with a sliding fingertip.

Schroeder saw a woman of large appetites and too little fear. Frau Ilse could be useful, but her lack of fear would become problematic. One day there would be a reckoning for those members of the Reich who confused the Aryan birthright to empire with Roman excess or unrestrained perversion.

"You are an art collector, Frau Koch?" The *skin* rumors.

The commandant bellowed, thrashing his hands, the words unintelligible. Servants approached to assist him to the stairs. Ilse Koch barked, ordering them out. Both veered as if on rollers. She smiled at her husband, his head rolling on stooped shoulders.

"My husband tells me you are Reichsmarschall Göring's aide de camp? His man in America and the Middle East. An important position for such a young man."

She was younger than he. Schroeder smiled and sipped a bland Riesling.

Ilse Koch continued. "I have heard . . . other things. That you may be a man to be feared." She grinned as a wolf might. "And in our Führer's Reich this would be quite an accomplishment, *ja*?"

"What is it like, Frau Koch, for a beautiful young woman around the camps? Do you spend most of your time away, riding in the forests? The commandant must be a lonely man."

She purposed a small shiver and then a smile. "A woman and her horse have a . . . rhythm, Herr Schroeder." One finger toyed with a throat locket. "But a horse and a man's leather saddle is not a man." She showed him her teeth and her neck. "A horse would be better, if not for his weight."

Schroeder watched her lean back and sip the Riesling, and her husband sink deeper into the alcohol. She was flushed and only partly by the wine and tossing her red hair.

"You have an interest in . . . art, Frau Koch?" He glanced at her table lamps. The rumors.

"Tattoos." She wet her lips. "Skin."

"And you have some to show me?"

A wry red line smiled across her face. "We do not yet know each other that well."

"But we could?"

She glanced toward her husband asleep in his chair. Her hand slipped below the table and her eyes locked on his at the table's other end. "There is a . . . texture to skin." Her breath shortened. "A taste." The rhythmic movement of her hand beneath the table was mirrored in her shoulder. Schroeder watched her and she let him, working faster as she gained his full attention, the flush filling her face.

"And you like this taste, Ilse?"

"Yes." She almost couldn't get the word out. "*Ja.*"

Schroeder's participation was measured, enjoying Frau Ilse's sexual gambit as one might a Berlin cabaret performance. She pressed forward hard against the table, her arm and hand feverish below. Schroeder felt the beginnings of an erection. Did Frau Ilse want him to rape her while her husband watched? Schroeder registered "rape" and retreated instantly into his military persona. Frau Ilse saw the anger in his eyes at his loss of control and mistook it for participation. She climaxed with a yelp, her blue eyes rolling almost to white.

The commandant slurred unconscious nonsense in response, then screamed in a nightmare. Servants charged into the dining room. Ilse Koch was a brilliant red and unembarrassed. The servants assessed commandant and wife, then Schroeder. Ilse Koch beamed at him from across the table, a bitch satisfied that she had drained the strongest male, stronger now because she had prevailed.

The commandant yelled again and was patted into quiet submission by the servants. Ilse allowed him to be led away by waving her hand. When the servants were gone, she said, "Reichsmarschall Göring should know the full possibilities of this camp and others. My husband struggles..." She glanced at his wineglass. "I do not. We have learned there will be newer, more modern *Vernichtungslagers*, annihilation camps. I would be well placed there."

Schroeder nodded and concentrated on being king. His assessment of Frau Ilse had been accurate, but her possible participation as a spy in Himmler's camp must be managed with due caution.

"What do you know of these annihilation camps?"

Ilse Koch leaned at him, uncompromised and bold, her breasts squashed against the table. "I know that only Himmler's apostates are being considered to manage these camps."

Schroeder stared and she returned it, the heat still in her face but her interest transposed to matters beyond the reach of her fingers. Schroeder said, "These . . . special camps could be constructed throughout Germany or beyond . . ."

Frau Ilse stiffened, defiant and proud. "And they will be . . . Wherever the Reich is forced to go in defense of the Fatherland, there will be Jews who own the banks and control the population."

"And?"

"Those Jews will meet the same fate as Jews who come here to Buchenwald. Their property will revert to the Reich."

Schroeder nodded, his concern hidden. Either Frau Ilse had read his mind or she was bolder than even he had estimated. She was offering a partnership, a spy who would know Himmler's and Eichmann's gambits against a Palestine solution long before Schroeder would. Frau Ilse was willing to side with Göring against Himmler, a very, very risky proposition, and likely willing to sacrifice her husband in the process. Something she'd happily demonstrated at dinner.

Schroeder stood to excuse himself. Whores were useful but rarely good partners. Ilse rose with him, smiled, and offered her hand. Schroeder grabbed her hair and slammed his free hand between her legs, then her against the wall. He spoke to her quietly and from one inch away. "I am . . . willing to consider your generous offer." He squeezed at her crotch until she winced her eyes shut. "As will the next man through your generous bed. When you know Eichmann's plans, we will do our business." Schroeder let go and her knees buckled. There seemed to be a smile under the pain.

CHAPTER 26

November, 1938

E rich Schroeder had flown all day and much of the night to America and now stood outside Madison Square Garden at the 50th Street entrance. Massed around him were twenty thousand American Nazis preparing to attend Fritz Kuhn's German American Bund rally inside. Ringing the American Nazis were fifty thousand agitators of every color and political persuasion. They jeered with bats and clubs and placards. Two thousand armed New York City policemen formed a skirmish line, all of it being documented by reporters from every major paper in the United States.

From the left: "Nazi bastards!"

From the right: "Rosenfeld's Jew Republic!"

The early stages of riot. Schroeder had warned Fritz Kuhn earlier today in his Yorkville headquarters that tonight's rally must not happen—a direct command from Reichsmarschall Göring. Kuhn had argued and lied and finished a fifth bier. Kuhn said his mandate came direct from Hitler, that the Führer wished America to know it

need not kowtow to the Jews, that soon Roosevelt would be dead and his Communist-dominated Jew trade unions with him.

"Nazi murderers!"

Shoulder-to-shoulder with the police, German-Americans in storm trooper uniforms rushed past Schroeder to push back the Communists, Jews, and New Yorkers looking for trouble. The photographs would be front page. Schroeder did not see how the spectacle could be worse.

Inside the hall, it *was* worse. The mammoth stage was backed by one hundred uniformed Nazis and a five-story banner of George Washington embraced by Bund flags. Martial music blared. It was Hitler's Nuremberg rally recreated in New York. The crowd roared at Fritz Kuhn proud and bold on the stage:

Sieg Heil!

Sieg Heil!

Salutes snapped—stiff arms, black uniforms, and red swastikas. Twenty-five thousand screamed, "*Sieg Heil!*"

Fritz Kuhn boomed: "Henry Jew Morgenthau takes the place of George Washington! We are in trouble, my friends."

"*Sieg Heil!*"

Kuhn shook his fist, mimicking Hitler. Schroeder scanned the crowd, as angry and bitter as the poorest sections of the Fatherland. A man lunged onto the platform, clawing toward Kuhn, and was beaten to the wood, subdued, then thrown off to the police.

Kuhn railed: "The Jews! The Jews send their assassins!"

Schroeder made a field decision amid the shouts and shoulders. It would be "Jews" who would murder Fritz Kuhn and his top lieutenants, the lieutenants first. Göring's message would be clear within the Bund leadership. And the remainder of the world would see the International Jew defending "his" territory.

Schroeder stopped at a new thought, stunned he hadn't come to it previously—the same "Jew-Communist agitators" should injure Eddie Owen's family. Burn down the farmhouse, kidnap or kill a sibling, possibly a parent in the hospitals. Eddie had not delivered the Jews their salvation, the Mendelssohn papers, and now, he could not. The Jew would punish Eddie mightily for this transgression and his work for the Fascist oil companies. Schroeder nodded, surrounded by bellowing American Nazis. Additional murders in America required sanction; Reichsmarschall Göring understood murder.

Schroeder shoved through the hall toward the exit nearest Jack Dempsey's restaurant on Broadway. Over dinner, a plan could be constructed, then a phone report to Berlin that Kuhn had not listened to reason. The sanction to kill or kidnap a member of the Owen family could then be requested, adding further pressure to the FBI's threats Schroeder believed were about to land on Eddie on Tenerife. Collectively, that should be sufficient to push Eddie Owen gratefully to Berlin the day after Tenerife was finished. And once there, Erich Schroeder would again be Eddie Owen's salvation.

From his long set of windows at the St. Regis Hotel, Schroeder sipped a sherry and marveled at how Central Park resembled Tiergarten in Berlin. Jack Dempsey's restaurant had proven too close to the rally and its inevitable riot. Behind Schroeder on his desk, CBS radio broadcasted Father Charles Coughlin and the final minutes of his *Golden Hour of the Little Flower* live from Royal Oak, Michigan. Schroeder was not a Christian, nor a devotee of radio preachers, but he listened anyway.

The Catholic priest sounded much like Fritz Kuhn pounding his podium, the priest railing at a radio audience Father Coughlin claimed was 40 million: "Roosevelt is the great liar and betrayer! Must the entire world go to war for six hundred thousand *German* Jews? Jews who fail to use the press, the radio, and the banking house— where they stand so prominently—to fight *communism* as vigorously as they fight *Nazism?* These Jews *invite* the charge of being supporters of communism."

Schroeder snorted at the radio. Jews. They multiply like vermin; now there were six hundred thousand, not four. Always the Jews—Schroeder glanced at the briefcase that held the Nazi plan for the Jews. And smiled. The radio changed voices. A self-important newsman intoned that today had been a banner day for speeches: Adolf Hitler had spewed an astonishing anti-Semitic diatribe in the Reichstag, warning the world that he would "exterminate the Jewish race in Europe if another world war broke out—for they alone would be the cause."

Schroeder was dumbstruck. Impossible. Hitler, even in his rage, would not undertake such an enormous tactical risk. Yes, it was true the Jews would be the cause, but the concept of "extermination" was to forever be the "Zionist lie," not Nazi *policy.* Nazi ambassadors and conspirators still had to deal with skittish Capitalist profiteers who lacked a commitment to *solution*, committed only to *money*. Schroeder palmed a letter opener as he would a fighting knife. He would swear Hitler had been misquoted, that was the answer. Misquoted by Jews who controlled the airwaves and newspapers.

Thankfully, there were prominent Americans who agreed with Father Coughlin. On the front page and inside the three newspapers that covered the desk in Schroeder's suite, Texas Congressman Martin Dies—chairman of the powerful House Un-American Activities Committee—strongly supported Hitler's stance on the Bolshevik threat and said nothing to demean the Fascist agenda.

A free thinker, Congressman Dies, unafraid of Jew influence. Illinois Congressman Stephen Day and Senator Burton Wheeler of Montana had waffled on their anticipated support but vehemently underwrote neutrality, adding that the globe already had 35 million men under arms and needed no more. Schroeder gouged the letter opener into the senator's eye.

Tomorrow, before boarding a train to Detroit, Hermann Schmitz would "pacify" his Jew bankers worried for their investments with steel magnate Fritz Thyssen and the remainder of the Ruhr Valley coal and steel monopolies, investments underwritten with the profit opportunities Hitler and Göring had promised in a war with Russia but had not delivered. And could not deliver without the final components for aviation gas. Schroeder smiled and kept the letter opener's point in the senator's eye. Schmitz and his Jew bankers and the Detroit industrialists would be a difficult mission. Rich men always feigned armor whether they had it or not. Mendelssohn's papers and Eddie Owen would reduce that armor to fishnet.

On Tenerife, Eddie was making his second call using Erich Schroeder's billing number. There'd been a fair amount of anger over Eddie trashing the phone cabinet, but not enough that Foreman Paulsen felt like tossing Eddie to the PJs. After the refinery was final tested might be another matter. The foreman's phone rang. Eddie jumped. The international operator said she had Eddie's party on the line.

"Pop! Dad? It's Eddie. How are you?"

The phone crackled. Newt's voice was weak, almost a whisper, not the man behind the plow. "We're fine, Eddie, just fine. Just fine."

"Mom? Is she okay?"

Static. "She's at the sanatorium. Good, I understand, but hard for her to talk, and I'm stuck in this machine. We'll be good again, you'll see. Lois and Howard were up yesterday. Good family they're with. We'll be good again, Eddie, don't you worry. The farm, too."

"I love you, Pop." Eddie was crying. "Tell Mom."

"We know, Eddie, we're proud; you pulling these strings from so far away. Proud, Eddie, proud."

"I've got it, Pop. Don't worry. Just get better. I've got everything else. Stay as long as you want. Just get better. I can call next week."

The operator said, "One minute remaining."

Newt coughed. The phone was silent. A woman's voice said, "Mr. Owen, your father needs to rest now; thank you for calling long distance."

"Wait—" The phone went dead. Eddie wasn't done; he needed to know more, to understand, to make it better—

Forman Paulsen's assistant shouted and pounded on the door. Eddie slowly cradled the receiver. His hand shook and he wiped his eyes. Since Schroeder had been gone, Eddie'd been on station sixteen hours a day. A series of his predecessor's undiscovered, unsanctioned shortcuts had come close to killing everyone at the refinery three times. The cataclysmic possibilities kept Red Beret at bay and Eddie's thoughts out of Doña Carmen's basement where Saba had been trying not to die for thirteen days. After Foreman Paulsen's repeated requests, the PJs had allowed Eddie to bury D.J. One of Tom Mendelssohn's people may have been at the cemetery. The man attempted to engage Eddie. The PJs drew guns and arrested the man. Eddie asked after him the following day; the man had not made it to the jail. If the man were from Tom Mendelssohn and still alive, any further interest from Eddie would surely get him killed.

The refinery's three trips to catastrophic implosion also kept Eddie's thoughts out of the file cabinet that no longer held Mendelssohn's papers. The foreman's assistant was the likely culprit—at the very least the little bastard was on somebody's payroll to spy on the foreman. Or it was Foreman Paulsen himself who'd found the papers. He could've stumbled onto the file by accident. The trailer door bowed from the pounding. Eddie swept open the door, brushing Forman Paulsen's assistant back. The assistant shouted rapid-fire demands at Eddie's back as Eddie walked toward the canteen.

Two sweaty blue suits arrived at Eddie's table before he could inhale a fast lunch. The foreman's assistant and two PJs escorted them. Both men showed IDs signed by J. Edgar Hoover. The taller of the two explained they were special agents of the FBI, sent here at the request of three United States senators, gentlemen from the nonindustrial South who held strong beliefs concerning the Dies Committee—the House Un-American Activities Committee.

Eddie motioned the men to sit if they chose. "Never heard of the Dies Committee, sorry."

Both agents glanced at the German submariners at the next table, then sat, and the taller agent continued his introduction. "The three senators believe we face a Fascist threat wielded by major US business interests north of the Mason-Dixon Line. Mr. Dies and his committee are whitewashing this threat. The senators have evidence that you, Mr. Eddie Owen, late of Texas—as is Representative Dies—is in league with the Nazis to the expanding detriment of the American way of life. The senators demand your return to the US by consent, or *otherwise*, where you will testify in person." The agent sat back. "While neither myself, nor Special Agent Johnson, are anxious to violate any US laws, in time of great peril to the nation we are Mr. Hoover's to command."

Eddie considered the indictment, the fact he was the piñata, not the captains and the kings. "Tell Mr. Hoover I won't be missing work to play political football."

"The choice isn't yours to make."

Eddie felt the anger rising with the color in his face. "Thirty-five hundred miles is a long trip to threaten one engineer. Maybe you protectors of the nation should've gone to New York."

The shorter agent said, "Meaning?"

"Where the goddamn money is." Eddie went back to his lunch.

The shorter agent tapped in front of Eddie's plate. "We have bank records and hospital records from St. John's hospital in Tulsa,

Oklahoma. Start with those, Mr. Owen. Make us believe you won the money downtown at the casino."

Eddie narrowed his eyes at the connection to his family. "Can't say I'm that interested in making you believe anything." Eddie dropped his fork. "And if you'd like to finish today with all your teeth, I'd leave my family out of whatever else you have to say."

"I would've thought you smarter." The agent's Princeton accent matched his words. He flipped three pages of a folder. "Class president, valedictorian, top engineer, light heavyweight boxing champion. No trouble to speak of . . . Wait, what's this, an oil derrick *explosion*? And you received substantial compensation?" He looked up. "Was that your *first* workplace explosion, Mr. Owen? Before the Sitra refinery and the Haifa refinery?"

Eddie said *fuck you* with his eyes.

The agent nodded and returned to his folder. "Then— Wait, what's this?" The agent touched his partner's arm. "An outstanding warrant in Montague County, Texas? And serious, too. Felony manslaughter. And damn, a fugitive warrant to boot. That's federal, unless you haven't left Texas." He smiled at Eddie. "We're not in Texas, are we?"

Eddie nodded at the volcano. "Nope."

"Mr. Hoover will allow you to return by consent. Or in handcuffs if you decline."

Slight rumble from Mount Teide. No response from Eddie. Behind his anger, Eddie had just been hit with the last nail in the coffin. Like D.J. had said, Eddie Owen and AvGas could end up being everyone's solution or everyone's villain. The line would be so fine it wouldn't bear trying to hold it.

The agent screwed his eyes into confusion. "Did I miss something in my presentation?" The agent turned to his partner, who shook an athlete's blockish head, then back to Eddie. "Crossing state lines in flight makes your Texas offense federal. That makes you ours. Pack your bags; we're leaving."

Eddie said, "We're in the Canary Islands—if I had a map I'd show you. So far these belong to General Franco, so you'll need a note or something from him."

Hard frown and squared jaw, just like in the newsreels. "You won't go willingly?"

"My people are in the hospital. Remember?" Eddie worked on a civil tone he didn't find. "You don't pay their bills; this job does. I intend to keep it."

"Erich Schroeder. German national. You know him?"

"Yeah, I know him."

"And what is your association?"

"He saved me from some Brits who thought drowning me would help save the Empire."

Both agents waited, the athlete with his pen near a pad.

"I ran into him in Iran last year; our plane crashed coming from Bahrain. Then I ran into him here after Haifa. Far as I know, he's gone."

"That it?" The athlete made notes.

Eddie didn't answer.

"Mr. Schroeder is Reichsmarschall Hermann Göring's man in America. Hermann Göring runs the Nazi Luftwaffe. To start a war and win it, Göring's Luftwaffe requires aviation gas." The agent chinned at the refinery's cracking tower Eddie was retrofitting to safe and productive. "Aviation gas is what you do."

"Classified, sorry."

The agent reddened. "Should there be a war, anyone dealing with Mr. Schroeder—aiding and assisting the enemy—would be an act of sedition, treason. That's the death penalty, Mr. Owen. Here, Texas, or anywhere we can find you."

"Good to know you speak for President Roosevelt, that we're not neutral anymore. We've sided with the Russian *Communists* against the Nazis. Do I have that right? When does the war actually start? Mr. Hoover knows, right? He told you?"

The agent rolled another page. "What is your association with Floyd Merewether and Lester Benny Binion?"

Shrug. "I write them a letter once a month, but you probably know that, the mail being federal and all."

"Mr. Merewether is the prime suspect in nine gangland shootings. Mr. Binion is a bootlegger and a gambler, but they both seem to maintain a continuing interest in you. How could that be, Mr. Owen? Could it be that you are selling Texas oilfield information that they gather to the Nazis?"

"You read my letters. You know what's in them."

"Are you a Communist, Mr. Owen?"

"Are you a Fascist?"

The agent's frown flattened and he removed an envelope from his jacket. Eddie recognized his mother's handwriting. The agent riffled it through his fingers the way card players at Pappy Kirkwood's did poker chips. The letter had been opened. The agent folded it back into his pocket and smiled.

Eddie glared. "Ever been in Oklahoma? Got any goddamn idea what the Dust Bowl's like?"

"Have you ever been to prison, Mr. Owen? The Luftwaffe just test flew their Messerschmitt Bf 109 with 'Grade C3' fuel. Dark green, 100 octane. Their plane ran four-hundred-plus miles per hour armed heavy, and four hundred miles before it blew up. I guess the gas you're making here is just about ready?"

Eddie said, "Maybe Bahrain gas runs dark green; you're FBI–know-every-goddamn-thing; maybe somebody stole some; you should ask. Whatever we're doing *here*, we're still *testing*. We haven't made a drop. And for the record, this plant belongs to CEPSA, Standard Oil, and others. If you don't like what they're doing, or who they're doing it with, talk to them."

"The owners of this plant's problems are theirs. Yours and mine, Mr. Owen, are ours, and they require your attention. Now."

Eddie nodded at the submariners. "You won't be doing the Lindbergh baby. I've been through that with your good guys, the Brits. They grabbed me right where we're sitting. I can assure you that won't happen again."

"Mr. Owen, you are going to the embassy in Morocco, then to Washington to appear before the House Un-American Activities Committee. The dissenting southern senators will put you under oath. If you do not cooperate fully, the FBI will deliver you to Texas to stand trial for unlawful flight and felony manslaughter." The agent closed the folder. "Your physical condition when you begin your trip to Washington is up to you."

The two FBI men shared a cell in the Santa Cruz jail. Eddie went to see them on the third evening of their incarceration. Two PJs and two German submariners followed Eddie inside. Eddie spoke through the bars. "I warned you not to grab me. You're lucky the submariners put you on the ground. The PJs would've killed you. May still, since all they got to do was kick on you some."

The tall one looked thinner already but no friendlier.

"Food's good, huh?" Eddie pushed two pounds of wrapped beef and peppers through the bars. "From the canteen."

The agents accepted without saying thanks. Eddie pushed an opened bottle of Madeira wine through. The tall one shook his head; his athlete sidekick grabbed it.

"Show me my mom's letter and you can ask me the rest of your questions." Eddie pulled a stool close to the bars so the Armada jailers he'd bribed couldn't listen.

The FBI agents checked the same two German submariners who had protected Eddie in the canteen. The tall agent held up a piece of beef. "Not bad." His sidekick nodded agreement. "How much are those Nazis paying you?"

"Show me the letter."

The agent pushed it through the bars. The letter was dated a week after his father's surgery and written with the lightest touch of his mother's hand Eddie had yet seen. Newt had survived thanks to Mr. Schroeder's doctor and friends. Eddie's mother added that she was in "quarantine" because of the consumption and about to have her lung deflated so it could heal, and that the Germans seemed to be really fine fellows who couldn't be who the government men said they were. She guessed these government men might be working for the bank even though their wallets said FBI. She'd heard about the FBI, of course, some years back chasing and killing the Floyds' boy, Charley, all the way from Oklahoma to Ohio for burning bank mortgages and running wild with John Dillinger.

Eddie heard his mother's soft voice in the weak handwriting, her need to see hope and goodness in almost everyone. Her letter went on to say that the weather was still killing everything; God had moved to somewhere else who needed Him more, God bless those poor souls. But even the tractor cotton on the bank farms here was going black. A few folks had straggled back from California saying they was the meanest people God had ever made. Bitter mean like February, called everybody "Okie" or "Red," paid almost nothing, and burned you out or beat you senseless if you complained.

Praise God and Eddie's hard work that they'd held on in Oklahoma and that the federal bank hadn't been able to run the family out. Eddie's mom didn't mention Howard or Lois, who at that time were lost in the orphanage system as wards of the state. She thanked Eddie again for his paycheck and the German's help; asked about the islands, volcanoes, and the desert, and his great friend D.J. Bennett; told Eddie she loved D.J. like D.J. was rain and to be good as he could.

The agent snatched the letter. "How much are the Nazis paying you?"

Eddie waved the agent to return his mom's letter and all it didn't say.

The agent slid the letter into his pocket. "Aid and assistance, Mr. Owen. Mama does like her Germans."

"Yeah? Did you offer to help save her husband or children? Her farm? Her life?"

The agent winced sympathy. "Treason is treason, old woman or young . . ."

Eddie leaned back, the violence in him less a surprise now than three years ago. "You, ah, may not want these fellas to let you out."

"Why, Mr. Owen, are you considering an assault on a federal agent?"

"No, I'm thinking about killing the coward motherfucker and his partner. That's how we Nazis do it out here in the bush."

"How much are your new friends paying you to sell out your country?"

Eddie wiped his mouth with the back of his hand, eyes hard and narrow, thinking very bad thoughts. "I. Didn't. Sell. Anyone. Anything."

The agent shook his head. "Two problems with that. First, the Nazis gave you at least two thousand dollars. Second, Göring had enough AvGas to test his planes—set a speed record, by the way."

"So goddamn what? Why's that illegal?"

"Eddie Owen is a *very special* petroleum engineer. As I informed you, it is against federal law to provide aid and assistance to the enemy."

"Did the FBI somehow miss Standard Oil and Vacuum Oil?" Eddie pointed out the small cell window toward the refinery. "They own the goddamn place *and* the formulas."

"Mr. Hoover is aware of that. William E. Dodd, the US ambassador to Germany, recommended Roosevelt try them for treason. Ambassador Dodd is that dead-sure we are going to war."

Eddie jolted. That was news.

The agent ate a bite of beef and chinned toward the refinery. "What do Binion and Merewether have to do with Tenerife?"

"Nothing."

"Merewether got you out of Texas. He works for Binion in Fort Worth, just like you did. The southern senators on the House Un-American Activities Committee tie all of you in with Representative Dies, all of you from Texas. Dies is directing the Committee exclusively at Communists. Not a single substantive investigation of the Fascists. Harold Culpepper is on the record as favoring the Fascists. Erich Schroeder *is* a Fascist, and you're taking money from both Culpepper and Schroeder."

"Floyd Merewether and Mr. Binion have nothing to do with whatever it is I've stumbled into back home and over here. Floyd and Mr. Binion put gas in their cars, that's it."

"Is Binion taking money from Culpepper and Schroeder, too?"

"No. I mean—"

"You mean you are and Binion isn't." The agent continued. "Your family in Oklahoma isn't the only one suffering. So when you take the Nazi blood money, think about the planes, the bombs they'll carry, how many are going to die to keep your people healthy and happy." The agent stood to the bars to back Eddie away. "The US ambassador will have us out shortly and your Spanish Fascist friends will put us on the ferry. But forty-eight hours after that, you can count on us being back and we won't be talking then."

Eddie hadn't moved. "I didn't tell or sell anyone anything."

"The Nazis gave you money because you're pretty? Or was it the Communists, Mr. Owen, the International Brigades favored by your dead friend D.J. Bennett and his Zionists?"

"See what I mean? You guys are doing Abbott and Costello's routine, *Who's on First?* How am I supposed to know the difference between the Nazis, Communists, and run-of-the-mill Fascists? How would I know if you experts can't tell?"

Eddie leaned into the bars, his teeth bared.

"I've been over here three years—Bahrain, Iran, Palestine, Tenerife—I can't tell the *teams*, let alone the players." Eddie jerked the wine bottle back through the bars and smashed it on the floor. "And neither can your fucking boss, J. Edgar." Eddie jammed his face into the bars. "And know this, motherfucker: you come after my family and I'll make a deal with whomever I have to. You'll be dead the same goddamn week."

Eddie stormed out of the Santa Cruz jail into one of the two PJs and knocked him down. His partner drew. The German submariners charged. Eddie bolted into a side street and ran till he hit Calle San Jose. Les Demoiselles was across the street. He started to cross, intending to kick in the alley door and demand a goddamn answer about D.J.—

A man huffing and puffing stepped in front of him. Between breaths, the man said, "Tom Mendelssohn"—huff, puff—"you must talk to me."

"Me? I'm not Tom Mendelssohn."

"Dinah Rosen, you, Tom Mendelssohn. Standard Oil."

Eddie pulled him into the alley and looked both ways. "You gotta be careful. I have PJs all over me."

"Our papers. You have them ready to use?"

"No. I hid them. They're gone."

"Gone?" The man straightened into Eddie's face. "This cannot be. No, you have them."

Eddie stepped back and looked both ways again. "Man, I'm sorry, but I couldn't keep them on me forever. I had to hide them and—"

The man aimed a gun at Eddie's chest. He was no longer panting or challenged in any way. "You will give me the papers."

"You're right, I would, but I don't have them."

"Who, then? Who has our papers?"

"*Maybe* my foreman's assistant. I hid them in the office. I think he found them and . . . Shit, I don't know what he did with them, *if* he's the one."

The man wagged the pistol. "Come with me."

"No. If I go anywhere with you, you're dead."

"Doubtful. But you will be dead here if you do not come."

The two German submariners sprinted into the street. Behind them, two of the PJs struggled to keep pace. Eddie turned back to the man with the gun and he was gone.

An hour after Edie's return to the refinery, Foreman Paulsen told Eddie that if he left the refinery again, for any reason, he would be docked two days' pay and upon his return he would be held under house arrest.

Schroeder and I.G. Farben's president boarded the New York Central's *Twilight Limited* together. Schmitz remained aloof, livid over Schroeder's presence in the banker meetings, chose to dine alone, and retired to his Pullman sleeper compartment immediately after dinner. It was not surprising that Herr Schmitz was troubled. The bankers for the Ruhr Valley Capitalists had not been "pacified." The bankers suspected what Reichsmarschall Göring suspected and made it clear that no more capital would be advanced for factories and infrastructure until I.G. Farben could produce *all* the agreements for the promised aluminum, synthetic rubber, and high-octane gasoline. "Germany," it was said in the meeting, "will not survive the spring thaw of the coming Russian winter. Germany's only defense against Stalin's three-million-man army is Hitler's blitzkrieg offense, an offense that cannot be sustained without proper materiel."

The *Twilight Limited* arrived Detroit on time. Schroeder and Schmitz stepped off the train; Hermann Schmitz was received with great veneration. Erich Schroeder was not. Unknown to Schroeder, he had been deemed an attaché by Schmitz. Schroeder was forced to demand a seat at the meetings, announcing that he was a direct emissary of the Third Reich and Reichsmarschall Göring. Schroeder's treatment improved to a quiet, if distant, respect. A greater, somewhat personal surprise was that he was not lauded nor welcomed by Irénée DuPont's representatives from Adam Opel.

For two days, Hermann Schmitz argued, cajoled, threatened, and bribed and finally secured the agreements for aluminum supply, synthetic rubber formulas, and "war volume" production quotas for truck and Panzer equipment. During the heated exchanges, there had been open criticism of Hitler's rhetoric, a demand that Hitler tone down relative to the Jews and remain focused on the Communists. A *demand*? Schroeder was shocked but hid it. These industrialists were not fools— And then he saw it. Hubris. These captains of industry believed their corporations would still hold power when the Nazis completed their rise. So, in the end, the industrialists were fools. Men like Göring and Himmler were the new gods, men who could march armies and incinerate races.

The final components and formulas for AvGas production were an unknown. Schroeder conveyed this to Reichsmarschall Göring by diplomatic courier, and that as Göring's direct representative, he had been excluded from a private meeting last night where AvGas and its ramifications had been discussed. Schroeder also conveyed that when confronted, I.G. Farben's president had denied any such meetings had taken place, and he refused to discuss AvGas further.

Schroeder quoted Schmitz as saying, "You are an *emissary*, Herr Schroeder, a placeholder for Göring, not a decision maker. You have no seat at the table with the true hierarchy of the Reich."

Schroeder had masked his anger and deep offense at the rebukes.

"Adolf Hitler, *the Führer of the German people*, sees the world's future in the same clear light as Reichsmarschall Göring and those of us who have spilled and shed blood for the Fatherland. Blood that you and your partners now wade in to reap your rewards."

Schmitz's answer was sharp and remedial. "Hitler's tone must be muted or the Jews in America will continue to gain ground, slandering Germany, robbing the Reich's industrial partners of the will required to . . ." Schmitz had stopped short of discussing the assassination of Roosevelt and the crematoria plans. Plans that Schroeder knew firsthand to be the International Jew's future.

The *Twilight Limited* trudged east toward New York through the first blizzard of 1938. In the dining car, Schroeder read Detroit newspapers and sipped cognac, watching America silenced in white. The newspapers reported that Franco's war with Spain's crumbling government was proceeding well, although the reporters were confused by the Red Cross charge that Tenerife held none of the Republican (Communist) prisoners and dissidents the Fascists had sent there. The Red Cross charge estimated more than 100,000 prisoners were missing.

Fritz Kuhn and his disastrous Bund rally were no longer on page one, at least in Detroit where the International Jew was less popular and powerful. The wayward Herr Kuhn would be dealt with after Eddie Owen and Berlin were called from the German embassy in New York. Reichsmarschall Göring would be pleased with the three contracts from Alcoa, Standard Oil, and Opel. But gauging the Reichsmarschall's reaction to the AvGas status would hinge on what had actually transpired in the secret meeting. Schroeder's supreme and divine hope was that the final AvGas elements had been withheld by Standard Oil, making the Mendelssohn papers and Schroeder's hold on Eddie Owen valuable beyond calculation.

Schroeder unfolded a copy of the *Dearborn Independent* procured while in Detroit, Henry Ford's "private" weekly suspended in 1927. A shame the Jews had forced the newspaper out of publication. The Jews' response to Ford's exposure of the worldwide Jew conspiracy had reduced Ford car sales in many US cities. Schroeder ordered another cognac; no doubt that would change shortly. Being a Jew inside and outside Germany was about to become a liability on par with having leprosy.

CHAPTER 27

December, 1938

Saba prepared for her confrontation. Her fever was gone. The gunshot wounds were closed and free of infection. She was weak compared to her normal condition but much stronger than when the fever had broken twenty-three days ago. The fever's delirium had worn on her more than the wounds. And the thoughts . . . All the thoughts she wished to blame on the delirium had not abated. Her basement room at Les Demoiselles that had hidden and healed her was in part responsible. Les Demoiselles was not a hospital. Les Demoiselles was a brothel that sold sex, liquor, and hashish. All in copious quantities, more than Saba had witnessed in any of her trips through the capitals of Damascus or Beirut. The smells and sounds of whoring had been constant in the dark hours, fueling her delirium with images and fears and faces and fire in her skin.

The brothel's *patrona*, Doña Carmen, a dark, intense woman, was at first Saba's mother reborn in the fever, then a nurse who became harsh, very harsh, and unused to disagreements. But in the days since the fever had broken, Doña Carmen began to temper her tone, adding distance, speaking little, and no longer looked directly when they spoke. Saba began to exercise and eat. The *patrona* made it clear she had a business to run. When the *patrona* was in her barroom, Saba could climb to a loft in the *patrona*'s apartment and a two-way mirror that allowed a view of the barroom and its brazen stairway to the sex rooms above. There the women serviced Spaniards and Germans and even English businessmen on occasion, men who would be paid handsomely for the Raven's head.

Doña Carmen was nervous when the English and Germans were in the brothel. The whores never seemed nervous. Saba quailed every day at the men fondling them and yet she watched until she could not. It was as if the delirium that had consumed her in the first days was now pushing her into an abyss populated with the horrible faces of England's troopers and the sweet smile of Eddie Owen in America. The feelings were corporeal, sexual if she would admit it. She was alternately terrified of her own thoughts and hungry for them. Then so angry she would grab and brandish her weapons at her own fantasies. And the stronger she became, the worse it became. Her salvation would be that the world outside the brothel's basement demanded her attention. *Those* thoughts she knew how to process.

On this, her thirtieth day in the brothel's basement, Saba finished an hour of exercise and silent plotting. She had found a better plan: kidnap Erich Schroeder wherever he might be cornered, then ransom the Nazi to arm her partisans. While she held Schroeder captive, he would provide the necessary information to trap Ghazi bin Faisal and his Army of God. And then she would kill them all.

The plan was a good one, but it would require partners.

Saba exited her basement room, the black keffiyeh in hand. Her face was naked for the first time since she had arrived the brothel. Saba climbed the loft stairs to Doña Carmen's desk table and stood before her. "You are not the Canarian you say."

Doña Carmen continued to count the evening's money.

"An Arab, yes? A Palestinian."

The sharp look was short and uncontrolled, the eyes scanning only Saba's hands.

"Please look at me."

Doña Carmen did, but not fully and not long.

"You think I am her?"

Counting. "It is not for me to know."

"But you do?"

"No." Curt. Almost a shout. Doña Carmen hesitated, dropped the money, turned her head, and stared without waver. "If you are not an impostor—a whore like us, who makes a living being what we are not—then . . . then, yes, I worry who you may be. What you are."

Saba had not expected that from the woman who had kept her alive instead of selling her for a decade of whore's profits. "You fear I will hurt you or your house?"

The *patrona's* eyes jumped away and stayed away. "I fear the poison in your blood that allowed your survival, the violence in your soul, where you have been and where you will go."

"Yet you allow me to stay?"

Doña Carmen shrugged and told the table, "They say she was raped as a child by many, her family butchered. She wandered unwanted by her own blood, was buried dead in the mountain camps of the French, but rose and became a spirit, *a demon*, a soul dark enough to kill a man without touching him." Doña Carmen nodded at her tabletop as she repeated the legend. "She rode as an equal with Khair-Saleh, the Raven. He gave her his name and the desert to bid for Palestine. And some say she does."

"And this you believe. That a woman can rise from the grave?" Saba was moved, embarrassed as always by those who believed she was so much more than she was.

Doña Carmen looked at Saba. The often harsh, always confident voice cracked. "Are you . . . her?"

Saba hesitated a long moment, unsure if she was. "Yes."

The *patrona* clenched as if shocked by an electric current. The jolt passed. She straightened her back and raised her chin. Her eyes closed and she whispered, "*Insha'Allah*. Then we will have Palestine."

From that day forward, the trade between the two women was a simple one, one Doña Carmen knew well but rarely indulged. She saw in Saba the terrified desire to become a woman, to understand a man and to drown honestly in his affection. Whoring taught the opposite, to steel one's self from affection while acting it, to give without giving, to feel pleasure unfelt. Both were truths; one was dangerous, the other profitable.

Saba Hassouneh al-Saleh, the Raven, wished to become a woman.

The desire was unspoken but apparent to them both. At first they argued, albeit carefully; the Raven had a temper when confronted with her weakness. Twice Doña Carmen feared she would die. Since then they had their discussions after Saba placed all her weapons in an open drawer.

Today they were discussing what a kiss might entail, how Saba's breasts might brush the man's chest, her lips linger on his neck near his ear, a word she might whisper . . . Saba was crimson as usual and unable to hold the *patrona*'s eyes.

Doña Carmen laughed. "It is good to be excited. The man will feel your temperature, know your interest. For you, this is a victory."

Saba covered her face with her hands. Doña Carmen carefully pulled the hands partly away but not entirely. "You hide too much, everything. The heat is . . . is the invitation you feel but cannot say."

Doña Carmen waited until the resistance left Saba's hands. "Good, now look at me."

Saba refused.

"Look at me."

Saba did, through her eyelashes, the timidity reaching to her shoulders.

"Chin up, as mine. You are proud to display this temperature, this invitation. Your eyes in his, but not a threat as you do." Doña Carmen eased Saba's face out of her hands. "There, see his eyes; yours should say, 'strong but not angry;' you know how. Show me."

Saba's lips tightened, her eyes said, "Stand back."

"No. Soften your mouth. Show me you appreciate my help, yes? Chin up. Now show me appreciation with your eyes."

Saba smiled and far too much, but her eyes were . . . beautiful. A young woman who for that moment hadn't been to Palestine.

Teacher and student spent one hour every day for the next thirty attempting to openly enjoy the attention of a man. Doña Carmen used a great deal of patience, a mirror, and her hands. She touched Saba often, on her arms, hands, and hair. They hugged with the *patrona* facing away at first and Saba applying the pressure. Saba had great difficulty with this contact and complained. Doña Carmen spun once in frustration and grabbed. She finished on the floor with Saba's hands hard on her neck.

Saba apologized and they tried again. And again. And again until after many days they hugged facing each other. Something little girls could do as soon as they could walk. For Saba it was draining, the harshest part of her recovery. Clothes would be next if she ever mastered the basest elements of the womanly arts.

As the days progressed, Saba's mastery of the womanly arts did not happen and the stronger Saba became the less malleable she became. The brief rise of the woman was being replaced by the soldier. If the woman were to survive, there would have to be motivation, motivation that could not be faked.

Eddie turned his back to the refinery fence, studied his hands, then the sky, then the two PJs and two submariners watching him. An hour ago there had been news from Les Demoiselles. A small, rugged Canarian laborer who Eddie saw every day inside the refinery stopped his wheelbarrow next to Eddie, shifted the wheelbarrow's load, and whispered, "The *patrona* says you may call this evening at 22:00. Do not be late."

The rush of emotions shouldn't have been a surprise, but they had been. And fear was up there near the top. Foreman Paulsen's assistant was the reason. He'd vanished on November 18, not that Eddie missed him, but the little bastard had disappeared two days after Eddie had mentioned him to the Zionist with the gun as a possible culprit for the Mendelssohn papers. The assistant's room had been ransacked the same night he disappeared. The news this evening was that on the night he disappeared, the assistant had dinner with a Canarian woman at the Gran Hotel Taoro in Puerto de la Cruz. Five hours ago his bloated body had floated ashore on a storm tide crossing the north end of the island. Both hands and ankle bones were broken and he'd been shot once in the back of the head. The rumors were it had been Canarian smugglers, or Communists, or the *Policía Judicial*.

Eddie scanned the fences that protected and imprisoned him, wondering at the timing of a dead refinery worker washing ashore who'd met with a probable Canarian smuggler on the same day this Canarian laborer was telling Eddie to be somewhere specific at a specific time. Eddie's Canarian would have no idea who or what was going on or if Eddie would make it back alive. Someone was paying the laborer because he could get next to Eddie. Could be anybody—English, Zionists, anybody. Eddie had all of an hour to decide whether he would go—and that would be *if* the refinery allowed him to step outside the fences—and if he did go what he would say to Saba, what he would do. Forgiveness was out of the question if Saba were guilty, *at a minimum*. Schroeder's concept of wartime morality and anticolonial agenda was way past anything Eddie planned to understand or ever entertain. For the last sixty days, Eddie had made that decision every day. If Saba *hadn't* shot D.J., then any future they could carve out of this madness was possible. Eddie had made that decision every day as well—Schroeder couldn't be positive; he hadn't been there. Eddie had replayed that night so often—what Saba had said, the gunfire from three directions. Pirates? Smugglers? Zionists? Brits? FBI? Arabs? Eddie was no longer sure what he knew, what he remembered, and what he didn't. It had been hell and it wasn't over.

Paulsen forbade Eddie to leave the refinery. "You're aware of what happened to my assistant?"

"I heard."

"Then I don't need to explain, *again*, why these fences keep you alive and working."

Eddie said, "How does *I quit* sound?" They argued; both knew Eddie was going nuts from sixty days of confinement and both knew he couldn't quit and both knew he was going into town with or without permission. House arrest wouldn't help anyone.

An hour later, Eddie walked through the coral blue door of Les Demoiselles trailed by two German submariners and two PJs. A folk guitarist strummed a smallish guitar called a Canary Islands timple. The light above and around the musician was an uneven, dullish amber from glassed lamps high on the walls. Nine wine-barrel tables were topped with Canarian cotton cloth, all occupied save one. In this light there was no way to read the faces for threat. The bar itself was polished teakwood with four stools, girls on each, all facing Eddie and the door.

A reasonably attractive brown girl leaped off her stool, grabbed Eddie's hand, and led him to the only empty table. Eddie sat; he read the room for the Zionist hoping to recover the Mendelssohn papers, who'd likely killed the foreman's assistant. A waiter approached the table. "You wish to buy Beatriz a cocktail, yes?"

Eddie guessed he did and bought the girl who held his hand a honey rum cocktail and himself a Las Palmas Tropical Beer. She spoke a steady stream of Canarian Spanish as if he understood, and didn't seem to care that he didn't. She clutched both Eddie's hands with both of hers, then smiled across her young face and urged him to take her up the stairs. Eddie glanced at the PJs watching him and nodded to the submariners. Neither pair looked pleased, and all four followed Eddie and Beatriz up the stairs.

Beatriz pointed Eddie into a small room, followed him in, and was not allowed to shut the door until the submariners inspected the room. With the door shut, she tapped her wrist as if it had a watch, then flashed her five fingers three times. The armoire door opened. Doña Carmen waved him in. Eddie ducked through the clothes, through a false wall, and into a narrow hallway. The hallway led to another false wall, then the back stairway that led to the basement.

Doña Carmen stopped outside the closed door, then gestured Eddie in, adding a finger across her lips. Inside, a small, empty table and two chairs were alone in the middle of the room. Eddie wasn't sure if this was the room he'd been in eight weeks ago; that night and the one before it were a blur. On the table, a tall candle soft-lit two wineglasses and an open bottle. Doña Carmen pointed to one of the two chairs, then disappeared through another door. Beyond that door, Eddie heard a brief commotion, then muffled words, then silence. Doña Carmen reappeared, walked past Eddie, and exited via the stairway door they had entered together. Eddie waited, D.J.'s .45 cold against his back. And wondered what he would do.

In the deep shadows of the far wall, a shape stepped to the outer edge of the candlelight. The silhouette moved no closer. Flickering candlelight added and subtracted detail—a woman, hair brushed out to her shoulders . . . Carole Lombard from the Lucky Strikes ad.

The woman came forward. Saba, no keffiyeh. A wide-neck peasant blouse wrapped her shoulders and hinted at the curve of her breasts under the gauzy linen. She shook her hair off her shoulder, turned the empty chair away from the table, and sat on it backward, one arm over the top. Her eyes never left his. Slowly, her other hand eased a revolver onto the table, then withdrew from the grip.

It was like watching Sally Rand prepare her feathers before she took the stage. Or Marlene Dietrich tie her tuxedo's tie. Eddie was too off balance to be cautious, or angry, or confused, or whatever the hell he was. He nodded at the bottle. Maybe liquor would help.

Hazel eyes, long lashes, olive skin. *Man*, she was something. Electric. Eddie said, "You remember me, right?" He edged a hand toward the bottle. "I'll pour us some wine. Don't shoot me."

Her chest rose and fell, and made it difficult for Eddie to pour. Most of the wine went in the glasses. Saba's eyes stayed locked on his. Eddie swallowed, flushed with . . . everything. His mouth tried to blurt the D.J. question/accusation; his hand jammed the wineglass into the words and forced his mouth to drink. He swallowed the wine, coughed, and said, "Try some. Say hello or something?"

Slow candlelit silence, then, "Hello . . . Eddie Owen."

Eddie lowered the glass. Was she . . . frightened? Or was it . . . fearless? Eddie made his lips move. "Um, could you move your hand away from the pistol?"

She moved her hand.

Her lips had . . . lipstick? "I'm thinking about touching your hand."

Her eyes cut away.

Eddie touched the top of her hand. Her skin was smooth and hot. His palm covered her fingers. His fingers reached almost to her wrist and stayed there. Exhale. "Standing up now."

Her eyes cut back to his.

"Been thinking about holding you on the beach before . . . everyone got shot. Think about it every night. Stand up, okay?"

Saba stood using just the strength in her legs, her back straight, breasts high, chin higher.

Eddie gulped and reached both arms around her as if dancing with a porcupine. Saba didn't flinch or move. He hugged. Her hands were at his waist, near the .45 but not on it. Gently he squeezed the distance out between them until her breasts were soft on his chest. Chestnut hair brushed his face and smelled of lemon. She trembled and might have tugged him an inch toward her. Perfume. Then strength? Her hands moved up his sides.

The embrace may have lasted a minute or an hour.

Eddie leaned back to look in her eyes and she let him. That in itself was a shock. "Okay, this is the big one. I'm going to kiss you on the mouth. Just a little."

He did. She didn't.

"Good. Good. Now this time you kiss back, okay?" Eddie tried again. Her breasts cushioned his chest. Her lips trembled but made a kiss.

Eddie grinned on her lips. "Wow, where'd we learn that?"

She tensed, as if it were a critique—

He kissed her again until she softened. "Feel strong enough to do this till morning?"

Her lips widened under his.

Eddie slid his hand deep into her hair and kissed her again, trailing the tip of his tongue across her lips. She softened further, arching her back, both hands gripping into his shirt. In another life it would have been fifth grade behind the barn. Here it was the most erotic moment Eddie'd ever spent. The swelling in his pants was proof. Eddie eased back and her body came with him until she realized she was pressing against him and stopped. Her eyes were luminous and right there, her lips parted and . . . Eddie lowered his arm to scoop her off her feet.

She snapped back and away.

They stared, confused, from three feet instead of three inches. Eddie reached with just his hands and palms up. She met him halfway, then all the way, pressing against each other again, harder than before, and kissed urgently, mouths open. The power in her body radiated through him and almost buckled his knees. She had a hand in his hair, the other full of his shirt.

And then she pushed him hard away and he stumbled.

"Whaa?"

She was breathing through her mouth, her chin up and eyes flashing, maybe processing lust for the first time. Either that or they were about to find out who was the toughest. Saba was making a big effort not to look below his waist. Eddie flushed on top of the flush.

"Sorry. It's natural, kinda, you know? It's what happens when a beautiful girl you just can't wait to see kisses back like she . . . she cares about you, too."

Saba was three shades of crimson and all looked stunning on her, alternately confused, angry, and excited.

Eddie had sole responsibility for saving the moment. The truth was probably his best shot. "I will never, ever do anything that forces you. Ever."

She glanced at his pants, then his eyes.

Eddie smiled. "Someday we'll have children, on the ranch in Texas. If you'll give me a chance between now and then, I'll explain how it happens."

A small grin fought through her armor and across her face.

"Really. Step by step. We call it show-and-tell in school. First I tell you, then I show you."

She blushed to the point he could almost feel it. Eddie offered his hands again. She took only one and kept her distance. No way to tell if she was afraid of him or herself. "Maybe some wine?" Eddie pointed at the table.

They took their seats, Eddie moving his closer, forcing their knees to touch. Saba allowed it, might even have pressed back. Eddie tried for nonchalant, but the jolt from her was like having sex with a movie star. Her touch, the perfume, the eyes . . . Man, those eyes were scorchers. Her breasts in the candlelight. There was a good chance Eddie would pass out.

"You seem weak, Eddie Owen. Are you ill?"

He blinked, remembered to breathe, and palmed his face, hoping it would help. "Ah, you have a big effect on me. Not exactly sure how much I can take."

She cut to her wine, but there was the beginnings of a smile.

"No, I'm fine. I'm fine. How are you?" *Change the subject, drink, move your feet. Don't look at her yet.* God, he felt like a child. A really warm one, but a child.

"Better. I exercise. Eat a great deal. Practice . . ."

Eddie glanced at her sideways. She reddened again. His turn to smile and it blossomed into a grin.

Saba noticed his enthusiasm and glared, but fiery like the woman, not the man she had a habit of becoming.

Eddie fingertipped at his wine. "What?" They didn't speak until it became too awkward not to. "Like I said, you look good as new, gotta be the strongest woman on planet Earth or this place is the best hospital."

"Doña Carmen is a good woman."

"I'll drink to that." Eddie did. "And to Texas." Eddie's voice came out louder than intended. "You and me."

"America is a dream. For Americans."

"*No.* Americans are just people who used to live somewhere else."

Saba frowned at his tone. "There is no good time for me to leave my country to the Europeans. My people die because the Europeans deem it so. Palestine needs fighters, America does not."

Tough to argue with that, but he tried. And the more Eddie argued, the more Saba became less the ingénue and more the soldier. She finished the transformation by leaving the table for her room and returning with a worn blue book she'd been given by Doña Carmen, placing the book at Eddie's hands.

"*The Protocols of Zion.*"

Eddie held the book.

Saba sat with sad assurance, teacher to student. "The right of world conquest by the First Zionist Congress. There are twenty-four protocols, each defining the Zionists' divine mandate. Palestine is to be their national homeland, so says their God."

The book was a British government translation of *The Protocols of the Elders of Zion.* Eddie read the date, 1920, and the London publisher, then flipped pages and looked at her. "It's a lie, the whole book. I read it in college as part of my senior curriculum. The *London Times* actually printed a series about how it was plagiarized from some French fellow."

He should have hit her; it would've been kinder.

"The Zionists are not invading my country? The English and the Haganah do not kill Palestinians and deport them to the camps?" She stood and started yelling. "They did not murder my family? And, and rape—"

Eddie tried to slow her with his hands but she was backing away, betrayal burned into her face. "Wait, Saba, wait. It's not what I meant. I—"

She smashed her chair against a column. Eddie blocked wood splintering in three directions.

"Listen to me. I didn't mean that. I meant the book was faked. Only that, not that what's happening isn't real. I didn't say that. Think. *Please*. I'm not taking sides against you. I'm not and I won't."

She might have heard him; it was hard to tell. Next to the Bible, the *Protocols* were supposedly the most widely read document in the world and considered just as accurate by millions. The *Protocols* were notes of the Zionist Congress meeting, or supposed to be, detailing Jewish divine right to subjugate the planet. Many of the major political events detailed in the original 1905 Russian document had come to pass, including the Great War in Europe and the Russian revolution—all stated in the *Protocols* as the future plans of International Jewry.

Except it was a sham. Not the predictions of the events—that had been awfully impressive to recent historians—but the fact that it was Jewish conspiracy at the root. Tell that to the Russians, Germans, and Turks, and you were likely to get a vastly different response than from the reasonably neutral historians working at the University of Oklahoma.

Saba spoke through her teeth. "The book is not a lie. My father knew this book at his college. What it says has come to pass thirty years after the words were written. How can it be a lie?" She threw the chair leg at him. "The *London Times* prints a report? And you believe the *London Times* cares about the rights of Palestine?"

Eddie was in a nasty box. Like D.J., Saba saw the world through a gun sight.

"I will never betray you, Saba, ever. Even if we disagree, I won't go against you. You gotta believe me. I can't mean anything more than I mean that."

Her eyes were screaming.

"Please?"

"Enjoy the American world. Few gain the chance. Go to Texas. I am ashamed to have touched you. Be sure, this will never happen again."

Eddie stepped toward her.

Her knife was in his face before his second step hit the carpet. "Touch me and I will kill you."

"Listen, please—"

"*No.* I am now a whore. But not for you. Out. Now, or I will end this as it did for Bennett."

Eddie jolted, her knife throat-high between them, her words almost knocking him sideways; she didn't mean . . . Professional murder filled her eyes, her hand in D.J.'s death as real as—

"Out or die."

She meant it; he was absolutely sure. The woman was gone, the Raven in her place, affection turning to poison. The Raven saw only his betrayal.

He glared back, trying to read her admission . . . D.J.'s death. *No.* No, *fucking* no. Eddie dropped his hand, reached behind his back for the .45. Saba already had her revolver off the table. Eddie stopped. Time stopped. The goddamn world stopped. He shouted, "Goddamn you," spun on his heel, ripped open the door, and stormed out.

Saba stood back from the light, heart pounding, her breath trapped in her throat, and burst into tears.

CHAPTER 28

January, 1939

E rich Schroeder was en route to Tenerife. He had one stop to make—ensure that I.G. Farben's president, Hermann Schmitz, remained comfortable not delivering the AvGas formulas and modification expertise that Schroeder owned in one Eddie Owen. Schroeder left Hermann Schmitz in New York unprotected, boarded an unscheduled Deutsche Luft Hansa flying boat that flew to the Baltic coast, then a Luftwaffe plane to Berlin. A gleaming Daimler-Benz general staff car drove Schroeder directly from Tempelhof Airport to a private meeting with Reichsmarschall Göring at the Ministry of Aviation offices on Wilhelmstrasse.

The Reichsmarschall was quick to the point. "Herr Schmitz is at this moment boarding a flight for Berlin. He will be in this office in forty-eight hours to explain why he cannot deliver what you say you can. He will have Himmler or Heydrich at his side. You will draft a report of your meetings in New York and Detroit and I will demand that Schmitz answer. I would prefer your presence here but time is our enemy elsewhere. You will transit immediately to Iraq, then Palestine, where you will secure the selected sites and review the final budgets for the Final Solution in the desert. The Arabs must begin construction immediately if the public relations disaster favored by Himmler and Heydrich in Europe is to be averted."

"*Jawohl*, Reichsmarschall. It is a mystery that the SS does not see what you so clearly present."

Göring answered, "I.G. Farben and its Capitalist partners want the Jews kept in Europe as slave labor for their factories during all phases of the war. The Capitalists care about nothing but profit. Himmler and Heydrich are blinded by their inclusion at the Ruhr Valley's feast."

Schroeder did not ask Reichsmarschall Göring a second time for the permission to kill Eddie Owen's family member, a murder that Schroeder had already set in motion. Nor did Schroeder think it wise to burden the Reichsmarschall with details of the plan to kill German American Bund Bundesführer Fritz Kuhn's top two lieutenants instead of Kuhn himself—Schroeder saw a future use for Kuhn should Schroeder's private plans for the American industrialists and oil men require American fingerprints. And Schroeder did not mention his final New York meeting with a senior Irénée DuPont representative whose proud, pompous bearing ashened considerably when shown the Mendelssohn papers. Schroeder's bold move was in no part due to the rebukes in Detroit. The timing was proper to put his new *partners* on notice: Erich Schroeder would have his kingdom in the desert and his rightful seat at the table with the captains of industry, or he would destroy them.

Schroeder did not spend the night in Berlin. A Luftwaffe Fieseler 156 Storch flew him to Istanbul, then Baghdad and the Final Solution meetings with King Ghazi bin Faisal. But in Baghdad, the king was focused on Kuwait, demanding its annexation. Schroeder bit back his anger and spoke at length with the king's mullahs. They were more than accommodating, well versed in the extermination plans, and fully prepared to finalize their participation in the Jewish Question and all it would bring them.

The mullahs believed the Jews of Europe would go willingly to Palestine. And when the English empire had shrunk back to their island in Europe, the Jews could be landed in Haifa or Jaffa, then shipped by rail to the selected sites. There, they would work building roads until they no longer could. Their smoke and ashes would be the cleanser of the sand that their Zionist lie had defiled.

The mullahs saw this and the extension of their power with great clarity but were no longer confident of Schroeder's ability to keep his promises. Rumors were spreading that Saba Hassouneh, the Raven, was not dead—as Schroeder had cabled them eighty days ago—a death the mullahs had announced to all of the Middle East. In response to these rumors, black wings had reappeared on the walls of Janîn, then Haifa, Jerusalem, and now Baghdad this very week. And in Wadi Rum, the star *Minchar al Gorab* had blazed in the sky. Proof, the Bedu said, the Raven had *again* risen from the grave. She would unite the Arab against the invader. Bring vengeance and destruction against the betrayers of the desert people.

Schroeder assured the mullahs that Saba Hassouneh was flesh and blood and could not rise from the grave or fall from the sky. She was dead. He had shot her, personally, and watched her die. She would not return to trouble them.

The mullahs lectured Erich Schroeder—European—on the realities of the desert. The desert was full with many factions. Should the desert factions, especially the Bedu, unite around a godless *woman* who did not hate all Jews but only their Zionists and militia, then the Pan-Arab Army of God could not possibly bring the Nazi Final Solution to be.

Schroeder accepted the rebuke. The mullahs were his architects, builders, and champions, but they were also mystical men, mired and empowered by the insanity of religion. One day he would incinerate them in their own ovens. But that day was far in the future. For if by some impossible circumstance Saba Hassouneh was *not* dead, her reappearance now would be a disaster for Schroeder and, by default, Reichsmarschall Göring, of un-survivable proportions.

A Luftwaffe plane with one passenger took off south into the desert moonlight then banked west toward Morocco. Schroeder would land at Casablanca, board a waiting seaplane to Tenerife, and be at his hotel in time to dine with Eddie Owen. Eddie would be effusive in his thanks, his poor, pitiful family in Oklahoma saved again by the Third Reich. If Saba were alive and Eddie knew it, Eddie would lack the skill to hide it. Nor could Eddie hide from the vise about to be closed on him and everyone he cared about.

Schroeder arrived at Tenerife at eight p.m. The island was its usual cauldron of heat, humidity, and sulfur. Tired and brittle from the seaplane, Schroeder had been on island and in his suite at the Hotel Mencey thirty minutes. He had not had time to unpack, only to hear reports on the refinery's progress, the PJs' rancor over Eddie Owen, Eddie's day-to-day movements, and not a word or even a rumor that Saba Hassouneh was alive. Schroeder dismissed his submariners through a private exit, then swallowed a glass of port. Eddie Owen was late. Theirs would be a delicate moment.

A knock at the door. Instinct trumped logic; Schroeder stepped away and drew his Luger. If Saba Hassouneh was alive she was not in Wadi Rum with the Bedu; she was here and common sense said he was her next target. Schroeder climbed atop the small table in his entry and looked down through the door's transom. And the mullahs were correct; if Saba Hassouneh were alive she would return to Palestine and Iraq and kill as many of those who had betrayed her as was humanly possible. That was the only good news—she was human. And if so, she had to be dead.

Eddie Owen stood in the hallway. No expression on his face, two submariners behind him. Schroeder jumped down, switched the Luger to his left hand, hid both behind his leg, and opened the door. "Eddie! Come in. Come in."

Eddie walked past and began talking before he turned. "Getting really strange here. Thanks for seeing me so quick."

"Any time." Schroeder shut the door, beamed, but read Eddie carefully. "The world has become too irrational to describe."

"Thanks for the phone money. And thanks for taking care of the hospital again. Be a while before I can pay you back, but I will."

Schroeder nodded, satisfied now that Eddie had not spoken to Saba. If Eddie had, he would know it had been he, Erich Schroeder, who had shot D.J. Bennett.

"Have you seen her?"

Eddie fumbled, "Seen who?"

"Saba Hassouneh."

Eddie looked confused, then shook his head.

Schroeder saw the lie, or thought he did. He employed a patient, practiced calm he did not feel. "In the desert they say she is alive, that Bennett's bullets did not kill her. If she is alive and you seek her out, remember my advice and your dead friend D.J. Bennett—Saba is what she is, not who or what you wish her to be." Schroeder stopped Eddie before he could answer with another lie. "I was your age once, fifteen years ago. I know how it feels to be blinded by a woman."

"You said she shot D.J.; no way I'm blind to that." Eddie walked to the terrace doors, stopped, and turned. "The papers I told you I had are gone. I hid them and someone stole them. One of Mendelssohn's people came after me. I screwed up bad, told him I thought the foreman's assistant might have them. The Zionists murdered him. Tonight's only the second time I've been outside the fences since you left. Maybe the Zionists have the papers now; maybe they don't."

Schroeder grimaced. "If Saba is here and you know where, never allow her to know you carried these papers for the Zionists. She will . . . never understand your good intentions."

"Hell, you do, why couldn't she?"

"I know the papers to be a lie. I asked when I was in Berlin, toured the detention camp they call 'Buchenwald.' No ovens, no graves, none of what you described. And the camp is not for Jews alone, but all criminal and political adversaries of the Reich. No different than your great penitentiary Alcatraz that will soon release Al Capone."

"Mendelssohn's papers are fakes? You're sure?"

"Yes." Schroeder slid his Luger under his coat into the back of his pants and reached for a tray of glasses and a bottle of Portuguese *Vinho do Porto*. With enough liquor Eddie might offer what he knew of Saba, dead or alive. Schroeder nodded Eddie out onto the terrace and set the tray on the large table. "Please, sit." Schroeder poured them each a glass of ruby port.

"Similar documents were intercepted secreted on the persons of Zionists in Vienna and Prague. Soon, more of these forgeries will be common in the world's capitals, all claiming to be the 'only' copy." Schroeder pointed at the telephone inside. "Once the 'only' copy can be verified in ten places at once, the world will know it is yet another ruse of the International Jew. Buchenwald can be visited and my country will be vindicated."

Schroeder toasted with the port.

Eddie was slow to respond, but he did.

"Eddie, I know you worry. The winds that blow around you are confusing even to me and I have been in this world far longer than you. Trust your heart first, not your head. If I am the evil incarnate the Jews and Communists say I am, then you feel it." Schroeder tapped his heart. "Here."

"You saw the camp. It was a prison. Nothing more?"

"Not at all unlike what America builds to house those who would do her harm."

"And the Jews of Germany?"

Schroeder exhaled. "Always the Jews, never the Communists." Schroeder shook his head, turned away, then back. "The voyage of the MS *Saint Louis*, you know of it?"

"No."

"The MS *Saint Louis* is a German ocean liner, a pleasure ship. At immense cost to the German citizen, the Nazi government granted one thousand Jews free transit to Cuba *at their request* and paid for their visas. When the Jews arrived, a Cuban official demanded a bribe of five hundred dollars per person. The Jews would not pay. The Nazi government sailed the Jews to Florida in America, but America would not accept them, citing racial balance and quotas. The Nazi government sailed the Jews to Canada and she also declined to grant them landfall."

Eddie's jaw had dropped an inch.

"Yes, Eddie, as I told you, we, the Nazis, only want them out. The world who complains so bitterly about our policy refuses to grant assistance when it is their sovereign soil that must support the International Jew. Tar my country with the same brush you tar yourselves or not at all. This is only fair and proper, yes?"

Eddie believed what was good for the goose was good for the gander.

"The German economic miracle is not an accident. We as a people dug ourselves out of the carnage of the Great War and, in the last five years alone, have built our nation into one of the few on the planet where the population does not suffer as they do in Oklahoma. Your people have suffered concurrent disasters, as have we. There are those who say America's Dust Bowl is the result of failed government farming schemes and that the Great Depression is the fault of Wall Street and your bankers. In Germany, our leaders and our Jews also schemed. They plunged the world into war as a result. But Hitler and the Nazis do the opposite. We build; we do not destroy. We embrace who and what we are, and where we are.

416

We covet nothing that isn't our birthright. We do not seek empire as England and France do. And we mean no harm to anyone who allows us our prosperity within our borders."

Eddie said, "I'm beyond grateful for your help. My family is alive because of you . . . maybe because of the Nazis, but, for sure, because of you. And I know I'm in a pot full of trouble—here, England, and now back home—"

"At home?"

Eddie explained the FBI and the House Un-American Activities Committee.

"Congressman Dies. Yes, I know him."

"You know him?"

Schroeder nodded. "An honest man, denigrated by the Communists, but hoping to set the record straight by showing President Roosevelt the real enemy."

Eddie rubbed his face.

Schroeder said, "You are not alone, Eddie. The world is confused to the point of war. Who is right? Who is wrong? *Is* there a right and wrong? Or just history's . . . force of arms?"

Eddie uncovered his eyes. "And?"

Schroeder drank the port and poured another. "If I knew that answer with absolute certainty—"

"How about 'Do unto others . . .'?"

Schroeder smiled and offered a toast. "When you complete your contract for this refinery, we will vacation together. It shall be the national motto on our flag."

Eddie finished a second glass of port, thanked Schroeder again, and said he'd have to pass on dinner. Eddie's reason was, "I'm beat-to-death tired and can't afford to lose any more sleep. The refinery's on schedule but it's taking damn near double shifts every day."

"I understand, Eddie. Other than a brief business trip, I'll be on Tenerife every day until you're done. You can focus on the refinery;

I'll do everything I can to keep the PJs away and anyone else who might wish you harm. I can do that as long as you make sure my men never lose sight of you. Okay?"

"Sure. Thanks." Eddie's face was confused again. "Thanks." And he left.

There had been no further comment on Saba Hassouneh or an opportunity to question Eddie that wouldn't overplay the questioner's hand. Given what Schroeder already knew, further risk wasn't worth it. Other than Eddie's one visit to a whorehouse on Calle de Miraflores, a visit that the submariners had monitored as closely as possible without remaining in the room, Eddie had seen no one for two months other than people at the refinery. If Saba were alive and Eddie had seen her, it would have been at the refinery and that was impossible. Schroeder tried to imagine how a woman he had shot to death could crawl off a deserted road and recover inside the refinery. He could not.

But Eddie's face had been a lie. If not about Saba, then a lie about what?

CHAPTER 29

March, 1939

S aint Patrick's Day on Tenerife lacked the pageantry of its repu-
tation. Eddie didn't care and the Irish didn't seem to, either. In
fourteen days, Eddie's AvGas modifications would be complete. The
Irish would get their bonuses and move on and Eddie's contract
would end. Erich Schroeder had kept his promise to keep the PJs
at bay and for the last six weeks the rabid bastards had hovered and
glared and been everywhere Eddie had been, but hadn't tried to lay a
glove on him. The same couldn't be said for Eddie's loyal employer,
Culpepper Oil Products Company.

The telegram in Eddie's hand was from Harold Culpepper. It
said Culpepper Oil wanted to renew Eddie's contract, but given the
FBI intervention (Eddie's fugitive warrant in Texas and a federal
fugitive warrant), Eddie could not return to the USA and expect to
stay un-arrested on any job until something had been worked out.
Nor could Eddie be contracted to anyone outside the USA where
Great Britain could reach until Great Britain dropped their extradition demands. Culpepper was looking into a solution and if

Eddie would cease all the friction he was causing Foreman Paulsen and stop making demands for loans and threats to quit if he didn't get them, *maybe* Culpepper could work something out.

Eddie wadded the telegram. He'd only seen Three Card Monte once but he could recognize it in a telegram. Something was way off line here. How could he be "vital" *and* unemployable? It didn't make sense, not for companies whose disregard for "the rules" seemed the norm. The Owen family was stable but by no means safe. One missed payment to the hospital and sanatorium and . . . Eddie had two weeks' pay coming and two weeks more till he finished. Hard to believe, and all he'd tried to do was the right thing.

Mount Teide *harrumph*ed.

The tremors were fairly regular now and sharper over the last several days. Eddie looked up from the canteen's short stretch of beachside railing into what should have been Tenerife's sunrise. Today the horizon was behind the bow of a huge Spanish troopship aiming for the Santa Cruz dock. Behind the troopship and to its starboard was an equally immense Standard Oil tanker. The troopship's deck bristled with uniforms and weapons.

Ryan Pearce took a spot next to Eddie and nodded toward more Fascist authority about to land.

Eddie added reaction distance and wondered out loud, "Takes an entire army to guard a refinery?"

Pearce said, "Been more'n a little problem with the other plants producing your fancy gas. I imagine the generalissimo sees it proper to keep this one."

Each day for the last week, more Spanish Army security had materialized. More Germans, too, not in uniform but well trained and dead serious, and respectful to everyone so far. Foreman Paulsen and the CEPSA managers seemed grateful to the Nazis for their attention.

Pearce said, "The Brits' Lord Chamberlain is bat-mad today. Hear the London radio this mornin'?"

Eddie didn't listen to the BBC if he could help it. And he wasn't that interested in listening to Ryan Pearce, either.

Pearce continued anyway. "Nazis invaded the remaining part of Czechoslovakia last night after promisin' the peace in Munich less than six months back. Made a fool outta the British prime minister and German nationals outta the Czechs and Bohemians. The high-an'-mighty Brits got their faces in it now."

Eddie's jaw dropped.

Pearce nodded. "And Hitler's wantin' part of Poland, too, all the territory occupied by his poor ethnic Germans he says the Poles are terrorizin'. Hitler says he'll war with Poland's angels—England *and* France—if he has to. England and France can sign 'mutual defense' treaties with the whole bloody world, but Germany's defendin' her people."

"Jesus Christ, no wonder all these soldiers are pouring in here. Maybe Spain got dragged out of their civil war and into—"

"Nah, lad, Spain's still neutral, if ya call this neutral." Pearce nodded at sixty German submariners who were now sharing the camp. "You can count on your gas going German if these brave Spaniards ever have to fight to keep it for Franco or he tries to sell it to England."

D.J. had predicted this would happen. How could D.J. have been so wrong about the Germans and so right about almost everything else? Eddie un-wadded Harold Culpepper's telegram to make sure it said what it said. The telegram was clear; Eddie was unemployable. Impossible but true.

Pearce said, "*Lá 'le Pádraig Sona Duit*," some kind of reference to St. Patrick's Day; spit over the rail; and walked away. Ryan Pearce remained a troubling puzzle but not a serious problem, since Erich Schroeder had involved himself in Eddie's safety. Eddie remained vigilant because Pearce was a mercenary. Pearce clearly leaned toward Ireland and against England, but for the right amount of money, Eddie believed Ryan Pearce would shoot whoever was in front of his gun.

Maybe there was a job where Erich Schroeder had people? Schroeder had left the island unexpectedly, but not before he'd come to the refinery to say not to worry and that he'd be back in a week. The Germans needed gas. The USA wasn't at war with *anyone*. As long as the Germans used the gas for . . . *For what? Like you'd have a say?* Eddie exhaled. He didn't have a say in the USA, either, and he damn sure wouldn't in Great Britain. Eddie quit Schroeder and Culpepper and allowed himself to think about Saba instead, go far away to where the world wasn't a fucking nightmare. His parents and little brother and sister would be fine there. The place would have palm trees and smiles in equal amounts; he was sure of it, saw some vision of it every night on his cot. Saw Saba's chestnut hair, olive skin, and . . . killer instinct.

Eddie spit where Pearce had. *Yeah, we'll all live happily ever after on D.J.'s ranch.*

Seven days till final.

Every day would be double-shift, a textbook plan for miscalculation and mistakes. Add sleepless nights because you were a lovesick fucking Boy Scout and you could almost guarantee the cracking tower would incinerate the whole place and everyone in it. Eddie checked the armed submariners trailing him through the labyrinth of pipes and tanks shadowed in moonlight or floodlit with blazers. The first load of light crude had come in yesterday and was already in the oil depot's tanks. In seven days Eddie as Dr. Frankenstein would transform the "Mexican" crude into 100-octane gold or death sentences to millions, all depended on whose story you believed. Eddie checked the docking schedule with his flashlight—seven more tankers en route, all Mexican flagged. According to Foreman Paulsen, the oil wasn't Mexican; it was from a Texan, William R. Davis. D.J. had said the oil companies would become a nation unto themselves. It might be their oil, but Generalissimo Franco wasn't taking chances with *his* refinery.

In the last week, the guards and patrols outside the fences had tripled. All British and Moroccan nationals were being deported off Tenerife to Rabat and Tangiers in French Morocco. Nine "Communists" and four "foreign agents of destruction" had been shot or cage-drowned by the PJs. Eddie had been hauled out of his room at gunpoint by Red Beret and six PJs with machine guns—a first. Both Eddie's submariners had radios in their left hands and Lugers in their right aimed chest-high at Red Beret. Red Beret had paid no attention to the Lugers, cocked the pistol in his right hand, leveled it at Eddie's head, and demanded Eddie give up the Raven of Palestine's location. The Raven had killed the foreman's assistant as part of the *Comité d'Action Marocaine*'s plot to destroy the refinery. Eddie had helped her. When and where was the *Comité*'s attack? Eddie was still alive because nine submariners with submachine guns had answered their radios. The O.K. Corral ended without blood. Saba's situation probably wouldn't. Suddenly, Schroeder, the Brits, the entire goddamn population thought she was on the island.

Eddie shook his flashlight and rechecked the docking schedule.

For the three days since he'd been at the O.K. Corral, he'd wrestled with what to do. No way Saba would survive a house-to-house by the PJs . . . if Red Beret really believed she was here to blow the refinery. The other possibility, the one Eddie was wrestling with tonight, was that the PJs had been fishing when they'd pulled him out of his room, building their case to kill him the second the refinery was finished.

Mount Teide rumbled. Eddie checked the moonlit volcano against the night sky. No glow, thank you Baby Jesus. If the volcano decided to "attack," there wouldn't be much Generalissimo Franco's refinery and his PJs could do but die. Day and night for the last seven, Mount Teide had rumbled deeper and deeper, like distant thunder you could hear and feel on the ground. Eddie glanced at his watch, then out over the water. His eyes rose to Saba's stars. He'd forgotten how to sleep more than a few hours at a time. How do you fall in love with a woman who killed your best friend?

Saba did not kill D.J.

How do you fall in love with a woman you don't know? Eddie spit on the sand. Hell, guys fell in love with pictures. Saba was the most three-dimensional woman he'd ever seen. The Arabian nights . . . The attraction made him shiver, longing he couldn't shake. He was in love and lust and . . . and adventure. She was the ten-pin for all of 'em. How does a guy go back to college girls or chorus girls or . . . after he's seen a princess?

But she killed your best friend.

Bullshit. *Maybe* she killed D.J.— Eddie started to laugh and would've if it wasn't so fucking sad. How many of his classmates would ever have this conversation about who to date or marry?

Marry?

Jesus, he *had* lost his mind. D.J. was right. Eddie checked Saba's stars again. No way she killed D.J. She just wouldn't. *I can't be in love with her if she shot D.J.* Eddie tried to spit again and couldn't. Pretty damn tough duty for a farmer's son.

So? So, Eddie replayed the seventy-eight rpm denial record in his head then responded to a combination of his anatomical parts and real fear for Saba's safety if she were still here. Eddie told his two submariners, "I'm going into town to get laid, then to meet Herr Schroeder's seaplane when he arrives at the dock."

One submariner who spoke reasonable English said, "There could be trouble."

Eddie said, "Yeah. But I don't give a fuck," and an hour later stood outside the front door of Les Demoiselles. The brothel had closed for the evening. Eddie knocked, then knocked again and again until the *patrona* herself appeared at the door. She opened it a crack, saw the submariners scanning the street from its opposite side, and stepped into her doorway. Doña Carmen grinned for the Germans but snarled: "No. Go away."

Eddie grimaced his apology and didn't move. The *patrona* eased her weight into his ribs as if she would kiss him. A pistol barrel dug into Eddie's gut.

"We do not play a boy's game. The PJs threaten a house-to-house. Go away." Doña Carmen circled his back with her empty hand.

"She's still here, right? I gotta see her. Have to. Sorry."

The pistol dug deeper. "She is gone. Implicate me and I will kill you."

Eddie hesitated, no idea what to do or how to do it. "Tell her I was here. I'm coming back. I love her. I'll be gone in seven days. Just wanna hear her say she didn't do it before I go."

"Do what?"

Eddie told the *patrona*'s ear, "She'll know," and turned toward the docks to meet Erich Schroeder's seaplane due in at dawn. The submariners followed.

The docks of Tenerife's main harbor had just moored the Casablanca Ferry. The tall ferry blocked dawn's first glare from Saba's eyes. She sat at the far end of the dock across the wharf road and in disguise. The ferry's gangway slid to the dock between two empty "man cages." Spanish Army soldiers aimed rifles at the ferry from their shoulders. The passengers, all men, were waved to single-file off the ferry. Armada police confronted each man at gangway's end. Behind the Armada police were the plainclothes secret police, the *Policía Judicial*. Documents were checked and rechecked. All baggage was being searched. There were no shouts of anger from the passengers.

When Saba had landed here nearly five months ago, Arab anger on the ferry had been nearly a riot.

Saba's disguise was a fisherman's hat instead of a keffiyeh, fisherman's rags instead of beggar's rags. Her face was naked underneath the hat because it had to be, her first purposed foray without keffiyeh or veil in the ten years since the Raven had snatched her from the camps. This dawn she was not an Arab; she was a Canarian *pescador*, too old and too full with drink to work, but here on the docks cross-legged in the confusion of the wharf's ropes and barrels just the same. This dawn was practice. Practice that would, if successful, kidnap Erich Schroeder, murderer of Haifa, within the week. Her presence here and later in the city was to prove or disprove that she could allow her face naked and not be questioned. No veil or keffiyeh could be worn at Schroeder's hotel without drawing undue attention. The Grand Hotel Mencey had a proud, *European* tradition.

"Drunk" in her grubby huddle, Saba worried the wine bottle in her lap and watched the Arab passengers at the opposite end of the long dock as they were bullied and browbeaten. The Spanish fear of attack here was substantial. Troopships in the bay, soldiers and submariners on the ground. Saba purposely quit her recon, allowing her focus to slip so as not to be too interested, deciding she would wonder about the passengers, not the men at arms, wondering where the passengers had been.

Soldiers bumped her toes. Some bumped her knees. None commented, speaking Spanish to one another in the rough tones of soldier camps. Saba thought of the mountains in Lebanon and Syria and her years surrounded by men. How different the men were in the camps than when in Les Demoiselles. Women and sex changed everything—for a short moment—the men were easily controlled with nothing but promises. Threats and religion and nation were tools of another trade.

A seaplane cut through the glare and splash-landed in the bay. From a seawall pier south of the long main dock, a small wooden boat motored out toward the plane. Germans in white T-shirts clustered on the seawall pier. Two were not watching the plane; they scanned the main dock then the wharf and looked right at her. Saba cut her eyes left.

Eddie Owen.

Heat warmed her face, possibly the dawn that now lit the entire wharf. Was she in love with Eddie Owen? Was that the heat? Or with America far away? Or with just far away? Because she was in love with something; Doña Carmen had made that clear. The thought churned Saba's stomach just as it had when it had been shouted at her and almost brought her to tears. Eddie Owen. It had been three months since she'd sent him away. In those three months, she had regained all the physical strength lost to the Nazi's bullets but lost much of her fatalistic armor. Dreams of Eddie Owen's words clouded her sleep—of him and her in America, of them in a soft bed without clothes. Doña Carmen had taught her a woman's secrets, as Khair-Saleh had taught her a soldier's secrets, and as the German had taught her Abwehr secrets. Doña Carmen's secrets were the only ones that shamed her.

She could not, and would not, have Eddie Owen. She would have Palestine so another young girl could one day have these dreams and make them real. Her father had given his life for these dreams, as had the Raven, and, with great pride, now so would she. A raindrop from the stars where this was written splashed her hand. She noticed the drop was blackish, and that she was crying.

●●●

Sixteen hours later, an explosion rocked Eddie off his cot. His room window was fire. "No, goddammit!" Eddie bolted upright, jerked open his door, and— No oil tanks were on fire. *Volcano.* Eddie spun to Mount Teide. The volcano wasn't red; Tenerife wasn't Atlantis. Beer splashed him in the face, Spanish soldiers spraying with Las Palmas Tropicals. Another explosion boomed, this one behind him. Eddie spun to the water. *Fireworks?* Looked like fireworks, but *huge*. Eddie asked a soldier. The soldier was too drunk to answer. Eddie asked another soldier. He said Generalissimo Franco's Fascists had just taken Valencia and won Spain's civil war. The soldier shouted toward the harbor: "*Victoria Generalissimo! Arriba España!*"

Eddie turned. At the harbor's mouth, two night-lit Nazi submarines rode blatantly on the surface. The Nazi crews stood the decks in white T-shirts and uniforms, arms extended rigidly, saluting the shore. Ryan Pearce stepped between Eddie and drunk Spanish soldiers. Pearce pointed at the harbor. "There's your parade, lad, red and black." Pearce smiled but his eyes had the quick shifts of a caged animal. "Spain's in for the Nazis now; Nazis got Italy with 'em as well, the Czechs, and Japan. Strong group of combatants Hitler's built. Lord high-and-mighty Chamberlain's on the pot now, wishin' he'd stopped Hitler back at Munich. But Lord Chamberlain sent his troops over to kill the lads in Ulster and Belfast instead. Biscuits'll be payin' the piper soon and proper."

Eddie checked the volcano a second time, then the submarines, then Ryan Pearce.

Pearce said, "After ya final this baby tomorrow, the CEPSA bigwigs will be comin' for their christening. You'll have built Franco and his mates the grandest AvGas plant in the world." Pearce toasted the fireworks but didn't look that festive. "If they can keep her safe, our gas will be lightin' up the sky everywhere these dumb bastards have the bad word." Pearce swigged his beer. "Here's hoping London's the first fire."

Eddie thought about that. He probably had forty-eight hours left on Tenerife, free and alive. Eddie bolted for the city.

Santa Cruz was street drunk and half crazy; no telling who was an overjoyed Fascist and who was a beaten Communist pretending and plotting. Midstreet, Erich Schroeder clasped Eddie's shoulder. "My congratulations, Eddie. And perfect timing on the completion and the peace in Spain." Schroeder gestured at the fireworks. "Your success has begun and Spain's bloodshed has finally ended."

"Yeah, but what about the rest of the world?" Eddie had to play this nine ways from careful. His mission with Schroeder was about Saba.

"Together, we must help them see a future written in food not famine. Come, we will avoid the madness of the street, drink a toast to a day many feared might never happen."

Upstairs in Erich Schroeder's suite, the German was jovial but guarded. "My men keep the PJs at their distance?"

Eddie shook his head "The O.K. Corral three days ago was something. Your submariners have been a gift, let me tell you."

"Their job will not be complete until you are safely off this island and its maze of smugglers, Communists, and pirates."

"That'd be swell. Two days, three tops."

Schroeder nodded. "So, you have news of Saba Hassouneh?"

"Me? I haven't been out of the refinery."

Schroeder sipped wine from the table between them, on it a letter signed "Ilse" in red and Eddie's two promissory notes, his signature prominent below the imperial eagle and swastika letterhead.

Eddie lied to his benefactor. "I haven't seen Saba since . . . Iran? If I had, there's no reason not to tell you."

Schroeder's face saddened. "Eddie, I have been in this business, a bad business, a long time. I know people; it's my job. She is alive in your life—I saw it in your eyes the last time we spoke of her, and I see it now. If she is alive, I believe you know where she is. I do not press because Saba is not important to me other than she may harm you." Schroeder hardened. "And she will, Eddie, if she determines you brought the Mendelssohn documents here. She will believe you intended to somehow benefit the Zionists who steal her land and kill her people."

Eddie had no answer for that. If the documents had been real and he hadn't lost them, he would've used them. For something.

"Your safety is important, Eddie. Your refinery, Germany and America becoming partners against the Communists—*like Spain and America and Germany are here*—these are the things that are important."

Eddie fumbled his hands. In two days he had to have a paying job, and it would be great if the job were with the good guys . . . when the world figured out who the hell that was.

Schroeder continued. "I know you think Saba part of your future, but if she is alive and recovers from her wounds, she is far better off in my world, away from you and with her own people." Schroeder frowned. "I fear for her here; these Canarians wish to continue their centuries of killing. Their motives and relationships go far back and cross many lines. Your friend D.J. Bennett fell into this pirate/smuggler maze, as did Saba, I fear. To the Canarians they faced or employed, the Mendelssohn papers were merely contraband to be bought and sold, the lives of those involved all expendable. It is the way of the pirate."

Eddie had lost his affection for pirates, movie version or otherwise.

"Saba killed D.J. Bennett. I am sorry, but your affection or infatuation will not change that. And she likely killed the two Zionists. There are more Zionists here searching and killing for these same documents. If Saba is captured by the Canarians and sold for the bounty into British or Zionist hands, it will go very, very badly for her."

Eddie believed that. "Let's say I do find her, and she's alive. What then . . . ?"

Schroeder shrugged, his expression confused, then glanced at the wall as if he'd heard something through the plaster and wood.

"You'd help her get out?"

Schroeder's attention returned slowly from the wall. "Pardon me, you said?"

"You'll help Saba get out?"

"Of course, this is best for everyone. Although I do not agree with her violent tactics, I do agree, as does my government, that she has a birthright to her country that the European Jew does not."

Eddie wrestled with the words. They sounded right, reasonable, accurate in a world that was way beyond what he'd been able to figure. But it wasn't what he wanted to hear. That was the goddamn problem.

"Think about it, Eddie. You will come to the proper decision for you. These are difficult times for all of us—you, your family, our countries."

"You got that right." Eddie detailed his contract with Culpepper, his standing with the FBI and the Brits. "Basically, I can build a refinery, but anywhere I can build it, I'd go to prison or the gallows. Either one of those happen, my family's done."

Schroeder blinked confusion at Eddie. "You will not go to prison or the gallows, and your family will not suffer for lack of capital. Not while I am alive. Trust me in this, Eddie, America and Germany will be partners, and you and I will be there to cheer."

"Meaning I have a job next week?"

Schroeder laughed. "Yes. And likely with the great *American* company Standard Oil, but somewhere in Germany or one of our partner nations." Schroeder held out his glass. "To Eddie Owen, President of Standard Oil!"

Eddie drank, lightheaded, his family kept off the road to California yet again.

Schroeder stood. "I apologize but I am quite tired from my travels." He walked Eddie to the door. "If you must find Saba, be very, very careful. The PJs." Schroeder grimaced his entire face. "If they track you to her, it would be very, very bad for all of us." Schroeder grimaced again to make his point. "But if you must, please see to it before the refinery christening with CEPSA, yes? If Saba is alive and requires help, I will see to her personally, you have my word. Promise me this so I may put it from my mind."

Eddie nodded, exhaled, and said, "Talk to you in the morning."

"Good, Eddie, it is for the best."

Downstairs in the lobby, two PJs leaned against either side of the front door, their shoulder holsters worn over their white shirts with no coats. Probably another four or more outside. Eddie and the submariners walked toward them, the younger of the two PJs stepped into Eddie's path. Behind the PJ, the street was raucous. Eddie should've been happy—he had a job, he might get off the island alive—but happy wasn't what Eddie felt. He leaned into the PJ's nose before the submariners could stop him. "*Mano a mano*, Chiquita. Two days, you and me. I put you in the fucking ocean."

The German submariners pulled Eddie backward and drew their Lugers.

The PJ smiled. "*Si, amigo. Dos dias.*" He showed two fingers.

The submariners escorted Eddie to the street. Two women arm-in-arm passed and smiled. Why wouldn't Saba talk to him and just say she hadn't done it? How goddamn hard was that? Doña Carmen had to have told her he'd been by last week. *Why hasn't Saba tried to get back to me? For chrissake, I saved her.*

The submariners flagged a cab. Eddie hesitated at its open door, looking south toward Les Demoiselles. *Really, Eddie? Really? If she wasn't so pretty, so exciting, so . . . everything, would it be easier to* believe she *had* killed D.J.? The taxi driver smiled across the convertible's seat. Eddie wanted to puke. Of course it was. Can you say *femme fatale*? A jolt from Mount Teide shook the street. Eddie steadied against the taxi door.

Maybe that was the answer. Jump in the fucking volcano.

Saba's hands were fists. She'd heard the entire conversation from the maid's closet that adjoined Schroeder's suite, a common design element of the hotel. Doña Carmen had arranged access through the Arab girl Beatriz who whored at Les Demoiselles and also cleaned rooms at the Mencey. Like many whores and maids, the girl also sold information to the *Comité*, British MI6, the Nazi Abwehr, and the Communist Spanish Republicans. Saba was here to eavesdrop, a reconnaissance she would do every night until she was comfortable with a kidnap plan.

Eddie plans to betray me? He had been with Schroeder at the dock and now here? Discussing Eddie "finding" her? Saba's palms were wet among the string mops and bleach. *And what had you expected? You exit your life to become a woman and the world stops spinning? Men become honest and honorable? All you have learned can be forgotten?*

Saba listened to Eddie's footfalls heavy in the hallway. She did not peek. The footfalls quit. Her breath calmed. Schroeder's door rattled. She startled, bumping a mop, and froze, then squinted through the hinge seam at a middle-age man of military bearing. Schroeder answered his door. Saba vise-gripped the inside of her door handle. The military man introduced himself, ending the introduction with "Reichsmarschall Göring." The military man clicked his heels, reached inside his jacket, and produced an envelope. Schroeder accepted the letter, signed a booklet the man produced, then shut his door.

The man pivoted with precision and walked to the elevator with the care of someone who believed he was being watched. Saba watched until the man had disappeared into the elevator, then pressed her ear against Schroeder's wall. Footfalls sounded in the hallway. Saba jerked from the wall and again squinted through the door seam. Two men approached. Saba clamped her door handle with both hands. The men stopped at Schroeder's door and knocked, one white-haired and senior in his posture, the other younger, also in a suit and carrying a manacled briefcase. Schroeder's door creaked open. He said: "*Guten abend*, Herr Sturmbannführer, the SS takes a far vacation."

The man with white hair spoke German in an abrupt military cadence, introducing the younger man with the briefcase, finishing with "SS Reichsführer Himmler" as if it were "Himmler" who had sent them.

Schroeder granted the men entry to his suite. Their voices continued in German from the other side of Saba's closet wall. She released her door handle. The man with the manacled briefcase must be a courier of some sort. A muffled discussion followed, then a demand made by the older voice, firm but polite.

Silence.

The demand again. Harsher but still polite.

Silence. Schroeder's voice switched to English. "Do you speak English?"

The courier's voice answered, "*Nein*, Oberstleutnant."

Schroeder barked, "Remove your courier. We will continue in private."

The older voice answered: "*Nein*. He is SS Reichsführer Himmler's personal courier, dispatched here *with me* to retrieve the Jewish Question documents you have withheld. You will produce them. Now."

Silence. Then movements, then the two Nazis continued in English. The senior SS man moderated his tone, saying he enjoyed the practice. Saba knew the SS man's agreement to speak English was an Arab's disguised retreat, one the SS man would use as an attack platform when the first opportunity was presented.

The SS man and Schroeder discussed America in forced comfort—Roosevelt, the Communist labor unions, the eternal Jew bankers of New York and London. Saba imagined the two Nazis circling each other. The SS man added sharp concern—the US industrialists who had attempted Roosevelt's assassination were now warning that should Roosevelt's policies continue unabated, the results would crush the US and German reconstruction.

Saba heard a noise in the hall, peeked through the hinge crease of her closet, saw nothing, then pressed her ear harder to the wall. The Nazis were fencing, returning every few minutes to SS Reichsführer Heinrich Himmler and his Gestapo. Schroeder acknowledged that while in the United States, he, too, had heard these opinions of Roosevelt's policies and reported them to *his* superior, Reichsmarschall Göring. There was also a rumor that another coup against Roosevelt might be mounted in the very near future.

The suite conversation was muffled for two minutes until the SS man mentioned Himmler again. "Two German American Bund lieutenants were murdered in New York. A tactless affair that the Reichsführer believes was perpetrated by you. Reichsführer Himmler is most unhappy, as are others in the Reichstag concerned with our image in America."

"The SS is now concerned with image?"

"The Wehrmacht's autumn plans for Eastern Europe will be met with resistance. This will bring pressure on France and Britain to declare war on the Fatherland. Murder and ritual torture done in America do not propel the Americans toward our goals."

"The SS no longer practices ritual torture?"

"The Jewish Question documents trouble our friends in Detroit and New York. The documents must be returned to Berlin, *with* an explanation on how they were acquired and why they were kept from Herr Göring."

"Documents?"

"Documents *you* showed, threatened during your last trip . . . abroad. Our American friends have asked I.G. Farben to intercede; Herr Schmitz has asked Reichsführer Himmler, who now offers you a chance to . . . clear yourself of these accusations."

Silence.

SS man: "Of race treason and blackmail."

The floor creaked, then: "You mistake me for a woman. One who fears your black uniforms, who bows to threats from Jew-loving Americans."

The floor creaked again.

"*If* these documents exist and I had procured them in America before returning here, they are too important to be trusted to a defenseless SS courier."

"Reichsführer Himmler—"

"Commands you, not me."

Saba imagined the men glaring, separated only by reaction distance, Schroeder the more capable of lethal violence.

"Reichsführer Himmler commands Hitler's bodyguard and defends the German state. He offers you a chance to survive your . . . indiscretions. Something Herr Göring will not."

Schroeder laughed. "You would turn me? A Krupp? To work for a chicken farmer chasing homosexuals?"

"I caution you, Herr Schroeder. Reichsführer Himmler is not pleased with your clumsy attempts at dominion. For his own reasons he will pardon you, provided there is . . . inside access to Göring's camp *and* the documents are returned. If not—"

"*Gehen Sie raus!*"

The floor creaked toward the door.

"Now!"

"Until tomorrow, Herr Schroeder. Reichsführer Himmler's courier and I leave on the seaplane in two days."

The door shut quietly. Saba peeked beneath the hinge at the SS man adjusting a pistol under his jacket then walking down the long hall. The courier who had been dismissed trailed him. In Schroeder's suite the silence lasted until the SS man disappeared and two legs of a chair slammed partway through Saba's wall. Plaster showered her. She ducked, crouched tight below the hole. Another blow, this one higher, smashing the chair.

Erich Schroeder was stunned. Impossible, but his plan for dominion had been derailed. Worse, he'd been reported. Where had the American Capitalists found the nerve? Jew lovers! He would bury them, let the genteel aristocracy of Detroit's Grosse Pointe and New York's Hamptons watch their children fucked to death. He would build camps in America and burn the Jew lovers alive! Schroeder ripped open the sealed letter from the first courier and read instructions under Reichsmarschall Göring's seal. The prose was curt: *Immediately after Tenerife's AvGas equipment is tested with success, bring Eddie Owen by submarine to Bremerhaven where he will begin converting the Reich's refineries.* Included in the order was the long-awaited sanction to deal with Eddie Owen's family in Oklahoma. Schroeder thin-lipped a smile, not the least bit calm or happy. Himmler's representatives, the SS Sturmbannführer and his courier, should go missing, now, tonight—

Schroeder bit into his lip. Killing Himmler's SS envoy would solve nothing. Himmler may be a "chicken farmer," but at heart he was a butcher, a grinder of meat who never shut down the slaughter line once the process had begun. The term "race treason" had a special meaning to the Reichsführer, nothing Himmler hated more. To be classed as one who might violate those laws was to invite a public or private death sentence that could not be overturned. Even by Göring.

Schroeder chewed at a plan, then replanned. He paced, kicking furniture debris, and sidestepped out onto his balcony. Palm fronds whisked his railing; the air had more sulfur. He cold-eyed the volcano, then the suite behind him and the hole he'd put in the wall. A shadow? Behind the hole— The balcony shook hard under his feet; Schroeder's eyes cut to the volcano, then Eddie's refinery to the north. Now that the sanction was in place, Eddie's family could be abducted by "Jews" and taken to Mexico. This would be better than a killing and undertaken as soon as the refinery modifications were finished and he and Eddie had left Tenerife for Bremerhaven. When Hitler's Blitzkrieg scorched across Europe, Eddie would develop a conscience. His family would be the lever.

At Bremerhaven, Eddie would spend a sandy resort stay at the Villa Aegir on the island of Rügen under the watchful eye and propaganda of Schroeder's best people. Schroeder and the Mendelssohn papers would immediately continue on to Göring in Berlin where their use could be explained . . . The papers were a test for the American industrialists that they had failed.

Tested for what? For what?

Schroeder slammed the balcony table, levitating the oil lamp. It crashed and set the table afire. Mount Teide rumbled the building, shaking the oil fire onto his shoes. His shoes ignited. Then his pants cuffs. Schroeder ran for the bath, stumbled and fell, and saw the shadow move this time. Fire crawled up his hip, both legs flaming. He charged for the shower, twisted knobs, and grabbed the shower-head. Water blasted. Hot water. His hands slapped at the flames; fire bit into his shirt, then died under water. Steam. From the hot water. Schroeder bolted out of the shower onto the tile.

Smoke. *The papers.*

Smoke filled half the suite—the balcony table was burning. Schroeder ran blind and coughing through the smoke, grabbed the one table leg without flames, and threw the table over the railing into the celebration below. Puddle-fire nipped at his feet and he stamped it dead with soggy shoes. He spun, saw the papers were safe. What about the shadow? Schroeder drew his Luger and focused on the jagged hole he'd put in the wall. He stepped through the remnants of his living room to his door and eased it open. Straddling the doorjamb, he glanced at his suite's side of the hole, then on the other side of the jamb at the door that now faced him. Through that door would lead to the other side of the hole.

No number on the door—a maid's closet, the door slightly ajar. Schroeder had noticed the door when shown this suite but had forgotten to inspect it. He stiff-armed the Luger at the maid's closet and squeezed the trigger. Then stopped. Better to interrogate, see what tonight's occupant knew, then shoot. First a knee, then an elbow, cut out an eye . . .

The closet was empty. Down the hall, the elevator engaged. Schroeder ran to the cage. It was rising, not lowering. He hid the Luger. A uniformed bellman was in the elevator cab with the operator. He bowed three inches; made no comment on Schroeder's singed, wet clothes; and handed him a note. The note was from the SS Sturmbannführer. A satisfactory agreement could be made between them. Could they meet again on the hour?

After telling the taxi driver "no thanks," Eddie had walked into the street party celebrating the Fascist victory in mainland Spain, then decided to get blind drunk. The submariners weren't happy. The PJs had looked ecstatic. Eddie didn't give a fuck. His second final test was scheduled for tomorrow morning. The CEPSA bigwigs would be in on the first seaplane at nine a.m., then the christening celebration a day later on March 31. Then it's *auf Wiedersehen*, for and to, everybody. Eddie sighed, searching for sympathy pills—in truth his modifications were already done and tested, but he hadn't shared his results. Why? Who the fuck knew? Something was wrong—with him. Really, really wrong.

Eddie veered through the street crowd, coughed sulfuric air that hurt his eyes, rubbed his face, and turned toward the bottom of Calle Miraflores. Might as well go out in flames. He waved the submariners to keep up, then began snaking faster through the mob, hoping to lose the PJs. It took five blocks, three turns past clots of drunken soldiers firing pistols in the air, and a fast climb over two courtyard walls.

Outside Les Demoiselles, Calle Miraflores was packed in both directions. Inside was no different, Carnaval for Nationalists. Doña Carmen stood on the third tread of the stairway, saw Eddie trying to crowd in at the door, and glared. Eddie shouldered through to the stairway end of the bar like he wanted a drink, waved at the bartender with several others wanting drinks, then settled for the *patrona* at his shoulder. Doña Carmen leaned over the stair railing to his ear and said, "Go away. Find an American girl to marry."

Eddie pointed at the bartender like he wanted help but told her ear, "No. I want to see her. I told you, before I go."

"You betrayed her. She is dead."

"I didn't betray her. What're you talking about?" Eddie cocked his head, fearing the worst. "What happened? Where is she?"

"Dead. The Nazi."

Eddie rocked on his heels. Gunshots at the doorway.

The submariners turned to the gun blasts. Eddie leaped over the stair railing and ran up the stairs. Down the hall, he tried the door he'd been in before and it opened an inch. A girl smiled but shook her head. Eddie pushed her aside, apologized, and Doña Carmen rushed in behind him. She spoke to the girl and hurried her out. Eddie opened the armoire, unlocked the false wall behind the clothes, ran down the narrow hall, through the second false wall, down the back steps, and ripped open Saba's door— Saba lurched. Her knife arched to her blind side and buried in the wall directly behind her. She spun away from a threat that wasn't there, a pistol stiff-armed at Eddie.

Doña Carmen yelled, "No!" from the doorway.

Saba's pistol was in Eddie's face. Eddie didn't move, his hands open at his sides. Saba stepped back and into the wall, the buried knife vibrating chest-high at her shoulder. Had a man been there, the blade and hilt would have broken his sternum. She glared. So did Eddie.

Doña Carmen said, "His Nazi guards are in the bar. He would not leave."

Saba growled behind the pistol.

Eddie barked: "Tell me you didn't mean what you said."

Saba looked like she might lunge. "Give me to the Nazi? Will that be today? Tomorrow?" One hand ripped the knife out of the wall. Her eyes and pistol stayed tight in Eddie's face. "Tell me *now* about our life together in America."

Eddie had no idea what she meant.

She screamed, "I heard your words!"

Eddie flinched. "What? What words?"

"Is he here?" Her eyes blazed. "Outside? In my hall? Is my life over, Eddie?"

"What? No. I haven't told anyone . . ."

Saba glanced hard at Doña Carmen, then back, the breath coming fast, the pistol still rock steady.

Eddie had to know. "Tell me you didn't shoot D.J."

"And if I did? What then, Eddie Owen betrayer? What then would you do?"

"I didn't betray you, goddammit—"

"I heard your words!" Saba lunged. Eddie ducked. She stopped short. He looked ridiculous; she looked like an assassin. Eddie retreated two steps. "What words? Okay? Whatever you think I said, I didn't. And if I did, whatever you heard you didn't understand."

"In Schroeder's suite. Me for the 'Mendelssohn papers,' your salvation for my enemies and a way home for you."

"*What?* Would I be here if that's all it took? Ask yourself that. They'd be here. I'd have the papers; you'd be dead." Eddie scanned the room, didn't move his hands. "But the Nazis aren't here and I am. Unarmed. Hoping you're not the killer you said you were."

"I am *your* killer."

"Bullshit. If it's true you killed D.J., then shoot me. If not, then come back to Texas—"

"You can't return to America—"

"Okay, then come to anywhere in the fucking world you wanna go and I'll go with you. Pick and I'm there."

"These Mendelssohn papers, the Jewish Question—"

"Did you kill D.J.?"

"The papers. Explain them."

"Why the fuck won't you answer me?" Eddie'd replaced fear with anger. "Just say you did or didn't, okay? Just say it."

"Stand back."

"You gonna shoot me, too?"

She glared like she was considering it.

"*Just say it* or shoot me." Eddie put his chest on the end of her pistol and his eyes as deep in hers as they'd go.

The pistol didn't budge. They were ten inches apart, both ready to die. She said, "No."

"No what?"

"I did not shoot him— You sold me to the Nazi. When does he collect?"

Eddie took a flyer. "If you somehow heard me with Schroeder, you know that I never told him yes or no. There is no time, Saba, that I ever, *ever*, mean to give you up—"

"If I had killed your friend?"

Eddie swallowed words he'd thought but hadn't admitted. "Maybe I'd have killed us both. But I wouldn't have given you up."

Saba hesitated, then glanced at Doña Carmen. The *patrona* nodded a small frown and slowly lowered her own pistol. She said, "He will kill you both. That, I will believe. I will be in the bar, telling his Nazi guards he takes a woman. Be quick." And she left.

Saba stared. Eddie stared back. *She didn't shoot D.J.*

They began by not moving apart. Slowly Saba lowered her pistol. Eddie's eyes glistened, but his posture was rock strong. He fumbled for words and settled on, "I love you."

Saba blinked and seemed to . . . recoil . . . Angry . . . Confused.

"I love you."

Saba blinked again. A smile trembled to her lips and softened the hardest edges of her eyes. "You do not know me; how can you love—"

Eddie smothered her. All of her, the gun, knife, violence, anger, chestnut hair, shoulders, and chest. She stood rigid in his arms, her knife hand a fist pinned to her hip . . . until the arm circled Eddie's back. Her fist quit and she dug fingers into his shirt. Eddie squeezed her forever. Finally he said, "We can do this."

Her breath was short and hot on his neck.

"We can."

"What?" Breathless into his neck: "What can we do?"

Eddie hurdled them forward to happily ever after, somewhere, anywhere.

Saba pulled away, her skin scarlet, and pointed him to the small divan. He kissed her without thinking, didn't want to risk moving. Eddie kept one of her hands. They stepped to the divan. Her smile was forced, almost tired. She faced the door, took her hand back, inhaled, and said, "Your benefactor, the man who feeds and protects your family, who protects you here, *he* shot D.J. Bennett. An execution, no mercy, no accident. An execution."

Eddie shut his eyes, saw D.J. cold and yellow on the table. And there it was. Eddie took the gut punch, one that in his darkest hours he had suspected would be coming. The revelation was what he'd felt, what he'd sensed deep down but wouldn't admit or face. Eddie swallowed bile, rocked on his hips, and used the divan to steady.

"Your friend was my bait. Schroeder paid me to kidnap him in exchange for funding my partisans in Palestine. But Schroeder murdered Haifa, for some reason sooner than he likely wished. He knew I would kill him, no matter what lies he told me. He knew my exchange of your friend was bait and he bettered me in the exchange. My death here was his plan from the beginning."

Eddie looked up, his eyes blurry. "*Bettered* you?"

Saba nodded an inch. "I am sorry, but that is my world. Schroeder executed your friend while Bennett and I spoke of you, then Schroeder shot me to death, he thought . . . but because of you, I did not die."

Eddie blinked his eyes clear but not his head. Erich Schroeder was a cold-blooded replica of a human being. *And my family—here and Oklahoma—I have placed in his hands.* Eddie pushed forward to stand. "I gotta do something. Get my family—"

"Wait." Saba tugged him back. "There are things you must know. I believe Schroeder kills me in a trade with King Faisal in Iraq. I am a woman and not of Allah, and therefore a threat. Faisal has a plan with the Nazis. I do not know this plan, but I suspect it has to do with something the Nazis call the 'Jewish Question' and 'the Mendelssohn papers.'" Saba searched Eddie's eyes.

Eddie nodded small and rubbed at the fear in his face, the realizations of just how bad things were about to get in Oklahoma and elsewhere. "There are documents, the 'Mendelssohn papers.' Let me explain." And Eddie did, carefully, eyes on Saba's reaction after every sentence. Eddie finished by detailing the system plans for how the Nazis would efficiently dispose of eleven million bodies, making diagrams with his index fingers on the divan fabric at Saba's knee.

Saba shook her head. "It is not possible. Even the European is not capable of slaughter on this scale, not even the English."

Eddie explained his meeting with Mendelssohn and Dinah Rosen and their bombing deaths in Haifa.

Neither seemed news to her. "And you believe this . . . impossible plan to be fact? That you are not being used for Zionist propaganda? Both Rosen and Mendelssohn were Zionists, yes?"

Eddie nodded. "Schroeder said the documents were propaganda. Offered to take me to Germany to prove it."

Saba cut her eyes like she was thinking. "But a Nazi would have no choice but to deny. He cannot have the world pity the Jews of Europe; better the Jews are despised as pariahs."

"The whole 'extermination camp' story could be bullshit. It's that terrible. And the Jews seem to want Palestine bad enough that any lie now would be worth the cost later." Eddie visualized the detail in the plans, the seals, the signatures, the *pride*. "You've seen what the English are capable of firsthand, and they're Europeans. The Nazis could—" Eddie shied and wished he'd said it softer. "I'm sorry"—and leaned to kiss her cheek—"I'm sorry."

Saba didn't move or frown. "Schroeder's business here finishes when you do. After you left his suite, he met with an SS officer and an SS courier. The men argued. Schroeder dismissed them, but they met again." Saba's tone militarized. "The Nazis are certain of war in Europe. England's prime minister and France's president have agreed to defend Poland if Hitler attacks as he has promised. The SS officer predicts this attack and England's defense will happen very soon, before the winter of this year."

Eddie reached for her hand.

Saba pulled it back. "You must listen. The SS man ordered Schroeder to produce the papers about the Jewish Question." Saba struggled with her English or the content, or both. "The SS man inferred that the papers depict what is true."

"You heard 'em say it was true? That they're gonna murder eleven million?"

"Had I not heard the words from their mouths, it would be impossible to believe. Even now I am not certain."

"But you heard two Nazis say it was?"

"Yes. And in a meeting one half hour later, I heard Schroeder speak in German on the telephone with a 'Reichsführer Himmler.' I do not know what was said. After the call, Schroeder agreed to trust the papers to the SS man and the safety of the courier's diplomatic pouch. They leave on the seaplane the day of the christening."

"*Schroeder* has the papers? Mendelssohn's papers?"

"So he said."

Eddie shook his head; he'd let Schroeder play him for a fool every step of the way. "We can . . . grab the papers from the courier, then—"

"My plans are for Schroeder. I stay . . . to kidnap him as before, ransom for arms. My fight is for Palestine, not for Europe's Jews."

Eddie didn't have a great answer. She seemed to notice, or had known from the start that they wouldn't leave Tenerife together. "I gotta bunch to figure out, a whole bunch. Whatever I do, I'm not letting go of you. Work backward from 'we're staying together.' Everything we have to figure, we'll figure it from there."

Saba smiled, but there was no participation in it.

Eddie squeezed her hands. "C'mon. There's a way."

Saba didn't answer.

•••

Erich Schroeder drew tight, hard circles with the Luger's barrel and swallowed an overfull tumbler of Pernod. Two hours ago he had finished the second meeting with Himmler's SS colonel, their dance a two-pawn exercise in entrapment and blackmail.

Schroeder's way out of Himmler's trap—if there was a way out—would be AvGas for the Luftwaffe and a plausible denial of the Americans' blackmail charges. A tightrope, but possible. But even if the rope were walked, the only true safety rested in Göring's triumph over Himmler. And Heinrich Himmler was a dangerous man on the scale of no other Schroeder had met. Schroeder poured another Pernod. His Luger continued to groove Frau Ilse's signature. In dull euphemisms, her airmail letter of last week described Reichsführer Himmler's renewed and serious interest in Buchenwald. It had been Himmler's first camp, built and named by him in 1933. She said her husband was touring other sites in Germany with a small SS contingent. There had been extensive discussion of the railway systems in Central and Eastern Europe. Her husband's conversations with her—more guarded with her than usual—suggested that these railways would likely decide the locations of the camps. Poland was frequently mentioned.

Schroeder should also know that Poland was much discussed in the Berlin and Munich papers but for more public reasons. *As if those of us solving the Jewish Question are not sufficiently noble to be public?* Frau Ilse also felt strongly that Himmler's solution would center on Poland and not Palestine, and that Himmler's choice was gaining momentum. She added that the foundations for Buchenwald's test crematorium were being poured outside her window as she wrote.

Schroeder burned the letter.

CHAPTER 30

March, 1939

T he ocean was loud, the moon hidden. They had been apart only hours. Saba listened to Eddie, hearing most of his words. He was a handsome man, and, better, he was a good man. Honest. She felt that strongly now. His admissions were raw, his needs clear, his options limited. Sadly, Saba saw his and her situations as separate, as were their goals. She had analyzed all of it as a soldier would— what could be accomplished and what was a dream for another day. Her mission was arms for Palestine; his was to save his family in Oklahoma, the Jews of Europe, and himself and her if she would allow it. To accomplish all, or any of his plans, Eddie first had to escape the island *and have* the Mendelssohn papers.

"You ask me to take up your cause. Would you take up mine?"

"Lots simpler"—his hand squeezed hers—"if I just think about you on the divan."

Saba the soldier did not blush.

Eddie straightened and quit flirting. "I'm sabotaging the refinery."

Saba processed the tactical implications to her plans.

"I'll pour acid into the switches and three other spots. The refinery won't blow; she'll melt, and big. Serious sabotage—might even be treason if I'm wrong and the Nazis are really the good guys."

"They are not. They are Europeans, and in Europe there are no American 'good guys.'"

"So you'll help me? Even if it means the ferry?" *The ferry* meant give up her plans to kidnap Erich Schroeder. She would help Eddie recover the Mendelssohn papers from the couriers, then deliver the papers to America.

Saba had arrived at her decision moments after Eddie had left Les Demoiselles. Saba the soldier determined there was no way to successfully kidnap Schroeder off the island. She could kill him. That would deliver her personal retribution for Haifa but would do Palestine no good. In truth, the Mendelssohn papers could be bartered for arms more readily than Schroeder's life. The papers were the prize. *Palestine's* prize.

"If we do your plan, Eddie, your family will be at great peril."

"Yeah, I've been thinking on that."

"The first place your enemies will go is your weakest spot." For an instant the woman replaced the soldier. "And *I* am here."

Her admission went unnoticed. The surf splashed and Eddie said, "I know fellas in Texas, used to work for them. I owe them a small fortune for a car I wrecked, but they understand family. They could get people up to Oklahoma pretty quick if they were willing, and I'm thinking they would be." Eddie frowned. "They'll be mad about the call, though. Wasn't supposed to use the phones. Ever."

Saba produced a pen and paper from her sock. "Give me the Texas names and telephone numbers. Doña Carmen will use her network."

Eddie wrote out a phone number and two names: Lester "Benny" Binion and Floyd Merewether, then the address at Saint John's Hospital and the sanatorium, and finally a foster residence in Tulsa, Oklahoma. Eddie added the four names of his mother, father, little brother, and sister.

Saba read each name, thinking of her family buried unmarked somewhere in the marl rock and dust of Jerusalem. She checked the stars, then looked at Eddie and started to speak— The soldier replaced the woman and said their time tonight was short. The soldier asked when the refinery sabotage would become obvious. Eddie explained that the acid was part of a catalyst he worked with regularly. In the right mixture it would take roughly thirty-two hours to eat through the metal and just seconds to consume the circuits. The downside was that this acid was a "give-or-take" type of clock, one that could become a big problem. Saba saw the problem before Eddie finished explaining. The sabotage would be a major blow but it would also add severe risk and complications.

"You are correct that the SS couriers will be the most vulnerable on the ferry. To force them and the papers onto the ferry, both seaplanes must be damaged, one here, one on the mainland."

"Can you do that?'

Saba nodded. Doña Carmen could likely do both.

Eddie brightened, adding energy to his hopes. "I'll attend the CEPSA christening . . . At the last possible minute before the ferry leaves, I'll make an excuse, sick or something; pour the acid; don a disguise; and make a run for the dock."

"PJs will be on the dock. And make no mistake, Eddie, the *patrona* says the PJs mean to kill you."

Eddie shrugged.

Saba read his eyes, then continued. "The ferry for Casablanca— with the papers aboard—will depart one hour into your celebration. You say the acid will require thirty-two hours to melt the refinery . . . The ferry requires thirty hours to make Casablanca; we will be trapped aboard if the acid is faster or the ferry is slower."

"You smell like tangerines tonight."

Saba saw the divan in his eyes and possibly reflected in hers. Mixing these emotions and sensations would not improve their chances of survival. She tried for anger, then shame, and felt neither. Truly a new day in her life. She recalled the bluff above the college ten years ago in 1929, her father speaking . . . For a moment she felt the pride and affection and . . . happiness. She kissed Eddie on purpose.

Eddie fell, shocked, to his elbow. He remained half on his back in invitation, no longer shocked, and she wanted to join him. It was so new and so strong. My God, these feelings! Saba stood instead. "I go. We have eleven hours."

Eddie started to rise.

Saba signaled him down. "No. I will arrange the seaplanes and the ferry. You will board at the very last moment as an Arab man, as will I, but bent over; you are too tall. The PJs will have finished with their searches and be drawn to the wharf by a diversion, an argument during *Asr*, the fourth Muslim prayer. At the boat ramp, I will speak for you. A disturbance there, too, possibly; pay no attention and come to me. Yes?"

Eddie's face said a great deal more than *yes*.

"*Stop*. We risk our lives in this. If the PJs at the wharf do not kill us, the SS will possibly have others on the boat, men who kill as a profession. Thoughts of me without clothes will cease quickly then."

"Haven't yet."

The compliment lingered, unthreatening and warm, a combination never felt or allowed. A day of firsts. And one that must end. Saba said good-bye in Arabic, and before she could stop her hand or lips, she blew him a kiss. Her keffiyeh slipped across her face; the black cloak she wore swirled like a magician's and she was gone.

•••

Eddie grinned. Tangerines. He'd never quite realized how much he liked tangerines. Eddie remained on his back staring at where she'd been, then her stars. Had to be the strongest attraction ever between a man and a woman. How could you shift from certain death to lust by holding hands? If he ever got her in bed, he'd have a heart attack. Be worth it. Just the one time.

The ocean commented with a breaker. He grinned at the foam; *Eddie the college boy marries the Raven of Palestine. Robin Hood marries the fair Maiden Marian—wonder how I'll look in the dress? Probably not as good as Olivia De Havilland.* Eddie tried to whistle at Ms. De Havilland's image. *Shit, I need to live through this just to tell Benny and Floyd the story.*

Benny and Floyd. He should've called them first. The car money mattered and the instructions not to call mattered, and not bringing the FBI down on them mattered biggest of all, but Benny and Floyd would've helped with both surgeries. They'd have been mad as hell, but they would've helped.

The beach shook. He grabbed for balance. A line of pebbles tumbled past him to the water. Eddie craned over his shoulder at Mount Teide backlit by the moon. A thin cloud layer cut across the crater at 10,000 feet, well below the peak. Clouds near the summit, too, but different and not a layer.

More like a puff. Eddie tried whistling again, this time "Song of Atlantis," and scrambled for the road.

The third Muslim prayer had ended an hour ago at noon.

The refinery workers who prayed were now wide-eyed at the sky with everyone else. Eddie checked his watch. The outbound ferry would be almost finished loading its cargo. A lone Messerschmitt roared low, tipping a wing and burning Eddie's AvGas. The CEPSA gentlemen ducked toward the patch of lawn where they stood, as did others in gaudy Spanish uniforms. Erich Schroeder did not.

Schroeder stroked a pink orchid boutonnière and matched cocktail glances with the women in their gowns.

A decrepit Spanish biplane followed the Messerschmitt and the crowd ducked again. Tenerife's closed airport had been partially cleared to land the planes earlier. Both planes had barely survived the runway holes; a third had not. The two surviving aircraft had been refilled with Eddie's gas to do these flyovers before heading to the mainland. The CEPSA bigwigs were giddy. Eddie checked his watch. Now or never. He became Benny Binion at the poker table, pulled Erich Schroeder aside, and clinked glasses.

"Done."

"My congratulations. You have accomplished much for your country and, hopefully, the world."

"I found Saba."

Schroeder nodded, his interest unreadable.

"She was badly injured, shot twice, and can't speak. You were right; if you can't get her out of here she won't get out."

Schroeder nodded, his eyes calm but intent on Eddie's face. "I am sorry."

"I'll take you to her tomorrow night, after we're all done here." Eddie gestured at the dignitaries and fanfare. "She's at a house by the Volcán de Güímar."

Schroeder draped one arm around Eddie's shoulders. "Your decision is difficult but for the best. For all of us." He eased Eddie toward the closest bar. "A drink to Saba's survival, your accomplishments, and our future together."

Eddie drank one, ordered another, excused himself by saying he had to run to the latrine and would be back after he'd met with the Standard Oil and Culpepper people who were late but due in any minute.

In his room, Eddie gathered items provided by Doña Carmen— a hooded *jellaba*, a keffiyeh, old shoes and pants, a ferry ticket, and travel papers no six-year-old would believe. Eddie put the clothes in a bag, belted D.J.'s .45, took a deep breath, knocked wood for a gambler's chance at survival, and went to work.

Sneaking past the guards or overpowering them would be impossible. Eddie feigned hurry and concern, ordering those who saw him every day out of his way. General Franco's soldiers understood loud and officious.

D.J. would've been proud.

Probably.

Eddie fumbled the first quart of acid into a transmission tube, then beakered another that filled the bulkhead reservoir above the main circuit panel. A floor tremble shook acid from the beaker. Acid smoked his shirt cuff and dotted through but missed his wrist. Sweat soaked his jacket. Outside the steel housing, guards asked nervous questions through the closed door. Eddie coughed at the fouled air, capped both beakers, and caught himself before he wiped at his eyes.

"Almost fixed."

It would be a chain reaction, not unlike a boulder rolling down an ever-steepening hill. At the bottom of the reaction, the cracking tower would rupture, metal would acid-weld, heat would cease. The door behind Eddie jerked hard against its latch. Eddie spun; the beakers crashed. Toxic air. Shoes smoking. *"Son of a bitch."* Eddie ripped off a shoe. Mount Teide shook the ground again. Eddie staggered into the door and away from the smoking beaker shards, coughing as the acid began to eat.

"Calm down. I'm coming out." Eddie checked the sabotage. The volcano had spilled a large glob of the acid on the outside of the main panel. Watch check: one thirty p.m. The thirty-two-hour time clock had probably just changed, how much there was no way to know. Eddie popped the door. In the distance, the ferry horn boomed. Make the boat or be in the cage.

CHAPTER 31

March, 1939

The ferry horn boomed again. Saba stood the crowded steerage deck. The boarding was complete. Eddie was late. The main dock below had only dockworkers, PJs, and soldiers. No crowd to hide him. An out-of-place Arab woman approached the ferry's gangway-passenger ramp. Saba made a small signal with both hands. The Arab woman stopped under the high, corrugated roofing of a boarding area now shading only her and blowing litter.

Mount Teide rumbled. Saba shouldered through passengers and angry Spanish elbows toward the deck's gangway gate. A Tenerife harbor official pointed up from the dock to the pilot's bridge, then signed a clipboard and wound his hand in the air. The ferry's foghorn boomed.

No Eddie, no Nazis couriers; Saba had to get off.

A clot of men and PJs collided at the wharf end of the dock. Their arms waved at the ferry; voices shouted to wait. The PJs blocked the men and inspected documents—if Eddie were among them, he was doomed. A group of six was allowed to pass and rushed up the pier—the SS courier and SS officer among them, each waving an arm. None carried luggage other than the courier's case. No Eddie. The ramp paused and the six men single-filed at its base to board. Saba checked the wharf, saw Eddie's keffiyeh pass the blue barrel.

Now the diversion fuse would be lit. In five seconds the barrel would explode, rice and chicken blood would splatter the dock entry. Eddie's keffiyeh hesitated at the protected side of the dock. The barrel exploded—PJs fell, began to yell in the fog of rice and chicken blood, stood, and charged off the dock into the wharf. Eddie ran onto the dock. Mount Teide boomed. The Arab woman dropped to her knees at the ferry gangway and began to wail a prayer. Mount Teide boomed again and shook the boat. The crowd at the rail shrank back, pointing. "*Volcán!*" The gangway bounced. The men trying to board flailed for balance. The Arab woman was knocked over. A tall, hooded Arab stumbled past her and up the gangway ramp behind the Nazis, his striped *jellaba* only reaching his knees. Saba elbowed to the ramp. The Nazis climbed onto the deck, fumbling out their tickets; the too-tall Arab did the same. Sailors tried to load the gangway before it was clear. Mount Teide added a long, low rumble then thundered a vertical cloud. The passengers flinched and began to yell. Saba grabbed Eddie away from the stewards taking tickets. She shoved him behind her and his ticket at the steward, her eyes hard in his.

The foghorn boomed twice. Mooring ropes were released and the gangway ramp tilted up, dumping a sailor and a passenger to their knees and into the steward. Deck passengers grabbed for balance and the boat slid sideways into the open harbor. Saba shuffled Eddie farther from the gangway gate. Mount Teide thundered again and the entire harbor shook.

Eddie said, "Jesus, Teide is gonna go."

Saba twisted a sharp hand into Eddie's side for speaking English, then pushed them farther toward the bow. The boat veered left to face the ocean. All eyes stayed right and high on the volcano.

"Say nothing. You are deaf."

"Hi."

She claw-twisted his skin under his *jellaba* and glared into his eyes. Life or death and he was still a boy. Eddie winced again and went silent. The ferry found its line and motored out into two-foot seas. Passengers crowded to the deck rail, gawking at a disaster they'd likely escape. Saba watched the SS Nazi and his courier enter the covered seats of the first-class cabin, sweat pouring off both. The courier had his case manacled at the wrist. Both Nazis took seats with a prominent view, showing some disregard for seats with better protection. Saba had been on this boat before; her plan for the SS courier was based on the reconnaissance her partisans had done, partisans now dead, left behind on a beach road in Tenerife.

Near the Nazis, an attractive girl removed her scarf, exposing naked shoulders. She shook out her hair and seemed oblivious to the prominence the movement added to her bosom. Both Nazis noticed. Saba smiled. In five hours the sun would be down behind their stern if Mount Teide did not light the sky. The ferry had been at sea eight hours when Eddie had delivered the bad news—the refinery fuse was now an unknown, but almost guaranteed to be faster than the ferry. They would still be aboard when the refinery imploded.

Saba reset the weapons under her tunic. The two Nazis shared wine and conversation with the young girl. She seemed to captivate them, more so every hour, sharing her glances with each and the occasional touches of her hand. Saba saw the girl's movements as magic—to be so comfortable with men, so sexual, and yet . . . Thoughts of Eddie made her shiver. And that made her angry. She glared at him.

Eddie noticed, and floated his eyebrows.

Saba said, "Quiet," and checked beyond his shoulders at passengers who might hear them over the thrum of the ferry's engines. "Soon now, when the remainder of the boat sleeps, Doña Carmen's girl will lead the Nazis one at a time to the crew deck below. There is a crew cabin at the bow. Both its occupants have been paid a rental. She will take them there; you will create a diversion on this deck—"

"I will?"

Saba stood on his right shoe. "Do you wish to die on this boat?"

Eddie frowned and removed his toe from under her shoe.

"Fall into a Spanish man and knock him down. Say nothing. Bow again and again, then shrink away while the Europeans insult you. *Do not* stand straight and reveal your height."

"What are *you* gonna do?"

Saba squinted her increasing displeasure. "I will kill two Nazis for your papers."

The words leaned Eddie backward. His keffiyeh slipped and he quickly reset it, his hand struggling with a simple movement.

"If I lose this fight for your papers, you are on your own. The girl will be arrested. Do not seek her out; she does not know you."

"Wait a minute. I should go down there with you . . . to help. If you need it."

"You wish to kill a man? Two men?"

Eddie grimaced. "No. But if it's them or you, they're dead."

"It is always that. European blood or ours."

Eddie leaned closer. "You forget to tell me you're glad I made it aboard, alive?"

Heat reddened Saba's cheeks. "These men I will kill have families, children or lovers or parents who will never see them again. Do you wish to watch, see me end their lives?"

Her words and tone straightened Eddie an inch. "Listen to me, okay? I'm not you, but this ain't my first day off the farm. I don't have to dwell on it or eat it all day. I see other stuff in you whether you like it or not. I can use a gun, and will, if that's my part. But when it's over we'll take a bath—together—and forget all this shit." Eddie looked past both her shoulders. "And if this boat wasn't full of people trying to kill us, you'd be on your back right now."

Saba burned at him with her eyes. Her boy-man accomplice would not know whether it was love and lust or the Raven's teeth coming out. She didn't, either.

Movement in the first-class section. The young girl led the SS officer through the aisle to the stairway door. Another man filled the officer's seat next to the courier. Military bearing, strong hands, and hard eyes. Saba checked for others she'd missed and saw none.

"There are three. We have a new plan." Saba's eyes lost their fire. "Now you will go to war."

The SS officer returned after forty-five minutes. The girl fifteen minutes later. A drink was shared and the girl now favored the courier with most of her attention. At eleven thirty p.m., the courier and the girl rose into the aisle, then moved toward the cabin door. The SS officer hand-directed the third man to follow.

Saba said, "Now."

On the crew deck below, she stopped Eddie under the pipes just short of the portside gangway wet with the ocean's spindrift and lit with silvery moonlight. "I will go alone. Draw your pistol. Shoot only if I am assured to die."

"Bullshit. It isn't going that far—"

Saba put a finger hard on his lips, then removed her keffiyeh and shook chestnut hair to her shoulders. She unbuttoned her tunic, displaying her breasts almost to the nipples. Eddie gawked. Saba turned the corner into the gangway, attempting a swish to her hips she had not mastered. The Nazi at the bow cabin door turned. He dropped a lifejacket he had been inspecting, leveled a Luger at her chest with his right hand, and barked: *"Halt."*

459

Saba stopped, both hands open and visible, the knife in her sleeve. The Nazi added words in a commanding tone and waved her back. She shrugged confusion and walked toward the gun. He leaned into a one-handed shooting stance and barked the command again. Saba stopped and feigned bewilderment, then pointed meekly at a cabin door past the one he guarded.

The Nazi growled, "*Lassen Sie!*"

Saba squinted and shrank into her shoulders. She pointed, moving only a fingertip. The Nazi threatened her with his body. She shrank under a raised arm. He swung to knock her sideways and overboard. Saba drove her knife under his arm and her head into his chin. His Luger clattered to the deck. Both hands ripped at her neck, their bodies wrenching into the rail. Saba's knife came free but not her neck. She lunged with her hips, bent the Nazi backward over the rail, and her feet left the deck— Hands grabbed her shoulders and jerked her free. Saba pressed backward into the hands and kicked the Nazi in the chest. He went over the side into the dark. She spun to stab— The hands were Eddie's. He stumbled backward into the cabins' outer walls, grabbing her with him and back around the corner. Both were panting. Eddie started to speak. Saba drew her pistol, ran back onto the gangway, and burst through the bow cabin's door.

The courier and the girl were half naked on a bunk, heads twisted toward the door. The girl rolled to the floor. Saba stiff-armed her pistol at the courier's head, stepped over the girl to the bunk, and slammed her fist into the courier's nose. Blood splattered the pillow. The courier's hand reached to his face. The death's head ring of the SS glittered. Saba smashed his hand and head with her pistol butt. Blood splattered and the Nazi moaned. She mounted him and rammed the pistol into his forehead. "The key, Nazi, and I do not kill you." Saba's breasts heaved; the pistol was rock steady.

The courier mumbled in German, his head shaking that he had no key. Saba slammed a fist into his solar plexus. Air and foam whooshed in her face. The courier swallowed his tongue and blacked out. Saba patted him for the briefcase key, found a key in his money belt. The key unlocked the wrist manacle, not the case. The courier was turning blue like his shirt. Saba flipped him onto his stomach. The flip forced a cough and the tongue out of his throat. She glanced at the girl on the floor then at Eddie, pistol out at the door. Doña Carmen's girl was scared white. Saba rolled the Nazi to his back and pumped on his chest. He began to gasp. Saba pointed Eddie at the case. "Pry it open." She produced a second knife.

The courier tried to speak.

Saba fixed the pistol barrel to his chest below his chin. "You are pigs. The English in different suits. What life you have is only if I give it." The tone was cold and absolute, no mistaking the veracity. "His name? The SS officer above."

"Herr . . . Rainer."

"His contact in Casablanca?"

Headshake.

Behind her, Eddie said, "It's here, all of it. Some other stuff, too."

"Take the papers, close the case if possible, and reattach it to this pig's wrist."

Eddie did that.

Saba turned to the girl. "Dress now. Remain here. I will bring new clothes. Do not return to the first-class section. Yes?"

The girl nodded.

Saba told the courier to stand. He did with difficulty, staggering. She said, "Are these papers true?"

He shrugged. She hit him as hard as she could, surprised at her anger. He crumpled to the floor, bleeding from his eye socket and cheek. "Are they true?"

He mumbled, "*Nein.*"

"*Nein?* So the Jews of Europe are to be spared? Shipped to Palestine to steal my country?"

The Nazi blinked through the blood in his eyes.

"Answer me."

He rolled his neck, confusion and pain in his face. "Palestine . . . *Juden* . . ."

"Up. Outside. A noise and I will kill you. Understand?" Saba checked Eddie, then pointed the girl out of the courier's path to the door.

The courier steadied. His case clanged against the other bunk.

"Out." Saba threw him past her to the door. The courier fumbled with the door latch, opened it, and stepped into the gangway's moonlight. A wave caught the bow. He stumbled over the dead bodyguard's bloody lifejacket, fell to his knees, rose, grabbed the lifejacket, and dived over the rail. Saba lurched after him, aimed, and— Only moonlight on the black. Saba spun. The girl was frozen. Saba steadied her. "Can you lure the SS officer here? The first man you had."

The girl tried to speak but couldn't.

"Can you?"

The girl stuttered, terrified. Saba pushed her ahead. "Hide. Now. Find a man, a sailor with a *different* cabin. The SS officer must not see you. Yes? You understand? He will know and they will kill you."

The girl stumbled forward. Eddie pushed the papers under his robe. "And?"

"Upstairs and stay away from the SS officer who remains."

"That's the plan?"

Saba grabbed and pulled at Eddie until he decided to follow her. They ran down a narrow passageway, some kind of storeroom tunnel, around an engine room thumping behind thin walls, and out onto a stern stairway. The stairs rose one deck and left them unnoticed in a crowd of Arabs either drunk or sleeping. Saba found them an unwanted corner with only enough room to sit against the humming bulkhead. Neither spoke while the adrenaline pumped. Both watched the dim lights of the first-class section.

The boat hummed and rocked as if nothing had happened. Saba reset her weapons under her clothes. Eddie Owen had watched her fight and kill a man with a knife. Now Eddie knew her. His playful boyish overtures would cease. In truth, she would miss them. Eddie sat with his shoulder and arm against hers, his eyes wide for threat. Saba hashed at options. If the SS officer were allowed to raise the alarm, Doña Carmen's girl would be found. The girl's silence would not withstand torture. Saba and Eddie would die in the water with the papers. The SS officer must be lured, killed, and dumped in the sea.

Sunrise.

The opportunity to kill the SS officer had not materialized. The first heat of the sun crossed the deck and her boots. Saba and Eddie had not spoken or slept. Male passengers began moving about, doing what men did when they woke in the morning. A Spanish Army officer told his ten soldiers near the bow to organize their gear and clean their weapons. The ferry would not dock for thirteen hours.

Soon the SS officer would sound his alarm. The Spanish soldiers would then search the entire boat. And every passenger aboard. Saba began to prepare for the outcome that Eddie would not yet understand was coming.

Erich Schroeder checked the sunrise from his hotel balcony and removed his tuxedo jacket. The refinery's christening had been a tiresome, sprawling affair that had gone well but had required countless skillful conversations with oilmen who mattered to

Reichsmarschall Göring now and who would absolutely matter to the new king of the desert, Erich Schroeder, in the very near future. The post-christening celebrations with his new oilmen associates had continued at the Los Paraguitas brothel and just now ended. When Eddie Owen delivered Saba today, as promised, her threat to dominion in the desert would finally end as well. Schroeder blew air through his lips. Thoughts of Saba alive and what damage she would cause had been his constant companion for months. Now he would focus on Himmler. Eddie would live a grand life as an honored guest of Reichsmarschall Göring. He would produce AvGas for the Reich and armor for Erich Schroeder.

The telephone interrupted kingly thoughts. An hour earlier, Schroeder had placed a call to Kansas City in the United States. This call back was the reconnection. Schroeder said hello, watching the sunrise illuminate the old colonial city of Santa Cruz, and listened.

There had been a problem in Oklahoma, a delay only, and now the "*Juden*" kidnap team was en route. Barring further unavoidable difficulties, they would have the Owen family in twenty-four hours. Schroeder swore and demanded an explanation that was not forthcoming. He was reminded that this line had many ears. Schroeder threw the phone at the just-repaired wall of his suite. Thankfully, the men assigned to Eddie and his disappearance from the christening to retrieve the Raven were submariners, not the German-American Abwehr rejects he had been forced to retrain and deploy in America.

At eleven a.m., a door knock startled Schroeder awake. He was still dressed; he had dozed in his chair. Schroeder opened the suite's door to one of the two submariners assigned to Eddie Owen. The submariner was sweating. In German, Schroeder asked, "The American is . . . here? At the hotel? Where is the woman?"

"*Nein.*"

Schroeder stepped aside and beckoned the submariner to enter.

"He, Eddie Owen . . . he is not in his room where last night's detail assures us he is. We wait for him to go to Volcán de Güímar as you say he will, but he does not. He is not in his room now and nowhere we can find him."

Schroeder's eyes widened. *"What?"*

The submariner stiffened.

Schroeder stepped into his face. Nose to nose, he said, "The PJs—"

"Nein. He is not in custody. I prove they do not have him."

"If my American is injured, harmed in any way by these Canarian pirates, I will kill your family. Find him. Now." Schroeder shoved the submariner into the door. "Use every man in your company. Go to the village below the Volcán de Güímar. Every house, door-to-door. Shoot as many as is required until you have my American safe in your hands."

Schroeder immediately engaged the smugglers and pirates he knew to canvass the island, then spent three frantic hours on the search himself, appearing first at the PJ commander's office, demanding Eddie be released unharmed or the commander who Eddie had nicknamed "Red Beret" would pay a price he could not conceive. Schroeder made the same threats to the Armada, both to no avail. He spoke with the *patrona* of Les Demoiselles, Doña Carmen, who knew nothing beyond her doors. He spoke to the whore Eddie had used and the girl knew nothing. Schroeder checked back with the smugglers. Nothing. He returned to the refinery to retrace Eddie's steps a third time. The refinery was awash in oil, some kind of catastrophic rupture.

Foreman Paulsen did not have time to explain until Schroeder and three submariners cornered him at gunpoint in a utility building. Paulsen was chalk white and said that the Santa Cruz d'Tenerife refinery had begun to melt two hours ago. It appeared that the electrical circuits of the cracking tower had welded first, causing a low temperature fire in the tower. The refinery firemen put out the cracking tower fire, not realizing that the damage being done was unrelated to the fire. Within minutes, the back-flow valves failed and the tank farm began to gush oil in a river of black. It was first thought to be the volcano. Eddie Owen could not be found. Foreman Paulsen said he suspected sabotage.

The all-day hunt had failed. The sun began its fall behind the volcano. Eddie had not been seen for twenty-seven hours. Exhausted, Schroeder paced his suite. The submariner Schroeder had sent to the village below the Volcán de Güímar where Eddie *had to be* returned without him or Saba. Neither was there and there was no evidence they ever had been. Schroeder used his phone to inform the Armada police that the saboteurs of the refinery were likely on the ferry. If left unimpeded, they would be loose on the mainland in a matter of hours. Schroeder replaced the phone in its cradle, turned, and the hard heel of his hand slammed the subma-riner in the temple. The submariner staggered sideways and over a low table, crashing the lamp and ashtray. Schroeder followed him to the floor, flicked open a gravity knife, and stabbed once using both hands. The submariner rolled. The blade missed and pinned his coat. Schroeder screamed and stabbed again. Until his arms and shoulders quit on their own.

CHAPTER 32

April, 1939

On the Casablanca Ferry, the Spanish captain and the SS officer stood on the bridge. Beneath them, Arabs crowded on the steerage deck. Saba and Eddie were backed into the bow rail facing the bridge from one hundred feet. Three Spanish soldiers moved into the crowd where the SS officer had just pointed. The soldiers forced three Arabs to remove their robes and keffiyehs. A fourth Arab refused, was shoved, then cut down by the butt stroke of a rifle. Arabs charged. Spanish gunfire forced the Arabs back and sorted the steerage deck into noncombatants and combatants.

The captain demanded a young woman be brought forward, a whore who hid among the passengers. The captain apologized to the angry Arabs for their beaten countrymen, then asked over their taunts and insults for calm and assistance with the missing woman who had murdered two passengers. The Arabs jeered at the Nazi demand and the captain's apology. The captain turned to a ships officer with a paper in his hand. The captain read the paper, spoke to the ten soldiers behind him, who quickly fixed bayonets to their rifles. The captain wadded the paper in his left hand and addressed the Arabs again, this time with a bullhorn.

"The Santa Cruz refinery has been sabotaged. The saboteurs are among you. You will produce them. If you do not, all passengers will submit to search. Those who do not submit will be shot and thrown into the sea."

The steerage deck jeered at the insult.

The captain switched to English. "The Palestinian terrorist known as 'the Raven' is among you. She is responsible. She travels with an American accomplice—"

"*Al Gorab!*" cheered a pocket of young Arabs close to the bridge. "*Al Gorab!*" Twenty more leaped up and down and pumped their fists. "*Al Gorab! Al Gorab!*" Eight of the twenty rushed the stairs to the bridge. The Spanish soldiers leveled their rifles and shot them dead in one volley. Eddie jolted backward and almost fell over the railing. Saba grabbed him back.

The captain shouted from behind the soldiers, "You will submit to a search and give up the saboteurs."

The Arabs shook their fists and yelled at the gun barrels and bayonets. Wind blew across the deck and flapped Eddie's keffiyeh. Mendelssohn's documents were hot against his stomach. The ferry had to be closing in on the Casablanca harbor. The harbor meant more authority. More authority meant more soldiers.

Under her breath, Saba said, "There will be no search here. The harbor is soon. French rule in Casablanca. They will sift the passengers; they know the Raven's wings." Saba turned away from the bridge and continued close to Eddie's ear. "The SS officer will demand action from the French until he has what he seeks. We will have a small chance when the fighting starts. These men"—she raised her chin at the Arabs—"have pride, if not arms. They will not be deported home and be humiliated in front of their families."

Eddie didn't see the boldness Saba described. He did see the anger, but the anger was in everyday Arabs—men who worked, who had found a way to function under the continuing colonial occupation. The boldness was in the eight young Moroccans dead shoulder-to-shoulder on the deck. If this ferry docked and the remaining ordinary fellows didn't rush down the gangway or riot, Saba, Eddie, and the Mendelssohn papers would end there.

Saba brushed the pistol under Eddie's robe. "Do not die a slave or servant. Farmers and shopkeepers in America defeated professional soldiers. I have done so since I was seventeen."

Eddie had seen her gut a professional killer before the Nazi knew what hit him. That same ferocity would roar when she was finally cornered. Saba had been distant since the killing, as if she expected him to loathe her. His response was the opposite. Her bravery and the honest commitment to her cause at all costs made her the Palestinian Joan of Arc. Eddie glanced down his shoulder. *Lotta woman; better find us a country where everything she does isn't life and death.* Eddie almost laughed, and would've if it wasn't so fucking tragic. War seemed to have a lot of life and death, just as D.J. had promised. He patted her hand next to his and she pulled it away.

Erich Schroeder was seated in his blood-splattered hotel suite but not because he wanted to be. He growled under his breath, his professional calm the sole reason he did not strike the third Armada inspector to interrogate him this hour. A terrified maid had reported the fight and the submariner hacked to death on Schroeder's carpet. The *Policía Judicial* were also in the room. Their commander, "Red Beret," was not interested in the murdered submariner. Red Beret was interested in the Nazi whose substantial influence had kept the

Policía Judicial away from an American who no one could find on the day his third refinery disintegrated.

Red Beret listened with his arms folded across his chest while Schroeder petitioned the Armada police to take action. "*Comisario*, I strongly suspect that the murderer of my friend, slaughtered here on my floor, is the Palestinian terrorist known as 'the Raven.' We believe her to be the bomber of Haifa and Bahrain, and quite possibly the saboteur of all our work here at your refinery. I do not believe the refinery's destruction is the fault of the volcano, as your more naive associates continue to suspect."

The *comisario* frowned. "Again, Herr Schroeder, the Armada's interest is the dead man at our feet and his blood on your clothes, not—"

"*And* that terrorist is likely on the Casablanca Ferry." Schroeder jammed his arm toward his open terrace doors. "She escapes as we talk *here*. Radio the ferry. We must board it."

The Armada *comisario* considered the demand and, when he had saved the proper amount of face, said, "This was done moments ago."

"What was done? How will you board it?"

"The ferry will be thoroughly searched when it docks in Casablanca."

Schroeder stood. "Casablanca is controlled by the French and rife with *Comité* terrorists who have no love for General Franco. Have CEPSA demand the ferry be diverted to a Spanish-controlled port where a proper search can take place."

The Armada *comisario* considered Schroeder's assessment and agreed, but ordered the demand be made in the name of the Armada police, not CEPSA, then told Schroeder to sit in his chair.

"*Nein.* I must go—"

"I will arrest you for murder the next time you speak." The Armada *comisario* waited until Schroeder spoke or sat.

Schroeder sat. In Spanish, the Armada *comisario* spoke to Red Beret. They walked out of Schroeder's hearing and continued to talk. Schroeder used the time to construct a plan. Take the seaplane. If the plane had not been repaired, take a seventy-kph smuggler's boat. A fast boat from Cabo de los Pescadores could have him on the mainland in . . . fourteen hours. His Luftwaffe agents were already inbound to Casablanca—that call had been made before the submariner's blood was dry. But to join the Luftwaffe agents, he had to go *now*. Schroeder glanced his watch. Eddie Owen was on the ferry. He was there to steal Mendelssohn's papers. That meant Saba Hassouneh was with him. The SS courier would be no match for her; the bodyguard would be, but he would not see her coming. No, Eddie and the Raven would have the papers when they disembarked the ferry.

Schroeder's jaw muscles rolled. He asked the second Armada inspector who had interrogated him, "Has there been trouble aboard the ferry?"

The officer considered the question. "Yes."

Schroeder shot to his feet. Red Beret drew his pistol. "Stop!"

Schroeder froze. Behind Red Beret, the Armada *comisario* opened the door, listened to a report, shut the door, and said, "The ferry captain has radioed back—he is already in French waters and lacks sufficient fuel to divert to the nearest Spanish-controlled port. The ferry will be searched in Casablanca."

Schroeder said, "The seaplane. We will use it—"

Red Beret barked: "The seaplanes are beyond repair. *And* the brave Luftwaffe Messerschmitt that graced our christening flew to Berlin ten hours ago."

Schroeder lied calm into his face. "My apologies. Much work has gone into this refinery, and this man is"—he glanced at the corpse—"was my friend. We have worked together since boyhood in the Ruhr Valley."

Red Beret did not lower the pistol. "Sit in your chair."

"Call your superiors. They understand my mission here. It is as an investment ambassador to your country. I have been betrayed, as have you. My friend is dead, my work ruined. All by the Palestinian and she gets away as we speak. Please, I must assist in her capture."

"And how will you do that in a foreign nation?"

"I have resources in Morocco. German resources in the French-occupied cities, Casablanca, Rabat, and Tangier. If the Palestinian succeeds in disembarking the ferry, it is possible I can facilitate her capture before the French hide her for their own purposes."

"First, you will sit; I will not warn you again. You will explain the American Eddie Owen's whereabouts. When I have him in custody, then I will make your call." Red Beret smiled. "If *my superiors* do not agree on your immense value—in light of all your promises that now smolder in ruin—then Herr Schroeder, you will go in the cage with Mr. Owen."

An hour later, Schroeder roared toward Casablanca, the sole passenger in a smuggler's V-hull for what would be a long, brutal fourteen hours. He pictured "the cage" he had avoided but didn't smile. There were many cages waiting in many countries, all with their doors open to him if he failed. The Casablanca Ferry would dock in one hour. Luftwaffe agents he had telephoned would be there. His instructions were ironclad: If Eddie Owen were identified or captured at the ferry dock by anyone but the Luftwaffe—and that included the Gestapo or the SS—the Luftwaffe were to gain the papers and Eddie Owen by *whatever means necessary*. The level of anger in Berlin and Karinhall at the refinery's sabotage had been blinding, most of it directed at Franco's refinery security and the PJs. But that would change if it ever became known or suspected that Eddie Owen, *Erich Schroeder's charge*, was responsible. Then there would be no way to escape a Himmler death sentence.

For that reason and endless others, the Gestapo could not have Eddie. Schroeder clenched his jaw tight at the pounding waves and glared at the black surrounding him. Eddie had been his, signed and sealed, and somehow Saba had turned him. But that would end when Eddie awoke to his family kidnapped. Eddie Owen would wear Nazi red and black and sing Munich Hofbräuhaus Bier Hall songs while he fed the crematoria. Eddie Owen would do whatever he was told or his family would die, slowly while he watched, one after the other.

The eight dead Moroccans on the ferry deck had begun to stink. Eddie glanced at Saba. Casablanca Harbor was dead ahead. The ferry passed the outer beacon of the harbor's 10,000-foot jetty and began a turn to port. Armed French Legionnaires were posted every one hundred feet along the jetty. The clay-brick buildings of Casablanca silhouetted in the mainland lights. The ferry reversed its engines to slow its approach. Bright deck lights popped on. Eddie ducked, shielded his eyes, and steadied against the deck rail. The wharf shadows became figures. More French Legionnaires, these with fixed bayonets. Eddie counted thirty. Saba nudged him with her elbow. A Spanish soldier craned his neck, staring at them over his shouldered rifle. The soldier bumped the soldier to his left and nodded in Eddie's direction. The ferry's foghorn boomed. The echo died, absorbed by the clay walls of a 1,300-year-old city. Behind the French Legionnaires, eight European men stepped out of the shadows—two groups of four. Saba told Eddie's ear, "From the Nazi embassy near the *Cathédrale*. When the search begins, we will have the one chance only."

A Moroccan on the ferry deck near the gangway gate threw his shoe at the soldiers. Four rifles fired. Everyone ducked. The captain yelled Arabic from his bridge: "Order! Or you will be shot. Two single-file lines at the gangway. Those who hide the Raven and the American will be hanged. Those with papers in order will be allowed to enter the kingdom of Morocco." The SS officer stood next to the captain and scanned the crowd. The deck passengers unbent with caution, then stood and began to shout and shake their fists again. The soldiers fired again over their heads. Saba pulled Eddie to midpack. The gangway dropped. They surged left, packed in with thirty men funneling to descend the gangway. Eddie eyed for the soldier who had eyed him. The pack inched onto the gangway. Eddie glanced at the dock. Both gangway lines ended at a French immigration officer backed by four French Legionnaires. Each passenger who attempted entry was separated from the front of his line and told to step forward, alone. Six additional French Legionnaires used bayonets to block the others in line.

The SS officer appeared near the ferry's deck rail, shouldering through the crowd toward the gangway. A Spanish soldier blocked his exit. They argued until the ferry captain shouted and pointed for the SS officer to be allowed passage. The SS officer descended through jeers and elbows and, at the bottom of the gangway, took up a position between the two descending lines to stare up at each passenger as he was confronted.

A French immigration officer ordered the SS man back. He refused to move. The immigration officer ordered two Legionnaires to shove the SS man out of the lines. Four Nazis from the embassy rushed to the SS man's aid. The Legionnaires and the Nazis went chest-to-chest. Shouts erupted on the gangway. An Arab in the left line refused to be searched. Jeers and support rained from the ferry's rail. Two Legionnaires charged up the gangway at the Arab. An Arab in the right line demanded the Spanish soldiers on the ferry be arrested for eight murders. The ferry rail yelled agreement and pumped their fists. A third Legionnaire butt stroked the Arab to the head and he tumbled off the gangway.

The crowd on the ferry deck roared and surged toward the rail. The ferry began to tip. Eddie grabbed Saba's shoulder. Two men on their left sprang at a Spanish soldier. He fired, then fought to keep his rifle. The hundred passengers still on deck flinched at the shot, then surged toward the gangway. The crush jammed Eddie and Saba into the gangway mouth. More shots behind them. Forty Arabs charged down at the French position already being overrun. The French and Nazis fired pistols.

At the top of the gangway, a Spanish soldier went airborne over the ferry rail. Rifles and pistols cracked. Fists and feet pounded in the bedlam. More gunfire—from the wharf and the ferry above. Saba shoved Eddie left and ran head down into a Legionnaire. Eddie knocked the staggered Legionnaire off his feet and was punched sideways by an Arab at his shoulder. Two Nazis with the Arab pulled the Arab and the SS officer out of the riot. The Arab shouted: "There! There!" Eddie sprinted a waterfront street behind Saba. Gunfire echoed off the old medina wall. Saba bolted through an opening in the medina wall. Eddie fell making the turn, rolled, made his feet, and bounded up wet steps. Saba waved from the top, then ran again. Eddie found her outside a keyhole doorway on Place de l'Amiral. Saba pulled him in, then two-handed a pistol at the opening, waited a five count, wheeled, and ran the steps behind them. They ran past the Hôtel Central, then past the Rue Central, until semi-interested Moroccans stopped looking. At a horse-stable bolt-hole they crawled in.

Eddie sucked enough air to pant, "Thanks."

Saba nodded. Eddie breathed all the air he could until he could swallow, then scooted to the bolt-hole's edge and peeked back at the street they'd run. No Legionnaires or Nazis. Eddie fell back next to Saba and panted, "Clear. We did it."

Saba showed no particular pride in their survival.

"C'mon, we did it—hundred to one— Pretty goddamn amazing."

"You have the papers."

"Yeah." Eddie tapped his chest. "Safe and sound. Now what?"

"I do not know."

Eddie glanced at their bolt-hole. "Damn, hadn't thought of that. Be daylight in eight or nine hours. Can't stay here."

Saba nodded. "Doña Carmen provides us a chance in Oran. She is known there, her father, after they fled Palestine. From Oran there are ships."

"How do we get to Oran?"

"A steam train from Fès. Twelve hours from station to station. I am told there is no other way. We take the train and our chances."

"Wait. Who all knows we'll be trying for that train? *If* we can get to Fès."

Saba smiled for the first time since she had killed the Nazi bodyguard. "My American boy grows to manhood." She paused. "If we are betrayed—"

Eddie reached around Saba's waist and pulled her to him in the straw. "I can *show* you manhood."

Her breasts were mashed against his chest. She didn't fight, wasn't fighting; her chin was high, neck exposed. "You think me yours now? To do as you wish?"

"You're the one who wishes."

Heat radiated through her shirt. Eddie couldn't tell if the heat was sex or violence, but it was hot.

"You burn from death avoided—"

Eddie kissed her hard on the mouth.

Saba kissed back, sort of, but didn't press into him. Her breath shortened but she didn't pull away. Lips brushing his, she said, "You would have your woman in a stable?"

Her breasts were lush against his chest. Eddie kissed her again. "Say *yes*."

Saba didn't. She said, "We must go. To Rabat while we have the night, then Fès, then the train to Oran."

Eddie said, "Say *yes*."

"Survive the night . . . and we shall see about your woman."

Doña Carmen's girl was seated on a bunk in the ferry's bow cabin. She had explained all she knew to the three Nazis and now explained it again, this time to a pale-white Gestapo officer dressed as a German embassy official.

"I meet Gerhard, the courier, at Les Demoiselles. Gerhard invites me to travel with him to Morocco. I am paid in full for the ferry trip and one night in Casablanca." She glanced at the SS officer she had also serviced. "But aboard the ferry, this man here, he takes me first. Gerhard was angry but did not show it until we became alone in the cabin. We were only out of our clothes when an Arab man and woman attacked from the door." She pointed. "They fought and Gerhard jumped overboard."

The Gestapo officer's arms remained folded across his chest. He glanced at the SS man, then back to the girl. "And what of Gerhard's briefcase?"

The girl repeated what she said the first time. "The case was attached to him."

"Did they open it?"

"No."

"The Arabs, what did they say? Everything."

She shrugged. "Nothing."

The Gestapo officer leaned closer. "Nothing?"

The girl leaned back.

"You will tell me what they said or we will take you to sea, tie you to a board, and drag you as bait." He wagged his finger. "The sharks. Very bad."

The girl shivered and looked to the others for help. The SS officer said, "Leave her with me. She will tell me."

The Gestapo officer lowered his arms, a straight razor in his left hand. "Your part in this, Herr Oberst, will be discussed at the embassy. Reichsführer Himmler awaits your call. You will please remove yourself from the cabin and allow the Gestapo our work."

The other Gestapo man unbuttoned his coat.

Schroeder's first five hours of open ocean in the smugglers' boat had been brutal. His radio headphones shut out the engine roar, but the sharp mainland static sung at his ears like bees. His Luftwaffe agents on the Casablanca dock reported the ferry riot and that no Eddie Owen had been identified or arrested. The Gestapo were aboard the ferry with a Canarian female believed to be somehow involved.

"Eddie Owen was on that ferry. He cannot be far. Find him."

At four a.m., Schroeder cupped his headphones and shouted into a radio call to the mainland. "REPEAT. Say again, REPEAT." Schroeder listened, then grabbed the boat captain's shoulder and shouted over the engine to veer due east for the fortified port city of Essaouira.

On Schroeder's radio was a smuggler and coastal operative in Schroeder's Luftwaffe network. The smuggler explained to Schroeder that an SS courier had been found naked but alive by a coastal fishing boat two hundred and fifty kilometers south of Casablanca near Essaouira. He had a case manacled to his wrist. Before falling unconscious, the courier had rambled in German but the Portuguese fishermen could not understand. The smuggler told Schroeder, "I am the only German speaker the police know in Essaouira. I go to the doctor's office, see the courier's death's head tattoo and the outline of a missing ring on his right hand. I search the briefcase. The only item I find is your card with the number at the Hotel Mencey."

In German, Schroeder yelled over the engine roar and wind. "Is he alive?"

"*Ja.*"

"You will be well paid. Does Essaouira have a seaplane?"

"*Nein*, but there is a smuggler's plane at Safi."

"Reserve this plane. Steal it, commandeer it, and fly to Essaouira. I will dock at Essaouira in two hours."

It took only ninety minutes. Inside the doctor's clinic in Essaouira, Schroeder spoke comforting German to the near-drowned courier, promising him a European doctor was en route from the German embassy in Casablanca. The SS courier coughed and shivered and rattled and said he was attacked by an American man dressed as an Arab and a woman dressed as a man. The courier's eyes rolled back and he coughed blood. Schroeder wiped the blood away and reassured the courier he would survive.

The courier spit and gasped and said the whore had betrayed him. It was the whore and . . . and . . . and she wanted to see Oran. Would he take her there? Doña Carmen had mentioned Oran to her often. Other girls from Les Demoiselles had been to Oran. Oran, the great gateway. From Oran she could go anywhere in the world.

Schroeder paid his operative twice what was expected. "I wish to buy your services and loyalty. If you sell both and betray me or the Fatherland, we will kill your family here and in Stuttgart, all of them."

"I am yours to command, Herr Oberstleutnant."

"Execute this coward. Cut off his hand, put it in the case, and deliver it to the embassy in Casablanca. Tell the *ambassador* that it is your belief the SS courier was taken for ransom by bandits on the ferry and was poorly protected by his SS companions."

"*Jawohl*, Herr Oberstleutnant."

"I will use your radio, *bitte.*"

The operative turned to the SS courier on the bed, placed a pillow tight on the courier's face, and suffocated him. Both feet kicked under the sheets. Schroeder's operative used a saw to sever the courier's dead hand, placed the hand in the briefcase, then drove Schroeder to the land-based radio. Schroeder contacted his Luftwaffe agents in Casablanca. "Eddie Owen was on that ferry. What have you found if not him?"

"Nothing. A possible sighting, but likely a lie for money. The Gestapo aboard the ferry argue with the French to explain the whore's screams. A Gestapo staff car waits. The driver thinks he drives to Rabat and possibly on to Fès."

"The whore. She must know." Schroeder considered Himmler's probable reaction to his vaunted SS losing the papers. Himmler would twist any testimony from the whore into fact and demand that Schroeder produce Eddie Owen. If Schroeder did not, Himmler would state that it had been Eddie Owen who had murdered the courier and stolen the papers. "Do you have good people in Rabat?"

"*Nein*. People, yes, good, no."

"In Fès?"

"*Ja*. Very good. From there we are strong across North Afrika—Tunisia, Algeria, Libya, Egypt to the Suez—and become stronger each day. We will be ready when the war begins."

Schroeder hoped that was true. "I will fly the Safi seaplane to Rabat. Meet my seaplane and we drive to Fès. Can you arrange a ground plane in Fès?"

"Unlikely that there will be planes whose privacy or safety you can trust. The Communists and the Islamic Nationalists pay close attention, but we will try. To where?"

Schroeder said, "Oran."

"There is a train in Fès to Oran. Twelve hours."

"I know of this train. Offer a reward at the train station in Fès. Any amount. Tell the Arabs there that the American works for the French, that the woman is . . . an infidel, her tattoo a lie. She is a defiler of the mosques in Mecca who has stolen from the Great

Mosque in Casablanca. Then reach to Oran; there your network must bribe the locals in the French police, anyone and everyone. Should our mice succeed in arriving in Oran, we must not allow them out."

"*Jawohl*, Herr Oberstleutnant."

Schroeder handed the radio mic to the operative. "The seaplane. *Mach schnell.*"

The operative called for the seaplane that would cut Eddie Owen's lead to zero *if* Rabat were his first destination. Schroeder stared out the operative's small window to the ocean and Tenerife to the southwest. So it had been Doña Carmen who had saved the Raven. The *patrona* and her whores. And now Saba Hassouneh was one. Fitting.

Schroeder balled one fist. Once he was past the customs dock in Rabat, he would dispatch the operative and the Safi plane to Tenerife with orders to bring the *partisan* Doña Carmen alive to Fès where she could be questioned. By a professional. Schroeder would use his fingers, possibly his teeth.

CHAPTER 33

April, 1939

Schroeder feigned calm while the French customs/immigration agent at Rabat made a series of helpless hand gestures designed to elicit a contribution of some negotiable amount. Rather than shoot the French agent, Schroeder eyed the river cliff high to his left. Atop the cliff, the pirate stronghold of Salé threatened the river's mouth. According to the two Luftwaffe men who had just met his seaplane from Essaouira, the Gestapo had already been here and gone. The Gestapo had searched for and found a Salé truck driver and his young son who had picked up two travelers on the road outside Casablanca. The truck driver and son did not survive their interrogation. The Gestapo car was now bound for Fès. The car had left one hour ago.

Schroeder dispatched the Luftwaffe men to recheck the Salé story for any other details of any kind, then commandeered the Luftwaffe car. He fought trucks, wagons, and camels on the 180 kilometers of damaged road from Rabat to Fès. Ahead of his arrival, three Luftwaffe agents combed Fès with a reward backed by news of the tattooed infidel who had sacked the mosques and murdered a *marabout* holy man in Salé. Himmler's Gestapo would be doing the same. Like everywhere, God was only slightly less powerful than money.

Schroeder swore at the Arabs who crowded his road. The reward in Fès must be *his* money, not Himmler's.

Alone, Saba approached the Fès train station. She would wait in silence until others discussed the steam train to Oran. The train station had spies, as did all such places in the desert. They watched her and she watched them. Finally she heard the train would not be until tonight. She returned to where she had instructed Eddie to wait and shook her head once. "We must hide in the medina. Fès el Bali, the old city. Now."

The old city was a fourteenth-century maze, much more intricate and confusing than Rabat. Saba was cautious but comfortable, drifting them toward the Andalusian Quarter and the Bein El Moudoun Bridge. On the tannery and dyer's side of the bridge would be much activity, few police, and no Europeans. Saba stopped just short of the bridge at a crumbling mosque, its cobbled courtyard dotted with elderly beggars sitting alone, praying worry beads with both hands and rocking. She pushed Eddie inside the courtyard and forced him to sit alone against a wall and abandoned him there.

Outside the courtyard, a woman on the sidewalk passed Saba's shoulder, walking with a foreigner's precision. Saba crossed the narrow street and bought flatbread in an Algerian storefront with the last of her money. She watched.

A European man strolled past, glancing in the storefront. Another European stopped uphill at the bridge and talked with two smaller Moroccans. The Arabs listened then hurried in opposite directions. Saba clenched her jaw. The truck driver and boy in Rabat had sold them; Eddie's clothes would be known. He would not survive long in the daylight. Across the cobblestone street where Eddie sat, Saba checked for beggars who were not beggars, found no imposters, walked to Eddie, and pulled him to his feet. She whispered to his ear: "You must change clothes. Now. There are men on the streets."

Eddie was looking at the bridge. She tightened her grip on his robe, twisted, and yanked him forward.

"Easy." He knocked her hand away.

Saba glared at his English, then hissed: "Go, then. Since you are long in the fight and know better." She released his robe and hurried into the shadows of a crevice alleyway. Hurried footfalls followed her. Saba ducked and Eddie stumbled past, his arm extended to grab where her shoulder had been. Saba rose behind him, her pistol in hand as Eddie pivoted fast to face her.

Saba glared behind the pistol. "You are good alone?"

Eddie exhaled. "Guess not."

"You will not be a bull and live. They are many and we are few. Do as I say or die on your own."

"I wanna get us out of here, that's all. We're this close."

She stepped to his face. "To death you are that close."

Eddie looked like a proud, brave man who wanted to say or do something but didn't. Saba relaxed behind her glare and thought they might live to see the train.

Schroeder arrived Fès at noon, hungry and sick. Amphetamines masked his pallor and temperament after fighting 1,200 kilometers of bad water, air, and road. Two of the three Luftwaffe men met his car. One said the Gestapo and their agents were well represented at the train station and in the Fès medina. There had been whiffs of the fugitives but no contact.

Schroeder pushed himself and his men through three more hours of bribes and threats. The effort produced nothing. At three o'clock p.m., a hungry hand opened and led them to a beggar near the Karaouine Mosque. The beggar there knew nothing of value other than he wished to lie for money. Schroeder fumed. *It has to be Oran.* For centuries, the port city had been the smugglers' gateway out of North Africa no matter which occupying power tried to stop them. It was clear; Saba was leading Eddie and the papers to Palestine. Palestine was where the papers would stay—whether Eddie agreed or not—until the Raven could ransom them for an arsenal of men and money that would underwrite her cause, a cause that would also include the death or destruction of Erich Schroeder if the opportunity arose.

It has to be Oran. The Gestapo were at the train station. It had to be the steam train to Oran. Or did it? Saba would not have told the truck driver. The Gestapo were guessing, just as his Luftwaffe was. The train was slow. Saba was resourceful. Her pursuers would be frozen here in Fès all day waiting for the boarding . . . *while she breaks for Oran on the highway.*

Schroeder bolted for the car. He left instructions with two of his three Luftwaffe agents: If Eddie and Saba did try to board the train, capture Eddie alive, shoot Saba, and shoot the Gestapo agents. If Eddie did not board the train, shoot the Gestapo agents and remain in Fès one day for the next train to Oran.

Sunrise. Saba and Eddie had now lived a full day longer than her expectation. Rather than board the train in Fès, she had secured transportation east one hundred kilometers into the desert. There she and Eddie had joined the Al-Maghreb steam train when it stopped for water at Taza. The train was six cars, one for freight, all wooden and painted maroon and completely full. The train was battered and dirty, having arrived at Fès late after plowing through a monumental sandstorm in the great desert between Taza and Guercif.

Saba and Eddie sat in two of the Al-Maghreb's dusty first-class seats—the only passage available and bought by selling the gold ring Eddie had given her. The ring had also bought food and a black *jellaba* with matching keffiyeh for Eddie. His disguise was solid, but they stood out in this car, the only "natives" who were not jammed into the trailing fourth-class "steerage" coaches. By comparison, the dusty, frayed seats in the lead car were luxurious and comfortable. Saba fought the comfort and the sleep she desperately needed. She could not risk sleep surrounded by Europeans.

The chase had been even harder on Eddie. Eddie was a civilian who knew none of the signs—friend or foe, fight or flee—for him every step of the last three days had been constant adrenaline. He had done well for a civilian, remarkably well, but the toll had finally drowned him in a fitful sleep. Saba dug a painful thumbnail into her finger. The heat and steel-on-steel *clickity-clack* that had lulled his eyes shut and his body limp would do the same to her if she were not vigilant . . .

Saba startled awake, both hands on her weapons.

Her eyes cut and scanned. The train was slowing. She pushed higher in her seat. Out the window across the aisle, a shack appeared in the rocky desert, then another, a sign read Taourirt. The train slowed to stop under an elevated water tank. Eddie startled awake. His hand went to his weapon. Saba touched his leg with her knee. Eddie cut to her calm in her seat . . . then . . . eased back into his, the muscles of his arm taut against hers.

Saba watched the windows, her weapons ready. From the trailing cars, second- and fourth-class passengers unloaded onto the dusty station platform crowded with hard-looking Legionnaires and black men in uniform. A passenger seated in front of her told another, "Mercenaries. French Senegalese." Doña Carmen had spoken of mines in Morocco's barren hills and the Nationalists' threats against them. Saba logged the Legionnaires' weapons. The black mercenaries also carried the full complement. It was obvious the French meant to keep this country and whatever was in the mines.

An hour out of Taourirt, Saba calmed and exhaustion again overtook her.

She jolted awake from the black. Eddie had her hand; she snatched it back, gripped her weapon under her tunic, scanned the car, focused on an Englishman in the forward seats, and— No movement, no eyes, no threat. She cut just her eyes to Eddie.

Eddie smiled, winked, and rubbed his face. The air in the car was thick with heat. Another hour passed. Eddie's eyes closed and remained closed. Slowly his neck relaxed his head into the seat. One hand sought her leg. Saba allowed it, then allowed her hand to cover his. *Her*, seeking a man's touch and so much less frightening when he slept. Her breast edged against his upper arm and her nipples stiffened. The instant arousal was dizzying. She admitted for the second time her desire to feel a man and flushed so completely she almost fainted. Eddie stirred and she jolted. He faced her, but thankfully still asleep. Bold was difficult with his eyes only a blink from hers. She imagined sex. Being a woman was—a smile inched on her lips—confusing.

Four rows forward in the car, the Englishman sat with his seat flipped to face to the rear. His view would be the rugged terrain after it was overtaken and then all the train's trailing cars as they snaked through the hills and mountains. He read a book with both hands that his bespectacled eyes never left. Saba stared at the rough hands and his mottled red complexion.

Across the aisle from the Englishman, another set of seats was flipped to face the rear. Two Europeans in businessmen's fedora hats shared a flask and an argument's ever-louder tone with a German pair whose backs were to her. The Germans spoke English and lectured the drinkers. The morning sun quit suddenly as the train entered a narrow crease in the 10,000-foot Atlas Mountains. A slurry, aristocratic Italian accent answered a question Saba hadn't heard. The Italian's hands fluttered above his head as he and one of the Germans debated each other's ability to rule foreigners. The German seemed unimpressed. The Italian shouted like a boy on a playground might and shook a fist.

An insulting German laugh rustled Eddie awake. The German said something unintelligible and waved pages of his newspaper as proof of whatever he'd said. Saba read the headline in the gap between the seats. The news pressed her back; her exhale was audible. Eddie blinked at her. The Englishman raised his eyes from his book, listened but didn't focus. The Italian shouted, "Palestine? She has no future, no oil." He waved his flask at the newspaper headline. "Iraq prepares to attack Kuwait for her oil. Then Palestine will be but empty desert in bin Faisal's 'Pan-Arab Empire.'"

Saba felt eyes. The Englishman was staring directly at Eddie in his black keffiyeh. She took a breath she needed, nudged Eddie's hand toward his pistol, and reached nearer hers. The Englishman quickly returned to the book now resting on his knees, a heavy cloth valise tight between his feet. Saba noted his boots. Military or miner. Then his hands again, large and too rough for a businessman.

She pushed deeper into her seat. *Bin Faisal is openly threatening Kuwait.* How had his Pan-Arab Army of God grown so bold? Even the newspapers knew. Now bin Faisal would be much harder to kidnap or kill . . . but infinitely more valuable. Saba's spirits brightened in spite of the shock. Eddie's papers would buy the bin Faisal betrayal and the arms for her partisans. Bin Faisal's ransom or death would swell a partisan army and earn enough money, arms, and men for a serious challenge against the British. She and the partisans would overthrow one entire city, wipe out the garrisons, arm the population, and call for an Arab revolt as her father had called for revolt in 1929. This time the death struggle could end differently—Palestinians would have proved the British could be beaten.

Eddie patted her hand. She clenched and checked the Englishman. His eyes weren't focused on the book. Saba used her knee, then jutted her chin until Eddie glanced forward. Eddie ceased further demonstrations of his affection.

Schroeder had been in the ancient coastal seaport of Oran for three and a half hours. Under its current rulers, Oran was a smoldering collision of European colonial power and Arab Nationalist illusions. The pirates and smugglers and religious fanatics had always been here.

At great risk, Schroeder had involved the Abwehr and now made a final check for the confrontation to come. His car limped up Boulevard Marceau a third time, the car beaten badly by a blinding sandstorm near Guercif and the almost useless frontier roads. The 450-kilometer trip had taken fifteen hours instead of five. If Eddie and Saba had attempted the frontier road, they were dead or dying buried in the frontier sand. But Saba Hassouneh was of the desert; she would have known not to drive. In his exhaustion and amphetamines, Schroeder had miscalculated. Saba and Eddie were on the steam train. His men had not seen her board in Fès, but somehow she had. That steam train would arrive here in Oran in four hours.

One of the two telephone calls Schroeder had been able to complete had further reduced his options but strengthened his belief that Oran via Doña Carmen was Saba's plan—the operative from Essaouira who Schroeder had sent to abduct Doña Carmen had been found dead with his Safi pilot. According to the Armada police on Tenerife, the victims had run afoul of "Canarian bandits" in the brothel district of Santa Cruz.

Schroeder's car clanked and banged the last of Boulevard Marceau toward Oran's grand arabesque train station and the gravel car park on its west side. In his car sat one of the Luftwaffe men who had met his car in Fès and a Luftwaffe agent based in Oran who was new to the network but well versed in the city. Schroeder squinted toward the train station. Saba, Eddie, and the Mendelssohn papers would be on the Al-Maghreb steam train. They would be.

Two Abwehr agents waited outside the Oran station. The Abwehr agents traded shade from the blinding sun for protection from the howling sirocco winds. When Schroeder had arrived he had invoked Reichsmarschall Göring's name and added bribes of his own, convincing the two Abwehr agents to reblanket the Arab Quarter and the medina with the same infidel/reward offers Schroeder and the Gestapo had used in Rabat and Fès. Oran's Muslim underground was strong—the *Étoile Nord-Africain* (the Star of North Africa)—but underfunded by its Communist benefactors. For a price, Oran's Muslims would be pleased to produce an infidel spying for the French, a tattooed whore who had murdered holy men and desecrated mosques in Morocco.

The infidel Muslim gambit had its risks, the most dangerous a potential confrontation with the French that Schroeder and the Abwehr agents would not survive. Oran was a major port dominated for the last century by the French navy. From here France ruled the southwestern Mediterranean. Now the French faced increasingly violent assaults from these Muslim Nationalists, much as the English did in Iran, and were in no mood to be gentle with provocateurs from any country, and especially not Nazis.

The Abwehr agents told Schroeder they had no leads on Saba's contact here. Schroeder threatened them back into the city, demanding they marshal any and all resources, even those designed to stay hidden for the larger conflict all knew would come in the future.

Schroeder did not mention the Mendelssohn papers. His story was that he and Reichsmarschall Göring had to know anyone connected to Doña Carmen and her network that had sabotaged the Tenerife refinery. Name them, find them. *Now.*

Schroeder and his two Luftwaffe men braced through the wind and entered the train station. The cavernous Arabesque structure was crowded with loud, sweaty Arabs, French soldiers, and sulfate miners of several nationalities. The air was tobacco, sweat, and spice breath. Eddie and Saba would arrive in four hours. Schroeder walked to the platform where the Al-Maghreb train would arrive. One of his two Luftwaffe men would enter the last fourth-class steerage car and move forward; the other would enter the front steerage car and move to the rear. Eddie and Saba would flee onto this platform amid the other Arabs and be forced into Schroeder's guns and waiting hands.

Unfortunately, the officers of the French police prefecture and the *Armée d'Afrique* of "Greater France" would not allow Saba's murder and Eddie's kidnap without a French response. Schroeder remapped his diversion. As the train's steerage cars began to empty, he would rush to the French police on the platform, tell them that the Raven (and the bounty) was aboard this very train. She would appear; he would point. Saba would engage the French police to their maximum capabilities.

Schroeder did not share his plan with his two Luftwaffe men. He told them, "Saba Hassouneh will be dressed as a man and is very fast, very dangerous. Do not allow her near you. Do not wait on the French police. *Shoot her on sight.* The American must be taken alive. If he carries a case of any kind, we must have it as well."

"*Jawohl.* And the French police if they wish to intervene? The French are not soft here, Herr Oberstleutnant. Our instructions have been to avoid engagement at all costs."

Schroeder nodded. "We have no alternative; this American is vital to Reichsmarschall Göring and to me. We must have the American alive."

The Luftwaffe man added tight leather gloves in spite of the heat. "And if we succeed?"

"If?" Schroeder peeled his lips thinking of Himmler and his Gestapo dungeons, of short trials and long torture for race treason. "Both of you will be well rewarded. Fail, and the price will be high, for all of us."

Saba stayed within herself, eyes everywhere and nowhere, as the Al-Maghreb rattled tense and wary into the mountains. A final stop was made at Oujda, the Italians in the forward seats describing it to the Germans as the "protected route to the manganese mines at Bouarfa." Loud Spaniards boarded, likely from the Melilla coast, all with weapons in their waistbands. When the train left here it would be bandit prone and become the "Fès-Algiers," passing into the vast and desolate Algerian frontier to Oran, then on to Algiers. Saba braced as the Spaniards shuffled to replace the German-Italian foursome rising to leave, still discussing Italy and Germany's plans for North Africa and Europe.

The Englishman eyed their departure.

The Italians seemed surprised to see Arabs in the car and so close behind them. The last of the foursome into the aisle was the sober German, young and blond but with hooded eyes and the small smile of a man who hid his importance poorly. Saba had seen many such men, pleased with their ability to frighten others. He reminded her of Erich Schroeder.

●●●

Eddie's stomach woke him, registering the train's steep, sudden descent off a treeless plateau. He glimpsed a cathedral dome; the dome vanished, replaced by a sheer drop to the sea below. Eddie craned at his window. At the track's edge, a rugged coastline plunged toward the Mediterranean and a seaport's long quays stacked with goods. Military vessels dominated the harbor, guns pointed ashore and to sea. Each ship flew France's *tricolour*, blue, white, and red. Eddie looked at Saba; this had to be Oran; he'd slept the entire way.

A long whistle sounded. The train braked hard, shrieking on the rails, then began to inch downward in lurches. The tracks curved at the base of a fortified peak and turned back on themselves as the train rounded the peak, then straightened into an amphitheater of low buildings beneath the plateau. At sea level, the train stopped.

Eddie whispered, "Legionnaires on my side. Lots of 'em."

Saba's hand disappeared into her robe. No passengers were allowed to disembark. No Legionnaires or *Armée d'Afrique* soldiers boarded the train. At the rear, the freight car was uncoupled and left on a siding. The remainder of the train backtracked higher on the same tracks they had descended, chugging around the peak, stopping to switch tracks, then lurched forward under and through the outer gates of Oran's train station.

The station looked like the Alamo with a five-story minaret clock tower. The Alamo reminded Eddie of his family. He'd put them in the Nazi's hands, a Nazi who at this moment would do just about anything to stop their son. Eddie shivered. He had to warn his parents, had to find a way to get to Benny and Floyd if Doña Carmen hadn't/couldn't get to them as agreed. But Eddie wouldn't be doing that if Saba's escape plans didn't work. She made it fifty-fifty—they escaped or they didn't. Her advice was what it always was: "Do not be taken alive."

A conductor walked the aisle announcing something in French. Eddie could make out only "Oran" and "passports." As planned,

Eddie stood from his window seat to join the passengers disembarking. Saba grabbed his arm and chinned at the window. Eddie bent and eyed the window.

Erich Schroeder.

The two men with Schroeder were splitting toward each end of the train. *That ain't good.* Eddie started to speak. Saba's hand covered his mouth. The European passengers in the seats behind them filed past toward the front of the car. The car was almost empty. Beyond the windows, Erich Schroeder spoke to a French policeman. Schroeder's men were gone. Police whistles shrilled on the platform. Loud, shouted French commands followed. The four fourth-class steerage cars disgorged three hundred ill-tempered passengers and their goods. Uniforms rushed through toward the train. Inside the first-class car, the last passenger cleared Eddie and Saba's seat aisle. Saba nodded toward the rear of the car while the front exit was still jammed. "Now. They will think us in the steerage cars."

"My absolute pleasure."

The coupling between the rear of the first-class car and first steerage car was empty. Saba pulled Eddie out of their car onto the coupling. She shoved him airborne between the cars. Eddie landed on his back. The concussion knocked his air out. Gasping, he rolled to a shoulder. Saba landed on her feet and helped tug him between the wheels under the car and onto the tracks. Eddie sucked air but got steam, choked, covered his face, coughed, and gasped. Steam hissed from the engine and billowed on the track bed. Saba pumped on Eddie's chest. Eddie blinked back from blackout. Rats scattered from hot bits of oil and ran past Eddie's shoulders. Eddie caught enough air to breathe and rolled to his stomach. The station platform was four feet above him and the track bed's slick gravel. Feet thudded on and off the train above. Loud, angry arguments mixed with thuds and scrapes of goods landing and being recovered. French commands echoed, followed by Arabic and French profanity. The train lurched a foot forward, whistled, and geysered steam.

Saba told Eddie's ear: "Trouble on the platform; the train departs early." She rolled toward the car's opposite edge, then over the rail and out onto the railbed's bank. The Al-Maghreb lurched another foot. Eddie rolled toward the rail. The train whistled, lurched again, and Eddie rolled past the wheel before it cut him in half. He stood, stayed tight to the train, and ran with Saba along the tracks, keeping pace with the coupling where they'd dropped. On the inside track, another steam engine chugged toward them; signal poles and the workers manning the poles started to turn. The Al-Maghreb's momentum built. Saba jumped up and into the coupling. Eddie chased the opening until he could follow her up and in. Once aboard, he yelled: "Goddammit, don't do that again."

Panting, Saba pulled them to a crouch and pointed at the trailing steerage cars. "There are Nazis aboard. But they must come to us through the Legionnaires and mercenaries who boarded at Taourirt." Saba pointed with her pistol to the first-class passenger car door at her shoulder. "And there will be a Nazi in there."

Eddie pulled his .45.

Saba said, "This train is now named . . . the Express 101 to Algiers, 'the death train.' The Algerian Nationalists throw grenades at the Europeans in the first-class cars."

The Oran station disappeared behind them. Eddie grabbed her to jump off. "We're here to meet Doña Carmen's folks. C'mon—"

"No. We have been betrayed." Her eyes checked his. "We find another way."

Erich Schroeder scanned Oran's cavernous station crowded to its limits and the horde of angry passengers being blocked from exit. He turned and eyed the platform he stood, then the train tracks beyond. Eddie had been on that red wooden train. Schroeder lacked absolute proof but he knew it. The train billowed steam toward Algiers. Schroeder squeezed his fists white as the last of the angry Arab passengers filed toward and past him on the platform. The Europeans were grouped to themselves and being calmed by a uniformed railroad employee. One of Schroeder's two Luftwaffe men stood five feet away, caution evident in his distance. The other had not jumped off when the train emptied all but the Legionnaires and Senegalese mercenaries. A uniformed captain of the French prefecture station guards barked in Schroeder's ear, the captain furious that he'd been duped about "the Raven" and now threatened Schroeder with jail for the near riot he'd caused.

"The Raven was on that train." Schroeder spun and jammed his hand at the crowd. "And the Raven is in that crowd."

The uniformed police captain swore in French and spit on Schroeder's shoes. Schroeder scanned fast for an exit that would skirt the customs queue. He and his remaining Luftwaffe man must get to the gravel car park at the front of the station, where they could safely watch every passenger as he or she was processed through customs.

Schroeder pivoted away.

The French captain yelled: "*S'arrêter!*" and poised a whistle near his lips. He yelled more French, furious at Schroeder and his Luftwaffe accomplice. Near the back of the queue, an Arab shouldering a heavy box was knocked hard by another passenger. The Arab stumbled. His box fell and split. Grenades rolled like deadly marbles. Schroeder and his Luftwaffe man sprinted. The French captain drew his sidearm and shot the Arab. The crowded terminal erupted—men and freight swarmed at and over the customs queue. More shots. Schroeder and his man followed the other Europeans through a police gate to the outer car park, then turned and faced the mob trying to overrun the queue. Schroeder pulled his man behind the protection of an automobile fender. "Ours will be the tallest Arab! Search for tall! Bent over!"

Sirens wailed. More police and *Armée d'Afrique* soldiers charged past. Arabs who successfully fought out of the station were beaten to the gravel. Schroeder palmed the Luger under his coat. "They were on that train." Schroeder squinted through the wind and riot for tall or bent over. The Luftwaffe man did the same, his Luger in-hand behind his leg. No one resembling Eddie Owen in size or color passed through the queue. Schroeder said, "But they are here. Somehow. On the train. And they make for Palestine."

The Luftwaffe man's eyes were intent on anyone and everyone. The queue emptied. No Eddie Owen. No Raven. Schroeder refocused on the port and its many ships. "Oran is a thief's clearinghouse. The Raven is wanted by the French, Spanish, and English. My American is wanted by the English. Algeria is a thousand miles of impassable desert in every direction . . . but one."

The Luftwaffe man pointed at the harbor below the train station. "Then she will take a boat. The whore's route—find a sailor or smuggler who will hide her." The Luftwaffe man added, "I know Oran one year. If her contact here is undefined, she will hide your American outside the city and come in alone. If her contact is known and trusted, he will be in the Arab Quarter or the labyrinth of the old city, where the commerce of the Arab traders and the European money can mix. There she could hide your American until dark, then find their way to the port."

Schroeder said, "Check for any ship bound for Lebanon, the Suez, or Palestine. Where can we meet in the Arab Quarter in one hour?"

"The Murad. Rue Megherbi."

Schroeder agreed. The Luftwaffe man departed on foot; Schroeder stayed to watch the last of the stragglers leaving the train station. The Abwehr agents he had employed were either working their contacts in the city or had chosen to keep their distance. Or they had betrayed him to Himmler. Schroeder watched a line of stooped Arabs carrying packages past the adjacent towers of a mosque and a cathedral. Schroeder spoke to himself. "Now we rebait our traps in the Arab Quarter, let the noble Arabs of Oran know the reward has risen, that there is one year's money to be made." Schroeder heard his own words and did not belt the Luger, his faith now stronger in the gun.

Clinging between cars, Saba and Eddie rode the "death train" three miles out of the Oran station. The train built speed in the deafening echoes from a tall gray wall that sealed off the right side of the tracks. Saba read VILLAGE NÈGRE painted there—the exact name of the area where Doña Carmen had instructed Saba to go— The train jolted into a sharp curve on a bad section of track; Saba lost her grip, grabbed for a handhold whose screws gave way, and she fell off the train. Her shoulder landed hard; she tumbled headfirst down the track-bed embankment, rolled twice, and bounced to her feet, marl dust swirling around her.

Hoots erupted from the fourth-class steerage cars. Arms of Arabs and Legionnaires pointed at her out the window holes. Saba ran with the train and yelled in Arabic for Eddie to jump. He did, landed solid, and slid down the track-bed embankment. They sprinted, trapped between the train and the gray wall, until they reached a switcher's shed fronted by squat palms and jumped behind. The train and the shouts steamed past.

Saba checked the tracks back toward the station. *Empty.* Then back at the train. A man—European?—leaned out of the passenger car, looking for the object of the shouts and the pointing. The train disappeared into the curve; she could not tell if the man jumped. Saba checked her weapons, then the high wall that trapped them to the tracks. Behind the wall, a hillside cemetery rose higher and spread in three directions for as far as she could see. She pointed

Eddie fifty meters down the long wall to a nine-foot plaster section. "We must climb there. You can do this?"

"Hide and watch, honey."

They scaled the wall's ragged brick ends and over, dropped inside without injury, then sprinted through Christian tombstones and blinding sunlight. Saba stopped running at the last stand of almond trees and motioned Eddie into a shaded crouch. To their left, a forty-foot arched gateway opened into the city. The neighborhood the gateway framed was a dense maze of white mud-brick and low-roofed buildings like the fellaheen slums of Janîn and Haifa. Arab children shuffled in the street between the donkey carts and storefronts lined with old men. Beyond the buildings, an elaborate multistory skyline rose and ringed the Arab area. Those elaborate buildings and their wealth would belong to the European masters. Saba spit sand.

Eddie nudged her. "You okay?"

Saba rubbed more chalk dust on the wings beneath her eye. "When it becomes dark, I will see to Doña Carmen's assistance. Please remain here in the trees. If for some reason you are forced out, return at midnight, then again at three a.m. If I do not return, then the betrayal I fear has proven true and I am dead."

Eddie grabbed her hand. "Hey. Can we just take a minute? You need to sleep—"

"There is no place for sleep." Saba knew what Eddie did not. Doña Carmen's connection was here in Oran's Village Nègre, part of a tribe that serviced pirates and smugglers, a tribe driven by money not loyalty.

Eddie pulled his .45 and braced up against a tree. "Lay down, rest your head against my lap. You watched me on the train; I'll watch you here."

"You will guard me?" Saba half smiled. "You will take no liberties . . . with my person?"

Eddie smiled and pulled her to him at the tree. "Put your head here." He laid her down, her body hidden by trees, her head against his thigh. "*No* liberties is asking a lot."

Saba did not sit up. She drew her pistol and folded it under her arms in one fluid motion. She made two adjustments with her body and head, and was asleep in an instant.

An hour after sunset, Saba walked the narrow streets of the Village Nègre dressed as a man. The streets were hard-packed earth that would run to mud when it rained. Shadowy gas lamps lit the storefronts and their sidewalk tables. The men at the tables smoked and sipped from small cups. More French was spoken than Arabic. Saba smelled strong coffee, then spiced oil and sweet peppers cooking in ginger-turmeric—her mother's food—and remembered her younger brother Rani's fondness for it. Between two busy cafés, an Arab man stopped her, his face too close. In Arabic, he asked directions. She shrugged and tilted her face slightly away. He gave his name, waiting for a response. The knife eased into her hand. The man blocked any exit and asked again. She didn't answer. He cursed her and walked away.

At the next street, Saba found food—lamb and peppers and flatbread, paid with the last of her ring money—then asked directions of her own. The directions led uphill through a drab, swelling population, then downhill through more of the same. Saba was never alone and could not be sure if she were being followed. Near a stone square, three Arab beggars fell in step with her, pleading for her food. One persisted, grabbing the sleeve of her free hand. She jerked away and sidestepped past him into the mouth of a long, narrow alley. At the alley's opposite end, a European suit passed. Then another—Europeans here at night was wrong; it would be dangerous for them at night.

Something bumped her from behind and splattered her food to the alley's hard-pack. She wheeled and slashed—a beggar in a threadbare robe fell to the ground, his robe split across his stomach. Saba fast-glanced the alley for the Europeans, then the beggar on his back. She jabbed him to not move and gathered her food one-handed. He crabbed back, then raised his hands, trembling. He wheezed beggar words for food in Hebrew and French. Saba glared at the borrowed language of the conquerors and checked the alley again. He was not bleeding. She growled and gave him a third of her and Eddie's food.

The food stayed in his hands, not his mouth, his eyes on hers. She checked the alley's far end again. In Arabic, she barked, "Eat if you are hungry. If not, return my food."

He shivered, eyes wide. Her knife was still between them. "You stare, beggar, but you do not know me."

His face was creased with terror. He swallowed, squinted at her, then elevated his eyes to the stars above her head. Saba's attention snapped to the alley's far end—two European suits and several Arab men craned in to look at her and the beggar. None moved toward her. Saba stepped to the beggar's thigh. "If I am what you think, know I can come from the sky, take a man from the inside out just as they say."

The beggar shut his eyes, hands shaking harder, and pressed the food higher between them.

"I grant you your life." Saba tucked the knife. "For seven days you do not know me. On the eighth, you may say you saw her. Tell them in every house the Arab Revolt has risen from the fires of Tenerife."

The beggar began to sob.

She helped him to his feet in order to sneak a glance at the alley's far end. The Europeans hadn't moved. Saba told the beggar, "Go. Now. Eat my food. The Arab dawn is at hand." She shoved him until he stumbled away.

Sharing their food was a mistake, leaving the beggar to talk was worse. The beggar either knew her by legend or, much more likely, by a European bounty that must be circulating. Saba hurried out of the alley, down a block, and deeper into the maze. Across another street and down the block from where Saba now stood, a sign read: *OPÉRATEUR DE CIRCONCISION*—a circumcision operator—the place of Doña Carmen's contact. Saba leaned against the outside wall of a still-crowded café and watched the street. The street activity was high, much higher than proper. Arab men walked in small groups, staring at shadows they saw every night and at building doorways they saw every day. The Nazis were in the Village Nègre, she was sure of it, but not at the *Opérateur de Circoncision*, where they would have waited had Doña Carmen betrayed her and Eddie. Somehow Erich Schroeder knew it was Oran and guessed the Arab Quarter, but not where. Schroeder was a murderer of the first order but a worthy adversary. Saba listened to the many conversations in the crowded café and finally overheard how it had been accomplished.

She eased into the dark and with great caution, back to the cemetery.

Saba handed Eddie his half of their food and sat across from him to eat. Eddie said, "So?"

"There are Nazis; a bounty is offered. The Arabs hunt on the Nazis' behalf. They know you are tall and that you wear black . . . A Nazi on the train saw you jump."

"Doña Carmen told them?" Eddie stood fast, looking left and right. "Then she didn't call Benny Binion and Floyd. My family—"

"No. We are not betrayed. There were no Nazis at the *Opérateur de Circoncision*. The Nazis know we are here but not where." Saba reached for Eddie's hand and tugged at him to sit. "We must find new clothes for you, not black. Bundle your *jellaba* and keffiyeh. I will go to the medina and make a trade, one item at a time."

Eddie disrobed and handed her the garments. "Waiting here is making me nuts."

"But you must. The city will kill you. I want you alive, for me."

A small smile broke through the frustration and worry. "Could you say that again?"

Saba felt the blush. "One time is enough, for now." She stood, turned, and ran into the dark. Oran's streets were almost empty, lit only with moonlight and what stars weren't hidden by the westward clouds. A storm was coming out of the desert. There would be no rain, only hot winds and sand. Saba kept the bundle under her arm, her pistol in hand but hidden. She could smell Eddie in his bundled clothes. How endlessly odd it was to be a woman and a soldier— A figure startled her. Hooded and small, it moved like a woman. Saba aimed from behind the bundle and stepped back into the doorway. In Arabic, a woman's voice asked for food or money. Saba shook her head. The woman asked again. Saba said to move on.

The woman spoke French. "*Étoile Nord-Africain.*"

Étoile Nord-Africain was Doña Carmen's code to be used at the contact point. Doña Carmen's father had been a founding member fighting against the French occupation.

Saba fast-glanced past the woman's shoulders.

The woman returned to Arabic. "You look for something?"

"No."

The old woman moved on, hesitated, and returned. "The *jellaba* is Moroccan. Black." The woman glanced at Saba's bundle, unable to tell anything about it other than it was black. "The man who wears the *jellaba* is an American."

Saba fast-scanned again.

The old woman showed her hands empty. "There are enemies roaming these streets, and friends. The friends search to help."

Saba sifted shadows, finger tight on the trigger, and took a chance she would normally not take. "Carmen Bishara al-Janîn."

The woman grinned and bobbed her head, then glanced at the sky. "It is said the American travels with the Raven of Palestine."

"And if this is so?"

"*Étoile Nord-Africain* will help her fly."

The doorway had shrunk to Saba's shoulders. Dying in Algeria, marked by an old woman, was not how Saba had fantasized it. One finger removed oil from her cheek. The woman leaned into the bundle and Saba's gun barrel behind.

The old woman gasped, then steadied. "I . . . I am honored. Many French soldiers die at your hand. We embrace you." And she did.

Saba jerked the pistol into the open over the old woman's shoulder and the hail of bullets that would kill them both. The woman told her shoulder, "Fear not. *Étoile Nord-Africain* will not betray you." Saba fanned the pistol. No attack. No men. No bullets. Only the night air of North Africa and the frail Arab woman.

Saba Hassouneh al-Saleh backed them deeper into the doorway, took a breath, and allowed herself pride in being an Arab.

Erich Schroeder resisted the impulse to kill someone with his hands. Fate had beaten him at every turn of the wheel. It was as if he were the player and his prey the house. But his prey's luck could not last; there were too many righteous men in Oran who wished to see an infidel and her consort captured or had good use for the French francs offered. And as his Luftwaffe man had stated, there was no good way out of Oran for foreign fugitives other than by train or ship.

Oran's train station now hosted as many informers as could fit in its baths and under its domed roof. Saba's exit would be a ship, the whore's route from the whore's network. She would abandon any further attempt to make contact. She would break for the Palestinian coast. Three ships were in Oran's harbor; each would eventually make port in either Haifa or Beirut. One was French-flagged, the other two English and Greek.

The Greek ship *Mustafa II* was the most likely because once aboard, Saba would not be wanted for murder or considered a brazen whore-infidel desecrator of religious shrines. The French ship was next likely and only because Oran was long steeped in the Byzantine politics of the French. If Saba had connections here, she would have connections in the port and by default on a French-flagged vessel. The English ship was highly unlikely, as it also carried a contingent of Royal Marines. Eddie and Saba were both wanted by the British.

Schroeder doubled the bounty, then tripled it, offering any man who could produce the prey more money than could be spent in Oran in three years. He drank two cups of Moorish coffee, then went to see the harbormaster's second-in-command, armed with a formal request from the German embassy in Algiers.

CHAPTER 34

April, 1939

Eddie paced a slow circle through the cemetery's almond trees and arid moonlight. Tom Mendelssohn's papers itched against his skin. Below Eddie, two figures appeared at the wide cemetery gate, then hugged the nearest wall after they had passed through. Saba? But her clothes were different. The hooded figure was small but not definable by sex or nationality. The two figures followed the base of the hill until it hid them from the gate, then climbed higher to where Eddie waited in the trees.

The taller figure signaled it was Saba. Eddie leveled the .45 and waved the figure to him. It was Saba. She offered Eddie a white robe and headdress. "We have a ship. French-flagged to Beirut."

"When?"

"Six a.m. Three hours." Saba touched the person on her right. "She will lead us through the harbor. There is a heavy-rail quay, *Quai de Marseille*. We board there in one hour, boxed with the last of the heavy-rail freight."

Eddie's stomach churned. Either the lamb he'd eaten or Saba's plan. Saba put her hand on his chest. "I have news from Doña Carmen." Saba swallowed, then raised her chin. "In Oklahoma." Saba put both hands on Eddie's shoulders. "The news is bad. Your father is dead, killed by Erich Schroeder's Nazis—"

"*What?*" Eddie stumbled. "*What?*"

"The remainder of your family is safe with"—she stuttered the name—"B-Ben E. Binion of Texas."

Eddie stumbled backward into an almond tree. "Newt's dead?"

Saba nodded, stepped to Eddie, and hugged him to her. Eddie fought the words until the shock registered as fact. "How?"

Saba eased back, her tone military. "Your friends from Texas arrived soon after Erich Schroeder's Nazis. The men from Texas prevailed in two locations. Your father died outside his iron lung saving your mother when she was put into a truck with him."

Eddie's eyes squeezed shut. His father, weak but not beaten, dies saving . . . always saving. Eddie saw his father behind the plow, his pride, his hope, his smile, his hat . . . the hat Erich Schroeder had given Eddie in Tenerife. Eddie's paycheck had saved the family only to kill them. His hands began to shake. He flexed to shove her off his chest.

"*No.*" Saba leaned into him, against his chest. "Have I not suffered the same? Are my losses less?" Saba grabbed tighter. Her eyes bored into his. Eddie inhaled to yell. He choked. Tears welled. Saba pressed her cheek hard against his neck. "I cry, too. For your father and for mine. For our failures. For the many who hope. Now, you must keep the anger within yourself, as I do. We must go. Prevail in quiet for now and we may have our reckoning."

At dawn, Eddie and Saba's crate was stacked on Oran's heavy cartage pier. They were crunched inside the six-foot cube of black-dark, oily tannery hides. Outside, Oran Harbor was already loud. Soldiers' boots tramped past the crate. Eddie was sick with the fumes and the confinement. If he and Saba made it off the *Quai de Marseille* and aboard the SS *Caubarreaux*, there would be no trace of them leaving Oran. The crate would be opened in the upper hold, then Eddie and Saba led above the propellers to a steerage cabin with toilet reserved for "Avatar el-Baidar."

Saba had said she did not relish the crate or the cabin name "Avatar el-Baidar" chosen by the *Étoile Nord-Africain*. But if she and Eddie could remain safe for the three-day voyage to Beirut, there was an excellent chance they could pass into Lebanon without arrest by the French. Saba repeated the warnings she had received— if there were difficulties aboard, make no attempt to hijack the ship. There were traps. All vessels on the contraband routes were well prepared for interference.

Voices.

Eddie blinked, inches away from the whites of Saba's eyes, all he could see. She squeezed his hand. The crate moved a little, then a lot. Then up and juggled at an increasingly odd angle. More voices, louder, shouting. The crate righted and swung to Eddie's left and out toward the water. They hung there. He whispered, "Hope they don't drop—"

They did. About ten feet. Eddie would have puked but it happened too fast, stopped, then continued lowering, orderly this time and without the yelling. In three minutes they were packed away, just the noise of little clawed feet scrabbling in the dark.

Three French soldiers ringed Erich Schroeder at the gangway of the SS *Caubarreaux*. An hour ago Schroeder had stood in the assistant harbormaster's office and told him to either take the money offered, or honor the German embassy's *formal* request, or get his superior out of bed. The officious little man had called his superior. The superior declined to intercede, saying the decision was the assistant's. The assistant had refused to speak German or English, and he'd refused Schroeder's request. "The passenger manifest is confidential, as is the cargo manifest."

The three French soldiers who now ringed them near the gangway had appeared when Schroeder had followed the little man out of his office and began to shout. Schroeder calmed, adding unfelt sincerity. "My apologies for my manners. It is so . . . tragic, so important. Please, two of your passengers must be recalled. It is an emergency in their family; the ship will take too long; they must fly."

"You have checked the other ships, *monsieur?*"

"Yes." That was the truth, and the Greeks and English had been far more industrious and amenable.

"If they must fly . . . there is a plane, *monsieur?*"

Schroeder lied. "Yes. Waiting at the airport now. Please."

"What are their names?"

Schroeder took the one chance this officious French ass was allowing. "Eddie Owen and Calah al-Habra."

The Frenchman scanned his papers. "*Non.* Not aboard." He signaled the stevedores to cast off the ropes.

Schroeder beseeched, then blocked the Frenchman's exit. The ship's horn boomed. Schroeder offered money again. "Please take this, for your children. Check again. Any passengers going to Beirut."

The Frenchman smiled at the money, then the three soldiers who politely looked away. The Frenchman accepted the bills, rolled them into his pocket as a professional would, and rechecked the list. "*Non.*" He sidestepped Schroeder and escaped behind the uniforms, his personal victory against the Nazis.

Schroeder glared at the ship and the laughing soldiers. Cunning helped him reach for more money instead of his pistol. Behind the guile, he knew something those brass-buttoned uniforms did not— they would revisit this day on the battlefield, and it would be soon, and it would be in France. The French were just Jews in disguise and Jews did not fight. France's prodigious array of tanks and artillery pieces required soldiers to feed the breaches, soldiers willing to die. And when the time came, the egalitarian French always had far fewer of those.

More francs bought a cabin for Schroeder's most trusted Luftwaffe man, the man who had ridden the red wooden train until he had proven Saba and Eddie Owen were not on it and jumped off. Eddie and Saba had to be on this ship . . . not on the train, not hiding in Oran. They were on a ship, this ship . . . probably.

At eight a.m., Schroeder watched the SS *Caubarreaux* slide out from the pier. He and his local man would remain to squeeze the Village Nègre, then break into the harbormaster's office and scan the manifest. His man on the *Caubarreaux* would hunt, cabin by cabin if necessary. Eddie and Saba would be found, here or there; the luck that had propelled Eddie this far would eventually falter. And then . . . then Eddie and his whore would pay a price, a price that—no, *Saba* would pay the price, naked and begging and bleeding. Her plan to rob Eddie of the Mendelssohn papers would vanish with her clothes, then her life. Eddie would continue on to work, like all Germans would work, hard and for the Fatherland. And the Mendelssohn papers would work hard for Erich Schroeder and Reichsmarschall Göring.

Schroeder wanted to smile but couldn't. The farther Eddie got from the desert and the North African states, the more vulnerable Erich Schroeder became. Himmler's Gestapo could not be certain that Eddie Owen was who they had chased to Fès, no matter what the whore on the Casablanca Ferry had told them. Himmler would make that assumption, but without proof, Himmler would have to worry that Eddie and the Mendelssohn papers were now with Erich Schroeder, en route to Berlin. And without proof, Himmler would not dare confront Göring. Himmler's dead SS contingent in Fès had sealed Himmler from Oran, but not forever and not without speculation over who had killed them.

The SS *Caubarreaux* sounded a horn. Himmler's Gestapo was vastly stronger on the European continent and the SS *Caubarreaux* would make its first stop in Bari, Italy. If proof of this fiasco leaked, Himmler's Gestapo would meet the ship. That would be the last of Eddie and the papers. And of Erich Schroeder.

CHAPTER 35

April, 1939

For twenty-four hours, the SS *Caubarreaux* battled to hug Algeria's coast, but the ship's engines were no match for the sandstorm boiling out of the Sahara. The storm had pushed everything that floated deeper into the Mediterranean. Gritty crosswinds and battering southern seas kept the decks clear and the tiny cabins full. Luck and cover for some, twenty hours of illness and fatigue for others.

The old ship shuddered. In their tiny cabin, Eddie wobbled to the porthole and Saba's cheek. She said, "Sardinia," to the glass and a distant island coastline lit by a late, hazy sunrise. Eddie had never seen Sardinia. The only islands he'd seen were Bahrain and the Canaries. He liked Saba's cheek more than Sardinia, even though she still smelled like new leather and so did he. During the night they had awakened from the sleep of the dead comfortably in each other's arms. Saba's shock was total and she had jolted out of the bed—a fully dressed mountain lion, her chest heaving, hands up and ready to fight. Eddie converted his current leer to confusion. If he could only get her to put that energy into *any* attempt at sex . . . Maybe just part of her energy to start, until he got used to the beating.

Saba said, "We will need food for tonight." She reset her pistol. "The bread from the crate will not last."

Eddie kissed her instead. His .45 was on their bed, seven feet from the cabin's barricaded door.

"Stop. I smell like a cow."

"Fine with me." He kissed her again.

"No." She pushed him away, demonstrating her strength. "Food. A bath. Then we must plan a way off this boat."

Eddie grinned. "I'm not getting off. We're sailing into the sunset."

"You have a fever."

Eddie leered.

"I will go for food. Do not leave. If there are police or Nazis aboard, they will look for a tall man. Whoever has provided the *Étoile Nord-Africain* this cabin may or may not know who sleeps in it. If money is offered, many will accept."

Eddie smiled, not thinking about storing food.

"Give me what money you have."

He did and tried to hold her hand.

"No." A tiny flash of smile in her eyes.

Eddie wanted to pin her to the wall, mash his chest to hers, and kiss her until she couldn't breathe.

Saba shoved her hand between. *"No.* You forget this is not a game. They wish to kill us. Death forever, like your father and your friend Bennett."

Eddie eased back as the grin faded. She lowered her hand but didn't move, then turned and left the cabin. Eddie read the closed door and didn't move toward the lock. His father's image stared back: the knotted workingman's hand gentle on a plow handle, the overalls, the years of work blowing around him—

The door opened. Saba said, "I meant no disrespect. Lock this," and withdrew. Newt's image lingered as if he had something father-to-son to say, then melted away into the swirling dust of Oklahoma. Eddie didn't know how Newt died, how Schroeder's men had killed him. Eddie palmed the .45 off the bed . . . heard Walter Winchell on the oil derrick's radio six years ago just before the Cochise No. 1 blew apart and sent Nazis to Oklahoma.

"I'm sorry, Pop. This was bigger than I knew how to handle." Eddie locked the door and returned to the porthole. Best he could remember, Sardinia was almost to Sicily, maybe two hundred or three hundred miles west. To cross the Mediterranean, the SS *Caubarreaux* would have to pass between Sicily on the north and the Tunisia coast on the south—maybe get to see Malta—then steam due east for two days and nights, past Libya and Egypt to Palestine. Libya was ruled by Fascist Italians, not Libyans; Egypt was ruled by a seventeen-year-old Egyptian king backed by the same British warships, tanks, and rifles that controlled Haifa. Neither Libya nor Egypt would be good places for fugitives to land if the old ship had trouble. Eddie hefted his pistol and laughed at the porthole. Like there *were* good places for him and Saba to land. Eddie rechecked the door and wondered if seven shots were ever enough. He started to pace but there was no room.

Oberstleutnant Erich Schroeder sat in a cramped, private office deep within the Nazi embassy in Lisbon. To get here from the ship docks in Oran, he had fought through his second sandstorm in three days, arriving on a weather-beaten Luftwaffe plane that had almost crashed into the Mediterranean on takeoff. Schroeder was behind the embassy's grand facade on Campo Mártires da Pátria, to bet his life on three final moves. His knuckles were white. He was on a private call to Reichsmarschall Göring at Karinhall. Göring was livid over the implosion of Tenerife's AvGas refinery, railing against "the Spanish peacock" Generalissimo Franco and his "weak-kneed army of drunken dilettantes." Göring had not been informed Saba Hassouneh or Eddie Owen was responsible. Schroeder reported that Eddie Owen had disappeared in the aftermath—an escape from the volcano that many still believed had crippled the refinery.

"Disappeared!" The telephone boiled for a full minute with Göring's epithets.

"*Ja.* The American has contacted me for assistance. I will recover Eddie Owen within thirty hours and have him in Berlin by midnight Friday."

Göring calmed to controlled anger.

Schroeder had to buffer the "Mendelssohn" revelation to come. He hinted at the papers and his use of them in America to force the industrialists' participation, and then his gambit with Himmler's representatives in Tenerife, all "on Göring's behalf."

Göring exploded. He demanded an immediate explanation— but not by phone—in person, on the next plane.

"*Jawohl,* Reichsmarschall. But Eddie Owen must be secured first. A full report on the Mendelssohn papers will be made on Friday when I arrive in Berlin with the American."

Göring growled but concurred, adding: "You will explain the Mendelssohn papers, their use in America, and this 'gambit' with Himmler via today's courier from Lisbon."

"*Jawohl,* Reichsmarschall." Schroeder tried to continue but the phone went dead—loud, like a firing squad.

A ring tapped the glass of his hallway window— Two Gestapo officers, one glancing in at Schroeder without regard or respect, the other tapping his ring on the glass in annoyance.

Ruthless little pimps. And higher placed than their two counterparts dead at the Luftwaffe's hands in Morocco. Thankfully, it would take more nerve than these two Gestapo had to openly obstruct Göring's man. But Himmler and Heydrich *had* been notified of Schroeder's presence, that was assured. Erich Schroeder would be followed everywhere that the Gestapo could manage. The two Gestapo at his window wished a meeting; a formal request had been submitted in writing and under Himmler's seal.

Schroeder used the phone again instead. He commissioned a Luftwaffe plane from Lisbon to Rome. Once in Rome, he would organize another plane, this one from outside Luftwaffe channels. Unidentified, Schroeder would fly to Bari, Italy, where the SS *Caubarreaux*, battered by the same storm that had almost killed him, would dock if the weather did not force the ship elsewhere. What had finally convinced Schroeder that Eddie and Saba were aboard the SS *Caubarreaux* had been a passenger name on the Oran harbormaster's manifest. The name was "Avatar el-Baidar." In Arabic "Avatar" meant "bird" and "el-Baidar," among other meanings, was the name of a refugee camp in the Lebanon Mountains.

Schroeder had confirmed this information to his Luftwaffe man onboard via a coded ship-to-shore telegram. Schroeder also informed his man that the Italian embassy in Lisbon had secured the following guarantee from their counterparts in Bari—the SS *Caubarreaux* would not leave Bari until it had been thoroughly searched and all passengers accounted for. Schroeder checked his watch. His flight left in one hour. From Lisbon to Rome to Bari would require more than half of today once he could arrange the flights, but he would be in Bari on the pier and well prepared when the SS *Caubarreaux* arrived.

The Gestapo officer tapped the window again.

Schroeder ignored him. With luck, his Luftwaffe man would locate "Avatar el-Baidar" on the ship. His man would exercise caution; the French officers and crew were not to be alerted until the ship was in Italian waters. If luck were with Schroeder's man, he would isolate Eddie and kill Saba before they docked in Bari. If not, the Luftwaffe man would bide his time and when the ship docked, he and Schroeder would kill her.

Eddie balled his fist and squeezed the .45. It had been almost six hours. Saba had to be dead. But she couldn't be. That's not how it was supposed to end. His dad wasn't supposed to be dead, either, or D.J. The knob on the cabin door turned. Eddie leveled the pistol. No voice. Remaining in the cabin had been hell and had required all of his self-control. The knob kept turning. The ship pitched and the doorknob stopped. Eddie stiff-armed the .45 head high on the door. *C'mon.* His lip ached and he quit biting. *C'mon.* The ship pitched then rolled like they'd slammed open water. French voices argued in the hall. A body bumped into the wall and more voices followed. Someone rapped on the door, sharp, like a ring or a pistol. He didn't know any French and couldn't use English.

"Les Demoiselles."

Shit, it was Saba! Eddie fumbled at the lock. Saba ducked through and he shut the door behind her. She pointed at the lock. He locked the door and added the barricade. "You're . . . okay!"

She produced food from a large ship's-galley waterproof bag, then a bottle of wine, then her pistol. Eddie kept grinning, then realized he'd opened the door sans keffiyeh. "You do love me." He grabbed for the bottle. It was a trick; he grabbed her instead, wrapping both arms around her so tightly she couldn't move. He kissed her through the cloth until she kissed back. Soft, but she did.

"I love you . . . more, now that you're alive."

"Put me down."

"Say it."

Her keffiyeh fell away. "What?"

"That you love me, or I'm not letting go." He squeezed, hoping she wouldn't head-butt him.

Saba blushed and shut her eyes. Then kissed him. "Let me go. I must eat."

"Say it."

She mumbled something in Arabic.

"That's it?"

"What I have . . . for now."

Her eyes were so hazel, so warm he put her down but couldn't stop staring. "You have to be the prettiest woman in the whole world, this ship for sure."

She pointed him away to the only chair. "Sit. I will explain. Have the wine."

Eddie worked on the bottle, wishing he had two so he could get her drunk, after he hid her weapons. Get them both drunk. Forget the world's nightmare for an hour.

She explained while she ate. There was a German aboard and the large Englishman from their car on the train.

Eddie stopped working on the wine. "From the train?"

Saba nodded. She said neither man had recognized her. There was much talk of war, and soon. Italy was massing ships to invade its neighbor, Albania. Hitler and Mussolini had signed a new treaty with Japan, threatening Soviet Russia. England and France were feverishly building planes and tanks while they talked of peace.

"Jesus. Quite a report. How'd you get it?"

"Six hours with men and their newspapers. Men enjoy bragging about themselves and what they know."

"The German and the Englishman told you?"

"The *Times*. The rest was conversation with the ship's crew. These sailors hear; some listen for others. If we had money we would know more."

"How'd you get the food?"

Saba raised her chin. "I am not pretty enough?"

Eddie fumbled the bottle. "What?" She was laughing at him as he attempted to catch the bottle and stare at her face. "What'd you say?" The bottle hit the floor and rolled past her. Eddie corralled it on his hands and knees. "Jesus."

"Quite a man, Eddie Owen."

He jumped to his feet. "Yeah, I am," he said, laughing at her and him. "To us." He toasted and sipped the wine before he remembered he hadn't pulled the cork. "I was so much better with women until I met you. So much better."

"Yes, I would hope."

"I'm gonna open this, take a big drink, then kiss you on the mouth."

She didn't say no and that's what he did.

Saba made the wine last; the food they finished in the first hour. She felt his eyes and the heat of his intentions. His intentions weren't much different than hers, just more comfortable. He'd talked her out of her top three buttons by examining them with the interest of a gem trader. She knew better. Each one had added night air to her skin and weight to her breathing. He leaned to her mouth and kissed her softly. Just a wisp at first, then longer and longer. She felt his tongue trace her lips, then push past and enter her mouth. His hand was in her hair, too, then one threatening at her waist. No, it wasn't threatening, it was soft and resting on her hip. His tongue withdrew. She licked at it, shocked. He kissed back and searched for her tongue. Her neck bent and his lips trailed down its length. She gasped, her skin alive with his. Seated on the bunk her hands were buried in the bedclothes, the cords in her forearms iron tight.

Eddie pulled back one inch and kissed the tip of her nose. "I want you to show me something."

"Whaa . . . t?" She was trembling everywhere.

"See if you can put your weapons in the drawer." He pointed within her reach. "If you do that, we're going to lay down and just see what happens. I don't wanna die if you get excited."

Saba flushed, redder if possible.

"C'mon. Try it. If you say stop, I will."

Saba glanced at the door, stood, and checked the chair under the knob. She returned to the bed, avoiding Eddie's eyes. The heat in her was like sudden fear, only concentrated in her skin. Parts of her body demanded attention that had just begun to confuse her ten years ago as a teenager. No. She would say no, push him away.

"Just try, honey. I'm pretty sure you don't want to kill me by accident." Their legs touched. He stroked through her hair and touched her ear without demand. He whispered, "Just try."

Short of breath, she said, "I . . . I have not been without weapons since I was eighteen."

Then she did, first the pistol, then two knives. The blades clattered on the table, unsteady in her hand. She finished but faced forward, almost frozen. Eddie leaned her back into the bunk, his arms gentle around her. She laid on her side, eyeing the weapons, then Eddie behind her. Her breath was so short she was light-headed. Eddie squeezed assurance and asked for no more. She calmed and straightened one leg, then the other. Eddie matched her movements.

A man had her. In bed. His arms over her breasts, his lips in her hair and at her neck. She could feel his hips, his . . . She bolted, ending two steps away against the wall, facing the bunk. The alarms in her head pounded with her heart, her hands extended to stop the charge. One breath. Two. Then a third. Chest still heaving but eyes sharp. No imminent threat. No attack—

Eddie hadn't moved.

Saba burst into tears. *"I can't."* She slammed her fists into her thighs. "I can't."

"Not yet. That's all." He smiled so warmly, she felt it cross her face.

"I . . . I am ruined for a husband—" She choked on the word, never dreaming of saying it, not since the alley—

"Rape's a horrible thing. But the English rabble did it, not you."
Eddie's face went from somber to sunlight. "I think you're the single
most fabulous woman who ever walked. And if you ever wanted a
husband, there'd be a line to Dallas, me at the front."

He knows? About the soldiers in Jerusalem, in the alley? Was this
to shame her? Mock her? Blood rushed into her face. She kicked
the chair aside, grabbed clothes and weapons, and ripped the cabin
door almost off its hinges.

Eddie jumped up to chase her. Three steps into the dark passageway,
he realized he had no robe or keffiyeh. He backtracked into the
cabin, added costume, then stooped thirty degrees and back out.

The ship's foghorn boomed.

On deck, Saba stood at the stern rail with her back to the water.
Her hands were hidden but for sure one was full. She eyed him
every step or seemed to. When Eddie got to five feet, he realized
she wasn't eyeing him, just fast glances and not at his face. Eddie
checked his shoulders. "I'm gonna say this quick so we don't die out
here with the spies and Nazis. Marry me."

Saba sprang partly off the rail and stopped. "You cannot want
me. No man takes a wife ruined by others."

"I love you. No matter where you've been, what you've done, or
what's been done to you. To me you're a princess and I'd have you—
if you let me—for as long as you want. Here, there, anywhere."

Saba glared.

"C'mon home." He put all the smile and "aw shucks" he could
into his voice. "It's small and only got the one window, but it's ours."

The bow of a huge gray warship passed between them and the
moon. Saba said, "Italian."

Eddie looked at more dim shapes in the distance. The Mediterranean Sea was a big place to be crowded. Something must be up.

Thank God he and Saba didn't matter to the Italians. "Tell you what. Come home, downstairs, we'll get some sleep—just sleep, I promise. Tomorrow when you wake up, I'm gonna say these same words again. On my father's grave, I mean every syllable."

Saba blinked. Everything in her posture changed. The strength of the words "my father's grave" was written on her face. She seemed confused, wanting to come to him and not. Finally she eased off the rail, lingered at his shoulder only long enough that he could smell her hair and see the glisten in her eyes, then walked past to their passageway's door.

Eddie took that as an "okay," grinned at her stars like they were in this with him, checked the deck in both directions, and followed before she changed her mind or pulled a gun.

The French sailor who had watched the exchange thought it interesting. He could not hear from his working perch, buffeted by the wind gusting down the rock-and-foam Sicilian coast, but the postures were strange. Two Arabs, one tall like the German passenger had been asking about—the offer a year's pay if the Arab could be located.

This one was tall *and* an Arab—an Arab the sailor had not seen during the first two days of the voyage. The sailor wanted to follow but these were dangerous times, filled with desperate people; a history with such people told him to remain on station. There was time, and only ten lower cabins were reachable by the stern-passageway door. Spray peppered him and drew his attention to Sicily's eastern coast. He felt the beginning of a gentle northern turn into the Adriatic. In eight hours his watch would end. He could narrow the options then, long before they made port in Bari. The sailor set about dreaming of his own boat, one that could fish the Corsican banks or run processed opium to Marseilles.

• • •

At eight a.m., Erich Schroeder stood alone at the top of Italy's Adriatic boot heel. His trek to the port of Bari had required twenty-three hours. He was here but his situation was perilous; his Luftwaffe network compromised by Himmler . . . or possibly Reichsmarschall Göring himself reaching down, sensing threat from Schroeder's maneuvers and artifices. A storm front's chill blew in over the dirty harbor. No merchant ships were docked in Bari's Gran Porto, only Mussolini's Italian navy. Beyond the harbor's outer breakwater, the Adriatic Sea was rough with whitecaps and thick with packed Italian troopships wallowing low in the rough water. If Mussolini's threatened attack on Albania two hundred kilometers directly across the water was a bluff, it was well supported.

Schroeder walked out on the rail pier to the one empty berth that awaited the SS *Caubarreaux*. Behind him, a ceremonial cannon fired. Schroeder turned, following the cannon smoke to the high ground and *Castello Normanno-Svevo*, the walled fortress/prison facing the port. Santa Claus was buried here somewhere, maybe in the prison, his bones stolen from the Arabs. How fitting. Now Bari was a transit point for rich Jew refugees hoping for Palestine instead of Himmler's death camps in Poland. Possibly Santa Claus would help them.

Behind the fortress, the ancient city climbed a steep limestone outcrop—another walled labyrinth of alleys and streets built and rebuilt by each new conqueror. Schroeder wondered how Hitler would use it when he tired of *Il Duce*'s vain stupidity. Schroeder glanced south across the width of the pier. Two German embassy officials approached, passing a brick stationmaster house that sat at the center. Jew refugees were crowded behind the building, standing and sitting in nervous bunches. Both embassy men would be Gestapo or privately in their pay. As a forced amendment to his plan, Schroeder had requested the German embassy's assistance when the SS *Caubarreaux* docked. He had done so in Reichsmarschall Göring's name.

"Herr Schroeder." The official gave a curt, officious nod.

Schroeder offered his hand.

The embassy official did not take the hand. "The Gestapo will be responsible for the American."

Schroeder's neck flexed, jutting his chin. "The American belongs to Reichsmarschall Göring. The Gestapo has no interests on this pier today."

The embassy official exhaled a tired frown at his associate and sprinkled the dock with cigarette ash. The wind blew ash across Schroeder's jacket. No apology accompanied the ashes.

Schroeder resisted striking him. "Your failure to secure the American for Reichsmarschall Göring will not be tolerated. Nor will interference of any kind after the American is found. Do you understand, Herr . . ."

"Doebler." Herr Doebler sprinkled the dock with ashes again. "I answer to the ambassador, not Reichsmarschall Göring's Luftwaffe."

Schroeder crowded Herr Doebler, chin to chin. "You fear Himmler's cutthroats. But Himmler is in Berlin and I am here. Should my American 'disappear' from this ship, the Gestapo will reward your treachery, then feed you to the wolves—*know that*, Herr Doebler. And here in Italy, where you stand in your Italian shoes, the Luftwaffe are the wolves. Il Duce's wolves."

Herr Doebler was a sufficiently seasoned embassy official to know that a Reich power struggle at the top was not survivable at his level of influence. And like bureaucrats of all systems, he would fear the devil in front of him—one that cheerfully bombed Il Duce's enemies—more than the devil in the shadows, no matter how nightmarish.

The cigarette again. "The American's name is available? His description so the Italians might detain him?"

"*Might?*" Schroeder wanted to gut the presumptuous bitch *puff-mutter*. "The Luftwaffe was able to detain his family *a continent away*." A lie that now made Schroeder want to vomit. "I will have the American here and now, if your embassy men know their business. And for the sake of your family, they had better."

Herr Doebler coughed. "The Italian authorities have instructed their stationmaster to impound the ship when it arrives. Those 'citizens'"—he nodded toward the Jews on the pier—"'wishing to board for passage to Beirut will be processed by Italian immigration but held in quay until the ship is searched for 'contraband and stowaways.'"

"You will lead the search?"

Herr Doebler shook his head. "The French captain will not allow Nazis to search. Only the Italians may board, and then only with the French captain's permission."

Schroeder snarled. The Italians were inept bunglers further distracted by their impending conquest of Albania. Italy was quite the ally, wasn't she? A grand partner for the Führer, capable of almost striking fear into Ethiopia *and* Albania. How horribly operatic that after all the effort, Erich Schroeder, *a Krupp*, now risked his demise and that of his far-reaching plans on this miserable pier hoping for the performance of mindless bureaucrats and gutless Italians. They would be no match for the Raven. She would utilize the contacts who had secreted her aboard in Oran to hide herself and Eddie somewhere on the ship. And when the *Caubarreaux* docked in Beirut, she would be ten-fold stronger, capable of marshaling partisans and guerrilla fighters to the dock who would never allow her capture.

The confrontation had to be here.

Schroeder swallowed bile. His only remaining option was obvious. Conscript his competitor. He would add a twist to the lie he had told Göring and involve Himmler's E-6 Gestapo. The E-6 were the ruthless police Himmler placed in foreign countries. With the E-6 would also come battle-armed Waffen-SS. The E-6 could scheme on Saba's scale and the Waffen-SS could outgun and outfight her.

Schroeder spit the bile burning his throat. And then he would face down the Gestapo for his prize. He would find a way. Corrupt them or kill them. He was Erich Schroeder, a Krupp—not a *bastard* Krupp—a *Krupp*. Eddie Owen and the Mendelssohn papers were his.

Lying in the bunk, Saba faced Eddie, fully clothed, feverish at his proximity.

"Sure hope you're not pregnant."

She gasped and curled her back to him, arms hugging her chest. The things he said! There had been no sex, but she had slept with him and felt naked the entire night. No shame, only pleasure. She was lost in a dream and had allowed it, listening to him sleep, feeling his hands and arms caress her. She would try again—if there was an again—and hope she could accept his affection. The thought made her shiver. She felt Eddie rise to an elbow behind her. Saba focused on the porthole. "We sail a new course, more north than east," then cut to the barricaded door. She stood and belted her pistol from the nightstand. Eddie's attention seemed divided between her belt and the pistol.

"I think you'd feel better lying down."

"North could be the stop—"

"Lying down means happily ever after." Eddie reached but his hand only brushed her thigh.

She wanted to devour him, to swim in his taste, his skin, his . . . He was smiling at her as if he'd read her mind. She covered her head with the keffiyeh. "I go to see why we change course. Lock the door behind me."

"Wait—"

Outside their cabin, the passageway was empty, as were the stairs up to the deck. The wind there was strong and off the bow. That would be out of the north. Saba stood portside looking left at a gap between two rocky landmasses.

A voice above and to her left said, "*Reggio di Calabria*. The toe of Il Duce's boot."

She ducked back and almost fanned the pistol. Eddie had her thinking about things other than survival. The voice again, in French-accented Arabic, identifying the speaker as a European she had met yesterday when scouring for food. He had given her the wine, thinking she was the son of a Bedouin trader gone to learn the ways of the West. Westerners liked to believe such things. Saba stepped out and the European waved. The Englishman from the train was next to him. The Englishman wasn't waving. The European pointed off the bow. "U-boats."

Saba squinted until she saw two submarines.

The Englishman said, "Med's thick with 'em."

Saba shrugged as if she didn't understand. The Englishman repeated his comment, his eyes on her, not the U-boats. The European translated badly. She nodded and turned back to the sea, glancing at both ends of the deck. If they were near the toe of Italy and changing course to the north, the stop could be anywhere—Italy, the Balkan coast of the Adriatic, even Greece. She knew nothing of these places other than her schoolbooks in another life, wanted to ask, absolutely had to know, but could not maintain a man's tenor in her voice if she yelled. Her back was exposed, a position only amateurs held. She had grown soft with Eddie and his dreams—her dreams—

A sailor approached from a distance, carrying a box. He nodded as he passed but his eyes were wrong, searching. She guessed the box was empty but carried as if it were not. He disappeared into her passageway door.

Were the two men above her *with* the sailor?

Saba imagined the ploy—the sailor causes the ten cabins on her passageway to empty to the deck via a fire threat or a ship's drill. The occupants parade for the men above. She glanced forward again and saw three sailors, then aft and saw three more. Mercenaries for the men above? If Eddie left the cabin or answered the door, he would be captured.

Eddie tried to pace Cabin No. 9 but it hadn't gotten any larger. "Hide and watch" made sense—what D.J. would've done in these circumstances—but it was murder on the muscles that wanted to beat the problem. Eddie rubbed his face, the .45 in his hand. "Hide and watch" was an old insult in Texas and Oklahoma, saved most often for partners who thought caution had more merit than action.

The door rattled. A knock?

Another rattle, this time with French commands attached. Eddie reached for the knob but stopped short. Saba knew he didn't speak French. More knocking and the knob turning. Eddie aimed the pistol. Voices in the passageway, either angry or confused. Answers in French. He had locked the door, thank you God. Maybe the ship was sinking. Sounded like they were rounding up anyone still sleeping. The French weren't Nazis, so how bad could it be? Eddie reached. *Real bad, idiot.* French words didn't mean French men. *Get some blood above your waist if you wanna live another hour.* Eddie aimed head high and waited. Lots of footsteps. One more series of knocks and a rattle of the knob.

Hide and watch . . .

Saba watched the passengers climb out of Eddie's stairway and onto the deck. More than half were Arabs and none was Eddie.

She glanced higher without raising her neck. Both the Europeans were intent on the crowd of fifteen. The sailor, sans box, approached her and in French asked if she were in Cabin No. 9. She shrugged confusion, her pistol ready. The sailor drew a "nine" in the air and pointed below.

Saba nodded.

He moved away, looking higher to the two Europeans as he did. The Englishman had no expression; the man next to him stared right at her—possibly a German and not the Frenchman he sounded now that she felt the trap. Saba moved only her head, reasonably sure that she was suspected. Two passengers arrived at her shoulder. In Arabic one told the other, "Bari, Italy, at one a.m. tonight. It is a military port on the Adriatic."

Saba checked the rail above; both men were gone.

Then she saw him, the German, approaching from the stern, slowly and with both hands visible. He moved with precision, like Erich Schroeder moved. She glanced past her shoulder without letting him see. Clear. The other passengers had dispersed in several directions.

The German stood the rail but stayed ten feet away, seemed to brace, then told the ocean, "The Reich has no quarrel with the Arab, just a mission I must complete to benefit us all." His glance at her was furtive. Both hands stayed on the rail but his knees were bent. "I can pay handsomely for the American, wages that would please a sharif or raise a small army."

Saba noticed the Englishman approaching from the far end of the deck.

The Nazi followed her eyes and said, "A bounty hunter. We play cat and mouse. He follows me and hunts the American for his crimes against England. The Englishman is a danger to us both."

The Nazi hid his mouth. "Stateroom Twenty-six after the noon meal. I will wait." And walked toward the English bounty hunter, both men feigning friendship. The two men met middeck, the Englishman looking over the Nazi's shoulder, the Englishman's interest in her distant but there.

Shoot them.

Her hand hesitated. The men disappeared.

Six months ago, both would already be dead. Saba frowned. Six months ago, she protected no fairy-tale future. She had become weak. Stateroom 26 would be close quarters and likely a trap—a bold one, but a trap. Trap or not, her confrontation with the Nazi was inevitable, in his stateroom or elsewhere on the ship, and Eddie would not survive without her. Saba projected a series of future moves. If she prevailed, the Nazi's money might be the difference. The Nazis would hold sway in Bari, Italy. *This* Nazi knew her clothes and her cabin. Money or not, when they docked in Bari, there would be no escape.

She would kill the Nazi and, if possible, also the Englishman who hunted Eddie, then devise a plan to hijack the ship or steal a lifeboat. The antihijack traps her Algerian benefactors had warned about were not apparent, but the French captain would not want to die to maintain his course. If a hijack were not possible, they would wait until they neared land and jump. Once in the water, she would learn to swim, or drown.

The ship's noon meal ended early. By two p.m., the SS *Caubarreaux* had cleared the sole of Italy's boot and the *Golfo di Taranto*—the boot's high, blue-water arch. The temperature dropped as the ship approached the boot's narrow heel—this would be the last landmass before the turbulent entry to the Adriatic Sea. The far northeastern horizon of the Adriatic was graying to black, announcing a storm ahead that would already be hammering Albania and the Baltics some hundred kilometers north. A shear wind rocked the *Caubarreaux*, weather the passengers said had littered the coast with wrecks for centuries. Very, very bad if she and Eddie were forced overboard into the sea. Saba checked her weapons, then the sky where her stars would be tonight, and went to Stateroom 26.

Panting from the fight, Saba used the back of her hand to wipe the blood off her face. Stateroom 26 was smashed. Blood dotted the walls and carpet. The Englishman lay dead on the cabin's floor. Saba wanted to kill him again, could still feel where his strong hands had choked her, still see the surprise on his face when he realized the Arab boy he'd seen on the rail was a woman. A woman with black wings under her eye and a knife he felt but never saw. The Englishman died with her knife in his heart, blood in his mouth, and "Janîn" in his ears.

The Nazi was also on the floor. He had been tortured, then shot twice by the Englishman just as Saba had arrived. The Nazi was not quite dead. Saba straddled him on her knees, then ripped at his clothes. The Nazi was slack-eyed, in deep shock from the Englishman's torture. Saba finished her search. His money belt had packets of German marks, French francs, and British pounds, and identification that included the word "Luftwaffe."

One of Erich Schroeder's killers.

He tried to speak but couldn't. Saba dismounted and he curled fetal to die. She riffled the Englishman's pockets. He had money that she took but no record of whatever he had learned from torturing the Nazi. Their weapons she would leave for the French sailors to find, hoping the murders would be viewed as an argument or robbery. The ship's foghorn sounded. Saba ducked, then checked the porthole. The ship was turning more north into high waves and a blackening sky. The foghorn boomed again and a bristling warship slid alongside, gray on gray, deck guns high, and a red Nazi flag at its stern. The Nazi warship continued past but on a matching course. She began searching the Nazi's cabin for any clue to Schroeder's plans— Whatever Schroeder's plans were, she and Eddie could not be aboard when this ship docked. They had to get off.

CHAPTER 36

April, 1939

E rich Schroeder smiled into the storm. The Balkan storm had churned into a gale and now howled west across the Adriatic toward Italy—God's windy present to the Italian navy wallowing off the coast as the brave Italians prepared to sack Albania. Schroeder steadied against the gusts buffeting the rail pier and dipped his hat against the rain. The SS *Caubarreaux* was due into the pier's only berth in two hours. Apathetic Italian soldiers from the 47th Bari Division crowded the pier, their necks bent against the rain, their presence more threat than capability. Schroeder glanced at the pier's brick stationhouse, the windows full at eleven p.m. with nervous Italian bureaucrats and his two German embassy officials. They were safe from the storm but not the possibility of catastrophe.

The *Caubarreaux*'s landing would be a major confrontation of three nations about to go to war in central Europe—France, Italy, and Germany. A mistake here by a petty official could fire the first shot. It had happened that way the last time. The ship-to-shore radio argument with the *Caubarreaux*'s French captain was into its fifth hour. The captain was adamant that German Gestapo or SS would not board his ship when it docked. It would not happen. The *Caubarreaux* would load its Bari passengers under maritime law and sail for Beirut unmolested by Italians or Nazis. The French embassy in Rome had been alerted—the captain's sailors would be armed with orders to shoot all boarders. The SS *Caubarreaux* would not be another Rhineland surrender.

Across from Schroeder on the wide pier's south side, two hundred moneyed Jews in their fine coats and family huddles remained quarantined behind a fence, pretending with their travel cases to be holidaymakers. Some stood under sheet-metal roofs. Others had shied back to the rear fences, exposed in the thunder, rain, and wind. Schroeder smiled at the Eternal Jew's reaction. Hours of weather were the lesser threat. Between the Jews and safe passage to Lebanon aboard the *Caubarreaux* stood two men under a rain-dimmed lamp. Both wore the black leather overcoats and black fedoras of Himmler's utterly ruthless E-6 Gestapo. To the Gestapo's right, a uniformed SS officer stood erect and ready with twenty Waffen-SS in formation. The jagged lightning bolts on their collars shone sharp and crisp in the Italian murk.

Cold wind and sheeting rain whipped the decks of the *Caubarreaux* as it steamed north along a rocky coastline. What lights Saba could see in the storm were too far to judge distance. Saba was wedged into a bulkhead two levels above their steerage cabin on the Stateroom Deck, hoping for options she had not found. She and Eddie had searched the ship for ways to debark, found none other than life vests and life-preserver rings. Eddie was below in their cabin attempting to engineer them into a design that would keep them alive if they were forced to swim for shore.

Passengers sickened by the rough seas emerged from their cabins on the Stateroom Deck—Arabs in cloth robes unaccustomed to the cold rain, Europeans in slickers. Eventually all began to retreat for their staterooms, furious and sodden and muttering. As the last of them left, Saba heard news of Ghazi bin Faisal in Iraq. The impossible stumbled her to her feet. A bow wave bucked her sideways. She righted, slipped on the wet deck under an isolated overhang, and squeezed in under its rigging.

Movement on her gangway—it was Eddie, bent almost to half apologizing when he arrived but clear he wasn't leaving. After a long silence, Eddie used one finger to gently turn Saba's face to his. He studied her expression. "Are you okay?"

Saba exhaled. "Ghazi bin Faisal has been assassinated. A 'car accident' two days ago saves Kuwait."

Eddie brightened. "The Iraqi Army of God guy?"

Saba clenched her teeth. "Bin Faisal was my hope for Palestine." She turned away. "I would kidnap him, raise an army with the ransom, capture a city, show the Arab states the Palestinian can outfight the British. Make amends for my participation in Janîn and Haifa."

Eddie touched her hand. "Sorry it messed up your plans."

Saba glared. "Understand *this*. My *plans*, *if* we survive this ship, are not to save Europe's Jews, the English, or the French from the Nazis. The Nazis are *Europe's* fight. I fight for Palestine. And now I must find another way."

"I'm sorry; don't know what else to say . . ."

"Your life preservers and lifejackets are our only option. *Face what that means.* The French crew is now armed and stationed at all control points. There will be no hijack. Stealing a lifeboat without being shot or captured will not be possible."

Eddie looked toward a shoreline neither of them could see. "You can't swim. We've got war, weather, and money. We'll find a sailor or two we can bribe, or trust."

Saba looked away, struggling with the finality of her aspirations. Now came the pragmatic betrayal for *cause*. She would sell him and the Mendelssohn papers to the Nazis for her freedom and arms to fight for Palestine. Or Eddie would strike first, betray her to the French in hopes of saving his family, the Jews of Europe, and himself. Such was the way grand dreams always ended. "What I can or cannot do does not alter our circumstance. See it for what it is."

Eddie stepped forward half a step and clutched her arm. "Are you trying to tell me something?"

Saba was calm. The decision had been made long ago.

Eddie ripped the Mendelssohn papers out of his shirt. "Here. However you want to use them, they're yours."

Saba took the papers. She slid them under her shirt, her eyes tight on Eddie.

Eddie's face was red, his gaze resolute. "I'm not choosing you over my family, not if it kills them. Tell me you'll save them from Schroeder. *Promise me*. On your *goddamn* stars. And I'll go with Schroeder when we land."

"You would betray your country?"

"One of us has to. Mine's gonna put me in prison or execute me. I love my family." Eddie swallowed. "And you. But you gotta promise." Eddie jammed his hand at the storm. "On every fucking thing that matters to you."

Saba nodded. "I promise."

Eddie exhaled hard. "Then let's get to it." He stood.

Saba grabbed his sleeve and pulled him back underneath the rigging. She had tears in her eyes. "If selling you were my decision, Eddie Owen would long ago be in Nazi hands."

Eddie blinked. "Meaning what?"

"The Nazi cannot be trusted, by me, by you. There is no bargain with him." She pointed at the waves they could not float, waiting for Eddie to understand. "The water will kill us both. Only you can be saved. The motives of the French who command this ship will allow it. Sell me to them; you and your papers are free."

Eddie leaned back, slowly shaking his head. His lips trembled, finally he said, "Never happen," then reached to rest one wrist on her shoulder, his fingers light on the back of her neck. "I know where you've been, so I forgive you for thinking I'm like the other men you know. We go in the water together, you and me. We make it for us and everyone else or we don't."

Saba remained in his grasp, a hand light on her neck, the other clutching her arm. To her complete and utter surprise, she nodded, in what must be love for the first time in her life. "Then together is what it will be."

"See?" Eddie beamed. "See. I knew it! Mrs. Eddie Owen. Forget princess, you'll be the queen. Benny and Floyd will have you—"

"Stop." Saba stared until his grin faltered and the tears in her eyes ran down her cheeks. "There will be no Texas for us. Just here. And now. This is all we will have."

"But—"

"Be a soldier; I have seen you do it. We are lovers, that is true." Saba reddened again. "And . . . that must be behind us. Now we fight—the water first, and if we somehow survive what we cannot, then the colonial masters who will await us on the shore."

Eddie's grip tightened on her neck and arm. "We're not gonna die. I won't let you drown and no colonial master is killing us. We're gonna have children, five of 'em after we practice a lot. And if it isn't in Texas then it'll be in Palestine. But you and me . . . we ain't over."

Saba smiled through the tears at a man who wanted her as she was, who knew her history, her shame, and saw no damage. A man she could marry under her stars. The impossibility shook her. A young girl's imagined future, standing in front of her now. It was . . . was almost as good as having it to live. She nodded. "For us, then, Eddie Owen." Her right hand unpinned the ten franc note from inside her pocket, pulled Eddie's hand to hers, and pushed both at the sky. "And them, yours and mine."

Erich Schroeder squinted into Bari's Gran Porto, searching for the running lights of the *Caubarreaux*. The ship was due but the shore, sea, and harbor were obliterated in rain, the pier itself only partially visible in the murk. Once the *Caubarreaux* appeared and was docked, the Italian stationmaster would counter the French captain's threats by saying the Adriatic was not safe with war imminent. The Italian ministry would declare an impound—all passengers and crew would be confined to the ship until further notice. Possibly weeks, the Italian ministry would speculate.

Two large maritime lamps ignited with a *pop*. Both lights rotated, glowing steam, splashing the pier with wide, milky beams. The moneyed Jews behind the fence on the pier's south side remained huddled with their "holiday" luggage and hope for secret transit from Lebanon to Palestine. Proof, yet again, that the extermination camps should be in Palestine not Poland. The Eternal Jew *paid* to reach Palestine. It was . . . perfect. Lightning drilled into the harbor. The Italians next to Schroeder shrank. Thunder pounded the pier. Only the Aryans stood erect in the rain. One of the two maritime lamps exploded in white sparks. The other remained focused on the Jews being segregated five at a time for preboarding inspection.

A phalanx of gray and black SS uniforms marched up the pier toward the smeary lights of the stationmaster house. The two E-6 Gestapo stood outside in their long leather coats. The SS phalanx marched past the Gestapo to the Jews' fenced quarantine. At the quarantine's double gate, an Italian soldier struggled with the lock. The gate swung open. The SS officer in command sent eight of his ten SS in to the Jews. The soldiers grabbed three and returned them to the lights of the stationmaster house. Two women ran to the fence, shouting their men's innocence.

Schroeder laughed. *Innocence? Have you not seen Europe? The Jews' toilet?*

The three men were placed in front of the Gestapo. Questions were asked. The Jews answered their innocence. Facts were stated; accusations were made—capital crimes against the Reich, embezzlement, treason. The Jews protested. The Gestapo waved them silent and signaled for the SS to take the Jews off the pier. The smaller Jew drew a pistol and fired twice. The Gestapo landed flat, splattering the pier. The Jew ran through the surprised SS. A maritime light spun and splashed his path. Five SS soldiers opened fire; the Jew pancaked on his belly. Jews in the quarantine shouted and surged at their fence. A section wavered and collapsed. The SS soldiers pivoted and fired into the quarantine. The first row fell. The other Jews ducked or froze.

The SS officer shouted, "*Einstellen!*"

The SS ceased fire. The officer stepped forward, leveled his Luger at a standing Jew. The Jew did not retreat. The SS officer fired one round. The Jew's head bucked on his neck, his knees crumbled, and he fell in a pile. The SS officer barked a command. His soldiers advanced in a tight battle line, rifles butted to their shoulders. The Jews ringed back. Dead and wounded littered the pier. Three children remained, each clinging to a different corpse.

Cold-blooded, pitiless, efficient. Schroeder could not have been prouder. This was how the British had ruled when they had successfully subjugated the world. Will. Resources. Destiny. The Reich was ready. Schroeder smiled in the rain; the operatic irony had shifted in his favor. These Jews had killed a Gestapo. They would be the perfect diversion when it came time to extricate Eddie Owen from Himmler's grasp.

Flashes to Schroeder's left. Out in the Adriatic, the darkness glowed red and white. Muffled concussions followed. More flashes. More concussions. Schroeder watched the staccato lights and spoke to the remaining Gestapo officer he would later murder to secure Eddie Owen. "Navy cannon. Italy invades Albania. The world finally has its war."

Eddie explained to Saba what he knew about oceans and current. The drop from near the stern of the ship would be thirty feet into fifteen-foot seas. If they could time the jump to the top of a wave, the fall would be half as far. But they had to jump *away* from the ship or they'd be sucked down and under into the propellers. *Away* was the most important. Eddie would carry all the weight—the pistols, the money belt, the papers wrapped in the ship's galley bag and waterproof lifejacket fabric. He could swim; Saba couldn't.

Saba and Eddie steadied on the wrong side of the deck rail, lashed together at the wrist, pounded by wind and rain. Each wore two lifejackets wrapped around a halved life preserver on their backs. Two French sailors appeared on the aft deck. One shined a light. The other shouted, aimed a pistol, and shouted again.

Eddie yelled, "Jump!" and jerked Saba off the rail. The gale wind hit them and blew both back into the ship's side. As they were being sucked under to drown, a fifteen-foot wall of black scoured them off the steel and hurled them into the Adriatic.

The *Caubarreaux* dwarfed Schroeder as it slid into its berth on the Bari pier. The portholes below deck poked lifeless ghost beams into the black. Dim yellow lights hollowed the decks empty of the armed French sailors who should have manned them. Schroeder shielded his eyes from the rain. There would be dead French sailors aboard. Two Italian maritime police boats bobbed in the harbor chop, guns and floodlights trained on the *Caubarreaux*'s aft deck and propellers. A group of Italian soldiers took their position at the ship's stern. The Gestapo and the SS had control of the pier. The Italians would board. The Raven would kill them first. A search onboard had been agreed, the French captain influenced by the artillery shells raining down on the civilian population of Albania and the private notification that the *Caubarreaux* had "the Raven" aboard. Unspoken to the passengers was that no passenger would disembark without a gunpoint Gestapo/SS inspection. Schroeder stood with the ten Waffen-SS at the bottom of the gangway. If Saba was smart—and she was—she would use Eddie as a hostage shield, then bargain him away when the opportunity presented itself. If Eddie had the Mendelssohn papers, Schroeder would support and facilitate the exchange. How the remaining Gestapo officer would react was unknown.

Schroeder was scanning the ship's decks when he was informed that two passengers had jumped into the sea some thirty minutes ago.

CHAPTER 37

April, 1939

Roiling surf spit Saba facedown onto a rocky coastline. She puked saltwater, clawed the rocks. Surf pounded her back. She clawed higher, spit blood, pushed with her feet and knees until her head and shoulders were out of the surf. Panting and puking, she gripped tight, waited for the next wave to hit. It did, receded, and she scrambled out of the froth.

The wave that had slammed her and Eddie into the ship's hull had ripped Eddie away, sucked her down the backside wave, and rolled her underwater. She'd thrashed above and below the surface, was pounded almost unconscious until . . . somehow she was here. Saba rolled to her back. Rain pounded her face. Part of a lifejacket was cinched to her chest. Eddie's engineering had saved her. She yelled into the dark, "Eddie!" coughed saltwater, and yelled again, "Eddie!" The storm was too loud. She crabbed across the rocks, yelling at the surf. "Eddie!"

A voice yelled back.

"Eddie! Over here." Saba stood. "On the rocks!" A light blinded her. Saba ducked, spun, her foot wedged a rock, the knee buckled, and she pitched forward into the surf.

The voice was not Eddie's.

Saba knelt the wet stones of a natural boat ramp. Her wrists were handcuffed; her face bloody and swollen. Erich Schroeder and two Italian Carabinieri policemen stood over her, their silhouettes black shapes in the rain. A third Carabinieri lay dead beside her. Schroeder told the two Italians who had survived her capture to add the shackles he had brought. One Carabinieri sat his weight on her back. The other Carabinieri clamped the shackles to her ankles, then stood and demanded the reward that Schroeder had circulated to the police up and down the coast.

Schroeder kicked Saba hard in the ribs. "Take her to the castle."

The Carabinieri barked: "The reward first."

Schroeder snarled. "She does not have the papers. I must talk with her. She will tell me. We will find the papers. You will be paid your reward."

"No. You will pay now. Or she goes to the *stazione polizia*—to the Gestapo."

Schroeder reached for his pistol and pointed it at Saba curled in the rain. "She is the murderer of *hundreds* at Haifa and *hundreds* at Janîn. She and her kind plan the same for Bari. Do you wish to answer for that if the Gestapo fails? They and the SS are busy with the Jew conspirators on the pier. I know this Arab. I know how to extract the answers we require. Castello Normanno has . . . privacy and proper equipment, yes?"

The Carabinieri policeman hesitated, then nodded that this was so. It was the last place an enemy of Il Duce saw. The Carabinieri turned away as he said to his fellow officer, "Castello Normanno. *Avanti. Rapidi!*"

Saba's interrogation cell at Castello Normanno was five walls of cold, medieval stone and one of iron bars. The cell was narrow and deep with a drain at the center and smelled of strong cleansers. Iron eyehooks protruded from the ceiling. A hanging bulb dangled from a rusted chain strung just above her head. Muffled voices echoed somewhere in the prison and the storm howled beyond that.

Saba blinked in the harsh light. Her lips were swollen; blood caked her cheeks. She sat a death chair, stripped to a soldier's sleeveless T-shirt and her belted pants. Painful leather ligatures circled her neck, wrists, and ankles. At the cell's bars, five men leered at her face and body, each taking her in as if the liberties were their due. Her legs were spread almost to their limits and invited more focused attention; the black keffiyeh was gone, her face uncovered. It was Jerusalem again. The first gate of hell.

Her eyes jumped for information. Across from her, Erich Schroeder sat a bench in silence, staring between his boots. Schroeder had remained silent while the men of the prison had come to look at her and leer. Schroeder stood, gathered himself, and un-holstered his Luger. At her chair, he bent to a knee and placed his empty hand near her crotch, edging it slowly forward until it brushed the fabric of her pants.

Saba held her breath.

Schroeder began the corner of a smile. "I should continue?" His Luger rose to caress her breast and flatten a nipple. "This is good, yes? Or you would prefer the British way?"

Saba said nothing, but reddened so much that Schroeder eased back and added to the smile.

"I will allow the Italians to have you first." He tapped at the wood in front of her crotch. "Two or three of the youngest while their fellows watch. Then one prisoner at a time—would five or six be sufficient to satisfy you? When they are finished, you will smell like them, like their saliva and *excretions*. Then we will talk, *ja*? And by then I will have your boyfriend, too."

Saba tried to spit in Schroeder's face but choked. She hoped Eddie was alive. If she had survived the waves with his engineering, he could be safe somewhere.

"Did he fuck you, too? Of course he did. Was it good . . . in the mouth? Yes, yes, you liked it didn't you? Sadly, these gentlemen will likely be nervous about your teeth." Schroeder patted near her teeth and ran a fingertip over the wings. "You will have to be satisfied with other pleasures."

Saba retreated deep into her family, to Khair-Saleh, to her partisans with whom she'd shared the fight. They were all now stars in the sky. She would will it and be there, too. The slap rocked the chair. She kept her eyes shut tight, her mind buried in the stars, in a soft, cool grave when this was over. Another slap rattled her teeth. She rushed deeper, saying good-bye to Palestine, saying she had helped Palestine by helping America, that Eddie Owen is a good man who won't forget her, who will tell others what had happened. Two hands gripped her ears and slammed her head against the wood. Soon her people would defeat the colonial ruler, British, Nazi, Zionist. Soon. The stomach punch opened her eyes.

Schroeder spit in her face. In his teeth and glare she saw her salvation; she could die before they raped her, when they attempted to remove her from this chair. She would make them kill her. Schroeder dug a punch deep into her liver. Saba coughed blood across them both. *Stay awake.* Saba fought the comforting edges of blackout. Pain and death did not compare to rape. *Stay awake. Stay awake. You will have a chance.*

Schroeder straightened, trying to read her eyes. Italian voices echoed at the cell bars. A doctor in a white lab coat split the young men and only he entered. The doctor carried a leather medical bag and sat it on Saba's lap. His face had no expression. His hands were white and he used both to open the bag. Saba did not look in the bag; bumps rose across her arms and neck. The doctor removed a syringe.

Schroeder smiled at her body's betrayal. "It would be hard for these gentlemen to enjoy you in the chair. Better I relax you, then move to a more comfortable position."

The doctor pumped a clear stream from the syringe that showered her knee.

"Herr Schroeder?" One of the two Carabinieri policemen Saba had not killed on the shoreline extended a document through the bars.

Schroeder signaled the doctor to wait, then walked to the bars and accepted the paper. The policeman spoke in whispers. Schroeder brought the document back to the light above Saba's head, stood next to her, and studied it.

Saba recognized the document, a page from the Mendelssohn papers. Across the top was written: "Piazza Mercantile. Now. *No more than two guards with you.* We trade—I get her; you get all the pages."

Schroeder smiled down at Saba trying to read the document. He nodded and holstered his pistol. "It appears our American is alive. Do you wish to tell me how? With whose assistance?"

Saba rocketed through possibilities that seconds ago were only rape, torture, and death.

Schroeder leaned back from her reaction, then signaled his two Carabinieri at the cell door. They pushed along the bars and disbursed all the leering men clustered there. Saba controlled her breath, pushed down the adrenaline, and gauged the odds she might face, the mistakes these men would make now that they had profit to protect. Her eyes cut from the cell bars to Schroeder at her shoulder. Any chance. Die fighting.

Schroeder pivoted into Saba's face. He squatted so they were eye to eye and said: "So, my Arab friend, there may be a bargain for you and me after all . . . that is, if you still burn to save

Palestine . . . more than your man." He smiled. "Bin Faisal is dead in Iraq. This changes my plans. I must have a warrior in the desert. A lion the Bedu and others will follow. You will trade me this *one* American—who can never return to America anyway—and I will give you your army in Palestine."

Schroeder waited for her ultimate dream to take hold. "Agreed?"

THREE HOURS AGO

Ten miles south of Bari, two maritime smugglers fought chest-high surf and spray to reach their boats and secure them against the storm. The two brown men were brothers, Italian-Portuguese, fifth-generation members of an Adriatic and Mediterranean network uninvolved with the grand politics of Europe. Like most who made their living on this coast—forty miles in either direction from Lamandia to Casalabate—the brothers were "long ago" Jews, nonreligious and nonsecular, focused solely on the small-boat politics of all coastal smugglers and squeezing a small profit from the movement of goods; money; and, on occasion, people.

Wedged between the brothers' wooden boats and the breakwater, a man flogged surf for air. The brothers ducked underneath him then shouldered the man onto the rocks. The man was beaten ragged but seemed unwilling to die this close to the shore lights. One brother pumped the drowned man's chest. He vomited saltwater, coughed, choked, and tried to roll to his knees. The older brother tried to calm him. The man gasped, and spit, and again tried for his knees. "My wife, she's out there—" He jabbed an arm that didn't work into the storm. "I gotta find her—"

Thunder hammered. The rain was blinding.

"A woman," one brother yelled in broken English. "A woman they find by the town. Alive, with the detention of Carabinieri, the police."

The man fought up from his knees, staggered, and passed out.

•••

The wives of the brothers were worried. They had worked almost two hours to revive the feverish young American—his body was strong, but as was always the case on this coastline, the Balkan storms and the sea were stronger. This American and his wife—if she survived the Carabinieri—would thank only the angel Adriel for their lives.

While the women worked, their husbands considered Eddie's fat money belt, his pistol, and the bagged papers wrapped in life-jacket fabric that had been stuffed down the back of his pants and belted to his body. The brothers understood the foreign money and pistol, but the papers were another matter. It was clear the papers were important—the raised seals, the swastikas of the Nazis, the same Nazis who now had power in Italy. This American and his wife had risked the sea with these papers, so close to the dock at Bari . . .

Eddie was conscious but hiding it. The two men who had saved him seemed to be brothers. In the last ten minutes, they had involved other men, dangerous men by their appearance. Men with dots tattooed on their right little finger, dots that were prison code Eddie had seen in Haifa. One man removed his shirt to let it dry. He was badly scarred and under his arm was a faded mark in the same dots:

דמעמה

The mark was Hebrew or close. These men were very likely Zionist militia, Saba's mortal enemies. They would kill her if they found out who she was, or sell her for the bounty and let the British kill her. Eddie plotted; he listened for words he might understand. The man who had not removed his shirt pulled a chair to Eddie and sat, the women and brothers behind him. The man looked into

Eddie's eyes and spoke when he saw Eddie's eyes were clear. His accent was thick and Balkan but educated. He said, "I am Hirsh. I am a Jew, not a German, not a Pole, not a Russian. I am a Jew."

Hirsh pointed to the larger, shirtless man at his shoulder. "My associate, Anistazio. He is a Jew. Our business is weapons. And Palestine is a customer." Hirsh tapped the Mendelssohn papers in his right hand and smiled. "I know of Tom Mendelssohn in Palestine. His network once passed through Bari, before the Nazis were here, also just across the sea in Croatia, the islands Krk and Cres. Mendelssohn pays well for the cargo he moves . . . before he dies."

Eddie nodded, watching Hirsh's eyes for clues that the Zionist knew Eddie's wife was Saba Hassouneh.

Hirsh tapped the Mendelssohn papers again. Hirsh's hand was oversize and strong. "We also know talk of these papers, but I never believe *I* would see them. Please, you will explain how you have Tom Mendelssohn's papers."

Eddie explained, gilding his future participation in Tom Mendelssohn's blackmail plan against Standard Oil and its partners, the Jews that the plan might save, the money it might earn. Eddie offered a bargain—if the smugglers would help rescue Eddie's wife, he could carry out Tom Mendelssohn's plan or whatever reasonable version the smugglers might decide.

Hirsh nodded. "And you did not kill Tom Mendelssohn for these papers?"

Eddie's stomach tightened. Unarmed, he would not leave this room alive.

Hirsh answered himself. "You did not, or why have the papers with you here, so many months after Mendelssohn dies, when the sale to many parties could have been made long before." Hirsh chinned at his associate. "Anistazio and I will talk. Please, for us, a few moments."

The two brothers and their wives remained with Eddie. Eddie began to sweat, probably a fever. Or a vote on his and Saba's future. Eddie continued to sweat until Hirsh returned without Anistazio.

Hirsh said, "We will assist you and your wife. Anistazio begins this now with a message to her captors. The Carabinieri on our coast can be dealt with provided your wife has no . . . other value?"

Eddie said, "No. None. She's Jordanian, a teacher. Her name's Calah al-Habra. She teaches kids in Amman. It's the papers everyone wants."

Hirsh nodded once, but without agreement. "Your wife has been taken to Castello Normanno-Svevo; we know this before we arrive to you. An important Nazi, Erich Schroeder, is there. Her imprisonment in the castle is . . ." Hirsh searched for a word he couldn't find. "Your wife has no special meaning?"

"No. None. It's the papers." Eddie swiveled to look at the brothers and their wives, selling them the story. "She's really pretty, beautiful. Maybe they took her to— I gotta go get her. Now. Whether you help me or not."

Hirsh glanced at the low ceiling. He was a smuggler of weapons, and in Palestine. No doubt he had strong survival skills and believed almost none of what anyone told him. Leading him to Saba could be the ultimate betrayal. Eddie weighed options he didn't have. But if he had a gun . . . Not *if*, he'd make sure he had a gun.

Hirsh said, "I will make for you later a Photostat copy of the papers; there is a machine in Bari. But these, the originals, and three-quarters of the money in your belt will remain with me. You, and papers you will not have, will be the bait. If you survive, you will assist us with Standard Oil and the other Americans. Do we agree?"

"Deal. Hand me my gun and let's go get her."

•••

Gale-force wind battered the plaster and stone buildings of Bari's Piazza Mercantile. Eddie could see only thirty feet into the storm. His standing heart rate felt double, almost enough to make up for going fifteen rounds with the Adriatic. In minutes, Eddie and Hirsh would attempt the exchange for Saba. Saba's captors were Nazis—professional killers—and her rescuers were ex-convict Zionist militia smugglers. Eddie squeezed D.J.'s pistol grip in his belt—probably not enough bullets. Probably not enough luck. The exchange of original documents for Saba would be based on improvisation and those bullets—there were no documents for Schroeder.

Eddie swallowed. *If we somehow get past this gunfight alive, move number two will be to cover Saba's tattoo with her hair and hope for the best.* Hirsh nudged Eddie. They were inside a deep doorway on the abandoned piazza. Hirsh pointed southeast into the sheeting rain and thunder. "The Nazi will have more than the two guards when he enters. Two will side him, the others are searching for position now—Il Duce's Black Shirts, OVRA secret police, Waffen-SS, I do not know. Anistazio and his rifle will take the first he sees."

Rifle? Eddie scanned the buildings surrounding the piazza. All the windows were shuttered. The rooftops were socked in. *Rifle from where?* Eddie counted six, maybe eight streets feeding Piazza Mercantile.

Hirsh continued. "The women who revive you will appear on the street, rushing from the weather. The women and the brothers will seal the piazza behind Herr Schroeder with a car we borrow. You and I will then take Herr Schroeder and the two guards he shows us. If you or your wife survive the fight, run for the rendezvous at the top of the piazza." Hirsh pointed. "A car waits—Sicilians, associates of the brothers—but you must be quick. If the Sicilians are told of dead Nazis, they will melt away."

Eddie wanted to be sure he'd heard all the good stuff and asked again. "That's it?"

Hirsh loaded and checked a second pistol, then nodded Eddie out of the protected doorway. "You must show yourself to Herr Schroeder and his guards but appear to be hiding. If you are too bold, the Nazi will know you are here to kill him, not trade." Hirsh waited for Eddie to nod. "The Nazi will not suspect you have friends here. You are out of the water, alone, and desperate. This is how Anistazio delivers your note. Yes? You understand."

"Yeah." Eddie wished he were D.J. or Floyd Merewether. Gunfight 101 had more nuance than he had anticipated or could process in his current condition.

"When you recognize the Nazi, Herr Schroeder, do a full circle with your head. You are fearful and check the entire square. This is a signal to Anistazio. Trust Anistazio's rifle to find whomever Herr Schroeder has placed behind you."

Eddie said a dazed, "Good, yeah, okay."

"I will be there, in the café doorway." Hirsh pointed under a red awning flapping in the wind. "One of Herr Schroeder's guards will hold secure on your wife with a weapon at her head. Should this guard be on my side, I will take him. If the guard is not on my side, Anistazio will take him."

Eddie nodded.

"Should the guard stand *behind* your wife, you will begin for us. You will shoot Herr Schroeder, *not your wife's guards*. Do not waste your one moment on a guard; you will shoot Herr Schroeder. And you will shoot Herr Schroeder as soon as he speaks. Our hope is that the two guards' first instinct will be defense. Anistazio and I will then shoot at them and hope for the best result."

Eddie had seen Tom Mix do similar and lose and that was a goddamn movie. "And you guys are still alive? This kind of shit actually *works?*"

Hirsh frowned and waved Eddie out.

Eddie was too beat and inexperienced to conjure anything that might improve Saba's chances. He wanted to offer that she could fight but that might get her killed when the fight was over. He inhaled deeply, set his shoulders, and stepped out of the doorway into the piazza. The gale wind and rain slapped him from three directions. His shoes sloshed over limestone pavers sheet-draining across his path. Uphill was to the north and toward the blurry outline of a cathedral dome. The dome could be Anistazio's perch—Anistazio would be shooting down. That was good. What Anistazio could actually see probably wasn't.

Eddie stepped behind a scrubby tree planter midpiazza. Schroeder could sneak in a battalion and no one would see them. Eddie patted two pistols, one front and one back. His left arm clamped a heavy steel lockbox tight to his chest. The fake pages inside were wrapped and bound and blank. The lockbox was Hirsh's idea—it might stop a pistol bullet. Eddie liked the shield, but the box also guaranteed he couldn't shoot with that hand.

Hirsh said Schroeder would slide toward Eddie's weak hand as he approached. Eddie would have to step like a boxer—keep Herr Schroeder outside the right foot and facing Eddie's right hand that could and would draw the gun. Eddie understood a boxer's footwork, but he'd never killed anyone and he wasn't sure how he'd do. He wanted to kill Schroeder; that wasn't open to discussion. *Wanting* to do it was one thing, out-drawing a professional killer might be another.

Thirty feet downhill at Via Manfredi, Saba appeared in the rain, hands cuffed at the waist. At twenty feet, Eddie could tell she had been abused and badly. On her left side, a square-jawed Italian policeman had a leather belt tight around her neck and a gun at her head. Another policeman slid to Saba's right when the policeman determined Eddie was alone in the piazza. Torrential rain tinted everything an undersea green. A shape silhouetted directly behind Saba, then slowly materialized into Erich Schroeder. Schroeder remained behind Saba and his two gunmen and shouted through the rain: "We find ourselves in difficult circumstances, Eddie. Before you attempt whatever heroic action you have planned, please . . . allow me two minutes."

Eddie's heart pounded. Lightning drilled behind the buildings. Gargoyles flashed in the light, spewing rainwater from their mouths. *Be calm.* Eddie gripped the box tighter with his left arm and hand. He added his right to keep both hands in plain sight.

Schroeder continued. "Saba may go free. I have fought off those here who would rape and assault her. *She*, you can save, if her safety is your wish."

Eddie flashed on D.J., Newt, the farm—none saved. Rain battered Eddie's face and eyes. His hands were slick. Either gun he drew would be slick. Green air choked his throat. *Offer the box, pull the gun. Shoot Schroeder.*

Lightning cracked through the green murk. Thunder pounded. Eddie flinched and the thunder echoed through the piazza.

Offer, pull, shoot.

Offer, pull, shoot.

Schroeder stepped half his torso just outside the shoulder of the gunman who had Saba's neck. "Saba and I wish the same result for her homeland. Whether *you* truly understand that or not, *she* understands. If we all die here in the storm, it serves none of our countries. Only England and the world's Communists win."

Rain gusted and splashed and blinded. Eddie's left arm clenched on the box. Adrenaline shortened his breaths. *Offer, pull, shoot.* Eddie's right hand eased down from the box toward his side . . . Schroeder opened both hands to show them empty. He smiled, soliciting permission to close the distance. "Eddie, if you will come to Berlin willingly, I will guarantee Saba's safety *and* the funding of her partisans." Schroeder eyed Eddie's right hand and took a careful half step closer. "You may be in contact with her by radio phone as often as you wish, for as long as you wish."

Eddie cut to Saba. Saba's face was swollen and black. Her eyes burned into his.

"Your family in Oklahoma will be supported and protected—"

Eddie snapped, drew the gun behind the box—

Schroeder ducked to the stones. Eddie fired. Anistazio fired from the dome. The Italian policeman on Saba's right exploded backward. The policeman with Saba jerked her sideways and fired. His bullet creased Eddie's hip. Schroeder fired from the stones. A bullet slammed into Eddie's lockbox and knocked him off his feet. A concussion grenade exploded. Hirsh jumped over Eddie's legs, shot Saba's guard, aimed at Schroeder but blew backward and across Eddie's legs. Schroeder rose to a knee, shot Hirsh again, then spun on Eddie. A rifle cracked from the dome. Saba had a dead man's pistol and fired at Schroeder. He pivoted, shot at Saba, stood, and staggered, and two rounds boomed from the dome. Schroeder stumbled, turning toward Eddie. Eddie was up, almost square. Saba rushed Schroeder. He spun. Eddie slammed his pistol into Schroeder's neck and pulled the trigger. Schroeder crumpled, gushing blood into the rain. Saba kicked the pistol out of Schroeder's hand and shot him in the chest until her pistol clicked empty. Eddie collapsed. Saba dropped the pistol, grabbed Eddie's shirt. "Up. Now." Her hands were cuffed. "Eddie. Look at me. We must go. Now! Stand, I cannot carry you. Stand."

Eddie smelled cordite, could almost see, but couldn't make his knees work. Saba propped him to her shoulder and they staggered uphill.

From behind. *"Halt!"*

Anistazio's rifle cracked from the dome. Pistol fire behind them made Saba duck. Eddie fell. The pistols fired again. Saba struggled Eddie to standing and into an alley. He said, "Higher . . . a car up there." Eddie's shirt was pink. Saba looked back at the piazza, then patted his side. Eddie winced; he was shot at least once. Saba pushed them up the alley and into another. Their second alley crested a hill in the maze of streets. Sirens wailed from three directions. The alley was the width of a cart and too narrow to hide either of them. At the top of the next rise, Anistazio waved, then staggered left.

The Sicilians' car was a truck, the driver a brownish boy. Anistazio was bloody and gray-pale with his rifle slung over his back. He whispered foamy words to Eddie's ear as they piled into the truck's cab. The driver bounced them west then south, looping the city. Eddie felt sick, saw glary headlights spin, and passed out.

Saba crushed her hand and fought it bloody out of one cuff, then ripped the leather belt off her neck, read the road behind them, then their driver hunched tight to the wheel, head barely high enough to see. He eyed her handcuffs, then Eddie and the rifleman bleeding, then quickly back to the road. Lightning lit the narrow street awash in rain but getting wider. Saba felt for Eddie's pulse; his breathing was ragged but better. Rags were tied to the rifleman's neck, arm, and leg. The rags were soaked red. A police siren wailed close by but invisible in the storm. The boy asked something in hurried Italian blanketed by thunder. Saba didn't answer. The boy asked again.

Gale hammered the road and truck. Saba barked: "No Italian."

The boy shouted Hebrew—

Saba jerked back into the passenger window. The rifleman's arm bounced limp over his head and across her leg—he had a faded blue tattoo under his armpit. Saba's breath caught in her throat; she smeared at the blood:

דמעמה

Irgun. The letters were Hebrew and meant "The Stand," an Irgun identifier from the murdering militia's earliest days in Jerusalem. Saba grabbed the rifleman's bloody hand and found blue dots on his little finger. The boy driver grinned yellow teeth, nod-ded big, and started to speak. Saba reached over and across Eddie and the Irgun rifleman and ripped the pistol out of the boy's belt. The boy wild-eyed her instead of the road. His truck veered into a wall, bounced off toward the sea. Saba jammed her foot across the gearshift to the brake. The truck skidded, grabbed, and everyone smashed forward into the dash. The truck crashed back into the wall and stopped. The boy's hands were on the wheel. Slowly, he raised one hand above his head and spoke apologetic Italian: "*Alto grande.*"

The Irgun rifleman was spread across Eddie and Saba's lap. He spoke in wheezy broken English: "Anistazio. My name is Anistazio."

Saba aimed the pistol at the boy and glanced down at Anistazio's face. Death crept into the Irgun murderer's eyes. Irgun had killed many of her people and she had personally killed five of his kind. Rather than cut his throat, an odd reaction filled her. "You are a good soldier, Anistazio. You have saved us." She hesitated, then smoothed his forehead, the same as she had done three of her own fighters in their final moments.

Anistazio coughed blood, blinked, and tried to speak again. His eyes clouded and focused on hers. He said, "Yes, I am good soldier," and died.

The boy reached over Eddie for Anistazio's face and cried out in Hebrew. Eddie mumbled blood into Saba's shoulder. She pushed Eddie into the boy, fought the passenger door open, pulled out Anistazio's body into the gale, and got back in.

The boy shouted: "No!"

Saba pulled the pistol and slammed it across Eddie into the boy's head. His other cheek flattened against the driver's window. She shouted, "Doctor. For him."

The boy's eyes were sideways to their limits.

"Doctor!"

The boy stuttered, "*D-Dottore?*"

"Yes. *Dottore.*" Saba pulled back. "Now!"

The boy started the truck. The windscreen was green with wind-blown water. He said, "*Dottore,*" to the steering wheel and windscreen and inched the truck uphill, over a crest, then downhill toward the seafront. "*Dottore.*" The boy had tears in his eyes and on his cheeks. Saba braced with her feet, wrapped her left arm around Eddie against her shoulder, and wiped the blood off his mouth.

"Breathe, Eddie." She twisted the skin on his face.

Eddie jerked with the pain. His eyes fluttered.

Saba yelled at the boy, "Faster!"

CHAPTER 38

April, 1939

The doctor's office was the front rooms of his villa. Saba stood with her back to the locked door, pistol in hand. The boy sat cross-legged on the floor, Eddie on the operating table, the doctor over him. Through his mask the doctor said, "Two bullet holes, no bullets. He can live, if he is not moved."

Saba did not answer. If they were still here after the storm passed, she would die at the hands of the Irgun, the Italians, or the Nazis. Without the papers, Eddie's value was Eddie—a price on his head by the British and the Spanish for sabotage. The Nazis would want him for their refineries. The doctor's office had a telephone. Saba had Eddie's money belt. She said, "We cannot stay and survive. He and I are fugitives."

The doctor turned his head to her, then went back to work.

Saba continued. "We will leave you safe. But you must show us an exit from Italy."

The doctor spoke while he worked. "You are Albanian? Caught in Il Duce's war?"

Saba didn't answer.

"No? You are Jew? A fugitive from the Nazis?"

Saba didn't answer.

The doctor said, "My patient is not a Jew, not of the kind I have seen. If you are not Jews or Albanians, then why are you with—" The doctor stopped, his hands busying with Eddie's wounds. "The boy and his family are Gypsies, Jews, smugglers, the 'old family of the coast.'"

Saba was unsure what the doctor meant.

"Pirates. Is your American a pirate? A gangster like our Lucky Luciano? If your American is Mafia, they can get him out of Italy. The Mafia does not love Il Duce." The doctor worked until he finished, then removed his gauze mask and washed his hands. He faced her from his side of the room and did not demonstrate fear. Saba wanted to look at Eddie but did not.

The doctor said, "You require a doctor's attention as well." He touched his face to mimic hers and shook his pants. "And dry clothes. And likely food and water." He paused, inspecting her. "But you ask for none."

Saba waited for the Italian doctor to arrive at his destination. The boy on the floor shot glances between them.

"And you are comfortable with your gun. And the manacles that hang from your wrist." The doctor paused. "You are no pirate, no mafia. You are a soldier." He paused again. "But whose?"

"American."

The doctor smiled a cautious inch and shook his head. "No." He tapped the cheekbone beneath his right eye.

The boy craned from the floor. Saba glanced at his movement. The boy could not know, could not be sure; her face was too dirty and bruised. The boy pushed himself deep in the corner, eyes locked on her face. The doctor said, "There is a legend here among the pirates and smugglers, the Jews in particular. The women use it to scare their children into order." He touched his cheekbone again. "This legend can do many things to those who incite her."

Saba stared at the doctor.

He said, "I have heard this legend. And know it cannot be true, no woman could be this powerful."

Saba nodded. With two fingers she removed the ten franc note inside her pocket, pinned there with the numbers Eddie had given her for Doña Carmen, and placed the note and money on the sheet by Eddie's feet. "These are numbers in America, in Texas." She glanced at the phone. "You will call them, yes? And I will see to my man."

The doctor picked up the note, not the money.

They waited an hour while Eddie fevered for his life.

The doctor's phone rang. He answered in Italian. Saba shouted, "English!" and aimed the pistol. The doctor went silent, listened, his eyes on her, nodded, handed her the phone, and backed away. Saba held the phone to her ear. "Yes?"

Through the transatlantic static, a Texas accent said, "And who might you be, honey? Calling Texas from Bari, Italy?"

Saba answered, "State your name."

Silence, static, then, "Floyd."

"Floyd Mer-weather?"

"Close enough."

"I have Eddie Owen. Alive but shot. We are fugitives. Can you help him?"

"How bad's he shot?"

"Cannot travel well, but we must."

"He's there with you?"

"Yes."

Static shrilled the line. "Hold on a minute."

Saba glanced at Eddie immobile on the table, then the boy terrified in the corner, then the doctor watching her on his phone.

The phone said, "Where's Bari?"

"The eastern coast."

"Hold on." Two minutes passed. "Can you get our friend to Naples? Supposed to be their big port on the west coast?"

Saba asked the doctor. He shook his head.

"No. Eddie is not strong enough."

"Naples is the best I can do, honey. Pretty damn good, considering middle of the fuckin' night in a goddamn foreign country. Maybe you work a little harder on your end or go back to your kitchen."

Saba squeezed the pistol in her hand. "Where in Naples?"

The doctor said, "No. He cannot—"

Saba waved him silent. "*Where* in Naples?"

"The harbor. Main dock. Eddie can get a ship with a hospital; big passenger ships from all over dock there in Naples. Go inside the harbor station. If there's an ocean liner in the port, I'll know the name by the time you get there. You and Eddie will have a cabin booked for 'Mr. and Mrs. Benny Binion.' If there's no ocean liner in port, hide till one arrives. Won't be long; supposedly, they sail in and out all the time."

"You can do this? From Texas?"

"Where the fuck you from, lady? I said it, didn't I?"

The drive to the outskirts of Naples was an endless series of turns, dips, and climbs. The gale stayed just to their south, walling off the entire of Southern Italy and Bari's dead policemen and Nazis. Eddie coughed blood onto Saba's pants the entire way. Saba had the boy in front of her in the front seat of the doctor's Fiat coupe and the doctor's wife behind the wheel. Eddie was in the back with the doctor and her. The doctor picked the lock on her handcuffs and constantly admonished his wife to drive slower. The almost six hours had not been easy on Eddie. The doctor's drugs masked Eddie's condition. He was pale, his breathing ragged, and Saba could do nothing about it.

The Naples harbor station was large and new and beneath a castle. Saba blinked. All of Europe must be ports and castles. Ships were in the port. Soldiers were everywhere—Italy was sixteen hours into her war with Albania. The doctor, his wife, and the boy were on the outskirts of town, unharmed but isolated, for how long, Saba couldn't know, other than they had been good to her and would be free soon.

Saba drove the doctor's Fiat down the seafront road past the street vendors and merchants of the docks. Behind them, an enormous, awe-inspiring vessel held the main berth. The flag was French, an ocean liner, the SS *Normandie*. It was the finest vessel Saba had ever seen, slung high to low, the bow a sharp, towering, deep *V*, three red smokestacks, and black-and-white hull trimmed in red. Saba could not imagine what it was like aboard. The Europeans lived in a world so foreign their palaces could travel.

Saba parked the doctor's Fiat away from the harbor station's grand entrance. She checked Eddie resting in the backseat, donned the long coat and scarf provided by the doctor's wife, and walked inside to be Mrs. Benny Binion. Saba had one pistol, a knife from the doctor's office, boots that had been in the sea, and no travel documents. As instructed, she would state her name to the ship's purser. He would assure their boarding or he would betray them. One or the other. It could all easily end here.

The harbor station was as grand on the inside as the SS *Normandie* was on the outside. The lobby bustled with well-fitted passengers—men in vested suits, women in lace hats, tailored coats, and dresses with matching gloves, their servants better dressed than Saba had ever been. Porters in maritime uniform pushed carts of leather valises and wardrobe trunks across the marble floor. Ceremonial Royal Italian soldiers lined the monumental walls . . . an amazing, surreal grand ball from *The Great Gatsby*. In better times, Saba would have gawked. Walking through the money of Europe, she smelled the perfume and the coffee, listening to the lilt of dignified voices, men of position who would soon sail away from the war.

Saba read the queue for travel documents she did not have, gripped her pistol under the coat, and presented herself as Mrs. Benny Binion. Immediately Saba was passed through the queue. Without touching her, two uniformed crewmen spoke nonstop at her shoulders of their deepest wish to be of service for the entire voyage. Saba stopped them when she was willing to believe this was no trap. She explained she must return for her husband, Mr. Benny Binion. He was briefly ill, under a physician's care—

Both crewmen said they were aware and a place had been made in the ship's sickbay, a hospital. All would be well.

Saba hid her surprise. Who were Benny Binion and Floyd Mere-Weather? She asked the two crewmen to provide porters who would assist when her husband arrived in a few short minutes. Could they meet her at the main entrance? Both crewmen said they would see to it and escorted her back through the travel documents queue. She asked if they could remain, so that her husband's process through this queue could be as simple as hers.

The men said that this was their honor.

Saba thanked them and walked through the station, past guards and passengers who had seen the flurry of activity around her. They would wonder about her clothing beneath the woman's coat—that of a man, rough and unfashionable. Possibly they would think her an actress or an eccentric heiress of some type. Saba stepped outside, walked past the street vendors to the doctor's car, and slid in the backseat with Eddie. He was up and sitting. She was shocked.

He said, "Where are we? The ocean's on the wrong side."

Saba stared. Eddie stared back. "What?"

Saba checked his pulse, then his forehead for fever, then his eyes.

Eddie said, "Maybe you should kiss me."

Saba found a smile that surprised her. "You are under a doctor's care. Such an act may kill you."

"Try me."

"We are at a ships' berth in Napoli, the coast away from the Italians' war. We are Mr. and Mrs. Benny Binion of Dallas, Texas—"

"You talked to Floyd and Benny?"

Saba nodded. "I believe it is safe, although I cannot promise this. The ship is French, bound for New York City. You will be met there, possibly by police if the phone call was overheard. If not, then a train to Ne-va-da"—she had trouble with the word—"not Texas; you cannot go to Texas now."

Eddie's eyes added light and focus. "No shit, we made it?"

Saba nodded. "Possibly, yes. If we can get aboard . . . and I believe we can. Your Mr. Binion is an important man."

Eddie grinned to his limits, reached, hugged Saba to him, winced at the pain, and held on anyway. "I don't know what to say. Thanks. For everything. Now it's my turn. I swear to God I'll make you happy."

Saba didn't answer; she held on.

"Nevada's a desert, like yours. They just built this gigantic dam, the Hoover Dam. Mr. Binion has his eye on a gambling town, Las Vegas; maybe that's what we'll do first. I don't know. I'll get my family out there—you'll love them and Benny and Floyd, too—it'll be good, Saba, better than you can imagine. Mr. and Mrs. Eddie Owen." Eddie was out of breath and stopped.

Saba pushed back from him and smiled best she could into his jubilant blue eyes. "I love you, Eddie. You know this, yes?" She nodded for him to nod.

He kissed her instead. She kissed him back, intending the kiss to be soft and short. Her lips pressed into his; both her hands gripped into his clothes. Tears formed in her eyes. She squeezed, hoping to stop the tears from her cheeks, but could not.

Eddie's lips told hers: "Don't cry; you can still be a cowboy in Nevada."

Saba swallowed a small laugh, pushed back, and wiped at her eyes.

She started to speak and Eddie said, "God, you're beautiful."

"I cannot go with you . . . to America."

Eddie pushed back in the seat, breathed deep against his arms clutched across his wounds, and didn't speak. Silence filled the space between them. Eddie swallowed again and nodded small. He curled his lips against his teeth and said, "I know."

Saba's face blanked, unable to hide her surprise. Eddie was a boy, but he was not. She had seen it clearly when they were in the worst of times and she saw it now.

Eddie grabbed her hand. "I know. But you'll marry me. Here, right now."

Saba laughed in her throat and the tears welled again. "You would have a wife who is only a memory? Who you will never know in your bed? Her and no other?"

"Not a memory. I'll see her again. At first, it'll be every night in those stars." Eddie pointed at the roof of the Fiat. "And when the war is over, and Palestine is free, I'll come and get her, wherever she is, whatever she's done."

"You are a boy—"

"Yeah, a boy who scares the Raven with just his fingertips."

Saba reddened at the challenge, then exhaled and said a breathy, "Yes. His hands *and his heart* frighten me." She swallowed. "And I wish them both."

"Get on the boat."

Saba leaned back. "I will send two porters to the car. They will take you to the crewmen who will take you aboard your ship to America. My fight is in Palestine, not our bed. Not in this lifetime, but in the next."

"Marry me or I'm not leaving."

Saba shut her eyes. She believed him, Eddie the American who believed in dreams. "Stay, then," she said, and stepped out of the driver's side into the merchants and street vendors.

Saba returned with two simple gold rings and a priest who spoke English. The priest knelt in the front seat facing them. He removed his hat, explained she must wear it, then asked, "He has a ring for you?"

Saba put her ring on Eddie's finger. Eddie put the ring she gave him on hers.

"Hold the hands with the rings."

They did. The priest spoke Italian and made motions with his hands. He finished with the Christian sign of the cross and pointed Eddie at Saba's lips. "You must kiss your bride."

Eddie grinned. The priest grinned.

Saba cried. The priest excused himself.

Eddie said, "C'mon, get on the boat. We'll figure it out."

Her hands were on his cheeks. She wished to climb inside his clothes, to feel Eddie's heart against her skin, to begin their magical trip to the American desert in Ne-va-da. "You are my man, a man I never believed I could allow or have. For that there is no . . . loss." Her thumbs caressed his cheeks. "But Palestine is my country, Eddie, as America is yours. To leave is to betray my people. They have little now and no leaders."

"We get aboard, stay together."

Saba acknowledged the two porters behind Eddie's window. "The porters are here; you must go. Too much attention and I will be caught."

Eddie coughed and shrank at the pain. "Get on the boat. I swear to God I'll go back to Palestine with you as soon as we get the chance. I promise."

Saba slid out the driver's side and circled to the passenger door. She opened it and asked that the porters assist her husband. The porters helped Eddie out of the car. Pain he'd been hiding racked his face. He leaned against the fender, caught his breath, and told the porters, "Give me a minute. *Un momento*."

"*Sì, sì,* but the ship . . ." The porters pointed at the SS *Normandie*.

Eddie turned to Saba. Her finger went to his lips. She didn't argue or speak, just stayed in Eddie's eyes, hoping hers said what she could not. She stepped to him, touched the wings hidden beneath her eye, and trailed the fingertip on his lips.

"Look to the stars each night, Eddie Owen. You and your wife who loves you very much will be in them."

Eddie tried to stop the porters. "Wait. Wait a sec." But it was their feet that propelled him. He turned his head— "Stay alive. I'm coming back. I promise."

Saba nodded. Then dropped the coat in the car and melted into the working people dressed much the same as she. Uphill and away from the station, she found a place to await the SS *Normandie*'s departure. After an hour, Eddie appeared at the ship's rail. Being the foolish romantic boy that he was, he propped himself into a tall chair and searched the shoreline that might hide his wife. At sunset the SS *Normandie* sounded her horns. Eddie waved at what he could not see. Saba squeezed her hand and Eddie's ring as her husband and her dreams left the harbor. The grand ship turned for the sea. Saba waved small and whispered to her husband, "I am Saba Hassouneh al Saleh, the proud bride of Mr. Eddie Owen."

Eddie's last words to her had been, "Stay alive. I'm coming back." And Saba decided it would be the one little girl's fairy tale the Raven would believe.

EPILOGUE

The bloodiest, most profitable war in human history began five months after the SS *Normandie* sailed. The opening salvo was a radio broadcast in Upper Silesia orchestrated by Reichsführer Heinrich Himmler. The war lasted six years. When it ended in 1945, there were 60 million dead, 6 million of them murdered in the extermination camps depicted by the "Mendelssohn papers." Thousands of the world's cities were rubble; 10 million more would die of famine and disease; fortunes had been made—most a direct result of Nazi Germany and the Empire of Japan's ability to manufacture and deliver munitions.

> *Mr. President, I recommend Standard Oil and its board of directors be tried for treason.*
>
> —William E. Dodd
> US Ambassador to Germany

> *The Appeal is denied. Standard Oil can be considered an enemy national . . .*
>
> —Charles E. Clark
> Chief Judge, US Court of Appeals

Not one officer, stockholder, or banker of Standard Oil, Vacuum Oil, General Motors, Ford Motor Company, Alcoa, or DuPont spent one day in jail. Nor did any member of the reigning Wall Street banking families.

On May 14, 1948, the State of Israel was founded in Palestine. That same year, Benny Binion moved the last of his Texas gambling operations to Las Vegas. Some said Saba Hassouneh al-Saleh had survived the war, as had Eddie Owen and his little brother and sister. Many more said the Raven had not survived—how could she?

Or that she had never existed at all.

In the refugee camps, in the most desperate of times, black wings would appear on the walls and tents. Those who had no other hope but the Raven never quit believing. Eddie Owen made three trips to Palestine and found no trace, but at night, when the stars were out, he, like the others, refused to let her go. A promise was a promise, and sometimes, no matter what the odds, sometimes . . .

APRIL 7, 1952
LAS VEGAS, NEVADA

Binion's Horseshoe Casino was a huge hit—movie stars, torch singers, cowboys—and had been from day one. Ava Gardner and Robert Mitchum drank and gambled here. Eddie had taught Ava to shoot craps and a .38 Colt. Ava had her actress pals look Eddie up when they came to town for their four-day divorces. At Benny's request, Eddie had driven Ida Lupino to the Douglas County seat in Minden for Ida's second breakup. Hard to imagine that the Jacksboro Highway led to Fremont Street and Hollywood, but it had.

Tonight Eddie had the night off from making gamblers and movie stars happy, and leaned against the fender of his 1951 Nash-Healey two-seat breezer. On his radio, Patti Page sang her "Tennessee Waltz" to the desert stars while Eddie sipped red wine from a bottle Benny Binion gave him every April 7th.

The wind in Eddie's face was hot, even at night, even hotter than it had been in Iran and Lebanon and Tenerife. Saba's stars were always there, so she had to be, right? Some desert? Somewhere? Saba knew about Nevada and Benny Binion. It could happen. Eddie didn't ask Benny and Floyd for the odds; they made odds for a living. Eddie just believed, because he said he would.

Eddie sipped again and held the bottle to the stars. "Hey, baby." Reddish dust answered. Eddie was parked off Highway 95, a good thirty miles from the Proving Grounds that President Truman had renamed the "Nevada Test Site." Six times in the last year, B-50 bombers from Nellis Air Force Base had dropped atomic bombs out there, the most recent earlier this week, the flashes so bright they were seen in San Francisco. The US Atomic Energy Commission assured everyone the area was "safe" but Highway 95's new concrete now rippled like a washboard. Any wind at all and the top layer of desert on either side jumped into the sky like a carpet of flies.

Atomic bombs may have ended the war, but they were front and center to start a new one—an atomic Armageddon faceoff between the USA and Russia. Wisconsin Senator Joe McCarthy was on the rise, riding the "Red Scare" like a warhorse. McCarthy had ferreted out Russian Communist spies and American traitors in Washington, DC; Los Alamos; and Hollywood. According to the senator, America was again on the verge of destruction, assaulted from within by fellow travelers who would destroy democracy and pave the way for the Communists. Government-approved bomb shelters were being built in backyards across the nation. America had fought a second world war only to lose her mind in the peace.

Eddie toyed with the ring Saba had put on his finger thirteen years ago. Tonight was their wedding anniversary. He knew a great deal more about his wife now than he had before the war started. The Israelis in the USA who were snooping around anything "atomic" had privately told him the Raven was a ghost, a Robin Hood legend that every culture manufactured in their darkest hour. They said the woman Eddie had known was an imposter, one of many, all of them dead.

Eddie turned to the sound of a distant engine. No headlights fanned in the dark. His free hand trembled and that was unusual. His hand held a ten franc note that had been bet on a roulette table in Binion's three hours ago at midnight. The bet won and no one collected. Pinned to the note was a hand-drawn map to this spot and Eddie's name. The map smelled like tangerines.

AUTHOR NOTES

The novel covers the ten years between 1929 and 1939. Three events in the timeline have been juggled for clarity in the plot: the voyage of the MS *Saint Louis*, Hitler's formal threat in the Reichstag against the Jews, and the German-American Bund rally in New York City.

ACKNOWLEDGMENTS

F.O.N., Simon the Lionhearted, Sharon and Doug, Easy Ed Stackler, Major McQuinn, Pack, Murad, Saudi, Miami Jon, Lt. Dennis,Maurice, BT, King Hamad, Abdul Lateef, Khaldoon, and Julio Rancel-Villamandos in Tenerife. The biggest thanks possible for the backstage passes, critiques, and support of every imaginable type.

For two years this novel traveled me from the Jacksboro Highway through Sitra, Beirut, Amman, Wadi Rum, Aqaba, Jerusalem, Haifa, Ramallah, Nablus, the Golan Heights, Damascus, Tenerife, Casablanca, Oran, Algiers, Bari, Naples, Bastia, and Marseilles. Lots of stops, some I'd made before; lots of people, many of them new; all of it the best part of the writer life.

ABOUT THE AUTHOR

Charlie Newton is the author of two previous novels, *Start Shooting* and *Calumet City*. His work has been a finalist for the Edgar, the Ian Fleming Steel Dagger, the Macavity, and the International Thriller Writer's Thriller Award. Born in Chicago, Charlie has built successful bars/restaurants and resort apartments, raced thoroughbreds that weren't quite so successful, and brokered television and film in the Middle East. He lives on the road.